D0284804

AMERICAN *Baby* BOOMER

AMERICAN *Baby* BOOMER

LUCAS CARTER

To order additional copies of this book, contact:
Xlibris
1-888-795-4274
www.Xlibris.com
Orders@Xlibris.com
799386

CHAPTER 1

I am one of several million baby boomers born in the late 1940s. I was born on the front edge of the baby boomer generation, being born in 1948. The following is just one account of what it was like to be born, grow up, and retire during this period. There are thousands, if not millions, of other stories, all unique to the lives of their individual authors. But this is my story.

My generation has seen more change than any generation before it. I, for one, have never been convinced that all those changes were quantifiably better for the world or the country in which I was born.

In retirement, I've had time to contemplate several of those modifications or shifts in culture regarding government, individual freedom, rights for the masses, and spirituality. As well, I'd had time to think about my own life; the joys, the sorrows, those things I controlled, and the decisions that I had limited or no influence over as I've made this journey we call the aging process.

I have also reflected on the seasons of my life and where I am currently in that cycle. I have always believed that there are four distinct stages of life that are concurrent with the seasons of the year.

If we should be fortunate enough to live a full-term life to normal life expectancy numbers, each of us will enjoy (or endure) the spring, summer, fall, and winter of our lives. Much has been written about this, and after reading many articles, both secular and nonsecular on the subject, I agree that the comparisons of the seasons coincide with all living things in creation.

The season of spring starts at birth and ends for most of us in the early twenties. It is in this season that each of us will learn 90 percent of all we ever learn in our lifetime. We are inexperienced in the ways of the world, and each of us will be enriched by our individual experiences. In this season, you develop your personality; your libido is formed, with its insecurities and strengths, and you develop a sense of self and individuality, which may be positive or negative depending on a multitude of direct and indirect factors that affect an individual's life to that point.

Summer begins at twenty and continues into the midforties. In this season, your adult life and future are formed. You will most likely find spouses, have and raise children, expand your established families, and build new traditions. You will acquire friends based on them having similar ambitions, aspirations, and social status to yourself. You begin to accumulate personal wealth. Homes, furniture, and automobiles will be purchased, all with a distinctive style that becomes part of your family makeup. You will find jobs, hopefully, careers that you are passionate about and want to pursue for a lifetime. And if you are some of the most fortunate few, you will start saving a few dollars for the future.

These are also the professional formative years in which you work hard, try to be noticed by your superiors, and strive to move up the food chain of life. In the early years of summer, you will be moving at lightning speed, concentrating on your marriage, raising children, and working long hours to move forward with your career. In the later years of summer, many of us begin to look forward to the autumn or fall season and what we have done to set up for this next season, while still others will slow down, looking back with regret and wishing they had a second chance to start over after spring's completion. Their mantra will be the regretful "If only I had it to do over again!"

Fall and winter are usually the shortest of all the seasons of life. Fall begins somewhere in the mid to late forties and continues into the early sixties. This is a time for building stability in your life. Career is still very important, and job security is paramount at this stage of your life experience. Most people in this season are making the most money they have ever made to this point in their lifetime. In the fall season, age starts to become a major factor in your marketability. You can no longer leave a job and quickly get another based on your knowledge, ability, or track record, regardless the strength of your skill set. Irrespective of your standing within a company, at this point in your career, your name is part of most, if not all, succession planning conversations. Your main contribution from this point forward will be to mentor and develop the leaders who will follow in your footsteps, ensuring the future strength of your company. You will become a trainer for the next generation. And for the first time in your work life, you are likely to be working for a boss or supervisor who is younger than yourself. That person will likely not be a baby boomer but, rather, a millennial or from generation X or generation Y, with ideas and a management style that is not in line with your own.

This is a season in which many of the baby boomers have been forced off a cliff based on economic conditions, salary reductions based on high unemployment in their industry, and a difference in management philosophy. Your opinion because of your past management experience will most likely be dated and irrelevant moving forward.

The final season of life is winter. This is when we are hopefully able to retire and enjoy family, grandchildren, travels, and giving back to society. This should be a season for enjoying the fruits of our labors.

Unfortunately, and sometimes because of circumstances beyond our control, this becomes a season of loneliness and regret as some reflect on those things they could have or should have done to prepare better for winter. Most of us will spend an inordinate amount of our time in winter reflecting and reliving both the good and bad times we've enjoyed and endured as we grew older. We will, at some point, all resign ourselves to the fact that we are old and that our end-time is near.

I am in the winter of my life. My hopes and aspirations for retirement had been what inspired me to continue working harder than I probably needed to in my last years of employment.

Since a very young age, I've always known that life is simply a matter of choices. Some choices reaped reward, while others only harvested regret. But I had plans and was confident that everything I had planned for would come to fruition as my work career ended and I entered the winter of my life. But none of us really know what the future holds for us.

I, like all of you, am a product of my parents. So to understand my story, you must go back a little further and see what influences they had in my life. They are the real start of my story.

"Welcome to the United States of America!" This phrase has greeted millions of incoming immigrants to the bountiful U.S.A. for over two hundred years. Whether they come by land, sea, or air, everyone enters this land of opportunity with a smile on their face and the hope for overwhelming prosperity in their heart. It was no different for my mother and father.

My parents came to the United States through Canada. My father was born in Canada, and my mother in Norway. Both sides of my family are deeply entrenched in their Scandinavian ancestry. The family surname, Larsen, has a lineage that dates back prior to the times of Erik Thorvaldsson, better known as "Erik the Red," who lived in approximately AD 900. I would learn early in life that Viking blood runs deep in all of us born under the Larsen moniker.

For as far back as I can remember, I've been told stories of my grandfathers, my uncles on both sides, and my dad detailing a magnitude of adventures and crazy dilemmas they were involved in over the years prior to my birth. All these stories, at some point, would include a reference to Norsemen superiority that all family members seemed to truly believe existed purely based on our genealogy.

Both families were devout Lutheran Christians, and they loathed those who practiced the Catholic faith, although they couldn't articulate why. When asked why, the only answer that seemed consistent was that it had been that way for generations. Another Norwegian tradition was a built-in animosity for any person of

Swedish descent. Deserved or not, Swedes were the butt of many, if not most, Norwegian jokes.

Thinking back on those stories now, I have a better appreciation for how easy it has always been to brainwash young children. Because these narratives come from the ones we love and trust most, the gullibility of our youth causes the offspring of all ethnicities to not question their parents. As I have matured over the years, I have come to believe that this may be one of the essential elements and the root causes of bigotry, religious wars, and gender inequality throughout the world.

I am of the opinion that if you were to take children that were less than six months old from one culture and dropped them anywhere in the world, they would learn that language, develop that area's belief system, and adopt that specific culture as their own. Muslim babies could be brought up as Christians and vice versa. Asian babies would thrive in African American or Caucasian families, taking on the cultural differences in stride because of their current and unique life experiences.

For me, this manifested itself primarily because my parents and grandparents were so deep seated in their traditions and heritage that I bought into their illusion of race superiority for the first season of my life.

Both sets of my grandparents uprooted their families in Norway and traveled to Canada in the late 1920s. In 1926, my mother's family settled in Calgary, where my grandmother worked as a nurse and my grandfather worked in a butcher shop. On my father's side, his family moved to the small town of Kindersley, Saskatchewan, in 1928. This was farm country, and they were able to buy and cultivate three hundred acres of land as they had done for generations in Norway.

Both families had huge households by today's standards. My father was the youngest of sixteen children, and he was one of only three children born in Canada. All his other siblings were birthed in

Norway. My mother had fourteen children in her immediate family. She and one other sister were adopted in Canada by the Jorgensen family after her birth parents were killed in a tornado. She had been two years old when this misfortune had occurred.

Both patriarchs, based on their long-held cultural roots, were extremely chauvinistic and controlling. My grandfathers were the masters of their own clans, and no one in the household dared challenge their authority. The boys and young men of both families worked either in factories or on farms. The girls and women worked around the home, cooking, cleaning, or doing whatever tasks they were instructed to do by parents or older siblings. Everyone lived at home, and if they worked, they contributed a substantial portion of their earnings to the household coffers until they were ready to marry. Only then were they allowed to leave the nest and start new lives away from the family. For the girls, courting was much more difficult because of the scrutiny being exercised by not only their fathers but several of their older brothers as well.

Life was far from glorious for either of my parents as they grew up in the '30s and very early '40s. In 1929, the Great Depression gripped first the United States and then the remainder of the world. They didn't know it at the time, but the two families may have been fortunate to be living in Canada as the Great Depression wasn't quite as severe there as it was in the United States. With unemployment at 27 percent nationally in Canada, they all felt blessed to put food on the table during those turbulent years.

My mother grew up in the city with many more comforts than my father had on their family farm. She was able to easily walk the short distance from home to school. She was also competent in helping with chores around the house. She did much of the cooking for her family from an early age.

My father, however, lived a much different lifestyle. On the farm, my father's clan had a well for fresh water in the backyard, and they used an outhouse as their only toilet for as long as he lived there.

Indoor plumbing, a commode, and a septic tank weren't installed until 1943 at the Larsen farmstead.

Dad rode a horse twelve miles to school every day, regardless if it was raining, snowing, or beautifully sunny outside. As some of the older brothers left to start families of their own, my father spent more and more time working on the family farm, which continued to grow as they continued to purchase more land when farming was good.

My father quit school after completing the seventh grade because my grandfather needed him to work full time on the farm. Several of his older siblings had struck out to start families and begin lives of their own. It was simply a matter of needed hands to work the farm that caused my father to stop his education at the time. He thought he would be going back to school, but instead, he worked diligently for the next six years on the farm.

Being the youngest in the family, Dad had learned early on how to scrap and hold his own with his older brothers. He was pound for pound one of the toughest kids in Kindersley. Very few lads, including boys much older than himself, wanted to be involved in an altercation with him. As he continued to grow in years and strength, not even his older brothers wanted to provoke him.

Unfortunately, on occasion, his older brothers would give him some of the alcohol they made from fermented corn as the weekend began. He didn't always handle alcohol well. His Viking heritage seemed to kick in a little too intensely when he drank hard liquor. If he was drinking and went into town on a Saturday night, trouble usually found him, even if he wasn't looking for it. He was escorted out of town by the Kindersley constable on more than one occasion for fighting and being disorderly.

One night, he made the mistake of hitting the constable during one of those trips. He was put in jail, and one of his brothers was sent to bring their father back into town. When my grandfather arrived, he apologized for his son's behavior and plopped down half of a suckling pig on the constable's desk. He then politely asked if he could take his son home, assuring the constable that he would punish his boy accordingly.

And punish him he did. My father was forbidden from going into town for six months after that fracas. He worked seven days a week for the six months before he could have a break from his chores and duties on the farm. Eventually, the incident blew over, and farm life began to normalize for everyone.

However, things were not going as well for my mother's family. First, Grandpa lost his job at the butcher shop because of a severe slowdown in business. Few people could afford to pay the price for meat as the depression deepened in Canada. They couldn't have had any idea at the time that circumstances were going to get much worse before they got better. My grandfather searched for employment daily, but it was a very difficult time to find work in Calgary. He worked some odd day jobs, but steady work was not available as the depression continued its stranglehold on the world.

As well, because of the depression, the general public had little or no money to pay for medical services they received. Still, no one who needed medical attention was turned away by Grandma's hospital in Calgary. But the hospital had to make huge layoffs to their staff if they wanted their doors to remain open for the sick and needy. Grandma became a casualty of the ever-increasing unemployed about eight months after my grandfather lost his job at the butcher shop.

My grandparents were frugal people, and even without jobs, they were in better shape than most of the families around them. But with so many mouths to feed and minimal money coming in, they knew they had to do something different quickly if they were to survive.

A nurse who'd become a good friend and had also been laid off from the Calgary hospital wrote a letter to my grandma telling her of good-paying nursing positions at a new hospital in Bothell, Washington, in the United States. Bothell was a small farming community about twenty miles north of Seattle. She suggested that my grandmother get a work visa and come to the United States, where she could work and send money back to her family. After much discussion between my grandparents, my grandmother did move to the United States for what she assumed would be a temporary period. She'd applied for the position, was accepted, and began her nursing assignment two months after receiving the letter from her friend.

It was a stressful time for the entire family, but particularly for Grandma. Here she was in a foreign country without any family and friends. She told my father several years later that she worked as many hours as she was allowed, ate sparse meals, and cried herself to sleep for the first four months she was in America. But she was able to send money back to Calgary weekly to help the family with housing and food costs. As uncomfortable as she was being separated from her family in this new country, she knew in her heart that this job was truly a godsend.

While working one day at the hospital, Grandma overheard a doctor she'd grown to admire and respect tell another physician that his father had passed away, leaving a rather large farm to him. He was complaining that he couldn't sell it because no one had the money to buy it, and he didn't know anyone who could run it and keep it in working condition.

In passing, my grandma asked how big the farm was and what he was looking for in a caretaker. It turned out that the living quarters consisted of a main house and two bunk cabins for hired hands. It was easily large enough for Grandma's entire family, and the location was only seven miles from the hospital in Bothell.

The farm consisted of various livestock that were being raised for their meat. There was even an on-site butcher shed that was used to prepare the meat for market.

Grandma asked him if her family could manage the ranch, noting that her husband was a butcher by trade. After some negotiating, they came to an agreement that was beneficial to all parties, and her family prepared for the move from Calgary to the United States. It was an answer to all my grandparents' prayers! Once acclimated and after living in their new residence for two years, the whole family applied for United States citizenship and became American citizens some years later.

My mother had a pretty good grasp of the English language by the time her family left Canada and moved to Washington State. She started high school in Bothell. She'd made a lot of new friends at school in her first two years in Bothell, but she always felt guilty for not contributing financially to the family finances. She had two younger sisters and one younger brother who were also in school, which put an enormous stress on her two older brother and three sisters to help Grandpa on the farm. The rest of her siblings had already left home.

One day, while walking home from school, she noticed a sign in the window of one of the two cafés in town advertising for a waitress. She applied and was hired immediately. My mom quit school in the middle of her junior year of high school to go to work at what was to become her life's calling. She felt blessed to have stumbled onto this opportunity with so many people still out of work because of the economic plunge, both locally and around the world. But she was even more grateful to be bringing home some money and helping provide for the family.

World War II started for Canada on September 10, 1939. Within two months, the first contingents of Canadian troop arrived in England to supplement the British Expeditionary Forces. The war marked the end of the depression era as all countries began opening factories to fuel their individual war machines.

Even though he knew it would put a strain on the farm, my father told my grandpa that he was going to enlist and fight for Canada. He had just turned eighteen, and he, along with his older brother Alfred, joined the Royal Canadian Navy. After boot camp, he was assigned to the RCN Pacific Fleet at Esquimalt base, on Vancouver Island, BC. The base was home to fifteen vessels and six thousand sailors and support staff. Dad was assigned to the HMS *Uganda*, a cruiser that patrolled the West Coast searching for German submarines.

The Royal Canadian Navy took on an even more important role after December 7, 1941, when the nation of Japan all but destroyed the United States fleet in Pearl Harbor, Hawaii. The fifteen Canadian vessels were now the remaining protection for the West Coast from not only Germany but also a Japanese invasion. Their job was to protect the coastline and ensure that the major west coast harbors of Vancouver, Seattle, San Francisco, Los Angeles, and San Diego remained open and were protected from submarine attack.

Years later, when asked about what happened during those years on the *Uganda*, my father would say very little. Generally, he would praise the use of flushing toilets and speak of his intense distaste for mutton, which was the main protein source while they were at sea.

While on a seventy-two-hour shore leave in Seattle, my father and a couple of his compatriots partied and caught their first glimpses of America. Coming from the small town of Kindersley, Saskatchewan, Seattle was amazing and awe inspiring. My father had never seen so many buildings, so many people, so many automobiles, so much activity, or so many lights in and on buildings and streets in his life.

As they explored the city and surrounding countryside, they decided to stop for a quick lunch in the small town of Bothell, about twenty miles outside of Seattle. Pulling into town, they stopped at the first café they came to for lunch.

As the three sailors sat down, the waitress, who, some years later, would become my mother, came over to wait on them. To his dying day, my father's eyes would light up when he recounted their first meeting. He said that the first time he heard her voice, it was as if he were listening to an angel.

"Here are some menus. Can I get you, gentlemen, anything to drink while you decide what you would like to eat?"

Looking up, he saw my mother for the first time, a smile on her face and the brightest blue eyes he had ever seen. Both of his companions asked for coffee, but my father was dumbstruck and did not respond. Still waiting for an answer, she asked again, "And for you, sir?"

One of his buddies elbowed my dad and then looked back at the attractive waitress and responded, "He'll have a cup of coffee too!" With that response, her smile broadened as she turned and started back toward the kitchen.

"What's up with you?" asked one of his fellow sailors, as Dad sat and stared after their server walking back around the lunch counter to get their coffee. He didn't answer as he continued to watch for her return.

The waitress returned shortly with three cups of coffee, set them on the table, and pulled out a pad and pencil to write down their orders. "What would you like to eat, guys?" she asked.

Before he knew he'd said it out loud, my father muttered, "Hun er vakker!" Norwegian for "She is beautiful!"

My mother blushed, smiled faintly, and replied, "Takk skal du ha," which simply means "Thank you!" The other sailors looked questioningly at each other, hearing a language they couldn't identify.

My father's mouth fell open, and he responded in English, "You speak Norwegian?"

She crossed her arms and replied in English, "Of course, I do. I am Norwegian."

"So am I!" said my father excitedly. "Can I ask your name?"

"My name is Lila," she responded. "What is your name?"

"Eirik, Eirik Larsen," replied my father. "I and my family live in Kindersley, Saskatchewan. We have a farm there."

"I grew up in Calgary, Alberta!" responded my mom excitedly.

"Wow, small world," stated Dad enthusiastically, smiling up at my mother. They both stared smilingly at one another, neither saying a word for several seconds.

"I'll have a ham sandwich with some potato salad, if it's good," said one of the other two sailors.

"I'll have the same," said the other.

The lunch orders broke the uncomfortable silence, and Lila started writing them down. Looking up, she said, "And what would you like, Eirik?"

"I haven't looked at the menu yet, so I'll have what everyone else is having. Oh, and a piece of apple pie for desert, if you have one," responded my father.

My mom smiled again and said, "I think we can do that." Putting her pad and pencil back in her apron pocket, she turned and headed back toward the kitchen.

"What's gotten into you?" asked one of Dad's companions as the waitress walked away. "You're acting like a kid who has never seen a girl before!"

"Are you kidding!" Dad responded. "She is gorgeous!"

After finishing their lunch, Lila brought the bill. "Will there be anything else, gentlemen?"

Everyone at the table shook their heads no. The sailors divided the bill so each could pay his share and then gave the money and the bill back to Lila. As they got up to leave, my father walked over to the lunch counter, waiting for Lila to finish with other customers and walk back toward him. As she neared him, he asked, "Would it be too bold to ask what time you get off work today?"

"Why?" she answered inquisitively.

"I was hoping we could talk, and maybe I could walk you home, if that's OK."

"I don't get off work for three more hours," she countered.

"If I wait, can I walk you home, then?" asked Eirik.

A sheepish smile crossed her face and her cheeks reddened as she softly replied, "I guess that would be OK."

As she walked away from the counter, she felt her heart beating faster than she could ever remember. She had never had the time for a boyfriend, never been walked home by a boy, never even wanted to be walked home by a boy!

Her next thoughts were what her mom and dad would say if she came walking up to the house arm in arm with a stranger in a Canadian Navy uniform. How would she introduce him?

She suddenly realized she didn't know anything about him or if he was even a trustworthy person. As so many thoughts swirled around in her subconscious, she began to think that she had made a terrible mistake by agreeing to let him walk her home. Nothing could come of this, so why waste the time with someone she would never see again after today? But every time she looked in his direction, he was looking at her, and his smile only grew larger each time they made eye contact.

Finally, her shift ended for the day. To Lila, it had seemed that time had gone agonizingly slow for the last three hours. But now that her workday was finished, she felt a surge of panic knowing she had made a commitment to a stranger that she felt obligated to keep. Taking in a deep breath, she turned and walked to the lunch counter where Eirik sat and calmly asked, "Are you ready to go?"

"Yes" was the only word out of his mouth as he stood, put on his coat, and followed Lila out the front door.

Eirik took hold of her bicycle and steered it as they began the forty-five-minute walk from the restaurant toward the farm. Conversation came much easier than either one of them had expected. After only a few minutes, they were talking freely and laughing together as they made their way to Lila's house.

A short distance from the front gate, Lila's worst nightmare was realized as she saw her father standing in the front yard. When he finally noticed the two of them, he stopped what he was doing and walked slowly down the fence line toward the front gate. All three of them arrived at the main gate to the farm simultaneously.

"Good evening, sir," Eirik said in Norwegian, as he stuck his hand out to shake.

"Good evening to you," replied Lila's father in his native tongue as well, extending his hand and gripping Eirik's. They shook hands firmly, each measuring the strength in the other man's squeeze.

After shaking hands, both men turned their heads toward Lila, as if they expected her to put an end to their awkwardness with an explanation of why Eirik was here. Her cheeks flushed crimson, and she felt dampness on her upper lip as she realized her social ineptitude was quickly being replaced by unnerving terror while no one spoke.

Watching panic overtaking her expression, Eirik introduced himself to her father, again speaking in Norwegian. "My name is Eirik Larsen, and I am in the Royal Canadian Navy. I am assigned to the HMS *Uganda*, a combat cruiser. We have been deployed to ensure the Pacific coastline is safe from enemy attack. Before I joined the navy, I worked on our family farm with my father and brothers in Kindersley, Saskatchewan. I am on a three-day leave in Seattle, so a couple of my mates and I stopped to have lunch in the café where Lila works while we were doing some exploring. By accident, I discovered that your daughter speaks Norwegian, and we exchanged pleasantries. It was the first time I have spoken my native tongue to another Norwegian since leaving home over a year ago."

"What do you mean you accidentally discovered she speaks Norwegian?" he asked before Eirik could finish what he was saying.

Now it was his turn to blush. He looked at Lila, who was also blushing, and told her father the truth. "The first time I saw your daughter, I mumbled that she was beautiful in Norwegian, and she thanked me for the compliment in our native tongue." Looking back into her father's eyes, he tried to assure her father that he meant this in the most respectful way possible.

Her father slowly smiled as he responded, still speaking Norwegian, "I'll bet that did catch you by surprise." Still grinning, he continued. "We don't see many folks here that are from Canada or Norway. Have you got time to stay and have dinner with us?"

My father's response was a simple "Yes." And with that straightforward retort, the relationship between my mother and father began. Neither one of them could have known at the time that on that day, a love affair began that would last for the next fifty-seven years.

When the war was over, Eirik only stayed in Canada for three months. He applied for American citizenship and, six months later, moved to Seattle, found work in the Everett shipyards, and married Lila. They lived in Seattle for two years before my father decided the real opportunities for prosperity were in California. They had saved enough money to buy a reliable used car and some creature comforts in that relatively short time. With a few dollars in their pockets and little else, they left Bothell to make a new life in California.

My parents moved to a small town in Southern California, where I was born. Indio was in the California desert, just twenty miles from Palm Springs, which would become a favorite vacation destination soon during the winter months for people from around the world.

I was the first born of two boys. My mother tells the story that she and my father were having a "date night" and had gone to an outdoor drive-in movie theater in Palm Springs the night I was born. The outdoor theater was my mom's choice because she was so uncomfortably pregnant with me that she was having a hard time sitting still. They were watching the movie *Tarantula* when I decided to come into the world.

Mom always detailed that she'd been watching the movie for about fifteen minutes when a giant tarantula appeared on the screen; coming from the left side of the screen into a metropolitan setting. The people in the movie began screaming and running in all directions. The spider reached out and plucked a man from the panicked crowd and started rolling him up in spiderweb it produced with its saliva. It scared my mother so badly that she screamed, buried her head in my dad's chest, and jerked back in her seat, immediately realizing that the jolt had caused her water to break.

As she finishes the story, she always remembers to reveal that my father wanted to stay for the rest of the movie and asked her if she would try to be strong and make it through the movie, or at least hang in there until her contractions started coming closer together.

My dad always had a smirk on his face when that part of the story was brought up. But after knowing my father for a lifetime, I am reasonably sure that my mom's account was spot-on.

I had heard this story more than enough in my lifetime; but it seemed as though every time our family got together for my birthday, regardless how old I was to be, I would have to relive the tale as Mom narrated it to anyone who would listen to her tell it yet again.

On March 8, 1947, I was brought into the world as Michael David Larsen to my parents, Eirik and Lila Larsen. I was born in the Palm Springs hospital at 11:30 p.m., and based on my mom's recollection, I came into the world with only one mission—and that was to eat.

My father had been driving a taxicab in Indio, putting in long hours to try and make a decent living for the three of us when he got the news from Mom that there was another baby on the way. Unfortunately, he was having a hard time making ends meet no matter how many hours a day he worked driving cab to feed three, soon to be four, mouths.

Through a fare he'd picked up one day, Dad found out about a job working for a construction company. He applied as a truck driver and got the job. He lied and said that he could drive a truck and trailer combination, and in less than a week, he was driving dump trucks with trailers for his new employer, Redlands Asphalt. It only took a few days to become familiar with driving the truck. His experiences with farm machinery earlier in his life had shortened his learning curve.

Redlands Asphalt had multiple contracts with the state of California to build new freeways throughout the Los Angeles basin over the next several years. Just a short time after my little brother

CHAPTER 2

I had just turned two years old when we moved from Indio to Beaumont, California. At that early age, I obviously didn't retain many memories of occurrences happening around me. But my mother kept a five-by-eight framed picture of me sitting on her dresser for as long as I lived at home.

You could tell that my hair had been bleached blond from the sun and that I had a pretty dark tan for being a fair-haired Norwegian boy. As I sat smiling into the camera, it was also notable that my mom had been right about me being a good eater as my pose always reminded me of a little Buddha with my shirtless protruding belly with chunky arms and fat little legs.

When we would look at the picture together, my mother told me that in my early days, she'd had to watch me closely as I became quite the hunter. She voiced that I loved being outside, running around, trying to catch and eat cockroaches, spiders, and horny toads, which could all be found in and around our desert home.

But my first real cognitive recollections go back to about four years old. By that time, we had been in Beaumont for almost two years. My little brother had started crawling, and he was become annoying for me. My parents, my brother, and I all had our own bedrooms. My parents had either purposely or accidentally already provided a much nicer home for us than either one of them had lived in while growing up.

I remember making friends with the kids next door and playing outside with them until dark. Connie and Billy Marshall became my constant companions and close friends for the first few years of my young life. When my brother got a little older, he became the fourth in our band of renegades. We had our two yards and three hundred acres of wheat fields behind our houses to play in every day. Even though we weren't supposed to go there, we would crawl under a barbed wire fence and cross an irrigation ditch, which was dry most of the time, and we were free to roam acres of open space and create imaginary play scenarios in the wide-open spaces of the field. Sometimes, we played cowboys and Indians, sometimes it was war games, and if the grain was high enough, we played hide-and-go-seek or tag.

In the fall, after the crops were harvested and the fields were freshly plowed, we would dig deep holes to make individual forts. We would choose teams and play war, ducking into the first available foxhole, looking for cover when attacked. Dirt clods and dried cow pies were our weapons of choice as we aspired to achieve total world domination.

Billy was the oldest of our group, being three years older than me. I idolized him all through grade school. He taught me how to make a slingshot from a forked tree branch and a strong piece of rubber, usually a piece of inner tube from an old car tire. We also made our own bows and arrows to play cowboys and Indians from junk we found around our houses.

We would meet in the backyard between 8:00 a.m. and 9:00 a.m. on weekends, have lunch at one of our homes in the early afternoon, and go back out to play until one or the other's mom called us in for dinner. If we got thirsty, we drank from the garden hoses at one of our homes. Unless you needed to use the bathroom, there was no other reason to go inside a house during the weekends.

But my favorite times were when Billy and I would simply lie in the foxholes out in the wheat fields with our hands clasped behind our heads, talking to each other about life as we stared up at the sky. We would watch the clouds float by as we tried to spot an occasional airplane passing overhead and talked about what we wanted to be when we grew up. Billy always wanted to be an airplane pilot, but I jumped all over the place. I wanted to be a fireman and then a helicopter pilot and, finally, a veterinarian as I recall.

It's curious how things turn out in life. Billy joined the air force right out of high school, achieved his college degree while serving his country, and eventually became a fighter pilot. He stayed in the armed services for twenty years, retired, and became a commercial pilot for American Airlines as his second career. I, on the other hand, never entered any of the professions I had so strongly aspired to become during those conversations.

Those days are still wonderful memories for me, and when I reflect on them, they always put a smile on my face. But when I contemplate those memorable occurrences, it's hard to relate them to how my son grew up or to compare them to the even more drastic changes I've seen in the rearing of my grandchildren.

As an example, my father brought home our first television set when I was seven years old. Until that time, our evening entertainment consisted of simply talking with one another or maybe playing a card game with our parents. My brother and I learned how to play cards and checkers at a very early age, and we were formidable opponents by the time we were in grade school. After my father purchased and brought home the TV, we could watch an hour of television nightly before we went to bed. We only had three channels available, ABC, NBC, and CBS. That was it! No HBO, no MTV, no ESPN, nor fifty other channels to choose from. We watched the nightly news and kept up on a few selected weekly series like *Gunsmoke*, *Bonanza*, and *The Ed Sullivan* variety show, *Amos 'n' Andy*, and *Walt Disney* on Sunday nights.

Comparing my childhood to raising my son is almost incomprehensible. Making toys for himself was a completely foreign concept. He wanted toys for sure, but they were toys he'd seen advertised on TV while eating breakfast and watching a big purple dinosaur named Barney or the *Sesame Street* show. Toys like Hot Wheels cars, Three-Wheeler cycles, and Lincoln Log building blocks had all become necessities. He "needed" to have these items because his friends all had them. When my son was six and through his ninth year, he played outside for a couple of hours a day at best but spent most of his day playing in his room with the newest toy craze that we had supplied for him.

He spent two or more hours sitting in front of the TV, and that television time seemed to increase exponentially with each year that passed. By the time he was in high school, he would come into the house, walk straight over to the TV, turn it on, and then walk to the refrigerator, take out something to eat or drink, walk back to the sofa, plop down, and stare at whatever was his favorite program on that day until we either made him turn it off or called him to the table for dinner. From high school on, little changed in our household until he started college.

And as time marched on, he married, and my grandchildren were born. The world continued to invent more sophisticated toys and develop new technologies such as computers, smartphones, and tablets. In their early lives, our grandkids were literally raised by television as both parents worked to provide a better life for their families. The kids went to day care after school and were picked up by one parent or the other on the way home from work.

As this next generation continued to mature, they became more and more self-absorbed and isolated. Their entertainment, if not their very lives, became immersed in smartphones, social media, and online friends they would never meet face-to-face.

They were not assigned chores, never had to work or even look for gainful employment, rarely spoke to each other, hardly ever played outside, and seldom ate as a family unit, and fast food became a way of life for them. Thank God for progress!

Drinking water from a garden water hose? Yes! I drank water from a garden hose all my life as I grew up at home. But not my grandkids, and now not their parents either. They now only drank bottled spring or mineral water.

My grandfather would turn over in his grave if he knew that his offspring, those descendants of a fierce Viking heritage, would pay a dollar each for a plastic twelve-ounce bottle filled simply with water.

He'd pulled water up from a well, drunk it without boiling it, and then used the remainder to bathe or wash dishes. Now the Larsen bloodline wouldn't even drink water from a faucet that was coming through lines supplied by a water treatment plant. Instead, they bought case after case of water from a local Costco. How ridiculously soft had humanity become in just three generations?

I unfortunately followed in my father's footsteps in school. Every year, I seemed to get in more and more trouble from my teachers for either talking too much or acting up in class. We didn't have the availability of mental diagnoses in those days. But if tests had been available, I am sure I would have tested positive for ADHD or some similar prognosis. Academically, school was easy for me. But socially, it was much more of a test.

Unfortunately, I also drew the short straw by having Miss Buckman as my first-grade teacher. I'd been told by my neighbor Billy Marshall that she was a mean old woman who hated kids. It didn't take long for me to agree with his assessment.

She made me stay in her classroom and eat my lunch at my desk several days a week to ensure that I practiced my cursive writing. She constantly told me that I could be so much more if I would just put in the effort and apply myself.

Today, I am constantly complimented on what beautiful handwriting I have, so I guess I really should have thanked her for the time she invested in me early on.

If she caught me talking, she would march back to my desk, grab hold of and twist my ear, pulling me out of my desk, and then lead me to a desk in the front of the classroom she'd designated for "hooligans." The desk faced the blackboard, and whoever was forced to sit in it had his or her back to the rest of the class. It quickly became like my second home.

I didn't like most of the kids in my school, and I didn't like playing with other children if I didn't know them, so I pretty much stayed to myself. I did, however, make a lifetime friend with one other boy by the name of Jimmy Clarke when I was in the first grade, and we've remained friends forever. We were in different classes, but as we grew closer, we sought each other out at recess, and we sat together during lunch if I wasn't detained in Miss Buckman's class that day.

Jimmy and I were both reasonably smart, equally disruptive in class, and in trouble most of the time, but we became inseparable. We were both mischievous, and we tried to outdo each other with new cusswords we learned daily. Jimmy had an advantage because he had three older brothers and two younger sisters, and his brothers taught him all the newest cusswords as they learned them. Jimmy, in turn, taught them to me.

The two of us spent so much time together that I no longer played much with Billy and Connie Marshall on the weekends or after school; I now spent most of my spare time with Jimmy. We were at each other's house so often that our mothers finally met. They hit it off, and eventually, our parents went out to dinner together, and we all became family friends.

Jimmy and I hung out to the point that his older brothers were like my older brothers. They were a wild bunch, and they taught Jimmy and me a lot about life, mostly bad stuff, but they became my protectors if times called for such protection. That only happened once when I was bullied by some kids that were two or three years older than me. Jimmy's oldest brothers, a set of twins named Terry and Larry, had a talk, or so they said, with the offending boys to make sure the bullying didn't happen again. Those boys were as nice as could be to me after their supposed talk with the twins.

In our school system, corporal punishment was commonly used if you were guilty of misconduct. Not the type you see on television today where a school guard or teacher rips someone out their desk by the hair and starts beating the hell out of them while every other student in the room records it all on their cell phone camera. It was a much more civilized and progressive punishment. You were warned by the teacher for misbehaving. If a second warning came, it was usually with a promise that you were going to be sent to the principal's office. The third time, you would, in fact, be sent to the principal's office with a note from the teacher. The principal was the only person who doled out the physical discipline.

On a good day, I would be one of four or five kids waiting to see him. Depending on the seriousness of your crime, you would receive several swats from what the principal called his punishment paddle. He would have you bend over and put your hands on your knees and begin the discipline. He didn't really hit that hard, but I remember always walking out of his office with tears streaming down my cheeks.

At the end of swats, he would always have a conversation with you, trying to secure your commitment that you would become a better citizen and never come back to see him again. Unfortunately for me, that conversation turned more into "Until I see you next time, Michael."

I believe I still have the school record for the most swats in any given year. I achieved that recognition while I was in the third grade. I doubt the principal was ever in better physical condition than that year. I gave him a great workout, at least his right arm, for my nine months' stay in the third grade.

One Saturday night, my parents had Jimmy's parents over to our house to play pinochle. Jimmy and his two little sisters came over as well. While the adults played cards in the kitchen, we watched television in the living room. The girls were seated on one of our two sofas, while Jimmy and I were lying sprawled out on the floor in front of the TV.

When they finished playing cards, both sets of parents came into the living room as Art and Louise were ready to go home. The girls pleaded to stay until the episode of *Gunsmoke* we were watching finished. They agreed to stay for the short time remaining in the program, and both sets of parents sat on separate sofas.

In the program, Marshall Dillon was shot in the arm by an outlaw with a shotgun. He turned slightly upon being hit, pulled out his revolver, and shot the cattle rustler dead. Jimmy jumped up off the floor like he'd been shot out of a bottle rocket and yelled, "That is so fake! If he was shot with a real shotgun, it would have blown his whole fucking arm off!" Then realizing what he had just said, he followed it up with "Oops!" as he covered his mouth. I couldn't contain myself and cracked up laughing.

Neither one of us knew what the word meant, but we had heard Jimmy's older brothers use it more than a few times. A second after the outburst, Art was up off the couch, jerked Jimmy to his feet, and started swatting him across his backside while I continued to roar hysterically.

Once Art decided he had dished out enough punishment to Jimmy, who stood there wailing, he reached down, yanked me up to my feet, and began spanking me next! I assume it was because I was laughing, but in seconds, the laughter turned to tears as I danced around the room, trying to avoid the next smack from his big hand! The only thing that really got hurt that night was our pride. But I guarantee you that we were much more careful with our language around adults from that day forward.

It seems strange to me now how different adults were with kids in those days versus today's generation. One day, Jimmy and I were walking in downtown Beaumont, and he was talking about one of his brothers. He called Larry a son of a bitch. We had just walked past a man and his wife, not paying any attention to them as we talked. On hearing the swear words, the man whirled around and said sharply, "Hey, there is a lady here! You two apologize for using that kind of language right now, or I'm going to whip you both!"

Startled, Jimmy and I reeled to see the man making his way back toward us. Simultaneously, Jimmy and I replied, "Sorry, ma'am!" He stopped moving toward us and pointed at Jimmy.

"I know your dad, son, and if he knew you used that kind of language, he would wash your mouth out with soap! So clean up your language, and if I ever hear you cussing like that again in public, I will have a talk with Art myself! Do you understand me?"

We both replied, "Yes, sir." Then Jimmy added, "It won't happen again!"

Satisfied, the gentleman turned, took his wife's arm, and walked away from us, never looking back.

Contrast that to three boys on the news in Baltimore, Maryland, last week who were using much worse language in a crowded local mall filled with mothers, kids, and elderly Christmas shoppers. One man had heard enough and asked the boys to clean up their language or at least keep it down around the kids. His comments turned into an argument, which quickly escalated into an altercation in which the single man was beaten and stabbed three times and then left bleeding on the marble floors as the boys all ran out the nearest exit.

The respect for adult authority we had as a culture when I was young is all but gone today. You listened to every adult, not just your own parents, and you risked punishment if you disrespected them.

Parents and adults in today's world don't intervene in most situations out of fear for themselves. Even though many times adults know something should be done or said, fears of physical confrontations prevent most people from interceding.

I didn't realize it when I was younger, but Beaumont in the early '50s and for most of my time, there was a relatively segregated community. I grew up with Caucasian, Filipino, and Mexican friends. Most of the kids in my class had surnames like Lara, Dominguez, or Ricadio. I have no memory of even one African American family living in Beaumont as I grew up. At that time in my life, it didn't seem strange to me that there were no blacks in our schools.

But as we watched the nightly news, we did realize that there was civil unrest in most of the southern part of the United States as the civil rights movement for racial equality was heating up. My parents were already racist by nature in that they both believed the Norwegian race was superior to all others.

In 1950, the U.S. Supreme Court struck down segregation of African Americans in graduate and law schools. That was the beginning of a very turbulent time in America. In 1955, Rosa Parks refused to give up her seat on a bus to a white man, and she was arrested. Blacks launched the Montgomery Bus Boycott in protest of Rosa Parks's arrest. Martin Luther King Jr. rose to prominence as he became the face of the boycott and led nonviolent marches in Montgomery, Alabama.

The news became inundated with stories of violence after four African American churches were bombed in Montgomery, and the homes of civil rights leaders, Martin Luther King Jr., Ralph Abernathy, and E. D. Nixon were all burned to the ground. Those protests and the violence across the south were all brought to us every night on live national TV. While there were forces at work to promote equality, the network news coverage seemed to promote a white-versus-back mentality.

On the other side of the country, it was no different for us in Beaumont. People didn't talk about it out loud, but our white and brown community didn't want to add blacks to the color mix. More than once, I overheard my mother say, "Why won't those Negros just stop with their protests and all their riots?" Usually, the phrase was uttered while we were watching a group of police officers beating the hell out of defenseless African American men and women with clubs while the latter were peacefully marching in the street on the national nightly news.

There were no Lutheran churches in Beaumont, so my parents took us to a Lutheran church in Banning, which was approximately five miles east of Beaumont. In Banning, African American families were welcomed and lived in a mixed racial community. It was there that I first met and was able to interact with my first black family. I didn't think anything of Negros being in our church when I was young, but it was not lost on me, especially as I grew older, that the African American families stayed to themselves and that those of us from Beaumont were cordial but really had nothing to do with them if we could avoid it.

My brother and I were instructed not to eat the food brought by Negro families to our church potlucks. I asked why my parents felt that way once and was told that they eat differently than we do, and my parents didn't want us to get sick.

If we as kids started to play with black children at a church picnic or other church functions, we were usually told to stop horsing around by a parent, and not necessarily our own. Banning and Beaumont seemed to be as divided as the north and south were in their philosophies on civil rights.

In the summer, after completing the third grade, I started mowing other people's lawns for spending money. My parents had developed a good work ethic in both my brother and me at an early age. My daily chores consisted of making my bed every morning, doing the breakfast dishes before leaving for school, washing and cleaning our front porch on Saturdays, and trimming and mowing the lawn with our old push mower once a week.

Since I was used to mowing our lawn, I thought getting paid to do it for other people in the neighborhood over the summer made sense. Soon, I had eleven customers that I mowed lawns for on a weekly basis. I got used to having a little money in my pocket and started looking for other ways to make even more.

I took on a paper route delivering the *Riverside Enterprise* newspaper when I was nine years old. I inherited fifty-four customers when I took over the paper route. It was my responsibility to deliver papers to all fifty-four houses every morning, seven days a week, 365 days a year, before 7:00 a.m.

After having the route for a year, I had signed up an additional fifty customers, making my route 104 papers that needed to be delivered daily. On Sundays, when the papers were packed with ads and considerably larger, I had to make two trips to deliver papers to everyone because I couldn't carry them all at one time on my bike.

I was making good money for my age and at the same time winning various trips by signing up additional customers. I won trips to Catalina Island twice and Disneyland eighteen times during my paper route delivery business, which lasted about five years.

As I continued to sign up newcustomers, my paper route became unmanageable for one person. I split the route in half and gave the half that was farthest away from my house to my little brother. He wasn't nearly as good a paperboy as I was. He hated to get up early, and often, his papers were delivered late. I still mowed lawns for several of his newspaper customers, and they all stated that they wished I was still delivering their morning paper.

Life was simple in Beaumont at that time. We didn't go to the grocery store for all our food while I was growing up. Milk was delivered to our doorstep on Mondays and Thursdays from a dairy farm.

Three houses down, but on the other side of our street, Mrs. Clement raised twenty chickens behind her house. Every Tuesday, I would walk over to her house and buy three dozen brown eggs for a dollar and fifty cents. For some unknown reason, my mother preferred the brown eggs to the white ones.

One block the other way on Eighth Street lived Mr. and Mrs. Perkins. Mrs. Perkins baked bread and rolls every day and sold her goods to people in the neighborhood. We usually bought our bread on Fridays, because Friday was the only day she also baked cinnamon rolls. Bread was twenty-five cents a loaf, but eight fat cinnamon rolls cost fifty cents. I can still remember walking toward the Perkins's house and smelling the wonderful aroma of fresh baked bread and cinnamon rolls. Even now, seventy plus years later, the thought of those smells still makes my mouth water.

By the time I was in the fifth grade, I had become quite used to having money all the time. Jimmy was always borrowing money from me, mostly because he never worked to have any of his own. He never paid me back, but I didn't care. After all, he was my best friend. Life had been good for me so far, no real trauma, drama, or bad experiences, but that was all about to change.

It was in the early spring, and I had just turned eleven when I first experienced death on a personal level. Shortly after my eleventh birthday, Jimmy and I were in my backyard when we noticed several people jumping out of an airplane with parachutes on and floating down into the freshly plowed field behind my house. I assumed they had permission from the owner because the new crop of wheat hadn't been planted yet. We raced to the fence, crawled under it, and ran out into the field to get a better view.

The plane made big wide circles, and the engine was working very hard as it climbed higher and higher. Just before it was above our field, it would get noticeably quieter and seemed to level off. As the plane slowed, two or three people at a time would jump out and rocket toward the earth. They would fall at a high rate of speed for what seemed like an eternity, and then their parachutes would deploy, jerking them almost to a stop as their marshmallow-looking chutes filled with air. They floated with various bright-colored parachutes in tight circles as they moved closer and closer to the earth, finally touching down in the soft dirt of the field with a small poof of dust.

As the second set of jumpers hit the ground, Jimmy and I continued to run in their direction to get as close as possible. When we were only about fifty yards away, we stopped and looked up for the plane. The sky was a soft blue with a few scattered white clouds in it as we spied the plane making another approach toward the field.

Cupping our hands over our eyes to keep from looking directly into the sun, we stared up as the plane approached. When it was right over top of us, we saw three people jump out of the side door. I remember thinking to myself how exciting it would be to fly like a bird as they plummeted toward earth.

After a few seconds, one parachute opened, and we watched as his or her decent rapidly slowed. A second later, the second chute opened. But the third sky diver was still hurtling toward earth, and if it was possible, he looked like he was picking up speed as he plunged downward. We both watched, neither of us uttering a word as he got closer and closer to the ground.

I'll never know what happened that day, but as he neared the ground, it was obvious that his parachute was not going to open. He hit the ground thirty yards from where we were standing. A dust cloud shot up, and I could have sworn that he bounced three or four feet back up in the air before coming to rest in the mini crater he had created with his impact. I heard a woman scream and watched as several people came running in our direction.

We stood there, stunned. I couldn't believe how much noise he or she had made when they contacted the ground. It sounded like a small bomb had gone off. The dust was settling around the fallen jumper about the same time the other sky divers arrived to tend to him.

Jimmy and I slowly walked closer as several people tried to help him. They tried to lift him out of the crater, but it looked like they were lifting 150 pounds of Jell-O. We could see a mixture of blood and mud on the back of his jumpsuit, and we knew he was dead.

People were crying. One woman sat next to his lifeless body, screaming and trying to rock him in her arms. Suddenly, one of the men spotted us standing there and yelled, "You kids get out of here. This is no place for you to be right now!" Still in shock at what we had just witnessed, we stood there frozen in place and stared at the body. "Go on!" the same man yelled again. "Get the hell out of here and go home!"

We both ran as fast as we could back to my house. Barging through the back door, we found my mother in the kitchen. Even though we were both out of breath, Jimmy and I began talking fast, loud, and at the same time as we bushwhacked my mom, who was finishing washing dishes. Her look moved back and forth from one of us to the other and then back again as she tried to comprehend what was being said. Unable to make heads or tails of what was being verbalized, she put her hands up to stop us from talking and started asking short pointed questions.

"People were jumping out of an airplane?" she asked.

"Yes!" we both responded, almost yelling.

"And someone fell all the way to the ground?" she continued.

"Yeah, and he's dead!" responded Jimmy before I had time to answer.

"Show me," she said, quickly wiping off her hands with a dish towel.

With that command, we were all out the back door headed toward the barbed wire fence. Jimmy and I were running, and my mom was keeping up surprisingly well as Jimmy and I reached the fence. We started to go under it when we heard a firm "No!" behind us.

"That's close enough!" Mom shouted. As she caught up to us, we all stared across the field where there was considerable commotion now under way. We hadn't even heard the sirens of the fire trucks, but there were two parked on the road just west of the accident with all their lights flashing.

Two firemen were at the scene, while three or four more were making their way through the field in that direction. We watched for five or six minutes, no one saying anything. Finally, four of the firemen loaded the body on a stretcher and placed a white sheet over it. Each taking a corner, they lifted the stretcher and began the walk back through the unsteady terrain to their truck.

"Sweet Jesus," my mother said softly as she raised her hand to her open mouth. "I hope he was a believer and that he's already in heaven." Then looking down at us, she continued. "Are you guys OK? That must have been horrible to see!"

Jimmy and I looked at each other but did not reply. What had started as a great day had turned to one of tragedy that we could never have anticipated. We had been running on adrenaline for the past half hour, but the reality that we had watched another human being die today was beginning to sink in for both of us. My mother turned back toward the house, putting one arm around my shoulder and the other lovingly around Jimmy's shoulder. We began the slow walk back, no one saying a word, each of us lost in our own thoughts.

In May of that same year, May 18 to be exact, both Jimmy and I would experience death again, only this time on a much more personal level. May 18 was on a Saturday that year, and like most Saturdays, Jimmy rode his bike to my house, and we were playing in the backyard.

A couple of weeks earlier, I had helped Jimmy make a slingshot for himself. We made a makeshift target and taped it onto our burn barrel out by the barbed wire fence in the backyard. This was our third time practicing with our homemade weapons, and we were getting pretty good at hitting the bull's-eye if we were within twenty feet or so of the target. We had an endless supply of small dirt clods and rocks for ammunition.

While gathering a new pile of ammo, I glanced back to see both Jimmy's mom and my mom walking toward us. Jimmy's mom had been crying because her nose and eyes were red, and she kept patting a handkerchief to one or the other. When they reached us, Louise looked at Jimmy and simply said, "Come on, we have to go home now."

Jimmy asked, "What's wrong, Momma?"

Louise dabbed her eyes again and replied, "We can talk about it at home. Let's go, son." With that, she turned around, and my mother put her arm around Louise's shoulder as they started back toward the house.

Jimmy and I followed, not speaking but both scared because we knew something was awry. When we got to the driveway, Louise opened the passenger door of their car, looked at Jimmy, and simply said, "Get in."

"What about my bike?" Jimmy questioned.

"Leave it" was her cold response as she continued to hold the door open. "Just get in, please."

Jimmy got in the car, and his mom shut the door. Before she could walk around to the driver's side, my mother rushed up to her and gave her a tight hug, while tears continued to leak from both women's eyes.

"If there is anything I can do, anything that you need, please call me. I can be there in ten minutes," said my mom, kissing Louise on the cheek. Jimmy's mom just nodded affirmatively as she turned away and got into her car. Jimmy and I stared at each other through the door glass with similar looks of fear on our faces, both knowing something terribly wrong must have happened. Louise started the car and backed out of the driveway, and then they were gone.

My mom and I watched them drive out of sight before I spoke. "What happened, Mom?"

"Come inside the house and sit down. Then we can talk," my mom said, turning toward the back-porch door and entering the house. I followed her into the living room, where she sat on one sofa and motioned for me to sit across from her. Once we were both seated, she began.

"There is no easy way to say this, so I am just going to say it," my mom started. "Melvin died today."

"What!" I shrieked. My mom didn't answer immediately as I tried to comprehend what I had just heard. Melvin was one of Jimmy's brothers. He was the third born and the closest in age to Jimmy.

"I don't know all the details yet, but it sounds like he was bird hunting with Terry and Larry this morning, and when he attempted to go over a barbed wire fence, he slipped, and his shotgun accidentally discharged, hitting him in the chest, throat, and face. His brothers tried to save him, but he died before they could get him to a doctor."

It felt like someone had just punched me in the gut! I immediately felt sick to my stomach. It started regurgitating, and for a second, I thought I was going to throw up. I couldn't speak, but my mind was racing. All I could think about was the poor Clarke family having to deal with this enormous loss. Jimmy would be crushed! He had a stronger bond with Melvin than he did with any of his other siblings.

I kept thinking over and over, *I just saw him yesterday, how this can be possible! I just saw him yesterday, how can this be possible!* It felt so unreal, like a very bad dream that I couldn't wake up from. Oh my god! Poor Louise, poor Art! I felt tears welling up in my eyes and spilling over as I sat there in silence! After just a few seconds, I got up, rushed into my mother's waiting arms, and began to sob.

The funeral was on the next Tuesday. I rode Jimmy's bike home, and my parents met me there in their car. I hadn't seen him since he'd left my house on Saturday. When I did see him, we walked to each other and hugged. He looked like he had been crying for weeks. I asked softly, "Are you OK?"

"I guess so," he replied. "Everyone is pretty messed up by this. My brothers are blaming themselves, my mom thinks this is her fault, and my dad hasn't said two words to any of us since Saturday night."

"I'm so sorry," I said, looking down and away from him.

"I know," he said as we turned to walk into the house.

The service was nice, lots of nice things were said about Melvin, and there was a river of tears shed by all.

Jimmy never got over his brother death, but as they say, time heals all wounds. We became even closer after Melvin's passing, but for some strange reason, we never talked about that day. He was gone, and it seemed like Jimmy wanted to forget everything about that week, so we simply moved on.

They say bad luck always comes in threes, and for me, it was true. While I was still in the fifth grade, my father was seriously injured in an accident at work. He'd had a flat tire on his dump truck and had stopped to have it fixed. While a tire repairman was airing up the tire to check for a leak, the tire blew off the wheel, killing the repairman and all but taking one of my father's legs off as the tire hit him and then bounced off the wall behind him.

I didn't know what happened for several days, because my mom didn't tell us about the accident until after it was determined that my father would live, having almost bled out at the scene of the accident.

My father was in the hospital in Loma Linda, seventy miles away from Beaumont, for two months.

My mother would visit him on the weekends, while Ronnie and I stayed with Art and Louise. She kept us updated on his progress when she got home Sunday nights.

Money got tight very quickly. My father still made a portion of his wages because he was injured at work, but not nearly as much as he'd made while working. The doctor bills started coming in, and we had no way to even come close to covering them. My mom had been a waitress before, and she went out and found a waitress job nearby to make more money.

Being the oldest son, I felt it was my duty to help as well. I gave my mom the money I made from my paper route to add to the family coffers. I was making almost as much money as mom was as a full-time waitress at the time. The first time I gave her my monthly earnings from the paper route and told her to spend it as she needed, she didn't say a word; she just kissed me on the forehead and hugged me tightly. I was able to give her fifty dollars a month for the next two years.

Meanwhile, my father was struggling through rehab and trying to learn to walk with crutches so he could get out of his wheelchair.

He knew he would never be able to drive trucks again, and the longer he sat around the house with no prospects for work, the angrier and meaner he became. Everyone walked on eggshells when we were around him. No one wanted to cross him or disagree with him lest you be the focal point of a yelling rampage.

I remember one night at the dinner table; he told my brother to stop chewing with his mouth open. My brother sat on the left side of Dad, and he was chewing loudly in my dad's ear. He told him a second time in a raised voice to quit eating like a pig. To this day, I am not sure if my brother was deaf or just stupid, because he went about his business of shoveling food into his mouth and chewing it noisily.

My dad lost his temper and backhanded Ronnie like he was hitting a full-grown man, not an eleven-year-old boy. My brother flew backward, his chair hitting the wall, with one of his flailing arms hitting our dining room window and cracking it. My mom screamed at my dad and ran around the table to help her son. His lip and mouth were bloody, and he was dazed, but otherwise he was OK.

My mother yelled, "Get the hell out of here and go into the living room, you sorry son of a bitch!" My father sat there looking stunned. I know I was stunned, as Mom went after him again. "You heard me, get the hell out of here!"

Without saying a word in response, my father wheeled his wheelchair out of the dining room, while my mother cleaned up the mess he'd made. I don't know if I'd ever heard my mother raise her voice in anger, and I know I'd never heard her swear before that night. Oh, there had been the occasional "darn it" or "crap," but never would I have thought her capable of calling someone a son of a bitch, especially my father.

I learned three important things that night. First, my mom was a strong woman who loved her kids and would do anything to protect them. Second, if I was ever going to stand up to my father, I had better be prepared for it to progress into a physical confrontation.

And, last, never eat with your mouth open if you know what's good for you.

I didn't think of us as poor during this period of our lives because we seemed to have plenty to eat, had nice clothes to wear to school, and lived in a house that kept us dry and warm. I still look back on those days as character building, and I have no regrets about the way we lived during that period of my life. However, my brother didn't see it that way. He asked my mom over and over if he could have a Hostess apple pie when we were at the grocery store one day, and she told him, "No! We don't have enough money to waste it on junk food like that!"

That next Sunday, at our individual Sunday school classes, my brother asked his teacher if they could pray for us because we didn't have money for food. He forgot to mention the food we didn't have money for was Hostess apple pies! After church, we went home as usual.

We had just changed out of our Sunday church clothes, and Ronnie and I were playing in the front yard when a convoy of cars pulled up, filling our driveway and parking on both sides of the street in front of our house. There were at least twenty adults converging on our house, each with a sack of groceries in their arms. I ran to the door and called Mom as they approached. She came out onto the porch, followed by my dad in his wheelchair.

Our pastor led the procession and, once on the porch, said, "We know it's been tough for your family with Eirik out of work for so long. So as a congregation, we wanted to drop off some extra staples for you and your family while you work your way through these difficult times. It is important to us that all the lambs in our congregation have food to eat."

My father's face immediately turned crimson. I couldn't tell if it was more from anger or embarrassment, but I surmised that both emotions were strong and getting stronger as he sat there saying nothing.

Finally, he spoke. "Thank you, Pastor, but there's been a mistake, and we have plenty of food to eat. I appreciate the thought and all your wonderful Christian charity, but we don't deserve or need all this food. Please give it to a more deserving family. Really, we are fine!"

The pastor looked directly at Ronnie and asked, "Do you have enough food to eat, boys?"

My brother looked over to my dad, who was glaring at him, waiting for the answer he expected.

Sheepishly, my brother looked down and softly replied, "I guess so," in a nonconvincing voice.

The pastor smiled and turned back to my dad, "Eirik, pride is one of the seven deadly sins, and at one time or another, we are all guilty of it. But I am afraid I am going to have to insist that you accept this gift as it was intended, in Christian love from our families in Christ to yours."

With that, he set down his bag of groceries and walked away. Then one at a time, everyone came up on the porch and laid food at my mother and father's feet. The act was unanimously accompanied by a "God bless you." In fact, I don't think I have ever heard "God bless you" so many times in my life. When the last bag was set down and the congregation members were all off the porch, my mom relented and said a heartfelt "Thank you all so much for your kindness. Can I make some coffee for anyone?"

The pastor raised his hand in protest, lest anyone accept her offer. "Thank you, but no thank you, Lila. We will leave you and your family to enjoy the rest of your Sunday afternoon in peace. See you next Sunday in church." His raised hand turned and gave a cursory wave good-bye as he began walking back to his car. Everyone else followed like the good flock of sheep they were, and in less than two minutes, everyone was gone.

"What the heck was that all about?" my father said, looking directly at Ronnie.

"I don't know!" my brother snapped back. "Why is everyone looking at me? I didn't do anything."

After some awkward silence, my mother bent over and raised up with two bags of groceries in her arms. Following suit, I picked up two bags and followed her into the kitchen. One thing for sure, I thought to myself, *We are going to be eating pretty good for quite a while!*

About a month after the congregation visited our house, we went to church like always, and a man by the name of Bob Fey asked my father if he had ever considered car sales. My dad responded that he had never been in sales of any kind and didn't think that career choice was for him. Bob Fey owned a Ford dealership in Banning, and he asked my dad if he could come over to his business and talk more about the opportunity the next day before giving him a hard no. Dad agreed to talk, and when he came home the next night after visiting Bob, to everyone's surprise, he announced that he had a new job!

He'd gone to speak with Bob, and halfway through their conversation, two customers had come into the showroom at the same time. Bob asked Dad if he would speak to one, while he talked with the other. The person Dad spoke to bought a new car right there! Bob told my father he was a natural and asked if he wanted to give this new vocation a try.

Dad was so excited that he said, "Yes," and told Bob he would start the next day if that was OK. My dad sold twenty-three cars the first month he worked for the dealership. He seemed to catch his stride almost immediately and never looked back. After a year or so, Dad was making considerably more money selling cars than he'd ever made driving a dump truck. Nevertheless, my mom kept her waitress job, and our household seemed to be on its way back to normal.

It wasn't until several years later that my father learned his first car sale was a sham. He and Bob Fey were having a drink at the end of the day, and Bob told Dad that he had already sold the customer the car the previous day, but he'd asked for his customer's help in making my dad feel confident by allowing him to go through the motions of buying his car from my dad. My father was a little irritated when he heard the truth, but that was outweighed by his gratitude for Bob getting him into the business.

The upside was we were able to pay our bills and put some money into savings. The downside was Dad was missing more and more dinners because he was working late, and it seemed strange to only have three of us sitting at the dinner table, staring at an empty chair.

Over the next three years, I did my best to stay out of trouble and, more importantly, out of jail. Jimmy and I were still pranksters, and we were doing bigger and more dangerous pranks all the time as we tried to outdo ourselves.

Jimmy crashed his bike when we tried riding down Cherry Hill Road with no hand on the handlebars. He broke his wrist and collarbone on that outing.

My brother shot me with a real bow and target arrow in the leg because he was angry with me. He later told me he was aiming for my chest, but I jumped when I saw the arrow coming, and it hit me in the thigh. My mom had to take me to the hospital to have it removed, and I got my first stitches. The crazy incidents never seemed to end for me.

School was still easy for me, but it didn't hold my interest. I was at the age in which I was starting to become interested in girls, and the attraction went both ways. Jimmy had grown to be three inches taller than me by now, and he was the real lady killer. Blond hair, tanned skin, big smile with bright white teeth; he had everything going for him except money. I, on the other hand, was reduced to being his wingman, and on many occasions, I was his banker as well. But it wasn't all bad unless we happened to like the same girl at the same time.

My father steadily improved through continued rehabilitation. He eventually was able to leave the wheelchair behind and progressed to crutches. He was much more agile and moved quicker as he became familiar with his new mode of transportation. With mobility came a new sense of self-worth, and he smiled again, something that he'd been missing for many years following his accident. Car sales was a perfect vocation for my dad as he continued to be one of Bob Fey's top salesmen month after month.

CHAPTER 3

One day in early June, my father announced at the dinner table that we were going on an extended vacation to visit his and my mother's relatives during the upcoming summer. My mother was as surprised and excited as Ronnie and I were about the vacation opportunity. We hadn't done anything fun as a family since my father's accident some five years earlier.

My mother was able to get time off from her waitress job, and my brother and I found substitutes to deliver papers while we were gone.

Jimmy Clarke took over my lawn mowing that summer. However, when I returned three months later, I discovered that I'd lost four customers because Jimmy had done such a crappy job while I was gone.

The day after I graduated from the eighth grade, we loaded up our 1953 Cadillac with luggage, and we were off to our first destination, Bothell, Washington.

Ronnie and I had not met any of our relatives up to this point in our lives, so we were very excited as we pulled onto the road that led to my mother's parents' farm.

Coming from the Southern California desert, we were mesmerized by the huge pine and Douglas fir trees lining the road. As we made our way up the muddy driveway to the farmhouse, we were surrounded by trees, and it felt almost like we were in a tunnel as they blocked out the sky.

The weather was softly misting, and the skies were filled with angry-looking clouds as we pulled up to the quaint, moss-covered main house at the end of the short road. As we all got out of the car, the door to the house in front of us burst open, and what I assumed to be three of my mother's sisters came running and squealing toward us with open arms. They all stopped and hugged Mom first and then my father and, finally, Ronnie and me as they jabbered about how happy they were to see us.

While all this commotion was going on, a tiny but athletic-looking woman with totally gray hair came out of the house and approached us. My mother rushed to her, and there were lots of hugging and kissing between them before they turned, arm in arm, to complete the short journey back to our car.

My grandmother gave my father a cursory hug and welcomed him rather coldly. Turning toward my brother and me, she bent down and gave each of us a warm hug while telling us she was so glad to finally meet us.

We had just finished our pleasantries when the skies literally broke open, and it began to pour down on us. Everyone but my dad, brother, and me turned and made a run for the still open front door through the curtain of water.

My father opened the trunk and started lifting suitcases out with one hand, setting them by the rear of the car while he steadied himself on a single crutch with his other hand.

Before Ronnie and I got the first suitcases into the house, three large men came running from inside and passed us, headed for our car. One said, "Hi, boys," as he ran past. They quickly said their hellos to my dad, grabbed handfuls of suitcases, and had them inside the house before Ronnie and I were able to get up the steps.

Once inside, I saw the man I imagined to be my grandfather sitting in a wooden rocking chair next to a wood-burning potbelly stove. I was really wet and cold, but the heat of the room warmed me almost immediately.

And the smells, oh my god, those smells! Pinewood burning and crackling in the potbelly stove. Even though I couldn't see them, the sweet smell of hot cinnamon rolls baking in the oven immediately overwhelmed my olfactory system. To this day, if my mind drifts back to that pleasant memory, it still puts a smile on my face and lights up my salivary glands.

The main house was full of people, all of them laughing and talking at the same time. My grandfather motioned for me to come over, and I slowly started walking in his direction. Once I was close to him, he said, "And what is your name?"

"Michael," I replied simply.

"Does your father take good care of you and your mother?" he asked.

Again, simple seemed best. "Yes," I responded.

"Good," he said, nodding his head affirmatively. "Welcome to my home, Michael. It is a pleasure to meet you." With that, he held out his hand to shake, and I offered mine back. His grip was strong, and his shake was extremely firm. Once we shook hands, he pulled me close and hugged me.

The next week was filled with great-tasting food cooked over a real wood-burning stove. I also loved watching my dad and my uncles drinking more beer than they probably should have while playing guitars and singing. I had no idea that my father could sing, let alone play a guitar.

We got to know our aunts, uncles, and the cousins we didn't know existed prior to that week. We learned so much more than we had ever known about my mom and dad and their families as we sat around a firepit, listening to them reminiscing and telling stories of their childhood well into the night.

Except for having to walk fifty yards in the dark to an outhouse, I had a wonderful time in Bothell, Washington, and I was really looking forward to our next stop.

I had no way of knowing that this was the first and last time that I would see two of my uncles. One, married to one of my mother's sisters, was a bush pilot in Alaska. During a snowstorm two years later, he crashed into the side of a mountain while trying to fly back to Anchorage. The other was my mom's brother, who was swept overboard while fishing in the Bering Seas off the Alaskan coast the year after we met him.

Our next stop was Kindersley, Saskatchewan, in Canada where my father was raised. The greeting was no less exuberant when we arrived in Kindersley than it had been in Seattle. Several of my dad's brothers and sisters were there along with assorted cousins and family members.

However, the topography was much different here than it had been in Bothell—totally flat farmland for as far as you could see in every direction, very few trees, and it was as hot as Indio during the summer months.

On our second day there, my grandpa asked if I wanted to go to work with him. Not having any idea what he meant or what that entailed, I simply replied, "Sure."

The next day, at 4:00 a.m., my grandfather shook my shoulder and softly whispered, "Get up, boy. It's time to go."

I wanted to say, "Leave me alone," but I dared not verbalize the words. I had made a commitment, and I would honor it. "OK," I said in a groggy response.

Getting out of bed, I quickly dressed and headed for the kitchen, where I could already smell bacon cooking. Grandpa was already eating as Grandma asked, "Would you like fried or scrambled eggs to go with your pancakes?"

"Scrambled, please," I replied softly. In no time, I was eating like a ravenous wolf pup, while Grandpa sipped his coffee and watched me intently.

As soon as my plate was cleaned for the second time, he simply asked, "Ready?"

I nodded affirmatively, and we both scooted our chairs back. I thanked Grandma for breakfast as I followed my grandpa out the door.

It was still dark outside as we walked the short distance to his old pickup. Grandma had packed a big lunch for us, which she handed to me to carry to the pickup. Opening the passenger door and getting in, I saw there were two canvas bags filled with water already sitting in the seat between us.

After a twenty-minute drive, Grandpa pulled the truck over and said, "Here we are." Getting out of the truck, he put on a nasty-looking, dirty, old hat, grabbed our lunch, and stated flatly, "Don't forget the water." He then turned and started walking out into the darkness in front of him.

Quickly, I jerked both waters bag up and followed, hoping not to lose him in the darkness as we moved through the waist-high wheat and deeper into the field. Finally, we got to a larger truck and a combine. I'd seen both types of vehicles on TV and in books, but this was my first time ever seeing this type of machinery up close.

"Have you ever driven a truck, boy?" he nonchalantly asked.

"Of course not, I'm only thirteen!" I answered, finding his question to be absurd.

"Of course not," he repeated with a slight smile forming on his face. "I forgot you kids are city folk." Continuing, he said, "Well, if your dad ain't going to teach you how to drive, I guess it's up to me. Get on up here, and I'll show you how this works."

"Really?" I replied. "You're going to let me drive this big truck?"

"Of course, I am," he responded. "I can't drive the combine and the truck at the same time. You'll need to follow me in the truck on the left side of the combine. See that big dump chute coming out of the combine?"

Looking up, I said, "Yeah."

"Well, you need to make sure that stays in the trucks dump box at all times. The combine will be harvesting the wheat, separating the chaff, and dumping all the wheat through that chute into your truck box. If you don't keep that chute inside the truck bed, you'll be wasting all the crop we've been farming this year."

Suddenly, I felt an immense sense of pressure I hadn't dealt with before. "But, Grandpa, I told you I don't know how to drive a truck!"

"I heard you," he said sharply. "Get up here so I can teach you!"

Over the next twenty minutes, I learned to start the truck, turn the lights on and off, slowly let out the clutch to get the truck moving in first gear, and, finally, to turn it around when we got to an end off a row and realign myself with the combine for the next pass through the field.

We started harvesting at 6:00 a.m. I couldn't believe it! At thirteen, I was driving a huge dump truck and helping a combine harvest wheat! I was sure that no one in my class back home was doing anything as cool as I was today!

By 7:00 a.m., I turned off the lights on the truck. By 10:00 a.m., I was sweating through my shirt in the ever-increasing heat of the truck cab. By 11:00 a.m., I was starving, but I guessed it probably wasn't time to stop and eat lunch yet. Once the truck was full, Grandpa would take over, driving it out of the field, and bring it back empty twenty minutes later. I took these twenty-minute breaks to rehydrate before the next round began.

We made two more passes before we stopped for lunch. Looking at my watch as Grandpa jumped off the combine, it was about 1:15 p.m. The other thing I noticed looking at my arm was that my sweat had turned the dust into little ribbons of wet mud that slid down them and fell off, puddling on the floorboard of the truck. Grandpa brushed himself off and created a dust cloud as he walked around the front of the truck to my window.

"Are you hungry, son?" he asked as he jumped up on the running board and stuck his head through the open window. I shook my head yes, and he jumped back down into the remaining chaff straw, creating another puff of dirt. "Then let's see what Grandma fixed us."

I opened the door and followed him back around my truck to his combine. Opening a compartment by the cab, he pulled out the bag with our lunch in it. Grabbing a still full canvas bag of water, he went behind the combine and sat down in the shade created by the height of the combine. I sat next to him as he opened the homemade lunch bag. He pulled out fried chicken wrapped in towels, huge dill pickles, corn on the cob, and two big pieces of a homemade brownie for dessert. I ate in silence like I hadn't eaten in days.

We'd both been concentrating on our eating when Grandpa broke the silence with "Well, how do you like farming so far?"

I shrugged my shoulders and kept eating as I nodded my head affirmatively.

"What's been your favorite part of farming today?" he continued.

I thought for a second and then simply replied, "Lunch, I guess."

He started laughing so hard that he almost choked on the chicken in his mouth. When he finally calmed down and caught his breath, he said, "You're just like your father!"

We ate our fill, and each of us took a long drink out of the canvas canteen. We sat there quietly for a few minutes, and then he said, "Time to get back at it." I got up off the ground when he did and walked around the truck, got in, and was ready to go to work again.

The cab of the truck was hotter than I'd remembered as I hit the starter and heard it jump to life. I was immediately wet as sweat trickled down off my forehead into my eyes.

Once the combine was started, we were on our way again, making another slow but straight pass through the dusty field. We worked through the afternoon, and at about 6:30 p.m., Grandpa stopped the combine and motioned over to me to shut off the truck. Jumping down off the combine, I could see his shirt was soaked through with sweat, and it almost looked like he'd wet his pants as the stains of perspiration traveled down his lap toward his knees.

Taking a long pull from the water bag, Grandpa brushed his arm across his mouth, took off his now soaked hat, and wiped his head with a reasonably clean bandana. "I'll go dump this load of grain while you take our lunch box and the water jugs back to the pickup. I'll meet you there in a few minutes," he stated matter-of-factly. I nodded, and we traded places, him now in the truck and me on the ground. I watched him drive off, a cloud of loose dust forming a small wall behind him, making it impossible to see the truck after just a few seconds.

True to his word, Grandpa pulled the dump truck to a stop by our pickup less than a half hour later. We both jumped in and headed home.

The cool breeze coming through the open pickup windows felt refreshing as we traveled back toward the farmhouse. After a considerable length of silence, Grandpa said, "You did a real good job out there today, son. I'll be proud to tell anyone that you are a Larsen and my grandson. You should be proud of yourself too!"

I smiled up to him but didn't reply. I was proud of myself. I'd worked that hard before, but this was different somehow. It felt like I had really accomplished something special out there with Grandpa today.

After we'd had a chance to clean up and were eating dinner with the rest of the family, Grandpa bragged about what a good worker I'd been that day. He relayed the story about my favorite part of the day, and everyone howled when he said the word "lunch."

I laughed along but felt a little embarrassed at the same time. He asked me if I wanted to go again with him tomorrow, which caught me off guard. As all eyes turned to focus on me, I finally said, "Depends, what's for lunch?" Everyone started laughing hysterically again, including Grandpa.

He then said, "That won't be necessary, Michael. I've got all the help I need tomorrow."

I was relieved. Working thirteen hours a day was not my idea of a fun vacation. We stayed almost a month with my grandparents.

Mom helped Grandma can vegetables and fruits from her garden. As well, she helped prepare meals for the working men. Dad spent lots of time with his brothers and sisters. He couldn't really do that much physical work because of his bad leg and the crutches, but he tried to help wherever possible.

Ronnie and I rode horses, milked cows, chased chickens, and explored new territories with our cousins. Our favorite place to play was always the barn. We hid in the hay, swung on ropes from one floor to another, and played tag or hide-and-seek for hours at a time.

I did help Grandpa harvest one more day while we were there because he needed help and there weren't enough people to go around. He was very grateful, and the second day seemed to go much easier than the first one had. I was tired at the end of the day but satisfied that I had really been able to contribute more this time.

And then it was time to move on to the next stop, Calgary, Alberta. As we were leaving, both grandparents gave me a big hug good-bye, and I noticed tears forming in Grandpa's eyes. We had bonded, and I believe he was proud of me as well as my dad, whom he hugged fiercely before spinning and walking back in the house. I don't think he wanted us to see him cry because he never looked back.

Calgary, Alberta, was almost a full day's drive east from Kindersley, Saskatchewan. There was nothing but miles and miles of flat farmland and straight, boring roads to look at as we continued east. Sometimes, we would travel for well over an hour before seeing another car on the road. It was a warm drive, and my dad had the windows down, creating a pleasant breeze throughout the car. With nothing special to look at outside and the hypnotic sound of the wind rushing through the car, I found myself nodding off to a peaceful sleep several times that day only to be awakened by the sound of a passing truck or bugs committing suicide loudly on our windshield.

Pretty late into the night, we arrived at my uncle Severyn's house. Unlike the relatives we had visited so far, Uncle Severyn lived in a major city. Pulling up and parking in front of his home, I saw that all the houses on the block looked pretty much the same. The only real distinguishable differences were the house color and the various types of yards. From the outside, they looked big, but they were all so close together it was almost claustrophobic after being on the two farms.

Before we could get out of the car, the front door opened, and my aunt and uncle were down the steps and headed toward our car. With quick introductions to all of us and warm hugs all around, everyone took a piece of luggage and started back into the house.

Once inside, I was surprised to see two girls, one heavy and not very attractive, the other tall, thin, and beautiful. My aunt's name was Irene, and my two cousins were introduced as Verna and Marie. They both seemed very nice, and we immediately began talking with one another like we'd been old friends for years. It was late, so we were directed to our rooms, quickly made up makeshift beds, and called it a day.

I was used to getting up early because of my paper route at home, and my sleeping habits hadn't changed just because I was on vacation. I was as quiet as I could be while making my way to the bathroom the next morning. Just as I was about to open the bathroom door, my cousin Verna came out in a short little nightgown.

She said, "Excuse me, I didn't know anyone else was up yet."

Verna was the least good looking of my two cousins, and if I were to venture a guess, I'd say she was three to five years my senior. But I will confess that as I stared at her very well-developed breasts through the sheer material of her nightgown, I couldn't take my eyes off them, nor could I speak.

She watched my eyes, smiled, and said, "You're a nasty boy, staring at your cousin like that!" With that, she turned and walked past me, back toward her bedroom. I was stunned! I had never seen boobs that large, that close, shaking in random directions as they skimmed past my face. And as good as this day had started for a thirteen-year-old, the day only got better from there.

It turned out that my uncle Severyn was a conductor for Via Canada Railroads. He was the conductor on a run from Calgary, Alberta, that went all the way to Vancouver, BC, on the West Coast. The trip took twelve hours one way, and he had to stay in Vancouver for twenty-four hours, and then he would make the return trip home the third night.

We all found this new information out over breakfast together. It was interesting to me, but not all that exciting. Well, not that exciting until Uncle Severyn asked Ronnie and me if we would like to take the trip with him the next day! Having never been on a train, we immediately turned to Mom and started begging for her to let us go.

She seemed as shocked by the offer as we were. She began asking questions like they were being shot out of a machine gun. "How much will this cost? Where will the boys sleep if they get tired? Where do you stay in Vancouver, and what will you do with the boys while you're there? Are you sure it's safe? Will you get in any trouble for doing this by the railroad?"

Uncle Severyn, who started by asking all of us to call him Sev instead of Severyn, which is what his close friends called him, spent the next twenty minutes answering all my mom's questions and trying to put both my parents at ease concerning his proposal.

It wasn't until Verna broke in and said, "It's very safe, I've done it several times. The first time is the best, but I've done it so many times that it's kind of boring for me now." She looked at me and smiled. I felt myself blush as I remembered our run-in earlier that morning. I couldn't hold her gaze, so I looked back to Mom, hoping for a positive response. Finally, after an agonizing amount of time, she relented and agreed. "I guess it's OK if you want to take them, Sev," she said timidly.

I tried to act more grown-up than I felt. "Thank you, Mom," I said, trying to sound older than I was in front of my cousins. "We will do exactly as we are told, and we'll stay out of trouble, I promise!" She just looked back at me like some alien had invaded the body of her firstborn. Nothing I was saying sounded like anything that would normally come out of my mouth.

After breakfast and once everyone was dressed for the day, we four kids all ended up in Marie's bedroom. We were listening to records and talking about the kind of music we liked and what the differences were between going to school in Canada and the U.S.A. After comparing notes for a while, I was convinced that the school systems in Canada were well advanced over our own in the United States. The courses I would be taking as a freshman were courses both girls had finished prior to entering high school.

Out of the blue, Marie asked, "Do you have a girlfriend, Michael?"

"Not right now I don't," I responded a little too quickly.

"Well, I do," Marie replied confidently.

"You mean you have a boyfriend!" I said with a soft snicker.

Marie shot me a look and said, "No, I mean I have a girlfriend. I don't like boys that way."

Verna barged into the conversation. "Marie is a lesbian!"

Never having heard the word before, I said, "She's a what?"

Verna continued. "A lesbian. You know, a gay person. Someone who likes people of their own sex."

Looking at Marie, I blurted out, "You mean you're queer?"

"That is an ugly word, and I'd prefer you'd not use it, but, yes, I am as you so maliciously called it—queer."

My brain went immediately into overload. How could a person who was so gorgeous not be attracted to boys? I wondered. How do you know if you are queer? Why is someone queer? Was my other cousin queer as well?

Not meaning to hurt her feelings, I apologized. "I'm sorry, I haven't heard those other names. I only knew the name queer. What do you want me to call you so I don't irritate you repeatedly?"

"Marie will be fine," she said, a little smile forming on her face. We sat in silence, and I'm sure she could see the confusion on my face. "For God's sakes, it's not a disease. You won't catch it, if that's what you're worried about," she continued, clearly put off by my repugnant reaction.

Again, I apologized. "I've just never known anyone who admitted that they were"—I started searching for the correct word and then kept going—"a lesbian before. Do your mom and dad know?"

"Of course, they do!" Verna interjected. "They've known for a long time."

I looked at Ronnie, who had been completely quiet throughout this big reveal conversation. I couldn't tell if he understood, didn't care, or was just thinking about the train ride with Uncle Sev the next day.

"Well!" I finally said, breaking the awkward silence. "One in a thousand people might be queer—I mean, gay, sorry! And I have one in my own family tree! That's pretty"—I was looking for the correct word—"unique," I continued. "Let's keep this between us four right now," I said finally. "Our religion believes that people like you go straight to hell, and my parents are pretty religious people. I think it would be best if we just keep this quiet, OK?"

"Do you think I'm going to go to hell, Michael?" Marie asked.

"How the heck do I know?" I exclaimed. "I've done enough bad things that if you do go there, we will most likely meet up again. What I really think," I continued, "is what a waste for mankind! You have to know you're beautiful."

Marie hadn't expected the response as she unconsciously ran her left hand through her hair while trying to smile with her ever-reddening face blushing.

Sixty years later, I now know that a huge number of Americans identify with being gay, lesbian, bisexual, or transgender. Hate by the general population for gays in the early years of my life eventually turned to tolerance, which, over the years, turned to acceptance as gay marriage became legal throughout the United States. There is really no reason for me to believe anything has changed in the numbers of gays as a percentage of America's population when I first spoke with Marie. The only difference that seems logical to me is that my cousin was one brave girl, while others walked in the darkness and hid their sexuality for fear of reprisals.

The train trip was as much fun as Ronnie and I had hoped it would be. Uncle Sev was truly the master and commander of the train. We could go anywhere, eat anything, and sleep in cool berths if we desired.

Except for bugging other passengers, we were free to do whatever we wanted to do on the train. At the first stop, Uncle Sev let Ronnie stand next to the train and yell as loud as he could, "All aboard!" We both had the pleasure of doing that a few times before we reached Vancouver, BC.

We'd been up virtually all night, and now we were only half an hour from Vancouver, when Ronnie said, "I'm really tired all of a sudden." I didn't respond, but I felt the same way.

It was about 9:00 a.m. when Uncle Sev finished and turned in his trip paperwork to the stationmaster. We grabbed our overnight bag, and Uncle Sev hailed a cab for us. Twenty minutes later, we were in an apartment, and ten minutes after that, both Ronnie and I were sound asleep. It was almost 3:00 p.m. when I felt Uncle Sev shaking my shoulder and telling me to wake up.

"We've got some sights to see if you guys get up and shower."

I looked over to see Ronnie getting out of bed and heading to the bathroom. In less than thirty minutes, we were back in a cab and headed to Grandville Island to sightsee and enjoy a very nice dinner at one of the many restaurants.

Getting back to the apartment at about 10:00 p.m. with full bellies, we had no trouble going back to sleep. The next morning, we had breakfast, and Uncle Sev took us to a place called the Capilano Suspension Bridges Park. It was one of the coolest things I'd ever done in my young life. The bridges were built in 1889, and they were suspended seventy feet above ground, being anchored to treetops. We walked over the Capuano River, and the bridges seemed to go on and on. We were in a rainforest, and we went over seven total suspension bridge spans with viewing platforms between them. We ate a late lunch at the restaurant in the park and then caught a cab back to the railroad station for the trip home.

The return trip was as much fun as the trip to Vancouver. On the way home, my uncle arranged for Ronnie and me to ride with the engineer between different legs in the journey home. Everyone with the railroad was kind, informative, and easy to talk to as we made the twelve-hour trip back to Calgary.

We spent the next week getting to know our cousins better and going to the local swimming pool most afternoons. I even got to meet Marie's girlfriend one day at the pool. I don't know what I expected, but she was the same as any other girl I'd met, nice, polite, cute, easy to talk to, and all around very pleasant. I told Marie later that I thought her friend was very nice, and she seemed to appreciate the comment. And then it was time to say our good-byes and move on.

Verna asked me if I would write to her, and I said I would. Interestingly, we stayed in contact for the next thirty years, sending letters back and forth, as well as Christmas and birthday cards, etc. It's curious to me now that I was only able to see her one more time besides our summer visit, and yet we had somehow bonded so strongly.

She unexpectedly suffered a severe stroke in the summer of her forty-seventh year of life and passed away two days later. We'd spent so little time together, yet I cried like a baby when I received the horrible news of her death.

Our next stop was Billings, Montana. This was home to two of my father's older brothers. Uncle Orvil was married but had no children. The other uncle, Uncle Ed, was single and a wild man of sorts. I had already heard stories of his craziness, but I certainly didn't expect to be involved in them.

We stayed with Uncle Orvil and his wife for our time in Billings. My aunt Astrid was two bricks short of a full load as far as I was concerned. She had old newspapers stacked up in piles throughout the house. Every room was filled with newspaper stacks except for a narrow path left empty so you could walk through the rooms. She was also up all hours of the night doing weird stuff, like mopping the kitchen floor at 3:00 a.m. with the radio playing rather loudly while the rest of us were trying to sleep.

We were invited to Uncle Ed's house, which was more like a cabin in the woods, during our second week of the visit for a family dinner. When we arrived, Uncle Ed walked a crooked path to our car so he could greet us all. When he got to the side of our car, Dad rolled down his window, and Uncle Ed asked, "Where the hell have you guys been? Get your butts in here. Dinner's ready." He stepped back, turned, and headed to Uncle Orvil's car, which was behind ours.

My dad rolled up his window, and my mom said, "He's drunk! This should be lots of fun." We all got out of the car and went inside the cabin. It was sterile inside, and it was obvious no woman lived here. The only decorations on the walls were multiple sets of elk antlers and a stuffed eight-point deer head above the fireplace.

One couch, two chairs, and a dining room table, plus two picnic benches that looked like they were stolen from a schoolyard were all visible from the front room. That was pretty much all the furniture I saw between the kitchen and myself. I watched Mom as she quickly scanned the room, and I could almost feel her disgust as she started toward the kitchen. Just then, my two uncles and Aunt Astrid came walking in.

"Let's eat!" said Uncle Ed a little too loudly. "If you're coming to my house, you know you're getting venison. Everything's ready, so let's dish up!"

I had never eaten venison before, and I didn't really have any preconceived opinion about the taste, but I was very pleasantly surprised at how good it tasted. It had been cut into small cubes, drenched in egg and then flour, and fried in a big cast iron skillet with plenty of butter. It was delicious. Two very good side dishes completed a wonderful meal. There was very little talking during the meal as everyone seemed to be caught up in the same food euphoria as myself. There were, however, several unintelligible sounds like "mmm," signifying pleasure and appreciation coming from various people around table.

After dinner, Uncle Ed wanted to go out by his firepit and have a cigarette. The women offered to clean up, and my dad elected to stay inside for a while. Uncle Ed, Uncle Orvil, Ronnie, and I went outside. It was dark, but Uncle Orvil had a fire going strongly before Ed could finish his cigarette. Ed asked Orvil to go in and get him a fresh bottle of whiskey. I don't think Orvil wanted to do it, but he didn't want to start a confrontation with his brother either.

After Orvil was gone, Ed turned to my brother and said, "You're a quiet one, aren't you?" I don't know why my brother didn't respond, but he remained silent. "You can speak, can't you?" he asked again.

"Yes," Ronnie replied timidly.

"Come over here, son," Ed said, waving to my brother to come join him on the other side of the now blazing fire.

Ronnie rose to his feet, looked at me like a scared fawn, and started a slow walk around the fire toward Uncle Ed. When he was almost there, Uncle Ed reached out and grabbed him, pulling him close in a tight bear hug as he said, "Come on, boy, I'm not going to bite you!" With that, he shook my brother a little and made a growling noise like a bear. Ronnie tried to break free, but my uncle continued to hold him tightly.

"You're pretty strong for your size," my uncle said as he tightened his grip on Ronnie. My brother said nothing, but his face started to turn noticeably red in the glow of the yellow licks of fire that made their way up into the blackness of the night.

I could tell he was having trouble breathing, and I yelled, "Let him go!"

"Oh, he's all right," Uncle Ed responded.

But I could tell he wasn't! I rose to my feet and started toward my uncle.

As he watched me approach, his eyes narrowed. "What's on your mind, boy?" he asked menacingly.

Watching my brother struggling to take in air, I responded sharply, "I said let him go!" The same second that I yelled at Uncle Ed, Uncle Orvil walked out the front door of the cabin with a full bottle of whiskey in his hand.

"And if I don't," Ed started, but before he could finish his question, I swung the piece of log I'd picked up on the way to them and hit him hard on his left shin. He screamed in pain, let go of my brother, and grabbed his leg, belting out a steady stream of profanities.

"Holy shit," I heard Uncle Orvil say as Ronnie ran past him into the house crying.

I dropped the club I'd just used on Uncle Ed and started back to the house myself. Ronnie was crying and telling my mom and dad what had just happened as I walked through the door. I was barely inside when Uncle Ed came limping through the door and scanned the room until he spotted me. He took two steps before my mother was between us and yelled, "Leave him alone, you drunk asshole."

"Shut the hell up, Lila," Ed said as he started to push Mom out of the way. I balled up my fists and prepared to defend myself. But the second my uncle's hand touched my mother, my dad was up. He'd dropped his right crutch, and using his left crutch for balance, he threw the fastest punch I'd ever seen. It caught Uncle Ed under his chin and literally lifted Ed's feet off the ground as I watched his eyes roll back in his head. Uncle Ed hit the floor with a sickening thud and didn't move. My dad was standing over him with clenched fists and even tighter clenched jaws when Orvil came busting through the front door.

"Oh, for Christ's sake!" he spouted.

Before he could say any more, Aunt Astrid blurted out, "He asked for it, and I don't blame Eirik one bit for hitting that jerk!"

We all stood there for a moment, no one saying anything; everyone staring at Uncle Ed's sprawled-out body on the living room floor. Finally, Uncle Orvil said, "You guys take Astrid and go back to our house. I'll clean up this mess and doctor up Ed. I'll see you all later."

With that, we all grabbed our stuff, loaded the Cadillac, and left. Ed was still lying on the floor when I walked out the door for the last time. I started to wonder if my dad had hurt him so bad that he might get in trouble with the police.

We were all silent as we drove back to Aunt Astrid's house. We spent another week with Aunt Astrid and Uncle Orvil, seeing the sights and visiting. The incident at Uncle Ed's cabin was never mentioned, at least never in Ronnie's or my presence, for the remainder of our stay.

We said our good-byes at the end of the week and headed to our next stop, Cut Bank, Montana.

We were several hours into our next leg of the trip when I couldn't help myself as I asked, "Dad, is Uncle Ed going to be OK?"

Dad never looked away from the road as he responded, "He'll be fine from the fight." He paused before beginning again. "He's always been a crazy man who drank too much, but I think he is in real trouble with alcohol now. I know I never want to see him again unless he stops drinking. It makes him too mean to be around."

My father had no idea how prophetic he'd been that day. Seven years later, my uncle Ed left a tavern at 2:00 a.m. and ran into a tree on his way home, killing himself instantly. The Montana Highway Patrol said he was traveling at over eighty miles per hour when he left the road, hitting a giant fir tree dead center. Sadly, I fear there were few tears shed for him after his passing.

Cut Bank was home to one of my mom's brothers and his family. His Christian name was Jason, but everyone called him Dobbie. I often wondered but never asked or heard the reason for his nickname. He was a much bigger man than my father, with a full mustache, and hairy chest that crept out of his loosely buttoned cowboy shirt. When he put his right hand out to shake mine, I first noticed a large ornate silver bracelet on his wrist adorned with a large piece of turquoise at its center. Then looking further down at his extended hand, I noticed that his index finger and the finger next to it were missing. As I put my hand in his and began to shake it, it became painfully obvious that the missing digits had no effect on his strength.

He and his wife, Marie, had two young girls, and the four of them lived comfortably in a relatively new double-wide mobile home. They were both happy people, seeming to always be laughing or giggling, and they were extremely excited to see my parents.

Dobbie was the closest in age to my mother of all her siblings. As I watched them interact, it was obvious that they had grown up close. While Dad drank beer, Uncle Dobbie liked whiskey, and he had several pours every evening from a Jack Daniels bottle that never seemed to be very far away from him. He especially liked drinking whenever the adults played cards or strummed their guitars and sang. I was quite surprised how well Uncle Dobbie played the guitar given the lack of fingers on his right hand.

While sitting around a fire outside the trailer most evenings, we all enjoyed the music the men made with their instruments. As the liquor flowed, the men were inevitably joined by Aunt Marie and my mom as they harmonized with them and sang one favorite country song after another. Some fifty years later, those star-filled nights still bring back wonderful memories for me. I loved those moments in time.

Cut Bank was pretty much the same topography as where Dad grew up in Canada. Few trees, hot during the day, but cool at night. In the winter, it was just the opposite with temperature well below zero for several weeks in a row.

When watching the national news at home as I grew up, Cut Bank, Montana, was the coldest spot in the nation more than once. I think the only reason they lived there was because Uncle Dobbie had a good job with the Caterpillar Corporation making heavy equipment for roads and construction. For whatever reason, Cut

Bank was one of three manufacturing sites for Caterpillar in the United States.

Dobbie, Dad, Ronnie, and I went fishing a few times during our two-week visit. My favorite part of the fishing trip wasn't fishing at all. It was riding in Uncle Dobbie's car. He had a black-and-white 1955 Ford Crown Victoria with a Continental kit on the shining rear bumper to carry the spare tire. Everything that wasn't black or white was a highly polished chrome, including the spinner hub caps. The interior was all hand-stitched tuck and roll leather, also done in black and white to match the outside. On the steering wheel, he had a clear plastic brodie knob with a beautiful red rose that looked like it was still alive in its center.

As we drove to and from his favorite fishing spots, I loved just riding in the car with the windows down, listening to the loud country music playing on the radio. I coveted that car and hoped to have something that nice myself someday.

While visiting Dobbie and Marie, Ronnie and I were exposed to Norwegian foods we had never previously eaten. Marie was a wonderful cook, and it seemed like we were always eating, even between meals.

One night, she served a fish dish called lutefisk. It smelled horrible and looked terrible. My aunt, uncle, and parents all ate like they were tasting their favorite desert. Ronnie and I just looked at each other as we ate everything on our plates around it. Noticing this, my uncle Dobbie said, "Why aren't you kids eating your fish?"

"It stinks," I responded.

Dobbie smiled slowly and said, "We all grew up on this dish. Normally, it's reserved for Christmas and special occasions. And this is a special occasion, so at least try it."

Ronnie and I both sat, staring at the fish, neither of us saying a word.

Finally, Uncle Dobbie said, "Which one of you pussies is going to try it first?"

Aunt Marie yelled at her husband, who had consumed quite a few drinks before dinner, "Hey! Watch your language around the kids! If they don't want to eat it, they don't have to!"

Dobbie was silent for a time, and then he addressed my dad without looking at him. "Are you sure these pups are yours? They don't seem to have a Norwegian bone in their bodies, if you ask me."

My dad quickly rose from the table, fire in his eyes. Both my aunt and my mom were on their feet immediately as Dad started around the table without his crutches.

"Stop it! Just stop it, Dobbie!" my aunt screamed at her husband. "You leave the damn dinner table and go to bed if you're going to sit there and be an asshole in my house!" By now, the two girls were crying, and Ronnie and I were out of the dining room, waiting to see what was going to happen.

My mom jumped in. "Sit down, Eirik, before you do something stupid again that you'll regret later!" Turning to her brother, she continued. "And you listen to your wife and just shut up and eat!"

Everyone slowly sat back down at the dinner table in silence. No one spoke for a long time, and then Aunt Marie said in a cheery voice, "I have strawberry shortcake for dessert."

Everyone looked at each other as slow grins broke out, turned to light chuckling, and progressed into hysterical laughter as all four adults practically doubled over with tears now streaming down their faces.

They were laughing so hard, my aunt Marie farted loudly, which brought about an even louder uproar. She apologized several times, saying, "I'm so sorry, I don't know how that happened," which had my dad pounding his fist on the table as he tried to catch his breath. After about five more minutes of pure hysteria, they all slowly calmed down.

Finally, when it was quiet again, my aunt asked nonchalantly, "Well, now, who wants strawberry shortcake?"

That night had to go down as one of the strangest meals I've had in my entire life. I did try lutefisk some years later only to discover my initial instincts were correct. It is herring soaked in pickling spices and lye for about three months and then soaked in water for another three months to get the lye out. I have never had such a rotten taste in my mouth as I did in that one bite! I had to apologize to all who were eating at my table that night for spitting it back onto my plate after being unable to swallow it. If liking lutefisk was mandatory to being Norwegian, then I would confess to be a Swede!

I also began to wonder if there was going to be a fistfight on the remainder of our vacation stops. Was it the Norwegian bloodline, or were these two families just not good with alcohol consumption? I couldn't tell which the case was yet, but it seemed tempers flared quickly for the men on both sides of my family tree if alcohol was involved.

On the one hand, I was proud of my dad for standing up for our family, but on the other, I wondered why he couldn't come to a compromise with any male family members without it becoming a physical confrontation. I also wondered if I would follow in his footsteps, or would I be the one to break the chains of our Viking linage and become more rational in my approach to conflict? Only time would tell.

Our last stop was in the smallest town yet, Minot, North Dakota. About ten miles outside this sleepy little town, we came to a small sign that simply said "Jakobsen Ranch." Turning onto the dirt road next to the sign, we began a dusty drive toward the ranch, which looked to be a mile or so away. My mother's sister Alicia and her husband, Hagar, had lived here for about ten years.

We had been driving through desolate terrain for hours prior to reaching Minot, and this country was more of the same. As we drove down the lane leading to the main house, there were wheat fields that seemed to go on forever on both sides of the road. They were massive compared to what I'd witnessed on my grandpa's farm in Canada. I wondered if I would have to help with the harvest here as well.

Finally reaching the ranch house, my father stopped the car as a cloud of dust kept moving past us toward the building. My aunt and uncle came walking out of the house toward us. Both were in Levi's, hers formfitting, his with the largest buckle I'd ever seen on his belt.

Uncle Hagar was so bowlegged that I could see the barn door through his legs. He had a toothpick hanging out of his mouth and a big white cowboy hat on his head. Aunt Alicia had a tasteful red scarf in her raven-black hair, which hung to her shoulders as they approached our car.

Once we were out of the car, Mom ran up to Alicia, and they hugged affectionately for a good amount of time. Hagar and my dad smiled as they came together, shook hands, and slapped each other on the shoulder after a quick embrace. Then my uncle turned to Ronnie and me, saying, "And who are these two fine gentlemen?"

"I'm Michael, and this is my brother, Ronnie," I replied, sticking my hand out to shake his. He clutched my hand in his large hand and shook it more gently than I had imagined he would. He was a pretty large, fit man who I knew was stronger than his handshake implied, but he was restrained as he then reached over and softly shook my brother's hand.

"It's a pleasure to meet you both," he said, tipping his hat slightly with his other hand. Suddenly, two bare-chested boys came running out of the barn. They were sweaty, without shirts, and only wore Levi's without belts, and both had on beat-up cowboy boots and hats.

"Hi," the one who appeared to be the oldest said to Ronnie and me as he slid to a stop in front of us. The second boy, who was obviously younger, slid to a stop behind his brother and continued. "I'm Bjorn, and this is my big brother, Jonas. What's your names?" We told them our names, and then we all went silent.

"Did you boys finish your chores?" asked Uncle Hagar.

In unison, they replied, "Yes, sir!"

"Then let's help these folks get settled in. Each of you grab a suitcase and take it up to the house." Both boys ran to the back of the car and waited for my dad to open the trunk.

Soon, we were all in the farmhouse, and my aunt was showing my mom and dad to their room. Uncle Hagar took Ronnie and me out onto a back porch that was completely screened and set down our suitcase.

"Boys," he said, "we only have so many bedrooms in the house, so you two will have to sleep out here on a couple of cots. I hope you don't mind."

"Sounds fine to us," I answered for both myself and my brother. Just then, Jonas came running from inside the house onto the porch.

"Dad, they can have my bedroom. I want to sleep out here!" he said disappointedly. His father shot him a look, and Jonas said no more.

"Maybe all four of us boys could sleep out here together a couple of nights, if that's all right, Uncle Hagar," I said, breaking the silence.

Uncle Hagar smiled, roughed up my hair with his big hand, and said, "That sounds like a great idea, Michael! We'll definitely do that."

Jonas and Bjorn seemed starved to have someone else to play with and talk to. After Uncle Hagar left the porch, the boys sat there like anxious puppies waiting for us to unpack, hoping we would ask them, "What do you want to do now?" We did not disappoint and soon found ourselves running behind our new cousins toward a horse corral some forty yards away from the farmhouse. We spent the next couple of hours getting to know one another before our aunt called for us all to come in for dinner.

The tone was happy around the dinner table, the food delicious, and the talking was nonstop. I think everyone had seconds, and then Aunt Alicia brought out a huge blueberry pie from the kitchen for dessert. We told our cousins we would help them with their chores the next day and then we could all explore.

Uncle Hagar told his sons, "You should take your cousins to the lake tomorrow."

"That's a great idea, Dad!" shouted Bjorn. "Maybe we can catch some fish!"

The idea certainly appealed to Ronnie and me as we piped in on the conversation. "That sounds great to us," I answered for both of us.

By the time we finished dinner, it was starting to get dark outside. I don't know if it was the long drive that day, the excitement of meeting new family members, or simply a food coma that was fast overtaking me, but in an instant, I felt so tired that I could barely keep my eyes open. We helped clear the table, and I asked if I could go to bed.

"Sure, you can," said Aunt Alicia. "Sounds like you guys have a big day ahead of you. By the time you finish the chores, I'll have a lunch ready for you, and then you can go to the lake." She smiled and brushed my face softly as she spoke.

With that, both Ronnie and I gave all the adults a good-night hug and headed out to the porch, where our cots had been set up and were made up with sheets, blankets, and pillows. The rest of the household was not far behind us.

Thirty minutes later, all the lights were off in the house. I was struck by how bright it remained as the stars illuminated the sky through the light screens on the porch. As well, this was the first time I'd ever been serenaded to sleep by a chorus of frogs and crickets. I'm sure I probably had a smile on my face as I drifted off to sleep.

I woke up the next morning to the smell of coffee brewing. As I opened my eyes, I could see it was almost daylight, but the sun hadn't made its way past the horizon yet. I rolled over and saw Bjorn sitting on the floor by my bed, just staring at me. I reflexively jumped up to a sitting position and pointedly asked, "What are you doing?"

He rose and simply replied, "Waiting for you sleepyheads to get up! Wake your brother up and meet us in the barn so we can get the chores done." With that, he was gone, running out the screen door like he was on fire as he headed to the barn.

I woke up Ronnie and told him we had to help our cousins with the chores. He looked around groggily and asked what time it was. Scanning the room for a clock, I found none. I had no idea what time it was, and I told Ronnie so. I just barked out, "Get up! We said we'd help, and we are going to do our share."

Ronnie rolled out of bed and got dressed, and we both put on our shoes and quietly stepped out of the screen door. When we entered the barn, I was shocked to see how much bigger it was inside than the one I'd played in just a couple of weeks earlier at Grandpa's. There were multiple stalls, and I guessed I was looking at eleven or twelve horses as they all turned their heads to watch us coming through the large barn door.

"Good morning," Jonas said cheerfully as he acknowledged our presence. "We feed and water the horses in here first. Then we go outside and feed the pigs and chickens. Bjorn, go show them where the water buckets are. You and I can feed hay and grain, and they can water the horses."

"Sounds good," responded Bjorn. He waved for us to follow, turned, and ran out a back door. Ronnie and I ran after him. When we were outside, I watched Bjorn pumping a handle that pushed water into a waiting water bucket below the faucet spout. Water gushed from the pump every time Bjorn pulled up and pushed down the handled. After filling one bucket, he set it aside and put a second empty bucket under the spout. Seven pumps later, the second bucket was filled. Picking up one bucket with each hand, he started back toward the barn door. "Come on, I'll show you what to do next!" he shouted over his shoulder as he went through the door.

When we were inside, Bjorn put the water down, opened a stall with a horse in it, picked up the water, took it inside, and shut the gate behind himself. The horse moved to one side, letting him pass without incident, and Bjorn put one bucket down, lifted the other to chest level, and poured it into a stainless-steel tub about four feet off the floor. Once finished, he hefted the other bucket and dumped it in the tub as well. Walking out of the stall with the empty buckets in hands, he again shut and locked the gate. The horse turned around, took three steps, and was immediately taking long drinks of the fresh, cool liquid.

"There are fourteen other horses to water. There are also two more buckets next to the well outside. You guys water the rest, while Jonas and I feed them grain," Bjorn stated matter-of-factly. "Then we'll move outside and feed the rest of the critters." Bjorn was off running again, leaving the two of us to fend for ourselves.

As we started our chores, I realized a couple of facts rather quickly. First, these two boys were wicked strong for their sizes. Pumping the well handle took a lot of strength. Ronnie had a very hard time pulling it down, so I helped him fill his buckets. Carrying two five-gallon buckets full of water was close to eighty pounds, which had to be about what Bjorn weighed. Ronnie and I were a couple of years older and twenty to thirty pounds heavier than our cousins, but these two were every bit as strong as, if not stronger than, we were.

The second fact that I noticed immediately was that as soon as these two got out of bed and until they returned to it at night, they were running. I had no idea where all their energy came from, but it seemed to be endless.

It took almost an hour to feed and water all the animals. "We made great time," Jonas announced. Then he started running toward the main house with the three of us close behind.

"Wow! That was fast!" exclaimed Uncle Hagar. "That's about forty-five minutes quicker than normal! You guys hungry?"

We all nodded affirmingly.

"Wash your hands and let's get some breakfast," continued Uncle Hagar.

Between slurps of coffee, my parents were having a lively conversation with my aunt and uncle, while the four of us ate our fill of hotcakes and eggs.

I found out that wheat wasn't their main crop. The main crop was alfalfa hay. They also owned two hundred head of Hereford beef cattle.

Uncle Hagar had twelve farmhands who worked full time for him. Today, he and most of his cowboy crew were going to drive the cattle from one pasture to another where they would graze for the next month.

After breakfast, we helped clean up our dishes. Then Ronnie and I put on shorts and clean T-shirts for the day. Jonas came into our room and asked, "Are you guys ready?"

We nodded yes and followed him back into the kitchen. "Is lunch ready, Mom?" he asked as he approached the grown-ups.

Aunt Alicia took a quick sip from her coffee cup and rose to her feet. "Yes, it is," she responded, walking to the counter next to the sink. She handed each of us a sackful of food. "Make sure each of you has a canteen of fresh water before you go," she said, looking at Jonas. "Be home before dusk, because you still have evening chores to do before dinner."

"We'll be back in plenty of time for chores," Jonas replied. "Thanks for the lunch, Mom!" And with that, we were off and running back toward the barn. As I said, these two never walked anywhere!

Once inside the barn, Bjorn dragged a platform composed of a set of four steps made of wood over to one of the stalls. Jonas was already inside and was guiding a horse to the stall door. Once the steps were in place, Bjorn jumped off the steps and ran into the tack room, walking out a short time later carrying a western saddle with both hands, and he had a bridle thrown over his shoulder. The saddle and blanket looked bigger than him as he struggled to make his way back to the platform. Once there, he dropped the saddle and took the lead rope from Jonas as they switched places. Jonas first took the halter up and secured it over the horse's head. Then jumping to the ground, he picked up the blanket and ran back up the steps to place it on the horse's back. Jumping down again, he lifted the saddle with little difficulty and made his way slowly back up the steps. Once at the top, he leaned back and threw the saddle over the horse's back, landing it directly on the center of the horse blanket.

The horse jumped a bit as he felt the full weight of the saddle settle on him. Bjorn pulled the halter hard once and then started talking softly to the horse. "Whoa, boy, take it easy," he cooed in a soft voice as the horse threw his head back and forth a couple of times.

Jonas was off the platform in a second and was now under the horse, cinching up the gear that held the saddle to the horse. Once finished, he came out from between the horse's legs and said, "He's all ready to go!"

Bjorn walked the horse down about six stalls and then tied the reins to a portion of fence, turning and running back to us. "One down and three more to go," said Jonas matter-of-factly. "Bring another horse," he continued, pointing at Bjorn, who turned and ran down three stalls, opened the gate, went in, and came out leading a second horse. Fifteen minutes later, all four horses were ready to go.

I knew it probably went without saying, but I had to make sure our cousins knew. "You guys know neither one of us has ever been on horse, don't you?"

They both stopped what they were doing to stare at us. Finally, Bjorn said, "Really, neither one of you?" I just shook my head, signifying he was correct.

"That's OK," said Jonas. "One of you can ride my horse, Jellybean, and the other can ride Mom's horse. Star is very gentle and kind of old, so she's really easy to handle."

With that, Jonas put our lunches in the saddlebags on the horse he was riding and put a canteen on each of our saddle horns. "Let's mount up, guys!" said Jonas. He cupped his hands together, and I put one foot in them as he boosted me up into the saddle. Once he had adjusted my stirrups, he helped Ronnie get up on Jellybean. Ronnie and I walked the horses out of the barn, while Bjorn and Jonas led their horses outside, only stopping to grab large-brimmed cowboy hats and putting them on.

Once outside, Bjorn asked, "Does either one of you have a hat?" I simply replied, "No."

He dropped his reins, leaving the horse free to roam, and ran back inside the barn, coming out with two more cowboy hats. Giving one to each of us, Bjorn said, "You don't want to fry your brain out here! I think these should fit OK."

Jonas led the way, Ronnie was next, and then Bjorn, and I was bringing up the rear as we left the barn and headed north. Jonas asked Bjorn if he'd brought the fishing gear, and Bjorn responded, "Yes, sir!"

We rode in silence for about an hour when Ronnie finally asked, "How far are we going?" I hadn't asked, but I was wondering as well.

Jonas turned in his saddle to face us and asked, "You guys doing OK?" We both nodded affirmatively, and he continued. "It's about another hour and thirty minutes to the lake. If you need to pee or anything, just say so, and we can stop." Turning back to face forward, the silence resumed.

The country we were traveling through was beautiful. Wheat fields, high plains, and rolling hills with various-colored flowers accompanied us to our destination. The sky was a brilliant blue, and I was very glad to have the hat on as the heat seemed to have increased exponentially as we got closer to Velva Sportsman's Pond. Once we arrived, we followed Jonas's lead and took all the gear except the saddles off the horses and made a little campsite next to the water.

"You guys want to try your luck fishing?" Bjorn asked.

"Sure," Ronnie and I said in unison. Ten minutes later, we all had lines in the water, waiting for a monster fish to bite. We had a few bites, but no one was able to land a fish in the next hour and a half. Bjorn, clearly tired of fishing, yelled, "It's hot. I'm going swimming!"

We had no bathing suits, but that didn't seem to faze Bjorn. He reeled in his line and started undressing. Boots came off first, and then shirt and Levi's, and, last, his underwear. He went running into the water, screaming and totally naked! There was no one in sight except for the four of us, and I thought, *What the heck.* Jumping to my feet, I quickly reeled in my fishing line, ran back to our campsite, and started stripping down myself. Once naked, I followed Bjorn's lead and ran into the water. It was cooler than I expected, but it felt so refreshing. Soon, Ronnie and Jonas joined us, and we swam around for the next hour or so.

After getting out of the water, we sat on our clothes and let the warm sun dry us off. The longer we were naked, the more comfortable I became with my nudity. Soon, it seemed as comfortable for me to walk around nude as it would for any aboriginal tribe member somewhere on the other side of the world.

Finally dry, we all put on our clothes and sat back down for lunch. The afternoon was filled with more of the same, a little hiking, a little fishing, and one more long dip in the lake to cool off. Then we mounted up for the ride home.

Being on the back of the horse this time was a little more uncomfortable than riding into the lake. My body wasn't used to being bounced around, legs spread, while I clenched tightly to stay on top of an animal four times my size.

I did become more comfortable riding back as we trotted, galloped, and ran the horses for a couple of short bursts on our way home. Jonas and Bjorn looked like they were one with their equine partners as they had them moving any direction they wanted with seemingly no effort.

Once we were back at the farm, we began the events of the morning only in reverse. We took off all the saddles and gear, put the horses back in their stalls, and started feeding and watering all the animals again. By the time we finished, Ronnie and I were both beat and hungry. But none of the day's events seemed to have fazed Bjorn as he ran from the barn to the main house, this time without us running behind him.

After dinner, I rose from the table only to find I could hardly walk. The pain in my butt and legs was excruciating. I asked Aunt Alicia if she had any aspirin and explained why I wanted it. She smiled and gave both Ronnie and me two aspirin and some salve to rub on our sore parts before we went to bed. After some talk about our day, we were excused to go to bed. I can't remember ever being that tired. We both put on the ointment as directed and got into bed. I think I may have been fast asleep before my head had sunk into the cool comfort of my pillow.

More of the same happened over the next two weeks. We had some great times with our cousins, and we worked right alongside of them if there were chores to be done. Uncle Hagar was very funny, and he was always kidding around with the four of us.

We were leaving on Sunday, so my aunt and uncle decided to throw a little going-away party for us that Saturday night before we left. He invited several neighbors and all his workers and their families to join us. And was it ever a party!

We were in the open barn, and everyone was talking, eating, and drinking. A four-piece band that included Uncle Hagar played some western music, and several couples and kids alike danced on the straw-rich barn floor. Jonas and I put a little vodka in our Cokes, and before long, I was feeling pretty good myself!

The night flew by, and the noise got louder with laughter and singing as the liquor flowed freely. One time, when Jonas and I were spiking our drinks again, Uncle Hagar caught sight of what we were doing. He walked in our direction, and I knew we were in big trouble. When he reached us, he simply said, "Don't get sick, boys! Both your mothers will be pissed if you guys start puking."

At about 1:00 a.m., I was done. The barn and everyone in it were starting to spin, and I could feel myself starting to weave when I walked. I told everyone good night and half walked, half stumbled to the porch and my bed. Ronnie was already asleep, and I was only minutes behind him.

It seemed like I had just fallen to sleep when I was awakened by Uncle Hagar. He'd sat down on the edge of my cot and was pulling his cowboy boots off. "Sorry, little buddy, but I've been cleaning up a bit, and everyone else is in bed already," he slurred. "I don't want to wake everyone in the house, so I'm going to bunk with you, if it's OK."

"That's fine with me. What time is it anyway?" I asked.

"It's about three," he responded. Then standing, he took off his belt but left his Levi's on. "Get over, buddy, I'm coming in," he said before plopping down on the cot next to me. He instantly started breathing heavily.

I tried to go back to sleep but was having a hard time with the heavy breathing, crickets chirping, and frogs croaking. Then the breathing turned to snoring, and within minutes, it was so loud the crickets and frogs stopped trying to compete and fell silent.

At some point, I did go to sleep, only to wake up to the morning sun streaming through the screen directly into my face. I rolled over and discovered I was alone on the cot. I could hear people talking in the kitchen along with the unmistakable smell of coffee brewing. I got up, dressed, and went inside for the last time before leaving.

We spent the day helping with chores and getting ready to go home. I'd had a wonderful time here, and this was the first place we'd visited that I really didn't want to leave. We said our good-byes, and there were hugs all around. Then we drove down the dirt road to the highway and set a course back for Beaumont, California, and home.

I had no way of knowing at the time how this trip would affect the rest of my life. My heritage, my demeanor, my courage would all be tested in various ways as I matured, and I was able to tie the way

I handled those situations directly to one or more of the events that had occurred on this vacation. In the last three months, I'd grown from a boy into the beginnings of a young man.

Thirteen years later, Uncle Hagar drowned trying to rescue a cow in a flash flood next to the lake we'd swum in that summer. Jonas and Bjorn took over the day-to-day running of the ranch, and Aunt Alicia stayed on with them to help manage it and cook for the family.

CHAPTER 4

By the time I became a freshman in high school, Billy Marshall, my next-door neighbor and childhood friend, was a senior. He was also the hero of the Beaumont Spartans football team. As the Spartans starting quarterback for the second year, he was well on his way to leading Beaumont to another league championship. He'd been having an outstanding year so far. Last year, he'd been the passing yardage leader for all high schools in California, with 2,867 passing yards, and he had thrown thirty-three touchdown passes. And it looked like he might beat those accomplishments this year after an outstanding first game against rival and perennial powerhouse, the Banning Warriors.

Billy was a great friend to have on the first day of school as a new freshman. Hazing was not only practiced but also a rite of passage in our small town for the incoming freshmen class members. And unless there was physical harm being done, the teachers pretty much looked the other way on this one day. You weren't allowed to take off someone's clothes, but you could make a mess of them. Lipstick was used for writing on clothes or skin, Limburger cheese was used as hair conditioner or shoved up your nose, and dish soap was smeared anywhere and everywhere. These were the more traditional and predominant forms of torture dished out by the seniors for this once-a-year tribal ritual.

Jimmy Clarke and I were both targets this year because Jimmy's older twin brothers had hazed several of the outgoing seniors when they were freshmen. Jimmy was the major target, and I was simply guilty by association for hanging out with the Clarke brothers. It was a great time for many seniors to get some payback for the mistreatment by their older siblings. Thankfully, Jimmy received a lot more attention that day than I did.

One of the main reasons was that I choose to hang around Billy as much as possible, and he didn't allow his fellow seniors to have their way with me. They would start to harass me, but after some light hazing, Billy would step in and stop them by saying, "All right, all right, that's enough. You've had your fun, now leave him alone." That ended it every time. It was as if they were hearing from one of the prophets in the Bible. He would speak, and everyone simply listened and obeyed. It seemed that no one dared to challenge the words coming from the mouth of the school's star quarterback.

When the bell sounded and we had to change classes for our next period, I would look for Billy, run to him, and then stick to him like glue until just before the bell rang again, signifying we should be seated at our next class. Then I'd run like hell to get into my next class before a senior could stop me in the hall for some fun and games at my expense.

Jimmy, on the other hand, got trashed! We had American history during fifth period together. Because we were friends, we sat next to each other, but on this day, I really wanted to move. He smelled horrible from the assortment of cheeses he was wearing. He had been made up by someone to look like a girl with lipstick, eye shadow, and sloppily applied blush on his cheeks. His white T-shirt had several statements on it written in lipstick or Magic Marker. The one that's stuck in my memory more than any others that day was "smear the queer."

I'd heard this saying many times before. Heck, I'd said it and played an aggressive game by the same name several times growing up with the Clarke boys. But with the discovery fresh in my mind, that one of my own cousins was gay, I found the saying offensive for the first time in my young life. I am also positive that phrase written on a T-shirt by an upperclassman wouldn't go over very well today. But then, neither would the physical hazing of incoming freshmen. Fortunately, we all got through the day alive, and another school year began.

Having multiple teachers was new to all of us in the freshman class. I had three female teachers and three male teachers. I enjoyed the male teachers more than the female teachers. Though it may sound like it, my preferences weren't based on gender bias but, rather, based on the subject matter they taught. The classes I had female teachers for were Algebra I, Spanish I, and physical science, all of which were boring to me. The men taught world government, English composition, and physical education. My favorite class and teacher was social studies/world government taught by Mr. Parnell. As the year went on and we talked about current events, I found out that he'd fought in the Korean War from 1951 through 1953.

Because social studies was my last class of the day, I would often stay after class and ask Mr. Parnell about his experiences in the United States Marines. At first, he was reluctant to speak about personal experiences, but as the year progressed and he became more comfortable with me, he opened up more and more. I was fascinated as I sat listening to him, learning his views on communism versus capitalism.

Through these conversations, Mr. Parnell enlightened me on both the reasons for the war, when it began, and how it had still never officially ended. I had studied this time in history in the eighth grade, but there was only a quick mention or two pertaining to this enormous world current event. I had no idea, until listening to Mr. Parnell, how little attention this war had received from the American press. Hence, it was given the nickname "the Silent War."

The Korean War was the first war that the United States participated in which they didn't win it outright. Unfortunately, I had no way of knowing at the time, but we, as a fighting nation, would, at best, lose or call it a draw in many more wars during my lifetime. Conflict after conflict, it seemed that regardless how mighty the United States military strength or how much money we threw at each campaign, victory would elude the most powerful nation on the face of the earth well into the twenty-first century.

Mr. Parnell had me do some research on the Korean War and present it to our class for extra credit. As I researched, I found that the war had begun between free capitalistic countries and those who identified themselves as communist countries. This started as a war of words and ideologies but soon escalated to a combative situation in Korea.

The country of North Korea bordered China to its north and South Korea to the south at the thirty-eighth parallel on the globe. With the help of Chinese reinforcements, North Korea invaded South Korea and captured a major city, Seoul, with a well-organized strike in June 1951.

The United States, under the direction of Pres. Harry Truman, sent in America troops to help South Korea fend off the North Korean/Chinese surge. Our troops were led by Gen. Douglas McArthur, an accomplished and outspoken military leader who had been a major contributor in leading the U.S.A. to victory in World War II. Our armed forces were soon joined by British and French troops with the assistance of their allied nations.

In a counteroffensive, South Korea and their allies were able to take back Seoul from the communist north. General McArthur wanted President Truman to declare war on communist China, which had backed and aided North Korea in this campaign. But Truman's only goal was to stop the communist onslaught into the Pacific where Japan would be the only sovereign nation left between communism and the United States. Truman and McArthur vehemently disagreed over China, and McArthur was ultimately relieved of his command. Truman was satisfied that the communist insurgents had been stopped, and with the help of the West, South Korea again maintained its sovereignty. There was a truce drawn in July 1953 between the two Koreas.

To this day, the thirty-eighth parallel remains the border between North and South Korea. There is a strip of land known as the demilitarized zone that is fiercely guarded and constantly blockaded by both countries to prevent invasion by the other side.

When I heard the numbers of human lives lost in this war, which only lasted two years, I could hardly believe them. Over five million people were killed in the Korean War. And the most tragic number, 2.5 million of those killed were innocent civilians from both countries. Men, women, and children who were caught up in a war and just couldn't get out of the way were slaughtered by the warring armies.

The United States forces paid a high price as well in protecting democracy with forty thousand Americans dying on foreign soil, and an additional one hundred thousand Americans wounded or maimed in this short period.

I knew it was extremely personal, but one day, when it was just Mr. Parnell and me, I asked him if he'd ever been on the front lines and had to kill one of his enemies. His eyes teared up, and he didn't answer for a few seconds. Then he spoke softly, "Hundreds, I'm afraid. It was a conflict of weapons against humanity."

Seeming to drift off into another world, he continued. "The North Koreans would send a mass of humanity at our front lines. Not trained soldiers but farmers and civilians who had no choice but to advance on us or be killed by their own army. We had machine guns, and we would mow down one wave, and another wave would come behind it. And then another and another and another, until the machine-gun barrels glowed red from the constant firing and started to melt. We would fall back as new guns were placed on the front lines, and it continued over and over and over, day in and day out. The North Koreans were climbing a mountain of their own people's dead bodies as they tried to break through our line, and still they kept coming."

Mr. Parnell's head had slumped down below his shoulders as he sat there with his arms resting on his knees. He was quiet now, and I wondered where his mind was as he sat there. Was he reliving those horrible memories that I had so nonchalantly dredged up? I broke the silence by thanking him for telling me about his experiences and left his room. We never talked about the Korean War again. I was sorry I had pried into his personal life and war memories, and I wished I hadn't push so hard for information.

I talked to my dad that night after dinner and told him about my conversation with Mr. Parnell. He agreed with me that I had invaded this man's privacy and suggested I not speak to him about Korea again. "War is hell, son, and for people who saw action on the front lines, it can be very painful to talk about to others who weren't there."

"Did you ever have any experiences like that?" I asked, wondering if I had overstepped my bounds for a second time in the same day.

"No, no, I didn't," he replied. "But your uncle Mel was in the Marshall Islands fighting the Japanese, and he witnessed death on a horrific scale. Of the sixty-two men that were deployed there with him, only twelve got back on the ship sent to take them home three weeks later. Your uncle has never been quite right since coming back from that mess. He can't hold a job, he's divorced, and now he's an alcoholic. Like I said, war is hell."

At my ten-year high school reunion, I was told that Mr. Parnell had gotten divorced about four years earlier, and two years after that, he'd committed suicide in his own garage. At the time I heard it, the news hit me hard! I had thought of him often, and the notion that he couldn't live with his guilt over what had happened during the war had crossed my mind several times. Even though he wasn't one of the original forty thousand casualties, I knew in my heart that as I watched him sitting there staring at the floor in his classroom that day, it was undeniable that this war had claimed many more victims.

I have always liked sports, and as with most people, I am better at some games than others. Even though I was still small in stature as a freshman, I was solid and strong. Football suited me, and I was pretty good at tackling opponents. I played first string middle linebacker on our freshman high school team. We had a reasonably good year, winning seven games and only losing two.

When football was over, Jimmy Clarke begged me to go out for the freshman basketball team. I was just starting my adolescent growth, and I was too short to play basketball. As well, I wasn't that good of a shot from the outside, and I didn't really possess the quickness necessary for court sports. But Jimmy continued to badger me until I agreed to try out. Based purely on a poor gene pool and a height-challenged freshman class, I somehow made the team. We didn't win many games, but we were surprisingly competitive in most. I played many more minutes than I had anticipated as the season progressed. The freshman and junior varsity teams played on Thursdays in the late afternoon, while the varsity team played on Friday nights.

On one of our away games in Palm Springs, we had finished our freshman game, and the junior varsity had just started their game. Gabriel Martinez and I decided to walk over to the Safeway grocery store across the street to buy a candy bar while the junior varsity team played. I asked Jimmy to come along, but he wanted to stay and watch the JV game. He was more serious about basketball than I ever was.

While in the candy aisle, Gabriel whispered to me, "I dare you to steal that candy bar and just walk out of here."

Looking down at the Almond Joy I had in my hand and then looking back to him and pointing to his candy bar, I responded, "I will if you will." He lifted his T-shirt and slipped the candy bar he was holding into the waistband of his pants and then pulled his shirt down over it. I looked around, saw nobody in our aisle, and did the same. We turned and headed for the front door. Just as we crossed the door threshold, a voice came from behind us. "I think you boys may have forgotten to pay for those candy bars." Gabriel took off running toward the high school, and I wasn't far behind him. Did I mention previously that I wasn't a very fast runner? Gabriel was putting some distance between him and me when I felt a hand the size of a meat hook latch on to my shoulder. I was immediately pulled to a stop.

"Tell your friend to get back here!" a voice behind me said forcefully.

"Gabriel, stop and come back here!" I yelled as he continued to put more distance between us. "Gabriel!" I yelled louder this time. He slowed, looked over his shoulder, and finally slowed to a stop. Turning back toward us and seeing that I was caught, he slowly started to walk back in our direction.

Once he was standing next to me, my captor simply said, "Let's go back to the store and talk about this, gentlemen." Never taking his hand off my shoulder, he turned, and we started back toward the store with Gabriel in tow. Once in the store, he marched us straight into the office and closed the door behind us.

"We lose about 1 percent of our profits annually to you punks from the high school. And it pisses me off that more and more of you little pricks think it is OK to come into my store and steal stuff!" he said, his voice raising with every word coming out of his mouth. "So I'm not letting any of you off the hook anymore! Sit still and be quiet while I make a phone call." With that, he picked up the receiver from the phone on his desk, dialed, and within seconds was talking with the Palm Springs Police Department.

When he hung up, Gabriel spoke up. "Sir, we're not from here. We are from Beaumont, and we are just here to play a basketball game against Palm Springs High School."

He shook his head in disgust. "Do you think that makes any difference!" he yelled.

"But what about our coach?" said Gabriel. "Who is going to tell him?"

Again, shaking his head, he retorted, "Maybe the police, and quite frankly, I don't give a shit if they do or not! Your coach will figure out something is wrong when they realize you're not on the bus home."

I looked at Gabriel, and he looked back at me with wide eyes but said nothing as we both realized we were in serious trouble.

When the police arrived, they knocked lightly on the office door and waited for the store manager to open it. The two police officers talked to the manager in a low voice with their backs to us and then turned and addressed us. "Empty your pockets, boys," one said matter-of-factly.

Both Gabriel and I stood up and took everything out of our pockets. Gabriel had his student identification and three dollars and some loose change. I also had my student ID and about thirty-four dollars in bills. Having thirty-four dollars in your pocket in 1962 would be the equivalent of having $340 in 2017.

The police looked at the money and then at each other, and, finally, one of them addressed us, "Why the hell would you steal a couple of candy bars when you have that much money in your pocket?"

Gabriel and I just looked at each other. Then I looked back at the police officers and simply shrugged my shoulders. Gabriel took it upon himself to speak for both of us. "I dared him to steal the candy bar, and then he dared me back," he said as his head lowered, no longer able to hold eye contact with the officers.

The store manager was so angry at hearing Gabriel's confession he couldn't keep his mouth shut. "You spoiled little fuckers are both going to jail!" he screamed, his face turning a bright red as he yelled at us.

The police officers looked at him, and one of them asked, "So you want to press charges against them?"

"You damn right I do!" he responded loudly, the veins in his neck looking like they were going to explode. "I'm sick and tired of being ripped off by these little punks. This is the only way I know to stop it."

Both officers shook their heads affirmingly in agreement, and then the smaller of the two said, "Stand up, boys, and put your hands behind your backs." We both stood and did as we were instructed. I felt the handcuffs close tightly around one wrist and then the other. After we were handcuffed, the two officers opened the office door and escorted us out of the office and through the store, while several patrons stopped their shopping to stare at us in disgust. When we finally arrived at the car, they took each of us to a different side and opened the back doors. Then one of them simply said, "Get in." Once we were inside, the doors were closed, and both officers got in the front seat, and we drove away, headed for the police station.

My head fell back against the seat as I thought about how much trouble I was going to be in! I was pissed at Gabriel for egging me on, and I was even more pissed at myself for taking the challenge when I knew better!

Once we arrived at the jail, we were booked and allowed to call our parents. The police told us that our respective parents would have to come pick us up. Gabriel got hold of his mother on the first call. I, however, was not as lucky. I tried to call my mom three times in the space of an hour with no success. Finally, one of the officers asked, "Where does your father work?"

"Bob Fey Ford in Banning," I answered. "But I don't know the phone number."

"What is your father's name?" he asked.

"Eirik Larsen," I responded, keeping it simple. I did not want a police officer calling my dad at work and, worse yet, having my father driving to Palm Springs to pick me up at the Palm Springs police station. *I am in so much trouble*, I thought to myself again as the officer turned and started back toward the office.

A few minutes later, a different police officer came out of the office and walked to our holding cell. Opening the door, he said, "Which one of you is Michael Larsen?"

"I am," I responded.

"Come with me, I have your father on the telephone."

My heart sank as I followed him to the office again. *Shit! Shit! Shit!* I thought to myself as we walked toward the telephone on his desk. I kept thinking over and over, *This can't be happening!*

Picking the receiver up off the desk, the officer turned and held it for me to take from him. Taking it, I raised it to my ear and spoke into the mouthpiece, "Hello."

I had not overestimated my father's anger as he began to scream into my ear. Every time he stopped yelling to take a breath, I would quickly insert an "I'm sorry." That at least gave him enough time to fill his lungs for the next barrage of demeaning statements delivered with a spattering of profanities as he screamed through the phone at me. Finally, he seemed spent and asked to speak to the officer again. I handed the phone back to the police officer, who listened and gave short answers to my father.

"Yes," he started. "I understand, sir." "Fine," he continued. "I will see you then, sir." With that, he hung up the telephone, turned to me, and waved me back toward the door we'd come through only moments before. We headed back to the jail cell, and he stopped to open the door, again motioning for me to go inside. As I moved through the door, I heard the loud clank of the door closing behind me, followed by the jingling of keys as he locked the cell door again.

"What did your father say?" Gabriel asked.

"He was so pissed!" I responded. There was nothing more to say.

About an hour later, Gabriel's parents arrived to pick him up. Looking first to her son and then to me, Gabriel's mom said, "So this is the boy who got you into this situation." My head snapped around to Gabriel, and I shot him a wicked look. He quickly broke away from my stare and looked down but said nothing. The cell door was opened, and Gabriel stepped out and followed his parents through the office door in silence.

I, on the other hand, continued to die a thousand deaths as I waited for my father's arrival. Two more hours passed before I saw the office door open and my father accompanied by a police officer walking toward my cell. I wasn't sure if I wanted to get out of the cell or if I should beg to stay in jail. But when the door opened, I made the only move available and walked out.

My father didn't speak at first; rather, he turned sharply started toward the office door and said as he walked away on his crutches, "Come on." There was no need for more to be said as I followed behind him like a beaten puppy. When we got to the car, he simply said, "Get in."

We drove the twenty miles home in complete silence. When we finally arrived and walked through the front door, my mother was waiting for us. Her puffy red eyes made it clear to me that she had been crying. Looking at me, she said in a low broken voice, "Michael, I will always love you, but sometimes you break my heart." With that, she turned, walked into her bedroom, and shut the door behind herself.

My father had moved into the living room, leaving me standing there by myself. I felt the tears well up and spill down my cheeks as I thought about my poor mother. She was right; she deserved a better son than me. She had done so much to make my life normal during very hard times, and this was how I repaid her? By disgracing our family name and being thrown in jail for theft at the age of fourteen. I quickly went into my room and shut the door softly. I couldn't stop the flood that followed as I cried in shame for what I had done to my parents.

No one said a word the next morning as I sat eating breakfast. As I got up to leave for school, my mother stopped me. "Don't forget your lunch," she said, holding out a brown paper bag for me to take from her. I felt like crying all over again as I reached out and accepted her gift. Even though I had embarrassed our family, my mother proved with that gesture that she still loved me unconditionally. I kissed her on the cheek, took the lunch sack, and left for school.

"What the hell were you thinking!" were the first words out of Jimmy's mouth when he saw me in the hall. "You are in so much trouble! I am so glad I'm not you right now."

"Oh, shut the hell up!" I responded. "I'm going to class."

As I headed to my first-period classroom, it was obvious that word had already spread about our misguided adventure. Walking through the halls, it became silent as I neared other kids, and they moved back toward the walls, letting me pass through them in silence. I felt like Moses crossing the Red Sea, when God held the water back for his safe passage. It was a relief to finally reach my room, and I hurried to my desk, intentionally not making eye contact with any of my classmates.

The rest of the day went as well as I could have expected. Very little eye contact and lots of whispers or snickers as I walked past various groups of students and so-called friends. I had only one period left in the day, and that was the mandatory pep rally we had on the second Friday of each month. I felt relieved that I was close to having this day from hell over. I had just sat down in the bleachers when Jimmy found me and hopped up the bleacher steps to take the seat next to me.

"How did the day go?" he asked, punching me in the leg as he moved closer.

"Not as bad as I'd imagined it would go," I retorted.

He smiled slightly and continued. "By next week, this is going to be old news, so don't sweat it."

I smiled back, neither of us knowing what was about to transpire.

The room was loud with the anticipation of our varsity basketball team's entrance. Just a moment later, they entered, followed by Coach Nicholas, with his ever-present clipboard in hand. The room seemed to spontaneously erupt in noise as the team came strolling in and took their seats on folding chairs already set up in a straight line on the basketball floor. Once seated, the cheerleaders in front of them broke into a Beaumont high school cheer.

"Two bits, four bits, six bits, a dollar, all for Beaumont stand up and holler!" The entire student body was up on their feet, joining them in the cheer and screaming at its conclusion, while the cheerleaders jumped around with their pom-poms like they were all on fire! The coach walked to center court, waving his hands for everyone to calm down, and slowly, the roar subsided, and eventually, the room fell quiet.

"Thank you all for your support of our fine basketball team," he started. But before he could get anything else out, the room erupted again in cheers and whistles. Motioning again for people to be quiet, he started talking over the roar.

"Before we get started with our pep rally today, we have some business to take care of," pausing before moving on. "Gabriel Martinez and Michael Larsen, please come down here and stand with me," he commanded.

Holy shit, I thought to myself for the second time in as many days, *this can't be happening.* Jimmy and I exchanged quick glances, and I rose to my feet and started making my way through the crowded bleachers toward the floor. By the time I got to center court, Gabriel was already there. I took my place next to him only to be motioned to the other side of Coach Nicholas. I quickly moved away from Gabriel and to the other side of the coach.

The room had gone deafeningly silent as the coach began to speak. "These two young men took it upon themselves to embarrass our school yesterday. After playing in the freshman basketball game, they decided to steal something while waiting for the junior varsity game to finish. They were caught, taken to the Palm Springs jail, and subsequently charged with shoplifting." He paused for effect and looked around the gym to ensure he had everyone's attention. Then he began again, "Each of you will learn in life that with every action, good or bad, there are consequences. The consequences of this action are that these two gentlemen will no longer play basketball on the freshman basketball team." His eyes swept the room once more, and he continued. "In fact, they are forbidden from participating in or attending any school functions for the remainder of this school year." With one last long look around the room, he finished, "Let this be a lesson to all of you. This type of behavior will not be tolerated at our high school." Then with a look of distain, he turned his head first to stare at me and then turned right toward Gabriel and finally said, "You boys can go take your seats now."

The room was completely silent except for the creaking of the steps as I climbed back up to my row in the bleachers. My face was hot, and I knew I'd turned a bright shade of crimson as I continued to make my way to my seat. All eyes seemed to be on me as I shuffled through the row toward the center and my destination next to Jimmy. Finally, I reached the open seat and slumped down next to him. He gave me a reassuring pat on the knee as we both watched the coach continue.

"Now, let's get on with our pep rally!" he yelled enthusiastically.

The crowd erupted again, and the focus was finally off Gabriel and me. I don't know if I heard another word in the gym that afternoon. I just wanted to get out of there.

I was forever changed by the embarrassment of that horrible choice. I kept to myself, and except for Jimmy, I spoke to no one over the next several weeks. I either ate lunch with Jimmy or ate by myself. I was no longer his wingman either. None of the girls who had smiled as adoringly as I walked by prior to this event wanted anything to do with me now.

In fact, the only girls that wanted to talk with me were a select few bad girls who smoked cigarettes and had winos buying them alcohol before cruising the avenue on a Friday night instead of going to the basketball game. They thought I was cool. I thought they were sluts.

With no social life, I became much more absorbed in my academic life. I started concentrating on my classes, and in no time, my grades improved dramatically. I also wanted to get ready for football next year when my suspension from sports was to be lifted, so I started working out like a madman. I worked out every day, and as luck would have it, I'd grown much taller by my sophomore year. By football season, I was twenty pounds heavier and three inches taller at five feet nine inches. And because of the workouts, I was almost twice as strong as I'd been in my freshman year. I tried out for the varsity team, and much to my and many other surprise, I made the team. I was one of only three sophomores that were selected to play with the varsity football team that year.

Outside the walls of our high school, there were many history-making events that were going on in the world at that time in my life that dwarfed my personal freshman drama.

The Soviet Union and China had become the faces of communism. The Soviet leader at the time, a boisterous man by the name of Nikita Khrushchev, was diligently working to rid the world of imperialism and replace it with communism. He was intent on replacing Stalinism, a repressive style of government, by abolishing the feared Soviet secret police. He was also on a mission to improve the standard of living in his country. He began what was coined by the press the space race by launching a Sputnik rocket before the United States space program was able to get a rocket into space. Two years later, Russia launched a rocket to the moon, again ahead of America. Then in early 1961, Russia launched the first Sputnik with an astronaut aboard, Yuri A. Gagarin, who will forever live in the history books as the first man in space.

Khrushchev and the West had a tenuous relationship at best during this time. Relations worsened in the early '60s when Russia shot down an America U-2 spy plane deep inside Russia's borders. As tensions grew between the Soviet Union and the United States, discontent also rose in many Soviet Union satellite countries. Khrushchev suppressed riots in Poland and Hungary as they tried to exit the Soviet Union. Poland was peacefully suppressed, but it took military intervention to stifle the protests in Hungary, leaving 2,500 dead and 13,000 wounded. As well, Khrushchev built the Berlin Wall to stop East Germans from defecting to the capitalist West.

In November 1961, the United States elected John F. Kennedy as the president of the United States. He began his tenure in January 1962. Kennedy was a fiery war veteran and navy hero who had risen to prominence in the late '50s and early '60s. He was also the youngest president ever to be elected to the office at the age of thirty-two. In his inauguration speech, the new president said, "Ask not what your country can do for you but, rather, what you can do for your country." He had no way of knowing at the time that the phrase would become a large part of his legacy.

Cuba's democratic government had been overthrown by a communist supporter, Fidel Castro, in the late '50s. After Kennedy's election, it was discovered in October 1962 that the Russians had placed nuclear missiles on Cuban soil, just ninety miles off the United States coastline. Kennedy demanded Russia to move the missiles from Cuba or suffer the consequences. The Russians began moving nuclear submarines toward the Caribbean Ocean in response to Kennedy's demands. Kennedy and Khrushchev became locked in exceedingly dangerous rhetoric that continued to escalate for thirteen days. The newspapers of the day called their feud the Cuban Missile Crisis. During those thirteen days of escalating confrontations between the two superpowers, the entire world understood that our planet was on the doorstep of complete destruction if they didn't come to an agreement.

Hiroshima and Nagasaki Japan were still fresh horrific images for the entire civilized world. Khrushchev finally relented and agreed to take the Russian nuclear weapons out of Cuba. In return, Kennedy publicly agreed to not invade Cuba as they had tried in a failed attempt one year earlier at the Bay of Pigs. Privately, Kennedy also agreed to remove nuclear weapons from Turkey where they bordered the Soviet Union.

During this same time, we were practicing nuclear disaster drills weekly at our schools. We were all instructed to get away from windows, drop down on our knees, cover our heads with both hands, while ducking under our desks as we waited to see if we were inside the blast radius. After watching several videos in which dummies were instantly turned into fiery ash if they were in the blast radius, Jimmy Clarke and I decided to add, "And kiss your ass good-bye!" to the end of every practice session. It was a ridiculous drill, and we all knew that if in fact there was a nuclear war, everyone would be dead, if not from the initial blast, then from the radioactive fallout. Nevertheless, we were required to practice the drill weekly because it was mandated by the school system.

Then an event that was unthinkable for America and our allies occurred. On November 22, 1963, only two years after being elected as president of the United States, John F. Kennedy was assassinated in Dallas, Texas, by Lee Harvey Oswald. I remember that day as if it were yesterday.

I was walking to my chemistry class, which began right after lunch, when one of my teachers ran by me, and she seemed to be crying. Not twenty seconds later, another female teacher who was also crying passed me as she hurried toward the school office. I continued toward my classroom. Upon entering, I found Mr. Abrams sitting at his desk, motionless, staring straight ahead, with tears in his eyes. All of us were wondering what was going on, but no one asked. And then it came over the school loudspeaker.

"Teachers and students, today, at approximately 11:00 a.m., central time, Pres. John F. Kennedy was shot by an unknown assassin. He was rushed to a nearby hospital, where he was pronounced dead from his wounds at approximately 12:30 p.m." After a long pause, the voice on the microphone continued. "Linden B. Johnson, vice president, has been sworn into the position of president of the United States. This is a very sad day in American history. Please keep the

Kennedy family in your prayers, and God bless America." Then the voice went silent.

Not a word was spoken by anyone in the room. Several of the girls in class began to cry, while the rest of us were left with our own thoughts, fears, and insecurities. Finally, dabbing his eyes with a handkerchief, Mr. Abrams looked up, cleared his throat, and spoke to the class.

"Ladies and gentlemen, the American public doesn't know much yet, but we do know our president has been assassinated. I am sure the whos and whys of this tragedy will come out over the next few days. The answers to all our questions should come to light quickly." He paused and then began again, "We have called the school buses in, and you are all excused to go home early today. I don't know if school will be open tomorrow or not—that decision hasn't been made yet. Go home and be with your families as we all mourn the death of a great American hero." Looking away for a long minute, he concluded his conversation with a simple "Class dismissed."

Most of us just sat there, stunned, trying to absorb what we had just heard. That ten minutes in chemistry class during my sophomore year would be forever etched in my mind as I moved through life. It was one of the saddest, most unnerving events of my lifetime.

However, it wasn't the only assassination during those trying times. Civil rights leader Medgar Evers was assassinated as well in early 1963. The next day, the NAACP went on record by stating that "no state in the nation could match the inhumanity, murder, brutality, and racial hatred of Mississippi."

From 1963 through 1968, civil rights activists and hard-line segregationists waged war in Mississippi. Much of the violence being directed at African Americans beginning in 1963 was organized by a group calling themselves the Ku Klux Klan. The racial terrorism ranged from cross burnings and church bombings to beatings and murders. In 1964 alone, a Mississippi journalist reported that Klansmen had killed six people, shot an additional thirty-five, and beaten another eighty activist. The homes, businesses, and churches of an additional sixty-eight civil rights activists had been firebombed.

As a sophomore, and still with no social life, I had become more involved in my church and a nondenominational Christian organization called Young Life. I don't know if it was because I felt guilty about being branded a thief and needed forgiveness, or because Young Life was in Banning, where I wasn't so well known for my transgressions. But I was now old enough to make my own decisions on race equality, and I found myself drawn into some very deep conversations with people of color at Young Life meetings and outings. My biblical upbringing reinforced that all people were equal in God's eyes. Even though in my heart I knew that to be totally true, I felt fortunate to have been born a blue-eyed Norwegian boy and not African American.

I continued working out religiously after football season was over. We'd had a pretty good year, but losing an all-state quarterback like Billy Marshall was hard to overcome. Still, I'd decided that I would only play one sport for the rest of my high school career, and that would be football.

I had continued my growth spurt between my sophomore and junior year, and I needed a completely new wardrobe because nothing fit anymore. By virtue of my paper route and lawn mowing jobs, I had plenty of money to spend for clothes. I had a favorite store, Jeremiah's Men's Wear, which had the newest trends and styles in stock before anyone else. I spent a lot of time there trying on clothes and talking with people who came into the store. I was in there so much that I began giving other patrons advice on color and style if they asked for it. Not just high school kids, even some of the businessmen from around town were asking my opinion on their clothing selections when they were in the store. The owner took notice and asked me if I would be interested in working after school and on weekends for him. The money was great, so I accepted with the understanding that I wouldn't be available during football season.

Thirty days later, I gave up my paper route and only worked at Jeremiah's. I began every day working out in the morning, showering, and going to school. After school, I would go to work at Jeremiah's and then go home to eat and do homework, and then I would go to bed. Life was busy, but it was simple.

At dinner one night, my dad told me he had taken in a clean low-mileage 1957 Pontiac Chieftain in on a trade, and he wanted to know if I would be interested in looking at it as a first car. I was both surprised and excited, knowing I still had eighteen months before I would be old enough to legally drive. We looked at the car, and I loved it! I had enough money in the bank to easily pay cash for the car, and three days later, it was mine.

We left the car at the dealership, and I had a lot of work done on it as funds became available. I had the car painted jet black except for the roof, which was painted pearl white. I had black-and-white tuck and roll leather installed on the seats. Chrome wheels and polished chrome bumpers finished off the appearance. Once all the work was completed, the car was beautiful. I am positive that Uncle Dobbie would have approved of my General Motors replica of his 1955 Ford Crown Victoria. Unfortunately, I still couldn't drive it for four more months.

The good news was that we were back to football season, and I was back on my strict regimen of working out, school, working, eating, and sleeping. I didn't have time for the car or anything else for that matter until football season ended.

School in my junior year began much easier for me. And because I was a part of the football team, the seniors didn't really mess with me. The embarrassing stealing incident of my freshman year was all but forgotten as time had helped heal that wound to both my reputation and my libido. Because of Jeremiah's Men's Wear, I was one of the best-dressed guys on campus, and girls were starting to take notice of my new and improved attire and physique. And for some reason, I had developed a thirst for knowledge and was really applying myself in all my classes, which translated into straight As. Jimmy and I stayed close, and in time, I became his clothing advisor as well. Now that we were pretty much the same size, he seemed to have half of my clothes in his closet. He was a very accomplished borrower, but he was never very good at returning borrowed articles of clothing.

That same year, our high school became involved in a foreign exchange program for the first time. We sent two students to different countries, and they, in turn, sent two students to Beaumont High School. The students lived with a host family for the year, and after finishing the year, all the students would return home with a better understanding of each other's culture. Our school sent Gordon Stiles to France, and a French student came to live with the Stiles family. Barbara Evans went to Japan, and a Japanese girl came here to live with the Evans family.

During the second week of school in my junior year, we were called to an assembly to be introduced to our new foreign exchange students. The principal gave us some information about each of them and then announced the first student, Miko Atawana, and asked her to come into the gym.

In came a slight raven-haired young Japanese girl dressed in a traditional Japanese kimono. She shuffled her feet quickly rather than picking them up and stepping one in front of the other as she made her way to the center of the gym. Once there, she bowed at the waist in a perfect ninety-degree angle and then took the microphone from the principal and, in a high-pitched voice, said, "Kon'nichiwa!"

She expressed to the audience in broken English that it meant "hello" in Japanese. She then gave the microphone back to the principal. After a few more words from Principal Adams, he asked her to take a seat in the bleachers with the other students. She turned, bowed to him, and then shuffled to the front row where two girls made room for her to sit.

Principal Adams then started speaking about the next foreign exchange student. "This next young man, Jean-Paul Bernard, comes to us from Paris, France," began the principal. "He was first in his class as a sophomore at a very prestigious school in Paris. We are very happy to have him here to share his experiences and give us a look into his culture and share ideas. Please welcome Jean-Paul."

Through the door came a six-foot-tall well-dressed African American man with a full Afro, who approached the principal and shook his hand. The anticipated applause by the student body didn't come as nearly everyone just sat there, stunned.

He's black, I thought to myself. Sitting next to me, Jimmy said, "So he is," which alerted me that I had unconsciously given voice to my thoughts.

"Bonjour," he said, taking the mic from the principal. "That is 'hello' in French," he continued. "I am happy and honored to be here representing France," he said in remarkably good English. "I hope to become friends with several of you while I am here in America," he continued with a thick French accent. Handing the mic back to the principal, he bowed slightly and started walking toward the bleachers to a smattering of applause.

Once Jean-Paul got close to the bleachers, a space large enough for three bodies opened in front of him. He took a seat, and only Miko, the Japanese exchange student, scooted closer to him. Everyone else kept their distance and simply stared.

Principal Adams began speaking to the student body again. "OK, Spartan Nation," he concluded, "I expect each of you to welcome these new students and get to know them. This is a wonderful chance for all of us to learn about each other's cultures firsthand. You are all excused to go to an abbreviated first-period class." With that, we all filed out of the gym with much less noise and fanfare than normal.

It turned out I had no classes with Miko, but in sixth period, I was in Spanish II with Jean-Paul. He came walking into the room just before the bell went off, signifying we needed to be in class.

The classroom went totally silent as he looked for a desk to occupy. As luck would have it, the only open desk was next to mine. Sitting down and taking out his study book, he looked over at me, nodded, and innocently said, "Hi."

I nodded back, returned the greeting, and introduced myself. "I'm Michael," I said, offering my hand to shake.

He took it, and as we were shaking, he reciprocated, "It's a pleasure to meet you, Michael."

We weren't far into the class when it became quite apparent that Jean-Paul was far ahead of the rest of us in his grasp of the Spanish language. I must admit that I was very impressed that a junior in high school spoke his native tongue, French, as well as English and Spanish almost as fluently as people from those other cultures. He was pleasant, participative, and very friendly with the rest of his new classmates.

Strangely, fifteen minutes after class had begun, the color of his skin ceased to be his identity, but rather, we all seemed to focus more on his positive attitude and outgoing personality. I found myself being drawn to him as he tried to fit in with a room full of strangers. When class was over, I asked if he wanted to have lunch together the next day and told him I would be happy to introduce him to a few people. He seemed delighted and graciously accepted my invitation. We set a time and place to meet the next day, and then we were off to our next classes.

The next day, I wasn't completely impressed by being stood up for lunch as we agreed. I had already told Jimmy about the lunch date with Jean-Paul, and he was excited to meet him. Now, as Jimmy sat next to me, he was giving me nothing but grief because of the no-show.

"You can count on me, Michael," he chided. "Throughout history, we Frenchmen have been men of our word. I'll never let you down."

"Shut up!" I responded. "I'm going to the restroom and then to class. I'll see you after school." Jimmy simply shook his head affirmingly and kept eating as I walked away.

Walking down the hall toward my next class, I ducked into the first restroom I came to. Once inside, I saw two of our largest senior linemen had Jean-Paul cornered on the back wall by the waste container.

"Hey, what's going on!" I yelled out.

They both turned back to look at me, and I noticed the larger of the two, Jake Conners, had his hand on Jean-Paul's throat, pinning him to the wall. "There's nothing going on here that concerns you, Larsen. Just turn around and walk back out that door," Jake said, pointing to the door I had just walked through.

I didn't know either of them well because I didn't hang out with many of the seniors on our team, but we'd always been cordial. Jake Conners was our first-string center, and Adam Sparling was our first-string right tackle. Both guys were three to four inches taller and had a minimum of fifty pounds on me. Jake's grip tightened on Jean-Paul's throat as I watched his mouth open, trying to get some air into his lungs.

"I can't do that," I said, followed by "You need to let him go now!"

Adam started walking toward me and said, "You a nigger lover, Larsen?"

Setting my feet and readying for battle, I responded, "No, but I'm not a bigot either!" Adam was quickly closing the space between us, and I knew I had to be first if this was going to happen. Remembering that Adam wore a brace on his left knee when playing football, I stepped to the side and kicked Adam as hard as I could on the outside of his left knee. It gave with a sickening pop, and he started to go down in what appeared to be horrible pain. As both his hands dropped to grab his knee, I hit him with a left hook that literally blew up his nose. Blood flew everywhere, including on me, as he crumpled to the tile floor. I turned at about the same time Jake

Conners let go of his prey and started for me. We ran at each other and collided with a mighty thud in the center of the bathroom.

Once, when I was wrestling with Billy Marshall in the front yard and getting my ass kicked, my father made a statement that I believe to be true to this day. "A good big man will beat a good little man every time in an even fight." As Jake picked me up and slammed me to the floor with the force of a dump truck, I was once again reminded of that saying. He came down on top of me so hard that it knocked the air out of me as my head bounced off the tile floor. Through blurred eyes, I watched him pull back his fist and cock it, ready to throw the ending blow. The worst part was knowing that there was nothing I could do about it.

Out of the corner of my eye, I watched as Jean-Paul jump into the air and spun counterclockwise, his leg extended as the heel of his foot struck Jake dead center in the middle of his face. Jake was knocked backward and rolled completely off me. Raising myself onto my elbows and still trying to get some oxygen into my lungs, I saw Jake lying on his back, out cold. Looking back to Jean-Paul, I said, "What the hell was that?"

"Do you mean why they attacked me or what kind of kick that was?" he responded, offering his hand to help me up off the floor.

Taking his hand and getting up off the floor, I replied, "Both. You can explain it to me on our way to the principal's office. We want to give our side of the story to the principal before they do."

"I understand," Jean-Paul responded as we left the bathroom and started toward the office. "I have been studying a French martial art form called savate since I was nine years old. I am quite good at it," he stated matter-of-factly.

"So it appears!" I returned enthusiastically.

"As for the reason," he began again, still using annoyingly perfect English, "I think you can figure that out. My parents warned me that there was a lot of discrimination against people of color in parts of America. However, I didn't expect that to be the case in California.

But when I walked into the assembly at your high school gymnasium and saw no other African Americans anywhere in the bleachers, I thought this might happen. You probably don't know this living in America, but your nation is the epicenter for news around the world. The whole world is aware of what is going on in Mississippi and the south with the fight for racial equality in much of America."

We had reached the principal's office, and I stopped to open the door. Then we both walked in. Our conversation stopped as a secretary asked, "Oh my god, what happened to you?" she said, looking at me. Not having a mirror to see myself, I forgot that I was wearing Adam Sparling's blood everywhere.

"We need to speak with the principal as soon as possible," I said in response, not bothering to explain the blood. Two minutes later, we were sitting in front of the principal and telling our story.

Principal Adams listened without interruption as Jean-Paul recounted the events in the restroom. When Jean-Paul finished, the principal looked at me and said flatly, "Do you have anything to add, Mr. Larsen?"

I simply shook my head no but continued to hold his stare.

"Where are the other two boys?" he asked questioningly.

"If they're awake yet, they're probably cleaning up in the restroom," responded Jean-Paul. His response struck me funny and brought an unwelcome chuckle that I immediately knew was inappropriate, given the circumstances. Principal Adams shot me a stern look as I watched his jaws tighten.

"Thank you both for coming here to explain yourselves," he finally responded. "Jean-Paul, I am very sorry this happened here at our school. On behalf of the entire staff, I apologize for this unfortunate incident. My staff and I will be vigilant in seeing that this does not happen again while you are here."

Then looking back to me, he continued. "Michael, I still have not heard the other side of this story, so we very well may be continuing this conversation later today. Do you have a clean shirt in your locker?"

I nodded, affirming. "Then put it on and clean yourself up before going to your next class. Understood?" I nodded again, and we were dismissed from the office.

After school, Jimmy ran up to me and declared, "What the hell were you thinking?" I was getting tired of him asking that same question every time I got in trouble.

I didn't respond, just kept walking.

"No, I mean it! Beating the shit out of two seniors on the football team to save a nigger's ass? What's come over you?" he continued.

I stopped in my tracks and turned to glare at him. "He's not a nigger! He's a French student who happens to be African American! And if you use that word again, I'm going to kick your ass too!"

Jimmy stood there, stunned, looking back at me with big eyes. "Whoa, buddy! We're still on the same team," he said, putting his hands up in a defensive posture as he backed away from me. "I didn't mean anything by it. I was just making a comment. Stop being so sensitive, for God's sakes!"

I didn't respond other than to turn and start walking toward the gym again.

"Where are you going?" he asked.

"Football practice," I replied curtly.

"That is going to be interesting," he responded. "Give me a call tonight and let me know how that went." Then he turned around and headed the other way, saying, "See you tomorrow, champ!"

When I stepped into the noisy locker room, it immediately went silent. I could only assume that word of the earlier altercation must have traveled like a wildfire in dry brush. I moved straight to my locker, knowing all eyes were on me. Opening the locker door, I sat down on the long bench and started taking off my shoes. I barely had one off when Coach Moffit came bursting out of his office toward me.

"What the hell is wrong with you, Larsen!" he yelled as he closed ground between us.

I knew one thing—I was sick and tired of being asked that stupid question, but before I could respond, he continued. "Sparling is going to need surgery on his goddamn knee, and Conners will be out with a broken nose for at least three weeks! Singlehanded, you've blown up any chance we might have had for a league championship!"

He turned in a quick circle next to me, took off his Spartans baseball cap, and threw it on the ground with all the force he could muster. "And for what! So you could help some nigger kid from France instead of just walking away like you were asked to!" he shouted, showering me with spittle as he screamed. "If you want to save the world, go do it somewhere else!"

I stood up, half angry, half afraid. "I hope you're just angry and don't mean what you're saying," I said in a controlled tone. "Because if you mean that crap, you're setting a hell of an example for everyone in this room!"

There was no immediate response this time, so I continued. "I'm through playing football for you!" I didn't wait for a response from the coach. I sat down on the bench, put my shoe back on, got up, slammed my locker door shut, turned, and walked out the door.

As I was walking toward the parking lot, I noticed Jean-Paul and his host parents walking toward me. *Now what?* I thought to myself. *Could this day get any worse?* I stopped and waited while they approached. Jean-Paul was the first to speak.

"I never got a chance to thank you for your help, and I wanted to say it in person before I went home today. I'm sure that was hard for you, sticking up for a stranger, but I truly appreciate you not letting those two beat the crap out of me."

A slight smile formed on my face by the time he was finished. His host parents both thanked me as well and told me how brave I was to stand up to what they termed "vicious thugs" in the restroom. We said our good-bye, and I headed home.

At the dinner table that night, my brother couldn't keep his mouth shut. "Has Joe Palooka told you about his exploits today yet?" he said with a smirk on his face.

My mom looked at me and said through narrowing eyes, "Did you get in trouble today, Michael?"

Ronnie had a Cheshire cat smile on his face as I relived the whole story of the day's events.

My mother was furious. "You're off the football team! You loved football! Can you apologize to Coach Moffit and get back on the team?"

"I'm not going to play football for that jerk!" I snapped, a little louder than I intended to.

"I can't believe this is happening," she said, rising from her chair and starting to clear the table. "And all this because you decided to step in and rescue one of those troublemakers."

I was pissed at the comment but decided not to escalate this any further. I gritted my teeth and kept my mouth shut.

Once she was in the kitchen and out of ear shot, my father looked at me and simply asked, "Would you do the same thing if you had to do it over again?"

The question surprised me, but I didn't need much time to answer. "Yes! Yes, I would," I answered.

"Then you did the right thing, son. Sometimes, it's hard to make the right choices in life rather than the popular ones. But if you do what's right, you can sleep at night, while others lie awake wondering why they were such cowards. I'm proud of you for being selfless today," he said, giving me a couple of light pats on the arm.

I don't think my father had any idea how much his words meant to me at that moment. But as I left the dinner table, I wondered how my mom and dad could hear the identical story and come away with such different perceptions of the same event.

Jean-Paul and I hung out quite often in school after that day. Jimmy came around, and once he got to know Jean-Paul, they got along well. We ate lunch together most days, and on many occasions, Miko would join us, lightening up the conversation around the table. She was quite the comedian, and I could tell Jimmy was developing a bit of a crush on her.

The year progressed and I spent more and more time working at Jeremiah's and spending money on my car. Finally, in March, I was able to get my driver's license and drive to school. From the very first time I drove to school, everyone was aware that I owned one of the coolest cars in the parking lot. Suddenly, girls who hadn't given me a second look were smiling and flirting with me. Guys who wouldn't normally give me the time of day were asking me how I was doing. I found this newfound acceptance to be both comical and a little ridiculous, but I always smiled and just kept walking as these comments were cast in my direction.

On the first day of my senior year, I had decided not to participate in the hazing of incoming freshmen. In fact, I was quite committed to stopping any incidents that I came across this first day of school. It turned out not to be as big a deal as I had expected, and I only intervened twice during the day to slow down a few of my fellow classmates.

The second most important event of opening day was meeting her. Sitting by myself in Senior Square during lunch, the most beautiful girl I had ever seen sat down close to me and began looking through a purple folder. I looked at her and smiled, "Are you a senior?" I asked.

"Yes, I am," she replied, smiling sweetly. "This is my first day here. I transferred from Chicago." She seemed so innocent, like a baby lamb without its mother, as she sat there waiting for me to respond.

"Well, then, welcome to Beaumont!" I replied. Her smile seemed to grow even larger. "Chicago's a big city. What part of Chicago?"

She smiled and looked into my eyes. "Well, actually, I live west of Chicago in a small town called Naperville. It's just easier to say I lived in Chicago because no one has ever heard of Naperville."

"I see," I responded. "So then if your logic holds, you can tell your Chicago friends that you now live in Hollywood, right?"

She laughed, and in that one instant, I fell head over heels in love with a girl I'd just met, and I didn't even know her name.

"I'm Michael Larsen. What do you call yourself?" I said, extending my hand to shake hers.

"Well, I call myself Snow White, but my given name is Linda Copenger," she said confidently, taking my hand in hers and shaking it lightly.

"Which name should I use when addressing you?" I joked.

"We probably need to stick with Linda, don't you think?" Again, those big beautiful eyes smiled in my direction, and I felt myself melt into them. We sat there for a minute, not speaking, when the bell rang, letting us know it was time for class.

We both rose to our feet, and I said, "It has been a pleasure to meet you, Linda Copenger."

Smiling coyly, she responded, "The pleasure has been mine, Michael Larsen."

I don't know if I can recall anything else from that day, but I do know Linda Copenger was imprinted on my brain, on my heart, and on my soul, and I wanted to see more of her.

At lunch, I sat with Jimmy as always, but before I could say anything about my first love interest, he blurted out, "I met the most beautiful girl today in psychology. She just moved here from Chicago, and her name is Linda something. I'm going to ask her out to the school dance this Friday night."

I said nothing in response. We ate our lunch and went to our fifth-period classes. I hadn't seen Linda for the next couple of days when I accidentally bumped into her, literally, in the hall on Thursday between classes. "I'm sorry," I said before realizing whom I'd bumped into.

She collected herself from the jolt and then looked up at me with those big eyes and said, "Hey there, Michael Larsen, fancy running into you!"

"Hello, Miss Copenger, how is school going?" I asked, smiling back at her.

"Good, really good!" she said. "Are you going to the dance Friday night?"

I hesitated for a second and then said, "Probably not. I'm not much for school dances."

"I'm sorry to hear that," she said, looking genuinely disappointed.

"Well, I've got to get to class," I said.

"Me too," she responded, looking away as she walked past me.

After the fact, I realized there were so many things I could have said that I didn't say. I was angry for not staying and talking longer with her. I wondered if Jimmy had asked her to go with him to the dance yet, and if he did, did she accept? What did it matter, she wasn't going with me!

Walking to my car after school on Friday, Jimmy yelled behind me.

"Hey, can I get a ride home today, buddy?" he asked.

"Sure, hop in," I responded. "I'm going to work, so it's on the way."

Once in the car, Jimmy asked me if I was going to the school dance. I gave him the same answer I'd given Linda and then asked, "You?"

"I would like to go, but I don't want to go by myself," he said.

My ears perked up. "I thought you were going to ask the new girl from Chicago?"

"I did," he responded, "but she turned me down. She said she wanted to get to know more people before she started dating. I told her I understood, but I do think she will be there."

I said nothing else as I pulled up to Jimmy's house and he hopped out. "Let me know if you change your mind," he said, walking up his driveway.

Work was busy, which was good because it took my mind off Snow White for a while. When it was time to close, she again consumed my thoughts. I went home, took a shower, changed clothes, and called Jimmy. "Hey, do you still want to go to the dance tonight?"

"Yah, sure!" he responded enthusiastically.

"Be ready in an hour and I'll pick you up."

"Sounds good," he replied, hanging up the phone.

We arrived at the dance at about eight thirty and walked over to the refreshments. Greeting several classmates on our way, I scanned the room for Linda and didn't see her. We went and sat about six rows up in the bleachers, listening to the music and watching couples dance on the gym floor.

"There she is!" Jimmy yelled above the music as he pointed at the front door.

I looked over to see her coming in, wearing a red sweater, perfectly pressed Levi's, and cowboy boots. Jimmy jumped up, ran down the bleachers, and accosted her seconds after she cleared the door.

She smiled, and they talked for a minute. Then he pointed up to me. I don't know if her smile increased or if I only imagined it, but she waved warmly up to me as they started up into the bleachers.

"I thought you didn't like dances," she said sarcastically once she reached me.

Jimmy gave me a puzzled look as he sat down next to me, seating Linda on his other side away from me.

"I'd rather sit between you two, so I can hear both of you," she said, standing up and placing herself between us. I scooted over to make room for her. Seconds later, she was locked in a two-way conversation with me, and I could feel Jimmy was uncomfortable with the situation.

Jimmy rose to his feet and put his hand out. "Would you like to dance, Linda?"

Looking up at him, she smiled politely and said, "I'm sorry, Jimmy. I would like to dance, but I want to dance with Michael. I hope you understand."

Jimmy shot me a look of unmitigated anger as I rose to my feet, took her hand, and led her down the bleachers to the dance floor. Just touching her hand had my heart pounding. Once we were on the dance floor, no one else existed. I could only see her, only smell her, and only enjoy holding her close to me. The music stopped much too quickly, and we started back up the bleachers to where we were sitting. Linda again sat between us, but this time, she addressed Jimmy.

"I didn't realize you guys were friends," she started, looking him in the eyes. "But I haven't been able to get Michael off my mind from the time I met him on my first day of school. I don't want to hurt your feelings, Jimmy, but I really like Michael."

Jimmy looked crushed, and my heart soared hearing her declaration of affection. I didn't know what to say or do as she looked back lovingly to me. Then the song "Sugar Shack" came on, and she jumped to her feet and pulled on my arm with both hands. "Oh, I love this song, come on!" I was quickly on my feet and following her down the bleachers to the dance floor. When we returned, Jimmy was gone. He got a ride home with someone else that night. I know how disappointed he must have felt, but at the same time, I'd never been happier in my life!

Linda and I became a couple and remained in love throughout our senior year. She received an academic scholarship from Stanford at the end of the year and was off to college late that summer.

We pledged our love until eternity, and for months, I thought we would still get back together and eventually marry. For a multitude of reasons, it didn't happen that way. Life got in the way for both of us, and the inevitability of failure to our long-distance relationship became a reality. Before the Christmas of 1965, we were no longer a couple.

At our twenty-year reunion, I saw Linda for the first time since we'd been sweethearts in high school. She had skipped the ten-year reunion to my total dismay. I had waited another ten years, hoping to see her, and she looked amazing! I can't explain why, but my heart was pounding the same as it had the first time I'd seen her when she turned and smiled at me.

After saying hello and giving me a quick hug, she introduced me to her husband, who was an attorney. He seemed nice enough and was both good looking and very confident. After a couple of minutes, I excused myself and moved away before my staring at Linda became uncomfortable for both of us.

Catching me at the bar by myself later in the evening, Linda asked about my last twenty years, and I gave her a very brief recap. I was in the military for a year, came home and got my degree in business, was gainfully employed, got married, and had a son. Then my wife was killed in an accident, and I'm raising my twelve-year-old son.

"Oh my god!" she said. "That's horrible! I'm so sorry!" We sat silently for a few seconds, sipping on our drinks, when she finally said, "You know I never really got over you, don't you?"

I smiled at her and responded, "And I've never stopped loving you! Sad to say, but you will always be the one that got away. Unfortunately, we can't go back in time and undo what's been done. Your husband seems like a nice man. I really hope he treats you the way I would have."

Taking one last swallow and setting my now empty glass on the bar, I leaned over and kissed her on the cheek, "Good-bye, Snow White. I'm glad I got to see you one more time." I turned and walked away, trying to control the tears that I could feel forming in my eyes.

As I was about to leave, I ran into Adam Sparling. It turned out that he'd married a girl in my class. I didn't remember or recognize his wife from my senior class. Hell, I barely recognized him. He was still three inches taller than me, but he must have weighed 450 pounds now. As we approached each other, I noticed a decided limp in his walk. I wondered if that was from our altercation twenty years ago, or was it the effect of having so much weight forced onto his poor knees over the years? I stopped him and introduced myself in case my appearance had changed as well.

"I know who you are," he stated flatly. "Good to see you." Without saying another word, he took hold of his wife's arm and made his way past me, heading toward the bar.

CHAPTER 5

I was a junior in high school when the United States entered the Vietnam War. It was 1964, and less than 50 percent of the American public had ever heard of or, for that matter, knew where Vietnam was located on a world map. We all knew it was far away, but few Americans realized that this war had started with the French ten years earlier than our entrance into this international conflict. And it was even less known that Presidents Eisenhower, Kennedy, and now Lynden Johnson had all been involved behind the scenes with our allies for years in supporting the war effort prior to our active engagement into combat.

Vietnam was the second war in as many decades in which an idealistic battle between democracy and the communist movement had again sucked the U.S.A. into a major role of involvement in Asia. The United States had backed the South Koreans against a North Korean invasion a decade earlier, and now here we were trying to fend off an overthrow of the South Vietnamese government by a communist Chinese-backed North Vietnam.

The first days of 1967 were just around the corner. A year and a half had gone by since my graduation from high school, and I was still struggling with what the future held for me. I had signed up for the military draft like every other male in the United States on my eighteenth birthday. But since we'd only been formally involved as a nation in the war for two years, there seemed to be a very small chance of being called up for serve.

I had given college some serious thought, but I didn't really have the means to pay for it without going in debt. Inflation had also grown as the United States continued to fund the war in Vietnam, making the cost of college even higher. My parents offered to help, but I didn't want to put the burden of my future education on them. They had already endured enough financial hardships to last a lifetime.

Statistically, only 18 percent of the Caucasian students and 5 percent of the African American students graduating from high school in 1965 went on to college anyway. Regrettably, I believe the percentage of Beaumont graduates that were going on to college was much lower than the national average.

We'd graduated during a time in our history when there were plenty of great jobs that didn't require a college degree. Manufacturing and industrial jobs were abundant and paid more-than-fair wages. There was a multitude of construction jobs, which included housing, commercial buildings, and road systems, available for anyone who wasn't afraid of hard work. In fact, there were more jobs than there were people to fill them. With the low unemployment came a rise in individual income, which gave America a boost in the economy, especially in retail sales.

I had unknowingly fallen into one of those niche retail positions while in high school. Mr. Kraft, owner of Jeremiah's Men's Wear, had promoted me to assistant manager of the store. I was compensated by a generous salary plus a small percentage of the store's monthly profits. Business was great, and at the age of eighteen, I was making almost as much money as my father, who'd been successfully selling cars for six years now.

My job was terrific, and my employer fantastic, even though I wasn't completely enamored with the fashions of the day. Fashion sense was being strongly influenced by England and what was regarded as the British invasion in both the clothing and music industries starting in 1966. Patterned bell-bottom pants, flowered silky shirts, and madras T-shirts that turned different colors when they were washed were all in vogue at the time. Lots of boots, shoes, and even hats were made of shiny fabrics like vinyl or plastics manufactured to look like shiny patent leather.

The music scene and artists, like the clothing, were shifting from American to British influenced. Many of the American acts like Elvis; the Temptations and the Righteous Brothers were being replaced by the Beatles, the Rolling Stones, and Bob Dylan. Even though I didn't care much for the clothes coming out of the British Isles, I loved their music.

I was sitting at home by myself as 1967 rolled in. My parents had gone out on the town to celebrate the New Year with Art and Louise Clarke. They were armed with several party favors to bring in the year with a bang.

My personal favorites were the large blue glass frames that my mom wore with the big 19 in large numbers over her right eye and the numbers 67 above her left eye. After she had a couple of stiff drinks in her, I believe my mom envisioned her glasses to be both fashionable and alluring for the upcoming night's festivities.

A taxicab picked up the two couples, all well on their way to feeling no pain, at around 9:00 p.m. to take them to the Elks club for dinner and dancing. I didn't expect them to return until the early morning hours of the New Year.

Jimmy had invited me to a party at the house he and two of his older brothers now rented together. I'd declined even though I had nothing else going on. We'd been very busy at my work for the weeks leading up to Christmas, and the retail activity had continued through the end of the December. I was tired and was looking forward to a little downtime and watching some football bowl games over the next two days, hopefully with minimal distractions.

About two weeks into January 1967, I received a letter from the United States government stating that I was being called to action and was being required to serve in the U.S. army. My date to arrive at boot camp was March 8, 1967. That was an easy date to remember, because it was my nineteenth birthday. I remember reading it over several times and thinking this seemed so surreal. It seemed like either a cruel hoax someone was playing on me, or maybe it was somehow a mistake.

When my mother got home from work that day, I handed her the letter. She took it, read it, and immediately began to cry. I tried to console her, but she, like me, felt this had to be a misunderstanding.

"Surely our government isn't drafting and taking eighteen- and nineteen-year-olds to fight in a war halfway around the world!" she shouted as tears streamed down her face. I must admit that listening to Mom become so panicked by the letter gave me pause and made me feel a sense of insecurity and fear myself.

My father was more practical when he read through the orders that night. He sat in silence for a moment after reading the document and then looked first at my mother and then to me. I saw his jaws tighten as he continued to look me in the eyes but remained silent. I watched his eyes narrow as he finally spoke. "This is not good news, Michael. I am afraid you are about to grow up faster than either your mother or I wanted you to. War is hell, son, and I am afraid you are probably going to see the worst that humanity has to offer in the next couple of years. It scares the heck out of me, but you have to go and do your duty for your country."

The next time my father and I talked about serving in the army was almost two months later as I was boarding a bus to begin basic training. "Be careful, be smart, be respectful, and above all, stay safe." With those final words, he and my mother hugged me, and I stepped onto the chartered bus to Fort Ord.

"Hello, you bunch of maggots!" a deep raspy voice yelled out as we got off the bus. The voice was attached to a six-foot-tall black man in uniform who seemed to be doing a quick appraisal of each of us as we disembarked on to the asphalt. Square jawed, his arms and chest thick with muscle, he had his hands on his hips as he gave each of us a long look before moving his eyes to the next recruit.

"Let's see if you can line up in three straight lines," he barked, pointing to the side of the bus. We awkwardly scrambled to try and fulfill his wish, only to hear him grumble. "This is going to be a twelve-week shit show! Where do we get you worthless assholes anyway? You can't even make three straight lines!" And with those words of instant ridicule, my military career had begun.

I had been anticipating this day for some time, but I was still apprehensive, not knowing exactly what would happen next. I and I am sure most of the other recruits were consumed by barely managed fear and an adrenalin rush all at the same time. The sergeant shouted for us to stand at ease, and everyone relaxed.

Looking around, I saw three jagged lines of men of every race, body type, and size our country had to offer. I don't know if I was more surprised by the individual size differences or the huge diversity that composed our group. As I said earlier, I had led a pretty white life, and the percentage of Mexican and blacks to whites in our group seemed unusually high to me. But even odder was the fact that the blacks were all standing together in the back row, and the entire front row, which I found myself in, were all white guys, except for one chiseled and striking black man. The middle row was a conglomeration of a few blacks, many Hispanics, and the overflow of white guys that didn't fit in the first row. It was as if each race had sought out those of a like ethnicity and gravitated toward them to line up without being told to do so. I also thought it seemed strange that the black soldiers had stepped to the back row voluntarily, as if they thought they belonged there.

The sergeant looked around and then walked over to the black gentleman in the first row. "What's your name, boy?" he asked, his face only an inch away from the black man's.

"Jessie Evers, sir!" he shouted in response to the question.

The sergeant stayed silent but never looked away from the recruit's eyes. After an uncomfortably long time, the sergeant spoke again. "You're not planning on being any trouble for me, are you, Mr. Evers?"

"Sir, no, sir!" the recruit responded loudly.

"Then why are you in this line with all these white boys?" Not waiting for a response and moving close enough that their noses were almost touching, he continued. "Mr. Evers, I think you are going to be a pain in my ass! Are you going to be a pain in my ass, son?"

"Sir, no, sir!" he shouted again.

The sergeant stood stationary for a long moment before backing off and walking back to the middle of the group. "I notice that you black soldiers all lined up together, and all you white boys did the same up front. But I'm going to let you in on a little secret. In this United States Army, we are color blind! There is no black or white, Christians or Jews." He paused. "There are only America soldiers here! I don't care if you are from Seattle, Washington, or motherfucking Montgomery, Alabama. You will treat each other with the respect and dignity American soldiers deserve in this environment." He paused again before continuing. "Or I will personally make your life more miserable than you ever thought possible! And I won't give a damn what color you are when I do it!" He slowly paced in front of the group before continuing.

"Now we are going to make three new lines. Starting with the first row and going from left to right. This is referred to as soldiers in rank. I want the shortest people in the front. If the man lined up to your right is shorter than you are, you are a dumb shit and you're not lined up correctly."

He turned and started back toward the middle again as he continued. "There will be thirty men in the first row, and then we will start the second row. Same drill, smallest on the left and progressively taller as you move to the right. Same thing with the third row. I want to see blacks mixed with whites, browns mixed with Asians, but the lines need to be correct in each row by height." He stopped for a second and turned to face the group. "Do any of you not understand these instructions?"

The response was mixed. Half of the men said, "Sir, yes, sir!" While the other half sang out, "Sir, no, sir!"

The sergeant put his hands together, and shaking his head, he looked toward the heavens. "Jesus, please help me to properly train this burlap sackful of idiots." He ended his short prayer with "Thank you, Lord!"

Looking back at us, he said, "You have five minutes to complete this assignment, and the time starts now!"

All hell broke loose as we began to try and find people close to our same height. Looking around, I knew I would end up somewhere in the second row, so I tried to pull people who looked close to my height to me.

As each minute went by, the sergeant would notify us. "You have four minutes left!" he shouted over the voices of a hundred recruits. "You have three minutes left!" Then, "You have two minutes left!" Then, "You have one minute left." And finally, "Time's up! Get in your lines and stand ready for inspection!"

Everyone stopped moving and stood at attention. The sergeant walked the first line from left to right and then went back to the left to walk the next line. After he had done this three times, he sauntered to the front again to address us.

"Gentlemen, you did a pretty good job!" Shaking his head affirmingly, he continued. "But unfortunately, I don't think it is perfect."

"I want the first soldier on the left in line two to step forward and come up here with me. Now, I want the last soldier in line one to come up here as well." Both men came up front and stood at attention in front of the sergeant. "Gentlemen, turn back to back and stand up straight." The two soldiers did as they were told and stood back to back. The soldier from the first row was easily an inch taller than the soldier from the second row.

The sergeant looked them over closely and confidently stated, "I believe you gentlemen lined up in the wrong place." Continuing, he addressed us all, "We know we have this one adjustment to take care of, but are there more? You two switch places, and then I want everyone to recalibrate to ensure we have it correct this time. You have one minute starting now!"

The second time, we were much more organized. As a group, we made some minor changes and were ready long before the minute was up.

The sergeant walked the lines again and went back to the front of the group. "OK! It took a while, but you knuckleheads finally got it right. Now starting in row number one, I want you to start counting off. Every two men will have the same number."

So it will go like this: he pointed to the leftmost soldier in the front row and said, "One." Then he pointed to the man next to him and again said, "One." Pointing to the next man, he said, "Two." The man next to him then shouted, "Two." The sergeant stopped speaking, but he kept pointing at each man in the row until he was finished. Then he moved back to the left and started pointing to each person in the second row. This continued until every soldier had a number.

Returning to the front of the group, he said, "There are two reasons for this exercise. Number one, the man with the same number as you is your training partner throughout basic training. The main reason for this is to ensure us matching each of you up to someone your own size for our hand-to-hand combat training. Number two, as I said earlier, the United States Army is color blind. We expect you to take care of your buddy regardless of their color, religious beliefs, or political affiliation." Pausing and looking at each soldier, he continued. "Your buddy depends on you, and you depend on your buddy, period!"

As luck would have it, the man with my same number was Jessie Evers, the black man the Sargent had singled out as his preconceived pain in the ass. I silently hoped that whatever issues the Sargent had with Jessie wouldn't roll over to me during the next twelve weeks.

The sergeant continued. "Grab your gear and put it in barracks buildings number three and four. Your training partner will be bunking with you. One gets the top bunk, and one gets the bottom bunk. You'll have to work out between the two of you who gets what. Stow your gear and meet me back out here in thirty minutes, lined up exactly as you are now. Understood?"

A chorus of "Sir, yes, sir!" came from the troops in response.

"Remember, 1400 hours, be back here and lined up!" Then he barked out, "Recruits, dismissed!"

I picked up my gear and started toward the barracks. As I briskly walked, I introduced myself to my training buddy. "Hi, I'm Michael Larsen," I said, offering my hand to shake.

"Jessie Evers" was the simple response as he grabbed my hand and shook it firmly.

Once we released each other's hands, I said, "Are you going to be a pain in my ass, Jessie Evers?"

His head snapped around to see a smile on my face, and a slight smirk appeared on his own lips. "We'll see, Michael Larsen. We will just see!" he answered with little emotion.

Once inside the barracks, we grabbed the first empty double bunk we came to, and I asked, "Do you want the top or the bottom?"

"It doesn't matter to me," he responded.

"Well, then, I'll take the top", I said. "I think I'm younger than you, and out of respect, I think the older guys should sleep on the bottom."

He smiled at me and threw his stuff into the bottom bunk. "Sounds good to me."

In short order, Jessie and I had most of our gear stowed away and were ready to go back outside to our designated lines. Suddenly, there was a large disturbance coming from our left, deeper in the barrack. It started with raise voices, and just as I looked to see what was happening, one of my fellow recruits came flying out into the middle of the main aisle.

He was a pretty large black man who'd hit the floor with a resounding thud. Walking out behind him was an equally large white man wearing a tight white T-shirt, standard-issue army fatigues and boots, with both of his fists clenched firmly. He slowly walked toward the soldier on the ground and finally stopped, towering over him.

Looking down with distain, he spoke calmly. "I said I don't want to be your buddy. I don't want to be your friend. Hell, I don't even want to talk to you, boy! But if we must do this, you just do what you're told. I want the top bunk, and I will have the top bunk, and that is that!" Staring down at the soldier, he continued. "You need to realize your place in the pecking order here, son! We can do this the hard way or the easy way, but we are going to do it my way!"

I knew better, but I started moving in their direction. "Hey!" I yelled out.

The white recruit turned to look at me as I approached. It was obvious he was the larger of the two of us. After taking his measure of my physical size, he responded, "Hey what?" Then he added, "You'd better stop right there and say what you've got to say, little man."

I don't know why, but his arrogance and the demeaning tone in his voice made my blood boil over. As I felt myself quickening my pace, I spat out to him, "So you're the one!"

"What?" he responded with a puzzled tone in his voice.

"You're that motherfucker from Montgomery, Alabama, that the sergeant was talking about, aren't you?"

I'd made up all the distance between us while speaking, and I hauled off and hit him as hard as I could in the face with, first, my right hand and then a left hook. I watched his eyes rolled up in his head and saw instant bruises where both of my fists had been only milliseconds before. He limply crumpled to the ground, and there was a loud pop as his head contacted the wooden floor. I stood over him, still very angry, but at the same time silently praying that I hadn't killed him.

It appears everything and everyone had moved in slow motion throughout the entire confrontation. But from the time I'd heard the two men arguing to me now standing over a stranger's limp form had only been a matter of a few seconds.

I switched my gaze from him to the other soldier on the ground. His mouth was bleeding, and his shirt had bright red streaks where blood had dripped down from the cuts in his mouth and his busted lips.

"I don't think there is going to be a better time for you to claim that top bunk than now," I said calmly. I offered my hand, and he looked at it for a moment before accepting it. Then as I pulled him to his feet, a new voice came from the front of the barrack door.

"Well, well, well," said our sergeant as he walked toward us. "It looks like some of you have too much energy after that long bus ride! I can help you with that, gentlemen! Lace your boots tight, men, because we are going to go for a little run and see if we can get rid of some of that pent-up energy."

He smiled slyly and continued. "Remember, everyone in line at 1400 hours."

Bending down and closely examining the still unconscious recruit, he finally said, "He's going to live. Which one is his bunk?"

The black recruit with blood all over his shirt spoke up. "This bottom bunk is his, sir. The top bunk is mine."

I had to really concentrate to keep a smile from forming on my face as I digested his brave, self-confident response.

"Is he your training partner?" the sergeant asked.

"Yes, sir, he is my training partner" came the response.

"Well, then, you'd better get your ass over here and take care of your partner!" the sergeant said sternly. "You depend on your buddy, and your buddy depends on you! Did I not make myself clear when you jerk-offs were standing in formation today?"

The young black man scrambled to his buddy and half lifted, half dragged his white buddy back over to his bunk. It took considerable effort, but the soldier was finally able to get his limp teammate's body completely into his bunk. Looking back at the sergeant and speaking with blood still covering his teeth and mouth, he asked, "Sir, should I stay here with him or go back outside to join the others?"

"He'll be all right there. When he wakes up, I'm sure he will remember what happened." He pause and then started again. "You go on outside and join your fellow recruits. We have some running to do, and I wouldn't want you to miss out on the fun!"

The recruit quickly ran past me headed for the door and exited the barrack. That only left the unconscious guy, the sergeant, and me in the otherwise empty barrack.

Turning and walking slowly in my direction, I watched as he squinted, and his once round eyes transformed themselves into small colorless slits while I waited for him to speak. My heart was pounding out of my chest as he approached. I was filled with fear and anger at myself, and I couldn't stop thinking repeatedly, *Why can't you mind your own damn business! Why are you the one who has to step in every time someone is in distress? You only create more trouble for yourself, you dumb shit!*

"I'm pretty sure of what happened here." He began calmly. "I don't see it often, but once in a while, one of you white boys stands up to defend a brother." He continued, still speaking softly. "I don't know what your reason was for this altercation, and frankly, I don't care why it happened. However, I do know that you struck a fellow soldier, and you did it in the plain view of several of your peers. I have no recourse but to punish you as part of my duty to the United States Army. Without rules and laws, this unit would be nothing more than a gang of thugs. And I will not have anarchy in my ranks!"

He paced around in a small circle and once again was facing me. "What's your name?" he asked in a calm voice.

"Michael Larsen, sir," I responded, standing at attention.

"Well, Michael Larsen, sometimes, life isn't fair. And I think this may be one of those times. I am going to write a report on this and send it upstairs. You will be given a hearing and will be able to plead your case in front of our ethics board. The very least you will receive is a written reprimand. But the punishment could include incarceration for up to six months in a military prison or even a dishonorable discharge. Nothing is off the table here."

He slowly walked away and then sauntered back to me. "The one thing I know for sure is that if you step out of line at any time during the remainder of your basic training, you will be out of the military with a black mark on your record that will follow you for the remainder of your life."

I didn't respond but stood there at attention as the words sunk in.

"But for now, go get in line with your fellow recruits. We have some running to do." As I started to leave, he continued. "By the way, don't think this garners any respect or special attention with me. What you did was wrong, and you deserve whatever punishment is handed out to you!"

Getting back to my place in line, I stepped in and snapped to attention. The sergeant was just exiting the barrack and was still some distance from us. Jessie, keeping his eyes forward, whispered out of the side of his mouth, "Remind me again who's going to be a pain in the ass?"

I stared straight ahead as I responded, "Shut the hell up!" Both of us had small smiles growing across our faces as we stood there in silence, waiting for the sergeant to reach us.

We did run that day! We ran the rest of the day and into the night. We ran until the least fit among us were bent over vomiting on the side of the road. Those few unfortunate souls were being ridiculed and humiliated by various sergeants who ran step for step with the new recruits and never seemed to get tired! We ran until, as a collective group, we couldn't run anymore.

I had expected the physical punishment and had been working out intensely for several weeks prior to coming to Fort Ord. I was exhausted but not to the point of getting sick. I was as well impressed with the endurance of my training partner, Jessie. He had obviously trained prior to coming to basic training as well. Both of us were hot, sweaty, and spent. But compared to most of the other recruits, we were in pretty good shape.

And so it began, one week rolling into another and then another as we trained to become efficient killing machines. We exercised a minimum of twice a day. That exercise was only interrupted by learning everything there was to know about the weapons we'd been issued. We took them apart, cleaned them, and put them back together multiple times a day. We were constantly at the firing range, improving our shooting skills. Obstacle courses, team building assignments, and hand-to-hand combat training rounded out each week. Oh, yeah, and we ran. Sometimes, we ran in shorts and T-shirts and sometimes in full combat uniforms with our weapons and a full sixty-pound pack strapped to our back, but we were always running.

My least favorite exercise was using the pugil sticks. The pugil stick is a heavily padded pole-like training weapon designed to replicate a rifle butt on one end and a bayonet on the other. Each end was marked with a different color to distinguish which end was which. We would be given a helmet with a wire face guard to protect our eyes and a lightly padded vest to protect our vital organs.

We would then line up faced against our buddy and ready ourselves for combat. The end goal was to strike your opponent with the bayonet end in a vital kill area of the body before your opponent struck you there. There were no rules, and you could use whatever means necessary to win. These battles were fierce, short, and often quite painful. You could kick, punch, and use your pugil stick in anyway necessary to achieve a victory.

In the sixth week of training, our sergeant surprised us by announcing, "If any of you have a grudge or dispute with another soldier here, today is the day to work through your differences. Today, I am going to allow callouts with the pugil sticks. You can call out anyone you want, but they must accept the call out. If they accept, we will have a match. If your callout person does not want to fight, I will not make him. He will have to live with his decision and the guilt of not being a warrior today." Looking over the group slowly, he asked, "So are there any callouts?"

From somewhere behind me, someone yelled, "I call out Michael Larsen!" I turned to see Ben Bolzer, the man I had struck on our first day of training, glaring at me.

As it turned out, Ben was from a small town in Mississippi, and he was in fact a bona fide racist. His black partner, Randle Jenkins, had been granted a change of buddies in the second week of basic training. Ben's new buddy was another white boy from somewhere in Georgia.

Ben and I had effectively avoided each other from that first day until now. We hadn't talked or had anything to do with one another since the incident. We'd made it a point to not ever be in the same place at the same time. We ate on opposite ends of the mess hall. We showered at different times and even made a point to use the latrine at different times.

The sergeant stood staring at me, waiting for an answer.

"I accept," I responded tentatively. After that, there were five or six other callouts, and all of them were accepted by their called-out counterparts.

The sergeant said flatly, "We are about to go to war, gentlemen. Ready yourselves for battle." Not looking at anyone, he continued. "Bolzer, Larsen, gear up and let's get this party started."

Once geared up, we stood facing each other, waiting for the whistle to be blown. Knowing that being first was a huge advantage, the instant the whistle blew, I took two quick steps and swung my stick at his head as fast as I could. He had anticipated my move and ducked with a speed I hadn't envisioned a man of his size would possess.

However, his first thrust found its mark before I could defend against it. My protective mouthpiece shot out through my now open mouth as I felt a searing pain starting in my crotch and radiating through my body. Quickly realizing I had been struck hard in the groin, my legs went slack, and I slowly slumped forward to my knees. Unable to breathe, I looked up just in time to see out of my periphery that his pugil stick was about to meet the side of my helmet. Then there was no conscious thought, only darkness.

"Wake up! You need to get up!" My mom was yelling in my ear. "Michael! Can you hear me? I said wake up!"

"OK, OK," I finally responded, feeling very groggy. *I must have really gotten smashed last night*, I thought to myself. But I couldn't remember exactly what had happened to make me feel so strangely. I was trying to clear the cobwebs from my brain while, at the same time, shaking my head, hoping to correct my double vision.

"Come on" came her voice again. "Time to get up, son!" She grabbed me by the shoulder and started pulling me to my feet. I didn't remember my mom having that kind of strength or grip.

My double vision was diminishing when I realized it wasn't my mom's hand that was holding me up but rather the hands of my sergeant. The flash bulbs that had been constantly bursting in my head were slowing now, and my surroundings began to come into focus.

The sergeant took hold of me by both shoulders and asked, "You OK, Larsen?"

Before speaking and finally realizing where I was, I responded, "I think so, sir." I knew I didn't sound very convincing as I continued to try to remember what had happened. Looking past the sergeant, I saw Ben Bolzer standing with his fighting helmet under his left arm while holding his pugil stick loosely in his right hand. He wore a sheepish smile as he watched me trying to regain all my facilities. As soon as I saw the shit-eating grin on his face, my mind defrayed, and I knew exactly what had happened.

"In case you're wondering," the sergeant began calmly, "you lost that challenge." There were chuckles and some light laughter all around me as the sergeant continued. "You go get back in line now," he said calmly. "We have some other callouts to address."

I didn't immediately move as I tried to comprehend what was being said in my still bewildered mind.

"Go on! Get back in line, Larsen. Your fighting is done for today," the sergeant said, letting go of my shoulders and assessing whether I could stand on my own.

All my body parts seemed to move as they were designed, so I turned and slowly walked back to my place in line. Once there, the next set of combatants was called forward, and a new battle began.

"You just got the shit beat out of you by that asshole!" Jessie began. "I hope it's not too late to ask for another training partner, because I'm not sure I want you covering my ass in a real conflict!"

Not knowing if he was serious or just screwing with me, I decided to remain silent as we both stood there watching the contest unfolding before us.

In training week number ten, the sergeant ordered me into his office. "Mr. Larsen, you will not be joining us tomorrow morning for drills." Looking me directly in the eyes, he continued. "Tomorrow, you will be in front of a disciplinary commission led by Capt. Blake Stone. This is concerning the incident between you and Mr. Bolzer. I have given the commission a full report from my perspective, and last week, Mr. Bolzer gave his testament on the record to the commission as well."

Our eyes remained locked as he continued. "This should take about two hours, and then you will be sent back to your barracks. There will be no verdict or outcome discussed with you tomorrow. Once you are dismissed by the commission and sent back to your barrack, change into your fatigues and be ready to join us in the mess hall for lunch."

I did as I was told to do the next day. A six-member panel of officers bombarded me with questions about the incident, about my views on life, my reason for being here, and a myriad of other questions. Five white and one black officer grilled me for well over an hour and asked relevant and seemingly irrelevant questions. I answered all their interrogations as truthfully as I could. After all the inquiries were answered to the panel's satisfaction, Captain Stone asked me if there was anything I wanted to say before I was dismissed.

"Yes, sir," I responded.

"The floor is yours, Mr. Larsen. But I want to remind you that everything you say will become part of the record of today's proceedings," he concluded.

"Thank you, sir." I began. "I would like to start by apologizing to Mr. Bolzer and to the United States Army for my involvement in the incident I have created here. I am embarrassed by my irrational actions, and I take full responsibility for them.

"I am a small-town guy, and I perceived an inappropriate action was being taken by one of my classmates against another. I grew up in a very white part of California, and we had no people of color in our community. Honestly, I have never seen as many black men in one place in my life as I did the first day I arrived here." I paused for a second before continuing. "But I am not naive concerning what is going on around the country regarding race. I, like you, watch the strife and rage play out on TV every night." I paused again. "I have experienced discrimination in this form only one other time in my life. In high school, a foreign exchange student of color was harassed by some of my upperclassmen. Unfortunately, and I am sorry to admit, the results were the same. I got in a fight defending the exchange student, which produced negative consequences for both of us."

Looking quickly into each officer's eye, I continued. "Something inside of me just snapped when I saw what I perceived to be bullying happening and no one responding to it. Rage instantly replaced rational thinking, and consequently, here we are. I am ready to accept my punishment, whatever it may be, and again, I am sorry for creating this issue."

After a short moment of silence, the captain replied, "Very well, Mr. Larsen. We will decide on what action needs to be taken over the next few days. Once we have a consensus on the appropriate penalty, we will have you come back before the commission to give you our verdict. You are dismissed to return to your training."

As soon as the words were out of the captain's mouth, everyone on the panel were standing, and most turned to exit the room with little or no conversation with their peers. I, too, stood and exited the room, heading for my barrack.

Once dressed appropriately, I met up with the rest of my squad in the mess hall. The rest of that week and the start of the next was simply a continuation of our weekly training drills.

Then on Thursday of the next week, I was told to return to the commission headquarters, where I would be informed of their determinations and verdicts.

Once everyone were in their places and seated, Captain Stone began. "Mr. Larsen, we have come to a decision regarding this event. We do find you guilty of striking a fellow soldier while in training. The army has a zero-tolerance policy for fighting among military personnel."

He paused before continuing. "You will receive a written reprimand that will be placed in your file. Also, you will not be eligible to advance from the rank of E-1 during your first year of duty. This carries with it some monitory consequences since pay raises go hand in hand with promotions. You will also lose many leadership opportunities because as an E-1, the army will never put you in any supervision roles." He went silent for a minute while shuffling through the stack of papers in front of him. Finally looking up, he asked, "Do you understand all the particulars as I have communicated them to you, Mr. Larsen?"

"Sir, yes, sir!" I shouted out loudly.

The captain had a small grin forming on his face as he continued. "On a side note, it was brought to our attention through our investigation that you were not the only recruit who struck another enlisted man that day. These same punishments have been given to Ben Bolzer for his involvement with Mr. Turner on that same day."

"Do you have any questions, Mr. Larsen?" the captain asked in closing.

"No, sir, no questions!" I blurted out, still standing at attention and staring back into his eyes.

"Very well," the captain finished. "You are dismissed, Mr. Larsen. And I would suggest that you keep your nose clean for the rest of this year because the repercussions of another incident within a year are very serious indeed."

During the last couple of weeks of basic training, Ben Bolzer and I maintained our distance from each other. It was obvious that we didn't like each other, and neither one of us was apologizing for anything that had happened to this point. But we both knew, with the score one to one, that settling our differences in any way would cost each of us a price we were not willing to pay. I always blamed Ben for my punishment and not being able to move up in rank, and I am sure he felt likewise.

As basic training was wrapping up, I couldn't help but notice that racially, very few things had changed over the twelve weeks. When we were given a fifteen-minute break, or during meals, the division between black and white soldiers was unmistakable. The buddy system the sergeant had put in place on day one had worked for training purposes, but it hadn't translated to the real world. The segregation between ethnicities was as evident today as it was on day one.

Jessie and I had become conversationally friendly, but even with us, if there was a choice of sitting, eating, or communicating with someone from the same family tree, we almost always took it.

As I look back on basic training now, one of the most inexplicable phenomena of my training was that after twelve weeks, I had not learned or, for that matter, even heard the name of my training sergeant. His name was and always will be "Yes, sir, Sergeant, sir!"

CHAPTER 6

We had completed our basic training and were waiting for our orders to depart. We'd been granted a two-week leave to get our affairs in order and visit family and friends prior to being shipped out. It was a given that we would be going to Vietnam. We just didn't know where we would be stationed.

"Oh my god, Michael, you're so skinny!" my mom squealed as I walked through the front door. "And you look so handsome in your uniform!" Then she rushed me, wrapped her arms around me, and began kissing my checks repeatedly.

She was correct; I had lost fifteen pounds and gained a substantial amount of muscle mass after twelve weeks of daily physical fitness training. I was proud of the new me and my improved physicality.

"Hi, Mom," I finally responded as she started to release her python grip from around my back and looked lovingly into my eyes. Her eyes quickly filled with tears that began to spill over as she reluctantly let me go.

My brother walked into the room, and a crooked smile started forming on his face. "Wow! What did you do with my brother?" he asked. As he closed the distance between us, he continued. "You look great!" And then we were hugging. He pulled me away from himself, holding me at arm's length, and gave me a second look. "I mean it, really great!"

Later that evening, my father came home from work, and there was one last greeting, embrace, and time spent catching up on the last three months. Mom had prepared a killer meal, and we ate until we were all stuffed. Then we visited and swapped stories well into the evening. After clearing the table, my father and I walked out onto the porch and seated ourselves in the lawn chairs. He took a sip from his shot glass full of bourbon and asked, "Was it as tough as you thought it would be?"

I told him all the stories that I knew I shouldn't repeat to my mom or brother. I unloaded everything that had happened once I began. I told him about the significant number of black soldiers in my squad, the segregation of the troops at meals and breaks, and anything else that I thought was relevant. I even told him about the fight that landed me in so much trouble, and what started it. He sat and listened without interrupting until I was finished.

Finally, he spoke. "Michael, lots of things are changing in this country today. There is a lot of hate that has been building ever since the civil war, and it's about to boil over." Taking another sip of his whiskey, he continued. "You need to be sure the person watching your back is trustworthy when you get over there to Vietnam. There is so much racial tension here right now, and it seems to be getting worse. You've got whites who hate blacks and vice versa. You need to try and steer clear of the most obvious troublemakers in both ethnic groups. When you pick your buddies, be sure you can trust them. Death by friendly fire can come from a white bigot's rifle just as easily as it can from a disgruntled black soldier."

I simply nodded my understanding and remained silent.

After I had been home for a few days, it seemed as if half the news was about Vietnam, and the other half was about riots, segregation, and inequality for black Americans. I don't know if I just hadn't been paying attention or whether I had changed my perspective on Vietnam and racial equality since joining the army. But after being a member of the armed forces and being away from home for such a short time, it seemed like there was a growing national outrage, especially on college campuses across the country, regarding the Vietnam War. I hadn't picked up on this animus prior to joining the army. But then again, there weren't any colleges or many people protesting in the small and very white community of Beaumont, California.

But being home now felt as if I had been on the moon for three years, with no availability to news. While we were training, none of us had had the time to keep up on current events or politics. Just twelve short weeks ago, everything seemed perfect in this great country of ours to me. But after basic training, it felt like the country was being torn apart by a multitude of issues and ideologies. I was more interested in what was going on around the country and, for that matter, around the world than I'd ever been prior to my induction into the army.

I read everything I could get my hands on pertaining to the war. After discovering that Pres. Lyndon Johnson had authorized "Rolling Thunder" air strikes in the jungles of South Vietnam, I realized the reason for so many ground troops being called up. We needed to protect our navy and land-based airfields while the bombings continued. As part of a strategy to end the war as quickly as possible, the United States had decided to send 125,000 ground troops, not only to protect our bases but also to go after the North Vietnamese army on search-and-destroy missions. I apparently was going to be a part of that force.

The United States began drafting thirty-five thousand men per month about the time I had received my notice to report to the army. What I didn't know at the time was that the U.S. government would send over 150,000 ground troops by the fall of the same year, only to be confronted by 275,000 North Vietnamese soldiers who had been patiently waiting for us to step onto their home soil.

While this was all happening abroad, the efforts against the war were ramping up here at home. Jeannette Rankin, an eighty-seven-year-old congresswoman from Montana, lead a five-thousand-women's march in Washington DC to protest the Vietnamese war. These ladies not only gave legitimacy to the "no more war" movement but also began what was to become a growing women's movement in the United States. They developed their own motto, which helped spark what would become the next fight for equality in this country. "Sisterhood is powerful!"

The war protests didn't stop there. Over one thousand men returned their draft cards to government offices all over the country. Several hundred others burned them and left the United States looking for a war free life in Canada and denounced their U.S. citizenship.

Students on the Columbia University campus took over five buildings and held the dean and his staff hostage. The protestors were calling for the university to cut all ties with any military research projects. The police were called, and over one thousand law enforcement officers were dispatched. More than 700 protesters were arrested, 132 of them being students of the university. Four faculty members and ten policemen were injured by the conclusion of the demonstration.

At the same time, students at the South Carolina State campus were protesting segregation at Orangeburg, South Carolina's only bowling alley that didn't allow Negros inside their doors. Three black protestors were killed, and twenty-seven more were wounded when police opened fire on the crowd of protesters. Nine police officers were tried and acquitted of all charges related to the use of deadly force in the incident. But the protest organizer, a black activist, was sentenced and served seven months in prison for organizing the demonstration.

Just before I was shipped out to Vietnam, North Korea reared its ugly head again by seizing the USS *Pueblo* off their coast, claiming it was a surveillance ship that had strayed into Korean waters. One crewman was killed, and eighty-two others were imprisoned in the incident. What I didn't find out until I returned home from my tour overseas was that there would be an eleven-month standoff between North Korea and the United States before we would get our sailors back to the United States.

In politics, Sen. Robert F. Kennedy entered the race for the Democratic presidential nomination on March 16, only one week after I'd begun my boot camp training. Having lived through the death of his brother, Pres. John F. Kennedy, I was very pleased by his announcement. I hoped the younger brother could continue what President Kennedy had begun just two years earlier in our country. I considered the Kennedy family to be great patriots who had a strong moral fiber bred within their DNA that could only benefit our country.

And then my orders came. I was to return to base no later than 800 hours on June 1. Reading the orders over several times, it started to sink in that I was really going to fight in a war. Not only a war but also a war in a foreign land where I could be seriously injured or even killed by an enemy that I didn't know and didn't have anything against on this day. Fear and adrenaline, apprehension and doubt, patriotism and pride were only a few of the emotions I was experiencing as I lowered the orders and silently took stock of what was about to transpire.

"And it's one, two, three, what are we fighting for? Don't ask me, I don't give a damn! Next stop is Vietnam! And it's five, six, seven, open up the pearly gates, well, there ain't no time to wonder why. Whoopee! We're all gonna die!

That was the chorus to the song "I Feel like I'm Fixin' to Die Rag" by Country Joe McDonald and the Fish, which became popular just after I finished basic training. He sang this song for the first time to an estimated four hundred thousand people at the Woodstock Music and Art fair in a farmer's field in upstate New York. And now, I was about to live out those catchy lyrics in real time.

The rest of my leave went by quickly, and it was finally time to say good-bye to my family. Dad drove me to the bus station, while Mom and my brother sat quietly in the backseat. Finally, my brother broke the uncomfortable silence. "Keep your head down and keep your feet dry. I read that if your feet get too wet from slogging around in the jungle, you can get foot rot or other types of serious diseases!"

My father glared at my brother through the rearview mirror. Unable to contain himself, he blurted out, "Shut up, Ronnie, the army will tell all these boys whatever it is that they need to know about survival in the jungle!" And with that terse statement, silence returned to our vehicle.

We said our good-byes, and I love yous. I received hard, meaningful hugs from everyone and turned to go up the stairs inside the door of the bus. I could hear my mom crying, but I didn't want to look back for fear I might start tearing up as well. With the noisy screeching of the bus's front door closing, we slowly pulled away from the bus station, and I was off—off to fight a war in Vietnam. Everything seemed so surreal as I and several others just like me made our way to Fort Ord, California, for deployment.

I'd never been on a ship, let alone one that held over five thousand troops in its belly. But here we were pushing away from the dock on the 608-foot *General Nelson M. Walker*. This P2 Admiral class troop transporter was built in 1945 but was taken out of service in 1957 after serving in several conflicts including the Korean War. During the middle 1960s, the *Walker* and a sister ship were taken out of mothballs and refitted for service again. The remainder of her career was spent making numerous round trips to Vietnam from West Coast ports before finally being retired for good by the navy after the war. Before her retirement, thousands of soldiers and their units had been transported, along with thousands of marines headed to Vietnam as replacements. My entire graduating boot camp class was part of a battalion of army and marine soldiers being sent to reinforce the United States troops already in Vietnam.

The bunk quarters on board the ship were very tight and almost claustrophobic. And as we got closer to Vietnam, the temperature below deck seemed to increase exponentially. The heat and increasing humidity were stifling. Our hammocks were located in the lowest of the six decks of this constantly tossing and groaning massive beast.

The journey took eight days, but during the last two days, we hit really bad weather. High winds and mountainous waves crashed into and over the vessel, and everyone was confined to their hammocks.

For thirty-six straight hours, the ship pitched and dove into valleys of angry, perilous seas. I, like almost every other person on the ship, became deathly ill with seasickness. By the end of the second day, all familiar smells on our deck had been consumed by the overwhelming stench of puke and vomit as we continued our confinement to quarters.

Finally, the ship that I had earlier thought might sink during the violent storm had proven itself to be seaworthy by battling the fierce squall to a stalemate. To this day, I believe that was the worst traveling experience I have ever lived through. But it turned out to be only a foreshadowing of what was coming next.

As part of the Ninth Division, I served in the Second Battalion, Thirty-Ninth Infantry. Our unit was assigned to serve with the Mobile Riverine Force and other U.S. Navy units that made up what was referred to as the Brown Water Navy. The Brown Water Navy's area of responsibility was to control the rivers and canals of the Mekong Delta. Our mission was to give U.S. gunboats on these tributaries support and assistance when they encountered enemy forces.

We also had several other operational missions in addition to supporting the Brown Water Navy. Operating deep within the Vietcong, the Ninth Infantry Division was charged with protecting the area and its population against communist insurgents and ensuring that the South Vietnamese government's pacification program was maintained.

Faced with unrelenting physical hardships, a tenacious enemy, and the region's rugged terrain, the Ninth Division established strategies and quantifiable goals for completing their missions against a cunning adversary. Our division would effectively write the blueprint for combating guerrilla warfare that would influence army tacticians for decades to come.

We were stationed at Bearcat Army base near the city of Bien Hoa in the Dong Nai Province of South Vietnam. This base was home to the largest concentration of American forces in Vietnam. And the Ninth Infantry Division was the backbone of the base. Besides supporting the Brown Water Navy, we would go out on combat missions looking for enemy troops to neutralize and annihilate. Our main objective was to find and eliminate enemy strongholds. We were also responsible for defending Saigon, the new capital of South Vietnam, from the communist-led guerillas.

Bearcat Base was much larger and more hectic than I had imagined once we'd arrived. As our transport truck pulled up to the entrance gate and waited for clearance to enter, the sixteen of us sitting in the back with all our gear were equally amazed by the immensity of the base's size and the feverish amount of activity that was taking place everywhere we looked.

There seemed to be fifty or more helicopters flying in every direction over our heads. Some loaded with supplies, some with what appeared to be wounded soldiers, and others with men carrying weapons, presumably coming from or going into battle. I felt perspiration beginning to drip off my forehead, and my pulse quickened as I watched the chaos unfolding in front of me in the stifling 105-degree heat.

As the truck lurched and began to move farther into the camp, we pitched forward in our seats right along with it. Slowly driving through the base, I realized immediately that when you're fighting together, an army is truly color blind. There were no separate groups of whites and blacks like I'd seen in boot camp, only soldiers and marines who were smiling, smoking, and eating together, regardless the color of their skin. Some were dressed in combat fatigues, while others simply wore shorts, boots, and no shirts as they sat giving us a quick glance as we rolled past them.

And the helicopters! I had never seen so many helicopters in one place. They were flying, they were landing in various spots around the base, and others were loading men or supplies in preparation for impending missions.

There was a plethora of different types and sizes of helicopters being utilized. In the next few days, I would learn that the Bell UH-1 Huey had proven itself to be the workhorse for air cavalry units in Vietnam. I would become very familiar with this bird over the next week. It was used to fly troops into and out of combat situation around the neighboring provinces. I wouldn't discover until long after my tour was completed that these helicopters would move over a million soldiers to and from the front lines during this campaign.

The second most prevalent piece of airborne equipment was the Huey Cobra attack helicopter. It carried multiple rocket launchers and had high-speed machine guns mounted in three separate locations. It looked like the lethal killing machine it was, whether it was in the sky or just sitting on the ground waiting for action.

As our transport truck finally came to a stop, we were told to dismount and were assigned a barrack to bunk in for the next twelve months. Since Jessie and I were familiar with each other's sleeping habits already, we decided to share a bunk again.

"I'll take the top bunk this time," Jessie mused. "Because you ain't getting any younger, sweet pea!"

I smiled back at him and simply agreed. "Fair enough!"

The next day, we met our new lieutenant and sergeant. The lieutenant wasn't much older than me, and we found out this was his first command since graduating from officer training school. The sergeant was a different story.

Sergeant Hudson was a man of about thirty-five years in age. He looked as though he hadn't shaved or bathed in a week. He was a large man, with tree trunk arms and a barrel chest. Just one look at him and you knew he'd been around the block more than once. And he was about to give us the most disturbing welcome speech I'd ever heard.

"Welcome, men!" he blurted out in a raspy, gruff voice. "My name is Sergeant Hudson, and my job is to keep you alive! If you do what I say and listen to me, you should be leaving this godforsaken jungle in a year or two. If you don't, chances are pretty high that you'll be leaving here in a casket or a body bag!"

He looked at each of us for a few seconds and began again. "Stow your gear, make yourself at home, revelry is at 600 hours tomorrow morning. Any questions?" There were no questions as he snapped, "You're dismissed!"

The next week was crammed with nothing but helicopter training. We were divided into squads of ten men each, and we practiced with only our squads. My squad consisted of four black and six white guys. I was familiar with everyone in the squad but was a bit surprised and mildly disappointed when the sergeant chose my old nemesis, Ben Bolzer, to be our squad leader. I could only assume that Sergeant Hudson didn't know or didn't give a shit that neither Ben nor I was supposed to be in any leadership roles for our first year.

We learned how to board the choppers consistently and in an organized and methodical manner. We practiced disembarking as quickly as possible and securing the landing zone around us until the chopper lifted off again. The goal was to not have the helicopter on the ground for more than two minutes. We became familiar with different colors of smoke and their meanings in drop zones. And we were taught how to get our wounded onto the choppers as quickly as possible in a combat situation.

Operation Speedy Express was a significant operation that the Ninth Division was spearheading. It was a major combat engagement with the North Vietnamese Army and a large contingent of Vietcong units. Operation Speedy Express had begun prior to our group's arrival, but now we would be unequivocally involved. There were a few major confrontations, but there would be thousands of smaller contacts during this campaign by troops from the Ninth Division and the North Vietnamese.

My first combat mission took place in our third week at Bearcat Base. Two squads were being sent to Dinh Tuong Province to ferret out enemy troops reportedly moving to reinforce the front-line fighters in the south. We didn't know the number of enemies we would encounter, but our mission was to prevent them from accomplishing their goals with the use of deadly force.

Once on the helicopter, everyone was quiet as we lifted off the ground. Each of us was immersed in our own thoughts, fears, and prayers. Our sergeant sat stoically in the front of the cabin with his head back against the helicopter wall, eyes closed, a half-smoked cigarette hanging from his lips. Every couple of minutes, the end of the cigarette would glow bright red as he sucked in smoke and, without moving, blew it back out through his nose.

The swishing of the helicopter blades was loud but somehow hypnotic as I watched rivers, jungles, and small hills rush by below. I was seated close to the door and would be one of the first out when we reached our destination and disembarked from the chopper. It seemed we were in the air for more than an hour before the chopper banked hard right and headed for a clearing below.

"All right, men!" the sergeant bellowed out loudly. "We are here! Stay close to each other, and remember your training and you'll be fine! Remember, anyone who doesn't have a U.S. military uniform on is an enemy! Man, woman, or child, your job is to kill them! There are no friendlies out here—just people who want to kill you!" Almost before the words were out of his mouth, our chopper touched down, and he barked, "Go! Go! Go!"

I was out of the door like a shot! Taking a defensive position with my rifle raised, I scanned the waist-high grass while crouching and waiting for the rest of the team to disembark. I heard the engine revving up and could feel the wash of the rotors as they began moving faster. I realized everyone must have successfully made it off the chopper as it lifted off and quickly disappeared over the trees to our west.

We were left in the clearing with only an unnerving quiet, except for a symphony of various bugs, insects, and birds. The skies were overcast and angry looking, almost as if they were matching the dark mood of our mission.

The sergeant used hand signals and had us moving toward the tree line to our north. We moved slowly, carefully, and purposefully into the jungle, all our heads constantly on a swivel. The temperature was easily over one hundred degrees, and the humidity coming up from the jungle floor made it seem even hotter.

We had all cut up a camouflage T-shirt and made a bandana to wear on our head but under our helmets. Our sergeant told us to do this before we went out into the field. The T-shirt served as a wick and kept the sweat out of our eyes by letting it run off the back of our heads. Clear vision was the most important tool we would have at our disposal in close quarters combat.

Splitting up into our two squads, one went to the left, while we took the right flank and slowly proceeded deeper into the jungle. Tensions were high, nerves raw, and the persistent heat unwavering. Every limb, every orifice, every wrinkle of skin on my body was unceasingly dripping with perspiration. We continued our slow and methodical canvassing of the area deeper and deeper into enemy territory. After three hours of tedious searching, our sergeant signaled for us to stop for a quick rest and water respite.

Dropping my backpack to the ground, I slumped down beside it and placed my rifle against the pack. I took my helmet off and hung it from the barrel of my weapon. Then grabbing my canteen, I took a long slow drink of the now lukewarm water. I don't know if it was because I was dehydrated and sweating so profusely, or if I was just thirsty, but plain old water had never tasted as good to me as it did in that moment. Lowering the canteen to take a breath, I heard a sound that I couldn't identify. It was a kind of high-pitched whistle but was not a sound I recognized or ever recalled hearing.

I turned my head in the direction of the noise just in time to see one of my fellow soldiers twenty feet away from me literally explode into pieces after being struck by an incoming mortar shell. I stared, frozen for a moment, as I watched the smoke clear, saw the crater the shell had left, and saw an arm now lying only ten feet from me. Then a second explosive blast struck behind me, throwing brush and dirt all over me. I fell on my face, trying to grab my helmet and my rifle at the same time. The mortar shells were hitting all around us, and everyone stayed flat on the ground, praying one wouldn't land directly on top of them. The noise of the constant multiple explosions was deafening, and it went on for what seemed like an eternity. And then as quickly as it had begun, it stopped.

Staying in a prone position, I pointed my weapon in the direction I expected to see enemy troops charging. I was gripped with fear, but all my senses seemed to be on high alert, and I was hyperaware of my surroundings and had already worked out an exit strategy if I needed to retreat from my position.

But no charge came, just more painfully uncomfortable silence. No birds singing, no bugs flying around, nothing that I could see moving in any direction, just the agonizing silence.

We'd been lying there for about twenty minutes when I saw the soldier next to me start crawling toward the crater of the first explosion. I didn't realize it at the time, but that poor soul disintegrating right before my eyes would be my most frequent nightmare for years to come. He would become the person I associated the word "Vietnam" with anytime someone asked me, "What was it like over there?"

About an hour after the mortar attack was over, we slowly made our way back together as a group. Our squad had one fatality and no other injuries. The other squad had two wounded soldiers, neither seriously, with no fatalities. The bugs began to fly again, and you could hear an occasional bird chirping as we attended to our wounded and took stock of the damage done by the mortar attack.

The sergeant sent two teams of three men each out to try and find where the mortar attacks had come from. They returned about two hours later, with neither team finding any hard evidence of the mortar's positions. We were supposed to stay out here for three days, but with two wounded and one fatality, our lieutenant decided we needed to return to base. We retrieved all the body parts we could find and put them in a body bag. Once the wounded were made travel ready, we backtracked our way to the clearing where we had landed just eleven hours ago.

The choppers had been called in, and we stayed just inside the edge of the tree line until we heard them approaching. Moving as quickly as possible with wounded men, we ran through the clearing toward the helicopters that were now almost on the ground. Boarding exactly like we had practiced, we were off the ground in a matter of seconds.

Sitting with my back to the helicopter wall, I looked around the cockpit at my fellow soldiers. They all had the same blank stare that I could feel on my own face. The mixture of sweat and dirt from crawling around in the jungle had manufactured a caked mud that each of us wore like a badge to commemorate the day's events. Dirty, expressionless faces with muddy arms were clinging to weapons we hadn't even had a chance to use.

I'd seen death before back in the field behind my home in Beaumont. But watching a parachute not open was a world away from witnessing a person blown into pieces twenty feet from you. I didn't know how I would feel once we were in combat and started to sustain casualties, but all I felt now was an empty numbness. I'd barely gotten to know this young man, and now he was gone forever, and I knew that except for the fickle finger of fate, it could have as easily been me.

Two days later, we had cleaned up and resupplied and were boarding another chopper for the next mission. We had three new guys in our squad to replace those we'd lost during our first operation.

On our third day out, we stumbled upon a small contingent of Vietcong troops. There was a hasty but brisk gunfight, and they were instantaneously overwhelmed by our larger force with superior firepower.

Six dead, no prisoners, and no one had been able to flee the scene. We searched the dead bodies and found a couple of maps we thought might be useful and started back to our rendezvous point. We left the bodies to be taken care of by the jungle and as a warning to any enemy that might stumble upon their bloated, rotting corpses that we had been there.

Six months later, I'd been on too many operations to count. Our normal schedule was to be out in the jungle three days, back at the base for one day, and then off on the next three-day mission. Being on high alert so much of the time begins to wear on your psyche. Psychological issues on the base ranged from the development of strange twitches and ticks to full-blown psychotic breakdowns among the troops.

But we did become a brotherhood. Race and economic difference didn't matter during a firefight. Black or white, we had to depend on each other to stay alive. I formed some very strong bonds with as many brave black soldiers as white ones in my unit. Of the twenty soldiers in our original team, there were sixteen still alive and well. Our small squad of ten had suffered two fatalities and had two wounded severely enough to not be able to return to the field. In six short months, 40 percent of our squad had been either injured or killed.

This was like no war the United States had ever been involved in. During WWII, the average soldier spent less than twenty days a year in actual field combat. But in the Vietnam War, the average soldier spent 240 of 365 days in combat situations. There was a sharp difference in kill ratios as well. For every America that was killed in action, twelve Vietcong and North Vietnamese soldiers died.

I also realized early on that you can't stay neutral in war. The killing became easier each time we went out on a mission, and my dislike rapidly turned to hate for the North Vietnamese soldiers and those civilians who sympathized with them every time a bullet whizzed past me or struck another team member.

In so many of the villages, the good guys who supported the South Vietnamese had to stay silent to stay alive. The villagers who sympathized with our enemies hid weapons and food for them and lied to us about sightings and enemy activities. It doesn't take long for your morality to unravel as you move from distrusting to despising people of a specific race.

Coming home from a mission, everyone on the base was talking politics. Finally, I asked one of the soldiers from another squad if something was wrong.

He responded, "Haven't you heard?"

"Heard what?" I replied.

I stood there with a foreboding apprehension as he started again.

"Robert F. Kennedy," he proceeded, "was gaining momentum in his presidential campaign race, and he won the California primary two days ago." He looked away and then back into my eyes. "As he was leaving the Ambassador Hotel last night, he was assassinated by some guy named Sirhan Sirhan, a Jordanian citizen who was captured at the scene."

I was stunned! For the second time in my life, a Kennedy, one of the only leaders whom I thought could help this country excel and heal the wounds of discrimination and segregation, had been assassinated. I couldn't believe this was happening all over again!

It had only been three months earlier that Martin Luther King Jr., while in Memphis to attend a sanitation workers' strike, was fatally shot while standing in front of his motel. James Earl Ray, a white supremacist, fled the country after killing Mr. King.

This outrage to a black civil rights leader had set off riots by African American citizens in more than one hundred major cities nationwide. Over the next week, at least 39 people would die, more than 2,600 would be injured, and there would be 21,000 arrests as protesters were enraged by his murder.

It had just started to calm down, and time had started to heal some of the wounds across the nation, and now, the most outspoken white advocate for racial equality had been struck down as well. My mind was reeling as I wondered for the first time what I was doing here in Vietnam while everything at home seemed to be either falling apart or on fire.

Two days later, we were back in the jungle. There was no time to think about politics or racial equality here. We were simply in self-preservation mode as we again hunted for enemy strongholds and combatants.

The rainy season had started, and there was a light consistent rain falling, only to be interrupted by cloud bursts that would last for twenty minutes every hour or two. With the heat still managing to stay above eighty degrees, we were soaked but still uncomfortably warm in the high humidity.

On this mission, we were part of a much larger force sent out to stop what was supposed to be a major enemy contingent moving into the southern provinces. On the second day, we made contact. It was about 1400 hours when I heard the high-pitched whistle of incoming mortar rounds. I knew what it was this time and yelled, "Get down, incoming mortars!" Then I dropped to the ground, making a splash in the wet underbrush and mud beneath me.

Loud explosions rang out all around me as I kissed the ground, trying to stay as low as possible. The pounding went on for well over half an hour. The barrage was so intense that I knew we had to be sustaining casualties, I just didn't how many. And then, just like in previous attacks, it simply stopped and went quiet.

I looked forward in the direction the shelling had come from and expected to see only empty space between myself and the now pelting rain. But that was not what I saw. There were North Vietnamese soldiers rapidly advancing on our position, too many of them to count as someone yelled out, "Here they come!"

I don't know who fired first, but our firefight quickly escalated into a full-blown battle for territory. I had emptied a second clip and was replacing it with a third when I looked up to see a North

Vietnamese soldier only twenty yards from me. Jamming the clip into my weapon, I started to point it at him when the left side of his face was blown off. Glancing to my left, I realized it was Jessie who'd delivered the lethal bullet that may very well have saved my life.

I began firing again as more of the enemy continued to try and overrun our position. The rain made it difficult to see more than thirty or forty yards in any direction. I saw one, two, and then three enemy combatants go down almost instantaneously with my next three pulls on the trigger of my rifle.

Our sergeant yelled from somewhere on my right to fall back one hundred yards and hold that line until we received further orders. I stuffed a full clip into my rifle and carried another full one in my hand as I prepared to retreat.

Sending six rounds out in front of me for cover, I jumped up and started running to the new rendezvous point. As I retreated, I immediately noticed most of my team was quite a bit ahead of me. Bullets were whistling by, and I turned quickly every few steps to fire indiscriminately into the rain behind me.

As I turned back around and started running again, I saw Jessie fall and limply go down, his weapon heaving out in front of him as he hit the ground.

Running to him, I bent down and asked, "Are you hit?"

He didn't answer me, but I could see a trickle of blood mixing with the water underneath him. He must have been hit somewhere in the back. Turning back toward the enemy position, I emptied my clip and quickly replaced it with the new one I'd been holding. Getting to my feet, I grabbed Jessie and hoisted him up on one shoulder. Grabbing one loose hanging arm, I again started back to where the rest of our team was directed to be.

I hadn't even gone fifteen yards when a bullet drilled into my right leg, instantly dropping both of us to the ground. I rolled onto my back to see four or five Vietcong advancing and only seconds away. Raising my rifle as quickly as possible, I shot eight rounds in their direction. At least two dropped, and then a millisecond later, a third dropped. But I hadn't fired the shot at the third man, and I couldn't tell where it had come from. I continued to fire until my clip was empty. I knew I was in trouble when, suddenly, I felt a second strike in my left bicep muscle. I screamed out in pain and crawled over to Jessie. His eyes were open but lifeless as I absorbed the horrible truth that he was gone.

A strong hand grabbed me by the back of my flak jacket and began pulling me backward toward our troops. "You got any ammo?" asked my sergeant.

"No, I'm out!" I responded with a panic in my voice that I didn't recognize.

"Take my gun and you keep firing while I do the dragging," his graveled voice proclaimed, his weapon heavily plopping into my lap.

Picking it up with my good arm, I pointed his rifle at the approaching troops and started firing. As we got close to our own forces, I could hear multiple shoots coming from a bevy of weapons behind me. I watched six or seven of the enemy drop instantaneously. The rest had stopped and fallen into a prone position to avoid being hit by more volleys from our side. The sergeant gave a mighty heave and flung me behind our firing lines.

In less than a minute, a medic was by my side, and he immediately gave me two quick injections of morphine. For the second time since joining the military, everything around me faded to black.

I kept drifting in and out of consciousness, and the sounds around me were all garbled. Opening my eyes, I saw several men carrying me on a stretcher. But I could only see them for a split second before everything started spinning, and I had to close my eyes to stop the nauseous feeling that welled up in my stomach. I thought I heard helicopter blades turning in my head, but I couldn't be sure if they were real or simply imagined. Then I must have passed out.

"Well, hello there!" an army medic said softly as I opened my eyes.

"Where am I?" I asked, quickly looking around at my surrounding.

"You are at Bearcat Base in Vietnam," he replied matter-of-factly. "You just came out of surgery to repair your shattered left arm. I'm not sure what you remember, but you were shot twice, and your arm was pretty much a mess!"

"Will I ever be able to use it again?" I asked apprehensively.

"Oh, sure!" he responded reassuringly. "It's going to take a while and a lot of physical therapy, but eventually, you'll be as good as new." He smiled down to me and finished. "You need to get some rest now. I will check in on you in a couple of hours." And then he was gone.

After two days of recovery, I was put on a plane with other wounded soldiers and sent to an army hospital in Germany for further evaluation and care. Enduring two more surgeries, one on my arm and another on my leg, I started to recuperate and, through daily treatments, got ready to eventually begin rehabilitation.

I'd been in hospital for almost three weeks when my doctor calmly informed me that I would be going back to the States in a few days. He said my warrior days were over and expressed a seemingly heartfelt appreciation for my service to our country.

Reading the newspaper one afternoon in my room, I came across a story that brought me back to the day of my last battle. On August 21, Pvt. First Class James Anderson Jr. died by diving on an enemy grenade to protect his fellow Marine's during a firefight. He was the first African American to receive the Medal of Honor in the Vietnam War. I wondered if Jessie Evers would receive a medal for saving my life. One thing I knew for sure was that he was a hero in my book, and I would be forever grateful for his sacrifice and friendship.

CHAPTER 7

As soon as I was back in the States, my parents and brother came to see me in the VA hospital. You couldn't really see any of my wounds through the heavy bandages. My left arm looked like it was three times larger than normal because of the large amounts of gauze that was protected by a thick see-through Aircast to keep it immobilized. Additionally, my arm was placed in a sling designed to keep it above my heart when I was lying down. The doctors wanted to ensure that there was a minimal amount of bleeding to affect their repair work. My leg was in a cast that went from my groin all the way to my toes.

The IV in my right hand had fluids dripping into it from three separate bags hanging behind my bed. One contained antibiotic, another dispensed pain medication, and a third was filled with saline to keep me hydrated. I knew that to the casual observer, my condition looked much worse than it was at the time. I also realized the reason I felt so casual about my injuries was mostly the pain meds.

The second my mom stepped into the room, she squealed and immediately began to cry. Rushing to my bedside, she tried to find a place where she could get close enough to hug me. Having found no such opening in the tight space, she had to settle for putting her hand on the side of my face while managing to blubber out, "Look what they've done to you! I'm so sorry, sweetheart."

"Mom!" I responded. "It's not that bad, and I am going to be fine!"

My father was making his way to the other side of my bed as he asked, "Are you getting everything you need, son? Are they controlling the pain?"

"I'm doing pretty good, Dad. The staff here has been fantastic."

He smiled down at me and said, "I'm glad to hear that, son." He tapped my thigh lightly and continued. "It's really good to see you, Michael."

I didn't expect it to happen, but hearing his reassuring voice made me instantly emotional, and I felt my eyes filling with tears. I responded in a shaky voice. "It's really good to see you guys too!"

I knew that, of all people, my father understood what I was going through because he had been through this same drill many years earlier caused by his construction accident. I could feel his uneasiness as he looked around the room and surveyed the various equipment and instruments that were attached to me. Realizing that I was watching him, he gave me a slight smile and another reassuring pat on my thigh and again focused his attention on me.

My brother stood at the foot of the bed and was softly caressing my right foot. "Who knew we would have a real war hero in the Larsen family! We are all very proud of you, Michael," he stated with sincerity in his voice.

"Thank you, Ronnie, but I am no war hero. I was just doing my job like everyone else over there," I responded, feeling slightly embarrassed by his compliment.

We spent the rest of the day visiting and talking with the plethora of doctors and nurses who were constantly coming in and out of my room. Then we talked about how soon I would be coming home and what that would look like for everyone involved.

The day disappeared quickly, and when my dinner was served, my father announced, "We'd better get going and let you eat your dinner and get some rest." With that, we said our good-byes, and they were gone.

My left arm was healing nicely. Although once the bandages were removed, it was obvious that my left bicep was now considerably smaller than my right. Not only was it smaller but also the recovery process had left several deep, angry scarlet scars that were still in the process of healing. Some were swollen, while others looked as though someone had carved out large pieces of meat with an ice cream scoop. It was anything but pretty to look at in the mirror.

I worked very hard over the next few weeks on rebuilding my arm and leg muscles to reduce the atrophy caused by the injury and the multiple surgeries.

Because of the nerve damage and disfiguring bone destruction to my arm, my left hand had also been negatively impacted. The dexterity in my hand and a couple of fingers left a lot to be desired. I had a hard time making a full fist, and I had no feeling in the second and forth fingers and on my left hand. The doctors told me that over time, I would recover my strength and be able to make a full fist if I faithfully continued my therapy. But they doubted that I would ever recover the feeling in my two fingers.

Finally, I was discharged from the hospital. I had spent a total of forty-one days in rehabilitation in the VA hospital in Los Angeles. After being released from the hospital, I had accumulated enough leave time to go home and recuperate for an additional seventeen days before returning to base to be mustard out of the army.

I had been back in the United States for almost eight weeks when I received my honorable discharge from the United States Army. I had been a paid soldier for 337 total days at the time of my final discharge.

A Purple Hearts was awarded, along with a 22 percent lifetime disability from the United States Army. As spring began to move into full swing, I was no longer a ward of the government. I was about to be just another unemployed U.S. citizen.

It was hard for me to comprehend that I had been drafted by the army, been through basic training, gone off to fight in a war, killed other human beings, watched friends die, been wounded, and finished much of my rehabilitation and was moving toward being a normal civilian again; all in less than one year.

That is, depending on what your idea of normal looked like after being in close quarters life-or-death combat. My own opinion of normal had mutated into something much darker and more sinister than it had been a year earlier.

It felt good to finally be back home. Jimmy Clark had been drafted four months after me and was now in Vietnam with his own unit. I wrote him a long letter that basically said to keep his head down and come home safe. I prayed that he would heed my words and come home unharmed. I wanted us both to meet girls, fall in love, get married, have children, and tell war stories to each other, just like our parents before us.

I knew I had morphed from a boy into a man in the nine months I'd spent in those godforsaken jungles. The loss of close friends, the first time you take another human being's life, and the constant fear that envelopes your every waking moment while trudging through swamp after swamp will instantly mature you.

After a few more weeks of recuperation, I decided that I needed to go back to work. I needed to start concentrating on my future and try to get the past nine months of war out of my head. I needed to get my life back on track and become a meaningful and productive citizen in the country I, and so many others, had represented in the name of freedom.

I contacted Mr. Kraft to see if I could have my job back at Jeremiah's Men's Wear. He was excited that I was home and told me I could come back as early as tomorrow if I wanted. I thanked him, accepted his offer, and began working the next Monday.

A few days into the job, I realized this type of employment was no longer my cup of tea, nor was it destined to be my career path for the next forty years.

Something had changed. It was probably me, but the work no longer appealed to me. I didn't really care about fashion trends or the next new look as I once had. Constantly smiling and acting like I was interested in everyone I helped quickly became a false façade that I didn't want to engage in anymore. In fact, I quickly discovered that dealing with customers was almost irritating to me, and I found myself avoiding contact with guests as they entered the store.

I spent most of my evenings after work and dinner sitting on the back porch and either staring up at the constellations or looking at various photographs I'd brought back from Vietnam. I couldn't seem to stop reliving my time over there through my photos.

I thought about Jessie every day, and I couldn't get him out of my mind. He'd saved my life and given his own for our country. But why him and not me? I'd been given this second chance because of him, and I had no idea what to do with it.

I was having trouble talking about my experiences in Vietnam to anyone else, even my close family members. I found myself increasingly avoiding others and staying home most nights by myself.

Knowing the clothing store no longer appealed to me, I knew I had to do something else to support myself. I wanted to do something in which I didn't have to openly interact with other people.

What had been so comfortable before my deployment—home, friends, and girls—no longer seemed satisfying or pleasurable to me. I couldn't decide if I wanted to go to college or just get a job driving truck and make enough money to rent a small apartment where I could drown out my memories of the war in solitude.

Truck drivers, especially the long-haul road warriors, seem to be a kind of subculture of old cowboys who could still ride freely wherever and whenever they felt the whim.

It seemed to me that many, if not most, of these cowpokes had traded in their horses and saddles for sixteen-wheel monsters with five hundred horsepower to continue to try and control their own destiny. Many of the truckers I had met in the service were a free-spirited, rebellious group who didn't care much for rules and, in some cases, the law.

I wanted to be a cowboy too. I didn't want to be responsible for anyone but myself. I only wanted to interact with humanity on my terms, and my strongest predisposition right now was to be left alone.

One night, my father joined me on the porch. He sat down next to me but remained silent. We both looked up at the stars, and for a good length of time, neither of us spoke.

Finally, I began. "Dad, I'm not sure what I want to do." Pausing for a long moment, I continued. "In fact, to tell you the truth, I feel a little lost right now. I don't really have any goals or aspirations, and all I can think about is Vietnam. And most of those memories and nightmares are not very pleasant. I'm filled with guilt for the people I've killed, and even more guilt for the guys who were killed on my team that I couldn't save."

Staring back up into the sky, we were gifted with the sight of a very bright shooting star as it streaked across the heavens. I wondered, was it a sign of things to come or just a beautiful coincidence God had given the two of us to celebrate this time together?

Feeling emotional, frustrated, angry, and confused, I rested my elbows on my thighs, buried my face in my hands, and began to cry. It started small, but within a few seconds, my shoulders were shaking as I sobbed into my open hands.

My father put his arm around my shoulder and pulled me closer to him in a comforting embrace. He didn't speak. He just held me and continued to pat me softly with his hand as I tried to get control of my emotions. After about five minutes, I finally calmed down and began wiping the tears from my face.

"Wow!" I stated with surprise in my voice. "I don't know where that came from, but it feels good to get it out!"

"That's a lot of guilt you're carrying, son," my dad said, his arm still around me as he continued to lightly pat my shoulder. "Do you think you should talk to someone at the VA and see if they can help get you some counseling or medication?"

I didn't respond to his question at first, but then for some unknown reason, I began to tell him about my last combat mission. I laid out every second of the event in graphic detail, hoping he might understand where my guilt came from.

Again, he didn't speak for several minutes, and then he began. "Michael, I'm not a doctor, but even I know that you must get past this, or it will destroy you! Please speak with someone who can help you recover from the horrors you've been through."

We both turned our gaze back to the heavens and watched for another shooting star. When none appeared, he finally said, "You'd better get some sleep, buddy. Tomorrow is going to be here before you know it."

We both stood, hugged, turned around, and made our way into the house for the night.

The next day, I told Mr. Kraft that I would be quitting. I gave him my two weeks' notice and thanked him for all the opportunities he had given me. When he asked me why I was leaving, I knew that I couldn't be honest with him because I didn't want to hurt his feelings. He'd been so good to me, and I really didn't have a good reason for leaving.

"I'm going to start college in the fall, and I need to get applications into several schools to see where I might be accepted," I blurted out.

"Good for you, Michael!" he said with a broad smile on his face. "I don't know if you've picked a major yet, but as far as I'm concerned, you can't go wrong with a business degree."

I smiled back and thanked him for the advice and started my work shift. I felt like a load had been lifted off my shoulders as I realized there were only ten more days of working at a clothing store.

I hadn't seriously considered going to college before, but now that the words were out of my mouth, I thought, *Why not at least give it a try?* My education would be paid for by Uncle Sam, and I might find something that really interested me as a profession. In that moment, I made up my mind that I was going to apply to several institutions of higher learning and see if I had the grades to get into a decent school.

Three weeks later, I received a letter of acceptance from Fresno State University. I was excited to be taking this next step in my life. Likewise, my parents, who had been very worried about me, were now excited for me. To our knowledge, no one from the Larsen clan had ever graduated from college, and I wanted to be the first to achieve the accomplishment in our family.

After I was finished working at the clothing store, I continued to keep up on national and world events. So much of the news was negative and the disasters so unimaginable that it became hard to pick up a newspaper for fear of what had happened the previous day. By the time I was ready to leave for the fall semester at Fresno State, the world seemed to truly be falling apart.

A cyclone in Bangladesh had killed over five hundred thousand people in the spring.

At the beginning of summer, a 7.8 earthquake hit Peru, killing sixty-seven thousand people.

There was a cholera epidemic in Istanbul.

There was a fire at a nightclub near Grenoble, France, trapping people inside; 142 nightclubbers, mostly teenagers, died in the fire.

Hurricane Celia made landfall near Corpus Christi, Texas, leaving fifteen people dead and over $400 million in damages.

There was severe flooding in Vietnam that had killed 293 people and left 200,000 more homeless while they were still at war with the West.

The *Pacific Glory*, a Liberian tanker, spilled one hundred thousand gallons of crude oil in the English Channel, creating a huge oil slick and an environmental disaster.

Pres. Richard Nixon and the United States Congress increased import duty taxes on all non-U.S. products to protect American workers.

Rocker Jimi Hendricks died of a barbiturate overdose in London. Janis Joplin died two months later in a cheap hotel from a heroin overdose. And the Beatles, the best musical group of all time, decided to split up the band.

Antiwar sentiment was nearing an all-time high at home as our troops remained in Vietnam. Over one hundred thousand people demonstrated in Washington DC against the war in Vietnam.

The National Guard was sent in to stop war protests at Kent State University on May 4. The confrontation escalated to the point that the National Guard opened fire on the protesters, killing four students and wounding dozens more.

There was very little good news to offset the horrific events going on around the world, but there was some.

The *Apollo 13* mission to the moon had an accident shortly after takeoff on April 11. After rationing supplies and oxygen, the crew made a successful splashdown in the Pacific Ocean with all crew members surviving.

The first Boeing 747 jumbo jet made its virgin commercial passenger flight to London.

The Aswan High Dam was completed in Egypt at a cost of nearly $1 billion. This was a major achievement for the Egyptian economy.

Japan became the world's fourth space power by successfully launching a rocket into space.

And, last, President Nixon signed a bill into law lowering the voting age from twenty-one to eighteen years of age. This piece of news brought a smile to my face. *Finally!* I thought. If you were old enough to die for your country, you surely should be old enough to vote for its representatives.

I grew increasingly restless as the summer began to heat up. The average daily temperature was now in the high nineties or low one hundreds. If you didn't have a job, there wasn't much to do Monday through Friday in Beaumont. Since I wasn't twenty-one yet, I couldn't even hang out in an air-conditioned bar and play a little pool while enjoying a cold beer.

There is an old saying that I believe goes something like this: "An idol mind is the devil's playground." In my case, no truer words had ever been spoken.

One night after dinner, I went out to sit on the back porch like most nights. After a short time, my father walked out and sat beside me on the first step.

"How are you doing, son?" he asked casually. When I didn't answer after a couple of minutes, he persisted. "Is everything OK, Michael?" This time, he turned his head to look at me and waited for an answer.

"Everything is OK. I just can't get Jessie out of my head," I responded. "This may sound crazy, but I'm thinking about going to see his parents before I go off to college."

We both sat in silence again as he digested what I'd just said.

"Why?" he eventually asked.

"I just want to tell them how brave their son was and what a pleasure it was to get to know him," I responded. "I want them to know he had family over there too. People who admired and respected him. People who lost more than just a friend with his passing. I just think it's important they hear that from someone who was there with him."

My dad sat silently for some time. Finally, he spoke. "How would you even find them?"

"I'm pretty sure I could get the information from the army quartermaster. At least that's where I would start," I responded.

More silence as he took a sip of the coffee he'd brought out with him, while we both looked back up into heaven's brilliant nightly display.

"Then do it," he said nonchalantly. "Although it may be more difficult than you realize, I agree with you that a visit with Jessie's folks would probably be a good healing experience for all of you."

The next day, I began my search. It wasn't that difficult to get the necessary information to find his parents. I didn't get a phone number, but I found the address for James and Latoya Evers in Los Angeles. They were less than one hundred miles from Beaumont, but unfortunately, they lived in the Watts area of LA.

Five years earlier, there had been an arrest of an intoxicated African American man that started an argument between the black community and the arresting officers in Watts. This altercation continued to grow as the police called in more support, and more and more people from the community arrived to protest the arrest.

Someone spat on a police officer, who then retaliated with force, and the standoff quickly turned from a confrontation between the two groups into a full-blown riot. The mayhem that followed lasted for five full days. Widespread rioting, looting, assaults, arson, and major property damage all occurred during that time frame. The firefighters were afraid to go into the community for fear of assaults and damage to their equipment, so a large portion of the downtown area simply went up in flames. There were thirty plus deaths, one thousand plus injuries, and over three thousand arrests during those five days.

It had now been five years since the riots, but developers and chain stores were reluctant to reinvest money into the area. Without development, Watts had become a ghetto with many burned-out buildings still standing as a testament to the social and racial inequality of the region. The community was not a very welcoming place for white people or the police, even now, five years after the riots.

In early August, I left on a Tuesday morning, headed for LA. I had drawn my route on a map that I'd picked up showing the Los Angeles metro area. I started out early, 5:00 a.m., to beat traffic and ensure I was there with plenty of time to visit with Jessie's parents.

The sun wasn't quite up yet as I dropped into the Los Angeles Basin, and the sight before me was awe inspiring. There were lights still lit from Los Angeles and the surrounding communities for as far as I could see. There were so many lights that they almost turned the dusky sky into complete daylight as the horizon before me lit up with an intense brightness. There was also a heavy haze that hung low over the lighted expanse like an unwelcome blanket. I knew immediately that this was a thick layer of smog that Los Angeles had become famous for in the summer months.

During the summer months, the weather created an inversion in the atmosphere that kept the smog down at ground level in all the valleys. The waste created by five million automobiles would remain until the Santa Ana winds began in the fall, releasing smog's hold on the surrounding area.

As I approached LA, I still hit more traffic than I had anticipated. It had taken me two hours to get into Los Angeles proper. But it was another three and a half hours of stop-and-go traffic before I was entering the area of Los Angeles commonly known as Watts.

It truly looked like a war zone in a third world country. The streets were filled with garbage, and as the temperature rose, the stench of rotting and decaying refuge became almost insufferable.

There were a few people walking on the sidewalk, mostly African Americans with a few Asian folks sprinkled into the mix. They all are looking hot, tired, poor, and defeated as I drove past them. I'd driven twenty blocks to my first left on Jefferson Street, and I hadn't seen one white person yet. As I drove down Jefferson, there seemed to be more burned-out buildings than open businesses, and the conditions in this part of town seemed to be getting worse.

When a stoplight turned red at the corner of Jefferson and 110th Street, I came to a stop, but the front of my car was just inside the extremely faded crosswalk lines. In the car that came to a stop next to me sat a middle-aged black man and woman, probably husband and wife. They both looked in my direction, and I could almost feel the hostility as their eyes narrowed while they stared daggers at me.

At the same time, two black teens were crossing in front of my car when one of them slapped the hood of my car and yelled, "You're in the crosswalk, asshole!" He gave me the finger as he continued past my car.

I'll have to admit I was starting to feel uncomfortable as I sat there, unable to move. Thankfully, the light turned green, and I was able to accelerate away from the intersection without any quarrels or further confrontations.

Following the directions on my map, I continued to view the decimated buildings all around me. No wonder Jessie was such an overachiever and had the balls to line up with all the white guys that first day in boot camp. Joining the army was probably the best chance he'd had of breaking away from this slum and improving his life. *Who wouldn't want to get out of this inner-city ghetto and never come back?* I thought to myself.

As I made the next left turn, the neighborhood changed into row upon row of small, old, but reasonably well-maintained single-family homes. There were kids on the street playing with footballs and riding bicycles. As I slowed and carefully drove by them, not only the kids but also the adults in the yards stared at me as I passed them. Everyone stopped whatever they were doing and studied me intently. I looked in my rearview mirror only to see everyone's gaze was still fixed on me even as I continued to drive away from them.

When I arrived at my destination, 1423 Culver Street, I pulled to the curb and parked my car. There were people in several yards, and like the others before them, they all stopped what they were doing to stare at me.

As I got out of the car, two large very muscular men stepped off their front porch across the street and started walking in my direction. I felt intimidated as they slowly approached me. Stopping, almost nose to nose with me now, one of them spoke.

"You lost, youngblood?" After asking the question, he turned slightly and spat in the street, just inches away from where I was standing. They both stood there, glaring at me as they waited for a response.

"No, I'm not lost," but before I could finish, the second man butted in.

"Well, then, you must be some kind of stupid, white boy!" he sneered, his eyes narrowing.

I noticed that both men were now standing with clenched fists as they watched to see what my next move might be. "I'm here to see James and Latoya Evers," I began. "And this was the address I was given to contact them."

"Do they know you're coming to see them?" the first man asked, a toothpick moving from one side of his mouth to the other when he spoke.

"No. No, they don't know I'm coming," I replied.

"What business do you have with them? They are just a couple of old people trying to make it day by day in this hellhole," he said, his tongue making the toothpick spin around in his mouth.

"You better not be a fucking bill collector from some collection agency here to harass my neighbors! 'Cause if you are, regardless the balls you have to come up here into this neighborhood, I'm going to kick your ass."

"I'm not a collector," I responded. "I want to talk with them about their son."

"Their son was killed in fucking Vietnam," he spat out tersely. "What makes you think they want to talk about their dead boy to you, cracker?"

"I served with him in Vietnam, and he saved my life," I said. "I just want to tell them what a good son they raised and that they should be very proud of him."

Both of their expressions softened immediately, and they looked at each other for a second before turning their attention back to me.

"I was with him the day he died, and I thought they should know he was a hero that day."

The man with the toothpick in his mouth finally said, "I don't know how they're going to take this, but let me go up first and explain the situation to them so you don't get shot when you ring that doorbell. You just wait here until I find out if you can come up on their porch or not."

I nodded my understanding, and he turned, heading for the front door of the small house. I was left standing in uncomfortable silence with the second man.

Wanting to break the quiet, I said, "My name's Michael Larsen."

He looked at my now outstretched hand and then back to my face and simply responded, "Well, good for you." He made no attempt to shake my hand but, instead, looked back in the direction of his partner, who was knocking loudly on the green front door.

A middle-aged gentleman came out onto the porch, and the younger man began to talk with him. I couldn't hear what was being said, but there was a lot of heads turning to look at me accompanied by pointing back in my direction. The middle-aged man, whom I assumed was James Evers, finally stopped talking. He straightened up, stood tall with his hands on his hips, and simply glared at me for several seconds. Finally, he said something to the other man, turned, and walked back into his house, closing the door behind himself.

My new guardian stepped off the porch and started back in my direction. "Mr. Evers said you can come into his house. He wanted a couple of minutes for his wife to freshen up first."

"That's fine," I replied. "They can take as much time as they need, I'm not going anywhere."

We stood there in silence and waited for Mr. Evers to reappear on his porch. It was starting to get hot. My guess was that it was somewhere in the low nineties already. Sweat was starting to glisten on all our exposed skin, and I had to wipe my forehead a couple of times with my handkerchief to keep the perspiration out of my eyes.

Finally, the man who'd been talking to Mr. Evers spoke. "What did you say your name was, son?"

His partner answered for me. "His name is Michael Larsen."

Never taking his eyes off me, he simply stated, "There's only two things I know for sure about you, Michael Larsen. One, you've got balls. Bringing your little white ass up here to Watts is straight-up crazy! And, two, what you're doing here is a good thing. These people lost a lot when their boy died. I don't know why you're doing this, but that old man and his wife deserve some relief from their grief, and I hope you can help give them that."

He stuck out his hand for me to shake, and I obliged. Turning to go back to their own front porch and not turning around to look at me again, he yelled over his shoulder, "Be out of here before four o'clock or you may not make it out, period. And that's not advice, that's the truth, Mr. Michael Larsen."

He had just finished speaking when the front door to the Everses' home opened. Mr. Evers stepped out on his porch and motioned for me to come in. I had started forward and was almost halfway to the porch when I realized I hadn't brought my photographs with me. Spinning around, I double-timed it back to the car, grabbed the pictures, and jogged back toward the porch.

Standing next to James Evers on the front porch, we sized up one another for a long moment before I finally spoke. "Mr. Evers, my name is Michael Larsen, and Jessie and I were buddies from day one in boot camp. I just wanted to say, first, I'm sorry for your loss, and, second, I'd like to better inform you about my experiences with your son, if that's OK."

Tears welled up in his eyes, and he turned to walk back into the house. "Come on in, Mr. Larsen."

I entered the dark room right behind him only to be confronted by a small, portly woman standing there with her hands folded as though she were praying.

"This is my wife, Latoya," Mr. Evers stated. "This is Michael Larsen," he told his wife, halfheartedly pointing in my direction.

"It's a pleasure to meet you, ma'am," I said, extending my hand to her. She gave me her hand, and I shook it softly.

"Would you like some iced tea, Mr. Larsen?" she asked.

"Oh, please, just call me Michael," I responded. "And, yes, iced tea would be very nice, ma'am." The first hint of a smile started to form on her lips as she turned and disappeared into the kitchen.

"Take a seat, Michael," Mr. Evers said, pointing at a rocking chair across from their sofa. I took the seat as instructed, just in time to accept the tall glass of iced tea from Mrs. Evers. Then she and her husband seated themselves on the sofa across from me.

I took a long drink as Mr. Ever asked, "The boys across the street said you wanted to talk with us about Jessie." Mrs. Evers wrapped both her arms around James's left arm as if she needed his support for whatever was to come next.

Setting the now half-empty glass on an end table, I looked at both and began my story, starting with boot camp and moving forward to our last firefight. I didn't spare any of the details up to and including Jessie saving my life by killing a North Vietnamese soldier who was about to kill me. I explained that he had been hit in the back while we were retreating to a more defensible location.

I saw Mrs. Evers clamp her hands tighter around her husband's arm as I relayed this part of the story. Both parents had tears running down their faces as they sat there and listened intently.

"I jumped to my feet and was following Jessie's lead back to our cover fire when I saw him go down to the right of me." I paused for a few seconds as I tried to remember the exact chronology of events that followed. "He was lying on his back, and blood was quickly pooling beneath him on the ground."

Latoya let out a high-pitched squeal and buried her face in her husband's arm as she began to cry in earnest. It was difficult for me to watch, but I needed to finish the story.

"I picked him up and threw his limp body over my shoulder and started running again. Then I felt a searing pain in my left leg, which gave out, sending us both sprawling to the muddy ground." I paused again and then continued. "I grabbed Jessie by the collar of his flak jacket and started pulling him back to safety. A second enemy round hit me in my left arm, almost blowing it off. I rolled over to where Jessie was lying, and I knew he was gone." As soon as those words were out of my mouth, a dam broke, and I began to cry along with Jessie's parents.

Jessie's mother sprang to her feet and effortlessly pulled me up from the rocking chair, hugging me to her bosom. She continued to cry, all the while rocking me back and forth, trying to console both of us. Mr. Evers was sitting on the end of the sofa with his hands folded on his knees. No longer able to contain himself, his head started bobbing up and down as he moaned and began wailing loudly. After several minutes of crying simultaneously, we all tried to compose ourselves so we could finish our conversation. I sat back down in the rocking chair, and Mrs. Evers again took her place next to her husband.

"My sergeant came after us and did a second vitals check on Jessie before announcing that there was nothing more that we could do for him. He dragged me back behind our defensive lines, and a medic pumped me full of morphine. I don't remember much after the morphine took over.

"I did find out later that Jessie had been hit twice before he had died. When I first got to him, he had only been struck by one bullet, which means the second shot had to strike him while I was carrying him, hoping to get back to our cover."

Looking directly into Mr. Evers's eyes, I continued. "That means Jessie must have taken a second bullet while on my shoulder. A second bullet that, had he not been on my shoulder, would surely have hit me. I tell you this because Jessie saved my life not once but twice that day. He is the only reason I'm alive today, and I owe him my life."

There was silence for a minute, and then I began again. "I'm so sorry for your loss, Mr. and Mrs. Evers. But please know you raised a great son whom I was lucky enough to know and develop a bond with while in Vietnam."

The second round of silence was broken when I offered to show them the pictures I had of our team while we were in country. Both parents seemed to snap out of their melancholy haze once the photos were mentioned.

We spent the next forty-five minutes looking at pictures while I told the story associated with each one. By the time we had gone through the entire stack, all of us had smiles back on our faces.

I passed the stack over to the couple and said, "Pick through these and keep as many as you want to help remember your son."

"I can have any of them?" Mrs. Evers asked.

"You can have them all if you want," I replied. "It's the least I can do to honor the memory of the man to whom I owe my life."

They kept several of the photographs and returned the rest to me.

It was time for me to leave, but before I did, I asked if there was anything I could do for them.

Mrs. Evers smiled and responded, "Michael, you have no idea how much your coming here and telling us about our son means to us. And the pictures to remember his last days on this earth are absolutely priceless."

Mr. Evers took over where she left off. "Michael, thank you for everything you've done here today. And stop beating yourself up about Jessie's death. Only God knows the time and place when each of us will be called before his throne to answer for the life we've lived. My son is gone, and if he saved your life, all I ask is that you make something of yourself to honor his sacrifice for you."

Tears again welled up in my eyes as I replied, "Yes, sir, I will." We exchanged addresses and phone numbers and promised to stay in contact with one another. Shaking Mr. Evers's hand and hugging Mrs. Evers one last time, I turned and exited their home.

The two men who had first accosted me were still sitting on their porch, their heads snapping up to glare at me the second I was out of the door. Walking to my car, I looked back to see Mr. Evers standing on the end of his porch, his arm was around Mrs. Evers, both waiting for me to leave. I waved one final time, and they both waved back.

Needing to turn the car around, I pulled across the street into the two men's driveway as they watched suspiciously. Then backing out into the street again, I began driving out of Watts the same way I'd come in. The guy with the toothpick in his mouth raised his hand slightly in a subdued good-bye wave to me. I returned the gesture, and for a second, I thought I saw a small smile on his face.

"Well, did it go as you expected?" my father asked that night after we were both home.

"It went so much better than I expected!" I responded. "They were very nice people who loved their son as much as you guys love us. It was such a sanctifying experience that I believe each one of us is better for having met yesterday. I am so glad I went to meet them!"

"Well, that sounds great, son," my father shot back. "I hope it helps you deal with the loss of your friend."

"But Watts is a shithole," I stated. "I don't ever want to go there again!"

"Watts!" my father shouted. "You were in Watts! That's a good way to join your friend in the next world! Those people hate whites!"

"Most do, but not all of them," I responded.

CHAPTER 8

Before leaving for college some three hundred miles away, I decided that I deserved a new car. I was ready to get rid of my Pontiac and move on to something newer, and a lot faster! I advertised my Pontiac for $1,500 in the local paper, and in less than a week, it was gone.

My father had switched car dealerships and was now working for John Higgins Chevrolet. They had just brought in a brand-new 1970 Chevrolet 396 Chevelle, and it was beautiful! A shimmering metallic maroon exterior color with matching leather interior. It had bucket seats in the front with a manual four-speed transmission mounted in a center console. It was finished off with factory five-spoke magnesium wheels and distinctive twin hood scoops. And was it ever fast! The 396-cubic-inch engine delivered 375 horsepower to the rear wheels, and I could smoke the tires in all four gears if I wanted to put all that muscle to the pavement.

With my dad's discount, I paid $5,142 for the car, which was almost a quarter of what an average home would cost. But I loved it and had to have it!

I had owned it for almost a month as I watched the odometer turn over to one thousand miles just before entering the Fresno city limits.

The California State University, Fresno, also known as Fresno State, was a much larger school than I had expected it to be. It's one thing to read about the size of a college but a totally different matter to experience that enormousness in person. There were approximately fourteen campuses on 363 acres of land at Fresno State. And I was about to become one of the 14,600 students who were here hoping to obtain a degree in a variety of disciplines.

As I drove around the campus trying to find the administration building, it was hard for me to comprehend that this one university held four times more faculty and students than the entire population of Beaumont, California.

Finally finding the administration building, I went inside for a prearranged meeting with one of the school's counsellors. Being early, it gave me a chance to roam around the bookstore and the student union building. I was struck by the diversity I encountered as I wondered through the aisles. Not just racial diversity—although there surely was plenty of that—but also a type of class diversity that I hadn't expected. There were hippie types with torn jeans and T-shirts, their apparel looking like none of it had been washed in weeks, a few people in sports coats and slacks, Ivy League types, and a multitude of folks who were much more advanced in age and who were obviously not part of last year's high school graduating class. I was comforted by this fact because it would allow me to blend in and not stick out in the crowd. Wanting to be inconspicuous, I felt as though anonymity would be a welcome companion for me until I found my bearings around the campuses and observed my new professors and classmates.

My counselor suggested that I take four courses, which would give me twelve credits for the semester. I, however, wanted to take five classes so I could receive fifteen credits for the semester. We quibbled back and forth over the classes a freshman should take, agreeing on very little. Finally, I expressed to Mr. Bennett that I would make up the required subjects in my second semester, but for this semester, I wanted to take classes that were of interest to me.

We finally came to an agreement on an English literature class, Trigonometry 1, a beginning French language class, Biology 101, and political science. Once my schedule was mapped out, we shook hands and I left, going back to my small off-campus apartment that the government was subsidizing for me.

Days turned into weeks, and weeks into my third full month, as I found myself acclimating to college life well. I had classes every day and studied every night. I called Mom and Dad on Sunday evenings, because I knew that's when everyone would most likely be home.

Not being in a fraternity or living in a campus dorm, I hadn't made a lot of acquaintances and even fewer friends. I had not done anything fun since arriving here, and I hadn't talked to a girl, one on one, for who knows how long.

It was Friday night, and Fresno State was playing their last home football game of the year against Boise State. Both teams came into the contest with undefeated records, and on paper, this looked like it was going to be a great game. I decided to go to the game and root for my Bulldogs.

It was the first time I'd been in Bulldog Stadium, and it was huge! I went to the student section and tried to make my way to my assigned seat, which looked like it had a great view of the field. There were lots of loud and rowdy action going on all around me as I squeezed past people heading toward the middle of my row. Most people were standing up, and I was forced to do the same if I wanted to see the game. The guy next to me glanced in my direction, smiled, and then reached down into a cooler between his legs, pulling out a can of Rainier Beer with small chunks of ice dripping from it and offered it to me.

"Want a beer?" he asked, holding the beer out for me to take.

"Thank you," I responded. "I don't mind if I do." After accepting the cold can, I opened it, raised it in his direction, and simply said, "Cheers!"

He raised his can in response and bellowed, "There's more where that came from! Help yourself when you're empty."

I smiled back at him and introduced myself. "I'm Michael Larsen. What's your name?"

He looked dumbstruck as he stared at me for a second before responding. Pointing to himself, his eyes wide as saucers, he responded, "You have got to be shitting me! My name is Michael Larsen!" His eyes seemed to grow larger and larger as he continued to stare at me before finally grinning and saying, "Well, I wanted my name to be Michael Larsen, but my parents named me Jack Anthony instead." Shrugging his shoulders, his smile grew as he continued. "I guess we can't all be Michael Larsens."

I forced a laugh, wondering if the guy was already drunk, was being a smart ass, or just had a weird sense of humor. While I was trying to make up my mind, he slapped me on the shoulder and said, "I'm just playing with you, man!" Offering his hand to shake mine, he continued. "It's nice to meet you, Michael Larsen." He tipped his half-empty can to me. "To new friends!" Then he drained the remaining beer in the can and grabbed my hand, shaking it vigorously.

I'd downed four of Jack's beers by the time the game was over. Fresno State had eked out a 28–27 win, and the student section had gone completely insane! A girl I hadn't ever seen before grabbed me and kissed me on the lips. I'd had enough beer to loosen my inhibitions, and I kissed her back with her same fervor. Once the kiss was finished, she turned and vanished into the crazy crowd of people. Jack had been watching me from his vantage point and yelled, "You go for it, Michael! What an animal!"

As the roar of the crowd started to quiet into more reasonable noise, fans began departing the stadium in large numbers. Now that he could hear me, I asked Jack if he wanted to get something to eat.

"Sure!" he replied quickly. "You have a car?" he asked.

"Yes, I do!" I responded with a slight smile on my face.

As we were approaching my car, Jack stopped, looked at it, and then began talking, "No way! No fucking way that sweet thing is your car!"

I felt myself smile as I unlocked the door, sat in driver's seat, and, with the turn of a key, listened to the beautiful rumble as my 396 Chevelle roared to life. "You are coming or not?" I asked matter-of-factly.

"Sweet Jesus, yes!" he yelled back, as he ran around to the passenger door, opened it, and jumped in.

Once his door was closed, I hit the gas pedal and dropped the clutch, sending the car bolting forward. In a second, the engine was screaming, the tires were squealing and smoking, and my maroon beast was swerved and twisted its way toward the exit of the stadium parking lot.

Jack was yelling and hollering at the top of his lungs every time I shifted gears. Finally, running out of parking lot, I took my foot off the gas pedal. "God almighty, this thing is fast! I've never been in anything this fast! Michael, I love this car!"

Simply smiling in response, I asked, "I'm not very familiar with Fresno. Do you know any good restaurants where we can get something to eat?" We sat staring at the red traffic light at the parking lot exit leading to the main highway.

"Oh, yeah, I know a place," he replied and pointed out the windshield to go straight ahead.

About to put a piece of steak, cooked to a perfect medium rare, into my mouth, I calmly stated, "Dinner's on me tonight, Jack!"

He shook his head affirmingly, and once he'd swallowed what he had been eating, he replied, "I know! After all, you drank all my damn beer!"

"Are you serious?" I shot back. "The gas I used in the parking lot to show you a good time cost more than your damn beer!"

We looked at each other and both laughed profusely for several minutes. After finishing dinner, I drove Jack home, promised to stay in touch, and headed back to my apartment. I'd had more fun and laughed more that night than I had in months. Being around Jack felt as natural as being around Jimmy Clarke. It just felt right. I didn't know it at the time, but that was the beginning of a lifelong friendship that I would cherish forever.

By my junior year, I had much improved time management skills, which made my life considerably easier. I woke up at 6:00 a.m. and either worked out with weights or ran five miles, depending on what I'd done the day before. A quick shower and shave, a light breakfast, gathering everything I needed for that day's classes, and I was out the door by 8:30 a.m. I attended my classes, bought a light lunch or brought my own from home, and was usually back in my apartment before 4:00 p.m. I worked on homework and reading assignments until 7:00 or 7:30 p.m. and then either fixed something for dinner or went out for a quick bite, usually to a fast-food joint of some kind. Most Mondays through Fridays, there wasn't much variation in the routine.

I had made a few friends, but for the most part, I stayed pretty much to myself. I would see Jack two or three times a month, and each time we were together, it was the highlight of my week. He was a funny man, and I always left him feeling lighthearted and content. Still no girls in the picture, but I was OK with that. I was in college to get a degree, not to party every weekend.

I bought a twenty-one-inch black-and-white television for about $200. I had wanted a new color TV, but the cost was ridiculous; most were about $800. I quickly chose a few favorite programs for each night of the week. *Charlie's Angels* and *Bonanza* on Sunday nights, *All in the Family* and *The Brady Bunch* on Mondays, and several other programs depending on the day of the week.

I had to be careful not to get too engrossed in watching too much television. It didn't take long for me to realize that TV was the number-one enemy of my time management. A couple of nights, I started by watching my favorite nightly shows, only to wake up at 3:00 a.m. realizing I still needed to finish a paper that was due later that same day. Not having to answer to or have meaningful conversation with anyone else while in my apartment made watching TV my main source of communication with the outside world.

I religiously watched the ten o'clock news just before going to bed. The world was continuing to change at a rapid pace, and the news was the only way for me to encapsulate what was happening all around me while I was working toward a degree.

Top stories started with the United States now invading Cambodia. The outcry from the American public was deafening. Even though President Nixon had just been elected to a second term in office, his approval rating plunged after it was discovered that we had secretly entered Cambodia. In addition to the war, the Watergate scandal began when White House operatives were caught burglarizing the Democratic National Committee.

Arab members of the Organization of Petroleum Exporting Countries (OPEC) announced that they would no longer ship oil to western countries that supported Israel in their conflict with Syria and Egypt. They further announced that oil prices would go up drastically. True to their word, oil prices quadrupled, while supplies of oil and gasoline diminished. The West had become dependent on OPEC for oil, and with no reserves of our own, the Western world was thrust into a recession and was now facing massively inflation pressures.

For me, gasoline in a one-year period had gone from thirty-eight cents a gallon to a dollar and nine cents a gallon. The cost of gas was so high that I thought about selling my gas-guzzling Chevelle. Unfortunately, no one else could afford the cost of fuel for the beast either, so it remained in my possession.

There was significant growth in the women's rights movement and women's role in society, including the ability to decide when, where, and if they wished to have children. A large part of this movement was driven by the availability and access to contraceptive pills. The choice whether to have children became even more cemented when the United States Supreme Court declared that abortion is a constitutional right in the landmark decision of the *Roe v. Wade* case.

During my relatively short time in college, I had sensed a transformation beginning with a more vocal and activist female population springing up around different campuses. Not that I thought that was a bad thing, but some of their numbers had gone a little too far left in their race for equality and were openly hostile to those not of their same sex.

My twenty-first birthday landed on a Friday, and Jack nonchalantly asked if I was going to be around or go home for the big day. I told him I would be staying here as I had a term paper due the next week, and spring vacation was only two weeks away. He asked if he could take me to dinner and buy me my first legal drink, and I graciously accepted.

I picked him up at 7:00 p.m., and he directed me to a bar in the small town of Clovis, about ten miles east of Fresno. He knew the family that owned the bar and told me you can't get a better steak anywhere in Central California.

"Sounds great to me!" I said as we went inside.

"Surprise!" came an almost deafening roar as we entered the dark room.

The loud surprise startled me, and I unintentionally jumped back and recoiled with trepidation. While waiting for my eyes to adjust from the brightly lit day outside to this much darker room, I simply stood still. While standing there, a chorus of "Happy Birthday" filled the room. It sounded like there were a hundred people singing. What seemed so bizarre was that I didn't know a hundred people in Central California.

Once the singing was completed, cheers, whistles, and screams filled the room, and then it went silent. My eyes had adjusted to the darkness of the chamber by the time they stopped singing, and I could see that everyone was waiting for me to say something.

"Thank you all very much," I began in a voice loud enough to be heard by everyone. "You only turn twenty-one once, and this will always be a special memory for me." The crowd remained staring as I continued. "My only question is, who the hell are you people?"

Everyone roared with laughter, and after a few seconds, Jack broke into the conversation. "These are all my friends! And you are my friend!" Waving his arm to make sure he encompassed the whole room, he continued. "So now these are all your friends too! Happy birthday, Michael Larsen," he said, handing me a short glass half filled with who knows what in it.

I took the glass and raised it, clinking it to the other half-full glass he was holding in his other hand and simply said, "Thank you, Jack!"

Having never been a big drinker, I didn't know what I'd just drunk. But I knew it was warm as I felt it making its way down my throat and into my belly. I sputtered a bit while I tried to catch my breath, which had somehow vanished once the liquor had left my mouth and began its burning trail southward.

"Wow!" I finally said after fully collecting myself. "What was that?" I asked.

"That, my friend, was a twelve-year-old single malt scotch whiskey," he replied. "You should celebrate every birthday from now on with that same beautiful drink! You're a man now, Michael!"

I hadn't shared much about my army life and experiences with Jack. He didn't know that I had been to Vietnam because I made sure the subject never came up. It was nothing I wanted to brag about or relive with anyone, not even Jack. But the memories and occasional nightmares from those days had convinced me long ago that I had already earned the right to be called a man.

I met a ton of people at the party, all very nice and very welcoming. Unfortunately, the more I drank, the less I remembered the names of those surrounding me. I could feel the room starting to spin, and I knew I was getting drunk. I asked Jack if we could sit down and eat something.

"Sure!" he replied and cleared a place for the two of us at a rather large rectangular table. There were six other people seated at the table, and all were immersed in conversation with each other. Jack introduced me to everyone once they'd completed their individual conversations. After saying, "It's a pleasure to meet you," two of guests at the table let me know we had already been introduced previously.

"Whoops!" I responded. "I'm so sorry, I forgot that we'd met already. Either too many new friends or too much to drink!" I said, shrugging my shoulders. They accepted the apology, and everyone returned to their private conversations.

A huge platter was placed in front of both Jack and me. "I hope you don't mind, but I ordered for both of us," Jack said, adjusting the plate in front of him. "It's prime rib, medium rare, along with garlic mashed potatoes and locally grown green beans." He had his fork and knife in his hands, and using his knife, he pointed to the small white mixture in the cup next to the meat. "I'll warn you right now, though, that horseradish is tasty, but use it sparingly or it will choke you to death. It's really spicy!"

I was ravenous and began devouring my meal. It was a dinner fit for a king, and each side serving on the plate was delicious and perfectly cooked. When I couldn't eat another bite, I pushed the plate away, realizing I'd really overeaten. I sat back, unable to hold my bloated stomach in, and concentrated on my breathing, praying that I would keep everything down that I'd just consumed.

"Well, what do you think?" Jack asked. "Did dinner meet your expectations?"

"Exceptional, Jack," I replied. "Absolutely exceptional!"

As the two of us sat there in a food coma, Jack spotted someone and waved for them to come over. A very buxom, dark-haired woman in a tight sweater and even tighter jeans made her way through the crowd to our table.

"Sarah!" Jack sang out, standing to give her a warm hug. Holding her at arm's length, he continued. "You look fabulous! The last time I saw you was in July of last year, and you are even more beautiful now than I remembered!"

"Cut the crap, Jack," she retorted. "Is this the birthday boy?"

"Yes. Sarah Seremban, meet Michael Larsen." Then looking in my direction, he continued. "Michael, meet Sarah."

She put her hand out, and I took it, shaking it softly. "It's a pleasure to meet you, Sarah."

"Likewise," she said. "Oh, and happy birthday! Your twenty-first is a pretty special birthday." She sat down across from me and just watched me without speaking.

Finally, she rummaged around in her purse and pulled out a pack of Salem cigarettes and a lighter. Sticking the filtered end of the cigarette in her mouth, she lit the other end while inhaling deeply.

I was mesmerized by the hot red glow at the end of the cigarette as she sucked the smoke deeper into her lungs. Then she blew it all out through her nose, taking me back to another time when my sergeant had smoked a cigarette that same way while in transit to one of our combat missions.

Still looking at one another and saying nothing, it was obvious she was beautiful, and she knew it. Her deep chocolate-brown eyes and full red lips were accentuated by high cheekbones and sparkling white teeth. Her hair looked like it was made of silk as it shone in the dim bar lighting.

Leaning back in her chair and taking another drag from her cigarette, she asked, "So what's your story, Michael Larsen?" Smoke was rolling out of her nose as she spoke.

"Not much of a story," I responded. "Going to Fresno State to get a business degree, and today, I turned twenty-one. There isn't much more to the story."

Taking one last long drag off her cigarette, she snuffed it out in the ashtray on the table. Tilting her head upward and exhaling the smoke toward the ceiling, only this time through her lips, she looked back at me and said, "There's always more to the story."

A small smile formed on my face, and then she started to smile back. I had my first glimpse of a pair of distinct and very sexy dimples forming as she smiled. "Can I buy you a birthday drink, Michael Larsen?"

"No. No, you can't, Sarah," I said sternly. "If my momma knew that on the day I was supposed to become a man, I let a girl buy my drinks, she'd disown me, and my dad would probably kick my ass. However, I would be glad to buy you a drink and have one with you if you would allow me to."

Her smile grew larger, and her dimples recessed even deeper into her cheeks. "I'd be delighted to have a drink with you, Michael. Oh, and just to clarify, I'm no longer a girl. I have blossomed into a full-grown woman in case you haven't noticed."

"Why, yes, I had noticed, ma'am." I called the server over and ordered a drink for both of us. I turned to see what Jack wanted to drink only to find him gone.

"He's been gone for five minutes," she offered up with a little chuckle.

"How do you two know each other?" I asked.

She pulled another cigarette out of the pack and readied her lighter. "I've known Jack since he was about four years old. We were next-door neighbors for most of my life. We played together, and at one point, I babysat him when his parents went out on an occasional date night."

"Wait a second," I interjected. "How old are you anyway?"

She lit the cigarette and continued to watch me through the wall of smoke she'd created. "I could ask you to guess how old I am, but if you guess too old, it'll just piss me off. So let's just say that I got to celebrate my twenty-first birthday before you graduated from high school."

After a few seconds, she asked, "You got a girlfriend or someone special in your life, Michael Larsen?"

"No. No, I don't." I chuckled. "I have barely talked to a girl in the last three years. There's school and there's homework and there isn't much time for anything else. How about you?"

"That's a tough question to answer," she replied after a few seconds of silence. "I've been with the same guy for about four years, but I think we both know our relationship has pretty much run its course."

Talk continued between the two of us, and soon, it was like there was no one else in the room but Sarah and me. After more drinks and more conversation, the bar was thinning out as patrons left, and I decided it was about time for me to leave as well. At about 1:00 a.m., Jack came over and sat down with us.

"Hey, guys, I snagged a ride with Jennifer Cummings, so I just wanted to say good night and happy birthday one last time." I stood and hugged Jack and thanked him for the incredible night. "You OK to drive?" he asked before leaving.

"Don't worry about him. I'll make sure he gets home tonight," Sarah announced, catching both Jack and me off guard with the statement.

Jack looked first at Sarah and then back to me and then back to Sarah. "Well, all right, then," he said excitedly. "I guess I'll just see you both when I see you! Can't wait to hear the details!"

"Get out of here, you jerk!" Sarah snapped, as Jack turned and exited the bar.

"How did you get here?" I asked inquisitively.

"I drove," she replied curtly.

"Well, then, we still have a problem," I responded. "Two cars and only one driver."

"We'll just leave one car here," she replied, suddenly seeming irritated with me.

"I'm not leaving my car here!" I spat out, looking defiantly back at her.

"That's fine. I'll just drive your car and leave mine here," she countered. "Don't you trust me to drive your car? Besides, my car has stayed in this parking lot more than once. I know it will be safe." She again wore a mischievous smile as she waited for my reaction.

"Can you drive a stick shift?" I inquired.

"Please! I grew up on a farm. I can drive a car, a truck, a tractor, or anything else you can think of!"

I liked her self-confidence but didn't know if she was telling the truth or not, having just met her. But still, I responded, "OK! You go park your car, and I'll pay the check and meet you outside." She nodded in agreement and got up, left the table, and walked out the front door.

After paying our tab, I headed toward the door myself. After only a few steps, it was obvious that I was truly too drunk to drive. My vision was blurred, and I could feel myself walking in a crooked line, bumping into people as I tried to make my way to the exit. Finally making it to the door, I opened it and felt a rush of cool night air hit me from outside. It felt so good that I just stood there, half in and half out of the doorway. Closing my eyes, I took a couple of long, deep breaths of the sweet, fresh air through my nose and exhaled it out through my mouth.

I felt someone grabbing my arm and prying me away from the comfortable doorjamb. Sarah said softly, "I've got you, birthday boy!" She threw my left arm over her shoulder and slowly started to guide me away from the bar entrance. "Do you know where your car is?" she asked as we stopped at the street curb.

"It's over there," I said, pointing across the street. "The maroon one."

Looking over, she replied, "Damn, Michael, that is a nice car!" Then putting one hand around my waist while holding on to the arm over her shoulder, she looked both ways, and we started across the empty street.

I'd felt OK when we were sitting in the bar talking, but now I felt more and more inebriated with each step. The streetlights were out of focus, and everything seemed to be spinning around us as Sarah guided me to my car.

Putting her hand in my pocket while she held me against the front fender, she foraged for the keys to the car. After not finding them, she reached into the other pocket and fished around until she snagged and pulled my car keys out. Opening the passenger door, she half sat, half dumped me into the bucket seat, lifting my legs in, and closed the door behind me.

Once she was inside and the car was running, I rolled down my passenger window to feel more cool air. As we pulled away from the curb, the cool breeze in my face comforted me to the point that I was again able to open my eyes without seeing a whirling world in every direction.

"You doing OK, Michael?" she asked, never taking her eyes off the road.

"Yeah, I'm doing fine," I replied. I scooted up in the seat to a more upright position and stared out the windshield. The car lights coming toward us seemed extra bright, but at least now they had stopped spinning.

"I'm going to need an address, Michael."

Giving her my address, my next recollection was of us walking through the front door of my apartment. She was still helping me walk, but I was better able to support myself now.

"Pretty spartan decor" she commented, helping me sit down on my couch.

I paid no attention to her comment and sat there smiling back at her like a fool. Finally, I said in a slurred voice, "I apologize, but I have to go to bed. Make yourself at home, and we'll talk in the morning." With that, I got up and stumbled into my room, taking my clothes off and dropping them where each item came off as I made my way toward the bed. Once there, my knees buckled, and I fell facedown on the bed. I'm sure I was snoring loudly thirty seconds later.

As I lay there, I kept smelling a fragrance that wasn't familiar to me. It was very pleasant, kind of a sweet floral smell with some lime scents mixed in. Then, all at once, I thought I could feel the light touch of someone's lips as they softly kissed the back of my neck. I instantly felt goose bumps rising wherever those sensuous lips touched. I couldn't tell if I was dreaming or if this was real, but it felt fantastic.

Becoming more conscious and alert, I realized I wasn't dreaming, and I wasn't in bed alone. Opening my eyes, the digital clock on the nightstand directly in front of me read 5:30 a.m. Slowly rolling over, I came face-to-face with Sarah, who immediately kissed me with an animal intensity. She was naked, and in less than two minutes, my underwear was off as well, even though we never stopped kissing. The next thirty minutes or so were simply transcendent, kissing, touching, and kissing again as our bodies tangled together in the dance of primal lovemaking.

Finally spent, I rolled over, lying on my back with one arm over my head and the other at my side. I was concentrating on controlling my jagged breathing. Sarah scooted closer to me and laid her head on my sweaty chest. She draped one arm across my chest, and I could feel the perspiration dripping off her and onto me. We were both silent as we each tried to catch our breath from the intense exertion we'd just experienced.

Raising herself onto her elbows, she glanced down at my disfigured left arm and asked, "I'm not hurting your arm, am I?"

The workout had made her hair stick to her sweaty face wherever it touched. I smiled up at her, pulled her back down so her head was once again resting on my chest, and simply replied, "No, you're not hurting me." We lay like that for a good length of time, no words needing to be spoken. I found myself slipping in and out of sleep as I softly caressed the female arm that lay across my body. I don't know if I have ever known more peace than I did at that moment.

Sarah walked out of the bedroom at about 9:00 a.m. the next day. She had on one of my long-sleeved shirts that was hanging on the closet door, and I was pretty sure that was all she had on. I'd woken up hungry and was in the middle of making breakfast for both of us. "Coffee?" I asked.

She shook her head yes, and I poured her a cup. As she sat sipping her coffee, I said, "That may go down as one of the best twelve-hour experiences I have ever had in my life!" She seemed shy now, but her dimples revealed themselves as a smile started to form on her face.

"I could have slept till noon if it wasn't for the smell of bacon cooking!" she blurted out.

I had on a white undershirt, and when I glanced over at her, I noticed she was looking at the scars on my arm again. She caught me watching her and looked away, embarrassed at being caught.

Wanting to get the thousand-pound elephant out of the room, I said, "I was wounded in a couple of places when I was in Vietnam. I hope that doesn't gross you out too much."

"Oh, god, no!" she responded immediately. Then catching my gaze, she continued. "But like I said before, there is always more to the story."

We ate, drank another cup of coffee, and had a very pleasant conversation. It didn't feel as awkward as I thought it would to be sitting at my dining table and eating breakfast with a woman I'd just met, made love to, fixed breakfast for, all of it being accomplished in the last twelve hours.

"What do you want to do today?" I asked.

"Well, I want to get my car, but other than that, I don't have any plans," she retorted. "What would you like to do today?"

I rose from my chair, cleared my dirty dishes, put them in the sink, and came back for hers. "Well, after I do these dishes, and since it's raining outside, and now that my head has stopped pounding, I'd kind of like to spend the rest of the day in bed."

I walked back to where she was sitting, bent down, and softly kissed her on the cheek while whispering in her ear, "You're sure welcome to join me if you want."

She put her arms around my neck and pulled me back to her for a second kiss before quietly saying, "The hell with the dishes!" We spent almost the whole day in bed or in the shower, except for a few short breaks for nourishment. Saturday was turning out to be an even better day than my birthday, and I knew I was smitten!

On Sunday afternoon, Sarah asked me to take her back to her car. I didn't want her to leave but knew she had a life of her own that she needed to get back to. Pulling up to her car, we sat silently like two lovestruck kids, neither of us knowing what to say or how to end this beautiful weekend. The awkward silence was finally broken by her.

"I want you to know that this isn't a normal weekend for me," she began. "I had a great time with you, Michael." She looked over at me and continued. "I'm going to leave Chuck this week. He hasn't made me feel this good and, for lack of better words, this loved in a very long time. Thank you for a wonderful weekend." She leaned over and softly kissed me on the cheek. Then looking away, she reached for the door handle. "I really hope we get to see more of each other." Then she was out of my car and was quickly walking toward her own vehicle.

I felt the same way but wasn't sure how to articulate it as she got into her car and drove away. I continued to sit there, my car softly growling in neutral as I watched her drive out of sight. How could I be so captivated by this person after being with her for a mere thirty-six hours? I couldn't answer my own question, but I was consumed with wanting to see her again, and as soon as possible.

I hadn't been able to get Sarah out of my mind as another week of school came to an end. I had to see her. I called Jack, and he gave me directions to her apartment. Early the next Saturday morning, I drove to her place, and with all the intestinal fortitude I could muster, I knocked softly on her front door.

She opened the door, and a huge smile formed on her face. "Hi!" she declared, moving forward and giving me a big hug and then kissing my cheek.

I hugged her back and responded with "I was just in the neighborhood and decided to drop by and say hi."

"Right!" she said confidently. "Come in. Would you like some coffee?"

"Sounds great." In an instant, she was gone, and I was left standing uncomfortably alone in her living room. As I scanned the room, there were boxes stacked everywhere, and she had obviously been packing. My heart leaped a little bit as I realized she was really moving out as she had stated last weekend.

Returning, and handing me a hot cup of coffee, she said, "I'm so glad to see you!" Taking boxes off the couch and piling them on the floor, she continued. "Have a seat."

I did as she asked, and she sat next to me. I took a quick drink of my coffee and said, "So you're really moving?"

She looked me in the eyes and said, "Yep! I'm really moving!" Her cheeks dimpled as the smile was returning to her face. "Chuck and I are calling it quits, and I'm pretty excited to be moving on!"

As much as I tried, I couldn't suppress the smile that was forming on my face. "I have to tell you," I retorted, "that is welcome news to me!" Then looking around the room, I asked, "Where are you moving to?"

"I'll probably move home with my parents for a while," she responded, her eyes following my gaze around the cluttered room. "Not sure just yet where I want to live. Eventually, I want to be closer to my work in Fresno, but I haven't really had much time to do any apartment shopping."

"How is Chuck taking this?"

"Oh, he's fine! He stayed in Vegas all week, and we pretty much decided over the phone that this was what was best for both of us. He's coming by today to talk to me about getting out of our lease because he's going to move to Las Vegas. I think he may have a new lady friend there."

I felt a slight tinge of panic at the realization her ex-boyfriend could be showing up at the front door at any moment. "Will he be pissed that I'm here?" I asked, a little more concern in my voice than I had intended.

"No, not at all!" she reassured me. "I've already told him I found someone I care about. He understands, and we'll still be friends, just friends without benefits." Her smile widened again, and the dimples deepened as she waited for my response.

"I think I'd better leave," I said. "This is all moving too fast!"

Her smile instantly disappeared, and I could see real hurt in her eyes. I smiled and said, "I'm just kidding!"

She pushed me over on the couch and started playfully hitting me on the arm with both hands. "You dick! I thought you were serious!"

"I am serious," I replied. "Why don't you just move in with me?" The second the words were out of my mouth, I couldn't believe I'd just said them.

We sat in silence for a moment, neither of us sure what to say next. "Wow!" she finally exclaimed. "I wasn't expecting that!"

"Michael, I think you need a little more time before making that offer to me. We've only casually known each other for a week, and we've only spent two nights together. We really don't even know each other. Our likes, dislikes, our families, aspirations, what we like in movies or music—we don't know any of these things and so much more about each other."

I was silent for a moment and then stood to responded, "Listen, Sarah, I don't know why we met last weekend, but I haven't been able to stop thinking about you since meeting you. I have never lived with anyone except my parents, and asking a stranger to move in with me is way out of character for me. I can think of a thousand reasons why you moving in with me is a bad idea. But I don't care about our age difference, or any other differences we may discover, because if you feel at all like I feel about you, we can adapt."

I saw tears forming in her eyes, spilling over, and running down her cheeks as I continued. "I didn't come here today to ask you to move in with me, but you're like a drug that I can't get enough of! When I'm with you, I'm happy. When I'm not, I'm wishing I was with you. I don't know why, but I think I'm falling in love with you." Again, my own words caught me off guard. "Oh my god! I have never said those words to anyone before except for family!" I asserted.

Sarah jumped to her feet and rushed into me, wrapping her arms around me. We hugged, softly kissed, and then hugged again, only to have the quiet romantic moment rudely interrupted by a loud knocking on her front door.

Sarah apologized with a simple "I'm sorry." Wiping the tears from her face with both hands, she pulled away from me and moved toward the front door of the apartment.

"Hi!" she said, trying to sound cheerful. She came back into the living room, pulling another man in behind her by the hand. Once next to me, she introduced us. "Chuck, this is Michael. Michael, this is Chuck!"

Chuck let go of Sarah's hand and stuck his hand out in my direction. I reached out and grasped his hand, and we both used a stronger-than-necessary grip to shake each other's hand. Neither of us had said a word yet as we stood face-to-face, sizing each other up.

Chuck was older than I thought he would be, and he had a lot of hard miles on him. He was thin, nice looking, but as he smiled at me, his eyes narrowed almost like an animal stocking its prey. Finally, he spoke. "So I guess you're the new guy in Sarah's life?"

Sarah quickly interrupted. "Be nice, boys!"

"I hope so," I responded flatly.

After a long moment, he finally said, "Well, you'd better be good to her, or I'm going to have to come back here and kick your ass, son!"

Letting go of each other's hands, I countered. "You mean you'll come back here and try to kick my ass, don't you, Pops!"

Still staring at one another, a grin started to form on his face. "Sarah, you might have yourself a good one here! He's got spunk, I'll give him that."

He turned away from me and went over to the couch to sit down. Opening a briefcase and taking out a handful of papers, he placed them on the coffee table. Looking at Sarah, he said, "Let's get this business over with so we can both go our separate ways."

I went into the kitchen, took out a cold bottle of beer from Sarah's refrigerator, and exited the house through the back door, giving them some privacy to do whatever needed to be done.

Sitting on the back steps, I looked up into the clear blue sky and watched a few marshmallow clouds floating past. Sipping on my beer, I wondered if I was making a mistake with this rash decision that could change my life forever. As I was deep in thought, Sarah stepped out the back door.

"Do you want to come say good-bye, Michael?" she asked in a tone designed not to make me feel pressured.

"Sure!" I replied, leaping to my feet and following her back into the house.

Chuck was waiting at the front door as we approached. Sticking my hand out for the second time today, I stated, "It was good to meet you, Chuck. I wish you all the best life has to offer."

He smirked, took my hand, and shook it, a little gentler this time. "Remember what I said, young buck. She's a diamond, and you need to treat her like one." He turned away from me, bent forward, and kissed Sarah on the cheek and then exited the apartment.

Once the apartment door closed, we were left standing there just looking at each other. "Do you want to hang around for a while, or do you need to go?" Sarah finally asked.

"Well, I guess I should stick around. It's going take both of us all weekend to get this stuff moved to my place," I replied calmly.

Sarah rushed into my arms again and started to softly cry, her face buried in my chest. "Michael, you need to be sure this is what you want before we make this leap," she said, her face still immersed on my upper body.

I rubbed her back as I spoke. "I'm sure! If I wasn't sure, I wouldn't make the offer. But if you come, I hope you will stay for longer than four years! Besides, moving sucks, and I don't want to have to move you twice! I'll probably have a bad back after just one move!"

She chuckled, gave me a light punch in the ribs, and then turned her head up to kiss me. Once our kiss was finished, we stood there in silence again, just holding each other and rocking back and forth.

"Well," she said, finally raising her head to look me in the eyes, "everyone already thinks I'm crazy, so let's give them something new to talk about!"

At 9:00 p.m., Sunday, I had no idea how prophetic my words had been when I first spoke about moving in together. But I was sure that I didn't want to do this move twice! My back was killing me, my arms ached, and I was completely spent. Watching Sara slowly walking around her new apartment, I could tell she was as tired as me. She moved a few boxes out of the way and plopped down on the newly created space she'd made on the sofa.

"Why don't we just unload the rest of this stuff in the garage tonight?" she began. "I'm ready to take a shower, eat something, and go to bed. We can finish unpacking and hit this again next weekend if you don't have school and if I'm off work," she stated.

"I don't have any classes on the weekends," I responded. Looking around the cluttered room, I continued. "Why don't you jump in the shower, and I'll run out and get us a couple of burgers? I'm really tired, and I don't feel like cooking tonight."

"Can I have a chocolate malt too?" she asked, a small smile forming.

"Yeah, I think you've earned a chocolate malt today. You're a damn good little worker, Sarah Seremban!" I continued.

Her smile grew. "Thank you! You're a pretty hard worker yourself, Michael Larsen!"

I walked over to her, kissed her quickly on the lips, and said, "I'll be back in a little while." I replaced the rental truck keys with the car keys sitting on the dining room table, and a second later, I was out the door.

My alarm went off at its normal 6:00 a.m. the next day, and I reached over and hit it, immediately silencing the obnoxious noise. Sarah raised up on one arm, looked at the clock, and said in a pouty voice, "Don't tell me you get up this early every morning!"

"Just Monday through Friday," I responded.

"Great!" she snarled, falling back to her pillow and rolling away from me.

I smiled to myself, realizing how little we really knew about each other's habits. Last night, we'd eaten dinner, I'd taken a quick shower, and we'd gone to bed.

Regardless how tired we were, as different parts of our bodies met each other's, nature took over, and we'd made love. It appears I'd just fallen to sleep when that damn alarm went off and Monday began.

In the following days, we developed the semblance of a daily routine. Through trial and error, we were also learning a lot of little idiosyncrasies about each other along the way. Getting through our first week, we decided to finish working on cleaning up the apartment and garage. The good news was that as Sarah had mentioned the first time she'd been in my apartment, the decor was Spartan. The bad news was that Sarah more than made up for the lack of decorations with three U-Haul truckloads of furniture, clothes, artwork, and, for lack of a better word, stuff.

By Sunday night, the apartment didn't look anything like it had two weeks earlier. Prints, paintings, and various artwork adorned the walls. The rooms all became better organized spaces with different pieces of furniture (almost all of it hers). Fragrant candles lay around in abundance in each room, giving off various aromas, all of which were pleasing to the olfactory senses.

Once done, we finally sat together on the sofa, enjoying a nice glass of wine and admiring our finished product. We were both pleased with the fruits of our labor, and as we eyed our completed work, it was hard not to smile. I looked over at Sarah, and she seemed to have the same satisfied look on her face as she panned the room with her beautiful eyes.

I broke the silence by saying, "Where are we going to put all the stuff that's in the garage? I really want to park my car in there if possible."

She reached over and placed her hand on top of mine, which was sitting on the arm of the sofa. Patting it lightly a few times, she looked back at me and said, "If it means that much to you, I'll find a place to put all our excess stuff."

It sounded as though she had already been devising a plan and, now being confronted about the garage issue, was ready to execute her strategy.

On Wednesday, while we were eating dinner, Sarah dropped a bomb on me. "I called home, and my dad has agreed to store the rest of our stuff on the farm. He has plenty of room in the barn where it will be safe and stay dry." She continued eating her dinner as if she hadn't just said something significant.

"What?" I said. "Do your parents even know you and I are living together?"

After swallowing what was in her mouth, she responded, "No, but Saturday, when we're having dinner with them, would be a good time to break the news."

A sudden rush of panic swept over me. "Are you suggesting that I tell your father that we have moved in together? 'But don't worry about us. Because even though I'm six years younger than your daughter, everything will work out fine because we think we're made for each other!'"

She gave me a look and then responded, "Oh, sweetheart, don't worry about the age gap! That's the least of our worries. I come from a very traditional Armenian family, and my parents would never allow me to date someone of another race! My poor mother would have a heart attack at the mere suggestion that we would consider living together!

"I have two sisters, one twelve years older and the other twenty-four years older than me. Both are married to Armenian men through family-arranged marriages. Papa had to approve of them, and then he paid their parents a dowry to complete the marriage process. My oldest sister was wed in Armenia, and the younger one was married here in the States. Both husbands treat my father with the respect that he demands because he not only runs our family but has a voice in their families as well. Buying a house or a car, purchasing real estate or farm equipment—none of that happens without Papa's approval."

Sarah chuckled softly. "It's almost comical that my sixty-three-year-old brother-in-law has to get Papa's permission to purchase a car." She became serious as she continued. "I don't want to be a part of that world. I make my own decisions and live the life I want, and I don't need my parents' permission to do so!"

I sat there stunned as I listened to her. Finally, I was able to respond. "Wow! That is some crazy stuff!" Then standing up and crossing my arms, I paced aimlessly around the kitchen before saying, "What the hell am I getting myself into here, Sarah?"

"Me, that's what you're getting, Michael! And you should feel honored," she responded. "I've never taken any man to meet my parents before. And, yes, they are going to be pissed that you are not Armenian, but I doubt my father will be rude to you. He is a stern but fair man, and if he's pissed, it will most likely be at me. He knows I'm the wild child of the family. He also knows that I don't come home often because I don't want to live by their established cultural rules."

"So they never met Chuck?" I questioned.

"They never even knew Chuck existed!" she retorted. "I knew from the beginning that he wasn't my happily-ever-after mate. I didn't want to hurt my parents by bringing him home, knowing we weren't going to make it."

"So you were with Chuck for four years and you never introduced him to your parents," I said, a small smile forming on my face. "And you've known me for two weeks and you're ready for me to meet your parents? I don't know how I'm supposed to feel about that."

Her eyes narrowed as she stared at me. "You'd better feel pretty damn thrilled!" Then her look softened. "Anyway, that's how I feel."

I suddenly felt like my heart was going to burst. I understood she was telling me she loved me without saying the words. I knew that I felt the same way about her, but I couldn't verbalize the words either, even though I wanted to shout them to her.

During the next week, I read everything I could about Armenian culture instead of studying for my classes. I spent most of my time at the library, preparing for the inevitable weekend meeting with Sarah's parents.

Time and distance flashed by as I pulled off the highway and turned into the farm's driveway. It was a dusty two hundred yards further on loose gravel to the main house. Stopping where the other cars were parked, we waited for the dust cloud we'd created to pass by before exiting our rental truck. People, several more than I had expected, started coming out of the front door of the cute, small farmhouse.

"Oh, crap!" Sarah sang out. "It looks like Mama invited both my sisters and their families!"

My response was simply "Great!"

As we exited the truck, a tiny gray-haired woman I assumed to be Sarah's mom walked swiftly toward us with open arms. Once she'd cleared the passenger door, Sarah ran into the open arms of her mother, and they embraced for several seconds. Then pulling away from each other, they began speaking in what I assumed was their native tongue. By now, there were several more people surrounding Sarah, and she hugged or kissed all of them as she made her way through the group. There were smiles and a few tears as person after person was recognized by her.

After what seemed like an eternity, she looked back and waved me forward. There were introductions to each and different responses from each. It appears the older the person, the less friendly they were. Sarah's sisters and her brothers-in-law were cordial, but not what I would call welcoming. On the opposite side, her nieces and nephews, most of whom looked to be our age or maybe a little younger, were very hospitable as they welcomed me using perfect English.

It was one of the strangest situations I'd ever been in. When speaking to me, they used varying degrees of the English language. But if they weren't addressing me directly, they spoke Armenian to each other, giving me an occasional glance and possibly a quick smile.

As Sarah became more engrossed in her family, I felt more and more uncomfortable just standing there. Suddenly, the front door opened, and a rather small man walking with the assistance of a cane exited the house. Immediately, all talking ceased as everyone watched him approach us. Sarah smiled and rushed to meet him before he'd made his way to the group. They hugged, and he lovingly kissed her on the cheek. Once they broke from their embrace, he spoke softly to her, again in Armenian. She looked back at me as they continued to talk, and then they turned and, arm in arm, started forward in my direction. People moved aside, forming an aisle for Sarah and her father to walk through as they continued their short journey toward me.

Once they were directly in front of me, Sarah said, "Papa, this is Michael Larsen." Then looking in my direction, she continued. "Michael, this is my father, Jacob Seremban."

Putting his hand out to shake mine, he said in broken English, "You can call me Jake if you want. That's what most people call me."

Grasping his hand and shaking it, I said, "It's a pleasure to meet you, Mr. Seremban." His grip was very firm for a man his age. His hand was rough, like that of a working man who spent time in the fields every day.

"It's nice to meet you as well, Michael," he responded, his expression sober with no sign of a smile coming. "Please come into my home, and we can sit down and talk. If you drink, we can have a drink while we wait for dinner to be served."

We all went into the house, and all the women including Sarah immediately went into the kitchen. Jake sat in what I assumed was his, and only his, recliner chair. The two brothers-in-law, three male cousins, and I sat on two sofas that were on either side of the living room. One of Sarah's brothers-in-law started the conversation.

"Tell us a little about yourself, Michael. How did you and Sarah meet?"

Right to the point, I thought to myself, *Screw the small talk, let's go for the jugular with the first question.* Fortunately, I had prepared for this question, and with a smile on my face, I tried to answer it in a positive manner. The questions kept coming with everyone in the room taking a turn at me. The only person who didn't ask a question was Sarah's father. He just sat there and listened to all that was being said.

Thirty minutes later, he finally broke in and asked, "Would you like a drink, Michael?"

"I'll have one if you'll have one with me," I replied.

I saw a smile for the first time, and then he yelled out something in Armenian. Seconds later, Sarah entered the room carrying a trayful of shot glasses with some type of alcoholic beverage in them. She smiled at me but moved past me to serve her father first. After each of us had a glass in our hand, he raised his, and we all followed suit. He said a single word in Armenian, and everyone echoed the word and then drained their glasses. I followed the rest, not wanting to stand out.

"To your health," Jake said. "That is what we said in Armenian before our drink." I nodded my understanding and continued to field questions about myself and my relationship with Sarah.

"Dinner is ready!" came a shout from the kitchen. Everyone stood, but no one moved until Jake made his way through the kitchen door. Once he had exited the living room, we all lined up and followed him out of the house and onto a nice brick patio in the backyard. The view was breathtaking, with an old homemade brick barbecue surrounded by row after row of grapevines, all overflowing with fruit.

Jake took his place at the head of the large picnic table and motioned for me to sit by his side. "Michael, you sit here," he said, pointing to the right side of the long picnic table. Then he said, "Sarah will sit here," pointing to his left, "when she is finished serving."

I took the seat next to him as I'd been instructed. Then food started coming out of the kitchen door, platters and platters of food. One tray of various cut-up fruits and lots of beautiful green grapes; another tray loaded with circular pieces of some type of a flat bread; two huge platters of still sizzling lamb chops with fresh mint sprinkled over them; a bowl of rice, which I would find out later was called bulgur rice, something I'd never heard of or tasted before; a second large bowl filled with cut-up tomatoes, red onions, and olives, all swimming in a spicy oil and vinegar dressing. And the smells were nothing short of decadent. Once the food was all on the large table, the women took their seats, each by their individual family members.

Once seated, everyone looked to Jake and waited. He lowered his head, put his hands together, and offered up a rather lengthy prayer in Armenia. I joined in with everyone else in saying, "Amen!" as the prayer ended.

Food was passed from person to person until everyone had full plates. During the next several minutes, there was no talking, just the sounds of knives and forks meeting plates and an occasional glass as it was placed back on the table. I looked over at Sarah and said, "This may be the best meal I've ever eaten!"

She smiled at me and replied, "Thank Mama. She's the one who's been working for two days preparing this meal."

I looked at Sarah's mother and suddenly realized I hadn't been properly introduced and I didn't know her name. Not knowing what else to do, I simply said, "Thank you, Mama! Your dinner is delicious!"

Sarah chuckled at my response, and I saw the semblance of a smile on Papa Jake's face as he continued to eat his meal.

"You very welcome," Mama replied. "I love cook for all my babies," she continued, her grammar off a little bit, but I could tell she was speaking from her heart.

"Am I one of your babies now?" I asked, and everyone laughed.

She laughed as well and softly said something in Armenian, which caused everyone including Jake to laugh with true gusto. I looked over to Sarah, who was also laughing, and waited for a translation of what had been said.

Sarah said, "Mama said none of her other babies have such soft hands. Maybe you will be her mama's boy!"

I smiled and responded, "If you cook like this every day, I would be honored to be your mama's boy!" Again, everyone laughed loudly.

Once finished with dinner, Sarah's father asked me if I wanted to join him in smoking a cigar. I declined the offer but told him that I certainly didn't mind if he did. He and one of Sarah's nephews pulled out large cigars, bit the ends off of them, and stuck them in their mouths. Each had his own cigar lighting tool, and they breathed in and blew out until the business end of the cigar was burning a bright orange.

Blowing a mouthful of smoke over his head, Jake asked me, "What do you know of Armenia?" Sarah sat there nervously as she and everyone else waited for my response.

"Well, I really don't know that much about your country or your culture," I replied. "I haven't really been around Armenians before coming to Fresno State to go to school. I do know about the genocide that happened in your country in the '40s. We studied it in high school." Pausing for a second, I continued. "I'm so sorry the rest of the world stood by and watched those massacres go on instead of coming to your aide."

Papa Jake interrupted me there. "My wife, my oldest son-in-law, my two oldest daughters, and I lived through that horror before coming to America." He was chewing on the end his cigar, and I could see his jaws flexing as anger rose within him. "I lost my parents and two brothers to those Turkish bastards! My wife lost her whole family. It is only by the grace of God that we escaped with our lives and made it here to America.

"When we got to America, we had nothing but the clothes on our backs. No money, none of us spoke English, and we had no idea where to go for help. Fortunately, we found an Armenian aide service that took us in and fed us until we could find work and start earning some money.

"After four years, we were able to make the trip to California to be with others like us who had fled Armenia. We worked for them, saved our money, and eventually bought property of our own to farm. We raised raisin grapes and were able to make enough to build on to our small farm, little by little. By most people's standards, we are successful farmers. But only a few close friends know what we had to endure to get to this position. We no longer have our country, but we still cling to our culture," he said, looking directly at me. "The thought of my daughter meeting someone other than an Armenian boy was inconceivable to me ten years ago."

He puffed on his cigar a couple of times and continued. "But times are changing in America. No one seems to stay true to their culture anymore. Several of my Armenian neighbor's children have started dating non-Armenians. It vexes us, but there is nothing we can do about it anymore." He paused, puffed on his cigar, and looked up into the vast evening sky.

I decided it was time to speak a bit about myself. "I do know how important your homeland and culture are for those who have come to America from another land," I began. "I am Norwegian, and my parents are naturalized citizens. They came to the States from Canada, and all my grandparents migrated directly from Norway. Culture is very important in my family, especially for the grandmas and grandpas."

"And what about you, Michael, how important is your culture to you?" he asked.

Thinking a second before answering, I replied, "My heritage and culture have made me who I am today. But my grandparents lived in Norway, I didn't. You and Mama lived in Armenia, but Sarah didn't. We were both born here in America! And even though our cultures are embedded in us, we are Americans first now. When Sarah or any of her nieces and nephews marry and have children, those children will most likely identify less with their heritage and more as Americans. With each generation that follows, the old cultures will slowly disappear, and a new culture will take its place."

Papa Jake sat back and absorbed what I had just said, all the while puffing and chewing on his now stub of a cigar. "I like you, Michael," he finally said, looking directly at me. "I hope we get to see more of you. Now you need to get your items stored in the barn before it gets too late. Ollie, Duran, help Michael unload his truck, while Sarah helps her mother clean up."

With those simple instructions, everyone jumped to the tasks they had been given. When we were finished unloading, I followed Ollie and Duran back to the house. Once inside, Papa Jake said, "You should start for home."

"Yes, sir," I replied respectfully. Sarah was walking out of the kitchen, holding her mom's hand.

"Thank you so much for a wonderful dinner tonight," I said, looking at Mama. I saw tears starting to form in her eyes as she looked lovingly at her daughter. "And I promise Sarah will come by more often to visit the two of you."

Papa Jake put his hand out for one last handshake, and I obliged him. Then he put his arms out, and Sarah moved into them. He said something softly to her in Armenian, and I saw his chin quiver as he fought the urge to become emotional. Sarah kissed him on the cheek, grabbed my hand, and led me out the front door.

We walked to the rental truck in silence, got in, and were on our way back to Fresno before either one of us spoke. Breaking the ice, I started. "I think that went as well as we could have expected, don't you?"

"My family loved you, Michael. That went so much better than I could have ever hoped! When we were leaving, Papa said, 'He's not Armenian, but maybe we'll just say he is someday!' I was blown away by his comment," she finished. "Thank you! Thank you! Thank you!" she said, sliding over next to me and laying her head on my shoulder as we made our way home.

Spring turned to summer and summer into fall as Sarah and I fell more and more in love. I'd taken her home to meet my family, and she'd been an instant hit! She and my mom started writing each other consistently, mostly sharing recipes and keeping up on what was going on in our respective lives. We spent every other Sunday out at the farm with Papa Jake and Mama. They made dinner, and sometimes we played cards, while other times, we just sat and visited.

Papa Jake kept up on current events, and he and I weren't always on the same side when it came to politics or world issues, but we always tried to respect the other person's viewpoint when we debated an issue. As he became more comfortable, he laughed more and really became a mentor to me. He had almost no education but an enormous amount of life experiences to share that were more valuable than anything I would ever learn from books.

Sarah's birthday fell on December 21, four days before Christmas. We went to the farm to celebrate with her parents. We'd had a great day, and on the way home, she asked me what I wanted for Christmas. I couldn't think of anything special, and I told her so.

Smiling over at me, she said, "It doesn't matter anyway, because I've already got your present. It's something you've never had before, and you'll never guess what it is."

"Really," I shot back. "If I guess it, will you tell me if I'm right?"

"Sure," she responded. "Guess away!"

"You're pregnant, aren't you?" I said, watching her expression change from confidence to complete surprise at my guess.

She was silent for a second and then asked, "How could you possibly know that!"

CHAPTER 9

"Hi guys!" Jack said as I opened our apartment door. He had a bottle of wine in one hand and a small bouquet of brightly colored flowers in the other. Stepping over the threshold, he was immediately rushed by Sarah. She wrapped her arms around him and hugged him firmly.

"You're in a good mood!" Jack stated, lightly wrapping his arms around her to reciprocate. Sarah stepped away from him and responded with a simple but cheery "Hi, Jack!"

Then it was my turn. I replaced Sarah and gave him a strong hug. "It's really good to see you, buddy!" I said, moving away from him.

"Wow!" he said. "Neither one of you has ever been this nice to me! If you're going to ask to borrow money, I don't have much, but whatever I have is yours!"

We all laughed, and Sarah was the first to speak. "No, we don't want to borrow money! We're just glad to see you! I haven't seen you since the night you introduced me to Michael."

"I haven't seen you either, but I've talked with Michael a couple of times since that night, and he said you just won't go home!"

"No, he didn't!" she said, giving him a playful punch in the arm. "Both of you know he got the birthday present of his life that night!" She curtsied and pointed to herself with her right thumb.

Then she continued. "Let me take those flowers, and you guys go have a seat in the living room." Taking both the wine and the flowers, she turned and headed toward the kitchen. As she was leaving, she said over her shoulder, "Thank you for the flowers, Jack! They're beautiful, and they smell wonderful!"

While we were making our way into the living room, Sarah yelled again, this time from the kitchen, "Jack! Do you want to open the wine, or would you rather have a beer or hard liquor?"

Jack looked at me and said softly, "What are you going to drink?"

"How about we have a couple of beers and save the wine for dinner?" I responded.

"Great!" he said before yelling back to Sarah, "Beer for now, please."

Sitting on opposite facing couches, Jack said, "You look good! How are things going for the two of you?"

I smiled back at him and replied, "She is incredible! And she's right, I will never be able to thank you enough for asking her to come to my birthday party!"

"It all seems kind of weird to me," Jack interjected. "I don't know if it's destiny, God's will, or what, but the odds of you two ending up a couple after spending one weekend together have to be friggin' astronomical!" He shook his head from side to side before continuing. "And that Papa Jake likes your lily-white ass and lets you date his baby girl is even more ridiculous!"

Sarah walked into the living room with two bottles of beer and handed one to each of us. "What were you saying about Papa?" she asked, sitting next to me and wrapping herself around my closest arm.

"I was just telling Michael that he's gone where no man has gone before him! To have dinner with your dad! And he lived to talk about it!"

"Papa is not the bad man you and your friends all make him out to be. Even though Michael is the only man I ever wanted to bring home, your friends and most of the guys in town were so afraid of Papa that none of them had the guts to ask me out on a date." We all laughed but knew she was stating a cold, indisputable fact.

"How's school going?" Jack quizzed.

"Pretty good," I responded. "I have less than a year to go!"

"Then what are you going to do?" he asked.

"Well, I'm actually looking for a job right now, something that's part time but a job that could work into full time once I finish school."

"So you do need extra money!" Jack stated firmly.

"No, no, no, Jack!" Sarah said, breaking into the conversation. "Between my job and what Michael gets from the government each month, we really are doing fine. But once school is over, Michael will need to work because the government funding will stop, and we can't live on my income alone."

"You got any leads, Michael?" Jack quizzed.

"Yeah, a couple. Nothing that relates to a business degree, but one or two that pay pretty good money until I can find something I really want to do," I replied.

Looking over at Sarah, he asked, "What about you, sunshine? What's new in your world besides Michael?"

"There's really nothing new. I think I'm going to get a promotion at work, which should come with a pay raise!" Sarah answered. "Family are all good—life is good," she responded, looking over at me, "and I'm really, really happy!"

Changing the subject completely, Sarah asked, "So are you guys hungry?" We both responded affirmingly, and she finished. "Well, then, let's eat!"

We all got up and went into the kitchen, and Sarah began serving us a wonderful baked halibut dinner. Jack opened and poured the wine, and we took our seats at the small dining room table. Sarah stopped him before he could set a glass in front of her place setting.

"No, no!" she said, waving him away to ensure he didn't set the wineglass in front of her spot. "I'm not drinking tonight," she said casually.

"OK," he responded, a quizzical look on his face. "That leaves more for Michael and me to drink." He removed Sarah's wineglass from the table and sat down, ready to eat.

There was some small talk while we ate, but not too much as we wolfed down our food. Sarah and I cleared the dishes, while Jack pushed his chair away from the table and patted his now full belly.

"I don't know why I didn't know this before," he started. "But, boy, you can cook, Sarah! That was delicious!"

"Thank you, Jack!" she responded cheerfully. "If you're a girl growing up in a traditional Armenian household, you don't have a choice—you learn to cook!" She refilled our wineglasses and sat back down.

"There was one thing I wanted to ask you," I said, looking seriously to Jack. "I'm going to sell the Chevelle, and I know you love that car, so I thought I would give you first shot if you're interested in it."

Jack stared at me, while Sarah's head snapped around, her eyes growing larger. "What!" she shrieked. "You don't want to sell that car! You love that car!"

Paying no attention to her remarks, I returned to Jack. "I'm going to sell it for $3,500, but if you want it, you can have it for $3,000," I stated matter-of-factly.

"Again, I say, so you do need money!" Jack replied. "I'm on Sarah's side. You love that car, and I can't imagine you selling it unless you were strapped for cash with no other options available."

"That's not it at all!" I said sharply. "The Chevelle was fun! I've had it for three years, and now it's time to move on. Sarah and I want to start a family, and we need to buy a station wagon or a minivan or something that is more practical for our needs."

I could see a little panic on Sarah's face as she realized I was about to share our secret with someone else for the first time. "Maybe you and I should talk about this before you do something you'll regret," she said quickly, knowing I would understand the double meaning in her comment.

There was silence for a moment, and then Jack spoke. "I still think you should take some time and really think this over before you make any rash decisions. Besides, you guys will need to get married before you can start a family." Silence again, this time almost an uncomfortable silence.

Standing up, I dug a half-carat diamond ring out of my blue jeans pocket and said, "Jack's right."

Dropping down on one knee in front of Sarah, I asked for her hand in marriage. "I promise to love you forever, and I will be eternally honored and thankful if you would marry me."

Sarah's mouth fell open, and she quickly covered it with one open hand as the tears began to flow from her eyes. Before she could answer, Jack uttered, "Oh my god!" not realizing he'd said it out loud.

Sarah leaped from the chair and into my arms, almost knocking me over, and in a soft voice replied, "Yes! Yes, Michael, I will marry you, if you'll have me."

"There's nothing that I want more in this world than to call you my wife," I responded. Then we were kissing, and tears were running down both of our faces.

"I should get going," Jack said, feeling uncomfortable as he watched our intimate exchange.

"Not yet, Jack," I said, turning my gaze to him. Lifting Sarah back to a standing position and getting up from my knees, we both returned to our chairs. "I haven't talked to Sarah about this yet, but I'm hoping to have a small wedding, just family and a few close friends. So I'm going to need a best man, and I was hoping that could be you."

Both Sarah and Jack stared at me again without saying anything. Finally, his eyes filling with tears of his own, Jack replied, "How could I ever say no to that offer!" Then looking at Sarah, he said, "When are you going to tell your parents?"

Before Sarah could respond, I interjected, "This weekend. We're going to tell them this weekend."

"This is moving so fast," Jack commented. "If you just asked her to marry you, you haven't even had time to discuss a date yet."

"It will be soon," I replied. "In the next three weeks, a month tops!"

I watched Jack's face as he finally put the pieces of the puzzle together. Looking over at Sarah, he half whispered, "So that's why you're not drinking! You're going to have a baby?"

Putting both her hands on her stomach, she simply smiled and affirmingly shook her head in agreement.

"Wow! Congratulations to both of you!" he said, raising from his chair and going over to give Sarah a lengthy but loving hug. "I feel like I'm in the twilight zone tonight—so many unexpected but wonderful revelations!"

"Well," Sarah replied, "I didn't have a clue that Michael was going to ask me to marry him tonight either!" Both looked in my direction and smiled.

Smiling back at them, I responded, "This is turning out to be a really good night!"

Getting out of his chair, I walked over to the two and gave them a group hug. A few pats on the back, and then we were all standing and naturally smiling at one another.

"It's getting late, and I should get going," Jack stated flatly. "Besides, I need some alone time to try and fully digest all this!"

Sarah and I walked Jack to the front door, where everyone received one last hug and said our good nights. Once we were alone, Sarah rested her head on my chest, and we just stood there for a long moment, neither speaking.

Raising her head off my chest, Sarah looked me in the eyes and whispered, "I'm so happy, sweetheart!" Then placing her head back on my chest, she said, "Thank you for asking me to marry you! We are going to have a wonderful life together."

My response was a simple "Yes, we will! Let's go to bed, baby."

Ten minutes later, we were in each other's arms and were making love to one another. Sarah once again laid her head on my sweaty chest after we had finished, both lost in the euphoric aftermath of our lovemaking. I could feel tears running down my chest as Sarah sniffed, trying to stifle her soft cry. I ran my fingers through her hair as she lay there, saying nothing.

Finally, she spoke softly. "I don't think I have ever been happier than I am at this moment." She squeezed his torso with the arm she had around my waist.

"Me too, baby," I responded. "Me too!"

The week went by quickly, and both Sarah and I were very nervous about seeing her parents and giving them the news. We'd spent all week discussing what exactly we were going to tell them. Would we just talk about the marriage proposal? We didn't know how Papa Jake would react to having the first non-Armenian in the family tree. Would our marriage announcement be further tainted by telling them that Sarah was pregnant? Was delivering both revelations too much to dump on them all at once?

We still hadn't decided on an action plan as I turned off the highway onto the gravel road entrance to the farm. I looked at Sarah, and she returned my glance with the panicked look of a trapped animal, knowing there was no escaping its inevitable end. I smiled and tried to reassure her. "Stop worrying, everything is going to work out perfectly."

Once the car was stopped and the dust had cleared, we both stepped out and began walking to the house. Mama walked out the door as we were approaching the front porch. She was wiping her hands off on a clean white apron as she quickly advanced in our direction. Reaching Sarah about halfway, they hugged, kissed each other on the cheek, and immediately started speaking in Armenian. I continued my journey toward them, taking my time, while they greeted each other.

Once I was next to Sarah, Mama released her grip on her daughter and stepped over, hugging me. I just looked back to Sarah, who was as shocked as I was at the kind gesture. Letting me go, Mama stepped back and said, "It's so nice to see you again, Michael. Thank you for bringing my baby home more often, just like you said you would."

"You're welcome," I responded, a smile on my face. "It's my pleasure, but I have to confess, I have an ulterior motive here! You cook like no one I've ever known, and we would come here every day if Sarah would let us just to eat another one of your wonderful meals!"

She smiled shyly and said, "Thank you, Michael. Let's go inside, I have a couple of things still on the stove, and I don't want them to burn." Following her, we walked up the front steps and entered the farmhouse.

Sarah and Mama went straight into the kitchen, leaving me to face Papa Jake by myself. He was sitting in his recliner chair but rose to his feet as I approached him. "Michael!" he bellowed loudly. "It's good to see you again. Would you like to have a drink?"

"No, thank you," I replied. "I think I'll wait a bit before doing any drinking." We were shaking hands as I was talking. "It's good to see you as well, Mr. Seremban."

"Let's go out to the backyard patio so I can smoke a cigar!" he said, already moving toward the kitchen door. I followed him, not bothering to reply. As we passed through the kitchen, I winked at Sarah, and she quickly smiled in response, her dimples in full bloom.

"Good luck!" she mouthed silently as we walked past her. Then we were outside and headed down the brick walkway to the patio. There was a soft, cool breeze, and a few leaves were falling from the trees, signifying the season change that was about to transpire. The few clouds in the sky were moving quickly as we both took a seat in matching wooden lawn chairs on the brick patio.

Papa Jake pulled a cigar from his jacket pocket and carefully unwrapped it. Wadding up the now useless cellophane, he stuffed it back in his pocket. He ran the length of the cigar under his nose, inhaling the smell of tobacco before moving on to the next step. Biting off one end and then licking both ends, he placed it in his mouth and pulled out his cigar lighter. Once lit, he puffed on it several times, ensuring it was properly burning. He sat there puffing contentedly, his entire head enveloped in a thick cloud of gray smoke.

"I don't have many vices," Papa said through the dense haze he had created. "But I allow myself to smoke one good cigar every day! I have enjoyed this guilty pleasure for more than forty years now!" Then he began puffing again, only this time inhaling the smoke before blowing it out through his mouth. "So! What's new with you, Michael? How is school going?" Another quick puff, and he continued. "How is Sarah? The two of you seem happy with each other."

Thank you, God, I thought to myself. Papa Jake had given me the perfect lead into what I wanted to discuss with him. "School's fine. It won't be much longer, and I'll graduate with a degree in business. Then I'll just be another working stiff, paying taxes and providing for a family like millions of other Americans," I responded.

"I am happy to see you finishing your school. You should be very proud!" He took another long draw on his cigar before continuing. "But your education will not be the deciding factor for successes or failures in your life. It will be your desire to succeed that will define you. I came to this country with nothing and almost no education, yet we have been able to scratch out a decent living because we refused to fail, and we worked very hard! With all my heart, I believe the American dream is there for the taking for anybody who is willing to work for it!"

I opened my mouth to respond when Mama came out of the kitchen door, almost singing, "Dinner's ready!"

"Are we going to eat outside or in the house?" Papa yelled back to her.

"In the house," she replied, quickly turning and disappearing through the open kitchen door.

Snuffing out the embers on the end of his cigar on the brick patio floor, he commented, "I'll save the rest of this for after dinner." He set the cigar down, now half its original size, on the table next to his chair, got up, and started toward the still open kitchen door. I followed him inside, completely intoxicated by the magnificent aromas emanating from within the house.

We enjoyed another spectacular meal! Mama asked if we wanted some coffee after dinner; Papa and I accepted, while Sarah declined the invitation. After some small talk while we finished our coffee, Papa Jake said, "Well, Michael, let's go back out on the patio so I can finish that cigar." Mama smiled as he rose from his chair, ready to make an exit.

"Jake, can you sit down for a minute? There is something I would like to speak to you and Mama about."

He stayed standing and then looked first at Sarah and then to Mama. Both parents' faces immediately were overtaken by serious expressions. Slowly sitting back in his chair, Papa said, "What do you want to tell me?" Again, he looked over at Sarah, who could not hold his gaze and looked away from his piercing eyes.

"Jake, there is no other way to say this but to say it," I began. "I know not being born Armenian is a detriment to Sarah and me having a serious relationship in your eyes. Believe me, I get it that we would be stepping across cultural boundaries. I also know that we have only dated for a very short time." Summoning all the courage I could muster, I continued. "But I have fallen in love with your daughter, and I want to ask your permission to marry her."

Mama immediately placed her face in her hands and began to cry. I didn't know if it was out of joy or complete disdain for what she'd just heard. Papa just sat there, his jaws clenching and releasing, clenching and releasing, as he stared at me. Finally, looking over to Sarah, he asked, "And how do you feel about this?"

"I love him, Papa," she responded. "You've always known I wouldn't be part of an arranged marriage. For your sake, I always hoped I would meet a nice Armenian man and, eventually, we would marry. But that didn't happen. Instead, I met Michael, and we unexpectedly fell in love."

She paused, grabbed one of her mother's hands, and held it in her own. "Mama, the heart wants what the heart wants! We hope the two of you will give us your blessing, but if not, we are still getting married. Michael is my life now, and as much as I love you both, I choose to be his wife with or without your blessing! I know that may sound harsh, but I believe with all my heart that Michael is the person God meant for me to find!"

Papa had tears running down his face, and he haphazardly dabbed at them with his handkerchief but said nothing. Mama stared at her daughter as if she were looking at a stranger, a look of sorrow embedded on her face.

"Michael!" Papa half yelled. "Sarah is the baby of our family, and she holds a special place in both of our hearts. Are you sure you want to spend the rest of your life with her? We don't believe in divorce, and it is important to me that you realize this is a lifelong commitment."

"I understand, sir," I responded. "I will live to the vows we take together—for better or worse, in sickness and health, through the good times as well as the bad, until death do us part!"

Papa searched my face for any signs of apprehension or doubt before speaking again. "I would rather have you in our lives, loving our daughter, than having Sarah despise us for the remainder of our years. I don't think we could live without seeing her. A piece of our hearts would be ripped out."

It wasn't the most endearing response I'd ever heard, but I grasped his meaning and didn't take offense to the way it was delivered.

"Michael," Papa continued, "I've gotten to know you a little bit, and I think you are a good man with a good heart. If Sarah loves you, then the choice is out of our hands anyway. She is strong willed, but you will find that out for yourself in the future. Besides, she said she is going to marry you with or without my blessing! She must be pretty confident that you are the right one for her to express that so strongly to us."

Finally smiling slightly, Papa continued. "The heart wants what the heart wants! And in our hearts, Mama and I just want her to be happy!" Pausing for a moment to again stare into my eyes, Papa finished. "You have my blessing, and we look forward to you becoming a part of our family."

Sarah jumped to her feet, ran over, and gave her father a strong embrace. "Thank you, Papa! You have no idea how happy that makes both of us!"

Meanwhile, Mama was up and around the other side of the table. Grasping my head with both hands, she pulled me to her breasts and hugged me tightly. Leaning over to kiss me on the head, she said, "Please be good to her and make her happy, Michael." Then she released me and stepped back to receive a hug from Sarah, who had been waiting patiently for her turn.

A few minutes later, I followed Papa back out to the patio, where he lit his cigar again. We didn't talk much as the women finished cleaning up from dinner. It was dusk when Mama and Sarah came walking out the kitchen door. Mama had a bottle and four small glasses in her hands. She sat the glasses on the table and filled each with the wine she carried. Handing a glass to each of us, she raised her glass and spoke in Armenian. When she had finished speaking, everyone touched glasses, and we drank the contents.

Sarah told me later that Mama had toasted our marriage and wished for many grandchildren soon. We both smiled, knowing her wish would come true much sooner than she expected.

We were both pleased with how the night had turned out. It felt like a weight had been lifted off us, and now we could move forward with making plans for the wedding.

"When do we tell them about the baby?" Sarah asked once we were on the way home.

"Not right now," I replied. "They have enough to handle with the wedding and the new guy in the family. I think we should wait until just before or just after we are married." Sarah shook her head affirmingly, saying nothing in response.

On our normal Sunday night phone call, I told my parents we were getting married. They seemed genuinely happy for us and wanted to know how they could help.

The next three weeks were crazy. Planning for the wedding, keeping up on schoolwork, looking for a job, and with Sarah's work and pregnancy, we were both physically exhausted and frazzled by our wedding day. But we, somehow, got through it all.

The night before the wedding, Sarah went home to stay with her family. My parents and little brother had made the trip to Fresno and had been staying with us in our apartment for the last two days. The morning of the big day, Dad helped me tie my bow tie. Grabbing my tuxedo coat, we checked to make sure we hadn't forgotten anything, and then we were on our way to the farm.

Once there, I was very impressed with how beautiful everything was decorated. I suspected that Mama and her other two daughters had been hard at work for a couple of days to make this a fairy-tale day for Sarah.

Mama met us in the driveway and was quickly smiling and hugging my family as if they were her own. She looked beautiful in a light blue dress that showed off her figure to its best advantages. It was easy to discern where Sarah got her looks from after seeing Mama all dressed up!

Once the introductions were over, we all made our way down the path that led to the patio behind the house. Turning the corner and clearing the house, even I was taken aback by the beautiful transformation that had occurred to their backyard and patio. It was spectacular! There were about thirty white folding chairs set up in rows, all facing the patio, where the ceremony would take place. There were several people already seated as we approached. Most stood and offered their congratulations to me as we passed.

Jack was standing toward the front, speaking to one of our school friends and his parents when he saw me. He quickly excused himself and ran over to hug me and give me a strong pat on the back. Looking around, to ensure none of Sarah's family were within earshot, he said softly, "You can still back out! But this is your last chance!"

"Shut up and come meet my family!" I said disgustedly. We strolled over to where my family was standing, and I introduced everyone.

"We've heard so much about you, Jack," my mom said after shaking his hand.

"Well, not knowing if that is good or bad, I just want you to know that I have some stories about Michael as well," Jack shot back. "Mostly good, but a few that may be a little sketchy."

"Oh my!" my mother responded. "I can't wait to hear them all when we have time!" Everyone snickered and again began aimlessly talking with one another.

The minister walked up to me, carrying a large Bible. "I think we are about ready to start, Michael. If you and your best man want to take your places, we will start the music."

The music, it turned out, was from a very beautiful white Yamaha piano. It belonged to Sarah's sister, and she'd had it picked up at her home in Griffith Park and transported to the farm some two hundred miles away by professional movers. She had also agreed to play all the music for the ceremony.

Once Jack and I were in our practiced spots, I gave Sarah's sister a soft nod, and the music began. The people that weren't already seated stopped milling around and quickly found seats for themselves.

Once everyone else was seated, the ushers walked my mother and father to the front row and waited for them to be seated next to my brother before turning and starting their walk to the rear again. Next was Sarah's sister and both of her brothers-in-law, who were all seated in the front row on the opposite side from my parents. Last, Mama was escorted to the front and was seated one chair in, leaving room for Papa Jake once he had delivered his daughter to the altar and handed her off to me.

As soon as Mama was seated, the music changed to the bridal procession, and Sarah and Papa appeared from the rear, stopping when they reached the center aisle. Sarah looked breathtaking! She was holding a bouquet of white roses in one hand, while her other arm was wrapped around Papa's left arm. As they slowly started forward, they were a contrast in expressions. Sarah had the biggest smile on her face, while Papa dabbed tears away from his eyes and bright red nose. He had confessed to me prior to the ceremony that he'd cried when giving away both of his other daughters to another man in marriage. And it appeared this time would be no exception to the tradition.

When they stopped, I walked to them, and he gave me Sarah's arm and then turned back and sat next to Mama. The two of us turned and proceeded toward the minister. Thirty-five minutes and two solos later, we heard the words we were there to hear and had been waiting for.

"I now pronounce you man and wife! Michael, you may kiss your bride!" Then the pastor announced us as a couple. Turning to the onlookers, he said, "Ladies and gentlemen, it is my pleasure to introduce to you Sarah and Michael Larsen!"

The music began again with Sarah's sister loudly playing the "Wedding March" as we turned and started to make our way back down the center aisle. Glancing first at Sarah's family and then at my own, I could see there were no dry eyes anywhere. Even my father was misting up a bit. People were clapping for us, shouting out congratulation, and throwing rose petals all around us as we exited the pathway.

The backyard and patio were transformed from a church-like setting into a reception area in short order by Sarah's family members. There were drinks, food, and a whole roasted pig brought in to feed the attendees. Sarah and I danced the first dance together, and then she asked her father to join her for the second dance. Papa agreed, and as they danced around the patio, you could see pure joy in his face as he danced with his beautiful daughter. Mama's eyes filled with tears again as she pulled her hands up to her chest in a prayerlike movement and watched them slowly move around the makeshift dance floor.

Sometime later in the evening, Papa caught up with me when I was standing by myself. "I couldn't be happier for Sarah!" he said, slurring his words a bit. It was obvious that he had drunk more than his normal share of alcohol. "If you treat her with respect, I will grow to love you like a son! Make her happy, and you will make me happy!" With that, he pulled me close and gave me a strong hug.

"I will, Papa," I simply replied. He slapped me on the arm, turned, and went back to the patio to mingle with the other guests.

Either late in the night or early in the morning, I'm not sure what the exact time was, Sarah and I left the gathering and went to the hotel room we had rented for this special night. The party was still in full swing, with twenty or so guests, including Jack, still going strong as we left.

After the wedding was over and all our guests were gone, Sarah and I settled back into our apartment, ready to begin our new lives together as man and wife.

With all the excitement around ourselves and the wedding, I had pretty much zoned out on national and international news. We'd stopped watching the nightly news, because we were going to bed earlier, trying to stay fresh for the chores we needed to accomplish before the wedding. Now, having a little time to catch up, I wondered how I missed all the huge stories of the day. I'd caught small portions of many of them but hadn't really read about the actual accounts as they'd happened on any of the lead stories.

I'd heard about the eruption of Mount St. Helens, but after studying it closer, I'd had no idea how extensive the damage was or the huge area that was affected by its blast.

The United States' attempt to rescue the American hostages in Tehran, Iran, had failed miserably, causing an outcry against the United States by several Arabic countries.

John Lennon, one of the Beatles, was assassinated outside his home in New York. As well, John Hinckley Jr. attempted to assassinate Pres. Ronald Reagan and came very close to accomplishing his goal. And given that all bad things happen in threes, Mehmet Ali Agca attempted to assassinate Pope John Paul unsuccessfully.

It seemed to me as though the world was coming apart at the seams. But we had our own lives to concentrate on now that we were bringing a child into this screwed-up world!

Jack didn't buy the Chevelle, but I did sell it for $3,500 to a veteran who had just been discharged from the service. He was as happy to get it as I was to sell it! I found a part-time job working at Master Tire Service, which provided some extra money for us to prepare for our baby.

In less than thirty days after we were married, we told both sets of parents that Sarah was pregnant. She started to show shortly thereafter. Everyone seemed excited by the prospect of a new baby, and no one was bold enough to question the quick timing between our marriage and Sarah's pregnancy.

I graduated in June with my business degree and was happy to have college over with. I didn't attend the graduation ceremony because Sarah had become big and was very uncomfortable if she sat in one place too long. Knowing the ceremony would take a minimum of four hours, I opted to have my diploma mailed to our apartment.

Sarah was so uncomfortable that she had to take a leave of absence from her work. For the last four weeks of her pregnancy, she mostly lay flat on her back in bed. Knowing I needed to step up and make more money, I asked my boss if I could have more hours or even possibly work full time. He accommodated me, and a week later, I was working Tuesday through Saturday every week. I worked hard, trying to convey my appreciation for the opportunity I'd been given. Maybe a little too hard.

Master Tire Service was a union shop, and I had to join the local warehousemen's union to work there. Every day I tried to change one more tires than I had the day before. In less than two weeks, I'd become so proficient at my new craft that none of the other workers could keep up with me.

In my third week of employment, several of my coworkers were waiting for me in the shower room, where we changed from our uniforms into street clothes. I was caught a little off guard as the union steward began to speak.

"I'm not sure what's in your head, son," he began. "But you need to slow down some." His eyes narrowed as he continued. "You are in a union shop now, and we look after each other here. If you keep changing tires at the rate you are now, you're going to make the rest of us look bad. So slow down a little, because if management sees some of us standing around with nothing to do, they start thinking about layoffs. And to be clear, you have the least seniority, so you would be the first to go. So if you're trying to work yourself out of a job, just keep doing what you're doing! Otherwise, slow the hell down and support the rest of your union brothers!"

With that, they all left the room and went back out onto the service floor. I sat there for a minute, trying to digest what had just been said. The more I thought about it, the angrier I became. We were making damn good money, and they wanted to ensure their jobs by slowing down our service? That wasn't fair to our customers, and it sure wasn't fair to our employer! I wasn't sure what I could do about it after only being with the company for three weeks, but I knew right from wrong, and this union thinking was wrong as far as I was concerned!

I grabbed my shirt and walked out into the parking lot, stepped into our new minivan, and left the property. I made up my mind that day that labor unions had served their purpose in the past, but now they were simply bloated bureaucracies trying to get as many members as possible to pay more in dues monthly. The union's purpose wasn't to help the working man anymore. Anyway, not a union that encouraged slow work so they could add more workers. The more workers, the more dues flowed into the union coffers. It was as simple as that.

Two more weeks had gone by when Greg, our union steward, informed all of us about a mandatory union meeting that Thursday night. He also let me know that mandatory meant just that. "If you don't show up, Michael, fifteen dollars will be added to your weekly dues. I hope you will attend so Master Tire can continue to represent 100 percent compliance in union meeting attendance," he stated, patting me on the shoulder like I was his new puppy. "Looking forward to seeing you there." Then he turned and went back to his workstation.

There were more people in the union hall than I had expected to see at my first meeting. It looked like there were roughly fifty or so men of various ages milling around the halls and conversing with one another. Finally, our union representative, a man by the name of Mel Tanos, banged his gavel on a podium at the front of the room and asked everyone to take a seat.

Once everyone was seated, he began to talk about union business—everything from new benefits that were being offered to us next year to recognizing a couple of new union stewards who were being promoted at various companies. Everything that came out of his mouth was met with applause by the workers in the audience. After about an hour, Mr. Tanos said, "Now I want to talk a little bit about the upcoming election for county sheriff. As you all know, we usually support the Democratic nominee for this position, and this year is no exception. We are officially backing Jerry Kramer, the Democratic nominee for county sheriff. Our union has pledged $10,000 to his campaign, and he has our official endorsement."

Pausing for a moment, he slowly looked over the room before continuing. "And we are asking each one of our members in Union 501 to donate ten dollars toward his campaign as well to show your support for both him and your union. We can take it out of your next paycheck just likes dues, or you can donate cash to our treasurer before you leave tonight."

"Do we have to donate ten dollars?" I yelled out, standing up to be recognized. The room fell silent, and every head turned to look at me.

"No, we can't make you donate the ten dollars, but it would show your support for the union that takes care of you," he stated matter-of-factly.

I could feel my blood starting to boil before I responded, "Good! Then I won't be giving you or the union ten dollars to support this man."

His face started to turn a crimson red as he asked, "Do you mind telling me why?"

Now I was so worked up that I couldn't contain myself. "No! No, I don't mind telling you at all!" I started. "I went to war, fought in a foreign country, and killed people to defend the freedoms democracy affords us here in the United States. One of those freedoms is the right to support or vote for any person I choose to! I don't like your candidate, and I'm not going to vote for him. So I guess it goes without saying, I'm not going to give money to help that fat bastard win the sheriff's job!"

There were several audible gasps throughout the room as the union rep slammed his gavel down on the podium. "You're out of order!" he shouted, pointing at me with his gavel. "We don't allow swearing in a union meeting, and I'm fining you twenty dollars for disrespecting our process and for using profanity in an open meeting!"

"Fine!" I yelled back. "As long as my twenty dollars doesn't go to support your candidate, I'm happy to pay it!"

Now he was almost out-of-control angry. "What's your name, sir?" he asked contentiously.

"It's on the sign-in sheet by the door if you want it," I replied sarcastically.

"Do you want to go for a fifty-dollar fine, wise ass?"

"No. I think I'll just go home," I responded, turning and walking out the main door. I could feel eyes burning through the back of my head as I exited the hall, but I didn't give a damn because I'd spoken up and said my piece to Mr. Tanos.

Two days later, Mel Tanos paid a visit to Master Tire Service. He recognized me but walked right past me without saying a word. Stopping by Greg, the union steward's desk, he began to speak in a subdued quiet voice. They turned their heads to look at me several times during their conversation. Each time I caught them looking at me, I made sure to have a big smile on my face—my way of sending a "screw you" back to them without saying the words. Then Mr. Tanos went into the office to speak with Bruce Dibbert, the general manager and second-in-command behind Mr. Lovering, the owner. A few minutes later, he walked out the front door and was gone.

I didn't know what he'd said to our union steward, but I had a pretty good idea after an hour or so. My fellow workers almost immediately stopped talking to me directly. When my lunchtime came, everyone exited the break room as soon as I entered it, leaving me there by myself. As I sat and ate my lunch, Mr. Dibbert walked in and sat down across from me.

"It appears you pissed off your union representative at last night's meeting. He asked me to keep a close eye on you because he thinks you are going to be a troublemaker." He paused, looking into my eyes, and said, "Want to tell me your side of the story?"

"Yes, sir, I do," I responded. I then went over last night's meeting in detail. I even used the same profanity I'd blurted out at the meeting. Once I told Mr. Dibbert that I called the union's endorsed candidate a fat bastard, Mr. Dibbert laughed out loud.

"Well, you've got guts, kid!" he said once he'd finished laughing. Looking seriously at me, he started again. "I don't care much for the unions myself, but Mr. Lovering doesn't want to try and break with the union because he doesn't want picketers outside our store trying to run off business if we try to break away. But I guarantee you Mel has instructed Greg to give you every dirty job and to ride you hard for any mistakes made." He softly smiled. "I'm aware of the silly little games these guys play, so don't worry. You have a job here for as long as you want because the union doesn't control our staffing—I do!"

"Thank you, sir," I responded, a sense of relief washing over me.

He smiled, shook my hand, and said as he was rising from the table, "Keep up the good work, Michael!" And then he was gone.

Mr. Dibbert had been correct in his assessment of the situation. Greg gave me every difficult job ticket that came through. I completed all of them, but he always griped about how slow or shoddy my work quality had become. In fact, he wrote me up for taking too long on a job that no one else wanted to touch. I was irritated by the write-up but signed it and returned it to him as instructed.

"Michael, you have an urgent phone call. Can you come into the office, please?" said one of our secretaries. I dropped what I was doing and quickly followed her back into the office. Pushing the flashing lit button on the telephones base, she handed me the receiver.

Taking the phone from her, I simply said, "Hello."

Sarah's panicked voice came back at me. "Michael, my water broke, and I'm starting to have contractions. I need you to come home and take me to the hospital. Our baby is coming!"

"I'll be right there," I replied, hanging up the phone. Running into the shower room, I changed my clothes as fast as I could and started toward my car.

"Hey! Where do you think you're going?" came a voice from behind me. It was Greg, and he looked pissed.

Stopping and turning to address him, I said, "My wife is having our baby, and I need to get her to the hospital!"

"Don't you have family or a friend who could do that? We're already short one person with Jim being out sick today, and we have a ton of work scheduled for this afternoon. Jason and I can't get all this work done by ourselves unless we work overtime, and you know management hates to pay overtime!"

"What?" I responded, feeling the heat rising within me at his stupid suggestion.

But before I could answer, Mr. Dibbert, who had just walked out of the office, said, "I'll authorize the overtime, Greg. You two just take care of everyone on this afternoon's schedule!" Then turning to me, he continued. "You better get going, Michael. Mothers having babies aren't very patient! You are in for a long night, but it will be worth it! Now go!" he said, waving me toward my car.

I ran across the parking lot and was in the van and gone in a matter of seconds. Sarah was waiting at the front door of our apartment with a small suitcase she'd packed for this very occasion weeks ago. Twenty minutes later, we were in the hospital and she was being transported in a wheelchair to a labor room. Her contraction wasn't that strong yet, and there were still several minutes between each of them. She handed me a piece of paper with a dozen names and phone numbers on it.

"Go out into the lobby and call the first four names on the list now. The other eight can be called after the baby is born!" Her face cringed in pain as she felt a new contraction beginning.

"Are you going to be OK while I make these calls?" I asked sincerely.

She chuckled in response. "I think the two doctors and four nurses right outside my door can probably handle any problems that come up until you get back."

I kissed her on the forehead, told her I loved her, and went to find a pay phone.

The phone numbers were to her parents, my parents, and both of her sisters. I was able to speak with all of them on the first call. Papa and Mama were going to come to the hospital in a couple of hours. The sister who lived in Fresno would be at the hospital as soon as her husband got home from work. The sister who lived in Griffith Park said she would be here sometime early in the morning, probably around 5:00 a.m. My mom and dad, though excited, were not able to come to Fresno immediately. But they wanted me to call with updates, regardless the time, until the baby was born.

As the afternoon changed to evening and evening morphed into night, Sarah's contractions increased in intensity and duration. Her sister and Mama were in the room with us, while Papa remained in the lobby. Finally, Mama said, "Why don't you go out and keep Papa company? Maybe the two of you can go to the cafeteria and get something to eat."

"What about you?" I responded. "Can I bring the two of you something to eat?"

Looking first at her daughter and then back to me, she said, "No, we're not hungry right now. We'll stay here with Sarah. Go on! She's in good hands!"

I walked over to Sarah, gave her another kiss on the forehead, smiled at my two helpers, and left the room in search of Papa.

Papa and I found the cafeteria, and both of us had their meatloaf dinner special. The food was much better than I had anticipated it would be. There was some small talk, and then Papa opened up.

"You know, Michael, it seems like it was just yesterday when Mama and I were here at this very same hospital, waiting for Sarah to be born. And now my baby is having babies!" He had tears in his eyes as he stared up at the ceiling. "I didn't think I would live to see any more babies born into our family, but I'm so glad God has granted me this special gift."

I smiled back at him, knowing his confession needed no response.

It had been eighteen hours since we'd entered the hospital, and the delivery nurse relayed that it was time to call Sarah's doctor and have him come to the hospital. Sarah's second sister had arrived, and the room seemed pretty cramped with the four of us plus nurses in there. Everyone was giving Sarah advice, talking over each other, and arguing with the delivery nurses about proper procedure.

After one of her hardest contractions yet, Sarah laid her head back on her pillow and, with her eyes closed, said, "I love you all, but right now, I just want Michael with me. Can the rest of you please wait outside with Papa?"

Mama started to say something in protest, and Sarah's eyes shot open, glaring at her mother, stopping her in midsentence. Instead, she said, "We'll be right outside if you need us, sweetheart." She motioned to her other two daughters, and they all left the room.

Once the doctor arrived, it seemed as though everything began moving at hyperspeed. Sarah was ready, the doctor was ready, and I was ready as the doctor said for the first time, "OK, Sarah, when the contraction comes this time, I want you to push!"

As the contraction hit her, she sat up and pushed with all her might. She was squeezing my hand so tightly that it was hurting me.

"Push, push, push, Sarah," the doctor repeated. "Keep pushing! Good girl, here we go! One more push!"

And then we were both looking at this wonderful new creation as our son was born! They cleared his nose and mouth with a suction syringe and then gave him a sharp pat on the bottom, causing him to let out his first cry. He sounded beautiful! One of the nurses quickly cleaned him up, wrapped him in a blanket, and put him into Sarah's waiting arms. Both of us had tears running down our faces as we stared at the miracle we'd created together. I was so filled with love in that moment that I audibly cried for a few seconds. I kissed Sarah on the lips and told her how much I loved her and how proud I was of her for being so strong through it all.

After spending a little time alone with our new son, I asked, "Are you ready to let your family see the baby?"

She smiled and shook her head affirmingly. I left her side and went out to the lobby to find them. Once they saw me coming, everyone was on their feet and rushing toward me.

"Well," I began, a huge smile on my face, "we have a healthy new son!" Everyone started jumping around, grabbing and hugging each other, and openly praising God for our new family member.

"Would you like to meet him?" I asked.

"Of course!" they all replied, following me back to Sarah's room.

Once inside the delivery room, everyone became quiet as we all approached Sarah and the baby. "He's beautiful!" Mama whispered, bending down to kiss both her daughter and her new grandson on their respective heads. One at a time, everyone congratulated Sarah and fawned over the newest member of the family.

"Have you guys picked out a name yet?" one of Sarah's sisters asked.

"We have," I said, looking at Sarah.

"His name will be Jacob Shane Larsen," Sarah said with authority.

Papa almost crumbled when he heard the name. He began to weep, and Mama went over to hold him as he cried in earnest at the honor of having a grandson named after him.

All the girls, including Sarah, immediately became emotional as well and were crying right along with Papa as his wife continued to hold his now sobbing body. Once he regained some semblance of control over his emotions, Papa stood up and, pulling his handkerchief out, blew his nose and wiped his face.

Walking slowly over to me, he wrapped his arms around me and gave me a big bear hug. Stepping back, he said, "It is an honor to share my name with your son. This is the best gift I have ever received. Thank you both for thinking of me when you named him Jacob!"

Once everyone had given us their best wishes and exited the room, I sat next to Sarah, both of us simply staring at the new little man in our lives. Sarah was dozing in and out of sleep as the nurse came and took Jacob to his nursery bed. I left and went back to our apartment, giving my brave, wonderful wife some time to finally get some sleep.

Jacob was a great baby! He only woke up one time a night, and it was pretty much the same time every night. He only cried when he was hungry, wet, or poopy. The rest of the time, he was either asleep or sucking on one of his tiny hands.

Sarah quickly developed a daily routine with him, and we were never happier! I couldn't wait to come home from work so I could hold him before he went to bed for the night. Just knowing what was waiting for me at home put me in a better mood while I was at work.

After he was three weeks old, my parents came up to spend the weekend and get acquainted with their new grandson! The second Jacob woke up, my mom had him in her arms. She changed him if necessary and walked around the apartment, singing lullabies to him. Sarah almost had to pry him away from my mom to feed him. When Mom and Dad left to go home, my mom cried and begged Sarah to take as many pictures as possible so she could share them on the next visit.

Thanksgiving was just around the corner when Mr. Dibbert asked me to take his pickup and go to a meat-packing company to pick up twenty-seven turkeys. I took his keys and did as I was asked. Pulling up to the front of the building, there were approximately thirty people picketing in front of the location. From the signs, it appeared to be a wage dispute between the company and its employees.

Getting out of my truck, I started for the front door. I excused myself as I made my way past two picketers in front of me. Going into the office, I announced who I was and what I was there for. They had all the turkeys boxed and ready for me to load. Signing a bill and taking one copy, I picked up two boxes and started back to my pickup.

When I got back to the picket line, everyone had stopped walking and were standing bunched up in front of my pickup. As I approached the truck, they stood firm, not allowing me access to the pickup.

"Isn't Master Tire a union company?" a large man directly in front of me asked.

"Yes, it is," I replied, still holding the boxes of turkeys.

"So you are a union member?" he asked, crossing his arms.

I nodded my head in agreement.

"Well, this is a union strike!" he continued. "What the hell are you doing crossing our picket line?"

"My boss just told me to come over here and pick up these turkeys," I responded. "I'm just doing what I was instructed to do."

The big man slapped the boxes, and they flew out of my hands, breaking open and scattering six turkeys across the sidewalk. "I don't think you get it!" he spat at me. "You're not going to take those turkeys anywhere!"

Rage instantly overcame common sense. I hit him in the mouth with everything I had and watched as his eyes rolled back in his head before he fell backward like a sheet blowing in the wind. The others said nothing but, rather, looked at their coworker and then at me and then back to him lying on the lawn unconscious.

"If any of the rest of you want to try to stop me from loading these turkeys, now would be the time to speak up!" With both fists clenched, I took a long, hard look at everyone in the crowd. "If not, I would suggest you get the hell out of my way and let me finish my business!"

I bent down putting the six turkeys back in their boxes. Lifting them, I started toward my pickup again. No one said anything this time; they simply moved out of the way, creating a path for me to the truck. Four more trips and I was done. I stepped over the man who was still lying unconscious on the ground and got into the pickup. Starting it, I headed back to Master Tire with a pickup bed full of turkeys.

I had no sooner arrived and backed up to the office door than Mel Tanos came screeching into the driveway and slid to a stop in front of my pickup. Jumping out of his car, leaving the driver's door open, he rushed past me and stopped directly in front of Mr. Dibbert.

Pointing back at me, he said, "I want this piece of shit fired immediately! He crossed a union picket line today and struck a union brother in the process. I am blackballing him from ever working in any union facility in this town again!"

Mr. Dibbert made no response.

"Did you hear me?" Mr. Tanos repeated. "He's no longer in the union, so fire his ass!"

"Well, Mel," Mr. Dibbert said calmly, "we've been looking at this young man for a sales position, which I'm sure you are aware is not unionized. We weren't quite ready to make him the offer just yet, but if he is no longer in the union, it looks like we will be forced to move him to sales now rather than later."

My head snapped to Mr. Dibbert in stark disbelief. I didn't know anything about sales! We hadn't had any discussions about me joining the Master Tire sales force.

Mel Tanos was livid! Before he even spoke, he was shaking his finger in Mr. Dibbert's face. "You won't get away with this, Bruce! I'm going to talk to Lovering directly and get this resolved!"

"Well, just a second," Mr. Dibbert responded. "Mike's here in his office today. Do you want to talk to him out here, or would you prefer to meet in his office?"

Mr. Tanos was so angry he was physically shaking! He clenched his fist and stood there red as a beet before speaking. "Fuck you, Bruce! Fuck you!" He turned, stormed out the door, and jumped into his car, laying rubber across the parking lot as he left.

After unloading the turkeys, Mr. Dibbert called me into his office. "Michael! Michael! Michael!" he began. "I would have given a thousand dollars to see that fiasco at the meat-packing plant today!"

He had a big smile on his face as he continued. "So let's get down to some business! Here is what I had in mind for you."

He then outlined that he wanted to start a wholesale route to sell tires to smaller dealers and truck stops. I would have a new two-ton truck with a large load capacity, and I would make my own route based on the business I acquired. He didn't want the wholesale business to compete with his end user commercial business, so he wanted my sales to be outside the Fresno area. My territory would be approximately a hundred-mile radius from our location.

He went on to explain that because this was a startup position, he would place me on a monthly guarantee for the first year. I would receive a $600 base and 15 percent commission on the profit of everything I sold. But for the first year, I was guaranteed $2,000 a month. The only exception was if my actual commissions in any given month added up to more than my base guarantee, I would be paid the higher amount.

As a service employee, I could make approximately $18,000 a year at my current wage, and he was guaranteeing me $24,000 for the next year! That was like a $500 a month raise! *Oh my god, what a sweet deal!* I thought to myself.

"What do you think, Michael?" he asked after explaining the program.

"It's a much more generous guarantee than I would have expected, especially having no prior sales experience," I replied. "If I'm being honest, Mr. Dibbert, the offer scares the hell out of me and excites me all at the same time!"

Smiling, he countered. "You'll be reporting directly to me from now on. Oh, and I go by Butch to close acquaintances. So you should call me Butch from now on and forget about the Mr. Dibbert moniker."

"I don't know how I can thank you enough for this opportunity, Butch!" I stated appreciatively. "But I will make you proud and make this wholesale route profitable, that I promise you!"

"I have no doubt that you will, Michael," he said confidently. "Now go home and come back in tomorrow dressed in nice street clothes, and let's get this project started."

He walked me to the door and stepped inside the service area. "We'll see you tomorrow at 8:00 a.m. sharp!" he said as I walked away from him.

"Thanks, Butch! I'll see you then!" I replied, not turning around to see the expressions on the other service employees' faces. I doubt if Greg or any of the other workers had ever heard Mr. Dibbert referred to as Butch! I smiled as I stepped into the minivan and started home.

CHAPTER 10

The dark sky seemed slightly lighter than the last time I had looked up through the windshield of my new two-ton truck. The stars still shone brightly, ensuring the night still ruled over this part of the earth as I made my way to my first stop on my wholesale route.

Cresting a hill and looking off to my right I caught sight of my destination, a rather large truck stop ahead. As I got closer, the huge sign lighted up the sky, displaying a single word, "Chevron."

Taking the next exit, I slowed and pulled off the freeway, mentally preparing myself for the first sales call of the day. I would also take advantage of this location to fill up with fuel, relieve myself, and get a cup of coffee to go once my business was completed.

I slowly pulled my truck with "Master Tire Service" in bold letters on both doors into the truck stop entrance. My eyes were immediately drawn to the fifty or sixty big rigs pulling all types of trailers and cargo that lined the lot on three sides.

Parking at the gas pumps for small trucks and automobiles on the left side of the convenience store/restaurant, I shut off the engine and stepped out of the truck for the first time in over three hours.

As I stood motionless for a minute, it felt like every joint from my ankles up, including my neck, popped in unison to emphasize all the sore connection points and aching muscles in my body. "Son of a bitch!" I said softly as I bent over slowly and stretched my back before walking to the rear of truck. Taking off the gas cap, I stuck the nozzle in and began pumping gas.

While the fuel transferred from the pump into the truck, I looked up and scanned the truck stop for movement. There was one other person getting gas and two men walking from the store back toward the line of trucks at the rear of the complex. Except for the driveway I'd entered, I now clearly saw that I was indeed surrounded by two rows deep of semitrucks and trailers on three sides. The running lights were illuminated on all the tractors and trailers, but none of the headlights were on, even though it sounded like most of the engines were quietly idling.

I assumed the engines were running to keep the air-conditioning running while the occupants in sleepers tried to get some much-needed rest before confronting this morning's highway battles. Moving my head in a 240-degree sweep, it was like I was observing an army of colorful dragons of various sizes and shapes, all poised and ready to strike out at the first hint of light in the new morning sky.

This was not my first time at this truck stop. I visited this and several other trucks stops weekly to sell them tires and batteries, which they, in turn, sold to truckers in need. I stopped here once every two weeks, and this Chevron had become one of my better wholesale accounts.

The handle on my gas nozzle clicked off, and I placed it back in the gas pump cradle. Walking inside the store, I stood in a short line to pay for my fuel. The smells from the adjoining restaurant instantly grabbed me, reminding my stomach that I hadn't eaten in a few hours.

I was early, and I knew the location manager wouldn't be in for another thirty minutes. After paying for my gas, I decided I had time for something quick as I moved into the restaurant and took a seat at the lunch counter. I ordered a cup of coffee and a piece of apple pie. Once served, I began eating while I waited to deliver my tires and pick up a check.

As I sat there enjoying my pie, I wondered if my decision not to drive trucks for a living had caused me regret or had garnered rewards for me over the years. In my heart of hearts, I believed it was truly a coin flip.

I still fervently identified with these anarchists of the highway, and I've always been in love with the idea of freedom of choice and the wandering cowboy ways.

But so many relationships would not have happened, so many opportunities would not have been presented, and my son and however many family members that come after him would not have been born.

Sipping my coffee, I smiled, realizing the perfection of God's plan for me. I had made the right choice.

So far, Jacob had been pretty much a perfect child. He was potty-trained by his first birthday, which made both Sarah and me very happy. He wasn't prone to temper tantrums, he got along well with other kids, he learned quickly and had no difficulties with reading or writing, and he loved vegetables and fruit. Case in point, he would rather eat an apple than have a cookie.

A few weeks after Jacob had been born, Sarah was supposed to go back to her job. She was on the last week of her nine weeks' maternity leave. In casual conversation with Mama and Papa one Saturday afternoon, Sarah told her parents that in a week, she had to start working again.

Papa's head jerked around to look at her before responding. "No! No, I won't have that in our family!" Pointing his finger at Sarah, he continued. "A mother's place is with her children at home!" Deciding to soften his approach a little, he added, "At minimum until the child starts school."

Then he pulled out a cellophane-wrapped cigar and started the ritual that accompanied every cigar. No one spoke as we all sat there, transfixed on the process, and finally watched the lighting of another panatela stogie. From behind his newly created smoke cloud, he addressed me.

"Michael, you know your expenses, and I don't. Above and beyond what you earn at your job, how much more money do you need to live comfortably each month?" Papa asked.

"We will be just fine," I responded, somewhat embarrassed by the directness of his question. "I don't want more of your money! We can make ends meet, with or without Sarah working. I can take care of my own family!"

"Why don't you want my money?" Papa asked. "When Mama and I are dead, all our daughters will split what money we have among themselves. Are you saying you don't want to let Sarah have her share of the inheritance money?" Again, he began puffing away on his cigar while waiting for an answer.

"No! Of course, that's not what I'm saying!" I answered incredulously. "But you and Mama are a long way from being dead, Papa, and who knows what could happen between now and then with your health. I can't let you give us money when the future isn't certain for either of you!"

Papa grinned and then turned to Sarah. "If you go back to work, how much money would you take home every month?" He waited for an answer.

"Papa, Michael's right! You raised me and took great care of me as a child, but I'm not a little girl anymore, and I'm not your responsibility," she responded.

"How much?" he kept pushing, never taking his eyes off her.

We all looked back at Sarah, and I watched her eyes going from side to side as she tried to work out the calculation in her head. Finally, she looked back at him and said, "About $1,100 a month, I think."

Papa sat there for a moment, contemplating her answer. "I will give you $1,500 a month until Jacob graduates from high school," he said, twisting the cigar around in his mouth with one hand. "The only condition is that you stay home and not work. You stay home and tend to your family and go to Jacob's sports activities or get him involved in Cub Scouts or something else he shows an interest in doing."

Again, puffing on the cigar, he finished. "This arrangement is not up for debate! I will give you the money in cash sometime during the first week of every month. That way, you don't have to pay taxes on the extra income." He reached into his bib overall pants pocket and pulled out his wallet. "We can start right now or in a week after your maternity leave ends. What do you want to do?"

"You don't have to do this, Papa!" I said, rising out of my patio chair.

"I said no debate!" he snapped. "This is my gift to Jacob. You have no say in this matter!"

We all looked over at Jacob, who was chewing on his right fist even though he was sound asleep in his car seat next to Sarah.

I turned back to Papa Jake and reluctantly gave in. "Thank you, Papa," I said. "That is very generous of you!"

"Maybe Sarah could bring Jacob over to visit us during the week once or twice a month, if he doesn't have school?"

"I will!" Sarah responded. "We'll see lots of each other!" Standing, she walked over to Papa, leaned down, and gave him a heartfelt hug.

He simply patted her arm a couple of times, looked over to Mama, and smiled. She was already smiling back, watching the two of them embrace.

Our home life had been heaven without Sarah having to work. The house and my clothes were always clean and orderly. She was able to use some of her Armenian culinary skills and made us great meals almost every night. We made Friday nights our date night, and I tried to take her for drinks and a good meal or a movie every Friday. No friends or family were allowed; it was just the two of us alone. She was able to help at Jacob's school and really participate in his education a couple of times a week. Our lifestyle was close to perfect.

"Happy birthday, Jacob!" I said, taking the new two-wheel bicycle out of the back of the minivan. Sarah stood there smiling on the front porch as Jacob came running over to accept his birthday present.

"This is so cool, Dad!" he blurted out. "It's the right color and everything!" He took the bike, ran down the driveway with it, and jumped on, pedaling for all he was worth as he moved up the empty street.

Sarah walked off the porch, put her arm around my waist, and said with a smile, "Pretty cool, Dad!"

It was Jacob's sixth birthday, and so many great things had transpired in the short time we'd been blessed to have him in our lives. Jacob had wanted this air force blue Huffy three-speed bicycle for over a year, and now it was finally his. As we watched him turn around and start back toward us, it was impossible not to smile at his excitement.

One Sunday night, when I was speaking to my parents on our regular Sunday call, my mom mentioned Jimmy Clarke. I had been getting updates on him regularly and knew he'd re-upped for two more tours in Vietnam. On his last tour, he was shot several times in a firefight that almost killed him.

He and I had written back and forth several times while he was in the military hospital in Germany. He'd been struck in the chest, the stomach, and in his left leg with varying degrees of damage. He'd undergone eight surgeries while there, one of them being the removal of a generous portion of his large intestine, which was replaced by an external bag on his lower stomach. He was in Germany twenty-six weeks before he was shipped home for rehabilitation and discharge from the army.

I could tell by the tone of his letters that he was bitter about the extent of his injuries. In his letters, he made not-so-subtle comments, like "I doubt I will ever get married or have children, because no woman in her right mind would want to be hooked up with a cripple who wears a bag to crap in."

He seemed to be in a deep funk, and no matter how much I tried to respond positively about his circumstances, he always went to the dark side with his responses.

Mom said that Jimmy was back home staying with his parents currently and that she and my dad had visited with him for the first time that previous Wednesday. Mom said he was ultrathin and looked like he'd lost fifty pounds or more. She also stated that she noticed a decided change in his demeanor and attitude. He couldn't sit still and was always fidgeting with his hands. She said he pulled away slightly when she hugged him and that he didn't smile once during their thirty minutes together. She also revealed that his parents were very concerned about not only his physical condition but his mental health and well-being as well.

All this was extremely concerning to me as I had gone through much of this myself, just to a lesser degree. I vowed that I would come home soon to see him and spend some time trying to help him recover from the traumas of war.

On the home front, things had worked out very well for me at Master Tire Service. With Butch's supervision, I had enjoyed almost immediate success on my wholesale route. By my third month in sales, my commissions were consistently higher than my guarantee. That year, we paid income tax on $31,500, which was $7,500 above my guarantee. My earnings the next year were even better, and the year after that, I continued to grow the wholesale business exponentially, reaping even greater rewards for my efforts.

I was no longer looking for a career where I could put my business degree to use. As my sense of accomplishment along with my income consistently rose, I felt more and more comfortable working for Master Tire Service and was happy to be there.

On a warm June day, Butch came to me and asked me if I would do him a favor. "Michael, I have a schedule conflict today, and I need you to do something for me, if you could."

"I'd be glad to help," I responded.

"First, you'll need to call your wife and let her know you will be home really late tonight. So I hope you don't have any plans later this evening, or this won't work."

"I'll call her, but I don't think we have anything scheduled for tonight." I was becoming more and more intrigued about his forthcoming request.

"Don't talk about this to anyone, but I have to go to the hospital this afternoon and have a series of test done on my heart," Butch said softly. "Some questions have come up as a result of my annual physical yesterday, and my doctor wants to take a closer look."

"I am truly sorry to hear that, Butch!" I responded, genuine concern in my voice. "How can I help?"

"Well, we have a customer, Jim Layman Logging and Lumber, and I've taken care of them personally for twenty-five years. I have a meeting set up with them this evening to talk about some irregular wear on the last set of Toshiba Tires they purchased and a possible order for the coming fall." He paused. "Because they are up in the woods working, I don't have a way to cancel the meeting with them. I don't want to risk pissing them off by simply not showing up, so I was hoping you could go in my place."

"You are aware that I've never dealt with end users," I started. "My title is wholesale salesman. But even if I went, I don't know my way around the mountains! How would I even find them?" Continuing to stare at Butch, I continued. "Wouldn't Larry Schmidt or Jim Pearson be a better option than me?"

"As far as finding their location, I have a map, and I can give you good directions," he stated. "I've been up there several times myself. It's very easy to find. Your biggest worry is not getting run off the road by one of their logging trucks. They roll pretty fast on some very muddy and winding logging roads!

"As far as sending a commercial salesman, I'm not too happy with either of them right now, and I don't want my relationship with Layman Logging to get screwed up because of them. I trust you, that's why I'm asking you to go in my place."

I knew Butch had just shared very confidential information with me about other employees that I needed to keep to myself. I figured he must have trusted me enough to feel comfortable sharing his feelings about his commercial sales crew with me. Because he'd exhibited confidence in me, I felt duty bound to give him the same respect in return.

"Whatever you need, Butch! Give me a minute and I'll call my wife. Then we can go over your plan of action," I said.

He nodded his head in agreement, and I went into his office to call Sarah.

I'd seen plenty of log trucks at our store previously. Some getting flat tires repair; others getting fully outfitted with new rubber shoes. I'd also sold logging tires to several of my truck stops, ensuring they could take care of emergency needs if a logger lost a tire and couldn't get back to his normal tire dealer quickly.

While fueling up, most loggers preferred to handle their tire issues at the truck stop, hoping to save enough time to make another load that day. An extra load of logs was worth more than enough to pay for the tire and the fuel they'd just purchased.

Butch and I met in his office, and he gave me directions, while one of the service crew put a couple of new logging tires in the back of his pickup. We had strategized somewhat of a plan as I got up to leave.

"Oh! Just a second," he said, opening a drawer on his desk. He pulled out a bottle of bourbon and extended his arm to hand it to me. "Jim likes to take a couple of snorts after a hard day of logging, so you need to go prepared!"

I reached out and took the bottle. "This isn't like any sales call I've ever been on," I responded, a slight smirk on my face.

"I'm sure it won't be," he said. "Just don't drink too much yourself! You'll have to drive home later, and I want my pickup back in one piece! If you get lost, just call in on the truck radio, and someone will help you get back on track. Several of the service truck operators have been up there. Good luck, Michael. I've put a lot of faith in you, so don't cost me this account!"

"I won't, sir!" I responded, turning to leave his office.

It was almost a four-hour drive to the log landing where Jim and his crew were working. Checking my watch, I realized I had arrived about thirty minutes earlier than the appointment time. I pulled out of the way, parked the pickup, and just watched as logs were cleared of branches, loaded into piles, and then loaded onto waiting log trucks. The process was fascinating, and the individual workers moved in unison like a well-oiled machine. At exactly 5:30 p.m., a loud whistle went off for several seconds, and everyone stopped what they were doing and started walking back to the main camp area and their pickups.

Getting out of my pickup, I also started in the direction of the camp. There was one large tent standing at the back of the clearing with a firepit in front of it. There were several logs lining the deep pit where many of the loggers took a seat.

Some were warming their hands and feet in front of the fire, while others were changing from boots to more comfortable footwear for their drive home.

I asked the first man I saw if he knew where Jim Layman was currently. He was a large man with a powerful built. He'd just taken off his mud-covered metal helmet as he turned to answer me. Noting that everyone was incredibly dirty and muddy from the day's work, I noticed a very distinct line where the mud and dirt stopped, and white skin appeared on his head as he removed his protective headgear.

Turning away from the fire and straightening up to address me, he said, "I'm Jim Layman. Who are you?"

"I'm Michael Larsen, sir. I'm with Master Tire Service, and I've been asked to come up here and see what I can do to help you with some tire problems you're having," I responded.

"Where's Butch?" he asked, a slight irritation in his tone.

"He couldn't make it today, so he asked me to come in his place."

"You seem a little young to be a troubleshooter for Toshiba Tires?" he said, noticing my clean street clothes and shined shoes. "I don't want to sound like an asshole, but you just don't look like you belong out here!"

"I can understand why you would feel that way," I replied. After a moment of silence between us, I added, "But I'm pretty sure you'll find I'm smarter than I look if you give me a chance to try and help you."

My self-deprecation brought a smile to his face. "What did you say your name was again?" he asked, this time seeming more interested.

"Michael, sir," I responded.

He stuck out his large and very dirty right hand for me to shake. "You can call me Jim, and forget the sir—it doesn't really suit me!"

I grabbed his extended hand and shook it. "Come on over here. Only one of the trucks with the tire problems is here right now. But maybe you can give me some answers as to why these tires are wearing so wacky."

We went over to the truck in question, and I began to inspect the tires. I discovered the problem, and it wasn't tires at all but, rather, loose parts in the front end of the truck. I spent the next hour explaining to him what needed to be done to correct the problem.

"When can you bring the truck back to the tire store so we can get this resolved?" I asked.

"We're on a tight schedule with this timber contract, and I'm working the crew six days a week trying to meet our contractual commitment," he said, running his hand over his sparsely haired head. "It's going to be a while before we can get this truck down there to fix it. I need all my trucks hauling logs every day or we won't make our deadline!"

I thought about his comments and started to develop a plan in my head. "Let's go back to the fire and talk about possible solutions." With that, we turned and headed back toward the firepit.

Once we arrived, he said, "I have problems on another truck as well, but it's not here right now."

"Where is it?" I solicited.

"That truck made three trips today, so it won't be back here for another three hours or so," he answered.

Thinking about it, I remembered telling Butch that I would do whatever needed to be done to resolve the issues out here. "I'm in no hurry if you're not. I'd be glad to stay here and wait for your truck to get back so we can find out if it has the same problem or something different."

He smiled slightly and replied, "I'm not going anywhere. I'll be sleeping in that tent over there tonight." He pointed to the tent toward the back of the camp. "But you are going to have one hell of a drive home if you stay that late!"

"I'll be fine," I said reassuringly.

We both took a seat on vacant logs and stared into the hypnotic flames while we warmed up. Everyone else had gone home for the day, leaving just the two of us to stoke the fire and keep it burning.

"How about Sundays?" I inquired suddenly. "Can we get these two trucks to the tire shop on a Sunday?"

"It would work, but you guys aren't open on Sundays," he countered.

"If you're willing to bring the trucks in this Sunday, I'll make sure we have the manpower to get both of your trucks straightened out. I'll even throw in a free front-end alignment after we fix what needs to be fixed. Could you work with that?"

"Aren't you guys union?" he asked.

"Yes!" I acknowledged. "To tell you the truth, that's the only drawback to Master Tire. I really don't like unions much!"

Shaking his head affirmingly, he agreed. "Me either! Those bastards were up here a couple of years ago trying to push the union onto all my employees. I was able to convince my guys that they already had a better deal than the union proposal, so, fortunately, we avoided unionizing."

"Because we're union, we'll have to pay my tire guys double time for working on Sunday. But if that's what it takes to solve your tire problems in a time frame that fits your needs, so be it!" I said convincingly.

Getting up and stretching, I said, "I'll be right back." I jogged to my pickup, opened the door, and grabbed the bottle of bourbon Butch had given me to take up to the camp. I turned and jogged back to where Jim was still seated and held the bottle out for him to take.

"Just a little something to keep the cold off us until your other truck shows up," I said. He took the bottle, opened it, and took a long swig. His face grimaced as he handed the bottle back to me.

"Your turn, Michael!" he said with a raspy voice. "That tastes pretty damn good after a hard day's work," he continued.

We sat there and got to know each other as we waited for his second truck to arrive. We seemed to be getting along better with each pull off the whiskey bottle. We were sharing stories and laughing, and in short order, I felt comfortable in this environment.

Waking up the next morning, I looked at the clock on the bed stand to see it was almost 10:00 a.m. "Shit!" I said softly to myself, not wanting to wake Sarah. After jumping out of bed, two realizations came to mind immediately. First, Sarah was already up and out of the bedroom. And, second, my head felt like someone was pounding on it with a sledgehammer! It truly felt like it was going to explode!

I stumbled into the living room and saw Sarah in the kitchen. "Want a cup of coffee?" she asked, seeming to be a little irritated with me.

"Why didn't you get me up?" I asked. "I was supposed to be at work two hours ago!"

She walked over, handed me a hot cup of coffee, and, with a look of indignation, said, "I tried to get you up for thirty minutes!" Then walking back into the kitchen, she continued. "Finally, I just gave up!" Before I could respond, she started again, only this time, the full brunt of her anger was on display.

"I thought you were working late last night! Anyway, that's what you told me over the phone!" She was pretty much yelling at me as she resumed her attack. "You come home at three in the morning and drunker than I've ever seen you, and I'm supposed to believe you were working late! That's a crock of bullshit, and you know it, Michael!"

"I was working!" I answered loudly, making my head throb in pain. "I was up in the mountains taking care of a problem for Butch with one of our best customers."

She shot me a dagger look before responding. "So you're telling me that you drove home from the mountains this morning as drunk as you were?"

"I guess so," I replied sheepishly, knowing now how stupid and dangerous I'd been. Then a small smile crossed my cheeks as I said, "I really don't remember driving home!"

Sarah rushed over to me and slapped me hard on the back of the head. "Don't ever do that again, Michael!" Pausing for a second, she pointed her finger at me and finished. "I mean it, dammit! You'll be sleeping on the street and paying child support if this happens again!" Then she was gone, and I was left standing there with my head throbbing even worse now and with spilled hot coffee all over my right hand.

After a quick shower, I went to work. When I walked through the front door, Butch was waiting for me. He simply looked at his watch and then put both hands on his hips, waiting as I approached.

I'd already been yelled at once this morning, and I wasn't looking forward to that experience again. I smiled and said, "Sorry, I'm late, but I didn't get home until early this morning."

"You look like you have a pretty good hangover. Do you want to tell me about it?" he said, turning and heading back into his office. I followed him and waited for him to sit down behind his desk before speaking.

"Before we talk business, would it be inappropriate to ask how your doctor's visit went yesterday?" I asked.

"We won't have all the test results back for a few more days, but the doctor seemed pleased with the results they were able to see. Thank you for asking," he responded.

Returning to business, I told him everything that had happened and the arrangements I'd made for Jim Layman's two log trucks for Sunday at our shop. He chewed on the information and finally spoke. "That's a lot of extra expense for us, Michael. I don't recall giving you the authority to make those arrangements."

"You said he was an important customer and that I needed to make him happy!" I replied. "And I think I made him happy!"

Turning to exit his office, I walked out the door and then stopped. Sticking my head back inside the door, I remarked, "Oh, and I forgot to tell you, Jim ordered one hundred new drive tires and twenty-four new steering tires for his rigs. He wants to be tired up going into the winter." Putting my finger up to my lips while contemplating if there was anything else to say, I said, "He also wants four new tires for his log loader. I believe he said L-5s, whatever that means."

Butch's mouth dropped open as he sat there staring at me in disbelief. "You're bullshitting me!" he finally said, still watching me.

"No, I'm serious," I stated. Reaching into my shirt pocket, I pulled out a piece of paper and laid it on Butch's desk. "There's his purchase order for everything!"

Picking it up and reading through it, all he managed to utter was "Unbelievable! Simply unbelievable!" He got up, came around his table, and held his hand out for me to shake. I extended my hand back, and he grabbed it, squeezing it tightly as he spoke. "That is one hell of a great first commercial call, Michael! Jim's never ordered these types of quantities from me! You guys must have gotten along very well! How did you do this?" Butch inquired.

I smiled and responded, "I'm not sure I can answer that. Turns out he's a veteran, and we talked about that a great deal. He was really interested in my Vietnam experiences. But other than that, we just talked shop for the most part. Not knowing much about his business,

I listened and pretty much just mimicked him. If he took a drink, I took a drink. If he spat in the fire, I spat in the fire. If he stood up and put one leg on a log, I did the same thing! Pretty soon, he was doing all the talking, and we were conversing like best friends. Then the whiskey hit me hard, and I don't clearly remember much after that."

"Then you drove home like that?" Butch scowled. "You crazy fool! You could have gotten a DUI or, worse, killed yourself!"

"You don't have to go there," I responded quickly. "Sarah already bitched me out this morning for that very reason! She was so pissed!"

Butch smirked. "I've been there myself! But she's right! Next time, get a motel or sleep in the truck. No sale is worth your life!"

"I didn't give him any prices because I don't know what kind of discounts you give him," I said, changing the subject. "I told Jim I couldn't price the tires, and he said, 'Just have Butch price them out, he'll treat me fair.' So I guess you need to price out the tire order yourself."

"Come back in here and I'll show you how I price this," Butch said, waving me back into his office. I walked in and leaned over his desk to watch what he was doing.

"No, not there," he said, motioning me behind him. "You need to see this close up and understand it so you can do it yourself next time."

"Wow!" Butch sang out after he'd finished pricing the tires. "$51,436 is the largest tire order ever accepted by Master Tire Service!"

I felt my grin grow into a full-blown smile of pride as his words washed over me.

"Outstanding job, Michael!" he exclaimed. "Truly outstanding!"

"Thank you, Butch," I replied humbly.

"How attached are you to your wholesale route, Michael?" Butch asked, quizzing.

"I really like it!" I responded. "It's kind of a game for me to beat last year's and last month's sales numbers. I love that challenge!"

"How would you feel about becoming a commercial tire salesman?" Butch asked.

"I haven't really thought about it," I answered. Thinking about it quickly, I continued. "One of my real concerns would be that I don't have enough knowledge about truck and earth mover tires."

"We can teach you that!" Butch countered. "We would send you to a six-week school that Toshiba Tire offers for their own personnel and any dealer that wants to send selected employees."

I was completely caught off guard. I'd never considered selling truck tires. I needed to bring Sarah into the loop before making this decision. I felt doubt and confusion starting to creep into my thoughts as I stood there, saying nothing.

Sensing my indecision, Butch said, "Michael, the commission on this sale alone is more than you'll make in commissions over a six-month period selling to wholesalers." He paused, waiting for me to digest his words. "Layman Lumber is a house account, but if you want to think about jumping into the unknown, I'll make it your first official account. In fact, I'll pay you the commission on this sale! It's just under $8,000, in case you were wondering."

I didn't know what to say. Finally, I responded, "Can I talk to my wife first?"

He smiled and responded, "Certainly! But I don't think today is the right day to spring this on her. My suggestion is that you take her home some flowers tonight and ask for forgiveness. I'd give it a couple of days before broaching this subject with her. Why don't you let me know your decision by next Friday?"

Sarah was on board with me changing jobs at Master Tire, with one caveat—no drinking to excess with any account managers ever! I agreed to her terms, knowing how foolish and lucky I'd been on my first commercial call.

I traded in my two-ton wholesale truck and now drove a brand-new three-quarter-ton pickup with a large "Master Tire" on the door in bright metallic red letters. The truck was mine to drive for business, and I could use it for personal purposes as well.

With Butch's coaching over the next couple of years, I was able to establish several new commercial accounts. The crown jewel in my portfolio was a large trucking company by the name of Interstate Haulers. After months of cold calls, I was able to put a set of test tires on one of their trucks. Tracking our tires against their present supplier's tires, we outperformed them by 35 percent over the course of a year. In the end, they switched tire suppliers, and we took over a fleet of 120 tractors and 235 trailers. They bought approximately four thousand new tires each year, and all those sales went through me.

Everything in my small world was perfect. I was making more money than I ever thought I would make. We'd stopped taking money from Papa Jake and Mama because we no longer needed it. Papa had started putting the $1,500 a month into U.S. savings bonds for Jacob's college once he graduated from high school.

While I was enjoying prosperity and a wonderful life, the outside world seemed to be spiraling in a downward tailspin.

The United States embassy in Beirut was bombed, killing several Americans serving there.

There was a huge gas leak at the Union Carbide's plant in Bhopal, India, that killed hundreds of people in the area.

The Iran-Contra scandal erupted, causing an investigation to be done by the U.S. government.

The space shuttle *Challenger* exploded shortly after takeoff, putting our space program in serious jeopardy and killing all those aboard.

In the USSR, the first nuclear power plant meltdown occurred in Chernobyl. Thousands died, and for hundreds of miles around the city, the land was pronounced to be uninhabitable for the next hundred years by scientist.

On October 19, 1987, the U.S. stock market plunged to its greatest drop since the depression. The day would later become known as Black Monday.

Pan Am flight 103 was bombed over Lockerbie, Scotland, by terrorists, leaving no survivors.

The *Exxon Valdez* spilled millions of gallons of oil on the Alaskan coastline, creating the largest environmental disaster in American history.

Hundreds of students protesting China's ruling party were murdered in Tiananmen Square by Chinese government troops.

There were, however, a few highlights that improved mankind in one way or another during this period. Most notably, on November 9, 1989, the Berlin Wall came down, effectively ending domination by the Soviet Union of multiple countries around the world.

George Bush Sr. was elected president of the United States.

Computer systems were just beginning to be used in many companies, and the Internet, although still fragmented, went global, allowing computer communication around the world.

Butch approached me on a Monday morning and asked me if he could see me in his office.

As always, I replied, "Sure! I'll be right there. Give me a second to wash my hands and clean up a bit."

He nodded his approval, turned, and walked back through the office door.

When I walked into his office, Mike Lovering was sitting across from Butch in one of the two chairs on the customer side of the desk. I immediately apologized for interrupting them and said I would come back later, after the two of them were through talking.

"That's not necessary, Michael," Mr. Lovering stated, turning his head to acknowledge my presence. He patted the chair next to him and continued. "Come on in! We're here to talk to you, not each other."

My mind raced as I entered the office and started for the chair next to Mr. Lovering, who quickly added, "Close the door behind you before you sit down, please."

Had I done something wrong? I wondered. I couldn't think of anything, so I simply sat down as I'd been instructed by Mr. Lovering. Mike Lovering and I had probably spoken to each other six times during the last eight years, and all those conversations were short and impersonal. This looked to be something more serious, I thought, as I sat down and turned to look at him directly.

"Michael, I wanted to tell you how pleased we are with your performance," Mr. Lovering began. "You and I haven't really gotten to know each other yet, but I'm hoping to correct that today." He smiled at me as he began to ask questions about me, my family, and how I liked what I was doing at Master Tire Service.

I answered them truthfully and wondered why he was asking. Finally, he asked a question I wasn't ready for. "So Butch tells me you're not much of a fan of unions. Is that correct?"

I looked first to Butch and then back to Mr. Lovering and meekly responded, "No, not really."

Mr. Lovering smiled and said, "Do you mind telling me why?"

It felt like someone had turned up the thermostat in the room because, suddenly, I could feel perspiration forming on my upper lip and forehead, and my hands became clammy. I didn't know what to say as I again looked at Butch, hoping for some support with this difficult answer. Butch simply smiled weakly and said, "Go ahead, Michael. Just tell him the truth."

"Well, it really started when I first started working for you, sir," I began. "I'd only been here a few weeks when some of the men on the floor cornered me and told me to slow down because I was working too fast. That irritated me because their logic was so flawed. Then at a union meeting, the local representative tried to tell me whom I should vote for in the upcoming sheriff's race, and that really pissed me off. And, last, the union rep tried to get me fired for crossing one of their picket lines. They were striking about something that had nothing to do with me or Master Tire Service!"

I sat there for a second or two, feeling myself getting riled up all over again, remembering my past instances. "I believe you have choices in life, and the people running these unions want to take that away from the average working man. I consented to working for your company for an agreed-upon wage, and you should expect an honest day's work from me in return. The union doesn't care about me, the worker, or you, the employer. Instead, they ask the workers to slow down so more people can be hired, and they can collect more dues from both of us! That's just not right, and it really irritates me!"

Butch and Mr. Lovering sat there listening to me, and once I was finished, they both continued to stare, neither of them speaking. Finally, Mr. Lovering said, "Butch is going to be retiring pretty soon, and I would like you to take his position with the company."

I almost fell off my chair as I thought about what had just been offered. "Me!" I spat out. "You want me to take Butch's place?"

"Yes, I do, Michael," he responded calmly. "But there's more to the story that you need to be aware of before you accept the offer. I feel the same way you do about unions, and I want to make a break between them and Master Tire Service."

He looked at Butch and then back to me. "Unfortunately, unions are very powerful, and it's hard to push them out. Do you have any thoughts on how we should proceed if we want to break our relationship with the union?"

I thought about it for a minute and then asked, "How much do you think the union costs Master Tire in total over a one-year period?"

"Ballpark, around $500,000 a year with wages and benefits," he responded.

"If you break the union, how much of that money would you be willing to reinvest in nonunion workers?" I asked.

Looking up at the ceiling and thinking for a moment, he finally responded, "That's a real interesting question, Michael. How much do you think I should reinvest in a nonunion workforce?"

"Most of it, but paid out in a different way," I replied. "Right now, I think we have two full-time employees too many on the service floor. But instead of laying people off, we should reward performers and starve out the slackers! We could go in with a lower wage and pay an incentive for added sales to the workforce. Maybe a productivity incentive for the entire crew if we hit a specific sales goal. And an incentive for additional sales such as brake jobs, front-end alignments, battery sales that would be paid to everyone based on their personal performance. I would say the incentive program should be guaranteed for one year to get it up and running. Then each person would be incentivized on their own merits after the first year with no guarantee."

Mr. Lovering thought on my offer for a few seconds. "That is a very interesting thought," he said.

Butch chimed in, finally speaking, "I told you he was smart!"

Getting more and more excited about the prospect before us, I jumped back in. "I think the wage and incentive guarantee would need to be about $1.50 more an hour than they are currently making on average." I thought about it and added, "Some would leave because of their tenure with the union, but I believe most would stay. And anyone we hire new to replace those who leave would have to earn their incentives, not have them guaranteed. And, of course, you would have to offer a benefit program that is comparable to the union's."

"How would you start this process, Michael?" Mr. Lovering asked.

I thought about it for a minute before responding. "I think I would do it on the down low first by approaching a couple of our guys who I know are not thrilled with the union already. Check their interest first, and if they like the idea, have them help sell the rest of the team on the idea. If they're honest, every one of our guys hates paying union dues, which keep going up every year. And I'm pretty sure no one will object to not having to contribute personal money to help their union brothers with political candidates!"

Mr. Lovering smiled. "The union won't just walk away quietly, you know that, don't you?"

"Yes, I know that," I answered.

"If we can make this work, they will want their pound of flesh," Mr. Lovering said. "And that's where Butch and you come into the picture."

I didn't quite understand his meaning as I looked at him, puzzled.

"Butch wants to retire, and I need someone to run the business once he's gone," Mr. Lovering started. "When the union comes around, angry as a worked-up bunch of hornets, Butch will be our sacrificial lamb. The deed will already be done, but we'll make it look like this was all Butch's idea, and I'll make it appear that I fired him over this transgression, and you will become his replacement."

Butch smiled devilishly. "Do you think we can pull this off, Michael?" he asked.

Before I could answer, Mr. Lovering said, "You will have complete control of all personnel, your own pickup, and I'll give you a $20,000-a-year raise over your last year's income. How does that sound, Michael?"

I didn't know which question to answer first! Deciding to respond to Butch first, I replied, "Yes. I do think we could pull this off, and I think the company will be so much more efficient by rewarding performance and promoting high performers from within."

Then it was time to answer Mr. Lovering. My demeanor was calm on the outside, but I was doing backflips on the inside! I knew I didn't have to ask Sarah about this promotion; how she could not say yes!

"I feel honored to accept your offer, Mr. Lovering. I don't know how to thank both Butch and yourself for putting so much faith in me," I answered.

Mr. Lovering rose from his chair, grabbed my arm with his left hand, and shook my hand with his right hand. "Obviously, we need to keep this between the three of us for now! We'll have several more meetings to formalize our approach before we start this campaign. I'll work on the insurance plan, and you two work on the incentive plan and head count needed to pull this off."

He paused for a moment, looked over to Butch, and said, "Let's meet next Friday, lunch, and block out the entire afternoon for the three of us!"

CHAPTER 11

Being promoted to general manager of Master Tire Service meant we now had enough income to qualify and buy a nice four-bedroom home in one of the nicer areas of Fresno. There were plenty of nearby parks for Jacob to play in; nice wide, well-lit streets; and some of the best public schools in the state.

When we told Papa Jake that we'd found a house, he and Mama came to look at it and give it their seal of approval. He took his time walking around the house, looking in every nook and cranny. He opened cupboards, drawers, and every closet door. He even used the flashlight he'd brought with him to look up into the attic. Then he went out into the garage and measured front to back and side to side with a measuring tape. Once completed, he asked Jacob to go for a walk with him around the neighborhood. Jacob agreed, and they headed east down the sidewalk. They were holding hands, which was impressive since Jacob was now eleven and thought he was a full-grown adult.

Papa Jake and Jacob came walking back to the house from the opposite direction about an hour later. They weren't holding hands anymore, but they were laughing as they talked back and forth. Once home, Jacob ran to Grandma and gave her a quick hug before asking permission to go back outside and play. Sarah nodded her approval, and Jacob turned and was out the door like a shot.

Papa Jake looked at Sarah and me as we stood together, holding hands, and said, "This is a very nice house." Smiling at Mama, he continued. "Much nicer than our first house!"

Looking back to Sarah and me, he continued. "I think this is a smart investment for the two of you. You should buy it! I think this would be a great place to raise Jacob!"

Papa Jake reached in his pocket and pulled out a cashier's check, walked over, and handed it to Sarah. "This will help with the down payment," he expressed with a matter-of-fact tone in his voice.

Sarah looked at the check and then to me and then back to Papa. "This is too much!" she shrieked, handing the check to me.

As I looked at the check, I was as shocked as Sarah had been! "We can't accept this, Papa!" I said, trying to hand it back to him.

He smiled, shaking his head from side to side, and said, "You two are the most difficult people to give money to! Just take it, use it for your down payment, and start your lives in your new home with lower house payments."

Knowing there was no winning this argument for us, I stepped over to Papa and gave him a big hug. "Thank you from the bottom of our hearts," I began. "You are the most generous man I think I've ever known!" Then I moved away and went over to hug Mama.

Sarah had taken my place with her father, and after hugging each other, they began to chatter back and forth in Armenian. I saw a tear run down Sarah's face, and I could almost feel the love she felt for her parents at that moment.

Moving from our cramped two-bedroom apartment into a four-bedroom house with 2,500 square feet was not only fun but also liberating. There was so much extra room—so much so that we could hear our voices echoing off the walls when we spoke to each other, even after all our furniture were situated in the rooms. But this move was a labor of love, and once we were settled, it immediately felt like home.

Our business at the tire store had been steadily improving since I'd taken the position of general manager. It took a full year, but we did finally break the union and become an independent dealer. I had changed several performance standards and behaviors to better serve both our retail and commercial customers once we no longer needed union approval for every change.

I always ran any changes I wanted to make past Mike Lovering prior to implementing them. To date, he had never questioned any of my changes or responded negatively. His acceptance made me comfortable with my position in the company.

Mike Lovering and I had worked closely together for about six months, and I felt we had developed a pretty good relationship. So I decided to invite him and his wife to our house for dinner on a Saturday night. After extending the invitation, Mr. Lovering's response was not exactly what I had expected.

"Thank you for the invitation, Michael," he began. "But my wife and I decided long ago that we wouldn't mix business with pleasure. Without wanting to come across as elitist as this may sound, we don't socialize with our employees. Involvement with those you supervise tends to create feelings—and feelings can be very dangerous for the owner of a business, especially if there are hard choices that need to be made regarding that specific employee."

He paused for a second and then said, "Thank you again for the invitation, but now you know that won't be necessary again. Oh, and no birthday cards or Christmas presents, please. I hope you can understand that ours is strictly a business relationship."

I was absolutely stunned! "I understand, sir," I stammered once I found my voice. I was feeling both embarrassed and angry at the same time. "I'd better get back to work. I'm working on our spring tire order, and it's not even close to being done yet!" With that, I returned to my office and closed the door behind me.

As I sat there, so many feelings were coursing through me. The first and probably strongest was a seething resentment! Who the hell did this pompous ass think he was talking down to me like he owned me and I was forever indentured to him! I could feel my jaws tightening and my breathing quickening as I sat there dwelling on his contemptuous response.

I took a few slow deep breaths and tried to calm myself. As my anger subsided and my emotions turned more toward hurt feelings,

I continued to mull over our conversation. After some reflection on the one-sided conversation, I decided that the most important lesson of the day for me was that there were only two columns in Mr. Lovering's ledger. You were either an asset to the business and his ultimate success, or you were a liability and you needed to be cut out like a cancerous tumor. In less than an hour, I had gone from a feeling of complete job security to the realization that I was just one of many pieces of meat that were disposable at any given moment by my employer.

Six months after we had dissolved the union, one of the office assistants knocked on my door.

"Come in," I said cordially.

Opening the door and sticking her head in, she simply stated, "Mr. Tanos is here from the union, Michael. He asked if he could speak with you for a moment." She stood there, waiting for my response.

"Send him in, please," I replied. Seconds later, he was walking through my office door, closing it behind him.

Advancing toward my desk, he put out his hand to shake and said, "It's nice to see you again, Michael."

I stood and we shook hands, but I made no reply.

He pulled one of the chairs on his side of the desk up close and sat in it, folding his hands and plopping them down on top of my pristine, clean glass desktop. "I think you and I may have gotten off to a rocky start." He was able to produce a fake smile as he continued. "I'm here today to try and rectify that."

"How do you propose to do that?" I asked, my eyes narrowing as I stared at him.

"Well, to begin with, I want to apologize for our first meeting. You pushed my buttons, and I got angry and lashed out at you," he said, shaking his head from side to side in a feeble attempt to show his remorse. "I'm sorry for that. It was very unprofessional of me. I am also aware that the driving force behind dissolving the union here was Butch Dibbert!"

He sat back in his chair, leaving two trails of slime as he dragged his sweaty hands across my desktop while moving backward. "So I wanted to come by and make sure you were aware of all the benefits the union has to offer to both your employees and upper management. Do you have thirty minutes for me to go over why the union is the best option for your business?"

"I'm sorry, Mel, but I'm working with a really tight timeline on a report I have to get finished and back to Toshiba Tire today. Do you think we could do this another day? Maybe over lunch?"

Mel smiled and shook his head affirmatively. I'm sure he felt he had made a great first impression with me.

"That sounds wonderful, Michael!" he responded enthusiastically. "How about a week from today, say, 1:00 p.m.?"

"I'll look forward to it," I responded, smiling back. My expression changed slightly as I added, "But I would like you to research a couple of items for that meeting if you would."

"We are actually paying our service team about $1.50 an hour more today than when we were affiliated with the union. That was made possible because management hasn't had to contribute to the union pension fund. I don't want to change our employees' new wage, but if we must contribute to the pension fund again, we will be spending more money out of pocket to become a union shop. How can the union assist us in keeping our costs the same without affecting our employees' wages?"

The smile on Mel face slowly eroded as I continued. "Also, union dues keep going up, which is constantly taking an increasing amount of money out of our employees' pockets. Can we get a contractual agreement that dues will remain at one level for a specific period of years?"

Mel's smile was now completely gone. "And, last, give me three reasons or examples of how being part of a union improves the bottom line for our company and how much additional income we should expect if we go back to being a union shop."

Mel didn't respond. Instead, he sat there glaring at me.

Placing his hands on the arms of his chair, he rose and started for the door in silence.

As he opened my office door to exit, I asked, "Should I pick you up at your office, or do you want to come by here next Wednesday?" He continued out of my office, closing the door behind himself and saying nothing.

Over the next few years, my life and the lives of my family members flourished. Jacob turned out to be a pretty good athlete and was involved in multiple sports throughout his junior high and high school years. He made good grades, had lots of friends, and was active in the youth group in our church. I'd purchased a late-model Jeep for him once he'd passed his test for a driver's license. The two of us spent several hours together either working on his car or buying new accessories to "trick out" his new ride.

He hadn't really shown a serious interest in those of the opposite sex yet, even though he did date a bevy of girls from his high school. He set his sights on following in my footsteps and enrolling at Fresno State once he'd finished high school. Sarah and I were both so very proud of him.

Sarah was very happy being a homemaker and wasn't too interested in getting back into the job market. She kept herself busy running around to various activities Jacob was participating in. She was his number-one cheerleader, and everyone knew instantly that she was his mother if he was responsible for a good play in any sporting event.

Sarah had also became pretty involved in several community projects. Right now, she was concentrating on a new state-of-the-art animal shelter that we desperately needed in our area. The estimated cost was $2 million, and Sarah was part of the finance committee trying to raise money to get it built.

Old age was quickly catching up with Mama and Papa. They were both starting to move around more feebly, and they repeated themselves several times in most conversation. Papa had to give up smoking cigars on doctors' orders, and Mama was now burning half the items she cooked, making many of her dishes inedible. It was a little sad to watch, but they seemed to accept that they were in the winter of their life cycle and made no excuses for themselves. They had lived good lives, and both were happy to be alive but weren't afraid of their inevitable end.

Master Tire Service was doing well, and we were in the process of opening a brand-new truck tire center right off the I-5 freeway. Toshiba Tire would build it, and we would buy it back on a lease to purchase program over a ten-year period.

I was not in favor of the idea because I felt it put too much financial pressure on the company. To me, it was too risky a venture because it increased our debt load beyond what our profit capabilities were.

However, Mr. Lovering expressed that if we didn't do it, Toshiba Tire would open the truck tire center as a company-owned location, and we would end up competing against our own product. He felt we had no choice but to agree and move forward with the project.

Sarah, Jacob, and I had managed to stay reasonably isolated from all the catastrophic events in the world as we lived out our perfect upper middle-class lives in Fresno. But as we moved through the '90s, the world and our country were continuing to exhibit signs of escalating insanity.

George Bush Sr. was the president as we entered another war in a foreign country. The United States led a thirty-five-nation coalition into Iraq. The Gulf War and Operation Desert Storm were in response to Iraq's invasion and annexation of Kuwait. In less than six weeks, the war was over with coalition troops freeing Kuwait and pushing Iraq back behind its own borders. The Iraq military capabilities were all but destroyed in the process.

For the second time in my life, Los Angeles became the epicenter of racial violence in our country. Four Los Angeles Police Department officers who were filmed beating Rodney King, a black motorist, were acquitted of all charges, setting off riots throughout the city. In the next week, there were over sixty deaths and $1 billion in damage caused by rioters in LA.

That same year, hurricane Andrew, a category five hurricane, hit the gulf coast and Florida, killing sixty-five people and causing $26 billion in damages. It was the costliest natural disaster in American history.

In 1993, Bill Clinton became the forty-second president of the United States.

That same year, a truck bomb exploded in the parking garage under the World Trade Center in New York City, killing six people and damaging the building.

As well, a religious cult full of Branch Davidians worshippers led by David Koresh stood strong against the United States government in Waco, Texas. The compound was burned down, and eighty-one followers, including David Koresh, were killed.

The "storm of the century" struck the Eastern Seaboard with blizzard conditions and severe weather conditions. Three hundred people were killed, and damage estimates from the storm were over $6 billion.

Massive flooding along the Mississippi River killed fifty people and caused $15–$20 billion in damages.

A massive earthquake in Northridge, California, killed seventy-three people and injured nine thousand others in the Los Angeles area, causing $20 billion in damage.

Even though the world was crazy around us, we had maintained a reasonably ordinary and contented lifestyle in our own little world. That lifestyle was completely shattered on June 2, 1994. I remember the events of that day as if they were yesterday. At the same time, I have never really been able to wrap my head around the thought that this inconceivably horrific event was real and not just a horrendous nightmare from which I never awoke.

It was a Friday, and Sarah and a girlfriend were going into town to have facials and massages, do some shopping, and have a nice dinner together. She had planned this for a couple of weeks and was looking so forward to some girl time with her friend. She had asked her sister to go to Jacob's baseball game so he had someone there to cheer for him in her absence.

Jacob and I were going to have some male bonding time of our own; a quick burger and a shake, and then we were going to go catch a movie together that evening.

Trying to get ready to leave the house that morning, I could see how excited Sarah was to be going out with her girlfriend. I was excited for her as I helped get breakfast ready for all of us.

Suddenly, the doorbell rang, and we both knew Sue Simmons was here to pick her up for their day of fun. She answered the door as I walked into the living room behind her. Greetings and hugs followed, and Sarah grabbed her purse and started out the door. Suddenly stopping, she turned and rushed back to me. Wrapping both arms around my neck, she kissed me quickly on the lips and told me she loved me.

I responded in kind, smiling back at her excitement! Then she was out the door and trotting toward Sue's car. She was dressed in a cute baby blue blouse and light brown khaki pants. She looked gorgeous as I watched her get into the car.

As they pulled away from the curve, Sarah looked back at me with a big smile on her face and waved. Her smile made me smile, and I waved back. I hadn't seen her this excited in some time. I was so pleased she was doing this for herself. She surely deserved it.

Looking up into the heavens, there wasn't a cloud in the sky, and it looked like today was going to be a perfect day. Knowing I had to get Jacob up, ready, fed, and out of the house for school, I went back into the house and called for him to come down for breakfast.

At two fifteen in the afternoon, one of the office secretaries came running back to the truck department office where I was at the time.

"There's a call for you on line two, Michael, and the woman says it's an emergency!" she said, her breath slightly labored because she had jogged from the office, through the warehouse, to me.

Running back into the service manager's office, I picked up the phone and simply said, "Hello."

Miriam, Sarah's sister, quickly said, "Jack! You need to come home right now!"

I could hear the panic in her voice and immediately felt my heart beginning to pound faster. "Is Jacob all right?" I asked, my panic now matching hers.

"He's fine," she replied. "He hasn't come home from school yet. He has a baseball game this afternoon at four o'clock."

"I was dropping off some pans I'd borrowed from Sarah, so I let myself into the house. Someone from the California Highway Patrol was leaving a message on your answering machine telling you to get in contact with them as I was walking through the front door. It sounds like Sarah and Sue were in a car accident. That's all I know! You need to come home now!"

The words were barely out of her mouth before I slammed the phone down in its cradle and started running toward the parking lot and my pickup.

I'd probably made the drive to and from work one thousand plus times, but it seemed as though traffic was the slowest it had ever been today. I caught myself honking at people whom I deemed were driving to slow and cutting off cars as I continuously changed lanes, trying to get that much closer to my destination, one car at a time if necessary.

It was normally a twenty-minute drive either way from home to work, but it felt as though an hour had gone by as I pulled into the driveway and jumped out of the truck, leaving the driver's door open, and began running to the front door of the house. While I bounded up the steps two at a time, I glanced at my watch and realized it had only taken fifteen minutes to complete the journey home, regardless of what my brain was telling me.

Throwing the front door open, Miriam met me on the front porch. She came running up to me and handed me a piece of paper. "I listened to the message again, and here is the phone number for Sergeant Ramirez from the Highway Patrol. Call him!"

Running into the house, I dialed the number that Miriam had given me. The call was answered on the second ring. "California Highway Patrol, this is Brenda, how can I help you?" she stated calmly.

"My name is Michael Larsen, and I received a message from a sergeant Ramirez stating that my wife has been in a car accident and that I needed to call him!" I spat out, hoping what I was saying made sense to her.

"Mr. Larsen, I'll connect you with his office now," she responded, still maintaining her calm demeanor.

"Sergeant Ramirez," stated the deep voice on the other end of the line.

"Mr. Ramirez, this is Michael Larsen," I began quickly. But before I could get any more out, he interrupted me.

"Thank you for getting back to me," he responded. "As I stated on the message, Mrs. Larsen and Mrs. Simmons were in a car accident at approximately 12:35 today. Your wife was very seriously injured. She was life flighted to the Fresno Surgical Hospital on North Fresno Street. Do you know where that is, sir?"

"Yes! Yes, I do, Officer," I replied. "What about the other woman?"

There was a short pause before he answered, "I'm sorry, sir, but she didn't survive. I'm told your wife was in critical condition, so you should probably get to the hospital as quick as you can, sir."

I hung up the telephone without responding to him. Looking at Miriam, I said, "You go get Jacob and bring him to Fresno Surgical Hospital. Don't say anything to him except that his mother was in a car accident. We can call Mama and Papa from the hospital."

I turned away from her and started toward the door when Miriam yelled, "Is she going to be all right, Michael!"

"God, I hope so!" Then I added, "But I don't really know!" With those words, I was out the door and running back to my truck.

When I got to the hospital, I ran up to the attendant at the emergency room desk and asked her if she could tell me where Sarah was in the hospital. She made a call and sent me down a long hall to the surgery wing. She told me that a hospital staff member would meet me there.

I arrived at the surgery waiting area, but there was no one there waiting for me, just four people who were obviously waiting for word on another patient who I presumed was also in surgery. Stepping back into the hallway, I grabbed the first person I saw in a white coat, praying he worked in this department.

"My wife was in a car accident! She was brought here! Can you help me either find her or get someone who can update me on her condition?" I begged, holding firmly onto the lapels of his lab coat with both hands.

He had a fearful look in his eyes as he slowly removed my left hand from his coat and said, "Let me see what I can find out for you, sir. What's her name?"

"Sarah, her name is Sarah Larsen!" I shouted to him.

"And your name?" he continued, prying my other hand off his coat.

"Michael Larsen," I responded. "She's my wife!"

"Just give me a couple of minutes, Mr. Larsen, and I will try to help you," he said calmly. Before I could respond, he turned and jogged down the hallway, disappearing behind a door fifty feet or so from where I was standing.

While I waited for his return, Miriam and Jacob came running toward me. "What have you heard, Dad?" Jacob yelled, still a good distance from me. Once he reached me, he locked onto me, and we hugged each other with everything in our being.

"I haven't heard anything yet, son," I responded, kissing him on the top of his head as I spoke. Looking at Miriam, I said, "You'd better call Papa and tell them to get here as quickly as possible. Call your sister too!"

"I was hoping we would hear some news before calling either of them," Miriam responded.

I shook my head in agreement. "That's probably a good idea." We all stood there, each of us lost in our own nightmare, waiting for the doctor to come back with an update.

A couple of minutes later, a doctor came walking down the hall dressed in light blue scrubs. He was taking off his protective mask as he approached us. I could see deep red stains on his shirt and pants as he closed the distance between us.

His face was solemn as he spoke. "Mr. Larsen?"

"Yes, I'm Michael Larsen," I replied.

"And these are family members?" he asked flatly, displaying no emotion.

"Yes!" I responded. "This is my son and my wife's sister."

"Let's have a seat in the waiting room," he said, walking into the room ahead of us. Once there, he asked the other four people if we could have some privacy, suggesting they go have a cup of coffee in the cafeteria. They all rose from their seats and exited the room.

Once we were alone, he began again. "Please have a seat." He motioned for us to sit where the people had just left. Then he pulled up a chair and sat directly across from us.

"Your wife was very seriously injured when she was brought in today," he stated. "She had multiple fractures to her arms, legs, and spine."

A sickening feeling was immediately overwhelming me as I listened to him. I felt like I was going to throw up, listening to his explanation of the massive damage done to my poor wife.

"But our greatest concern was an injury to her spline and kidneys, which caused significant internal bleeding," he continued. "We thought we had stopped it, but while closing up the incision, her bleeding began again." His tone had changed, and I watched as tears began forming in his eyes. "Unfortunately, we couldn't stop the bleeding," he said, unable to hold my gaze.

He took a few second to let his words sink in before raising his eyes and looking me squarely in the face. "I'm so sorry," he said softly. "We weren't able to save her."

Miriam let out a sickening screeching cry as her head collapsed into her hands. She began sobbing uncontrollably.

Jacob's face went completely white as he sat there, not crying but, rather, in shock from what he'd just heard.

I felt physical pain pulsing through my chest as I sat there trying to comprehend a life without my beautiful Sarah. Snapping out of my haze, I reached over to Jacob and pulled him close to me. He was my priority now. He was my responsibility now. He was all I had left of his sweet mother—my wife. We held on to each other, and both began to cry as we realized the devastating loss we would have to deal with from this day forward.

The report from the Highway Patrol cited the cause of the accident to be Sue's fault. It appeared, based on skid marks and eyewitness testimony, that she had veered into oncoming traffic and was struck head-on by a fully loaded semitruck going the other way. The truck driver had sustained injuries as well, but they were not life threatening.

The first time I saw Jack Simmons, Sue's husband, was at the funeral home where our wives were both being prepared for burial. My first response was anger because his wife had killed my sweet Sarah. But seeing the hurt and loss in his own eyes, anger was quickly replaced with profound sorrow and pity. He had also lost someone dear to him—someone who could never be replaced—and he looked completely broken.

I slowly walked over to him as he silently stood over his wife's closed casket. He looked up and saw me coming. With tears streaking down his face, he grabbed me and pulled me into a strong embrace, all the while repeating over and over, "I'm so sorry, Michael! I'm so sorry!" We both stood there crying together as everyone else left the room to give us some privacy during this excruciatingly painful moment.

The funeral was attended by over 120 people, all there to pay their respects to my wonderful wife. Papa and Mama were crushed at the loss of their youngest daughter, and both wept openly throughout the funeral.

Papa clung to Jacob from that day forward when we would visit them and wouldn't let him out of his sight. It was as if Jacob was all that was left to remind him of his daughter, and he had to be close to him, had to touch him, had to talk with him. Jacob seemed to instinctively understand his grandparents needed to be by his side, and he accommodated them without reluctance every time we were all together.

Once Jack found out about the accident, he took it upon himself to all but move in with Jacob and me. He cleaned up after us, fixed our meals, and made sure we both ate daily. He tried to take our minds off our extreme grief by talking about everything under the sun except for Sarah. He always listened to both of us with a sympathetic ear and never criticized our feelings or thoughts. He was also grieving, but he seemed to put his grief on the back burner as he tended to our needs first. I don't know how Jacob and I would have gotten through this tragedy without Jack being there to support us.

Loss of a close family member is always hard. I don't know how many times various people had told me, "Time heals all wounds," after Sarah's death. But from personal experience, I can tell you that the phrase is a complete fallacy.

It had been almost two years, and Jacob and I were both still lost without the glue that held our family together. We spent as much time as possible together, but no matter what the activity, the joy seemed to be missing without Sarah.

Jack had become more like Jacob's uncle than just a friend of the family. He helped Jacob work on his Jeep and took him to movies, football, or basketball games. He had been a godsend, and in many ways, he'd replaced me in keeping Jacob entertained and loved as I immersed myself in my job at the new truck tire center we'd opened.

Jacob and I continued to visit Mama and Papa on the farm at least once, if not twice, a month. We spent most holidays with them and remained in close contact with the entire family.

Papa never got over the loss of his little girl. He didn't speak of Sarah too often in Jacob's presence because it always made him so emotional. But if he and I went out on the back patio, where we could have a drink and talk freely, we had many conversations about her, God, and why this had happened. He either ended up with tears streaming down his face or crying openly as we relived the highlights of her life together.

In one of those intimate conversations between the two of us, he told me he was looking forward to seeing Sarah in heaven. Looking up into the sky, he said, "A father is not supposed to outlive his children." Still staring at the puffy white clouds passing by, he continued. "I would give a million dollars to just go to sleep one night and wake up with Sarah sitting there waiting for me when I woke up."

On May 30, three days before the third anniversary of Sarah's death, Papa's prayers were answered. He had remarked to Mama that he hadn't been feeling well that day. In the late afternoon, he called and spoke with both his daughters and said he was just checking in on them. He also made a call to Jacob to say hi and ask how school was going.

Reflecting on the day, Mama said she recalled that it was odd for Papa to talk on the phone that much on any given day. He had ended each conversation with "I love you very much," which was not something he would normally say over the phone.

She said he was quiet during dinner, and after watching a little television, he wanted to go to bed early. Once in bed, he kissed her on the cheek, told her he loved her, cuddled up to her, putting his arm around her, and held her close as they both drifted off to sleep.

When Mama woke up the next morning, Papa appeared to be sleeping peacefully on his back, his hands on each side of him. Mama got up quietly, put on her clothes, and was headed to the kitchen to start the coffee brewing and making breakfast. She had been through this same routine thousands of times previously. She smiled down at her sleeping husband and decided to give Papa a quick kiss on the forehead on her way out of the bedroom.

The instant her lips touched his cold forehead, she realized he was gone. Quickly checking for a heartbeat and finding none, she crumpled onto the bedroom floor and began to wail in despair.

Later that morning, Miriam called me to share the bad news. After listening to her explain the events as they had unfolded, I felt a sense of peace knowing that God had answered the prayers of this good and faithful man. He hadn't suffered, and now he and Sarah were together again. I was very saddened by our loss of him but at the same time almost joyous that his prayers had been fulfilled.

A few weeks later, Mama moved in with Miriam and her husband. The farm was put up for sale, and all that was left for any of us were memories of better days.

Three months after Papa's death, Mama passed away. In her grief, she had almost completely stopped eating. She had become so skinny that she looked like a concentration camp victim. The doctors couldn't give a valid explanation of what had caused her death, but we all believed it was simply a broken heart that had taken her to be with Papa and Sarah.

When the will was read, Jacob and his cousins were left a substantial amount of money in separate trust funds. The cousins had complete access to their money because they were adults with families of their own. But Jacob would have to wait until he was twenty-five years old before he could collect his. It comforted me to know that Papa had made sure Jacob's financial future was secure as he started life on his own after college.

CHAPTER 12

As I had predicted, the new truck tire center was putting a strain on the finances of Master Tire Services. Truck tire, off-road, and industrial tire sales were up 30 percent year over year after our first six months of being open. Unfortunately, because we carried a much broader spectrum of products, we needed additional stock to meet our customer needs and Toshiba Tire requirements. The additional stockpile of merchandise slowed down our inventory turns-to-sales ratio—meaning, we were paying for more inventory each month before it was sold.

In that same first six-month period, our inventory on hand costs had soared by 154 percent. That meant our cash flow was all tied up in excess inventory, which had ballooned from $190,000 to $407,000. Even though sales looked great now and for the foreseeable future, we had almost instantly become cash poor within the business.

Mr. Lovering went to our long-term banker and was able to get an increase of $100,000 to our line of credit, which helped us pay other bills besides the tire bills and ensured we made payroll each week. But it quickly became obvious that something needed to change for our new venture to be viable.

Mike Lovering wanted to sell his way out of debt and asked that I hire two additional commercial salesmen, bringing our total to four salesmen plus myself.

Again, I disagreed with this approach because it created a significant increase to our monthly expense side with no real evidence that we could outrun the inventory increases. But he owned the company, so I did as I was directed.

Three weeks later, we had added two new three-quarter-ton pickups, fuel and insurance for those vehicles, and two wage guarantees for our newly hired salesmen of $3,500 a month each.

The balance sheet was moving in the wrong direction, and I was skeptical that we could correct it quickly enough to stay solvent.

However, in our first month under the new sales format, Mr. Lovering proved he had been correct with this aggressive strategy. Our sales had increased by 124 percent over the previous years, and our income was up substantially. Even with the additional expenses and added inventory, we ended the month in the black for the first time since opening our doors, albeit barely in the black.

There was finally a light at the end of the tunnel, and I started to believe that we could be successful with the truck tire center.

But additional sales meant additional labor, and we had to hire additional workers. More service trucks, more wages, increased benefits; it was a battle every month to stay in the black versus losing money once all the expenses were deducted.

At the end of our first full year with the truck tire center, we now had $637,000 in owned inventory, and we booked a profit of $31,000 for the year. Our profits were still tied up mostly in inventory, and we continued to struggle with cash flow on a monthly basis.

I asked Mr. Lovering if we could meet with the division manager for Toshiba Tire and try to come up with a better plan to help our cash flow. Mike agreed and set up the meeting.

During our meeting, we were able to get the approval to return about $200,000 worth of inventory for credit against future tire bills. Then Walt Frank, the divisional manager for Toshiba Tire, agreed to put a consignment of the most popular selling truck tires into our inventory.

We would be limited to having a maximum dollar amount of $100,000 in consignment inventory. That inventory still belonged to Toshiba Tire, but it was housed in our warehouse. Twice a month, we would pay for whatever we sold from the consignment, and new products would be shipped to us to replace those items sold. The meeting was a huge success, and in less than three hours, we had freed up $300,000 in useable cash for our business. Both Mr. Lovering and I were ecstatic with the results of our presentation.

After we concluded our meeting, Mr. Lovering asked me if I wanted to go have a drink with him at the Fresno Country Club. I thanked him for the invitation but said, "No, thank you." I explained to him that I already had plans with Jacob for the evening and I couldn't change them.

He said he understood as I walked him out to his car. We stood in the parking lot of the truck center, and he again congratulated me on how well I had prepared for our meeting. I thanked him one last time and then watched him get in his car and drive away.

I didn't really have any plans for the evening, but his invitation had immediately brought back the harsh words he'd spoken after I'd invited him and his wife to my home for dinner. I could almost hear them verbatim as I stood there declining his offer.

"I'm sorry, Michael, but my wife and I agreed years ago not to socialize with our employees. Socializing with employees creates feelings, and feelings can be dangerous if they affect those who work for you." I seriously doubted that we would ever be having drinks together.

I had been working six and sometimes seven days a week trying to make the truck tire center successful. With our cash flow issue finally solved, I felt comfortable that we were making great progress toward profitability and a sustained business model.

But I was tired, both physically and mentally. I hadn't taken more than a couple of days off, apart from Sarah's funeral, in almost three years. I knew I needed a vacation to rejuvenate my spirit, my drive, and most importantly, my relationship with Jacob. I also knew Mr. Lovering would have no issues with me taking off for a week or two because he had been practically begging me to take some time off for over a year.

So I began thinking about what I might do to put some fun back into Jacob's and my life. A smile started to form on my face as

I began to formulate a plan. That night at dinner, I asked Jacob if he had any plans for Friday night. After responding that he didn't, I asked him if he would like to go out to a nice dinner with Jack and me. He quickly responded that he would love to go.

After a couple of minutes of silence, he looked at me, concern in his eyes, and asked, "Is everything OK, Dad? I mean, you're not going to tell us that you're sick or dying, are you?"

I laughed at his comment but was touched by the concern. "No, no, no!" I replied. "There's nothing wrong with me! I've just been so busy at work that I haven't seen or spent any quality time with either of you. I just want to get caught up on what's going on in everyone's life!"

Jacob shook his head affirmingly and simply replied, "OK, that sounds great!"

Later in the evening, I called Jack, and he, like Jacob, was very excited at the prospect of the three of us getting together.

Jack arrived at our house promptly at 7:00 p.m. on Friday. We quickly became a room full of smiles, followed by a few hugs and warm greetings, and then we were ready to go.

Work had consumed me, and just being with two of my favorite people made me realize there was still room for fun and joy in my life. As we walked out the front door, my spirits and mood were the best they had been in months. I felt genuinely happy for the first time in a very long time.

We drove to the Parma Restaurant, parked our car, and were seated five minutes later. The Parma was a well-known Italian restaurant on North Palm Avenue, and it was one of Jack's favorite places to eat.

"Now this is what I'm talking about!" Jack said, as the waiter stepped to our table and offered us menus. I just smiled back, knowing both he and Jacob loved Italian food.

Once we had ordered our meals and had our drinks, Jack asked, "So what's this dinner all about, Michael?" Both he and Jacob were staring intently at me, waiting for an answer.

"Why does this have to be about anything?" I stated. "I haven't really spent any quality time with either of you lately, and I just wanted to decompress and see what's new in your lives."

They both smiled and I asked Jack, "So are there any new love interests in your life?"

Jack snickered as he responded, "Are you kidding! Every day I go to work at an all-male accounting firm and then coach a boys' basketball team for the YMCA four nights a week, and we play basketball games every Saturday. There's not a lot of time left for love interests!"

He took a drink of his wine before continuing. "I haven't even talked to a girl, except my mom, for at least two weeks!" Looking over at Jacob, he said, "Jacob, I think your dad and I are depending on you for all three of our love lives. Do you have anyone special in your world?"

"Naw!" he responded. "I've dated a couple of girls, but there isn't anyone special. Besides, girls are friggin' expensive! I'd rather spend my money on the Jeep!" He paused for a second and continued. "I guess the Jeep is my favorite girl right now."

We all chuckled, knowing he was telling the truth. Just then, two busboys brought out our dinners on large flat trays and began placing the food in front of us. It looked and smelled delicious. Jack said a quick prayer before dinner, and everyone went silent as we concentrated on the meals in front of us.

"Oh my god, I'm full!" Jack bellowed, pushing his chair away from the table and the remaining food on his plate.

"Me too!" I said, following his lead.

Jacob, however, was cleaning his plate using a piece of bread to get every drop of sauce off it, leaving the plate empty and almost spotless. He quickly looked over at the remaining food on both of our plates, trying to decide if there was anything of value left for him. Seeing nothing that appealed to him, he sat back and simply said, "That was good!"

As we sat there digesting our meals, I finally broke the silence. "Jack, do you have any vacation time available?"

"I have lots of vacation time," he responded with a chuckle. "I just don't have anywhere to go, anyone to go with, or enough savings to spend money on a vacation."

Turning to Jacob, I said, "How about you? Could you get away during spring break if something came up?"

"I suppose so," Jacob replied. "I'm pretty caught up on everything, and I don't have any plans for spring break yet. Why?"

"Well, I've been thinking about taking a cruise to Saint Thomas and the Virgin Islands this year. I've never been to the Caribbean Sea, and I think it would be fun. Do you want to go?"

"Of course, I do!" Jacob yelled. "That would be so fun!"

Looking over at Jack, I said, "How about you, big boy?"

Jack was immediately shaking his head from side to side. "Thanks for the offer, Michael, but I can't afford that right now. I appreciate you asking me, though."

"No one said you had to pay for it!" I responded. "If it didn't cost you anything, would you go with us?"

The stunned look on his face was priceless! I watched his eyes grow large as he realized what I was saying.

Before he could answer, Jacob jumped into the conversation. "That would be so awesome! You've got to come with us, Jack! Scuba diving, deep-sea fishing, beautiful suntanned girls, and all the food you can eat! How could you turn that down?"

Jack finally answered, "I can't do that! I can't let you pay for my vacation, Michael! I won't take advantage of you like that!"

"Take advantage!" I snapped back. "When Sarah passed, you were about the only person that kept the two of us sane. We will never be able to repay the friendship and kindness you showed us during those dark days."

"I could not agree more," Jacob interjected.

"Listen, Jack," I started again. "We haven't been anywhere since Sarah, and I think it's time for Jacob and me to start moving on with our lives. You're a part of this family, and I want you included in the trip. I have plenty of money, if you have the time, and you already said you have lots of vacation time available. So what do you say? Are we going to be the three musketeers on a Caribbean cruise, or are you going to ruin the vacation for all of us by saying no?"

I could see Jack was still struggling with his decision when Jacob spoke up again.

"Come on, Jack! This could be the trip of a lifetime, and we both want you there!" he stated enthusiastically.

Looking first to me and then to Jacob and finally back to me, Jack responded, "I can't believe you're doing this, but I don't see how I can turn down your generous offer! I sure don't want to ruin your trip! Yes, I'll go!"

Jacob jumped out of his chair and ran around the table, giving Jack a warm hug, not letting him get up from his chair. Then Jacob moved to me and did the same.

"Thank you, Dad!" he said. "This is really going to be fun! I can hardly wait!"

Six weeks later, as we started to board the cruise ship, Jack looked up toward the main deck, several stories above us, and said, "Holy shit, this is a big ship! I thought it would be large, but this thing is like a floating city!" Looking around and seeing several other people around us, Jack excused his language. "Pardon my French!" he said to an older man and woman who were only a couple of feet away. "I apologize, but I've never seen anything this big floating on water before!"

"It certainly is a monster!" the elderly gentleman responded, a smile on his face as he addressed Jack's comments.

The organization of the cruise ship crew was truly impressive. In less than three hours, our luggage had been taken off the dock and were delivered to our rooms. All 2,400 guests had boarded the ship, had had pictures taken with the captain, had been handed a drink of their choice, and were personally escorted to individual quarters. Once in our rooms, the crew member gave us a fifteen-minute orientation about the ship, our dinner times, and dress requirements for various meals. They also left a map of the ship and several brochures of available side trips when we stopped at various ports of call.

I had booked two rooms, one for Jack and one for Jacob and me. Both rooms had a living area with large sliding glass doors that led out to an open-air patio with a small table and two chairs. Sitting outside, you had an unobstructed view of the ocean and any points of interest on that side of the boat. We were on the sixth-floor deck, and the view was spectacular.

I walked out, leaned on the railing, and inhaled the salty sea air as we prepared to leave port. Looking down, I saw several crew members taking off the huge ropes that were holding us close to the docks and throwing them toward the ship. It appeared the ropes were being pulled into the boat by some kind of very strong wenches. The crew members all moved in unison, and the ship was set free from its confinement in a matter of a few minutes.

A short time later, Jack appeared on the balcony next to ours and grabbed his deck railing. Shaking his head from side to side, he smiled and said, "This ship is insane! This experience is going to be incredible! What a day! What a great start to our vacation!" I simply shook my head in agreement, unable to keep the smile off my face.

Just as Jack stopped speaking, a deep, bellowing whistle came from somewhere above us. Jack and I both jumped at the incredibly loud, deep noise. It was obviously meant to alert crew members and the harbor crew that we were about to leave port. Looking back down, we could hear the propellers starting to move as we watched the water on our side of the boat start to froth and move at an ever-increasing rate.

As we moved away from the dock, I was in awe of how skillful the captain and his crew were at moving this behemoth in such tight quarters. The ship moved backward for several minutes until we were in a larger opening of the harbor. The engines stopped for a minute and then reversed direction as the ship began to turn around slowly. Once completely turned, we headed out to sea, picking up speed after exiting the harbor barriers.

Jack and I had been watching for over an hour as we stood on our respective patio decks, taking in the whole experience. The water passing under and beside the ship made it increasingly noisy as we continued to pick up speed. Jack looked over at me and yelled, "Let's go do some exploring and get a drink!"

I shook my head in agreement and walked through my cabin, meeting Jack in the hallway outside our rooms. Jacob had already left the cabin and was exploring the ship on his own. I wondered if we would even cross paths knowing how large this ship was and how many people were on board.

We took one of the multiple elevators to the second deck, where the ship's map showed there were several sizes and types of lounges, a gambling room, and three specialty restaurants to eat in, and all open twenty-four hours a day. Even with as many guests and crew members as I knew were aboard the ship, it certainly didn't feel crowded anywhere we went.

"How about this?" Jack said, stopping at a bar with sculptures of sea horses and mermaids surrounding the entrance.

"Looks great!" I responded as we walked into the brightly lit room. There was a solid row of floor-to-ceiling windows on the far side of the room. They created a breathtaking view of the ocean as we methodically bobbed up and down in the crystal-blue water.

Sitting at a table next to the windows, we were immediately approached by one of several servers in the room. "What can I get for you, gentlemen?" he asked after introducing himself.

"Gin and tonic for me," I responded.

Before Jack could speak, Orlando asked, "Is there a particular gin you would prefer, sir?"

"What kind of gin do you have?" I responded.

Smiling back at me, he simply replied, "We have all of them, sir! Perhaps I should surprise you with one of my favorites. I can assure you that you won't be disappointed."

"Sounds great," I replied.

As Orlando turned his attention to Jack, Jack quickly stated, "I would like a Budweiser in a bottle with a glass, please."

"Coming right up!" he responded, turning and heading back to the bar.

After we finished our drinks, Jack and I spent the next few hours familiarizing ourselves with the various floors on the ship. There was nothing you could want for that wasn't on this boat. Bowling alleys; three pools that we'd found so far; a water park with tube slides on the main deck; zip lines; a movie theater; two casinos; a video arcade room; and more restaurants and bars than either of us had imagined. We decided that you could stay on the ship and never step off at any port of call and still not do everything that was available or eat at every location possible.

Tired, we both decided to return to our cabins for a quick nap before dinner. Once in the room, I saw Jacob soundly sleeping on the sofa with the television blaring while two teams from Mexico played soccer. I walked over and turned down the volume and then went into my bedroom and crashed on the bed.

"Well, this should be interesting," Jack said as we walked through the door to our first assigned dinner of the cruise. We were led to table number eight and were seated by a crew member with white-gloved hands and in a full-dress uniform. There were eight place settings, so we knew to expect other guests to arrive soon and sit with us. The table was beautifully set, and each place setting had more silverware than any of us were used to using. Jack leaned over and whispered to Jacob, "You should be safe if you start on the outside with forks, spoons, and knives and just work your way in as each course is served."

Jacob shook his head, signifying his understanding, but remained silent.

Our other dinner guests arrived as one large group—two women I guessed to be approximately my age and two younger women and a young man who all looked to be a bit older than Jacob by a couple of years. All three of us stood up to introduce ourselves.

"Hi, I'm Gabriella Chase," a gorgeous blonde said, reaching for Jack's hand, who was closest to her. "And these two belong to me," she said, pointing to the two people closest to her. "This is my daughter, Aria, and my son, Thomas."

Both gave the three of us a small wave when they were introduced.

Turning to the others in her party, she continued. "And this is my good friend Judy Harper and her daughter, Hana."

Jack took it upon himself to introduce the three of us. "I'm Jack Anthony, and this is Michael Larsen and his son, Jacob." He paused for a moment and continued. "It is a pleasure to meet everybody!"

"So what occasion brings you all on a cruise, Gabriella?" Jack asked after everyone had taken a seat.

"Please, just call me Gabby, that's what all my friends call me," she answered. "Well, there isn't really any special reason. Judy and I just decided it was time for a vacation and asked our kids if they wanted to come with us. How about you guys?"

Before Jack could respond, our waiter walked up and stood directly behind Jacob. "Good evening, ladies and gentlemen, my name is Benjamin, and I will be your server for all meals in this dining room while you are on our beautiful cruise. Before I go over the menu, I would like to take your drink orders, if I may."

He looked around the table and, seeing no objections, started with the ladies. Looking first at Gabby, he stated, "Mademoiselle."

She ordered a glass of Cabernet, and Judy quickly said she would have the same. Aria ordered a vodka and soda with no lime, while Hana ordered a screwdriver. Next, Thomas ordered a dry martini. The waiter looked to Jack, who said he wanted a Budweiser in a bottle with a glass.

Jacob quickly spoke up. "That's what I'll have as well!"

Jack and I both looked intently at Jacob but said nothing. Finally, I said, "Make that three beers, please." Jacob gave me a sheepish smile and quickly looked away.

Benjamin bowed at the waist, thanked us for our orders, excused himself, turned, and left to retrieve our drinks. Aria, Thomas, Hana, and Jacob quickly engaged in conversation. Within minutes, you would have thought that they were all close friends who'd come on this trip together. It brought a smile to my face as I watched the four of them interacting with each other.

Jack was talking almost nonstop to Judy and Gabby. It felt as though he was trying to set himself up for a date with one or the other. They were smiling back at him, nodding their heads affirmingly at everything he said, but appeared slightly uncomfortable with his aggressiveness. I also noticed they were both drinking their wine faster than one would normally expect. I wasn't sure if they just liked to drink or if they needed to catch a buzz to tolerate Jack's verbal assault.

When Jack stopped talking long enough to take a drink of his beer, Gabby turned her attention to me and asked, "How about you, Michael? What do you do for a living, and what prompted you to book a cruise?"

I grinned as I started to address her questions. "Well, I work in Fresno, California, for a company called Master Tire Service. I manage a truck tire center for them."

"Isn't that a Toshiba Tire–sponsored truck tire center?" Gabby asked, cutting into the conversation.

"Yes! Yes, it is!" I responded. "How do you know that?"

"I've heard of your company before," she stated, smiling at me. "I'm an executive assistant for the northwest divisional manager for the Toshiba Tire Company in Portland, Oregon, and your company's name has come up a couple of times at our divisional meetings."

"How unbelievable is that!" I responded. "What do you suppose the odds are that two complete strangers would be placed at the same table, on a cruise ship, from different areas of the country, working for the same tire supplier?" I was smiling and shaking my head in disbelief as I talked. "Do you know the divisional manager in Southern California?"

"I sure do," she responded. "I probably talk to Walt Frank at least once a week when he calls to speak with my boss, John Warren." She continued. "We don't have meaningful conversations, but he is always cordial and friendly on the phone."

"As far as the odds of us meeting randomly here, right now, I would say they are about 100 percent," she said, smiling.

I returned her smile. "Maybe it's karma," I joked.

"Or perhaps it's destiny," she stated, her smile turning mischievous.

I felt my face flushing at her innuendo as our eyes remained locked. She was quite beautiful, and I was further drawn in as I held the gaze of her gorgeous green eyes.

Jack and Judy had been listening to our conversation intently and were now looking at each other as smiles formed on both of their faces. During my short conversation with Gabby, it appeared that we had unintentionally been divided into two distinct couples, Jack and Judy, and Gabby and me.

Dinner was served, and everyone at the table got to know a little bit about each other. Thomas had just graduated from Portland State University with a business degree and wasn't sure what he wanted to do with his life yet. Aria was in her sophomore year at the University of Oregon and was a communications major. She wanted to work in television as either a sportscaster or weather commentator. Hana was the quietest of the younger group. She had quit college after her first year and now worked at a high-end retail store. She and Aria had been best friends since grade school, and she seemed to be as much a part of Gabby's family as she was Judy's daughter.

After I finished my dessert and a great cup of coffee, I decided I needed to work off some of the calories I'd just consumed. Pushing myself away from the table, I said, "Well, ladies and gentlemen, I enjoyed our dinner and getting to know a little about each of you, but I think I'm going to do a little exploring and walk off some of this food."

As I was raising myself up from my chair, Gabby asked, "Would you like some company?" Smiling at me, she continued. "I could use a walk too!"

I felt myself flushing red at her request. I don't know why, but I looked over to Jacob, who was now smiling along with us.

"That is a great idea! I don't want you to be my anchor all night!" he said.

Everyone at the table chuckled at his comment. "Besides, the four of us already have plans for our first night of partying!"

Looking back to Gabby, I said, "I would love some company." Looking over to Jack, I asked, "Do you and Judy want to join us?"

Jack shook his head no. "Thanks, Michael, but I'm more of an after-dinner-drink guy than I am an after-dinner-walk person." Looking over to Judy, he asked, "Can I buy you a drink, Judy?"

She laughed and responded, "You know that all the drinks on the ship are free, don't you?"

Looking a little embarrassed, Jack replied, "No, I actually didn't know that." After a short pause, he said, "But if that's the case, I'd like to buy you anything you want to drink! Nothing but the best!"

She shook her head from side to side and simply said, "I'll have a drink with you, big spender!" Thirty seconds later, we were all up and going in different directions from the dining room.

As Gabby and I walked down the hallway from the dining room, I asked her if she'd done any exploring yet.

"Not really," she responded. "But this isn't my first cruise, so I pretty much know how the ship is laid out."

"Well, then, to save me from embarrassing myself, why don't you be the guide and lead the way and I'll just follow along?"

"Fine with me," she answered. The mischievous smile returned to her face as she continued. "Try to keep up! I'll stop when we come to something interesting to talk about, OK?"

"OK," I replied. For the next two hours, she familiarized me with the top three decks of the ship. I became completely absorbed in her tour. There was so much to do! So many beautiful staircases, ballrooms, restaurants, and boutiques. I found where the best twenty-four-hour restaurants were, where the medical center and hospital were located, and where the evening entertainment shows and dance venues were found.

Having walked off our dinner and not wanting to see another level of the ship, I asked Gabby if she would like to sit on the top deck for a few minutes. She said, "Sure."

We had only been seated for a few minutes when a crew member walked up to us and asked if he could bring us anything. The speed of our ship cutting through the ocean created a pretty good wind, and with the sun going down, I knew we would probably start feeling a real chill in the air soon.

"Do you make hot drinks?" I asked.

"Yes, we do, sir," he responded, bending slightly at the waist.

"Could you make us two hot buttered rums, please?"

Bowing again, he said, "Right away, sir. Will there be anything else?"

I looked over at Gabby, who shook her head no and responded, "No, thank you. Just the two drinks."

After he left and we were alone again, Gabby said, "I haven't had one of those in years! We used to drink them when we went skiing at Mount Bachelor."

I smiled and asked, "Who are *we*?"

"The kids, their father, and I," she answered.

"Why didn't the kid's father come on the trip?" I asked. I realized it was too personal and an intrusive question the second the words were out of my mouth. Trying to undo my invasion of her privacy, I quickly stated, "You don't have to answer that! It's none of my business, and I shouldn't have asked!"

"No, it's OK," she said, reaching over and touching my arm with her hand. "I know you were just being curious."

The server returned with our drinks before she could say more. We both thanked him, received his customary half bow, and then watched as he walked away.

"Cheers!" I said, raising my mug in her direction.

"Cheers!" she responded, clinking her mug against mine. We both took a drink of the hot liquid, and she murmured, "Mmmm, that is delightful!"

I turned to watch the sun disappearing into the sea, and Gabby did the same. As we sipped our drinks, the sun went from a bright yellow to orange and finally turned into a fiery red half sphere as it quickly sunk into the ocean at the horizon. Nature's show, more magnificent than any fireworks display I'd ever seen, had only lasted twenty minutes, but it had been spectacular!

With the deck, walkways, and pool all now lit up only by the ship's lighting, their effects seemed to change the look of our surrounding. Everything glowed as the lights hit the polished railings and bounced off the teak flooring. It was beautiful.

"This is unbelievably gorgeous," Gabby finally said, still watching day turn into night.

Looking over at her, the light highlighting her features, she looked fabulous as day turned to dusk. Her blond hair shimmered and looked as though streaks of light had been added to her already stunning tresses. There were shadows accentuating her high cheekbones and eyes. She was the vision of a Greek goddess sitting there looking back at me. I have no idea what came over me as I mouthed, "No, you're gorgeous!"

She smiled sheepishly before responding. "Thank you!" she stated softly and then continued. "Tell me the truth, Michael, how many girls do you think have heard those words from you in the last three years?" The mischievous smile returned as she waited for my response.

"None," I answered flatly, the smile leaving my face as I looked down at my hands cupped around my mug. "My wife, Jacob's mother, was killed in a car accident a little over four years ago. To tell you the truth, I've spent more time with you here than I have with all the women that I've known combined over the last four years. I haven't been on a date or, for that matter, had a meaningful conversation with someone of the opposite sex since Sarah's death."

Looking up from my hands and into Gabby's face, I said, "I'm so sorry for telling you that! My life is not your problem! That's way too much personal information to spew out to someone you've only known for a few hours! I apologize! I'm not very good at this, and I feel like I'm making a fool of myself."

Rising to my feet and putting my hand out to help her up, I said, "Why don't I walk you back to your deck, and we can just call it a night before I trip over my tongue some more!"

She pulled softly on my hand. "Sit down for a minute, please."

I did as she instructed, and she kept hold of my hand as she began to speak. "I'm sorry about my comment, and I'm so sorry for your loss. I know how painful that is, and I can tell you that it will become a little less painful with time." She was holding the palm of my hand in hers as she placed her other hand on top of mine, squeezing it softly with both of hers.

"My husband, Jim, was in construction, and he was killed in an accident about ten years ago. I moved from Anchorage, Alaska, to Portland after his death and started a new life for my kids and myself. It was six years before I went out on my first date. I still don't date much, with work and my involvement in the kids' lives,"—she chuckled—"and their drama. There never seems to be time for a relationship."

"I'm sorry for your loss as well," I responded. I realized the mood had become too somber for two people who'd just met on a vacation cruise. "Now that we know more than we should about each other, what do you say we start off tomorrow on a different foot and have some fun! Have you ever been parasailing?" I asked.

"No!" she quipped. "I don't know if I'm ready for that!"

"Please have breakfast with me in the morning. Then we can go watch people do it first! If you're not too chicken, we can try it after that. My treat!"

She gave me a playful push and said, "Yeah, well, how many times have you been parasailing?"

"I've never done it!" I replied. "But it's time we both did something out of our comfort zone, don't you think?" She just looked at me, fear and intrigue both obvious in her gaze. "Come on!" I said. "You and I deserve some fun! So let's check this off the bucket list!"

We walked to the elevator in the middle of the decks lobby, and I hit the number six for my deck, while she hit floor number seven. When the door opened, we stepped into the empty elevator, and the door closed behind us.

"I'll meet you up on the top deck, by the elevator, at nine o'clock sharp," she said as the door opened for floor six.

"That's what I'm talking about!" I said, starting out of the elevator door.

She gripped my arm with both her hands and pulled me part way back into the elevator. Pulling me down, she kissed me on the cheek and said, "I've had a really great time, Michael. Good night." Then she let go of me, and the door between us closed.

I stood there staring at my reflection in the high polished brass elevator door for a minute before turning to head down the hallway to my cabin. My heart was beating a hundred miles an hour, and feelings I hadn't felt in years were rushing to the surface of my consciousness.

But what about Jacob? How would he feel about me spending time with someone other than his mother? Was it too soon after Sarah's death to have these feelings? Could anything good come from developing a relationship with a person you met on a vacation cruise? Twenty minutes later, I was still struggling with those and many more questions as I drifted off to sleep.

Gabby was tastefully dressed as she stepped out of the elevator the next morning. She was wearing a peach-colored blouse and khaki shorts with matching peach sandals and handbag. She smiled broadly as she made her way to me.

"You look beautiful!" I said as she approached.

"Thanks!" she responded with a note of cheer in her voice.

"Did you bring a bathing suit?" I asked, wondering if she had prepared for my suggested venture.

"I'm wearing it!" she responded.

Looking into her eyes, I said, "I'm proud of you! I didn't know if you would do this or not!"

"I'm proud of me too! But I would be less than honest if I didn't tell you that I am scared as hell! I didn't hardly sleep at all last night thinking about what could go wrong today—flying off the back of a twelve-story cruise ship with a parachute strapped to my ass!" She smiled quickly again and continued. "But I'm here!"

I chuckled as we made our way to the closest breakfast restaurant and were seated almost immediately. After a light breakfast, we sat there looking at each other, still smiling like a couple of teenagers with their first loves, as we sipped our coffee.

"Gabby," I began as we continued to stare into each other's eyes, "I haven't been kissed by anyone outside of my family for a very long time. I didn't really have time to react before the elevator door closed, but I wanted you to know that I very much enjoyed it."

She looked away shyly but made no reply.

"I have to confess that I couldn't stop thinking about you until I fell asleep last night," I continued. "If I'm making you uncomfortable, I apologize, but I want you to know I really had a great evening."

"Me too," she responded timidly.

Changing the subject, I asked, "Well, are you ready to go give this a try?"

The smile disappeared from her face as she responded, "Not really! But I'll do it because I said I would."

We watched several guests go off the rear deck of the ship and slowly rise into the air. There was a light morning breeze, and the huge parachute looked very stable as it trailed behind the ship. Finally, it was our turn, and the crew members strapped each of us into our harness.

As we sat there waiting for the line to be let out, freeing us from the deck, Gabby reached over and tightly grabbed my hand. I could see the fear in her eyes, and I tried to reassure her with a faint smile. "This is going to be fun!" I said as we were lifted off the deck by the first gust of wind.

Gabby let out a little scream and clamped even tighter on my hand. Two or three minutes later, we were 150 feet above and behind the cruise ship. We were far enough away that the only sound was the slight whistle of the wind as we passed through it. I quickly discovered that we could speak to each other without yelling.

"How are you doing?" I asked, noticing she was now looking all around us.

Still holding my hand, she replied, "This is so cool! I'm not afraid anymore, and the views are spectacular!" She then went on, "Thank you for helping me have the courage to try this. It's the most fantastic experience I've ever had!"

I simply smiled back and squeezed her hand for a second. Then we were both lost in our own worlds as we soared behind the mighty ocean liner and gazed at the wonderful sights all around us.

As the ship's crew began winding us in, we both wanted to stay airborne longer. Gabby looked over at me and quickly blurted out, "Maybe we could do this again before the end of the cruise?"

I smiled at her excitement and answered, "I think that's a great idea!"

As we got closer and closer to the deck, we noticed that all the kids were standing in line, watching us being reeled in. I'd forgotten that we were still holding hands but, realizing it now, decided to remain in each other's grasp.

Once back on the deck and freed from our harnesses, we walked over to where our children were standing in line. They all started talking over each other and congratulating us on our bravery for parasailing.

Aria was the most vocal. "Mom, in a million years, I never thought you would have the courage to do that!"

Gabby reached over and took my hand in hers. "I had to prove to Michael that I wasn't chicken." Then she looked up at me lovingly.

I broke her gaze and noticed all the kids had smiles on their faces as they silently watched our interaction. Jacob winked at me and gave me a quick thumbs-up, signifying his approval. We told them to have fun and agreed to talk about our experiences at dinner that night.

Gabby and I slowly strolled to the largest pool on the deck and decided to catch some sun while we reflected on the morning's accomplishments. Gabby removed her blouse and shorts, revealing her bathing suit. I tried not to stare but couldn't help myself. She had on a one-piece dark blue bathing suit that complimented her figure perfectly. I had my first glimpse of her tanned, muscular legs, well-proportioned bust line, and shapely hips, which were only further accentuated by a very tiny waist. She was breathtakingly beautiful!

As I took off my own shirt and shorts, I regretted that I hadn't spent more time working out and better toning my body before coming on this cruise. I wasn't fat, but I was nowhere near the perfect build I saw beside me. For the first time, she saw the multiple scars on my left arm but said nothing about it. She smiled and we sat down on our lounge chairs, letting the warm Caribbean breeze blow over us.

We both had sunglasses on, and I had just closed my eyes and was almost asleep when I felt her hand softly grab mine as we lay there. I couldn't keep the smile off my face as I took hold of her hand and held it in my own. We played in the pool, had several drinks, lay in the sun, and lazily enjoyed our afternoon together.

At dinner that night, everyone talked about their day's adventures. Jacob and Aria had drunk a little too much and had retired to their respective cabins for a late afternoon nap prior to coming to dinner. Hana and Thomas had spent most of the day in the pool, and it was obvious that both were badly sunburned. Jack and Judy had spent some time at the pool as well, but they decided to go have massages in the afternoon, after a late lunch. Everyone was having fun and seemed to be getting along fabulously.

We were going to be docking on Saint John's Island sometime before daylight, and everyone was getting off the ship to explore the island. Jack, Jacob, and I had signed up for a snorkel tour on one of the smaller islands that would leave the main island at 1:00 p.m. and be back to the ship before 6:00 p.m.

Jack turned to Judy and asked if she wanted to join us. She looked at Hana and then to Gabby before finally responding, "That sounds pretty fun. Sure, I'll go!"

"What about the rest of you?" I said. "Why don't we all go? My treat!"

The kids were all in favor of the outing, but Gabby was hesitant. "I can't let you pay for all of us!" she said sternly.

"I'll make you a deal," I quipped. "I'll pay for the snorkeling, and you can pay for lunch and drinks! Will that work?" She reluctantly agreed, and Jack excused himself from the table to go make the additional arrangements.

I smiled to myself, knowing lunch and drinks were included in the excursion package. But nobody else needed to know that.

The dinner was great, the conversation light, and everyone was tired. We all agreed to go to bed early and save ourselves for tomorrow's adventures. Saying good night, we all headed to our rooms. Before entering the elevator, I asked Gabby if I could speak to her for a moment.

"Of course," she responded, a worried look crossing her face. We walked outside the ship, and I stopped at the railing, turned, and kissed her with all the pent-up passion I was feeling. She wrapped her arms around me and gave as well as she got while we stayed locked together in the moon light. Pulling away from her finally, I said, "That's really all I wanted to say."

She pulled my face back to hers and said, "Then say it again! Only this time, say it like you mean it!" The second kiss left me breathless as I looked down to watch her eyes slowly open as our lips parted. We both smiled, turned, and walked back to the elevator in silence. Once the elevator stopped at my floor, I pulled her hand up to my lips and softly kissed it before exiting the elevator.

"I'm looking forward to tomorrow," I said as the door closed, giving her no time to respond. I felt like I was walking on clouds as I quietly entered my berth.

Everyone was up and ready to go early the next morning. Jack, Jacob, and I ate a quick bran muffin and had a cup of coffee on the main deck. We were now fully fueled and anxious to step on dry land at our first island destination.

Judy, Gabby, and their kids found us before we disembarked, and we all exchanged "Good mornings." Gabby looked strikingly beautiful in her lime-green top, deep purple Bermuda shorts, and a wide-brimmed purple hat with a matching bag full of beach towels and, I assumed, the usual girl stuff. She walked over to me, a smile on her face, and leaned in to kiss my cheek. I could feel everyone's eyes on us as we clasped hands, but I didn't really care what they were thinking now. I just felt happy and grateful to be here with her today. I had already decided we were going to have a fantastic day.

Once on land, we planned to meet back at the snorkel boat by 12:45 p.m. Then we split up into groups. The four youngsters decided to explore together. Jack and Judy wanted to go into the open market downtown, while Gabby and I opted to walk down on the waterfront and look through the various tourist traps.

We each bought a couple of small souvenirs, which Gabby put in her large beach bag. Time passed quickly as we walked and looked around, all the while holding each other's hands. We started back toward the cruise ship at noon and stopped at a street taco vendor for a quick lunch. As we arrived at the excursion boat, we realized we would be part of a much larger group than we had anticipated. There were about sixty people by the boat waiting to board. Five or ten minutes after we arrived, all the kids as well as Jack and Judy showed up and found us.

Once everyone was on the boat, the captain, a very jovial, tanned Mexican gentleman, picked up a microphone and welcomed all of us aboard in perfect English. He spoke about the history of the area and wrapped in a few corny jokes as we left the bay and headed out into the open ocean. All the guests seemed quite excited as we cruised through the rough water in a much smaller boat than our ocean liner.

The captain asked if anyone would like to have a drink the traditional island way. Not waiting for an answer, several crew members moved forward with leather bota bags filled with some type of fluid. He explained that the bota bags were leather bags filled with margaritas, which would help loosen everyone up for the day's adventures.

He asked his crew members to demonstrate how these vessels worked. Each crew member took off the lid to the short snout at the front of the bag, held it above their head, and squeezed the bag. A stream of liquid shot out from the bag into their open mouths from a foot away. After several swallows, the crew stopped pressing the bags, and the streams stopped.

"Who wants to be first?" the captain asked, looking back through the guests seated behind him. Since no one volunteered, he pointed to a passenger and asked her to be adventurous and give it a try.

"How about you, senorita? Are you brave enough to try?" he said, pointing at Aria, who was seated next to Gabby.

Aria's face turned crimson almost immediately. Being a good sport, she replied, "Sure, I'll try it!" A crew member approached her, and she stood up, reaching for the bag.

"No, no, no!" the captain said loudly. "You just open your mouth, and we will squeeze the bag for you. All you have to do is swallow!"

Aria put her hands down and opened her mouth. With a smile on his face, the young crew member lifted the bag above her head and began to squeeze. She swallowed as quickly as she could, but the liquid just kept coming. Finally needing to breathe, she put her hand up to stop, and the crew member stopped squeezing the bag. She had been drinking for almost a minute, and everyone on board knew the amount of alcohol she had consumed would hit her in short order.

"Very good, senorita!" the captain yelled. "Who wants to be next?"

Several hands went up throughout the boat. I had not expected it, but both Jack and Jacob had raised their hands. More shocking for me was to see Gabby raise her hand as well.

"Come on, Michael!" she teased. "There's nothing wrong with getting a little buzz before we hit the island." And with that, she took hold of my hand and lifted it high in the air with hers.

About 80 percent of the guests on the boat drank from the bota bags. As time went on, the crew members squeezed the bags longer and longer for each guest. Our entire group participated; Jack, Thomas, and Jacob drank more than once by the time we docked at the island's pier.

As we stepped ashore, I did feel a pretty good buzz from the margaritas. Looking at Jack, Thomas, and Jacob, it was obvious they were well on their way to being inebriated. They were laughing a little too loudly and were weaving and wobbling as they made their way off the pier and onto the beach.

The girls seemed to be in the best shape of all of us as we gathered around a stand where we were each given a mask, a snorkel, and fins. After a safety talk, the tour guide gave us a basic idea of where the best snorkeling was around the small island and told us to be back to the pier on time to make the return trip home.

The four youngsters immediately went into the water, only a few feet from where we were standing. Jack and Judy, and Gabby and I watched them for a few minutes with smiles on our faces as they played in the water before walking away from the group. Then Jack and Judy set down their gear about a hundred yards away and headed for the water.

Gabby and I began walking hand in hand east on the expansive beach before us. We talked, looked for seashells, and watched the waves breaking only feet from where we were walking. As the tides washed the water over our feet and then back to the sea, I was struck by how warm the water felt on my legs and feet. The sun was starting to emit more heat as we casually continued our journey in the clean, breezy ocean air.

"How about stopping here?" Gabby said, setting her bag down on the warm sand.

"Looks great!" I replied, looking back to where we had just come from. I could still see people in the distance, but just barely. We had walked farther than I'd thought. Looking at my watch, I made note of what time we needed to leave our little paradise to get back to the boat on time.

Gabby had pulled out a light blanket and spread it out on the sand. Sitting down on it, she began removing items from her bag—a large beach towel, a nice bottle of wine and two glasses, two bottles of water, and two kinds of sunscreen for us to use.

"That's a lot of stuff for one bag!" I kidded. "I should have been carrying your bag, and you should have been carrying the snorkel gear. I think your load was much heavier than mine!"

"That's OK," she responded, rising to her feet. "I need the weight-bearing exercise at my age." First kicking her shoes off next to the blanket, she took off her blouse and then her shorts, revealing a bright orange bikini that gave me an unencumbered view of her figure. She had a nice tan, and I was completely awestruck by the perfection of her body as she sat back down on the blanket next to me.

Reaching over and picking up one of the sunscreens, she handed it to me and lay down on her stomach. "Would you put some sunscreen on me, please?"

I wanted to yell, "Hell, yes, I will!" but said, "Sure! I'd be glad to." As my greasy hands moved over the various areas that needed protection from the sun, I could feel my pulse beating faster and faster. I had covered every sun-exposed area, but I didn't want to stop touching her. Finally, she rolled over on her back and flatly stated, "And now the front."

I began applying lotion on her stomach first and slowly rubbed it into her flawless skin. It took every bit of restraint that I had not to jump her as I became more and more aroused by looking at and touching her taut body.

After a couple of minutes, Gabby smiled up at me and removed her sunglasses. "Am I imagining things, or are your hands shaking?" she asked, her mischievous smile still there.

Pulling my hands away from her as though I'd just touched a hot stove, I apologized. "I'm sorry, but, yes, I am shaking a little. It's just that I haven't touched a beautiful woman in so long! And you are so stunning lying there I can hardly control myself!"

She reached over, putting her hand directly on the crotch of my shorts, and said, "Oh my, you are happy to see me!" Taking her hand away, she sat up, unhooked her bikini bra, and let it fall to her side. "What can we do to relieve all that pent-up tension I feel in you?"

Instantly, our lips locked, and moments later, we were lost in the euphoria of lovemaking. We made passionate love, rested, drank some wine, and then ran into the ocean, both of us completely naked and needing to cool off. When we were chest deep and used to the feel of the water on our sun-drenched skin, she put her arms around my neck and lifted her legs, locking them around my waist as we kissed again. Before the kiss was finished, we were making love again, this time as wave after wave slowly washed over us in the clear blue water.

As we were walking back toward the pier, I started laughing softly. "What's so funny?" Gabby asked.

"I was just thinking what a waste it was to carry all this snorkel gear out here! Even though this is the best snorkeling trip I've ever been on, the gear was pretty useless."

She smiled up at me and said, "Well, we should get our stories straight for the kids. We saw a few beautiful fish and snorkeled over a reef full of coral and stuff."

"Sounds great!" I responded. As we started to approach the group, I stopped for a minute, and Gabby turned toward me. "Gabby," I began, "as silly as it sounds, I want to tell you that I'm falling in love with you."

She started shaking her head from side to side and boldly responded, "I don't know if you can fall in love with someone in three days! I have very strong feelings for you as well, but let's see if anything comes of this once we are back home or if it's just a quick vacation romance we both needed right now."

Although her words hurt my feelings a little bit, I knew she was correct. These were perfect conditions for a romantic interlude. I smiled back at her and responded, "Given the circumstances, I would like it if you assumed that I love you with all my being for the next seven days. We can see where it goes from there." We softly kissed and continued back to our rendezvous point to join the others in the group.

Except for our nightly dinner in the formal dining room, I rarely saw Jack and Jacob the rest of the trip. Jacob moved out of my room and into Jack's so Gabby and I could have some privacy. Gabby spent all her days and most of her nights with me. We'd become inseparable, and it was obvious to all our friends and family members.

I'd had a conversation with Jack and Jacob individually about my relationship with Gabby. Both were thrilled that I had found someone I cared for so strongly. Their approval was very important to me, and their acceptance of Gabby helped solidify my feelings for her.

As we sat in the formal dining room on our last night aboard the ship, there was a somber mood around the table. It was obvious to all that Gabby and I were sad to be saying good-bye tomorrow. Everyone was quiet as we ate what was to be our official and figurative last meal together. Jack finally broke the silence and proposed a toast.

"Here's to meeting people who become your friends from other places. I hope that we can all continue to stay in touch and remember this glorious cruise!"

"Here, here!" Jacob stated, raising his glass toward the center of the table.

"Cheers!" everyone else responded, raising their glasses and then drinking from them.

Jack looked at Judy and said, "Why don't we go around the table and each person say what their favorite thing or activity was in the last ten days?" Everyone seemed to like the idea, and Jack pointed to Aria first. "Why don't we start with you, Aria?"

"OK!" she responded excitedly. "Well, for me, it was probably the day we went snorkeling! I was the first to drink from the bota bag, and I got a little tipsy and had a great time in the water." She stopped and then began again. "But seeing the ear-to-ear smile on Mom's face this whole trip has made my trip very special!"

I looked over at Gabby, who had tears welling up and spilling over as she listened to her daughter. "Thank you, sweetheart," Gabby said softly.

I felt like crying with her, but before I did, Jack pointed to Judy and said, "It's your turn next, Judy!"

We went around the table, and everyone talked about their most fun experiences, bringing smiles and laughter to the table. When it was Gabby's turn, she said she really loved the parasailing, but the snorkeling was by far her favorite activity of the trip. She looked over at me and said, "So many beautiful fish and a gorgeous coral reef. That day was beyond anything I'd ever dreamed of it being!" The mischievous smile was on her face as I smiled back at her.

"Well, you're the last one. What about you, Michael?" Jack asked.

"This trip could be summed up in one word for me," I said. "Gabby! I've loved our time together."

CHAPTER 13

It had been four months since the Caribbean cruise, and the weather in Fresno had turned brutally hot. Large fires were popping up all around the county, and we hadn't had any measurable rain in over ninety days. Forested land and entire communities were being destroyed by a deluge of disastrous blazes. It was beginning to have a very negative affect on our business since all logging was now shut down because of the fire danger in the woods.

With farming in its peak harvesting cycle and log trucks filling up the mills with fresh-cut timber, August had always been our best sales month of the year. But the extended dry spell and accompanying blazes had created drought conditions that the farmers and loggers were virtually unable to overcome. As a result, our business was down almost 40 percent from the previous year. With only one week left in the month, we knew we were going to lose money in August for the first time since being in business. We just didn't know how much.

Toshiba Tire announced they were merging with Tahatsu Tire Company in the late summer of the year. This was a big deal in the tire world. The two companies turning into one made them one of the largest tire companies in the world. They were also now backed by the Bank of Japan, and their resources were bottomless. I didn't know at the time if this corporate merge would affect our company, but I was about to find out.

Mr. Lovering was spending more time than normal in his downtown office. At first, I thought it was because it was too hot outside to play golf. But with his repeated daily calls asking for sales updates, I soon realized he was genuinely worried about the solvency of his empire.

He had been involved in two other businesses; one he'd sold to free up money for the tire company earlier in the year. He was also a partner in a real estate development project, and he was in the process of trying to sell his shares to the other investors in that business as well. It was obvious that he was putting all his eggs in one basket, hoping to keep his tire company creditworthy and solvent.

However, his continual micromanaging of our business made it even more difficult for our sales force to be productive. He had started coming to our sales meeting and demanding better results from the team. Often, he ended his sales presentations with veiled threats of staff reductions if we couldn't improve our sales numbers.

Once he left the meetings, I usually spent the next hour trying to calm the team down by ensuring their jobs weren't in jeopardy. I could feel the stress he was under, but his participation in our meetings was not only unnerving but also dangerous, and I feared we would lose some very talented salespeople if his rhetoric didn't soften.

I was working harder than I ever had, trying to improve our company's bottom line. But the business wasn't consuming a 100 percent of my life. My relationship with Gabby had only gotten stronger since we'd met on the cruise. We spoke at least once a day, usually in the evenings so we could stay on the phone for an hour or two and talk about the events of both of our days. She had become my sounding board and the source of my sanity during the high-pressured workweek.

I worked six days a week every other week. On the weeks that I only worked five days, I would leave right from the truck tire center and drive through the night to be with Gabby in Portland. It was a 750-mile trip that was supposed to take eleven and a half hours, but I usually made it in closer to nine hours. I would leave the truck tire center at 6:00 p.m., or earlier if possible, and I would pull into Gabby's driveway by 3:00 or 4:00 a.m. on Saturday.

We would spend the weekend together smiling, laughing, eating, making love, and sleeping when we were too exhausted to do anything else. Then I would leave for home at 4:00 or 5:00 p.m. on Sunday.

Twice we'd decided to meet in Lincoln City on the Oregon coast. We spent those weekends walking on miles of sandy white beaches and enjoying the seafood at our favorite little restaurant, Mo's Fish and Chowder House.

I hated the drive to and from Portland, but I lived for those weekends to be with Gabby. They rejuvenated my spirit and continued to strengthen the bond between us.

It was late September before we saw some much-needed rain in Fresno. After a week of solid rain, flowers and green grass began to reappear where only parched earth had existed just seven days before. The rains also had a calming effect for farmers, loggers, and business owners who could finally get back to work.

In the middle of the month of October, Gabby took a week's vacation and came to Fresno to stay with me. It was wonderful. We had dinner with Jack and Jacob one night, and everyone caught up on what was going on in each other's lives.

During dinner at the Parma Restaurant, Jack nonchalantly asked, "So when are you two lovebirds going to move in together?"

We both stopped eating and looked at each other with blank stares, his question catching both of us by surprise. Up to this point in our relationship, we had avoided this two-thousand-pound-elephant-in-the-room conversation. We had never worked up the courage to talk about being together permanently in either Portland or Fresno.

I had invested years in developing a career at Master Tire, and the thought of leaving it all behind and starting over somewhere new wasn't very appealing to me. In that same vein, Gabby loved her job and her boss, and she was in no hurry to leave either of them behind to move to Fresno.

"I don't have an answer to that question, Jack," I responded after several seconds of uncomfortable silence.

"Something would have to change for either one of us to make a move," Gabby continued. "I think I speak for both of us," she continued, sliding her hand over to mine and grasping it. "The day will come when we are together, but it will definitely be sometime in the future."

Jack and Jacob both shook their heads in understanding gestures, not realizing the complexities of the question Jack had just asked.

Later that evening, lying in bed with my arm around Gabby's neck and her head resting on my chest, she asked softly, "Do you think we will live together someday?"

I didn't immediately answer her, so she picked her head up off my chest and looked into my eyes. "Do you even want to live together?" She paused and then started again. "I mean, we've never really talked about this, and I would like to know your feeling on the subject."

I smiled softly at her as I responded, "There is nothing I want more in the world than to wake up next to you every day for the rest of my life. But it may take a while to come up with a plan that makes that possible. Right now, I think we just need to be patient and see what plan God has for us going forward."

Placing her head gently back on my chest, she responded, "I like that answer." After a couple of minutes of silence, she said softly, "Thank you for loving me, Michael." Shortly after her words of contentment were uttered, we both drifted off to sleep with smiles on our respective faces.

Our lives continued with little change as we both tried to find a way to live in a single location over the next few months. As rudimentary as our lives had become, events on the national and world stage were changing faster than at any other time in history. The decade of the '90s was about to see changes that would reshape the world well into the next century, especially in the area of technology.

The '90s saw the growth of the World Wide Web and the first personal computer PCs. After the World Wide Web became available for public use, it grew dramatically with the number of users multiplying exponentially. By the middle of the decade, there were an estimated eighty million users on the Internet. Toward the end of the decade, that number had increased to an estimated 295 million users. The Internet, in turn, caused a perpetual revolution in the communication and business worlds that continues even to this day.

These new technologies created multiple companies that would develop operating systems for computers. The largest and most successful of these companies was Microsoft. From small beginnings, they were able to provide users with the technology they wanted at an affordable price. In short order, Microsoft had its operating systems in approximately 80 percent of all computers in the world, making it one of the fastest-growing and most valuable companies on the planet.

Apple Computers developed and marketed the first iMac computers, which was an instant success. Apple would quickly move to become the leading name in the infancy of the computer industry.

As this industry quickly ramped up, several companies made the personal computer more attractive. Java Programming Language was released. The online auction site eBay was founded and became an instant success. The Internet search engine Ask Jeeves was introduced. Intel Corporation developed and introduced the Pentium Microprocessor. The possibilities of this new computer age seemed endless.

The other huge technology leap was the mobile phone. Mobile phone technology began in the late 1980s, but by 1995, owning a mobile phone was simply a fact of everyday life for most Americans. People either loved them or hated them depending on their views on privacy between themselves and others. But it was obvious they were here to stay as this industry also exploded onto the world stage.

But before everyone had access to or could afford a mobile phone, there was an interim tool developed, the pager. The pager was used to contact a specific person and leave them a landline number to which they could respond. It became a very useful tool for anyone who traveled or was in their car without a way to communicate with others. The popularity and ever-plunging cost of mobile phones made this tool virtually obsolete in just a few years.

The '90s was also an important decade for television. Many of the shows developed in the '90s would remain available well into the future; *Seinfeld* and *The Tonight Show* are just a couple of examples. Other shows created a great deal of controversy; videos on MTV, *Beavis and Butt-Head*, and *South Park* as examples. Additionally, the 1990s began the genre of reality TV that still remains popular at the present time.

There were also huge changes happening on the world stage as well. In Rwanda and Zaire, genocide and civil war were responsible for an estimated five hundred thousand deaths. The conflict was between the majority Hutu and the minority Tutsi populations.

Nelson Mandela, who was released as a political prisoner in South Africa in 1990, became the country's first multiracial president in an open and free election in 1995. And with his election, the age of Apartheid was over in South Africa.

The American space shuttle *Atlantis* docked on the Russian Mir Space Station for the first time.

The Bosnian war raged in what was at the time Yugoslavia. Ethnic outbreaks between Serbs, Croats, and Muslims erupted as each group fought for power and control of the government. The fighting led to many atrocities and attempts at ethnic cleansing.

Czechoslovakia separated into the Czech Republic and Slovenia.

Scientists at the Roslin Institute unveiled Dolly, the first successfully cloned sheep to the world.

Stem cell research also began in the '90s. Stem cells derived from human embryos were first isolated and then used to help correct or cure many of the diseases or illnesses we suffer from today.

In the beginning, most medical professionals believed this was the stuff of science fiction. But as more successes were achieved, humanity would be left to wrestle with the moral dilemmas, as well as the social and political implications of this new technology.

The '90s also saw a worldwide increase of the use, production, and smuggling of destructive and addictive drugs. Many initiatives were tried to stop the expansion of the drug trade, but now it is still an increasing problem for society.

AIDS became a major world concern as it spread from Africa and into the developed world.

In the United States, Bill Clinton was elected to a second term as the president after defeating Bob Dole. He appointed Madeleine Albright to be the first female secretary of state in the nation's history.

The United States had a budget surplus for the first time in thirty years. And the Dow Jones stock market ticker closed over eleven thousand for the first time.

Looking at the big picture, the world was changing at a ridiculous pace. On the micro level, most of us were just trying to keep pace and not drown in all the new technologies that were coming so fast.

Households in which both spouses worked outside the home were becoming the norm if you wanted to stay in what was considered the middle class. Less time with family and more time working was a mantra that seemed to increase every year if you wanted to remain successful.

It was early January when Gabby called me to give me some bad news. "Michael," she began excitedly, "do you know Master Tire was just placed on COD?"

"What?" I responded. "What are you talking about?"

"I'm serious!" she replied. "Your divisional manager was just on the phone with my boss, and your company is over 120 days late on some pretty large tire bills. We sent an auditor to your truck tire location, and it appears your consignment is short several thousand dollars' worth of inventory!"

"I remember the auditor being here last week," I answered hastily. "When I asked him how everything looked, he just said, 'I'll have a final report for you next week.'"

There was silence on both ends of the phone line for a few seconds. Finally, I began. "Do you think that's why our consignment orders either have been coming in slower than usual or are back ordered?"

"I can't answer that question, but it sounds like Mr. Lovering may have been cooking your books for some time," she responded. "Can't you tell what's being paid for and what's overdue in your internal reports?"

There was a long silence before I responded, "When I went on my vacation to the Caribbean, Mr. Lovering took over all the ordering and accounts payable while I was gone. When I came back, he told me he had a much better idea of the profitability numbers as a result of his being involved directly." I paused again. "He went on to say that he was going to continue to manage the accounts payables and inventory ordering, freeing up time for me to concentrate on sales and outstanding accounts receivables."

"So you're telling me that you haven't seen any actual financial reports since March?" Gabby asked.

It was an embarrassing question to respond to because I immediately realized I had no idea where we stood financially as a company. "I've seen some internal sales reports, but that's really all," I responded. "I give Mr. Lovering the tire orders to process, and I concentrated on sales, service, and collections."

I could feel the heat as a flush of anger worked its way up my neck and onto my face. My mind was filled with a thousand thoughts, most of them bad, as I pondered my next move.

After another prolonged silence, Gabby asked, "Are you OK, Michael?"

"Other than being completely blindsided, angry at my own stupidity, and pissed about this whole ridiculous situation, yeah, I'm fine," I responded a little too loudly.

"Michael! This is not your fault!" Gabby blurted out. "If you think clearly about this, in the worst-case scenario, you just lose your job. I know that sounds bad, but at least you don't have a financial stake in the business!"

"I'm not the only one who would lose their job," I responded. "There are lots of people here who depend on this place for their livelihood." More silence followed.

"Do you think Tahatsu Tire would take this location over as a company facility if we don't make it as a dealership?" I asked, hoping for a positive response.

"I have no idea," Gabby replied. "But we're not there yet. I just wanted to give you a heads-up on what I overheard today. Please don't confront Mike Lovering about this information. If he finds out you know about this, it wouldn't take a rocket scientist to figure out where you got the information. And I'm certainly not in a position where I want to lose my job right now either!"

"Don't worry," I said reassuringly. "I won't do anything that puts you in a compromising position."

After another short silence, I exclaimed, "Wow! That is a lot of information to try and absorb! Thank you so much for telling me. I really appreciate it!"

"Of course, I'm going to tell you," Gabby replied. "I love you!" Her words came with such sincerity that I knew she meant them.

"I love you too, Gabby," I said. "I'll call you after dinner tonight. Have a great rest of the day." We said our good-byes, and I leaned back in my chair, still stunned and trying to process what I'd just heard.

Jack was over at my house having a beer with me the following Saturday when I told him about my work situation. After finishing the story, I simply stared at him as he digested it.

"Holy shit, Michael!" he finally said. "If Mike Lovering is in as deep as you suspect he is, you should think about jumping off that ship pretty fast! I've been the accountant in more than one situation like this, and they never end well! My guess is your company will have no available credit and even less cash as this thing starts to snowball out of control. And it sounds like that has already started to happen. I seriously doubt Master Tire will be in business six months from now. Anyway, that's been my experience with similar circumstances."

After pondering his statement for a few seconds, I responded, "Well, you know what they say! Every cloud has a silver lining."

"What do you mean?" Jack quickly replied.

"If I'm going to have to look for a new job, I could just as easily do it in Portland, Oregon, as I could here! Maybe this is God's way of allowing me to finally be with Gabby. There won't be anything holding me back. I'd just need to move, and I'm more than willing to do that if it means we can be together."

A large smile grew on Jack's face as he listened. "What a great idea!" he responded enthusiastically. "Does she know about this yet?"

"No, she doesn't. I just now came up with the idea. I've been concentrating on how to save the business, and while I've been talking with you, I just realized, saving the business won't make me happy. I'll still be working for a man I've pretty much lost all respect. I'll still be in Fresno, while the person I want to be with will be in Portland. This is my chance to make a move that benefits both Gabby and me."

"That sounds outstanding, Michael!" Jack said. "What about the house? What will you do with it?"

"I don't know yet. I'll have to give that part some thought," I responded. "Jacob may want to live in it until he finishes with his master's program. After that, I could rent it or sell it. It's free and clear, so it won't be a drain on my finances." I smiled, looked down at my folded hands, and continued. "Besides, I have a fair-sized nest egg saved up, so I don't need to go to work immediately. I can pick and choose and take my time finding the right job the first time. Portland is almost twice the size of Fresno, so the possibilities are endless!"

Jack got up, walked over to me, and pulled me up off the sofa. Wrapping his arms around me and hugging me tightly, he said, "And that, my friend, is how you turn lemons into lemonade! Even though

I'll miss coming over here to mooch free beer on the weekends, I think that is an absolutely great plan!"

Pulling away from me, he continued. "You've got to tell Gabby! She is going to be over-the-top excited to know you're coming to Portland!"

"I'm going up there next weekend, and I think I would rather tell her in person than over the phone," I responded.

"Good idea!" Jack countered. "You guys are going to be so happy! I couldn't be more excited for you!" He couldn't stop smiling, which caused me to smile back at him. For a long time, we just stood there smiling at each other like two kids who'd just gotten away with something they weren't supposed to do!

The following Thursday, I was sitting in my office when Mike Lovering drove into the truck tire center in an unfamiliar car. I got up from my desk and walked to the front door to meet him.

"Michael!" he said with cheer in his voice. "How are you doing?" He extended his hand for me to shake.

Taking his hand and shaking it, I responded, "I'm fine. Do you have a new car?"

He looked back out the window and responded, "Yes, I do! I sold the Cadillac before it got too many miles on it, and I wanted to get the most money possible out of it. I leased this Volvo for next to nothing, and I'll just write most of it off to the business!"

"Sounds like a good business decision," I replied, letting loose of his hand. "To what do I owe the pleasure of your visit, Mr. Lovering?"

"I need to have a talk with you," he said. "Can we go into your office for a few minutes?"

"Sure," I responded. "Come on in." I led the way through my office door, and Mr. Lovering closed the door behind himself after entering.

Sitting in one of the padded chairs facing my desk, he began. "Michael, I need to be honest with you. The truck center has underperformed pretty much since we opened it. I'm sure you're aware of that—you've seen the financial reports."

I cut in abruptly. "Actually, you haven't shared any meaningful financial information with me about our business since last March."

A puzzled look crossed his face. "Really!" he stated. "For whatever reason, I thought my admin sent you those reports monthly." Shrugging his shoulders, he continued. "Sorry about that! I thought you were reviewing them."

"But if that's the case, and you weren't seeing them, let me bring you up to speed. We were barely breaking even through May of last year. Then we were audited by the state on both payroll taxes and sales tax."

He paused for a minute, raising one hand and running it over the entire surface of his face before continuing. "According to the state auditors, we hadn't correctly held out the amount of payroll taxes that were required. To make matters worse, our computer systems were all programmed with the wrong tax rate, and we were undercharging our customers on all purchases by a half of a percent for a year and a half.

"The back taxes and fines levied against Master Tire were a little over half a million dollars," he said matter-of-factly. "Our accountant and I decided to keep this between us while we appealed the ruling. But we were still obligated to pay the sales tax penalties or close the business. So we took about $250,000 out of the business to pay that obligation."

He paused again, and then slinking down further in his chair, he continued. "Things went from bad to worse when Mother Nature killed the farming and logging this year. We were counting on our new product line and summer sales to bring us out of the hole. Instead, they only compounded our debt without the offset of sales."

Mike rose from his chair and began pacing back and forth behind it. "We haven't been able to stay on top of our tire bill or replenish our consignment inventory as we agreed."

Putting his right hand to his face again, he continued, still pacing. "Now we owe Tahatsu Tire $246,000 that is overdue, and we still owe the state $163,000 for taxes and penalties." He stopped, faced me, and waited for some type of a response.

"Wow!" I said finally, "That sounds like a real mess!" Tapping my hand on the arm of my chair, I asked, "What are we going to do now?"

"I don't really know, Michael," he answered. "Today, I found out that our appeal has been denied, and the state wants their money with interest. Last week, Tahatsu placed us on a cash-on-delivery basis, and they are requiring cashier's checks. They won't accept our business checks because two of our business checks bounced last month. I made them good, but their corporate headquarters is requiring cashier's checks at the time of any deliveries. They also want to work out a payment plan to collect the past due amounts we owe."

"This doesn't sound like a solvable problem, Mike," I said, realizing it was probably the first time I had ever referred to him by any other name than Mr. Lovering.

He began pacing again before he spoke. "I believe I can hold the state and the tire company at bay if I file Chapter 7 bankruptcy. If we could work off the inventory we have in our possession now, we might be able to sell our way out of this and negotiate our debt down with both the state and Tahatsu Tire."

"If you file bankruptcy, what happens to the employees?" I asked.

"Unfortunately, their insurances will lapse immediately. Legally, I won't be able to pay them until the bankruptcy is finalized. But then they are entitled to all their back pay," he responded nonchalantly.

I could feel my temper building as I listened to him speak about his employees like they were inanimate objects rather than human beings. "Do you still belong to the Fresno Country Club, Mike?" I asked.

"Yes, I do," he responded with a smile.

"And you just leased a new car, knowing you will probably declare bankruptcy. Is that correct?" I asked.

The smile left his face quickly, and he didn't reply.

"Mike," I began, "you may be the most self-serving human being I've ever known! Those people out there have been working their asses off to make you successful, and for that loyalty, you are going to ask them to stay and work for an additional three months or more without a paycheck or insurance for their families."

"Now just a minute, Michael!" he responded loudly.

"Shut up and listen!" I snapped back. "This seems to be as good a time as any to give you notice that I'm leaving."

"You're giving your two weeks' notice now?" he replied in a loud voice.

"Two weeks, my ass! I'll be out of here in two hours or less!" I responded. "I just need to get a few personal items and have a talk with my guys."

"You can't say anything about this to the other employees. Nothing is finalized yet," he said, his tone almost begging me to be quiet and just leave.

"Screw you, Mike!" I yelled loud enough that several employees and customers in the main office turned to see where that sort of language was coming from. "Before I leave here today, I'm going to make sure every employee hears the same story I just heard! You try running this place by yourself and see how that works out for you!"

He stared at me, clenching and unclenching his fist before he finally responded in a loud voice, "I have to say, Michael, I'm very disappointed in you and your attitude! After all I've done for you! I thought I could trust you! If you weren't leaving of your own volition, I would fire you right now on the spot!" The veins in his neck stood out prominently as he spoke, his face immediately turning red with anger as his hands again clenched into fists.

"You are such an asshole!" I yelled loudly. Everyone turned around again to see who was in my office.

"After all I've done for you, I thought I could trust you too! Now get out! I'll leave all my keys at the retail store later today."

With that said, Mike Lovering walked out of my office and out of my life forever.

True to my word, I ordered in pizza and asked everyone to stay for an emergency meeting right after work. All but one employee was able to stay. I ran to the store and bought a case of beer to share with my team for this one last meeting.

The news was not received well. There was anger, outrage, and, in some cases, tears as I blindsided them with the new truth about their jobs. I knew they felt betrayed by me for not staying and helping them find new employment. They also viewed me as a part of management, and I'm sure most believed I had known this was coming for some time and chose to remain silent until I was ready to leave.

Although none of those assumptions were true, I still felt as though I had betrayed all the people who had put their faith in me to provide a better life for them and their families. And if I was truthful with myself, I also believed it was partially my fault. If only I'd paid more attention, I might have seen this coming. As I said my good-byes to everyone that evening, I don't think I've ever felt more like a failure.

I had spoken with Gabby a couple of times on Friday as I was traveling to Portland. I hadn't said anything about my work situation or that I was on my way to see her earlier than she expected. We had agreed to have another phone conversation after she got off work and was tucked in for the night waiting for my arrival.

I was standing on Gabby's front porch when she drove into her driveway that evening after work. I had parked my car on the street, and though she'd driven right past it, she hadn't recognized it.

Not seeing me standing there, she opened the garage door with an automatic garage door opener and drove her car into the garage.

Getting out of the car, she popped the trunk lid and started to bring out the groceries she'd bought for the weekend.

I left the porch, walked toward the garage, and, trying not to frighten her, said in a soft voice, "Would you like some help with those groceries, ma'am?"

Her head jerked around when she heard me. Seeing me, a huge smile formed as she put the groceries back down and turned to run into my arms! "What are you doing here so early!" she screamed as we embraced.

I kissed her before responding. "It is so good to see you, sweetheart!"

"Oh, I'm so glad to see you too, Michael!" she replied, hugging me tightly again. Stepping back and looking panicked suddenly, she continued. "But I didn't expect you until early tomorrow morning! I was going to make some brownies and a lasagna for this weekend. And I haven't cleaned the bathrooms or changed the sheets on the bed yet!"

"Stop!" I broke in before she worked herself up anymore. "I don't care about any of that stuff! I'm here to be with you, and that's all that matters. Now how about you let me give you a hand with those groceries?"

"OK," she said, a smile still etched on her face. With that, she loaded me up with two bags and picked up the third before closing her trunk.

Once in the kitchen, we'd just put the bags down on the kitchen island when we heard someone else pulling into the driveway. A car door slammed, and seconds later, Aria burst through the front door. Without looking, she yelled, "Mom! Where are you?"

"She's in the kitchen," I responded. She quickly walked into the kitchen, a look of apprehension on her face until she saw it was me.

A huge smile formed on her face as she came running in and gave me a big hug. "Michael! We didn't expect you until tomorrow!" she said enthusiastically. "What a great surprise!"

Pulling away from Aria and putting an arm around her mother, I responded, "You look great. What brings you over to your mother's house on a Friday night? I thought you'd be out tearing up the town with your friends!"

"I came over to give Mom a hand with some cooking and maybe a little housework," she said.

"Do you guys only clean and cook on the weekends I'm coming over?" I asked, a smile on my face.

Gabby gave me a little poke in the ribs with her elbow as she responded, "No! We just wanted everything to be perfect when you come to Portland, even if it is just for a few hours." She put her arm around my waist and gave me a light squeeze.

"Well," I said, "that may be changing very soon."

Gabby pulled away from me a little, a confused expression on her face and asked, "What do you mean?"

"I quit my job at Master Tire Service yesterday," I responded. Both girls had a look of astonishment on their faces as the words sank in.

"What does that mean?" Gabby asked.

"It means I'm unemployed," I said. "It means that I need to find a new job, and I think I can find something to do in Portland as easily as I can in Fresno."

"Please tell me you're serious!" Gabby said, pulling me back into her embrace.

"I'm serious," I replied. Before I could say anything else, Aria rushed the two of us for a group hug, while Gabby started to softly cry. After a minute, we separated, and Gabby wiped the tears from her face with the back of her hands.

"I thought we might look for a place for me to live in Portland sometime this weekend," I kidded.

"Oh, knock it off!" she responded. "You're moving in with me, and you know it!" she stated firmly. Then she was back in my arms, hugging me tightly. "I don't think I've ever been happier! This feels like a very good dream that you never thought could come true!" She squeezed me even tighter as she spoke.

After everyone had calmed down a little, we all sat down at the kitchen table, and I told them the whole story of the prior day's events with Mike Lovering. Neither of them interrupted, but when I was finished, they both had a multitude of questions.

"I'll answer all your questions, but I'm hungry," I said. "Why don't we go have a nice dinner somewhere and celebrate? Then I can answer your questions, and we can talk about new beginnings."

"I should go home and let you two be alone," Aria stated.

Before she could finish her thought, I broke in. "Why should you go home? We are going to have lots of time alone together from now on. Your part of this family, and I really want you to come with us!"

Looking over at Gabby, I said, "I'll help you make lasagna tomorrow if you want." Then smiling, I continued. "I might as well make myself useful if I'm going to be around here, and I'm not planning on going anywhere soon."

Gabby got up from the table, walked around, and kissed me on the cheek, saying, "Give me fifteen minutes to change and we'll go. Aria, honey, I want you to come too."

Then turning back to me, she said, "I'm so excited to finally have you here with me! I can't even express how happy I am!" Then she headed for her bedroom.

It was just about 7:00 a.m. on Monday. I'd just returned from my first run in Gabby's neighborhood. I never really got lost, but I did have to backtrack a couple of times as I ran into a cul-de-sac with no exits.

I'd left a towel on the porch before taking off, and now I picked it up and hung it around my neck as I headed to the kitchen for a cup of coffee. Sitting down at the kitchen table, I opened the newspaper I'd found on the porch when I returned from my run. I was reading the headlines and sipping on my coffee when Gabby entered the kitchen.

"Good morning," she said as she walked past me to the coffeepot.

"Good morning," I responded. "You look gorgeous! Do you always dress that nice when you go to work?" And before she could answer, I added, "And you smell wonderful! I love your perfume!"

Pouring a cup of coffee and taking a yogurt out of the refrigerator, she sat down next to me as she responded, "Thank you! I do have a lot of clothes, and, yes, this would be pretty representative of my normal work attire." She opened her yogurt and began eating it between sips of her coffee.

"What are you planning on doing today?" she asked.

"First, I'm going to take a shower. Then I'm going to go open a checking account at a local bank. Then I'm going to go look for a new car for you."

"What?" she said, shocked by my plan. "I don't need a new car! My car runs fine."

"So just to be clear, you love your car?" I asked. "How long have you had it?"

Coyly, she responded, "Well, no, I don't love it, but it works fine. I bought it used, and I've had it for about six years."

"Well, how about this," I said. "I'll go looking, and if I find a car I think you would love, we can go look at it some evening or next weekend. And if you don't love it, we won't buy it. How's that sound?"

She put her spoon down, walked around the table, leaned over, and kissed me softly. "You don't have to buy me things to make me happy, sweetheart! I'd be happy with you if we were a pauper."

"You really smell good!" was all I said.

"Actually, your sweaty body smells pretty damn sexy to me too!" she replied. "But I don't have time to do anything about it right now. I have to get to work!"

Kissing me again, she went back and filled her coffee cup again and started toward the front door. Blowing me one last kiss as she stepped outside, she said, "Don't get into any trouble today, OK!" She quickly closed the door behind her as she left.

I got up and walked to the front window to watch her backing out of the driveway. She was driving an eight-year-old Honda Accord that was a faded green color. I knew it was time for her to have a new car but was sure that with house payments, utilities, and helping her kids occasionally, a car wasn't in her immediate future.

After going to the Oregon State Employment Office and signing up, I spent most of the rest of the week searching for a job and setting up interviews for the next three weeks. I'd set up quite a few interviews and was reasonably pleased with the responses I'd received so far. Even though I wasn't in a hurry to go back to work, I felt confident that I would be working inside of a month.

On Saturday, I asked if Gabby wanted to see the car I'd picked out for her to look at while we were still eating breakfast. She tried to hide her excitement and responded again that she really didn't need a new car.

"So you don't want to go look at it?" I asked.

I could see she was fighting an internal battle with herself. She didn't want me to spend that much money on her, but, of course, she wanted a new car! Who wouldn't!

Finally, she said, "I guess it won't hurt to look," trying to sound not too interested. "But if I don't absolutely love it, we're not getting it!"

"OK," I responded. "Why don't I do these few breakfast dishes while you go get ready to leave?"

"I'll only need ten minutes," she replied, heading toward the bedroom.

"Oh my god, Michael!" she exclaimed when we walked up to the car. "This is nicer than my boss's car! What is it?"

"This is a new 1997 Lexus 400GL," I replied. "It is supposed to be one of the safest and most reliable cars ever built. Do you like it?"

"Sweetheart, I can't let you buy this! It's too expensive!" she said as she looked the car over.

The car was a beautiful silver with matching silver leather interior. It had all the latest innovations that were available from any luxury car maker.

"Sit in it and see if it fits you," I said. She didn't hesitate and sat in the driver's seat. I showed her how to adjust the electric six-way seats and electric mirrors. Once she was comfortable, I asked if she wanted to drive it.

"Yes, I'd love to!" she said quickly. After a short drive and showing her a sampling of the car's interior features, we returned to the dealership.

"Well, what do you think?" I asked.

"Michael, I absolutely love it, but I can't let you buy this for me. I just can't!"

"Well, that's unfortunate," I replied. "Because I already bought it, so I guess I'll have to drive it myself!"

"Did you really?" she asked, wondering if I was teasing her.

"Yes, I really did buy it," I responded.

"Then I want it! I never thought I'd have a car this beautiful in my lifetime!" she squealed, her eyes pleading for a positive response.

"Then it's yours!" I said as she exited the vehicle and hugged me.

Two weeks had past, and I'd had four in-person interviews. After a short explanation of the job, two openings were of no interest to me. I thanked my interviewer for their time in both and expressed that I wasn't interested in their positions.

I spent about two hours in my third interview. I liked the proposed job description, enjoyed the person doing the interview, and was very interested until we started to talk about compensation. As he was trying to sell me on the benefits of working for his company, I had to interrupt him.

"Excuse me, John," I began. "The job posting said $60K under the compensation. You just stated that I would be starting at $45K. That's a pretty large difference."

"The $60K also said management experience," he replied.

"I have management experience. As you can see by my resume, I've been managing a large group of people for a number of years!"

"Yes, I did see that," he countered. "But you haven't managed people in this industry. That's what we mean by management experience."

"John," I said, trying to keep my cool, "someone needs to redo your ad to match your expectations. It appears we have wasted each other's time today."

I started to get up to leave, and he panicked. "Wait, Michael! I think you would be a good fit for us! How about if we start you at $55K?"

I continued to my feet and replied, "John, if you were willing to give me $55K, then that's what you should have offered me. But now, I wouldn't take the job at $60K. I have some disagreement with our opening negotiations, and, unfortunately, I don't think your company is a good fit for me. It's an integrity thing," I said as I turned and exited his office.

The fourth interview went very well. The company was a large beer distributor, and they were looking for a management candidate outside their business model. The thought was they could teach me how they wanted their warehouse and delivery drivers managed without having to break bad habits from a former manager of a distribution location.

The money was good, the location was only twenty minutes from Gabby's house, and it was pretty much a reverse commute, which meant I would miss rush-hour traffic both ways. It was a pretty large business, but I had no doubts I was up to the challenge. We set up a second interview with the owners the next Thursday, and I felt reasonably comfortable that my job search could be nearing its end.

When Gabby got home that night, I told her the news. She was more excited than I was about the interview. We drank a bottle of wine to celebrate and then lay in each other's arms, watching TV the rest of the evening.

At breakfast the next morning, I asked Gabby if I could take her to lunch today.

She seemed a little taken aback by my request but responded positively. "How about 1:00 p.m.?" she asked.

"Great!" I said as she kissed me good-bye. "I'll see you then!"

At twelve forty-five, I walked into the divisional office of the Tahatsu Tire Company. The office was well furnished and attractive and had the familiar smell of tires I'd come to know and love over the years. There were several tire displays scattered throughout the waiting area and office. Stepping up to the front desk, I was greeted by Gabby with a bright smile.

"Hi, sweetheart," I said as she got up from her desk. "I'll just take a seat over here until you're ready to go," I said, pointing to a row of chairs by the window.

"No! No! No!" she responded, coming around her desk and grabbing my hand. "We can go now, but, first, I want you to meet my boss."

As she led me through a door, she said, "You sure look nice! But you didn't need to wear a suit!"

"I only brought some very casual clothes and a couple of suits when I came to Portland this time. And I thought you might do exactly what you're doing and introduce me to your boss," I said. "I just don't want to embarrass you, so I opted to wear a suit."

Gabby stopped outside a closed door and knocked.

"Come in!" came the voice from inside.

Gabby opened the door, grabbed my hand, and led me into the office. A man behind a well-appointed desk rose to his feet, smiled, and extended his hand, saying, "You must be Michael Larsen." I shook his hand as he introduced himself. "I'm John Warren."

"Pleasure to meet you, sir!" I said in response.

"So I understand you're here to take the brains of this outfit to lunch, am I correct?"

"Yes, sir," I responded, smiling at his comment.

"Well, don't be gone more than an hour because this place goes to hell if she's gone for more than an hour at a time!" he said, and we all laughed.

"I'll bring her back in less than an hour, sir!" I said as we turned for the door.

"Enjoy your lunch, guys!" he said, sitting down again. "By the way, Michael, would you have a few minutes to talk with me when you bring Gabby back from lunch?"

"Sure," I responded. "I don't have any other plans." Gabby closed the door behind us, and I asked, "What do you think that's all about?"

"I have no idea," she replied, looking as puzzled as I was.

When we returned from lunch, Gabby again escorted me back to Mr. Warren's office. Knocking on the door, she was greeted by the now familiar "Come in."

She opened the door, stepped out of the way to let me pass, and closed the door behind me as she returned to her desk.

"Have a seat, Michael," Mr. Warren said, pointing to the two chairs on my side of the desk.

Once I was seated, he folded both his hands in a prayerlike motion and looked over them at me. "I think it would be safe to assume that you've had an interesting couple of weeks," he began. "Walt Frank gave me the news about you leaving Master Tire last week. It didn't sound like it ended too amicably."

"No, it didn't," I replied, shaking my head from side to side.

"Well, what are your plans now?" he asked inquisitively.

"First and foremost was to move to Portland so I could be with Gabby," I said.

"Judging by what I see, that seems to have already been accomplished," he replied. "What else?"

"Gabby loves her job her, and she is quite fond of you as her boss," I began. "So I don't see us moving out of this area anytime soon. I've started looking for work, and I have a pretty strong feeling that

I may have already found a new career path with Portland Brewing Company. I'll meet with the owners of the company for a second interview next Thursday."

"Interesting!" he responded. "So you would be getting into the beer business."

I took a couple of minutes and explained the opportunity to him and what the company was looking to do with me.

"That sounds like a great opportunity, Michael," Mr. Warren said after listening earnestly. "Do you think you'll miss the tire business at all?"

"Of course!" I responded. "For seventeen years, that's all I've known. In fact, working for Master Tire Service is the only job I've had since graduating from college. But venturing into a new industry and the unknown is both a little scary and exciting at the same time."

"Have you looked for any positions at tire companies in Portland?" he asked.

"I looked to see what was available at the employment office, but there were only entry level positions available, and most of those were outside of metro Portland."

"If something came up in our industry, would you be at all interested?" Mr. Warren asked. "Or are you ready to move on and try something new and altogether different?"

I was both caught off guard and surprised by his question. "I don't know?" I responded. "I'd kind of given up on the idea that there was anything available in the tire business for me in Portland. Why, do you have a dealer in the area who is looking for someone like me?"

John smiled, leaned forward, and placed his hands on his desk. "No, Michael, I don't have a dealer in mind. But I may have an opportunity that would appeal to you."

My interests were immediately piqued as I responded, "I'd be happy to listen."

"To begin with, you were right about Mike Lovering. He filed for protection under Chapter 7 bankruptcy on Wednesday. The business, as he now knows it, will be finished in the next ninety days or so. He won't find other suppliers willing to invest in him, and he won't be able to pay his bills. We do own the truck tire center building, so we will reopen it under the Tahatsu Tire corporate name. You and your team built up a pretty sizable clientele over a couple of years, and we don't want to lose that business."

"Before you go any further, Mr. Warren," I interrupted, "it was a godsend for me the ways things have worked out so Gabby and I could finally be together. I have a lot of sweat equity in the truck tire center, but I love Gabby, and being together with her is my number-one priority right now."

"Just hear me out, Michael!" Mr. Warren said. "I'm not going to ask you to move back to Fresno. You know we also have a truck tire center here in Portland."

"Yes, sir, I know that," I responded. "Kelly Barnes runs it. I've talked to him multiple times on the phone, transferring inventory back and forth between us."

"As you are aware, we call our company-owned locations by a different name," John continued. "Tahatsu Tire Center here in Portland does twice the business Master Tire did monthly."

Mr. Warren paused for a moment before continuing. "Company-owned outlets do things differently from dealer locations, and there is a learning curve to discern those differences. I wouldn't put you in as the manager of a Tahatsu Tire Center until you understood our systems, programs, and corporate goals."

I was a little confused as to where he was going but at the same time intrigued enough to hear him out.

"Here are my thoughts, Michael," he concluded. "I know from your reputation and what Walt Frank has told me about you that you have the skill set to run a large commercial tire center. I would like you to come aboard as assistant manager and learn our systems under Kelly Barnes.

"In ninety days, or however long it takes for us to take over the Fresno location, we will transfer Kelly to Fresno to take over that location. When that happens, you will be promoted to the manager position of the Portland location." Then he stopped talking.

In the moments that followed, I was utterly speechless! My head was whirling as I tried to comprehend what I'd just heard.

He smiled and said, "I know that's a lot to take in, but at least it gives you a second option to look at for your future employment."

"Would this have any negative affect on Gabby's job?" I asked.

"As long as you didn't directly supervise her, it would have no negative effect on her employment."

I nodded that I understood him and then asked, "I would like to know what the compensation package is, if you could tell me."

"Our Human Resources people would give you the entire package presentation, but I can give you the highlights. As an assistant manager, you would start at 70K per year. Once Kelly leaves and you take over the Portland center, your salary would go to $85K per year.

"Once you become the manager, you are also eligible for annual bonuses of up to 50K, depending on your center's performance to specific goals and sales targets. Obviously, you would be able to participate in our insurance programs and would be automatically involved in our retirement program."

I sat there dumbfounded!

"Why don't you take some time and think this over?" he finished. "If I were you, I'd go on the second interview next Thursday before making any decisions. You might as well hear what they have to say before you decide."

I rose from my chair, extended my hand, and said, "Thank you, Mr. Warren! I'm a little overwhelmed now, but I'm very grateful for the job offer. I will get back to you with my answer next Friday, if that's OK."

"That's fine," he said, shaking my hand. "Have a great weekend, and I'll look forward to hearing from you."

As I walked out of his office, I quickly looked at my watch to see it was 3:45 p.m. I'd been speaking with him for almost two hours.

When I arrived at Gabby's desk, she stood up and said, "That was a long time! What was that all about?" She walked around the desk and faced me, waiting for an answer.

"Nothing much, actually," I responded casually. "He just offered me a job."

"What!" Gabby shouted, knowing she had responded too loudly.

CHAPTER 14

"You shouldn't need any help with a Windsor knot at your age!" Jacob said as he stood there trying to achieve the perfect look for his father's necktie. After several seconds of adjustments, he finally stopped fidgeting with it, nodded his approval, and continued. "There, that looks better! Now that's how a groom's tie should look when he's getting married!"

I had been living in Portland with Gabby for over a year when I proposed to her and asked for her hand in marriage. I'd known for some time that I'd been blessed to have fallen in love with two great women in my lifetime.

After Sarah's passing, I never, in my wildest dreams, thought that I would find another love to share my life and grow old with. But God had replaced my pain and loss with an equaled joy and happiness in the person of Gabriella Chase.

There was no need for a large wedding this time. For both Gabby and me, this was our second marriage. But it was important to us both to have a simple ceremony with family present while we expressed our devotion and commitment to each other. So here we were, in one of our favorite places, Lincoln City, Oregon, getting ready to say our vows and profess our love to each other and the world.

Standing in my room on the seventh floor at the Inn at Spanish Head with Jacob, I silently stared out the floor-to-ceiling windows that overlooked the beach and the Pacific Ocean.

The sky was bright blue, making the ocean appear bluer than its normal green shade. There were very few clouds in the sky, and a mild breeze was blowing up the cliff face. I could see several boats of various sizes out in the ocean, hoping to catch today's limit of fresh fish.

The tide was out, and the two men silently observed several couples holding hands and walking on the beach as they watched wave after wave crash onto the shoreline and run right up to their feet. There were also a few families, parents and kids, rushing out to the newly exposed sand as the tide went back out, looking for seashells or colored glass to take home as souvenirs.

This hotel was one of Gabby's and my favorite places to stay. It was built into a cliff, and you entered the lobby on the ninth floor. The tenth floor was a full-service restaurant and bar, and everything below the ninth floor was guest rooms. Each condo, regardless the floor, had an unobstructed view of the beach and ocean from one side of the room. They also had individual balconies with a table and a couple of chairs to sit in outside on the small deck, weather permitting.

If you left the sliding door open slightly, the repeated sound of the ocean waves as they broke on shore was an extraordinarily relaxing sound. And the smell of the fresh salt air accompanied by the screeching of seagulls only added to the ambiance of this pristine beach setting.

I had rented four rooms for our weekend marriage—one for Gabby and me and one each for Thomas, Jacob, and Aria. They'd arrived on Thursday, and the wedding was taking place today, Saturday.

Gabby had found a quaint little church nearby and had hired a local pastor to perform the ceremony.

Last night, Gabby had stayed in Aria's room so they could do all the girly things necessary for the wedding. At 7:30 a.m., I surprised them with breakfast and mimosas and had them delivered to Aria's room. I wanted this to be a perfect day from start to finish.

Looking at his watch for a moment, Jacob asked, "Are you ready, Dad?"

"I am," I responded as we started for the door. Waiting for the elevator door to open on their floor, I continued. "I don't know why, but I'm a little nervous."

Jacob just smiled and replied, "I think that's pretty normal, given the circumstances."

Everyone met in the hotel lobby and waited for two cars to be brought to the entrance of the hotel.

Gabby looked beautiful in a light pink dress she'd bought for the wedding. It was my first time seeing it, and she was stunning. As we looked into each other's eyes, we both were wearing nervous smiles. I kissed her on the cheek once we were together, and she wrapped her arms around my left arm.

"Are you ready for this, sweetheart?" I asked, looking at her.

Her smile grew as she gave a short response. "I'm so ready!"

The wedding was nothing short of perfect. It lasted about half an hour, and all five people in attendance smiled throughout the entire ceremony. Once we were pronounced man and wife and I was instructed to kiss the bride, all the kids started whooping and hollering as we kissed. We signed our marriage license, paid the minister, and were back at the hotel by 4:00 p.m.

We had reserved a small section of the restaurant for four hours to celebrate our new extended family. We just wanted to enjoy each other's company, have a few drinks, and share a nice dinner together.

While we were sitting there enjoying our drinks, I made a toast to my new family. After the toast, I asked Thomas, "Well, what do you think about all this, Thomas?"

"I'm happy for you and Mom!" he responded. "I think she's been happier this past year than any other time I can remember." Waiting a few seconds before continuing, he added, "And I love the respect you show her and that you treat her as an equal. Your actions and caring for her speak volumes as to how much you love her."

I could feel myself tearing up at his kind words. As I looked over at Gabby, she was obviously touched deeply by his response as she dabbed at her overflowing eyes with a napkin.

"Thank you, Thomas," I said. "I want you and Aria to know that you are part of this family in every context of the word from today forward. The two of you have absolute equal standing with Jacob in our household. He gained a brother and sister today, and you both gained a brother and a father."

After a couple of drinks, the talk around the table became lighter. As dinner was about to be served, Gabby asked, "Jacob, what do you want to do once you finish school?"

"I'm not sure," he responded. "I have a bit of an entrepreneurial spirit, and I have been looking at a few possibilities to open up a business for myself."

His answer caught us all by surprise.

"But it's not just up to me," he continued. "I've been dating a girl who lives in Fresno for a couple of months, and I am developing pretty strong feelings for her. She wants to teach in the public school system, and starting a business may be determined by where she gets a job offer."

"What!" I said loudly. "You've been dating a girl for a couple of months and you're ready to move wherever she goes to teach? That sounds serious! Why haven't you mentioned her before? We talk at least once a week, and there has never been a mention of a girl to me!"

Realizing I was raising my voice with each question, I looked around the table to survey everyone's expression after my outburst.

"Well, I, for one, couldn't be happier for you!" Aria said with sincerity in her voice. "How about you, Dad?" she asked. "Are you happy that my new big brother has a serious girlfriend?"

I smiled before responding. "If I'm completely honest," I began, "I'm not sure which freaks me out the most, Jacob having a secret but meaningful girlfriend, or me realizing I have to get used to two new people calling me dad!" Everyone at the table laughed as I finished.

"What is this mystery girl's name?" I asked.

"Her name is Sophia, but she goes by Sophie," he answered. "The next time I come to visit in Portland, I'll bring her with me so everyone can meet her."

Looking over at Thomas, I continued. "Do you have a love interest we don't know about as well?"

Aria started laughing and cut in. "Come on, Thomas, tell them the truth! It's time you let the cat out of the bag!"

"What are you talking about?" Thomas said as his face was flushing crimson.

"Yes, I have been dating a girl, but it's not serious yet—at least not from her point of view. Her name is Elise Alexander, and she's a nursing student." Pausing, he added, "She doesn't know it yet, but she's going to have my babies someday."

"Oh my god!" Gabby interjected. "I feel like we're playing a game of truth or dare with you guys today! How come no one has mentioned any of this to us before today?"

"You guys have been pretty involved with each other over the past few months," Aria said. "That's not a bad thing, but you didn't need any of our drama while you were making plans for your future. But now that you're married, we can tell you everything and not worry about breaking the two of you up!"

Everyone laughed robustly at her comments.

"Trust me," Aria continued, "you're going to be hearing a lot more from all three of us now that you are officially our parents! Not that we'll listen, but we'll be asking you for all kinds of advice and money!" More laughter by everyone followed her comments.

"Do you like you job at the Marriott, Thomas?" I asked.

"The hours aren't great, but in the management trainee program, you get the crappiest shifts, so I work most weekends and holidays," he answered. "After working there for a year, I actually thought I would have advanced to the next level by now. I really expected to be an assistant manager after a year, working my way toward being a manager of my own hotel within three years."

"That's a pretty ambitious timeline," I responded.

"Maybe," Thomas countered. "But I watched you start your job with Tahatsu Tire as an assistant manager and become a location manager in less than a year. If you can do that, why shouldn't I be able to do it?"

"Well, that's not exactly what happened," I retorted. "I had worked for another tire company prior to hiring on with Tahatsu. I started at the bottom, changing passenger tires. I was fortunate enough to be promoted several times because of good performance and some luck. But it took me almost eight years before I became the general manager of Master Tire Service.

"By the time that dealership closed, I had developed a pretty good name for myself in the tire industry. Tahatsu's offer to bring me on board at the assistant manager level was based a lot on past performances and a set of management skills I'd already acquired in my previous position," I replied.

"I don't know much about your industry, Thomas," I continued. "But moving into upper management in a year, or even three years, may not be realistic. If I were you, I'd reconsider your timelines and work at doing your current job better than anyone else in the hotel. Performance creates opportunities. So you need to outperform your peers if you want to advance quickly."

Thomas shook his head affirmingly as he replied, "That's really good advice, Michael." Then correcting himself, he said, "I mean Dad!"

Everyone snickered, and I responded, "You guys can call me whatever you want. If Michael is more comfortable, please use my name. Hearing the word 'dad' coming from the two of you is going to seem strange for all of us for a while."

Corporate-structured business was much different than working for an independent dealer. The three major differences that were immediately apparent were company correspondences, conference calls and meetings, and a healthy dose of internal politics.

Correspondences: Every morning, we would open our location to a pile of reports, requests for information, sales ads, and announcements that had been printed during the night and were now sitting in front of the printer. The stack of paper in front of the dot matrix printer could be as few as twenty-five pages or a stack of so many pages that it stood four inches tall. Additionally, there were several pages of faxes waiting for us each morning as well. Within a day or two, everything that came across the printer would be duplicated in hard copy, arriving either by mail or Federal Express.

At one point, I was filling two five-gallon trash cans a week with shredded paper from either our printer or the mail delivery. More than one time, I joked that I worked for the Tahatsu Tire and Paper Company!

Conference calls and meetings: As managers, we were required to be on a divisional conference call each Monday from 10:00 a.m. to noon. The retail store managers in the division along with the truck tire center manager were all on the call. Seldom did we receive any information that would be helpful to our business at the truck centers as the calls were very heavily weighted toward retail store sales.

Additionally, the truck tire centers had a conference call every Friday that lasted well over two hours with our corporate management team in Atlanta, Georgia.

Regarding meetings, we were required to travel to the divisional office in the first week of each month to go over our business from the previous month. Sales results, collections, expenses, staffing, overtime, and inventory turns were just a few of the items we were expected to discuss at length.

This meeting took a day to prepare and a day to explain the findings. Or said differently, for two working days in the first week of each month, we were wasting time going over and justifying reports that were already available to everyone via the computer.

Additionally, all truck tire center managers mandatorily attended a quarterly meeting with our upper management in Atlanta, Georgia, to go over this same information. That trip took most of us out of our businesses for four working days when you included travel time.

In January, we had one big meeting in which all the store managers went to Atlanta for a full week of training and developing business plans and goals for the coming year.

In summary, in a normal 2,080-hour work year, we spent approximately 208 hours on conference calls, 192 hours in divisional meetings; 128 hours in corporate meetings; and 48 hours in a corporate planning meeting. That adds up to 576 hours, or 72 full working days a year of nonproductive time that could have been used for improved sales by each truck tire center manager.

Internal politics: Having never worked for an international company before, I had never been exposed to the politics involved once you attain a certain position within that company.

If the CEO was from the western United States, the president, COO, and most upper management positions were people chosen from the west. If that changed and a new CEO from the eastern United States was put in by the board of directors, all those people at the top changed in pretty short order and were replaced by individuals from the East Coast.

At corporate meetings or during our annual conference, it was almost comical to watch various people trying to jockey for position with the people they thought might ascend to a higher level in the next transition.

None of that mattered to me. I was quite happy being a truck tire center manager in Portland, Oregon. Our location was always in the top four out of twenty-six locations in performance every year.

Each year, our truck center increased its business, and I was fortunate enough to make max bonus three years in a row. My work life was good, my home life was great, and I was on top of the world.

But the world was not in a great place. There was a bombing in Oklahoma City that killed 168 people and injured 800 more. It was the worst domestic terror incident in U.S. history. Timothy McVeigh and Terry Nichols were arrested, found guilty, and sentenced to death for their actions.

Retired football star O. J. Simpson was acquitted on two counts of first-degree murder in the slaying of his ex-wife, Nicole Brown Simpson, and Ronald Goldman. The nine-month trial received worldwide publicity and had another damaging effect on race relations in the United States.

A heat wave killed 750 people in Chicago, bringing to attention the plight of the urban poor and elderly during extreme weather conditions.

TWA flight 800 exploded off the coast of Long Island, New York, killing all 230 people on board.

The Centennial Olympic Park bombing at the Summer Olympics in Atlanta killed one person and injured 111 others.

Sparked by a global economic crisis scare, the Dow Jones Industrial Average followed world markets and plummeted 554 points, or 7.18 percent, to 7,162. It would be two years before the Dow Jones Industrial Average would close above ten thousand points again.

Pres. Bill Clinton was accused of having a sexual relationship with a twenty-two-year-old intern, Monica Lewinsky. This led to his impeachment by the House of Representatives. He was later acquitted of all charges by the Senate in a twenty-one-day trial.

Gabby and I had settled into a very contented lifestyle after our marriage in Lincoln City. Both of us were happy with our work; we talked with the kids often, and we had enough money to live comfortably.

We were able to give each of the kids a little extra money from time to time. If we wanted or needed something, we didn't have to budget for it; we just went out and bought it.

Either Aria or Thomas usually had lunch or dinner with us one day during most weekends. Jacob came to visit us about once every three months or so, and he brought Sophie a couple of times so we could meet her and get to know her.

On a Wednesday afternoon, July 9, my mother called me to let me know my father had a heart attack and was in critical condition in the hospital. I caught a flight that evening and was in Beaumont before midnight.

Mom and Ronnie were both at the hospital in the ICU with my father when I arrived.

It was obvious my mother had been crying a lot. Her eyes were puffy and bright red. Hugging, first, her and then Ronnie, I asked about my father's condition.

"It's not good, Michael," she said, her voice catching in her throat as she answered. "The doctor said we would know if he was going to survive in the next twenty-four hours. And even if he does, they'll need to do emergency heart surgery to repair the damaged areas in a day or two." Tears were streaming down her face as she gave me the bad news.

Looking down at my father connected to so many machines and instruments, I felt as uncomfortable as I'm sure he had been when he came to visit me in the veteran's hospital many years earlier.

"What happened?" I asked, more out of frustration than wanting information about the event.

"He was working, actually waiting on a customer around lunchtime, and he got up to walk out and show the gentleman a car," Mom said. "The customer said he just collapsed and fell to the ground unconscious. They called 911, and he was brought here by ambulance."

She looked down at him and said in a shaky voice, "He hasn't regained consciousness since his initial fall."

She moved to me, and I put my arm around her shoulder as she gripped my neck. "I'm really scared, Michael!" she said softly, a tinge of panic in her voice.

"Me too, Mom," I simply responded. "Me too."

Time passed by slowly as we waited to hear news about Dad. I tried to talk with Mom about anything besides him, hoping to take her mind off the situation at hand. But she was lost in her own world of worry and seldom commented in our one-sided conversation or responded to questions I asked.

I left the ICU waiting area and went to get a cup of coffee. I called Gabby and Jacob and updated them both on my father's condition. Both were very sorry and expressed that they were praying for his recovery. Taking two coffees to go, I headed back to ICU.

When I arrived, there was a doctor in scrubs sitting there, speaking with my mom. She was crying as Ronnie tried to console her. Instinctively, I knew by the scene before me that my father was gone. Putting the coffee down, I joined my grieving family as we all tried to comfort one another.

The next few days were filled with funeral arrangements, planning air travel for Jacob and Gabby, and notifying relatives on both sides of my parents' families. It sounded like twenty to thirty extended family members were going to come and attend his funeral.

I told Gabby that there was no need for Thomas and Aria to come. They hadn't even met my parents and wouldn't know anyone there except Jacob.

I loved my father and respected him and the life lessons he'd taught me. But I found myself much less emotionally involved in his passing than I was in Sarah's.

His life had been cut short because his heart gave out, and he'd turned sixty-seven only weeks before his death. However, I was quite frankly more concerned about my mom and my little brother's well-being than his departure.

Gabby met my mom face-to-face two days before the funeral. They'd talked on the phone, but this was the first time we'd traveled to Beaumont. She was a welcome comfort to my mom as she grieved, and the two of them established a bond almost immediately. That same day, Gabby also met Jimmy Clarke.

Mom hadn't exaggerated; Jimmy looked awful. I didn't recognize him until Mom told me who he was. He was skinny as a rail, his clothes hung off him, he barely smiled, and he couldn't hold eye contact with me. I gave him a hug once I was next to him, and his response was lukewarm at best.

I introduced Gabby to him, and he immediately put his hand out to shake hers. His hand was out there so fast that it appeared he was trying to avoid being embraced by a second person.

Gabby shook his hand and said, "It's so nice to finally meet you! Michael has told me so many stories about the two of you when you were younger. It's nice to put a face to the name!"

"It's nice to meet you too, Gabby," he responded, no hint of a smile on his face.

Looking back to me, he said, "Well, I'd better get going. I'll see you two at the funeral. I'm sorry for your loss, Michael and Lila." With that, he turned and simply walked out of the house and left.

I was deeply saddened by our limited exchange. This was a different Jimmy Clarke than the one I'd grown up with. I realized there would be no point in trying to salvage a relationship between the two of us. Life and circumstance had changed us both, but in different ways. In that two-minute conversation, I knew all that would remain of our friendship was memories of better times long ago.

I stayed a few days after the funeral to ensure my mom was OK and helped her with life insurance paperwork, social security setup, etc.

Ronnie was still single with no real love interest. He lived with a couple of roommates in an apartment just outside of town. He decided to move back home with Mom for a while. I encouraged the idea, at least for the short term, until she could start to recover from the shock of her loss. Ronnie and I both thought it would be good for Mom to have someone to talk with, cook for, and give her a reason to go on living.

Dad had planned well for his death, leaving a nice-size insurance policy for Mom. The house was free and clear, and it appeared that she would have enough money to comfortably live out her life.

I'd been back in Portland about three weeks when John Warren called me and asked if I could come to the divisional office the next day. I responded positively, and we agreed to meet at one thirty the next afternoon.

Gabby greeted me as I walked in, and since there was no one else in the office, she came around the desk to give me a quick hug.

"Any idea what John wants?" I asked.

"No, I don't," she replied. "But Sharon Hall from Human Resources is in there with him right now. As soon as they're through meeting, I'll take you back there."

I nodded my understanding and took a seat in the lobby. It was almost one forty-five when Gabby's phone rang, and she picked me up.

"Mr. Warren, how can I help you?" she asked. Then listening, she simply said, "OK." Hanging up the phone, she stood and said, "Mr. Warren asked me to bring you back to his office."

I got to my feet and said, "Lead the way, Ms. Larsen!" We made the short walk, and she knocked lightly on John Warren's door.

"Come in," he said loudly. Gabby opened the door, stepped aside, and let me enter before closing the door behind herself.

There was a smartly dressed woman sitting in one of the two chairs facing Mr. Warren. She stood as I entered, stepped toward me, and held out her hand. "I'm Sharon Hall from corporate HR," she said, a smile on her face.

I took her hand and shook it softly, responding, "Michael Larsen. Pleased to meet you, Ms. Hall."

She remained smiling and said, "Likewise." Then letting go of my hand, she returned to her chair and sat back down.

"Have a seat, Michael!" John said, pointing to the empty chair. Once I was seated, he began. "Michael, do you remember a Tony Steward that worked at the truck center as a salesman about a year or so ago?"

"Yes, I do," I replied.

Ms. Hall cut in. "What can you tell us about him, Michael?"

"Well, it's been closer to two years since he worked for me," I began. "When I started as the assistant manager at the truck tire center, he was one of our five commercial salesmen. Kelly Barnes, the manager at the time, asked me to supervise all the sales crew, so I did.

"Tony was underachieving and not making his sales goals, and I had several conversations with him in my first month, hoping to help his sales efforts. By the second month, there was no improvement, and I had another meeting with him to see if he had put any of our previously discussed plans into action."

"His response was negative," I continued. "When I asked him why, his response was simply that my ideas wouldn't work, so he didn't waste his time implementing them."

"Then what happened?" Ms. Hall asked.

"The meeting was over at that point," I responded to Ms. Hall. "So I let him leave. Then I walked down the hall and talked to Kelly about what had just happened."

"What did Kelly say?" Ms. Hall inquired.

"He expressed that Tony Stewart had been part of our sales force for sixteen years, and I should focus my efforts on the newer salesmen."

"Did you listen to Kelly?" she asked, continuing to write on her legal pad.

"I didn't like Kelly's response, but I did as I had been instructed. However," I continued, "I did go back and look at sales for the entire sales force on a month-by-month and annual basis. In each of the past six years, Tony's sales had decreased year over year. Every other salesman and sales territory had increased in sales during that same period. Thinking he may be in a more difficult territory, I asked Kelly if I could change a couple of territories around.

"He told me we had a salesman who was retiring, and when that territory opened up, I could move Tony into the new territory and have the new salesman take over Tony's underperforming old territory.

"When Randy Cross retired, I brought Tony back into my office. I explained we were giving him a much-higher-producing territory and that it would probably double his monthly commissions."

"How did he react?" Ms. Hall asked.

"It shocked me!" I answered. "He was pissed! He stood up and started yelling at me that I couldn't do that and that he didn't want the new territory! The new area was too far to drive from his house, and he'd have to spend two to three hours a day getting to and from his territory.

"I again tried to explain that this new area did almost twice as much business as his current territory, which meant he would be making a lot more money.

"He continued to yell about the change. 'I don't care about the money,' he said. 'I make enough money to live on now! Why would I want to leave an area that I've built up and am comfortable with to go work harder and longer hours? If this is such a good deal, give the territory to the new guy and I'll just stay where I am!'"

"Was that the end of the conversation?" Ms. Hall asked.

"It was," I replied.

"Then what happened?" Ms. Hall asked.

"I had a conversation with Kelly Barnes about the meeting," I said.

"What did Kelly ask you to do?" Ms. Hall asked.

"Kelly asked me to leave it alone," I responded. "He went on to say that he would be out of here and transferring to Fresno in a month or two, and I would take over as manager of the truck tire center.

"'Once you're the manager,' he said, 'you can do whatever you'd like with Tony Steward. But for now, just leave it alone and don't ride him so hard. I don't want to deal with firing a sixteen-year veteran salesman who's in a protected age group on my way out the door! I just don't want to deal with it!'"

"And then what happened?" she asked.

"As much as it irritated me, I stopped trying to manage Tony and just let him do whatever it was he did during the day," I replied.

"When Kelly was moved to Fresno and I was promoted to manager, I had a different type of conversation with Tony. I brought him into my office and gave him a ninety-day plan of action that I wanted updates on every Friday."

"How did that work out?" she asked.

"He failed to show up at our scheduled time the first Friday," I replied. "The following Monday, I called him to come see me in my office. He did come in, albeit an hour after I had asked him to meet me. He said traffic had been bad.

"I asked him why he missed our meeting on Friday," I continued. "He said he hadn't felt well in the afternoon, so he went home sick. I checked his time card and asked why he hadn't put in for sick pay if he went home early."

"What did he say?" she asked.

"He said it was obvious that I had singled him out and was trying to get rid of him because he was older and black! Then he told me he wasn't going anywhere, so good luck trying to fire him! He stood up, exited my office, got in his pickup, and left."

"Then what happened?" she asked.

"I'm pretty sure you have all the documentation from that point forward," I answered. "Over the next six weeks, I wrote him up on disciplinary action forms for various issues—time clock manipulation, not using our action plan, and insubordination for refusing to meet with me on multiple Fridays. Then I sent all the documentation to your office and was given permission to terminate him, which I did."

Ms. Hall stopped writing and relaxed back into her chair. "Mr. Steward has filed a complaint with the EEOC claiming both race and age discrimination against our company, and you personally."

"I can't say that I'm totally surprised," I commented.

"He is also asking for $500,000 in damages and another $120,000 for lost wages because he has been unable to find employment at his age," she said. "He claims the $120,000 would compensate him for two years at which time he would turn sixty-two and be able to start drawing against his social security pension."

I made no reply because there was no question, just a statement by Ms. Hall.

After a few awkward moments, she asked, "How do you feel about that?"

I shrugged my shoulders and threw up my hands. "I don't have any feelings about it one way or the other," I responded. "We gave him several chances to improve his performance, and he was unwilling to make the necessary changes to accomplish that goal."

"We used the HR write-up policy by the book and still saw no change," I continued. "So I sent in my documentation, and your department gave me the OK to terminate him."

Silence again from both John Warren and Ms. Hall. I broke the silence this time.

"Surely, we are going to contest his claim?" I asked.

"Unfortunately, it's not quite that simple," Ms. Hall stated. "Our legal team has looked at this complaint, and even though you did everything correctly and by the book, they feel there is a 75 percent chance we would lose if this goes to a jury trial."

I could feel the Viking inside me starting to rise as I replied, "So what would you suggest?"

John, who had been quiet throughout the exchange, finally spoke. "There is an issue here that needed addressing, and you did that appropriately. But there are also extenuating circumstances that no one in HR caught when they gave you the OK to terminate Mr. Steward."

"Before we go any further," I said a little too loudly, "what is it the two of you propose?"

John started where he'd left off. "The two years to social security eligibility should have been a flag for HR to give Tony even more chances to improve his performance before terminating him. Two years without a paycheck or unemployment compensation is pretty rough when you're terminated at sixty after working for a company sixteen years."

"Two points, please!" I rebutted. "First, because he had worked for us for sixteen years, he was given one year's earnings as part of his severance package. For that money, he signed documents that he would not seek further compensation from the company. Is his lawsuit even valid given the signed documents we have on file?

"Second, that specific territory has doubled the business in one year over any sales numbers in the past eight years. A brand-new salesman went into his area and proved that Tony's performance was subpar. That's why he was terminated!"

"But he is still sixty, and he's still a minority," Ms. Hall responded. "And our legal team doesn't feel comfortable with betting against him with a jury of his peers."

"So what do you propose, and how do I fit into your plan?" I asked calmly, even though my blood was boiling on the inside.

Sheepishly, John answered, "We are thinking about a counteroffer to satisfy the EEOC." Putting his hands in the prayer position and holding them close to his chest, he continued. "Legal wants to offer him his job back and keep him aboard at least until after he reaches sixty-two.

"During those two years, you can continue to address any performance issue so that documentation could be used later if necessary. We will let him keep the severance money and bring him back with a three-month-wage guarantee until he can get his feet back on the ground."

"Legal has been in touch with his lawyer, and they believe he will accept that offer," Ms. Hall interjected.

I sat quietly, saying nothing.

"I know this is hard, Michael," Rick acknowledged, "but this really boils down to dollars and corporate exposure if we decide to fight this. Five hundred thousand could easily turn into $1 million or more by the time the lawyers are through with this."

There was an extended silence again before John spoke. "Do you think you could live with this if we make the offer?"

I sat there struggling with myself on how to answer. Finally, I countered, "Unfortunately, Rick, I can't."

I watched as both sets of eyes grew larger. "I don't have a racist bone in my body, but Tony using his race and his age to extort money from a corporation just doesn't sit well with me, and I won't be a part of it. He's gaming the system, and all of us know it.

"I know what discrimination looks like. I've seen it and read about it all my life. I can also see when someone who is underperforming is abusing the social system, simply because we've become too liberal and our government allows it. For me, I can see that this isn't a winnable fight, so I concede to our legal department.

"If you offer him a deal, please feel free to ad that Michael Larsen will no longer be with the company," I said. "That should seal the deal for the prick!"

"Michael," John snapped, rising from his chair. "For Pete's sake, be reasonable here. We don't want to lose you! You're doing an outstanding job! Please reconsider your stance on this, and let's revisit this Friday, when I hope cooler heads will prevail!"

"You've been very good to me, Mr. Warren, and I've very much enjoyed working for you. I won't leave you high and dry here," I responded. "If this deal with Tony Steward is accepted next week, it will take another two weeks before Tony returns to the truck center.

You send me my replacement as early as tomorrow, and I'll train him or her to the best of my abilities during that two-week window."

"Michael!" Ms. Hall stated. "I saw this conversation going a lot of different ways, but none of them ended with you leaving the company. Please! Please take the weekend to reconsider your position."

"Sharon, John," I stated, "it's all about money and circumstances. I believe those were the words you used. Well, it's not about money for me—it's about integrity! My father used to say, 'You either stand for something or fall for everything.'

"I understand the company's stance on this matter. I just don't agree with it. Besides, the first time Tony Steward would walk up to me with a shit-eating grin on his face in my store, I'd knock his teeth out, and I'm pretty sure he'd win that lawsuit as well."

I stood up, went to the door, and then turned back. "John," I ended, "I'd like to be the one that tells Gabby about this if you don't mind."

John shook his head in agreement. "Not a problem. What was said in this room will stay in this room."

Looking over at Ms. Hall, I finished. "It was a pleasure to meet you, ma'am."

With tears forming in her eyes, she responded, "Oh, Michael! I'm so sorry things are ending this way! I'm just so sorry!"

CHAPTER 15

We were all sitting around the dining room table as Gabby brought in a large platter of steaming sliced turkey and set it down in the center of the table. "That look's wonderful," Jacob said, as several around the table seconded his statement.

It was a full house with each of the kids bringing a friend for Thanksgiving with us. Jacob brought Sophie, who was now his roommate, since they'd moved in together six months ago. Aria brought her boyfriend, Todd, whom she'd been seeing for about three months and was meeting the family for the first time. Thomas brought Elise, the girl who was going to have his babies someday. Everyone except Sophie and Todd had already met Elise.

Gabby and I had invited my mom and Ronnie to join us for Thanksgiving, but they declined. Ronnie had to work the day following Thanksgiving, Black Friday, and Mom needed to be at work the following Monday morning and didn't want to have to rush home after a quick trip to Portland.

It was tight quarters as we squeezed eight people into the dining room and readied to eat our feast. Just moments before entering the dining room, we had been deeply engrossed in our first NFL football game of the day, which Dallas won 24–17. Now we were taking a pause between football games to enjoy the delicious-smelling meal Gabby and Aria had prepared for our Thanksgiving holiday.

Once everyone was seated, I said a prayer, thanking God for blessing us so richly. When I was about to finish my prayer, Thomas cut in and expressed his gratitude for all the wonderful blessings bestowed on us, especially family. Everyone said, "Amen," in unison once he was finished.

Once the bowls and platters had all made their way around the table, we ate and had a group conversation. Everyone took a turn updating each other about what was happening in their lives.

Thomas talked about his new job as a medical sales representative and walked us through what that meant. He seemed pretty excited about the job, but even more so about not having to work weekends and holidays anymore in the hotel business. He and Elise kept looking at each other and smiling as they ate dinner. It was obvious they were smitten with each other. As I watched them, for the first time, I wondered if she might, in fact, be the person to have Thomas's babies. The fleeting thought put a smile on my face.

Elise talked about her nursing school and how much she loved it. She had two more years of school, and she had decided she wanted to be a labor and delivery nurse once she graduated. She made the comment that there were multiple hospitals in the Portland Metro area, and she would be willing to work at any of them.

Aria asked her, "What if none of them are hiring when you're through with school? Would you look in Salem or Eugene so you could go to work?"

Looking at Thomas first, she responded, "No, I wouldn't. I would wait until something opens in Portland. Thomas's job is here, and I'm not willing to go anywhere else unless he does."

Everyone smiled at the comment, and Jacob started humming the "Wedding March" loud enough for everyone to hear. That was followed by several laughs and chuckles until Gabby lightheartedly put a stop to Jacob's humming.

Aria told us how she met Todd and that they'd had instant chemistry. They liked the same food and listened to the same music. In fact, both were musical trivia experts. They could hear the beginning music or just a word or two from almost any song, and tell you what the song was, who the artist was, and in which decade it had become a hit. As soon as a radio was turned on, both tried to be first shouting out the song and singer. They were very good at it!

Todd and his brother owned a small business, and he lived in an apartment with a roommate. Aria also lived in an apartment with a roommate. She commented, even though they didn't live together, they spent almost all their time at one or the other's apartment together. They seemed happy.

Jacob and Sophie might as well have been married. They'd rented an apartment and moved in together several months ago, and they acted like they were husband and wife already. Jacob would start a conversation, and Sophie would finish half of his sentences. She was bubbly, full of life, and quite athletic. They both had road motorcycles and dirt bikes; both snow skied; both played league soccer; and they loved hiking and dogs.

For Jacob's birthday this year, Sophie had given him a gift certificate for both to go on three skydiving jumps. He loved it, and they made three successful jumps together!

Jacob treated Sophie with great respect and was very kind to her. Gabby and I always wondered why he hadn't asked her to marry him yet since they'd been together for over five years now.

When it was Jacob's turned, he hit us all with another surprise. "I took some of the money that Papa Jake left me, and I've started a business of my own. I bought an invisible fence company that puts up electric fence monitors to keep animals in a specific area. It's a relatively new concept, but I have signed about 50 percent of the customers I made proposals to."

"How much does it cost?" Gabby asked.

"Depends on the size of the yard," Jacob responded. "If you and Dad were to install it in your front yard, it would probably cost about $800."

"That seems like a lot!" Gabby expressed.

"Not a lot for most people who ask for this type of fencing," Jacob countered. "The product is geared more toward high-end users and people who want to let their dogs out but don't want a fence to destroy the aesthetics of their home. And, trust me, there are a lot more people out there than you would imagine who are willing to pay for this!"

"Sophie and I laugh about it all the time, but I went to college for four years to get a degree, two more years to get a master's, and now I'm digging ditches for a living!"

Everyone laughed as soon as the words were out of Jacob's mouth.

Sophie broke in. "Don't let him make you feel sorry for him! He has a machine that digs a one-inch-wide, three-inch-deep trench to put the electrical line in. I've operated the machine myself, and it's very easy to use."

"How about you, Dad? Any luck finding a job you'd be interested in?" Jacob asked.

I looked over at Gabby, who smiled and put her hand over mine on the dinner table. Smiling back at her, I turned my attention back to Jacob and answered, "There are a lot of jobs out there, and I just haven't found the right one for me yet."

"Your father has always been a thrifty man, and we have a good amount of savings in the bank," Gabby interjected. "He's been keeping busy, looking for work, and had time to do a few things around the house. It's been good for him to have this time off."

"Gabby and I have decided to sell the house in Fresno," I stated flatly. "We don't want to have to deal with renters, and none of you want to live there, so we are going to sell it."

Looking back at Gabby, I continued. "That will give us a pretty good cushion until something comes along that strikes my fancy."

"Do you have any leads or ideas about what you would like to do next?" Thomas asked.

"Not really," I answered. "I check the want ads every day and go down to the employment office twice a week to see what's available out there. I've been doing the same routine religiously for eight months now with no offers—well, no offers I want to accept.

"I have come to the realization that my age has become a bit of a detriment as I look for gainful employment. Most of the other gentlemen and ladies applying for positions I'm interested in are younger than me. I have the advantage with experience, while they have the advantage with longevity.

"But this time off has given me a chance to spend some much-needed time with my mom and my brother in California," I said positively. "I've been back to Beaumont twice in the last six months to visit and check up on them."

"How is Grandma doing?" Jacob asked.

"She's fine," I replied. "She quit waitressing, and she got a job working for the school district in one of their cafeterias. She makes school lunches for the kids, and she loves it! She's made some new friends, loves her work hours, and is off the same number of days as the students. Plus, she gets off for spring vacation, Christmas vacation, and three months during the summer!"

"That sounds pretty cool," Aria said when I'd finished.

"It's perfect for her," I replied. "Just enough work to keep her busy and around other people, but not so much work that she doesn't have time for herself. She's also very active in her church, which exposes her to a whole other group of friends. She really seems happy with her life right now!"

"How about you, Gabby?" Jacob asked. "How do you like being married to this big lug?"

Everyone chuckled, and then she responded, "Best thing I ever did was marry your dad! Although I didn't know at the time that I was going be one of those women that would be supporting a dead-beat right after our marriage!"

Everyone laughed, including me, as she continued. "I'm just kidding! He is a wonderful husband. And while he's been off work, he's turned into quite the cook! Once or twice a week, I come home to a beautiful gourmet meal for dinner. He has quite honestly spoiled me, and when he finds work, I have decided he should still cook for us once or twice a week!"

Todd yelled from the living room. "Hey, guys, the second game is about to start! You'd better get in here if you want to watch the opening kickoff!"

After clearing the table, all the male members of the family retired to the living room to watch football, while the females made quick work of the dishes and cleanup. Then they joined us in the living room.

From out of left field, Thomas asked, "What do you guys think about Y2K? Is every computer in the world going to self-destruct? Are we only a couple of months away from the end of the world? Have you stocked up on food and water yet?"

Todd responded, "I don't believe in any of that crap!" Pausing for a second, he said, "But I am going to back up my computer at work and unplug everything on New Year's Eve just in case something unexplainable happens."

"Are you kidding me?" Jacob answered. "Sophie and I are going to a Y2K party at a friend's house, and all I know is that if the world ends, the world ends! I guarantee you, if that happens, we won't be feeling any pain at the end!"

Elise cut in. "The Bible says, about that day or hour no one knows, not even the angels in heaven, or the Son, but only the Father. I believe the Bible, not the propaganda a bunch of wackos are trying to spread. I plan on waking up on January 1, 2000, going downstairs, and watching the Rose Parade like I have for the last twenty plus years!"

After everyone had commented, I chimed in, "Guys, Y2K isn't about the world ending! There have been a number of survival boot camps that have sprung up as some radicals think Y2K will spark a worldwide disaster, but that's pretty much just science-fiction stuff!

"I've had a lot more time than most of you to read up on this, and it really boils down to a math problem. This is nothing more than a computer bug. Computer experts call it the 'millennium bug.'

"It has to do with a problem in coding of computerized systems that has been projected to create havoc in computers and computer networks around the world at the beginning of the year 2000. It was more about the metric measurement K, which stands for thousand than anything else. There have been feverish preparations and programming corrections to ensure nothing major happens. Despite all the hype and news this event has garnered, I'm pretty sure there won't be any major issues."

"Wow!" Sophie exclaimed. "Who knew you guys were related to Michael the science guy!"

Everyone laughed as I responded, "I told you I have too much time on my hands!"

As I continued my search for employment, I came across a small ad that simply read, "Looking for a district manager for a storage company. If interested, please call." And there was a phone number attached.

I wrote down the number, and later that afternoon, I made the call.

"American Trust Storage," said the voice that answered the phone. "How can I help you today?"

"I was inquiring about the district manager job advertised in the newspaper. Is the position still open?" I queried.

"Yes, it is," came the response, "but I'm not the one you need to speak with. My boss, Ken Hayes, is the person you will need to speak with, and he's not here right now. Can I get your name and phone number, and I'll have him call you back when he comes in?"

"Certainly!" I responded. "My name is Michael Larsen, and my phone number is 503-183-4533. He can call me anytime."

"I'll let him know," the voice on the phone answered. "Thank you for calling American Trust Storage," and then they were gone.

While I waited for the return phone call, I looked up American Trust Storage in the phone book. I was quite surprised to find there were probably twenty to twenty-five locations in the Portland area.

How was it possible that I'd never seen one of these locations or even heard of them before? I wondered after discovering so many locations if they were in industrial parks or some other obscure locations. I decided to go visit one and see what the storage business was all about.

Pulling into the driveway and parking in one of the many parking spaces available, my first impression was an amazement at the size of the building in front of me. It looked like a huge square warehouse that covered a full block in all directions and was at least four stories high.

The office, which was on the left front corner of the location, had several ceiling-to-floor windows that made it easy to see inside the brightly lit showroom. There were boxes stacked throughout the office area and a long customer counter with two people behind it, waiting for me to walk inside.

"Welcome to American Trust Storage," one of them said, walking from behind the counter to meet me as I approached them.

"My name's Gene. How can I be of assistance to you today?"

"Well, I don't know," I answered. "This is my first experience with storage."

Gene was now standing in front of me when he began again. "Do you mind if I ask your name?" he asked, sticking his hand out to shake mine.

"Michael," I responded, shaking his hand, "Michael Larsen."

"Michael, we have everything here for your storage needs. Whether you're moving from one location to another, cleaning up your garage, or downsizing from your current living arrangements, we have a size unit that will meet your needs. We also sell packing supplies and boxes to make your move easier. And we offer a free truck for half a day so you can transport your items to our storage location from your home or business."

"Wow!" I exclaimed. "That's a lot of information to try and absorb!"

"Well, Michael," Gene responded, "let's start with a few questions so I can help you determine what size storage unit would work best for you."

"I'm just looking to get some stuff out of my garage so I can park a second car inside," I said. "But for today, I'm just looking for prices. I don't want to tackle this project until next weekend."

"Sound's great," he countered. "Can we make a list of the items you think you will be moving into storage?"

We made our list, and he suggested a size unit and took me into the warehouse to show me the space. We took a larger-than-normal-size elevator up to the third floor. Exiting the elevator, we walked to the second aisleway and proceeded to the space. All the while, he was pointing out features and benefits of his property to further sell me on his location.

The place seemed very clean, and it was climate controlled, so there was a pretty constant and pleasant temperature inside the building.

Once his sales presentation was over, we returned to the office to complete the process. I had been very impressed by his presentation, friendliness, and explanation of how to load the unit to get the maximum use from the space.

I reminded him that I was only shopping today, and to my surprise, he had a sales response to that objection as well.

"Well, Michael," he began, "do you think the space I showed you would work for you?"

"Yes, I do," I responded. "But as I said, I'm only shopping today."

"Michael, we are 94 percent occupied at this time," he said. "I only have two spaces on the property that size, and I would hate to see you wait a week and have both spaces rented out from under you."

"How about this, Michael," he continued, "why don't we reserve this space in your name until next Saturday? There is no charge to reserve it, and you don't have to pay anything until you move into the space. There is really no other way I can guarantee this space will still be available next week."

"That sounds like a good idea," I responded. "But what if I choose not to take it next Saturday?"

"We are reserving it as a convenience to you," he retorted. "If you don't want the space, then simply let me know, and I'll cancel the reservation. There is no obligation to you if you cancel the reservation."

Realizing I could cancel the reservation with no monetary obligation, I decided to reserve it. "Let's do it!" I replied enthusiastically.

"Sounds great!" he answered. "I just need to get some quick information from you so we can make the reservation."

Once he'd thanked me, set up a time for me to use their free truck, and showed me what packing supplies he thought I would need to maximize the space, we shook hands one last time, and I exited his business.

Driving home, I couldn't get over how well he'd presented his product and that he didn't let me say no to anything but, instead, locked me into his location to stop me from looking at any competitor locations.

The next day, I received a call from Ken Hayes, who identified himself as a district manager for American Trust Storage. We set an appointment to have an in-person interview on Wednesday morning.

Arriving at the American Trust location where his office was located, I walked in and was immediately greeted by one of the staff members. I explained that I had an appointment with Ken Hayes, and they asked me to wait in the store while someone went to get him.

I had a couple of minutes to wander around the store and observe their retail presentation. This was the second American Trust location I'd been in over the last couple of days, and like before, I was quite impressed with the merchandising, the cleanliness, and the attitude of the staff I'd met.

A tall, slender, balding man entered through the front door accompanied by the employee who'd been sent to fetch him. He had on slacks, a white shirt with the sleeves rolled up to his elbows, and a tie.

Sticking his right hand out, he introduced himself. "Ken Hayes!" he said, forcing a slight smile as he watched for my reaction through his thick dark-framed glasses.

"I'm Michael Larsen," I responded, shaking his hand.

Letting go of my hand, he said, "Let's go back to my office where we can talk." He turned, walking toward the front door, and I followed him outside and around the side of the building.

Stopping at the first door we came to, he opened it, and I followed him into the small office.

His office, though small, seemed quite functional for one person: a desk with a computer on it, two chairs in front of the desk for visitors, a printer on a separate stand next to his desk, and a bookcase to his left full of three ring binders filled with what I assumed to be reports.

He looked over my resume for a few minutes and then, looking at me, said, "What do you know about the storage business?"

"Nothing!" I responded. "I was in one of your properties two days ago, and that's the first time I've ever really thought about storage."

Looking back at my resume, he said, "Michael, I think we should get a couple of things out in the open. First, this is not a glamorous business. We store people's stuff, they pay us a monthly fee, and if after a certain period they don't pay us, we sell their stuff at public auction.

"Your job will be to hire and train store managers, do monthly audits to ensure we are following state laws, handle customer complaints, maintain the properties, and deal with roof leaks or customer break-ins, if they should occur, cut locks off delinquent units, and inventory the items inside for auction. Then once a month, you'll advertise and sell the delinquent spaces and ensure the money gets to the bank. You will be the auctioneer each month during the sales. Like I said, it's not a glamorous job."

I had questions but decided not to ask them until he was finished speaking.

"Second, looking at your past compensation, I can tell you up front that we would not pay anywhere near what you are used to making. The starting wage for this job is $45,000."

"How many locks do you cut each month?" I asked.

"It depends, but usually between 75 and 150 each month," he replied.

"And how many units do you sell every month?" I continued.

"On a normal month, probably twenty, but it could be up to fifty units," he responded. "You'll spend approximately eight working days of each month with lock cuts and auctions. Those two tasks account for about a third of your time as a district manager each month."

"Interesting," I responded.

He smiled, looked down at his hands on his desk, and said, "Before we waste any more time on this interview, from what I've just explained the job is, are you still interested in the position?"

"I am," I answered.

"Why?" he asked.

"Look, Ken," I began, "I've been looking for work for almost ten months now. There aren't a lot of jobs out there offering the money I was making previously. And there doesn't seem to be an appetite to hire a fifty-year-old person by most companies. Everyone is looking for someone they can train and build on for the future.

"I feel that I have fifteen, maybe twenty good years left in me to work hard and add positive results to any company's bottom line. That's why I'm here.

"As for the money," I continued, "$45,000 is a whole lot better than $324 a week in unemployment payments! I just want to get back to doing something."

Ken sat back in his chair as we held each other's gaze. "Well, you look physically fit enough to do the job, and I have no doubt you have enough intelligence. Do you have any experience with computers?"

"I do," I responded. "I'm pretty proficient with them actually."

"Well, all right, then," he said, standing up and offering his hand again to shake. "I'm going to send your resume forward to Wendy Jones, our regional vice president, and she will set up a second interview with you. She is in Seattle—that won't be a problem for you, will it?"

"Not a problem," I responded, shaking his hand. "Thank you for your time, and I look forward to hearing from Ms. Jones." I exited the office with a pretty optimistic view of this first interview and started looking forward to the next one with Wendy Jones."

The American Trust Storage regional office was in their corporate headquarters. It contained both offices for company officers as well as a functioning storage site for retail customers.

It was in a prestigious area of waterfront property on Lake Washington, very close to downtown Seattle and the Space Needle. The most striking difference between this building and the one's I'd seen in Portland was its size. This monster easily covered three square blocks and appeared to be about twelve stories tall, clearly dwarfing any of the facilities I'd seen in Portland.

Entering the main entrance, there was a sign to the left that simply said: "Corporate Offices," in front of a bank of four elevators. Looking the other way, I was looking at similar floor-to-ceiling windows and a retail display of stacked boxes and merchandise just like I'd seen in the other American Trust locations.

Walking over to the elevator, I pushed the button for the twelfth floor, per the directory in the elevator lobby. When the door opened, several people got out and were replaced by me and three others as the doors closed, and the elevator started up.

As the doors opened, I walked into a very nice reception area with a semicircle desk manned by two individuals, both with computers and telephones in front of them. Above the desk in large chrome letters were the words "America Trust Storage Corporate Headquarters."

As I approached the marble-topped desk, a very attractive Asian woman sitting to the left side of the reception desk smiled and asked if she could help me.

After telling her I was here to interview with Wendy Jones, she asked me to take a seat and she would let Ms. Jones know I was here.

There was a lot of activity in the reception area with people coming and going both from behind the wall at the back of the receptionist desk as well as on and off multiple elevators. After about a fifteen-minute wait, the Asian receptionist stepped out from behind her desk and approached me.

"Ms. Jones is ready for you," she said, again smiling at me. "If you would follow me, please."

I stood as instructed and followed her down a long hallway to a beautiful mahogany door that had a plaque on it simply reading, "Wendy Jones," and underneath her name, it read, "Northwest Region Vice President."

Opening the door, the receptionist stepped aside and motioned me in as she held the door open. Once I had passed her, she walked forward to Ms. Jones's desk and laid down the resume I had brought with me in front of her. Saying nothing, she turned and exited the office, leaving the two of us alone.

The office was very well appointed and had floor-to-ceiling windows directly behind Ms. Jones and her large maple desk. I had a 180-degree view of Lake Washington with a multitude of boats, both large and small, bobbing about in the crystal-blue water.

Ms. Jones stood, offered her hand, and introduced herself. She was dressed in an expensive-looking dark blue pants suit. She was a fit woman of between thirty-five and forty, I suspected. She wore very little makeup, and her hair was medium length and quite curly.

Shaking her hand, I, in turn, introduced myself, and we both took a seat facing each other.

"So," she began, "Ken forwarded you to me because he felt you were capable of handling all the duties of a district manager in Portland. Is that correct?"

"Yes, ma'am," I replied.

"Please call me Wendy, if you would," she stated. "I don't like being addressed as young lady, honey, ma'am, miss, or any other slang term you may be familiar with! My name is Wendy Jones, and you can call me Wendy or Ms. Jones. Those are the only two acceptable monikers I respond to!"

Her directness caught me off guard, as I responded, "Yes, ma'am!"

She shot me a look, her eyes narrowing, as I quickly corrected myself. "I'm sorry, I meant, yes, Wendy!"

After looking over my resume for several seconds, she stated, "If I were to find you acceptable for this position, I would forward you for one last interview with our divisional vice president. Because you live 150 miles away and because we need to fill this position quickly, I would like to ask John Belk, our divisional vice president, to come in, and we can interview you together. Do you foresee any problem with a double interview?"

"No," I replied. "I'm fine with that."

She picked up her telephone, hit a couple of numbers on the base unit, and waited for an answer. "Hi, John, its Wendy," she stated flatly. "Do you have time to interview the DM candidate for Portland with me now?"

She listened as he answered her and then responded, "Sounds good! I'll see you in a second."

She had barely hung up the phone when a tall, slender forty-five-year-old-looking man walked through her door without knocking. He was nicely dressed in a gray suit and blue tie. Quickly walking toward us, he stuck out his hand to shake.

I stood and shook his hand as he announced himself. "Hi, I'm John Belk. It's a pleasure to meet you." Letting go of my hand but not waiting for a response, he picked up my resume off Wendy's desk and sat down in the chair next to me.

"Michael Larsen," I said simply, sitting down while he studied the resume intently.

"Mr. Larsen," he began, "it appears most of your work life has been in another industry. Why would you want to work in the storage industry?"

"I don't honestly know much about the storage industry," I responded. "But I believe I have developed a set of management skills that are transferable to any industry. Frankly, I'm just ready to get back to work!"

"In looking at your resume," he continued, "it appears you've been unemployed for a pretty lengthy amount of time. Are there any gaps in here that we should know about? You know, jobs you've done, didn't like, but decided not to put on your resume?"

"No, sir, there are no gaps," I answered. "I have been unemployed for almost ten months now."

"You made considerably more money than we start a new district manager at," Wendy said pointedly. "Did Ken explain our compensation package to you?"

"Not completely, but he did speak about starting salary, so I am aware of what the starting wages are."

"Why would you be willing to take that large a cut in pay?" John asked.

"As I told Ken, what I've made in the past is of no consequence now. I am receiving $324 per week on unemployment, and that is my reality today. So your starting wage is a 300 percent increase over my current income."

"That's an interesting way to think of it," John said, smiling for the first time. "Here's my biggest concern, Michael. Say we hire you and invest in three months of training before we turn you loose as a district manager. Then once we place you, someone offers you more money to come on board with them. Why would you stay if you could make more money somewhere else?"

"I don't currently have any other interviews or opportunities available," I responded. "And if you were to hire me, I would stop looking for work. My wife works, and we are living comfortably without me working. I don't have to work—I choose to work. I have a lot to offer any company, and I am happy to share my management experiences with any and all your team members. As you can see by my resume, I don't change jobs often."

"What would your last employer say about your work ethic and performance?" Wendy asked.

"On the record, they would say I worked from such a date to such a date. My wages were X amount of dollars. I am eligible for rehire. That's pretty much it!

"But if you spoke to the divisional manager, John Warren, he would more than likely give me a great recommendation."

"If that's the case," Wendy asked, "why don't you back there and work versus working for us for half the money?"

"That's complicated," I responded.

"It may be complicated, but I would like to know why you left your previous job if you were doing such a great job," John asked.

I knew I was about to step into a trap of my own doing, but I decided to tell the whole truth. I told the entire story about Tony Steward and his termination, the EEOC complaint that followed, and the company's stance on how to move forward versus my own thoughts. I ended my story with "I believe everyone deserves a fair chance at success. But whether it's the color of your skin, your age, or your sexuality, no one should be able to underperform and keep their job by yelling discrimination. It's not fair to the employer."

There was silence for a moment, and I decided to put an exclamation point on my comments. "And I still believe that way today!" I said sternly.

"Well, I've heard enough!" John said, rising from his chair, placing my resume on top of Wendy's desk, and scribbling something across the face of the document. Then standing and facing me, he stuck his hand out for a second time to shake.

I rose to my feet and shook his hand. "It was nice meeting you, Mr. Larsen. Good luck!"

Turning back to Wendy, he simply said, "Give me a call when you've finished, and we can talk." She shook her head affirmingly and then he was gone.

Sitting back down in my chair, my heart sank into my stomach as I realized I'd probably committed political suicide. I waited patiently for the rejection speech that was about to be delivered.

"Do you have any questions for me?" Wendy asked matter-of-factly.

"No. No, I don't, Ms. Jones," I replied dejectedly.

She was silent as she wrote comments of her own on my resume. Looking up, she said, "John and I would like to offer you the job of district manager for Portland. John asked me to increase your starting wage to $50K. Take a few days and decide if that is acceptable, and then let me know."

I sat there dumbfounded. I was overwhelmed, confused, and more excited than I'd been in months! I couldn't wait to tell Gabby the news!

CHAPTER 16

It had been a year since starting with American Trust Storage, and for the most part, things were going well. My training with Ken was quite interesting to me, being in such a different industry with zero experience.

After two weeks of training at a location with a district training manager, I was sent to run a location by myself. This was the same training all store managers would accomplish in their first thirty days of employment. Once the training was complete, Ken gave me a proficiency test to see if I could effectively rent a storage unit, overcome objections, do all the paperwork correctly, and enter everything into our computer system. I passed the test.

The next thirty days were spent learning the district manager's job. Doing store audits, handling maintenance issues, staff scheduling, and sales training were easy tasks to master. The lock cutting, inventory of items in a unit, and sale of the customer units were both time-consuming and lengthy processes.

The third month was spent running thirteen stores as if they were my own district. As I came across problems or issues, I would call Ken for help. I tried not to call him about the same issue twice if possible. But I was still a bit uncomfortable selling a tenant's personal items out of a space just because they were delinquent on their rent by ninety days.

Once training was completed, the Portland area was split up into two districts, and I was assigned one district, while Ken was assigned to run the other.

Wendy, my regional manager, came to Portland during my second week as a district manager and spent one day working and testing my skill levels and then spent the next day on a ride along with Ken, I assume doing the same thing.

At the end of the second day, Wendy asked that we all meet back at Ken's office to debrief. I felt comfortable that our time together had gone well, and I was looking forward to her feedback.

Knocking before entering, Ken yelled to come in. Once inside the office, I looked first at Ken and simply said "Hi," before turning to Wendy and saying with a smile, "Good morning, young lady. How are you today?"

As soon as the words were out of my mouth, I knew I'd made a mistake. Out of my peripheral vision, I saw Ken physically pushing his chair back away from his desk. He was shaking his head slightly from side to side, and I could see real fear on his face.

Wendy stood up, turned to face me, and said nothing at first. I readied to defend myself because it looked like she might try to slap me.

I started to apologize. "I'm sorry" was all I got out before she interrupted me.

"Shut up and sit down!" she yelled at me.

I did as I was told and sat in the second empty chair on our side of the desk.

She lit into me like I was a two-year-old child, and she did it with venom. She started with I obviously didn't respect women and then continued with how disrespectful I was to her personally and to her position within the company and then morphed into I had no idea how many asshole men just like me she'd had to deal with on her way to becoming a regional vice president and finished her five-minute lecture with a personal attack, calling me smug and arrogant. She also wanted me to know that she hadn't wanted to hire me but had been overruled by the divisional manager and that it would only be a matter of time until I proved her right.

Her hurtful comments made me angry, but I again tried to apologize by saying, "I truly am sorry for my callous remarks!"

She didn't accept or even acknowledge my apology but, rather, turned her attention to Ken. It only took a second to determine her fury wasn't completely spent yet!

"The Portland portfolio looks worse than I've ever seen it, Ken! There were dirty hallways, trash in and around the properties, buildings with interior lights out, sloppy offices with half-assed box displays, and too many maintenance issues to mention!"

She stopped, sucked air into her lungs, and then began again. "You two need to get your shit together, or you'll both be walking down the road kicking rocks and thinking, damn, that was a great job! Do you understand me?" she concluded for emphasis.

"Yes, Wendy!" Ken responded quickly.

"I'll be back here in two weeks, and both of you had better have your houses in order or there will be disciplinary actions written! Am I clear?"

Ken again said, "Yes, Wendy!"

At the same time, I said, "Yes, ma'am!" only in a softer voice. I thought, *Oh, crap, I didn't just say that, did I?*

Wendy must not have heard my response as she picked up her oversized purse and computer bag and walked out the door, slamming it behind her.

Ken and I just sat there staring at one another in silence. Finally, I asked, "Is she always like that?"

"No!" he answered. "I've never seen her blow up like that in the three years I've worked for her." A crooked smile formed on his face as he continued. "One thing for sure, she doesn't like you!"

"I'm just glad she didn't hear me call her ma'am at the end of that tirade," I confessed. Both of us laughed loudly once I'd finished my comment.

In mid-January, Wendy brought all the district managers in her regional office in Seattle for a two-day meeting. There were two DMs from Portland, two from Spokane, two from the Richland, and six from the Seattle market.

District managers were measured almost exclusively on performance of a few specific metric with our company. By the end of the calendar year, I was leading the region in every measured metric but one.

After we'd finished with our meeting agenda, Wendy presented the District Manager of the Year award to a Seattle district manager, Tamara Lacey. We all clapped, whooped, and howled as she received a plaque with her name and the district's number on it, along with a check for $500. This was a prestigious award, and everyone wanted to be recognized as the DM of the Year for the region.

John Belk, the senior divisional vice president, had joined the meeting to present Tamara with the award and the check. Shortly after the presentation ceremony, John left the conference room and returned to his office.

Ken and I had driven up to the meeting in Seattle together to save gas. We were about to leave the office to head back to Portland when Gloria, John Belk's secretary, caught me and asked me if I could visit with him for a couple of minutes.

I told Ken I'd meet him at the car as soon as I finished speaking with John. Gloria led me into John's office, and I was surprised to see Wendy sitting in one of the chairs across from him as John asked me to take a seat next to her.

"Michael," John began, "you've just completed your first full year with us. How do you think you've done so far?"

I looked over at Wendy, who was glaring at me, and thought, *Uh-oh, this can't be good.* Nervously, I responded, "I think I've done OK. Wendy asked Ken and me to fix several areas when she was doing property visits early last year, and I believe we corrected those issues to her satisfaction and brought the properties up to company standards."

Turning to Wendy, he asked, "Were they corrected to your satisfaction?"

Her face was crimson and became redder by the second as she responded with a simple "Yes."

Turning his attention back to me, he asked, "Do you know where you stand at the end of the year in the district manager metrics?"

I smiled and was happy to respond, "Our district ended the year first in every metric except year-over-year revenue. But I'll take winning eight out of nine metrics!"

"For your first year," he responded, "I would have to agree with you. That is an outstanding performance!"

"Thank you, John," I answered, finally realizing I wasn't going to be fired.

Turning back to Wendy, John asked, "Can you tell me exactly how you determine the District Manager of the Year for your region, Wendy?"

It was obvious that Wendy was nervous as she scooted around in her chair before answering. "Well, there are several factors," she began. "I look at the DM metric rankings, I look at property visit reports for each district when I do property visits, I look at who is taking on extra assignments when necessary, and I consider tenure and if I feel the person is promotable to the next level if needed."

"Do you think Tamara is promotable?" John asked pointedly.

"With a year or two of mentoring, I believe she could be," Wendy responded.

"I don't!" John said sharply. "How many metrics did Tamara place number one in the ranking?"

"Just one, revenue," Wendy said. "But increased revenue is our most important metric. That's bringing real money into the company coffers."

"Where did Michael rank in revenue?" he asked.

"Second, I believe," she replied. "I can check that," she said, looking through her briefcase. "I have the report right here somewhere."

"You don't need to check it," John said. "He did finish second in revenue."

"During the Christmas vacation, I visited with family in Portland," John said, sitting back in his chair and looking up toward the ceiling. "I had a little extra time on my hands, so I visited a couple of Ken's properties and a couple of Michael's properties.

"I thought Ken's properties looked pretty good, and his people were a little above average at best. But Michael's properties were pristine. All the lights worked, no paper or trash on the properties, nicely presented box displays in each office, well-trained, knowledgeable personnel, all in clean uniforms."

Turning his gaze back directly to Wendy, he continued. "What additional assignments has Tamara done for you this past year?" John inquired.

"Well, she's my go-to girl if I need anything!" Wendy responded.

"Like what?" John pushed.

"Because of her tenure, she's the one everyone calls if they have a question about truck rentals or auction issues. She has all the delinquency reports faxed to her office, and she sends me a spreadsheet every day, so I know exactly where we are," Wendy answered.

"Don't you get a delinquency report the next morning automatically?" he asked. "And why isn't your admin doing that for you instead of a district manager?"

Wendy didn't try to answer his question.

"So why is Tamara your Regional District Manager of the Year?"

Wendy looked a bit flustered, but quickly regaining her composure, she answered, "Tamara has been with us for five years now. She is always one or two in the metric rankings for district managers. She has passed her internal operations audit every year with flying colors. And as I stated before, she steps up to help myself and the region in any way possible!"

"Who was your District Manager of the Year last year?" John asked.

"Tamara has earned and received that award for three years in a row," Wendy replied.

John sat quietly contemplating her response and then turned to me and asked, "Michael, do you think you should have been the District Manager of the Year for last year's performance?"

I first looked to Wendy, who was starting to dab at some perspiration on her forehead with a Kleenex, and then back to John.

"I don't know the answer to that question," I replied. "I had a great year with the metrics, and I was rewarded very well through my annual bonus check. So thank you both for that and the opportunity to work for the company."

I looked back over at Wendy, who now had sweat free flowing down the side of her face, causing her to make up to streak. I knew she was in a horrible position as John asked me the question.

"But this being my first year, I know I made more than my share of mistakes," I answered. "Wendy came down on me pretty hard on our initial property tours, but I'm thankful for that now! She set the expectation for what an America Trust property should look like and gave me clear direction on what needed correcting.

"We also made two districts out of one in Portland, and we had to estimate what to use as numbers for the district manager metrics for Ken and my district," I continued. "We may have estimated too low based on the results our district was able to obtain. I guess the real test for the district will be this year when we have to beat our own numbers from last year to maintain our number-one ranking.

"But to answer your question directly, no, I don't think I should have been the District Manager of the Year for last year's performance. But I'm going to work hard and try like hell to win the award this year!" I said confidently.

John smiled and sat stoically for a few seconds before commenting. "Thank you, Michael, for your honesty and a unique perspective. I appreciate you staying after the meeting to speak with us. You'd better get going now—you've got a four-hour drive ahead of you!"

All three of us stood up, and I shook hands with both, said goodbye, and walked out of the office.

Thomas and Elise had asked to come over and have dinner with us on Wednesday night, which was a little out of character, since we usually saw the kids on Friday through Sunday most weeks. Gabby had prepared a nice pot roast dinner, knowing Thomas was especially fond of the dish.

The conversation was light, and each of us talked about the good, the bad, and the ugly going on in our workplaces or at school. Elise won the prize for having the worst start to her week by accidentally deleting a term paper on her computer that she couldn't get back. She almost cried as she expressed, "Ten to twelve hours of my life that I'll never get back. It was heartbreaking to have to start all over from scratch."

We all expressed our sympathy and continued to eat dinner. Finally, Thomas said, "We have some news for the two of you!" He looked to Elise first, and both had instant smiles on their faces.

"I asked Elise's dad for permission to marry her, and he gave us his blessing!" Thomas said. "Then I asked Mary to marry me, and she said yes. So we wanted your blessing as well before we start making plans!"

Gabby got up from the table and quickly walked around to hug, first, Elise and then Thomas. "Of course, you have our blessing!" she said, kissing her son on the cheek. "What exciting news!" she continued. "You guys will have to tell us all about the proposal! You know, who, what, where, and when! I want to hear every detail!" she gushed.

Rising to my feet, I hugged them both and simply said, "Congratulations, guys! We couldn't be more excited for you!"

Sitting back down, we all had happy smiles on our faces. I looked over at Gabby and said, "You owe me five bucks!"

"What for?" she asked, a puzzled look on her face.

"When we were having dinner on our wedding night with the kids in Lincoln City, Thomas said he'd met the girl who was going to have his babies, remember?"

"That's right!" Gabby answered.

Elise gave Thomas a playful smack on the arm and said, "Thomas, did you really say that to your whole family even though we'd only dated a couple of times?"

"Yeah, I did," Thomas responded.

I cut in, looking at Gabby. "If you remember correctly, that night when we had gone back to our room, I bet you five bucks that Thomas would be the first kid to get married and that I believed Elise would be the girl!"

"I do remember that!" Gabby said loudly. "How did you know?"

"He was pretty excited when he mentioned her, and he seemed very committed. I had a one-in-three chance with my guess, and the other kids never really talked about marriage."

"When are you going to tell your brothers and sisters?" Gabby asked.

"Mine already know," said Elise. Then looking over at Thomas, she said, "We'll tell Aria and Jacob tomorrow."

"When are you thinking for a date?" Gabby asked.

"We're not sure yet," Elise answered. "I want to finish nursing school first, so not until next year sometime. But I'm going to go to school this summer so I can finish early."

"That's so exciting!" Gabby squealed again. "I'm so happy for the two of you!"

After the conversation with John Belk while Wendy was in the room, my relationship with her improved dramatically. We never discussed the meeting, but from that day forward, she treated me nicer and with more respect.

She called me in my office one morning and asked if she could ride along and visit properties with me the next week.

I said sure, and we agreed to meet at my district office the next Tuesday morning.

I was in the shower, thinking about the route and the properties I wanted to visit with Wendy, when Gabby stepped into the bathroom and said, "Honey, Wendy's on the phone, and she said she needs to speak with you now! She sounded pretty upset!"

I quickly turned off the water, threw a towel around my waist, and moved into the bedroom, dripping water everywhere as I took the phone out of Gabby's hand.

As Gabby exited the bedroom, I said, "Hello," now standing in the puddle of water of my own making.

"Michael!" Wendy said loudly. "I was halfway to Portland, but I've turned around and am headed back to Seattle!"

"What's wrong?" I asked, hearing panic in her voice.

"Turn on your TV!" she spat out. "Something very bad is happening! A plane full of passengers just flew into one of the Twin Towers in New York City and exploded! So far, the government doesn't know if it was an accident or intentional."

"Oh my god!" I said, stunned by what I just heard. Then I yelled to Gabby in the other room, "Sweetheart, turn the TV on, please!"

Thinking about Wendy still on the line, I quickly said, "Drive safe, and we can talk later, and I have to go." Then I hung up the phone and went into the living room, where Gabby was standing in front of our television set with both hands over her mouth in disbelief at what she was seeing.

Like her, I stood there in full shock as they showed, first, one plane and then the second smashing into the buildings and exploding almost on a continuous loop. We watched it over and over, neither of us speaking, just listening to the news commentator.

"At 8:46 a.m. (eastern time), American Airlines flight 11 crashed into the North Tower of the World Trade Center somewhere between the ninetieth and ninety-ninth floors, killing everyone on board and hundreds inside the building."

He continued. "Within seconds, the NYPD and FDNY forces dispatched units to the World Trade Center, while Port Authority Police Department officers on site began immediate evacuation of the North Tower.

"After initially instructing tenants in the World Trade Center's South Tower to remain in the building, Port Authorities have now broadcast orders to evacuate both towers."

The commentator continued. "At 9:03 a.m., United Flight 175, which we now know was also hijacked, crashed into the South Tower somewhere around the eightieth floor, again killing everyone on board, and we can only imagine hundreds more who were in that tower."

As Gabby and I sat there watching in disbelief, she began to cry softly. I put my arm around her, and we sat down on the couch, me still dressed in only a towel but almost completely dry now.

As new information came in, it was released, and we sat there spellbound by every facet of this horrific event. A short time later, the FFA banned all flights going into or through New York air space. Thirty minutes after that, the New York Port Authority closed all bridges and tunnels in the New York City area.

Another half hour went by, and the FAA gave notice to all military installations that another flight, flight 77, had been hijacked and had turned around, headed to what appeared to be Washington DC.

Speaking from Florida, Pres. George Bush called the events in New York City "an apparent terrorist attack on our country."

Twenty-five minutes after the president spoke, hijackers aboard flight 77 crashed the plane into the western façade of the Pentagon, in Washington DC, killing all fifty-nine people aboard the plane and, at first estimates, well over a hundred military and civilian personnel who were inside that portion of the building.

For the first time in history, the FAA grounded all flights over or bound for the United States by 10:00 a.m. (eastern time). Over the next two and a half hours, some 3,300 commercial and 1,200 private flights were force landed at airports in Canada and around the United States.

After passengers and crew members aboard another hijacked flight, flight 93, contacted family and friends, they learned about the other hijacked planes that had hit New York and Washington. They mounted an attack against the hijackers to take back control of the plane. In response, the hijackers deliberately crashed the plane in a field in Pennsylvania, killing all forty passengers and crew who were aboard.

At 9:59 a.m., the South Tower of the World Trade Center completely collapsed. Experts believed that because the second plane hit lower on the building, it caused the building to implode.

We would later find out that the 767 jetliner that hit the building had almost twenty thousand gallons of jet fuel on board. The steel infrastructure could not withstand the heat of the burning jet fuel, causing it to fail and collapse.

At 10:28 a.m., only an hour and a half after flight 11 struck the North Tower, the unthinkable happened, as that building also collapsed in on itself, while America watched it all on live television. Gabby and I both grabbed for each other as we gasped at the carnage we were witnessing!

"Oh, dear God!" was all I was able to say as a combination of a dust and smoke clouds spread out from the buildings to engulf everything in their path for miles in all directions. The TV cameras caught hundreds, if not thousands, of people running away from the dense cloud, most of them gray with ash from the cloud covering their entire being.

At 11:00 a.m., Mayor Rudy Giuliani called for a complete evacuation of lower Manhattan. This order included over a million residents, workers, and tourists, as efforts continued throughout the early afternoon to search for survivors at the World Trade Center.

By 1:00 p.m. (eastern time), President Bush announced that U.S. military forces were on high alert around the world.

Neither Gabby nor I went to work that day. We didn't call in sick; we just called to let our supervisors know that we would be staying home, keeping up on the most current news about this unbelievable attack. It was almost noon before I finally pulled myself away from the television long enough to get dressed.

Gabby had already spoken with each of our kids, who all expressed the same shock and despair we felt. Aria and Todd, along with Thomas and Elise, were coming over to our house later in the day. We all just wanted to be together.

Jacob and Sophie had already gone to her parents' home and were watching the same horrible drama play out on every television channel like we were.

Aria and Todd arrived at about 3:00 p.m. Thomas and Elise showed up just before 6:00 p.m. Gabby prepared a quick dinner for us all, and we made up our plates and went back into the living room with our food to continue watching the rescue efforts.

That night on national television, Pres. George Bush addressed the nation, calling the attacks "an evil and despicable act of terror," and went on to declare that America and its allies would stand together and win the war on terrorism that had begun today in these United States.

As we continued to watch the news well into the evening, the size and scope of the attack and carnage continued to escalate with each passing hour. People trapped on the floors above both crash sites were unable to escape the building. Firefighters, paramedics, New York City police officers, and Port Authority police were trapped in the buildings as they struggled to evacuate the buildings as they imploded.

It was past midnight, and we'd been watching TV for almost eighteen hours when we decided to go to bed. We had plenty of room, so all four kids elected to stay at our house and go home early the next morning. I think everyone just wanted to feel safe with their family on a day when none of us could quite grasp the disgusting and repulsive events that had transpired.

As Gabby and I went to bed that night, I couldn't go to sleep. I kept thinking about how this day, September 11, 2001, would change America forever.

Until today, we had been a country that feared no one, a society that was confident in our own ability to protect our sovereignty against any nation or group of people who wished to do us harm. But on this day, our vulnerabilities had been exposed, and our defenses had been breached as a small group of terrorists accomplished what no army or country before them had ever been able to achieve on U.S. soil.

The initial estimate of those workers and visitors who perished in the Twin Towers was over two thousand souls. Additionally, almost four hundred first responders were feared lost as they were helping with the evacuation of the two buildings when they came down on top of them.

Over the next several weeks, the entire country seemed to be numb from this tragic experience. But we all still watched constantly as the rescue and cleanup efforts continued. Death tolls rose, stories of heroism were told, and the perpetrators were exposed.

The attackers were Islamic terrorists from Saudi Arabia and several other Arab nations. They were members of a terrorist organization known as al-Qaeda, run by a Saudi fugitive named Osama bin Laden. They were acting in retaliation for America's support of Israel and the U.S. involvement in the Persian Gulf War.

There had been a total of nineteen people involved in the 9/11 attack on America. The terrorists were able to smuggle box cutters through three East Coast airports and boarded four early morning flights for California. These flights had been chosen because the planes were loaded with extra fuel for the long transcontinental journey. Shortly after takeoff, the terrorists commandeered the four planes by force and took control of them. These ordinary passenger jets had now been transformed into guided missiles with madmen at the controls.

In response to this terrorist attack, on October 1, 2001, Pres. George Bush announced the establishment of the Office of Homeland Security.

On October 7, 2001, the United States, along with participation from other nations, invaded Afghanistan to try and find Osama bin Laden and destroy al-Qaeda. This began an unending presence by the United States at war against several Arab countries. Less than two years later, the Iraq War began with an invasion by the United States and allied forces.

Six months after the attack, Thomas and Elise set a date for their wedding. Elise wanted to be a June bride, and they settled on June 29 to be married. Their wedding plans helped put joy back into our family again. Everyone was included, but if truth were to be told, I believe Gabby may have been more excited about this wedding than Elise!

Elise, her mom, and Gabby were out of the house almost every day looking at bridal dresses and bridesmaid dresses, picking out flowers, signing up at various bridal registries, looking for the perfect wedding invitations, and tasting cakes from various bakers throughout Portland.

Jacob and Sophie took a week's vacation and came to Portland to spend some time with the family the week of the wedding and helped prepare for the big day in any way they could be of assistance.

During dinner one weeknight, when all eight of us were together, Aria asked Elise if there was anything she wanted or needed prior to the wedding. Joking, Elise said, "Just somebody to pay for it!" and everyone laughed.

"Well, Gabby and I haven't given you a wedding present yet," I said from the head of the table. "But whatever we do for you guys, we'll have to do for Aria and Jacob when they get married. We want to be fair with all of you."

"How about this," I began, "Gabby and I will give each one of you $30,000 as a wedding present."

Elise's hand immediately shot to her face to cover her mouth in shocked surprise.

"You can't be serious!" Thomas said, shaking his head in disbelief.

Even Gabby sat there staring at me, saying nothing, obviously stunned by the offer.

"I'm serious!" I responded. "We'll give each of you the money a week before your wedding, and you can use it any way you want. Use it for the wedding, for your honeymoon, or to buy a starter home for yourselves. We won't question how you use it! It's your money!"

Thomas spoke first. "I don't know what to say! That is so generous of you and Mom! I can hardly believe it!"

"I really only have one request," I added. Everyone stared at me, waiting for the request, so I continued. "Promise me that all three of you won't get married in the next six months!"

Everyone laughed loudly at the comment, and Aria responded, "I'm not getting married for a while, so you're safe, Dad!" Her comments were followed by more laughter.

The wedding was beautiful, and Elise was gorgeous in her wedding gown. As Gabby and I sat there in the front row, she had her arms wrapped around my left arm and was squeezing it tightly. She leaned over and softly said, "Look at my little boy! I have never seen him happier!" Then I a saw a single tear sliding down my coat to the place where our arms were locked together. I smiled and gently patted the arms that were wrapped around my own with my other hand, saying nothing.

My work life seemed to improve every day. I'd managed to hire some great sales associates, and space rentals and merchandise sales in my district were rocking! No other district manager in the region was performing even close to our numbers.

On Wendy's last property tours, she'd given me some very welcome praise for how far our district had come in such a short time. She stated that she was also impressed that I was, in fact, beating my own strong numbers from the year before. I felt as if we had finally bonded, and she no longer looked at me as her adversary.

I had developed a monthly routine, and by staying staffed with good people in the field locations, I was able to accomplish all my district manager tasks easily. Ken and I had become so efficient with our duties that we only worked a half day every other Friday. We played golf and had a couple of beers those other Friday afternoons, and life was good!

At our next regional meeting, Wendy informed us that we were going to have a corporate weeklong meeting in Seattle that would include all the field management as well as corporate personnel. The location managers would stay and run the properties while we attended the meeting.

The meeting plan was met with varying degrees of acceptance. I was fine with the idea. My people could run their properties very easily without me being there for a week. However, that wasn't the same for everyone. Some DMs were understaffed and thought they would have a difficult time keeping all the properties open and may need to work properties themselves. Others were control freaks and were so strongly micromanaging their district they believed everything would fall apart without their involvement!

The meeting dates were set for mid-November, and we were all told to get our houses in order, because this wasn't an optional request.

When the regional meeting was over and we were packing up to leave, Wendy asked Tamara and me to come into her office. Once we were in the office and the door was closed, she let us know we would have a more significant part to play in the meeting.

Each region had been assigned to give a thirty-minute presentation on various subjects. Because Tamara and I lead the country in merchandise sales, we had been selected to prepare and deliver a presentation on how to increase merchandise sales at the property level to everyone in attendance.

Wendy asked us to work on it together and give her weekly updates on our progress. Tamara seemed very excited to be taking on the task. I, however, knew we were in for some very long hours and hard work if we were to make a decent presentation that I would want to put my name on. Nevertheless, we accepted the challenge and decided to brainstorm individually for our first weekly update call.

On our first update call, I spoke about setting up a fake store with all the merchandise we sell and do a skit showing a manager selling each item we offer to a customer who'd walked into the store looking for merchandise.

Wendy loved the idea, and Tamara, though reluctant, agreed to our plan. She insisted that she would be the customer and I would be the property manager doing all the selling and answering her objections. I agreed to her terms, and we were off and running.

We agreed that on our next update call, I would have created rough scripts showing how to sell locks, boxes, and other merchandise for the three of us to go over and refine.

Because Tamara's district was in Seattle, where the meeting was taking place, she oversaw setting up the fake sales floor with all the appropriate signage and merchandise to make it look authentic. She was also responsible for getting it there in a timely fashion.

Everything seemed to be on track as we had our final update call, the week before the meeting. I'd made printed laminated copies of the scripts so each DM could take them home to use as a training tool for their respective teams. I'd sent copies to Tamara so she could practice her part, and I'd copied Wendy on everything.

Tamara and I agreed to go to the meeting one day early so we could set up the fake showroom and put all our props in place for the presentation. We were supposed to meet at noon that Tuesday. It was 3:00 p.m., Tuesday, and neither Tamara nor the merchandise had arrived yet.

To make matters worse, she wasn't answering her phone. I'd already left three messages and had tried to contact her a dozen times, so there was no point in calling her again.

I called Gus Rojas, a district manager whose district was next to Tamara's, and asked if he knew where Tamara was and why she wasn't answering her phone. He informed me that she had auctions today and probably still had units to sell in at least three more properties.

I was livid! Trying to keep my composure, I asked Gus if he could find out where the truck was that contained all our display material for the regional presentation, and he agreed to help me try to find it.

Five minutes after we spoke, Gus called me back. He had discovered that all the materials were loaded on a truck, but because a couple of people had called in sick today, she was short-staffed, and she didn't have a spare body available to drive the truck to the corporate offices.

Gus stated that her plan of action was that once the properties closed for the day, she would have a property manager drive the truck downtown and deliver the items to me.

Doing the math in my head, I realized that with rush-hour traffic in full swing by the time the property manager could leave, it would take a minimum of two hours to reach our meeting site. That meant the merchandise would probably be to me at between 8:30 p.m. and 9:00 p.m.

By the time Gus had completed his explanation to me, I was so angry that I could hardly talk in a normal tone. I thanked him for his help and politely hung up knowing there was nothing more I could do but wait.

Tamara called me at about 7:00 p.m. to tell me the display material was on its way to me.

As hard as I tried, I couldn't contain myself. I bombarded her with one question after another. "Why didn't you answer your damn phone all day? The merchandise was supposed to be here by noon, along with you! How or why would you schedule auctions on the same day we were supposed to be setting up our presentation? When are you going to be here so we can finish this project and practice for the presentation tomorrow?"

She was silent for a minute and then responded, "Why are you being such an asshole!"

"Me!" I yelled back into the phone. "I've done this whole project with little or no help from you! All you had to do was get the merchandise here and help set it up, and you couldn't even do that right! So when are you going to be here?"

"I haven't even packed for the conference yet, and I still have a few things to do!" she yelled back. "I'll meet you there at six o'clock in the morning, and we can practice then!"

Knowing that her comments meant I would have to set up the display by myself, I couldn't even answer her for fear of what I might say, so I simply hung up.

When the display material arrived, the property manager helped me bring it all to the stage. He offered to stay and help me set it up, but I told him to go home. He'd already been on overtime for three hours, and I didn't want to cost Tamara any more overtime than was necessary.

I finished the set up at about 1:30 a.m. As I made one last lap around the display area, I was quite pleased with my work. I walked to the back of the room to view the finished product and again was satisfied that everyone in the room would easily see the presentation on the stage.

The next morning, I got up, went down and had a quick breakfast, and then went to our meeting room. It was 7:00 a.m. as I walked in, and Tamara snapped, "You're late!"

I didn't bother to respond. "Do you have your scripts with you?" I asked.

"They're up in my room," she replied.

I was instantly angry again! I gave her a contentious smile and thought to myself how much I would love to slap her smug face and wipe off the stupid look she was giving me. Instead, I said curtly, "I have an extra set you can use while we practice!"

We ran through the presentation three or four times quickly, and I felt we were ready to competently present later in the day. "I think we're ready," I voiced.

She put down the script that I had loaned her on the counter, turned around, and left the room without comment. She never once mentioned that the office I had set up looked realistic or that it was well done or anything about it.

We had watched several presentations by other regions in the morning, and most of them were pretty good. You could tell how much work had been put in by the product they presented to the crowd. There were a couple of regions on the East Coast that did poorly, and those poor showings obviously reflected negatively on their regional managers.

We were the third presentation after lunch. Tamara and I gave our presentation, and it came off pretty much without a hitch. We received a nice round of applause, and then we were all dismissed for a midafternoon break.

As people were exiting out the main back doors, John Belk, our divisional manager, came bounding up on the stage. He shook first Tamara's hand and then mine and simply said, "That was very well done, guys! And your mock display looks fabulous!"

"Thank you, John," Tamara said before I had a chance to speak. "All the merchandise came from one of my locations. We wanted this set to look as realistic as possible! I think it looks pretty good, don't you?"

For the second time in the same day, I wanted to slap her!

"It does look very good!" John said. "Who wrote the scripts?"

"We both did," Tamara announced. "Michael wrote the original scripts, and then I helped him tweak them."

Looking directly at me, John asked, "What time did you finish setting up the stage last night?"

"I think it was about one thirty this morning," I answered.

"I knew it was pretty late," he responded. "I had a dinner meeting with the other divisionals at 9:00 p.m., and when I passed by this room, you were working on the setup. After we'd finished dinner and had a few drinks, I headed back to my room and saw you were still in here working!"

Turning his gaze to Tamara, he asked, "What time did you quit working on the display? I didn't see you either time when I walked by."

Tamara's face went instantly beet red. "Well, I had some things to finish at home, so I didn't actually get here until six o'clock this morning," she replied.

John turned back to me, winked slyly, and said, "You did a nice job, Michael!" Then he left the stage and headed out the doors at the rear of the room.

As we both stood there, I wanted to scream, "Yes! Yes! Yes! He knows she didn't do a damn thing to help with this presentation." But instead, I simply said, "That was nice of him to say." Then I left Tamara standing there as I jumped down off the stage and went outside to get a cookie and a soft drink before the break was over.

On the last day of the meeting, John Belk again found me on a break and asked if I could visit with him. I said sure, and he led me down the hall to a small business center in the front of the offices. As I stepped into the room Jeff Hall, the company CEO stood and offered his hand for me to shake.

"Jeff Hall," he said matter-of-factly. "I don't believe we've met before."

I shook his hand and replied, "No, sir, I don't believe we have."

He released my hand, sat down, and instructed both John and me to take the other empty chairs in the room.

"I know you have some more meetings to attend, but I wanted to meet you personally before you left to go back to Portland," he expressed. "I've been hearing some great comments from John and Wendy about you, and the numbers in your district are the best in the company."

"Thank you, sir," I responded shyly.

"Please, just call me Jeff," he responded and then continued. "Where would you like to be, and what would you like to be doing five years from now?"

The question caught me by surprise, and I didn't really have an answer. "Well," I joked, "I guess I'd like to have your job, but it shouldn't take five years to get there!"

Both men laughed with passion and surprise at my answer.

"I really don't have an answer for you, Jeff," I said. "I don't really know what's available with the company."

"Are you able to relocate?" Jeff asked pointedly.

"My wife works, but if an opportunity availed itself and didn't hurt us financially, we could move," I responded. "Our kids are grown, and they all live on their own, so schools and pulling them away from their friends are not a worry for us."

"If the money were right and the opportunity a huge challenge, is there anywhere you wouldn't consider moving?" he asked.

Knowing we had a separate division in Europe, I answered, "I would want to stay in the United States."

Standing, he again put out his hand for me to shake. I shook it as he said, "I like you, Michael! I think there may very well be a bright future for you with our company. You'd better get back to your meetings now!"

I thanked him for the time and turned with John to leave the office. "Keep those rental numbers up!" And then he added, "I'm sure we'll see each other again soon!"

CHAPTER 17

Fall had turned into winter and winter into spring when Jacob called me.

"Hey, Dad," he began. "How is everything going in your world?" he asked sincerely.

"Things are good here!" I responded. "My job is good, Gabby's doing great, and we're looking forward to some dry weather now that winter is over!"

"I hear yah!" Jacob responded. "We've been watching the weather reports, and you guys have been getting pounded with rain this year!"

"How about you and Sophie?" I said. "Is everything good with you guys?"

"That's kind of why I'm calling," Jacob responded. "I've asked Becky to marry me and make this relationship legal! I just wanted you and Gabby to know before we told the rest of the family."

"That's outstanding news!" I said enthusiastically. "I can't wait to tell Gabby!"

"If you don't mind, Dad, I'd like to be the one to tell her," Jacob replied.

"That's a wonderful idea," I responded. "She will love that you told her directly versus hearing the news from me. When are you going to tell her?"

"I'm going to call her at work, right after we hang up," Jacob responded.

"Well, tell Sophie congratulations for me, please! I think she's a wonderful catch, and you two make a great couple!" I said. "I couldn't be happier for both of you!"

"Thanks, Dad! That means a lot to me!" Jacob said. "I'll talk with you later." And with that, he hung up.

Fifteen minutes later, Gabby called me on my cell phone. "Oh my god! Oh my god!" she started as soon as I'd said hello. "Can you believe it? Jacob just asked Sophie to marry him!"

Smiling at her excitement, I responded, "I just heard the news myself. It's pretty exciting!"

"I'm going to call Sophie tonight and talk to her about her plans!" Gabby gushed. "So many questions to answer! Will they get married in Fresno or Portland? Will it be a small wedding or a big blowout affair? Does she need any help from me? I am available for anything she needs!"

I was almost laughing as Gabby continued the conversation, which was really with herself. I just happened to be on the other end of the phone connection, but she seemed to be rehearsing what she wanted to ask Sophie once she got home tonight more than talking to me.

"I'm sure you'll have plenty of time for all your questions to be answered," I said while she was taking a breath to get ready for the next volley of concerns. "But listen for a second," I continued. "I have a lot of work to do today. Maybe we can continue this conversation at home tonight."

It was obvious that she was reluctant to get off the phone until she'd asked all the questions in her head. She was quiet for a second and then said, "OK! We can talk about the rest of this tonight! I'm so happy for both of them!"

We said our I love yous and agreed to start up where we left off later in the evening. Then we hung up. I imagined that both of us had goofy smiles on our faces that would remain there most of the day. This wedding really was great news!

The weather had finally started to heat up as summer approached us in the northwest. It was a Wednesday in the middle of June, and I was cutting locks off delinquent units and inventorying spaces. The task was physical, and lock-cutting days were the only days that I didn't wear a white shirt and tie to work. I wore a dark polo shirt, usually navy blue, because I tended to sweat through everything during this task. I learned through experience that it wasn't quite so obvious how much I was perspiring against a dark-colored background. Some days, I would take two shirts just in case the temperature and the difficulty of the lock cutting soaked me to the point that I needed to change shirts.

I had just finished cutting locks at my third property of the day and was walking from the location office back to my car when my cell phone rang. Answering it, I was surprised to hear my mother's voice on the line.

"Michael?" she questioned, as if she might have mistakenly called the wrong number.

"Hi, Mom," I responded. "How are you?"

"Hello, Michael," she replied, and I detected a sadness in her voice.

"Is everything OK, Mom?" I asked.

"No, not really," she said. "I'm calling to let you know that Jimmy Clarke passed away yesterday."

My knees almost buckled underneath me as her news hit me. "Oh my god!" I said, "What happened?"

With her voice starting to break up slightly, Mom responded, "The police found him down by the railroad tracks where the bums hang out. They said he died from an overdose of heroine. They found several hypodermic needles lying next to his body."

I immediately felt nauseous and thought for a second that I might throw up right there in the driveway. Jimmy had been my best friend all through school. He grew up in the same kind of household I'd grown up in. He could be funny, crazy, or just fun to be around, and now he was dead, well before his time.

What went wrong in his life? I wondered. We'd both been to Vietnam and been wounded. We'd both come home to welcoming families. Was his experience so much worse than mine that he had to resort to drugs to block out the painful memories? Or did the drug addiction begin with pain medication that got out of control and replaced all normal reason? I guessed I would never know now.

"Michael?" my mom said after I'd been silently lost in my own world for a few seconds. "Are you going to be OK?" she asked softly.

"I just can't believe this has happened!" I responded. "How are his parents doing?"

"Louise is crushed," Mom stated. "Even though she and Art knew months ago that Jimmy was headed down this path, she's still beside herself that he's gone."

"Art is just angry! This is the second son he's lost, and he's angry at God but taking it out on everyone around him. He keeps saying over and over that a father is not supposed to outlive his children! 'Why is God punishing me through my kid's deaths?'"

I felt tears starting to run down my face as I could almost feel the anguish Art must be going through. My heart was breaking for both of Jimmy's parents.

"Are you going to come home for the memorial service?" Mom asked.

"They're not going to have a funeral, just a memorial service?" I questioned.

"Jimmy didn't look like the Jimmy you and I knew at the end," my mom stated. "He was skinny as a rail, his teeth had gone bad, and his personal hygiene was almost nonexistent. I saw him walking down the street about three weeks ago in filthy clothes, unshaven, with his hair all matted, carrying a torn-up backpack, heading out of town. I drove past him before even realizing it was Jimmy!

"His parents have decided they are going to have him cremated, and Art doesn't want a pastor or any references of God or a better place after death mentioned at his memorial service. His heart has really been hardened by this catastrophe."

I couldn't answer her as I began to cry softly. Finally regaining my composure a few seconds later, I simply said, "I'll have to call you back, Mom. I can't think straight right now."

"I understand," she said, her voice quivering as she spoke. "I love you, Michael! And I'm so sorry I had to give you this horrible news."

"I love you too, Mom," I replied just before disconnecting from the call.

With this appalling news, I was done working for the day. I started my car and drove home. At about six thirty, Gabby came home from work to find me on the back porch steps with five empty Budweiser bottles all standing in a row like little soldiers and a half-empty sixth soldier still in my hand.

Sitting down next to me before speaking, she softly asked, "What's wrong, Michael?"

I looked over at her, and the tears began to flow again, and the dam of my emotions burst as I began to sob uncontrollably.

Gabby grabbed me and pulled me close, trying to console me. "It's going to be OK, sweetheart! We'll get through this, no matter what it is! I love you, Michael."

It took four or five minutes before I regained enough composure to actual tell her what had happened. Once she knew the source of my grief, she pulled me back to her and continued to hold me, rocking back and forth.

I stopped crying, wiped the tears from my face with the back of my hands, and said, "It's kind of weird, but I've already cried more for Jimmy than I did for my own father's death. He was just so young and so lost! I should have tried to do more to get him straight!"

She pulled away but still held me, only now I was at arm's length as she looked intently in my eyes. "Don't put any of the blame for his death on your shoulders," Gabby stated firmly. "When I met Jimmy at your father's funeral, I knew he was fighting personal demons even then!" She then pulled me back and laid my head in the crook of her neck.

"Are you going to the funeral?" she asked, never lifting my head to look at me.

"I don't know," I responded. "His father is really angry that Jimmy died this way. His mom is brokenhearted and embarrassed because his death was a result of his involvement with drugs. I doubt the memorial service will be much of a tribute to his life."

I stopped for a few seconds before turning to Gabby and saying, "And that's not the way I want to remember him! I'd rather remember him as my fun, irreverent, cussing buddy who was always there for me when no one else was!"

Gabby got up, walked back into the house, and returned a couple of minutes later with two more open bottles of beer. Handing one to me, she sat down next to me, and we spent the next twenty minutes drinking our beers in silence.

Two days later, I called my mother to tell her I would not be coming to the funeral. I also let her know I'd written a four-page letter to Louise, Jimmy's mom, to relay some of my fondest memories of Jimmy and offer my deepest condolences to her and her family. I never heard back from her.

As we moved into the twenty-first century, the world continued to change at an ever-increasing pace. The euro was introduced and became the standard currency in twelve European countries, including Germany and France.

The first group of twenty terrorist prisoners arrived at Guantanamo Bay, Cuba, for enhanced interrogation.

The first cases of a new respiratory disease, SARS, emerged in Hong Kong and began spreading around the world.

Despite worldwide political demonstrations, the Iraq war continued.

An unexpected but massive heat wave engulfed Europe, leaving over thirty thousand dead in the month of August.

A Harvard university student by the name of Mark Zuckerberg founded a new Internet site, Facebook, which would change interpersonal communication forever.

A series of coordinated bomb attacks on various commuter trains in Madrid three days before Spain's general elections killed 191 and wounded more than 1,800 others.

While attending one of Wendy's regional meetings about six months after our company-wide conference, I again ran into John Belk in one of the office corridors. He was walking and looking down at some reports he had in his hands. Looking up and seeing me walking toward him, he stopped and said, "Hey, Michael! How are you doing?"

I continued toward him with my hand out to shake his. Shifting his papers to one hand, he shook my hand and simply said, "I forgot Wendy was having a region meeting this week. Is this the front end or the back end of the meeting?"

"Front end," I replied, placing both hands on my hips while we talked. "We just got here this morning."

"I've asked Wendy's permission, and I've set up a working lunch for you to join Jeff Hall and me tomorrow in Jeff's office. We should easily be done in an hour. Does that work for you?"

Surprised by the news, I simply responded, "Of course!"

"Good!" John replied. "I'll have Jeff's assistant come get you when we are ready," he said, taking his hand back before starting to move past me. "Looking forward to seeing you tomorrow!"

I turned and started back to the conference room where we were having the region meeting, all the while wondering why a divisional vice president and the CEO would want to have lunch with me.

As we were wrapping up the first day of our meeting, I approached Wendy when no one was around and asked her if she knew what the lunch meeting was about the next day.

"I have an idea," she said, smiling. "But I don't think it would be wise for me to answer your question." Still smiling, she continued. "I can tell you that you're not in any sort of trouble, but that's really all I can say."

That night in my hotel room, I called Gabby and told her about the events of the day. "I bet they're going to promote you," she said with conviction.

"I don't think so," I countered. "It hasn't even been two years yet! They're not going to promote me that quickly. I believe that most, if not all, of the region managers were district managers for a minimum of five years before being promoted."

"Well, what else do you think it could be?" Gabby asked.

"I really don't know," I answered.

"They are going to promote you!" Gabby said again. "I don't know why, but I just know that's what this is all about."

"I guess we'll see tomorrow," I responded.

We spent the rest of our hour-long conversation talking about Gabby's work and what was new with the kids and discussing how bad traffic was becoming to navigate through in Portland.

The next day, a nicely dressed woman came into our meeting room at noon sharp. She walked over to Wendy, and they talked for a short time. Then Wendy pointed in my direction, and the woman turned and headed toward me.

"Mr. Larsen," she began, sticking out her hand to shake mine, "my name is Gloria. I'm Mr. Hall's administrative assistant." I shook her hand, and she continued. "If you will please come with me, I'll take you to Mr. Hall's office."

She turned and headed for the door, and I followed her out of the meeting room. Glancing over at Wendy, I noticed she was watching us leave with a demure smile on her face as we exited the room.

"Michael!" Jeff Hall said as I walked into his office. "It's good to see you again!"

We shook hands, and a few seconds later, John Belk entered the room. "Sorry, I'm late," he said, looking at Jeff, "but I was on the phone longer than I expected to be with a dissatisfied customer."

"Did you end the conversation on good terms?" Mr. Hall asked.

"No! No, I'm afraid not," John replied. "It's a long story, but I'm sure she and I will have several more conversations before her issues are resolved!"

"I'm confident that you'll handle the issue to everyone's satisfaction," Jeff said. "Enough about that," he continued. "Let's get to the business at hand!"

Pointing to a round table a short distance from his desk, Jeff simply said, "After you, Michael."

I said, "Thank you," and sat in one of the chairs as I had been instructed. On the table, there were three takeout boxes with lids on them, real silverware, knife, fork, spoon, and a bottle of water.

I waited for everyone to be seated, and then Jeff and I opened our lunch boxes. Inside was a French dip sandwich, a small cup of sauce, and a side salad with dressing already on it.

"I hope this is OK," Jeff said just prior to shoving a huge portion of the sandwich into his mouth.

"It looks great," I responded.

John Belk hadn't opened his lunch box yet, but he took a quick drink of water and then addressed me. "The reason we asked you here today is to gain a little more insight into your future. I guess the first and most pressing question is, are you willing to move?"

"Where?" I answered after contemplating the question for a second.

"Where would you like to go?" John responded.

"Hawaii would be great!" I said.

We all laughed, and now that Jeff had swallowed the bite in his mouth, he said, "I'm afraid that's not going to happen!" Turning more sober, he continued. "Let's approach this from another angle. Where have you lived?"

"Always on the West Coast," I replied. "Grew up in Beaumont, California, a little town east of Riverside. Went to college at Fresno State University. After school, I stayed in Fresno for a few years. Then

I was struck by the lovebug, and I moved to Portland, Oregon, to get married and be with my wife."

There was silence for a moment while we all took a bite of our lunch and ate. "Would you move to Seattle?" Jeff asked.

Not expecting that question, I answered, "I'd have to speak with my wife, but I think Seattle would be at the top of my list if I were contemplating a move."

Pushing his lunch box back away from him, Jeff wiped off his face with a napkin and asked, "So what would it take for you to move to Seattle?"

I just let thoughts ramble out of my mouth as I tried to answer the question. "I would hope there is a moving or relocation package to help with the expense of the move. Obviously, I would want to know what salary and bonus potential came with the new position. And, last, I would like to know, how far in the future are we talking?"

Jeff smiled at me and then turned to John Belk and said, "Would Seattle work, John?"

John Belk seemed to contemplate the question of a moment before answering. "Actually, it may be our best move," he responded. "I could keep my eye on Michael, and Wendy has wanted to go back to Los Angeles for a long time. It could really end up working out well!"

Jeff turned back to me and said, "How was your lunch?"

I answered truthfully, "Honestly, I haven't even tasted it! I've been more focused on our conversation."

"This is what I'd like you to do, Michael," Jeff began. "I'd like you to go home and discuss moving to Seattle with your wife. Take your time and talk it over with her."

"If we move you to Seattle," he continued, "your new base wage would be $85,000, and your annual bonus potential would be $100,000 per year. In your first year of the new position, we would guarantee you a minimum of $50,000 in bonus. If you earned more, we would gladly pay you the higher amount."

"If you aren't good at math, which I doubt or you wouldn't be sitting here with us right now," he said, snickering, "a lot of figures were just thrown out, so I want to be clear. Your gross income for the first year would be a minimum of $135,000."

"Oh, and there is a moving budget, relocation agreement, etc.," he summarized. "So you won't be out of pocket for any expenses involved with the move."

"To be clear," Jeff said, rising to his feet, "before you respond, it is important that you sit down with your family before you make this decision. Take a couple of weeks if you'd like and then get back to John with your answer. And thank you for coming to have lunch with us!" he said, extending his hand for one last handshake before John and I exited the office.

Looking at my wristwatch, I realized I'd been in there for an hour and twenty minutes, but it felt more like ten minutes.

When we arrived back at the conference room where our regional meeting was, John stopped outside the closed door and turned back to me. "You've got some big decisions to make, Michael. The only thing I have to say is that you'll be making a lot more money, but you'll be earning it! You'll be responsible for everything that happens inside your region. Unless you put in sixty- to seven-hour weeks, you won't be successful! You'll be on call 24/7, 365 days a year. The buck always stops at your door. Do you clearly understand what I'm saying?"

"Yes, sir, I do," I answered.

John Belk patted me on the arm, turned, and walked away. I went back into the region meeting, acting as calm as if I'd just been on a bathroom break.

"It's a lot to think about," Gabby said as she set her half-empty wineglass on the coffee table in the living room. "It's kind of a double-edged sword for me. The idea of not working any longer is enticing! I'd love to stay home, sleep as long as I want, and do whatever I want to do for the rest of the day!"

She leaned over, picked up her wineglass, and took a drink from it. "But the kids are all here in Portland, and I don't have any friends in Seattle. And with you traveling two weeks of every month and working longer hours, how much time will we really have together? I'm afraid I'll be lonely by the end of the first week!"

I sat and listened to her patiently, knowing this transition was probably going to be rough for Gabby, maybe even more challenging than she was expressing to me.

"Happy wife, happy life!" I said jokingly but not really joking. "Look, this decision needs to be both of ours. Your happiness is much more important than a promotion, the additional income, or any other variables. Let's wait a few days and then discuss this again. If you're not 100 percent behind this move, I don't want to do it!"

We had a wonderful weekend, and Monday when I got home from work, Gabby said, "Let's go out to Fuji's for dinner tonight."

"Sounds great!" I responded. "What time do you want to go?"

"I'm hungry now," she said.

"Great! Grab a sweater and let's go!" I answered enthusiastically.

We had ordered our dinner and were sitting in a secluded booth, having a drink, when Gabby said, "I gave my notice to John Warren today!"

"What!" I said, shock in my voice.

"I told him I would work thirty days to give him plenty of time to find my replacement," she continued nonchalantly.

"Gabby!" I said, still somewhat alarmed by her revelation. "I thought we were going to talk about this some more. Are you sure this is what you want to do? Are you absolutely positive?"

"I talked with the kids about it, and every one of them said we should go," she said. "Aria said, 'You've worked all your life, and now it's your turn to have a little time for yourself.'

"Jacob said that if I got lonely, I could probably get a job in the Seattle area pretty easily. That made good sense to me.

"Besides, if I'm that lonely, two of the kids are only a three-hour drive away. I can just hop in the car and head south if I want!"

"Wow!" I exclaimed. "Now that you've started the ball rolling on your end, I just hope the job offer is still there!"

We both laughed while we waited for our dinners to arrive.

Having absolutely no idea where to start looking for a new home, I rented a fully furnished, two-bedroom apartment for six months. The company had agreed to reimburse me for the expense, including utility bills, while I was there.

Gabby and I had decided that I would jump right into the job, and once she was done working, she would move up to the apartment with me. We were letting a realtor sell our house, and my company was picking up our part of the realtor's sales commission.

The management team asked me to keep everything confidential until the day we made the changes. It was October 1, and Wendy had scheduled a two-day regional meeting in Seattle for all her district managers.

Ken and I always alternated who drove to Seattle for the regional meetings. It made it fair for gas if we both drove our own cars every other time we had to go to the corporate offices. It was my turn to drive, and at the last minute, I told him we would have to take separate cars. I could tell he was a little peeved when he said, "Fine! But you're driving two times in a row in the future!"

I apologized to him and agreed that I would drive the next two times we went to Seattle together. It was a bit of a white lie, since we would probably never go to the corporate headquarters together again. But I was comfortable that he would understand why by tomorrow.

At 8:00 a.m. sharp, Wendy walked into the conference room, where all fourteen district managers were seated. Looking around the room, she said, "Good morning, everyone!" We all responded in kind with our own "Good mornings."

John Belk walked into the conference room after her, and again, we all exchanged "Good mornings." Wendy said, "John has a couple of announcements to make, so I'm turning the floor over to him before we get started."

John walked over and stood next to Wendy before addressing the group. "We are making some management changes, and I wanted to fill everyone in on those changes."

He paused for effect, looking at each DM, and then continued. "Wendy is leaving the northwest to become the regional manager in Southern California, our largest region. I am sure you will all miss her as much as I will, but Southern California is our largest revenue-producing region in the country, and they're struggling right now. Wendy is a seasoned regional manager, and we feel she can put that region back on the right path!"

He turned to Wendy and said, "Congratulations and good luck on your new assignment." Then he started clapping. Everyone around the table clapped as well. One district manager stood up, and the remainder of us followed his lead as we continued to clap.

After a moment, John began again. "Her transfer is effective today." Everyone had a bit of a confused look on their face as he continued. "In fact, I'll be taking her to the airport in a few minutes for her twelve o'clock flight!" which only brought more confused looks.

"Michael," John said, and I stood up and started walking to the front of the room. When I reached Wendy and John, Wendy handed me her laser pointer and simply said, "Good luck! Don't mess up what I started here!"

"As of this moment, Michael Larsen will be the new regional manager for the northwest region," John Belk announced. There was no standing ovation. There was no clapping. As I turned to face my new team, there were only a couple of short gasps and an overabundance of totally shocked faces staring back at me.

"Let's give him a hand and a warm welcome to his new position," John said loudly as he started to clap. His very enthusiastic clap drowned out the combined clapping from the thirteen district managers, all of whom remained seated.

John shook my hand and then Wendy's and said, "Good luck to both of you!" Then looking quickly at his watch, he said, "We'd better go if you want to catch that flight!" With that, they turned and exited the conference room, which again had gone completely silent.

I had envisioned this moment for weeks and had prepared for it. I had been a peer with these district managers only a minute ago.

Some would be jealous that I was chosen to lead the region after being here for such a short time. My relationship with a few, especially Ken, would have to change dramatically.

If I wanted to be successful, I had to realize that these people no longer worked with me, but, rather, they worked for me. Their successes reflected on me, and their failures equally reflected on me.

I needed to be friendly, but I couldn't be friends with any of them if I wanted to hold them accountable to high standards. For the first time, I understood what Mike Lovering meant when he said he didn't socialize with those who worked for him because socializing created feelings, and feelings were dangerous if you want to accomplish your business goals. At the time, I thought he was just being arrogant and elitist, but now I knew he'd been right all along!

I spent the last quarter of the year traveling with each district manager and assessing their strengths and weaknesses. Their tenure with the company ranged from eight months for our newest DM to nine years for our most veteran district manager. Each of them had unique territories and a varying number of locations.

I spent more time visiting districts outside the Seattle area to ensure I had a good grasp of their business and that we had self-starters in all those remote markets. Some markets catered to a suburban customer base, while others were more inner city and catered to local businesses and apartment tenants. Still, others were heavily influenced by a large college or university and stayed filled all winter but were hard to keep rented up when students went home for the summer.

Gabby finished tying up all the loose ends in Portland and moved to Seattle a month after I did. I knew traveling as much as I needed to in these first three months could take a toll on her as we started our new life in Seattle. She'd led a pretty regimented life until now, and she would be leaving all that routine behind once she moved two hundred miles north.

The "happy wife, happy life" phrase kept popping up in my mind over and over as I readied for her arrival. It was important to me that she stay busy and feel she was a useful and meaningful part of this transition.

I asked Gabby to interview a few realtors and pick one she especially liked and trusted. I asked her to find the perfect new home for us with just a few stipulations of my own. It needed to be no more than a forty-minute drive to the corporate office. It needed to have three bedrooms and two full baths. And, last, no less than 1,700 square feet and no larger than 3,000 square feet. Everything else was up to her—style, color, size of yard, area, everything!

She was immediately excited to take on the challenge. With spirits high, she embarked on her quest, and I'd never seen her more excited or committed. We had plenty to talk about every night as she downloaded me on the events of her day. If I was traveling, we'd spend an hour or more every night on the phone talking about the gems she'd found that day. She became consumed in her search for the perfect house.

On the weekends, I would go with her and check out the week's top picks to visit. We placed a couple on the possible list but discarded most for one reason or another. But she wasn't daunted and continued her search with gusto and determination.

We were still looking for a home as another Thanksgiving was about to descend upon us. I asked her if she would be interested in inviting all our family along with my mom and Ronnie to come to Seattle and have Thanksgiving with us.

Immediately, she said no and that my idea was a huge mistake. Where would we put everyone? How was she supposed to cook and entertain ten people in our small rented apartment?

"I don't expect you to cook," I said. "See if we can make a reservation for dinner at the Space Needle for Thanksgiving. Eating up there would be a unique experience, and I think everyone would love it! And there are at least three motels within ten minutes of our house where the kids and their guests could stay for a few days, while my mom and Ronnie stayed here with us."

"Really!" she squealed. "Oh, that would be so fun! I'll start working on it tomorrow morning! I've got to call everyone, make flight arrangement, motel reservations, and dinner reservation! I am so excited! This is going to be the best Thanksgiving ever!" she shouted.

It was impossible not to have a huge smile and chuckle at her excitement. But more importantly, I knew she wouldn't be bored while I continued my travels to the various districts in my region and concentrated on setting up for next year's successes.

Her planning had been perfect, and it did turn out to be the best Thanksgiving I'd ever participated in. It was great to have everyone together from both sides of the family. Thomas and Aria had never met Ronnie and my mom, and after that first five minutes of awkwardness that accompanies every new meet and greet, they were exchanging stories and laughing together like old friends.

The Space Needle experience was a once-in-a-lifetime treat for all of us. The weather had cooperated, and instead of the constant rain Seattle is noted for, we were blessed by clear blue skies with small planes flying beside or below our viewing area.

In the hour and a half that it took for us to finish our meals, we had made a full rotation and had seen Puget Sound, Lake

Washington, Seattle, and ferryboats coming and going from the San Juan Islands. The weekend had been magical!

On December 4, Gabby informed me that she had found our new home. I was out of town but promised that, as soon as I got home, we would immediately go and tour it.

I could tell by the sound of her voice that there was no reason for me to even see the house. Her passion and exhilaration revealed to me that there would be no talking her out of this specific property. I was convinced after only five minutes on the phone with her that this would be our new home.

We were able to close on the property in just three weeks. It was two days before Christmas when we signed final papers and received our keys. Gabby had already coordinated the move, and on December 26, a moving van showed up to unload all our worldly possessions from our Portland home.

I took the last week of the year off to help move in. By New Year's Eve, we were settled and pretty much done with the move.

As we sat on our sofa in the new home, Gabby lifted her glass of champagne and offered a toast. "To new beginning, continued successes, and countless blessings!"

I put my glass to hers, and as they clinked, I simply continued. "We're on a crazy ride, but there is no one else that I would want by my side other than you! I will love you forever!"

CHAPTER 18

The second Monday in January, John Belk asked me to meet him in his office at 10:00 a.m. His administrative assistant showed me into his office about five minutes early.

He was seated behind his desk and rose to his feet when I entered. In a chair next to the one I would be occupying sat Doris Young, a middle-aged African American woman who oversaw our Human Resources Department. She also stood up and smiled at me as we locked gazes with one another.

"Michael!" John said exuberantly. "It's good to see you. How'd you make it through the holidays?"

"Fine," I responded, smiling back at him while I shook his hand.

"Have you met Doris from Human Resources?" John quizzed.

"Briefly," I replied. "She and I have been corresponding by e-mail. She has been of great assistance to me with the relocation program!"

"Are you all moved in, Mr. Larsen?" Doris asked with genuine concern.

"Yes, we are," I answered. "Thanks to you! My wife and I love our new home, and we love the Seattle area. By the way, please just call me Michael—Mr. Larsen isn't necessary."

She shook her head affirmingly and responded, "And you may call me Doris." Then she offered her hand, and I shook it lightly.

Gabby had expressed to me several times that she had met many an executive who, upon introduction, had crushed her hand when they were first introduced. She cautioned me that if I shook a woman's hand, to respect her femininity and do it softly, or risk the consequences that she would think I was just another asshole male figure who wants to exhibit power over the opposite sex. I'd found that to be valuable advice, and I've always practiced it with women I met.

"Michael," John said as we all took a seat, "we asked you here today to talk about annual reviews for all your district managers. You've only supervised your team for six months, and we wanted to ask you if you'd feel more comfortable having Wendy write the reviews for their performances last year."

I felt that I had observed and worked with each DM enough to speak to their strengths and weaknesses. As to how well they performed, we had monthly numbers to use, and the numbers were the numbers!

While I was deciding how to respond, Ms. Young added, "If you decide to do the reviews yourself, I'd like to discuss each of them with you prior to your delivering them to your team."

John interjected, "If you do them, we would both like to set aside a day to go over them with you. How do you feel about that?"

"I would like to do the reviews if I could," I responded. "As far as meeting with the two of you before presenting them, I welcome your input."

"Before I start them," I asked, "could I ask each of you in what order you would rank the district managers in the region?" I handed each of the list in alphabetical order with all my DMs' names and the district they managed, and I kept one for myself.

"If you could, just rank them from one to fourteen as you see them. Both of you have worked with my team longer than I have," I said.

"I don't know if I feel comfortable with this," Doris responded, looking over the list. "I have little contact with them except for recruiting, hiring, approving disciplinary paperwork, and terminations."

"Are they all equally good in all those areas?" I asked.

"Well, no," she replied. "Some are definitely better than others."

"That's the piece you have that I don't!" I said. "Your one through fourteen may be totally different than mine, and if it is, we should talk about those areas of concern before I spend several hours writing a review that John and you disagree with. I would like to only do these reviews one time, with a few tweaks after we next meet to discuss them."

"That sounds like a pretty good idea to me," John said, setting his list down on his desk. Then he quickly began putting numbers to the corresponding names.

Doris Young obviously wasn't thrilled with the idea, but she too sat her list on John's desk and began numbering the names. I did the same.

Once we were done, I collected all three lists to compare them. John and my list were close to identical. We had reversed number seven and number eight, or they would have been a perfect match.

However, Doris's list was dramatically different from ours. She had Tamara from Seattle listed as number one, while John and I had her listed as the number-five district manager. She had Ken, from Portland, listed as eleven, while John and I both had him listed at number four.

I handed the three lists to Doris and asked, "Why do you think there is such a difference in how you see my team members from how John and I see them? Why do you think Tamara is number one?"

She shot me a look before answering. "Her numbers are always pretty solid. She turns her paperwork on time. She seldom contacts me with problems or issues. And she's the only female DM in a region dominated by males, and she has performed right along with them despite her gender."

I looked over at John and watched his brows furrow a bit after the last comment.

"So she gets extra credit because of her gender?" I asked.

"Mr. Larsen!" she began, her voice raising a little with each word out of her mouth. "Your region has the least amount of female DMs and the least amount of ethnic diversity in the entire country, and that needs to change!"

Her tone irritated me, so I snapped back. "Don't you have to approve all DM hires for this region?" I asked.

"Yes!" she agreed aggressively.

"Since I haven't hired any new DMs yet, and you approved all the DMs hired," I asked with a snarky tone, "how do you think I should proceed to get us out of this mess you've put us in?"

I watched anger flare in her eyes as they narrowed. But before she could speak, John jumped in.

"Whoa, guys!" he said sternly. "Let's everyone just take a breath and calm down for a minute here! Doris, why don't you and I take a few minutes and add three positives and two negatives by each name to give Michael a better idea of our thinking?"

"Great!" I said. "That would be very helpful!"

"Well, I can't do that right now!" Doris snapped. "I have a staffing meeting with Jeff in about ten minutes." Looking at me with a bit of distain, she continued. "I'll e-mail my list to you tonight once I've had time to complete it."

"Perfect!" I responded, trying to sound perky.

Doris and I stood and shook hands again, only this time, there were no smiles. Needing to mend some of the hard feelings I'd sown, I offered, "I'm looking forward to working with you!" She made no response as she exited John's office.

Jacob and Sophie had been engaged for over a year before they finally set a date. They were going to be married on February 14, Valentine's Day. We'd only been informed of the date and the location of the venue three weeks before the event was to take place.

Gabby wrote a letter and sent Jacob a check with their $30,000 wedding present enclosed in it. We thought it would be a nice touch if the check was written and sent by her and not me.

Valentine's Day fell on a Thursday, so Gabby flew to Fresno the Sunday before the wedding, and I flew down on Wednesday, the thirteenth.

Jacob and Sophie had a bit of a different plan on how to best use the money versus Thomas and Elise. They wanted a small wedding with just a few family and friends attending and a simple reception dinner afterward. Jacob and Sophie were both very good with money, and I imagined that after all expenses, they would still have at least $20,000 left from our gift to put into savings.

My flight landed at 11:03 a.m. on Wednesday. After I'd collected my bags, I went out to the curb and waited for Gabby to pick me up. She had my flight itinerary, and we had agreed to meet just outside door number six in the passenger pickup area.

As I stood there waiting and watching for her, I noticed a couple who was oddly walking backward in my direction once they'd exited the building. They continued to shuffle toward me and were only a matter of a few feet away before they stopped. A very attractive woman turned around and asked, "Do you need a ride somewhere, sir?" The man remained facing away from me.

Not quite understanding what this bizarre situation was about, I simply responded, "No, thank you. I have someone picking me up anytime now."

"OK, Michael," she said and turned back the same way her male friend was standing, again with their backs to me.

"Excuse me," I asked. "Do I know you?" The question was a legitimate one since she'd called me by name.

She turned back to face me. "We've never met before, but I know a lot about you!" she replied. "For example, I know you went to Fresno State University. I know you had a very fast car in college. I know that you like Italian food!"

I looked back down the road, hoping Gabby was coming soon, before responding.

"Who are you?" I asked, feeling like I was living out a real-life episode of *The Twilight Zone*.

"My name's Harper," she replied. "And I'm with him!" she continued, pointing at the man with his back to me.

He started to slowly turn around, and I screamed, "Jack! You're a big jerk! You guys were starting to scare the hell out of me!" I'd dropped my bags, and by the time the words were out of my mouth, we were hugging each other.

"Hey, little buddy!" Jack finally said. "It's really great to see you!" He pulled back, held me at arm's length, and then hauled me in for a second embrace.

Once we were apart, I looked at him and simply shook my head. "You're still the sickest, weirdest, crazy person I've ever known!"

He reached into his overcoat pocket and pulled out a can of Rainier beer and offered it to me. "One for the road?" he said. "Just like old times!"

I accepted his beer, opened it, and took a drink. A second beer magically materialized from his other coat pocket. He opened it, and we bumped cans, both of us taking long drinks.

Turning back to the lady with him, I asked, "Is your name really Harper?"

"Of course, it is!" she responded incredulously. "Why would I lie about that?"

"Well, Harper, how do you two know each other?" I asked.

She looked up at Jack and smiled. "We met here in Fresno about six months ago. I am a real estate attorney, and I live in Anchorage, Alaska. I was down here for a seminar when I met Jack. I was having a drink at the hotel bar, and as I was leaving, I must have dropped my wallet.

"I'd just stepped into the elevator to go up to my room and had pushed the bottom for my floor. The elevator door was just closing when Jack stuck his hand in the door, stopping it, and the door opened again. At first, his action scared me, but then he smiled and said, 'I think you dropped this in the bar, miss,' as he handed me my wallet.

"He was cute, and I was extremely thankful to get my wallet back, so I asked him if I could buy him a drink as a reward. He said yes, and I guess it was just destiny from there. We've been together as much as possible since that night."

"Do you still live in Alaska?" I asked.

"Yes, I do," she replied. "I'm trying to find an accounting position for Jack up there, so he'll move up. I have too much time invested in my client portfolio to walk away and start all over, so I need him to come to me. Just like you moved to be with Gabby!"

"Wow! You know about my wife?" I responded.

"Of course!" she said. "I met her earlier in the week, and when I found out she'd lived in Alaska too, we immediately became best friends! She is a sweetheart!"

"I think so too!" I agreed.

"Grab your bag and let's go," Jack said. "Everyone's waiting for us to show up!"

When we arrived at Jacob's house, Gabby came out the front door to greet me. It had only been a couple of days since we'd last been together, but I was thrilled to see her, and I hugged her tightly, sealing our embrace with a kiss.

We walked hand in hand up the steps and into the house. All the kids were there, as were Sophia's parents along with her two younger siblings. I was introduced to everyone, and after a very short time, it felt as though we were all one big happy family.

I gave both Jacob and Sophie a big hug and told them congratulations in person for the first time.

"Were you surprised to see Jack picking you up from the airport?" Jacob asked.

"I was more than just surprised," I said. Then I replayed the whole airport story to everyone, causing chuckles and laughter as I talked about being spooked by Harper, who seemed to know a little too much about me.

It was a comfortable afternoon, and as with most weddings, everyone had an indelible smile on their face as we talked about plans for the next day. I was standing by myself in the living room, sipping on a beer, and watching Gabby and Harper talk. They were laughing and touching each other as they spoke like familiar friends and seemed to be genuinely having a great time together.

From behind me, Jack whispered into my ear, catching me by surprise. "I know what you're thinking," he said very softly. "How did a big ugly lug like me attract a beautiful, outgoing, professionally successful woman like that?" He put a hand on my shoulder, moved even closer, and continued. "My answer is I have absolutely no friggin' idea! But I couldn't be happier, and if this is a dream, I don't want to wake up!"

I reached up and patted his hand on my shoulder. "Well, that wasn't exactly what I was thinking," I responded. "But it is a pretty damn good question!"

Later that evening, we were all seated at the rehearsal dinner when Jacob made a toast to Sophie and pledged her his love forever. Once everyone had a quick drink, Jacob turned to Jack and continued. "I am so honored to be sharing this moment with my friend Jack Anthony! Jack was there for my dad and me in our darkest hour, and now he will be with us for this joyous occasion. I am humbled to call him a friend, a mentor, and my best man!"

Looking over at Jack, I could see alligator tears forming and then spilling down his face. He simply mouthed the words "Thank you." Everyone raised their glasses once again and took a drink.

The wedding the next day was beautiful! Sophie looked stunning in her wedding dress, and Jacob seemed to glow with pride as he accepted her hand from her father's before turning and walking toward the altar. They were a beautiful couple.

We spent the rest of the weekend together as a family and laughed, ate, drank, and enjoyed each other's company. On Sunday, everyone left to go back to their respective homes and careers except for Sophie and Jacob.

They flew out on Sunday as well, but their destination was a two-week trip to the Grand Cayman Islands for their honeymoon. It had been a wonderful week!

Once the reviews had been written and approved by both John Belk and Doris Young, I set up two-hour time slots to go over them with each team member in my office.

For the first two days, the reviews had gone well. There were some minor disagreements between me and a couple of DMs on their areas of opportunity, but I made sure we both agreed on a measurable action plan prior to completing the review with each.

Tamara was my ninth review, and we had scheduled her review for 8:00 a.m. on Wednesday. It was 8:30 a.m. when she knocked on my office door.

"Come in," I said loudly.

"Hi!" she said, sounding rushed but making no apology for being late. "I had some trouble getting it together this morning!"

I handed her a copy of her review and explained the process. "What I would like you to do is read through this, which should only take about ten minutes, and then we can discuss it together. Go ahead and read through it. Take as much time as you need."

Before she started reading, she said, "I hope this won't take too long. I have lots to do today."

"I believe I asked you to schedule two hours when we set up this time slot for your review," I replied.

She glared at me, picked up the review, and started reading. She'd only been reading for a short time when she defiantly said, "This isn't accurate! I'm not going to sign a review written about me this way!"

"Just finish reading it," I encouraged. "Then we can talk about it line by line if you'd like."

As she continued reading, her face changed from a pleasant look to the face of an angry monster. She was biting her lower lip, and I watched as her hands began to tremble while she flipped through the pages. Her coloring had gone from crimson to beet red, and finally, all the color had drained from her face, leaving it white, like she was going to pass out.

"This is a bunch of bullshit!" she said loudly. "I don't agree with any of this, and I'm not going to dignify this crap by discussing it with you!"

I sat back in my chair and stayed silent for a moment.

"Are we done here!" she snapped.

"No, I'm afraid we are not done," I said as calmly as possible. "But perhaps we should postpone this until later in the week. You take the review and go over it closely. Then we can meet again on Friday. Does that work for you?"

"Nothing is going to change between now and Friday!" she spat at me.

"Maybe not, but John Belk and Doris Young signed off on these reviews before I was allowed to present them," I said, again trying to sound calmer than I felt. "So to be fair to all persons involved, I'm going to ask Doris Young to join us when we go over this Friday. I want to make sure you feel you are heard, and if we continue to have disagreements on your performance, maybe Doris can assist us with her counsel."

Tamara was so angry that she was noticeably breathing harder, her chest rising and falling like she'd just run a full marathon. I could see perspiration forming on her brow and upper lip as she sat there trying to stare holes through me. She stood up, crammed the review into her computer bag, and turned to leave.

"Whatever time we set for this coming Friday, please be on time," I said. "Mrs. Young won't be as tolerant as I was if you're a half hour late on Friday."

She looked back at me, scowled one last time, and walked out of my office door, slamming it behind her.

I had asked Doris to bring three copies of the district manager job requirements with her for Tamara's review. I had also discussed our first meeting and the resulting confrontation, trying to set the stage for what may be coming.

"Michael," Doris began, "I've read through this review again, and there may be some minor areas to discuss, but for the most part, I think this is a pretty fair review."

I thanked her, and we sat in silence, waiting for Tamara to come into my office. She knocked on my door eleven minutes past our prearranged time. When she came in and sat down, she did offer a slight apology.

"Sorry, I'm a few minutes late," Tamara said with cheer in her voice, "but traffic was horrible this morning! There must have been a wreck or something causing it to be so slow today!"

I glanced over at Doris and quickly realized she wasn't buying any of the "late for the meeting" story. She was sitting in her chair, tapping the fingers of her right hand in sequential order as she watched Tamara without smiling.

"Well, let's get started," I began. "Tamara, have you had a chance to go over the review?"

"I have," she responded, the smile melting off her face. "Like I told you on Wednesday, I think this review is total crap!"

I was surprised by her directness with the HR director sitting in the room.

Before I could respond, Doris asked, "What parts do you think are crap?"

"Pretty much all of it!" Tamara said loudly.

"John Belk, Michael, and I looked at where each of you DMs were ranked by month for the entire year. How do you think you ranked against your peers just in pure metrics?"

"Either one or two," she responded confidently.

"You ranked number five in the region," Doris answered.

"That's not even possible!" Tamara argued.

Doris took out a report and plopped it on the desk in front of Tamara. "You're welcome to look at the data if you'd like to, but you did statistically rank number five in the region."

Tamara said nothing as she stared at the stack of paper in front of her.

"In addition to that, your district was understaffed compared to our staffing model for six months out of the year," Doris continued. "Turnover was another area of opportunity, and I believe the review addresses that shortcoming as well."

"We don't pay our property people enough money!" Tamara said loudly. "I hire people, and three months later, they leave because they can make fifty cents more an hour somewhere else! When are we going to raise our property manager wages to be competitive with other businesses?"

Doris didn't answer at first, searching her brain for the correct response. When she finally did speak, she said, "Maybe you're not selling the benefits of the position when you do your initial interviews? Do you talk about wages, when wage increases will be available, merchandise spiffs, health benefits, holiday pay, etc.?"

"I talk about all of that!" Tamara said defiantly.

"Maybe you and I should do a few interviews together, and I can see if I can be of any help in explaining the job better," Doris suggested.

"Ms. Young!" Tamara snarled. "I've probably hired two hundred people in my six years as a district manager! I don't think I need any training when it comes to hiring!"

Tamara didn't realize that she was proving Doris Young's point by admitting she had, in fact, gone through two hundred people while those districts around her had been able to maintain stable, tenured managers.

"How do you see yourself when it comes to your leadership role with your fellow DMs?" I asked, changing the subject.

"All the Seattle DMs call me for advice except Jim Daniels," she responded. "We don't agree on much, so we just keep our distance."

"What about DMs from Spokane, Tri-Cities, and Portland?" I inquired.

"They don't call me often," Tamara responded. "But if they have a question, I'm glad to help them if I can."

"Tamara, let me ask you a direct question," I started. "Do you cut your own locks, or do you have someone else do it for you?"

"I have one of my male property managers cut them while I do the paperwork," Tamara answered.

"Why don't you cut the locks yourself?" I asked.

"Because I'm a girl!" she said. "I'm not going to sweat and do the physical labor required to cut locks!"

Doris and I locked eyes as I repeated, "Because you're a girl?"

"So you use store personnel to cut the locks, which shorts your store staffing for that day. Is that correct?" I asked.

"I move my people around to where I need them!" Tamara replied. "Whether they are cutting locks, cleaning spaces, or renting spaces, it all pays the same."

Looking back to Doris, I asked, "Do women in other districts cut their own locks?"

"Most of them use power grinders, but, yes, they cut their own locks," she responded.

"Have you seen female DMs cutting their own district's locks, Doris?" I asked again.

"When I was in Chicago training, I traveled with a female DM on lock-cutting day, and she cut her own locks," Doris answered.

"What is your point?" Tamara snapped.

I handed both Tamara and Doris a copy of the district manager job requirements and asked them to turn to page 5.

"Look about halfway down the page," I said as I began reading. "All district managers must cut delinquent tenant locks by the fifteenth day of every month. Property personnel should not be used to accomplish this task. American Trust Storage will supply each district manager with the needed tools, including personal safety equipment."

Looking back to Doris, I asked, "Is Tamara violating company rules by having property personnel cut locks for her simply because she's female?" I knew I was on shaky ground, but I needed Doris to agree with my premise.

"Yes," Doris replied reluctantly. "She is required by company protocol to cut her own locks."

"Tamara," I said, "knowing now that you have been violating company rules and standard practices for a very long time, do you still believe a 'meets expectations' is an improper rating for your review?"

As she glared at me, I was thankful there wasn't anything sharp sitting within her reach. Instead of answering me, she put her review down on my desk and signed it and then slid it across the desk to me.

"Is there anything else to talk about?" she said, her tone now sounding defeated.

Doris said, "No," and I echoed Doris's statement.

Tamara stood up, turned, and left my office, closing the door softly behind her.

Looking at me, Doris said, "You know that's not going to be the end of this, don't you?"

"You have two problems now," she continued. "If you're planning on terminating her for cause, you'd better have airtight paperwork with disciplinary forms and action plans. And, second, if she goes, another female comes in to replace her. We have got to get more diversity in this region."

"I thought we were supposed to hire the best candidate for the job?" I queried.

"As long as that person isn't a white male, please feel free to hire the best candidate. I will not approve or interview any DM candidates that are not either a person of color or female. Do I make myself clear, Mr. Larsen?"

"Yes, ma'am," I responded as we both stood and shook hands before she left my office.

The rest of the reviews went well, and when I was done, I used a 20-60-20 method to rank the region team; 20 percent were above expectations, 60 percent met expectations, and 20 percent, I felt, were at a needs-improvement level.

I asked Doris to put in a district manager requisition so I could hire, train, and have someone ready if one of my lower-performing DMs didn't make it. She agreed, and we started a search for a relocatable district manager candidate.

Gabby and I had adapted to our new life after a couple of months. She was getting used to my travel, felt comfortable in our new neighborhood, and was even making a couple of friends with some of our neighbors.

My birthday, March 8, fell on a Wednesday, and I wasn't traveling out of town that week. Because it was the middle of the week, we were simply going to go to dinner that night. Aria and Todd asked if they could tag along. Gabby said sure, and we were now a foursome.

Elise was talking with Gabby on the phone and found out the four of us were going to dinner for my birthday, and she invited herself and Thomas. Gabby couldn't very easily say yes to one set of kids and no to the other set, so she said asked them to join us as well.

We were having a nice birthday dinner gathering when Thomas hit his water glass with his fork a couple of times. He asked if he could have everyone's attention for a minute, and the table went quiet.

He looked at Elise, who was smiling back at him, and said, "Today is a very special day for all of us. Michael was born today, and just look at how positively he has touched all our lives. We are all better for having him as a part of our family. And our family continues to grow as we add new members through marriage and relationships."

Looking at me, Thomas continued. "Elise and I have one last gift for you tonight to celebrate your birthday, Michael, or should I say *Grandpa!*"

CHAPTER 19

As we moved further into the twenty-first century, mankind and nature continued to change the face of the planet at an astonishing rate. The world community seemed to be at odds with itself. Wars, terrorist attacks, diseases, and illnesses were all on the rise. Natural disasters were happening all over the world, leaving thousands, if not millions, dead or displaced by their fury.

An enormous Indian Ocean tsunami devastates Indonesia in December, killing more than two hundred thousand people, making it the worst natural disaster in world history. Worldwide aid poured in to help the eleven Asian countries devastated by the tsunami.

A 7.6 earthquake centered in the Pakistan-controlled Kashmir region killed more than eighty thousand people and left an estimated four million homeless.

A major hurricane, Rita, ravages the Gulf Coast of the United States.

Hurricane Katrina wreaked catastrophic damage, again to the Gulf Coast that same year. More than one thousand people died in the storm, which left millions homeless. The city of New Orleans was almost destroyed. Americans were shaken not simply by the magnitude of the disaster but also by how ill-prepared all levels of government were in the aftermath.

Chechen terrorist took 1,200 schoolchildren and other hostages in Beslan, Russia; 340 people were killed and hundreds more wounded when extremist detonated explosives at the school on September 2.

As the Iraq war ended, the United Nations discovers that about 380 tons of explosives were missing in Iraq.

Pakistan admitted they had sold nuclear weapons designs to foreign countries, including North Korea, Iran, and Libya.

One year later, North Korea test-fired missiles over the Sea of Japan and exploded a nuclear device underground in the North

Korean mountains. The UN Security Council immediately passed a resolution banning the sale of all materials to North Korea that could be used to produce weapons.

The militant group Hamas won 74 of 132 seats in the Palestinian legislative election. In response, Israel leaders vote to withhold $50 million per month that was to go to Palestine for improving their territory.

In defiance to the UN Security Counsel, Iran announced that they had successfully enriched uranium and now had the technology to build nuclear weapons.

Hezbollah, a Lebanese militant group, fired multiple rockets into Israel. In response, Israel launched a major military attack, sending thousands of troops into Lebanon.

London, England, was hit by Islamic terrorist bombings, killing fifty-two people and injuring more than seven hundred others.

Cancer replaced heart disease as the number-one cause of death in people age eighty-five and younger.

However, not everything happening in the world was bad. There was an end to other wars, and computers and phones were now the number-one industry in the world.

The Sudanese government and the Southern rebels signed a peace agreement, ending a twenty-year civil war that claimed the lives of two million people.

About eleven million Iraqis (almost 70 percent of the country's registered voters) turn out to select their first permanent parliament since the overthrow of Saddam Hussein.

Israel began evacuating about eight thousand Israeli settlers from the Gaza Strip, which had been occupied by Israel for thirty-eight years and turned the land over to Palestine.

The *New Horizons* spacecraft was launched. It would travel three billion miles over a nine-year period to study Pluto's atmosphere and surface.

The Irish Republican Army (also known as the IRA) announced that it would end its violent campaign for a united Ireland and, instead, would pursue its goals politically through the Northern Ireland Peace Process.

The digital age was alive and expanding exponentially. In one year, there were more than 350 million digital songs purchased. It was an increase of 150 percent from the previous year. During the same period, album sales decreased by 4 percent, and the number of albums sold would diminish quickly over the next few years.

"Well, Michael," John Belk said, "are you ready to present your region to upper management for the first time?"

I smiled and responded, "I'm as ready as I'm ever going to be!"

"You'll do just fine," he said, patting me on the arm before turning and walking away.

It was our annual management conference, and it was my first time attending. We were in a pretty large ballroom at a very nice hotel in Los Angeles. There were sixteen region managers, and each of us had been given a two-hour time slot to speak about our region's performance for the last four full quarters.

In the front row sat the management team, who would be asking us questions at the end of our presentations. The CEO, CFO, the head of Human Resources, the acquisition manager, the vice president of Property Services, and the four senior divisional vice presidents were all sitting stoically, waiting to begin.

Behind them, there were a variety of other high-ranking corporate staff along with a few of our major stockholders. Three of the nine board of directors were introduced and were also in attendance to listen to the presentations.

Not knowing if it was good or bad, I was scheduled to be the fourth presenter on the first day of presentations. My time slot was from 3:00 p.m. to 5:00 p.m., leaving one hour for questions from the panel. Our meeting was to end at 6:00 p.m. on the opening day.

In total, there were probably sixty people in the room, and I only knew six to eight of them by name, which didn't make my presentation any easier.

Wendy, who represented the Southern California region, was the first presenter. She introduced herself and jumped right into her presentation. I thought she did a very nice job, and when she was finished, I, along with everyone else, clapped for her.

Then came the questions. They started innocently enough, but in short order, each question asked was more difficult for her to answer than the last one.

Why did you overspend your budget on repair and maintenance? We brought you to Los Angeles to improve our results. Why, after a full year, are the results in revenue only slightly better than the previous year? Have you made the personnel changes necessary to make the region successful? If not, why not? What are you going to do differently this coming year to improve these low numbers? And the last question asked by the CEO, Jeff Hall, was, are you satisfied with your results over the last twelve months?

Wendy did her best to put a positive spin on the few areas she'd been able to positively affect, but the panel was relentless as they pressed for more detail and a stronger commitment toward improvement in the future.

Ten minutes into the questioning, I was feeling bad for her. Some of the questions that were asked were impossible to answer. She could only speculate about the future with no real facts to back herself up.

The light green blouse she was wearing had ever-increasing circles of perspiration under each arm. Her face was damp, and a few stray strands of hair were sticking to her clammy forehead.

Finally, the panel quit asking questions, and the CEO summarized his thoughts on the region. He said he expected much better results by this time next year and thanked her for her presentation. Then we were dismissed for a thirty-minute break before the next presentation.

The next presentation from the Florida region manager was more of the same. The presentation seemed well done to me. But when the questions started coming, they focused on areas of deficiency that had not been mentioned in the region manager's presentation.

As the presenter made up excuses without facts to back up his region's shortcomings, the management panel seemed to smell blood in the water. They were like sharks after a wounded seal! Pointed questions about his business quickly seemed to turn into personal attacks.

At one point, one of the divisional vice presidents asked James a question and then quietly listened to his explanation. He looked at the region manager, shaking his head from side to side before responding. "Do you think we are all idiots?" he asked in a loud voice. "If you don't know the answer to a question, just say, 'I don't know'! Don't stand up there and try to bullshit your way through this when it's obvious you don't know what the hell you're talking about!"

For the next fifteen minutes, it seemed as though the entire panel piled on to marginalize this now helpless presenter. Mercifully, the time for questions ran out because a hot lunch had been set up in the ballroom next to ours. The CEO thanked the regional manager and asked everyone to join him for lunch.

For the first time, I was nervous. I hadn't expected to see one of my peers ostracized in front of the sixty people in attendance. I immediately thought to myself, *There but for the grace of God, go I.*

I decided to skip lunch and went back to my room to rework my presentation. After witnessing two that didn't go very well, I knew I had to rearrange my format if I wanted to get off the stage alive.

We finished lunch, and everyone went back into our meeting room to continue. The third presentation was from the New York regional manager. It was better than the first two, but again, the region manager concentrated on her successes and didn't speak to her areas of opportunity.

During the question-and-answer period, she handled herself quite masterfully. Some great answers to some very hard questions and a little something I decided I would use in my presentation. It was a simple but great line, "I don't have the answer to that question, but I'll research it and get back to you before we leave the conference." I thought it was a brilliant response.

At the completion of her presentation, we were excused for our thirty-minute afternoon break. Since I hadn't eaten lunch, I was hungry, and I could hear my stomach growling. Although I wasn't sure if the growling was from hunger or from dread of what was to come in the next three hours. I knew I dared not eat now for fear I would be placing myself in jeopardy if I put food into my already nervous stomach.

"Michael Larsen, from the northwest region in Seattle, please come up to the podium," Doris Young, head of Human Resources, said into a microphone without standing up.

As I rose to my feet, there was a round of applause while I walked to the podium with a couple of cue cards in my hand to begin speaking.

"Good afternoon," I began. "I'm Michael Larsen, and I represent the northwest region." Looking over the entire room, I continued. "I would like to quickly go over the metrics for our region for the last year. All of you have a copy of each region's ranking, and as you can see, we are number two in the country. The numbers are the numbers, and I'm not going to spend time discussing them.

"When I was promoted to region manager, Wendy, as all of you know, was the region manager in the northwest. She handed me her laser pointer on her way out the door and said, 'Don't screw up what I've started here!'" Everyone laughed, even those in the front row.

"That has been my goal this year," I stated confidently. "She had already put processes and procedures in place, and I simply tried to follow her well-laid-out plan.

"Our goal has always been and will continue to be to achieve a number-one ranking in as many metrics as possible, regardless what management decides to track. I would like our team to be the Region of the Year next year."

After a brief silence, I began again. "I've decided this job is not about metrics alone, although they are one of the major areas on which our performance is evaluated. I believe this job is really about people. In my case, not just the fourteen district managers I supervise but also the two hundred property personnel who are the face of American Trust to our customers.

"I believe it takes a year to screw up a district. It probably takes two years to screw up an entire region. Conversely, it should only take the same amount of time to fix a district or a region. The key to that fix is always people—committed, happy with their job, customer-friendly, helpful, cheerful people at every level, especially at the field level.

"As I sat in the audience and listened to Wendy's presentation, one of the questions asked was, would she have better results next year? Because we've kept in contact, I know she has replaced two low-performing district managers, who, in turn, have replaced several low-performing property personnel. It's always about the people! People are the key to our success.

"In my own mind, I have a healthy fear of Wendy and the team she is building because she will be working hard to take that number-one ranking away from me. I have seen what she started in Seattle, and she is on pace to completely turn the LA region around this coming year, her second year as a regional manager in Los Angeles.

"I am not going to talk about anything today except my plan to further develop my people to a higher level of competency at both the district manager and property personnel level."

With that introduction, I spent the next hour talking about moving my highest-performing property personnel to the properties where they could best help each district. I talked about a succession plan for my top-three district managers and an action plan to either improve or replace my lowest-three district managers. I spoke to the lack of diversity issue in my region and committed to fix it.

I spent another thirty minutes talking about what I thought a regional visit to a property should look like. My main goal on each property visit was to thank and congratulate each employee for a job well done. If there were issues with property personnel, I would not be addressing them with the employee on the visit. I would address them with the district manager and expect him or her to work with the field employee.

Finally, I spent about thirty minutes talking about areas of opportunity regarding some of the physical issues at a few properties and discussed a plan of action to fix them over time so as not to blow out our expense budget.

When I was finished, I looked at the CEO and asked, "What questions can I answer for you?"

Jeff turned first to his right and looked down the table and then to his left and did the same. Looking back at me, he shrugged his shoulders and said, "I don't have any questions." Then looking again to both sides, he continued. "How about you guys?"

Several heads shook, signifying a no, and no one responded. Looking back to me, Jeff said, "That was one hell of a job for your first time presenting, Michael! I see why John is so high on you! Thank you for your presentation."

As I left the podium to return to my seat, I saw the biggest smile on John Belk's face. The audience was clapping as I walked down the center aisle, and Wendy stuck her hand out as I walked by, and I slapped it as I passed her.

Jeff stood up, looked at his watch, and said, "How about that! We finished an hour early on the first day! That's got to be record!" Everyone laughed at his comments.

"You're all excused to go make calls if you need to or have a drink and relax. We have a cocktail party set up next door starting at six thirty, and dinner is at seven thirty in this room. Good work today, everyone! I'll see you for drinks and dinner!" Then we all stood, gathered our things, and started for the exits.

That night at the cocktail party, things seemed to have changed dramatically for me. I was no longer the new guy no one knew. People I hadn't met before were walking up to me and congratulating me on my presentation. Some who hadn't presented yet asked if I would look over their presentations and give them some constructive feedback. It felt awkward, but I agreed to look at two presentations because the authors were so nervous and were practically begging for help.

I was standing in line at the open bar, waiting to get my second Crown Royal on the rocks, when someone began whispering in my ear.

"You did a really great job today, old-timer!" she said softly.

I immediately recognized Wendy's voice and turned to face her. She was in line directly behind me, and she greeted me with a smile as I turned around.

"You also said some very nice things about me," she said sheepishly, "and I wanted to thank you for the kind words."

"I wasn't being kind," I responded. "I was being factual. Even though we didn't work together that long, you taught me a lot about the business and how to lead a successful team. I'm just trying to not screw up what you started!"

We both chuckled, and she said, "Well, I may have been a little hard on you, but it looks like it paid off. That was one of the best presentations I've ever seen given to this audience."

"I rewrote my presentation during lunch, after the panel handed both you and James your asses during the question-and-answer period," I replied.

"Shut up!" she said louder than she meant to. "I thought I did pretty good job of fielding those ridiculous questions that were coming out of left field."

"I thought you did too!" I emphasized. "You'll probably never be able to wear that sweat-stained blouse again, though, but you did try to stay cool!"

Her face turned crimson, and she looked away for a second before making eye contact with me again. "I owe you one, so when you need a favor, just make the call."

"Thank you, young lady!" I responded.

A smirk appeared on her face as she said, "Don't ever say that in public, old man!"

Then it was my turn to order my drink and go mingle with the crowd.

When I spoke to Gabby that night after dinner, I was excited and pleased with my day. I told her every detail of the day, the presentation, and how glad I was to have it behind me.

She was sweet, very supportive, and listened attentively. Finally, she said it was late and she wanted to go to bed.

I looked at my watch and realized for the first time that it was 11:30 p.m. I had been talking for over an hour. I apologized for talking so long, told her I loved her, and went to bed myself, with a smile on my face.

Gabby and I were having dinner and talking about our taxes, which were due the next week, when the phone rang. Gabby answered it, and I watched her face immediately light up. "How are you?" she said loudly into the phone. I couldn't hear the reply, but she laughed heartily and responded, "You nut!"

Hitting the speaker bottom on the phone base, she sat the handle back in the cradle and walked back toward the table. "It's Jack Anthony!" she said softly.

I was immediately smiling as I yelled out, "Jack! How are you doing, partner!"

"Good!" he responded. "I'm doing really well up here! Just enjoying life!"

"Are you in Alaska?" I quizzed.

"Yes, I am!" he answered. "I've been up here for about two months now!"

"Congratulations!" Gabby shouted. "I'll bet Harper is loving that!"

"She's right here with me," he said. "Let me ask her if she's loving me being up here." There was silence for a moment, and then he returned to the line. "She said it could be worse, but she doesn't know how!"

"She did not!" Gabby yelled back, chuckling.

"So how are you guys doing?" Jack inquired.

"We're good," Gabby responded. "We've just had our first grandbaby! Thomas and Mary had a little girl late last fall. They named her Michaela, and she is so cute!"

"That's outstanding!" he replied. "I couldn't be happier for you guys! I'm sure you'll be great grandparents!"

"Thank you!" Gabby said in response. "I just love her to pieces!"

"So the reason for my call," he began. "I was wondering if the two of you might be able to get off the week of the Fourth of July."

"Summer is the busy season in the storage business!" I answered after contemplating the date. "What did you have in mind?"

"We went to an animal shelter auction a couple of weeks ago," Jack began, "and Harper bid on a three-bedroom villa in Bermuda, and she won the prize! The issue is that the week of July 4 is the only open week we can use it this year. We were hoping that the two of you could come with us!"

"That sounds wonderful!" I said. "But that is a really tough time for me to take off. I'll have to see what I can do."

"The trip includes airfare for four people, so our only out-of-pocket expenses will be food, golf, and souvenirs!" Jack replied. "Oh, and by the way, we are going to get married while we're there, and I was hoping you would be my best man and Gabby would be Harper's maid of honor."

"We're going!" Gabby yelled emphatically.

I looked over at her and knew that whatever it took, we would be gone the first ten days of July. "It sounds like we're going!" I said excitedly.

The time passed quickly, and on June 29, Gabby and I picked up Jack and Harper at the Seattle airport. Lots of hugs, a quick meal, and back to our house for a short night's sleep.

We were in the car with all our luggage and headed back to the airport by 5:30 a.m. the next day. Our first leg of travel was to Miami, Florida. We had a two-hour layover in Miami, and then we boarded another smaller plane for the two-hour flight to Hamilton, Bermuda.

We switched seats several times on the five-and-a-half-hour trip to Miami, with Jack sitting next to me and Gabby sitting next to Harper. It was great to get caught up, and I was so thrilled to see how happy Jack was with his new life and soon-to-be wife.

The villa was unbelievable! It sat on a hill about three miles outside of the main city of Hamilton and had an amazing 360-degree view. There were views of the city to the west, the ocean to the south, and lush mountain sides spotted with beautiful homes to the east and north. As we made our way through the entryway, the furnishings were gorgeous, and the light fixtures were truly works of art.

The villa came with two mopeds that the owners gave us permission to use while we stayed there. Jack and I checked out the pool and the mopeds, while the girls started to unpack.

"This place is awesome!" Jack commented as we walked the grounds. Once we found the garage and went inside, we discovered the two mopeds, and Jack started singing "Born to Be Wild." "Get yer motor running! Get out on the highway! Looking for adventure, and whatever comes our way! Born to be wild!"

I just laughed and waved him off as I turned and started back up the walkway to the villa.

The next morning, Gabby and I had slept in late. Yesterday had been a very long day, and we both needed the sleep. I was instantly awake when I heard Harper scream, "Jack! What did you do?"

I threw on a pair of shorts and ran out of the bedroom to see what was going on. Gabby grabbed a robe and was only seconds behind me as we ran out into front yard where the scream had come from. Jack was sitting on the ground; his head and his arm were both covered in blood.

I turned back to Gabby and said, "Go get some towels and bring them out here!" She turned and ran back into the villa.

"Jack!" I said as I reached him. "What happened? When Gabby gets back with the towels, I'll have her call an ambulance!" Harper was on her knees beside him, crying but trying to stay calm.

"I decided to take one of the mopeds out for a quick spin this morning. I was coming around a blind corner when a car came at me in my lane!" he said. "I didn't really have a choice. He was going to hit me head on, so I drove into the ditch, and both the moped and I hit some jagged rocks that were sticking out of the mountainside pretty hard."

"Do you think you broke anything?" I asked as Gabby returned with an armload of clean towels.

"No, I don't think I broke anything, just the moped! I just have a couple of rock punctures in my arm and maybe one on the side of my head," Jack answered. "I don't need an ambulance. After we clean me up a bit, we can take a cab to the hospital."

I started wiping the blood off Jack and could see he was right. He had a couple of gashes on his arm and a large bump with a laceration on the side of his head. Once we applied a little pressure with the towels on those two wounded areas, the bleeding stopped, and we were able to clean him up a little.

"Do you think you can walk?" I asked.

"Sure!" he responded. "I walked here from the wreck. I just didn't want to go inside the villa and get blood all over the place!

The moped is about a quarter of a mile up the road. I couldn't get it out of the ditch by myself."

Harper and I helped him to his feet and started the short trip back to the villa entrance. "I think we should call an ambulance!" Harper stated firmly.

"I've already called the police, and they have an ambulance coming," Gabby said.

Jack had a pretty nasty road rash on his right leg, which I guessed had been caused by the same hillside when he ran into the ditch.

Once back in the house, we wetted several towels and gently started removing the blood and gravel from his head, arm, and leg. He was calm and started to joke with Harper. "Happy honeymoon, sweetheart!" he said, still able to smile.

"I'm just glad you weren't killed!" she said with sincerity in her voice.

In less than ten minutes, a police car and the ambulance arrived at the villa. The paramedics took over, and Jack answered questions asked by the police officer.

"I saw your moped in the ditch on the road. Can you tell me what happened?" the officer asked, taking out a pen and a pad of paper to write on.

"I was going to take a test ride on one of the mopeds, and as I rounded that blind corner, a car was coming right at me, and I had to run into the ditch to avoid him!" Jack said.

"Do you mean you crossed the road and ran into the ditch when you tried to avoid the oncoming car?" the policeman asked.

"No! I was in that lane, and I had no choice but to put the moped in the ditch or hit the oncoming car!" Jack reiterated.

He stopped writing and slowly lowered his hands. "You realize," he began, "this is Bermuda, and we drive on the opposite side of the road than you do in the United States?"

Jack was speechless as he realized he was the cause of the accident.

"You were driving into oncoming traffic in that lane when you should have been in the left lane," the officer explained. With a sheepish smile on his face, he continued. "It's not the first time this has happened, but I am thankful you weren't injured more seriously than you were!"

Jack was silent for a second. Then looking back to Harper, he said, "I'm so sorry!"

I don't know why, but the situation was so crazy that I couldn't suppress the laugh that was building in me. "You dumb shit!" I said, and then I bust out laughing.

Within seconds, we were all four laughing, and the police officer was looking at us like we were crazy.

Four hours later, we were leaving the hospital and getting ready to head back to our villa. Jack had his arm and leg wrapped and had a pretty big dressing on his head as we hailed a taxi.

He'd been given some pain medication, and he seemed to be dealing well with his discomfort. "We're not going back to the villa!" he said once we were all in the taxicab. "Let's do some exploring! Driver, take us downtown, please! A nice restaurant where we can get a good meal, please."

The driver nodded his understanding, and we were off to the local tourist traps!

We ordered breakfast, and the girls and I ordered mimosas with our breakfast. Jack said, "Make that four!"

Harper shot him a look and said, "Do you think that's a good idea to mix alcohol and painkillers together?"

"I'll be fine!" he answered emphatically. "I didn't come to Bermuda to be the only one not drinking!"

Harper didn't respond to his remarks, although I could tell she was a little miffed by his answer. The waiter turned and left our table. In short order, he returned with four mimosas.

Jack raised his glass for a toast, and we all responded in kind. "Here's to the little hiccups in life that create memories!" We all clinked glasses and took a drink.

"Well," I said, "you do create some unique memories, I'll give you that!" Everyone chuckled. Breakfast was served, and we all had a second mimosa with our meal.

Once finished eating, Jack asked, "What should we do now?" He was slurring his words, and it was obvious that the mix of pain medication and alcohol was having a significant effect on him.

Quickly realizing his condition was going to get worse before it got better, I offered up, "Why don't you and I go back to the villa for a couple of hours, while the girls go firm up the arrangements for the wedding on Thursday?"

Jack looked at me with a blank stare and said, "There's a wedding on Thursday?"

I looked at the girls and said, "I think I'd better get him home while he can still walk. You guys go do whatever you need to do, and we'll meet you back at the villa this afternoon. I think Jack is going to take a nap when we get home."

The girls agreed, and I asked for the check. We took two taxis and headed in different directions.

Jack looked at me and, with glazed eyes, asked, "Are we going to play golf now?"

"Maybe later today," I responded, "but not right now. I think you and I should go home and take a quick nap before we play golf."

He looked away from me, staring out his window, and simply said, "OK."

The girl's arrived back at the villa close to three o'clock in the afternoon. We sat in the living room and had a glass of wine while they told me about their day. Everything was arranged, and all the times, places, and flowers had been checked and double-checked. After the wedding, the four of us had reservations to have dinner at a very exclusive restaurant on the opposite side of Hamilton.

At about five o'clock, Jack came wandering into the living room from the bedroom.

Harper got up to meet him and walked over to him. "How are you doing, sweetheart?" she asked softly.

"I feel like I ran into a mountain at full speed!" he answered. "Oh, never mind, I actually did that! Has anyone checked on getting the moped out of that ditch yet?"

"That's all been taken care of!" I responded. "A wrecker came and picked it up, took it to their shop, and said it will be repaired and ready to go by this Friday before we leave."

Both girls looked at me with surprise on their respective faces. "Good job, honey!" Gabby offered up.

"How much is it going to cost?" Jack asked sheepishly.

"No idea," I answered. "It's going to cost whatever it costs! We'll just pay it!"

Once Jack was seated and comfortable, the girls went over the wedding details again for his benefit. He was pleased with the details, but I could tell he was feeling bad about the mess he'd created.

"If you're up for it," I tossed out, "I can run to the store and pick us up some fresh lobsters to cook for dinner. We can stay home, have a couple of drinks, and just take it easy tonight." No one responded.

"Or we can go downtown, find a club, and drink and dance until we can't stand up! What's your preference?"

Harper said, "I definitely vote for the first suggestion."

Followed by Gabby, "Me too! We've had enough excitement for one day!"

Finally, Jack spoke up. "I'm pretty stiff, but I think I could show you guys some new moves you haven't seen before on the dance floor if you want to go clubbing!"

"I'll take the moped and go get a few things for dinner," I said. "We'll see your dance moves another time if you don't mind. It's three against one. We'll eat here."

"Remember to ride on the wrong side of the road!" Jack yelled as I was leaving.

We had a great dinner, a few drinks, lots of laughs, and everyone turned in early. The next day, we had scheduled a catamaran ride out to a reef where we could snorkel for a couple of hours before being served lunch on the boat.

Gabby, Harper, and I went snorkeling, but Jack stayed on the boat. We were all afraid the saltwater would really hurt his still-scraped-up body. The boat captain agreed with us, so Jack started taking pictures of the three of us as we bobbed around in the water. It was a great day, and everyone had fun.

As we were sailing back toward Hamilton, Jack had his arms around Harper and her towel while we moved through the water. They both looked so happy that I couldn't help but smile.

Grabbing on to Gabby's towel, I said, "Come here, you!" and started pulling her back to me. Once she was in my lap and I had my arms around her, I softly said, "I'm so glad we came with them. This is a wonderful trip, and I love you so much!"

She leaned back and gave me a kiss before repeating my words. "I love you too, Michael!"

The day of the wedding, everything turned out perfectly. There wasn't a hitch in any part of the day. The sky was crystal clear, and there was a mild wind keeping the temperature bearable. It was Jack's and my first time seeing the venue, and it was nothing short of spectacular.

Harper, like all brides, was strikingly beautiful, and Jack looked dapper himself in his light blue suit. Gabby was also stunning in her dress, her blond locks blowing slightly in the breeze as she moved.

There were two witnesses, the minister, Gabby, and me as the ceremony began. It lasted for about forty-five minutes, but the time seemed to fly by as Gabby and I watched my closest friend take a partner for life. Once they were pronounced man and wife, Jack gave Harper a long and loving kiss!

Congratulations and hugs followed from Gabby and me, and we spent another thirty minutes being photographed by a professional photographer that Harper had hired for the wedding. Then it was off to an early dinner.

The restaurant, like everything else on this pristine island, was gorgeous, a stark white structure with a pillared, covered entry, complete with an outdoor chandelier. When we walked in, the interior was even more beautiful than the exterior. The chairs and tables look as though they had come out of a sixteenth-century castle owned by royalty. Beautiful deep blue velvet seats and backed chairs sat on meticulously hand-carved ornate mahogany frames. The tables had light gray polished marble tops seated on more carved mahogany legs.

We were seated and given menus to look over. Three things jumped out at me as we browsed the menus. First, there were no prices on the menu. Second, there were only two other couples in the main dining room that looked like it could easily hold sixty people. And, third, there were more restaurant staff present than there were customers. There were four waiters standing on the wall behind our table, and after Gabby had taken a drink from her water glass, one of them immediately stepped forward and refilled her glass.

I looked at Jack, and he smiled back, lifting his water glass, taking a drink, and setting it back down on the table. A second waiter instantaneously stepped forward and filled his water glass. We were both amused, and it was obvious as Harper said, "Stop it, you two!"

We ordered dinner and asked for four glasses of champagne. The champagne arrived, and I toasted to Jack and Harper's wedding and wished them never-ending happiness. Once we'd all drunk to my toast, we placed the champagne glasses back on the table while we waited for our appetizers. All four waiters stepped forward, each with their own bottle of champagne and filled the glasses again.

I looked over at Harper and asked, "Do you have any idea how expensive this restaurant is?"

She shrugged her shoulders and responded, "No, I really don't. When I made the reservation, I simply asked for the best restaurant in Bermuda, and this was their recommendation."

The meal was the best meal I had ever eaten in my life! From lobster claws served in a creamy but rich broth through the individual key lime pies served on top of the most delicious raspberry sauce I have ever tasted.

The more champagne we drank, the more Jack and I played with the waiters. Jack picked up his glass, brought it almost to his lips, which had his waiter starting toward the table, champagne bottle in hand, only to place his still full glass back on the table without taking a drink. We both laughed, and even though they tried not to, Harper and Gabby laughed as well.

We had been in the restaurant for three hours when Jack asked for the check. Jack took out a credit card as he was handed the bill. He looked the bill over for a couple of minutes before starting to laugh. Pretty soon, he was almost doubled over he was laughing so hard. We could barely understand him as he said, "Thank God you only get married once!" and then tears were running down his reddening face as he went into another laughing fit.

"Let me see that!" I said, wondering what was so funny. He handed me the bill, and I looked at it and immediately began laughing with him. The girls sat in silence watching the two of us and wondering what was so funny.

Jack finally stopped laughing, wiped his now wet face with his napkin, and said, "I got the bill on the moped this morning. It will cost $963 to get it out of the shop."

"How about this," he continued, trying to keep a straight face, "I could use a little help here! You either pay to have the moped fixed, or you pay half of this bill! Your choice!" Then he and I both literally lost it as we laughed so hard we were having a hard time catching our breath.

Harper had finally had enough as she said sharply, "Give me that bill, Jack!"

Jack handed it to her, and I suspect she didn't find the humor in it that we did as she muttered, "Holy crap! This can't be right." Her words sent Jack and me into another laughing fit, which lasted for at least two minutes.

Once I got my emotions under control, I wiped off my face, blew my nose, and said, "I think that's the hardest I've ever laughed in my life! Give me the bill, and it can be Gabby's and my wedding gift to you!"

"We can't let you do that!" Harper said firmly.

Finally, Gabby spoke up, being the only one at the table who didn't know how much the dinner bill was. "How much is that thing anyway!" she asked, concern in her voice.

"Well, each time they filled our half-full glasses of champagne," I started, "it was twenty seven dollars a glass." Gabby gasped at the number.

"Gabby, there are two favors I need to ask of you if I could," I said.

"First, don't ever sign us up for a free vacation again! Second, how much is the tip on a $2,100 bill?" Everyone except Gabby lost it again as she sat there in complete shock.

CHAPTER 20

We were the Region of the Year in my second full year managing the northwest region. As I had predicted, the Los Angeles region, with Wendy at the helm, took the number-two position, just barely behind us.

Two of my high-performing district managers were promoted to regional managers and moved to other areas of the country. I was fortunate enough to replace them with two outstanding prospects whom I felt could move to the next level quickly.

They both had several years of managing at the region manager level but were willing to take a step back to prove their worth to our company by starting at the district manager position. An unexpected perk for hiring them was that one was female and the other was a Hispanic male, with both having impeccable resumes.

Jeff Hall, our CEO, called me on my mobile phone one morning to personally congratulate me on that month's results, which had just booked.

"It looks like your region is off to another great start, Michael," he said with praise in his voice. "I couldn't be happier for you and your team! Do you think you would have time to meet me for lunch on Friday in the early afternoon?"

"I very much appreciate your courtesy in asking, sir, but I'm sure you realize no one in their right mind tells their CEO that they're too busy to have lunch with them," I stated, laughing as I said it. "Of course, I'm available! Just tell me where and what time to be there."

"I guess you're right about that," he said, chuckling as he responded. "I'll have Gloria set it up, and she can e-mail you the details once everything is set. Thanks for making yourself available," he said. "I've got to go—I have another call coming in that I need to take. See you Friday!" The phone line went dead before I could even say good-bye.

We met in a quaint little restaurant in downtown Seattle. The staff was very familiar with Jeff, calling him by name as we were being seated.

"Would you like a menu, Mr. Hall, or will you have your usual?" our waiter asked.

"I'll have the usual, please," he responded. "But bring a menu for my guest so he can decide what he'd like to have for lunch."

Still looking at Jeff, the waiter asked, "Iced tea with lemon?"

"Please," Jeff responded.

"I'll have the same," I said, inserting myself into their conversation.

No more than two minutes later, I was looking through the menu and we were both sipping on our iced teas. "If you don't mind me asking," I started, "what is the usual?"

"It's pretty boring, I'm afraid," Jeff answered. "I'm having a hamburger with lettuce, tomato, and onion on it, with no condiments. Also, a cup of homemade chicken soup. That's my standard fare at this restaurant," he finished.

The waiter returned to take my order. I ordered a tuna melt sandwich with a side salad.

"Michael, we have a chance to increase the size of our portfolio substantially in the next few months. We are looking to acquire over one hundred properties through an acquisition we've been working on for some time."

I sat and listened intently.

"With that many new properties, we are going to add a new division, probably in the northeast. After meeting with all the current divisional managers, HR, and our CFO, everyone seems to think you would be the perfect fit for that role!"

Jeff stopped talking and simply stared at me, waiting for a response. When none came, he began again. "The current divisions would have to be reconfigured. I would need you to move to the northeast, New York, Philadelphia, or Washington DC. You would answer directly to me if you accept this assignment." Our lunch arrived as Jeff Hall waited for me to respond.

"What an honor to be offered such a wonderful opportunity," I began, "but are you sure I'm the right person for the job?"

He swallowed a bite of his hamburger and then said, "There is always a chance of failure when a company makes these types of moves, but we all agree you are the best prospect for this new position." Picking up his hamburger and preparing to take another bite, he continued. "Do you think your wife would want to live in the northeast?"

"That is a great question," I said, staring at my lunch, which I hadn't touched yet. "I can't honestly answer that question until I speak with her."

"Before we go any further, that question needs to be answered," Jeff said. "Why don't you take the weekend and discuss this with your wife? If she isn't 100 percent behind this move, you shouldn't take the position. Be honest with her! You will be doing more traveling, having more work, and having to fly back here to corporate headquarters a minimum of once a month. She's going to have a lot of alone time."

I agreed to give him an answer the following Monday. We ate the rest of our lunch pretty much in silence. When we were both done, we got up and started for the door.

"What about the check?" I asked.

"They'll just put it on my tab," he responded. "I pay the tab on the first and the fifteenth of each month. I have lunch here most days when I'm in town. I've been eating here for about twelve years now."

The next morning, I opened my computer and started looking at real estate in various places on the East Coast. Being a Saturday, Gabby was still sleeping since she didn't need to get up and make breakfast for me before I rushed off to work.

We couldn't afford to live in New York; it was much too expensive. I didn't want to live in Philadelphia; the houses were old, and the area wasn't very appealing. Washington DC was out because their crime statistics were off the charts!

I couldn't be traveling and worrying that my wife might be in harm's way while I was gone! After two hours of searching, I was both discouraged and frustrated by what I'd uncovered. As I sat there drinking my third cup of coffee, Gabby walked into the living room.

"Good morning!" she said, still sounding groggy, and plopped down beside me on the sofa. She took the coffee cup out of my hands and took a drink.

"Good morning to you, sunshine! You finish that, and I'll go make you a fresh cup, sleepyhead," I said, getting up and heading toward the kitchen. As quickly as the Keurig could make the coffee, I was on my way back to the living room, a hot beverage in hand.

Gabby traded me cups and took a quick sip from the new cup. "Oh, that's good!" she said after tasting the hot coffee.

"Why were you looking on Zillow?" she asked. "New York, New Jersey, Washington DC? Are you looking for vacation spots for the summer?" she quizzed.

"No, not really," I answered.

I watched her eyes dart back and forth as she began to process the information she had already accumulated. Suddenly snapping her head around to look directly at me, she said, "No! I don't want to live on the East Coast! I like it here, and all the kids and our granddaughter are on this side of the country! The winters are hard and cold back there! I don't like being cold!"

I sat there saying nothing in response.

After a few minutes of silence and a couple of more sips on her coffee, Gabby asked, "What do they want you to do?"

I repeated the entire conversation I'd had with Jeff Hall the day before at lunch. I didn't leave out anything, even the part about "if your wife isn't 100 percent behind you, then say no to the offer."

Gabby sat with her knees up to her chest, attentively listening and drinking her coffee, saying nothing. We sat in silence for a while before I asked, "Would you like me to turn on the TV to watch some news or something?"

"No," she replied. "Let me just think about this for a minute. I need to process this slowly. It's a huge move for us and for our family if we do this."

I got back on my computer and continued my search for suitable housing somewhere on the East Coast.

"You'd probably be traveling more there than you do here," she stated.

"I'm sure I would travel more," I agreed.

"What would I do with myself if you were gone all the time?" she asked. "I don't want to sit around the house and cry all day because I'm lonely! That's not a life I'm willing to live just to advance your career! That's not being selfish, is it?"

"No, that's not selfish," I responded.

"How about this," I said. "Let's get dressed and forget about this for now. We should go have breakfast at the Original Pancake House and enjoy our weekend!"

Gabby's mood changed instantly. "I'd love to do that!" she responded exuberantly. "It won't take me long to shower and get ready. Thirty minutes tops!" With that, she was up and rapidly making her way to the bathroom.

As I sat there thinking about our conversation, I realized there was probably a 90 percent chance that this move wasn't going to happen. I was OK with every aspect of that decision apart from having to tell Jeff Hall that I wouldn't be accepting the position. But Gabby's happiness was far more important than the promotion. I kept thinking over and over, *Happy wife, happy life*, and in my heart, I knew Gabby would never be happy on the East Coast.

On Monday, I walked over to Jeff's administrative assistant's desk and asked when a good time would be to visit with him for a few minutes.

She smiled, picked up her phone, dialed one number, and was instantly speaking with Jeff. After a very short conversation, she hung up the phone and told me to go right into his office.

As I entered the office, Jeff stood up, shook my hand, and said, "Michael! It's good to see you this morning! I needed to talk with you anyway. Have a seat."

I was trying to muster up all the courage in my being so I could deliver my disappointing news when Jeff said, "I'm afraid there's been a bit of a change of plans. Greg Young, the current divisional vice president in Southern California, called me this weekend and asked if he could have the new division on the East Coast.

"He grew up in Annapolis, Maryland, and he and his wife have lots of family back there. Greg has lots of experience with acquisitions, and he knows his way around that part of the country. It is a much better move for us to send him back home. It's really a win for the company and a win for Greg and his family."

"That makes perfect sense," I said, not trying to sound very happy about the news. "I completely understand the reasoning for the change."

"Thank you for understanding, Michael," Jeff said. "I'm sure you're disappointed, but when one door closes, another one opens. Instead of going to the East Coast, how would you and your wife like to move to sunny California and take over the Southern California division?"

"Where is the Southern California divisional office?" I asked.

"It's in Newport Beach, about fifty miles south of Los Angeles," he responded.

"Can I have an answer to you in the morning?" I asked. "I still want to speak with my wife before making a commitment if I could."

"You don't need to get back to me tomorrow!" Jeff replied. "This move probably won't happen for another month or two, but we are trying to get all our ducks in a row early. Before you give me your answer, why don't you and your wife fly down there for the weekend and look the area over? I'll have Gloria make all the flight and hotel arrangements." With that, Jeff stood up and shook my hand again.

"Thank you, sir!" I said. "That could play a big part in our decision. I really appreciate the gesture!" Then I exited his office.

In the minute that it took to reach Gloria's desk, she was ready with questions. What is your preferred airline? What is your wife's middle name? Do you know your mileage rewards numbers? What kind of a car do you want to pick up at the airport? Do you have a hotel preference?

I tried to act calm as I answered all her questions even though I was so excited I thought I was going to wet my pants! When the questions were finished, I left the office and drove straight home to tell Gabby the news.

"What are you doing home so early?" Gabby asked as I walked through the front door. "Are you sick?"

I chuckled and told her I wasn't sick. Sitting down next to her on the sofa, I downloaded all the information I had been given. I could tell Gabby was still somewhat apprehensive about the move but excited to take the quick trip to check out the area.

"Think of this as a very short all-expenses-paid vacation," I said. "Oh, and for your information and for packing purposes, the temperature is expected to be in the high sixties to the midseventies with zero chance of rain this weekend in Newport Beach! Not bad for the middle of February!"

It was cold and raining when we stepped out of the taxicab at the Seattle airport. Once we arrived at John Wayne International Airport in Newport Beach, we could feel the temperature change the instant they opened the airplane's main door. Walking through the corridor to the main terminal, it felt like it was eighty degrees even though we both knew it wasn't that warm.

After picking up our car, we drove to the hotel where Gloria had made a reservation for us. She had booked us at the Hyatt Regency

Hotel near the Fashion Island Mall and just a short distance from the airport.

After checking in, we were led to a beautiful three-room suite with every amenity that's available. Looking out the large bay window in the main living room area, Gabby looked back at me and said, "I could definitely get used to this! Look at all those beautiful palm trees!"

After unpacking, we called down for our car and went out to do some exploring. It was warm enough to drive with the windows down, and the warm breeze felt clean and refreshing as it came off the ocean. We had seen heavy smog as we passed over Los Angeles in our plane, but there was none here. You could see for miles in all directions.

Neither one of us had ever been to a town or area like this. Unbelievably expensive cars, beautiful people, both male and female, jogging through town, with the Pacific Ocean only one block off the Main Street.

We pulled the car over and parked. Holding hands, we walked the short distance to the beach and stopped to admire the beautiful homes, ocean, and people. Walking to the water's edge, I placed my foot in the water, and Gabby did the same.

"Oh my god!" Gabby squealed. "It's so warm!" I simply shook my head in agreement.

The beaches looked endless. There was gorgeous white sand as far as we could see in either direction. A soft warm breeze was dancing off the water, and there was a surprising lack of people on the beach for a Saturday. We started walking south, and I said to Gabby, "So this is what heaven is like!"

She chuckled, put her arm around my waist, and responded, "It sure feels like it could be!"

After a couple of miles of walking, we stopped at a small bar that was just off the beach and ordered two beers and some nachos. As we ate our food and drank our beer, we watched rollerbladers and skateboarders whiz by the open window frames. Everyone walking or running past the windows was a varying shade of golden brown. The music was a combination of new rock and '60s and '70s classics, and it was loud.

We could see a few surfers off in the distance where the waves seemed to be larger than the ones directly in front of us. It was simply mesmerizing to see and experience the peacefulness of this moment.

Once we made it back to our rental car, we decided to go see the divisional office. It was larger than I had expected. A real perk was that it was just minutes away from two major freeways, Interstate 5 and, further west, I-405, which both went north to Los Angeles or south toward San Diego.

The building wasn't nearly the size of our corporate headquarters, but it was certainly large enough to accommodate several people. I'd found out that I, two of my five regional managers, and five district managers would all be officing here. There would also be three administrative assistants, one for me and one for each regional manager, bringing the total headcount to eleven bodies.

We couldn't go inside, but we got out of the car and walked the property. There was plenty of parking, nicely manicured landscaping, and Gabby's favorite, half a dozen huge palm trees lining the road. Looking through the windows with cupped hands, it appeared to have plenty of room even with all the office equipment we saw in various areas of the office.

As we walked back toward the car, Gabby said, "I think you'll love your new office."

Not realizing she'd just given her permission to move, I simply responded, "I think it would be a great office!"

"You would be the most senior person here, wouldn't you?" she continued.

"I suppose that is correct," I answered, not trying to sound to full of myself.

"Where do you want to go now?" she asked.

"Why don't we just jump on the freeway and see where it takes us?" I said.

"Sounds fun!" Gabby replied. "Let's go see the sights!"

There was a ton of cars on I-5, but the traffic didn't seem any worse than it was on a normal Saturday in Seattle. We'd driven about fifteen miles when we began seeing billboards for Disneyland ten miles ahead.

"Disneyland!" Gabby yelled. "I've always wanted to go to Disneyland ever since I was a little girl! All our kids would have so much fun when they come to visit!

"We could spoil Michaela and bring her down here every year during the summer!" she said, excited by the prospect of visiting Disneyland.

"Don't put the cart before the horse, sweetheart!" I threw out. "I still need to accept the job, and we'd have to move here before anyone visits Disneyland!"

"Do you have any reservations about taking this position?" Gabby asked.

"No, not really," I responded. "But this must be both of our decisions, not just mine. Remember, Jeff said, 'If your wife isn't 100 percent in favor of the move, don't do it!'"

Gabby looked at me with a smile on her face and took a deep breath before saying, "This is an incredible place, and I think we should do it! I can't wait to live here!"

I looked over at her and said firmly, "Are you sure?"

She shook her head yes while responding, "I'm sure! How could anyone not want to live here?"

"OK," I answered. "It sounds like we're on to our next adventure! Oh, and by the way, when I lived in Beaumont, about two hours from here, I went to Disneyland twenty-one times! So I'll be a pretty good guide."

"I didn't know that!" Gabby said. "We've never talked about Disneyland before."

"We haven't talked much about either one of our childhood years," I responded. "It sounds like maybe we need to get to know each other a little better!"

Gabby smiled, looked away, letting her head fall back on the seat's headrest and stuck her arm out the open window, allowing the warm breeze to blow over her exposed hand, and saying nothing.

I realized that I was being promoted in a relatively short career span based on my strong performances as a district manager and then as a region manager. I believe that Jeff Hall and the rest of the upper management team saw me as an overachiever and trusted I was ready to step up to the next challenge.

But I knew this role would be different than my last two assignments in many ways. I'd realized early in my career that the more broken a district or region was when you inherited it, the quicker the performance measurements could be turned around.

Fortunately for our stockholders, but unfortunately for me, the Southern California division was far from being broken. With the addition of acquisition properties, it would be very difficult to achieve the successes they had enjoyed over the past few years.

Second, never having been in either of my previous management positions for more than two years, I'd never had to go up against my own numbers from the previous year. Upon leaving those positions, I knew that both entities would lag in performance for a short period until the new management could get their teams and processes in place and functional.

When I'd accepted this assignment, Jeff had made it clear that I would be here for a minimum of four years. He also made it clear that I needed to constantly improve on my division's performance year after year to meet the company goals and stockholders' expectations.

To drive that point home, Jeff awarded me a good amount of restricted stock at the current price. He told me that if I wanted to increase my net worth in the shortest possible time, all I had to do was make sure I was always concentrating on improving the stock price.

Third, I believed in my mantra, "People make the difference." I was intent on moving some of the strongest-performing property personnel to the acquisition properties as soon as possible to ensure our desired results. I had the same plan for both the district managers and the regional management teams. I planned to put systems and processes in place to either coach and train the existing employees to be more efficient and effective, or we would recruit and replace them with better people.

I felt that my success as a divisional vice president depended 80 percent on how well I managed my direct reports and 20 percent on luck, good fortune, and economic circumstances outside of my control.

Once I'd accepted the promotion, Gabby and I began preparing for the move. We listed our home with the same realtor who helped us buy it two years earlier. The Seattle market had become one of the preferred markets in the country, and we had no trouble selling the house and turning a very reasonable profit in the process.

As time neared for me to transfer to Southern California, I took several trips to Newport Beach so I could spend some time with the current divisional and glean as much knowledge of the market as possible while I had the opportunity to do so.

Taking advantage of our relocation package again, I signed a three-month lease on a two-bedroom condo in nearby Santa Ana. That would give us enough time to look for permanent housing and complete our relocation while still enabling me to do my job effectively.

I went to my first divisional meeting on June 29 back at our corporate headquarters. The CEO, CFO, acquisition manager, Human Resources managers, all the divisional managers, plus several accounting staff were all seated in the conference room when I walked in.

As I observed my peers during the meeting, I felt a little out of place. Most had held this position for a few years, and they were very comfortable in this arena. Two out of the five divisionals were looking through today's edition of the *Wall Street Journal* as we waited for Jeff Hall to join us.

I did quickly note that they were all pretty affected by their own sense of self-importance. John Belk, my former boss, was the least arrogant, but in this environment, even his personality had succumbed to the powerful egos in attendance. The small talk at the table prior to the meeting starting centered mostly on expensive wines, who had the newest car, and who the Italian designer was that tailored their custom-made suits.

June 29 was also the release date of the new smart phone being introduced by Apple. Except for myself, all the divisionals had someone picking up their first iPhone while we were in the meeting.

At the time, I thought this was just one more high-tech toy that each divisional wanted to be the first to own. None of us could have known at the time the impact this new smart phone would have on the world in the coming years. In less than a month after its introduction, I owned an iPhone as well.

It was a bit of a culture shock as Gabby and I moved from the laid-back Seattle lifestyle to the hustle and daily grind of the third-largest city in the nation. When Gabby and I had visited on a weekend, two months earlier, traffic seemed bearable. I had no idea at the time how horrific traffic was from Monday through Friday until I experienced it!

My first trip traveling with Wendy, who now reported to me, in Los Angeles was a nightmare! I'd left Santa Ana at 6:30 a.m. to make the fifty-five-mile trip to her office with the anticipation that we would meet at 8:30 a.m. At 9:10 a.m., I was still fifteen miles from our rendezvous point. I called her to let her know I was stuck in traffic.

"What time did you leave this morning?" she asked.

"I left Santa Ana at six thirty," I responded.

She chuckled back into the phone and said, "No wonder you're late! You needed to leave at least forty-five minutes earlier if you wanted to be here by eight thirty!"

When I finally arrived at her office, I was surprised as she greeted me with a quick hug. I hadn't expected the warm reception, but I was even more taken aback that she would physically hug me versus shaking my hand given our history together.

Once we'd exchanged pleasantries, she said, "First things first! When do you want to leave to get home?"

"I don't know?" I answered. "When should I leave?"

"Well, you really only have two options," she explained. "If you leave before 3:00 p.m., you should be home by 6:30 p.m., if there are no wrecks. Or you could leave at 7:00 p.m. and be home by 8:00 p.m. It's a three-hour drive versus a one-hour drive, but you'll get home later if you take the shorter drive."

"Since I don't know how often we'll be able to travel together," I answered, "I will definitely leave at the later time, giving us more time to visit properties."

"Sounds great!" she said enthusiastically. "Let me make a couple of quick calls, and we can get out of here."

As Wendy was making calls and setting up our travel route, I wondered around her office. Regardless how friendly and hospitable she was to me, I knew she wanted and thought she deserved to be the divisional vice president in Southern California.

I couldn't really argue that she wasn't correct. She had more experience than I did. She had been successful in every position of her career. Her drive and work ethic were incredible. The only answer I could come up with for me being chosen over her was because she was female. We'd never had a female divisional, and as sad as it sounded, it appeared we would have to wait a little longer before we allowed a female into the "good old boys' club."

Gabby found a location in one of the most affluent parts of the coast as she searched for our new home while I continued to dig into my new assignment. There was nothing available in our price range, so we had started looking at rental property.

I agreed to look at a pretty expensive condo rental only because it was a ten-minute drive from the divisional office to its location pretty much anytime of the day. It was in a community called Newport Coast, about five hundred feet up a hill and on a plateau above Newport Beach and the Pacific Ocean.

Newport Coast was home to movie stars, sports celebrities, successful doctors (mostly plastic surgeons), high-priced lawyers, and hedge fund managers who had invested well and retired in this seemingly recession-proof bastion of capitalism.

The condominium was two thousand square feet and was in a very nice gated community. There was a workout facility, pool, hot tub, and multiple gas grills that were available for all the residents to use in the middle of the complex. The condo we were going to view looked down on a beautiful park to the east, and being an end unit, it was quiet, tranquil, and caught the morning and afternoon breezes coming up from the ocean.

We arrived a little early, but we'd been given the gate code by the owner so we could enter the complex. We were standing out in front of the unit, waiting, when a bright red Ferrari with its top off turned the corner and stopped less than two feet from where we were standing.

A very handsome six-foot-two young man stepped out of the car in gym clothes. "I'm sorry, I'm late, but I've been playing tennis, and I just couldn't quite put my opponent away! We ended up playing about ten minutes longer than I had planned."

He introduced himself, opened the door, and invited us in to look over the condo.

While Gabby and I were walking from room to room, we heard a second car drive up and stop. The car door opened and shut and was followed by a yell from a woman. "Michael!" she blurted out. "Where are you?"

"I'm on the patio!" he yelled back. We heard a gate open and close, and then there was silence.

After we'd examined the home to our satisfaction, we joined Michael and his guest on the patio.

The woman was much smaller than her voice implied. She was about five feet tall and may have weighed one hundred pounds, but I doubted it. She'd obviously had a breast augmentation, and as she quickly approached us, there were telltale signs of other work that had been performed to try and keep her as youthful looking as possible.

"My name's Monica!" she said with authority. "Michael's my son." She put out her hand and quickly shook both Gabby's and my hand. "I'm sorry for interrupting, but I needed to speak to Michael about some plans I have for us tonight! He never answers his damn phone when I call, so I called his assistant and tracked him down!"

Turning to her son, she said, "Remember, 8:00 p.m. sharp at the club! Don't be late, and you can bring what's her name if you want. Now walk me out to my car!"

They started through the gate beside the house, and Michael looked back and waved for us to follow him. "Her name is Alicia!" Michael stated sternly as he walked beside his mother.

As we rounded the corner, not only were we looking at a Ferrari but also Monica got into a new jet-black Bentley that looked like it had just been driven off the showroom floor. Starting the car and rolling down the driver's side window, she repeated herself. "Don't be late!" The window went up, and seconds later, she was gone.

Gabby couldn't contain herself as she asked, "What do you people do?"

Michael smiled before he answered. "Well, I run a hedge fund that my father started years ago. He passed away last year, and now the business is mine. My mom owns three totally unrelated businesses and is on the board of directors at one of our local banks. She stays busy!"

"How old are you?" Gabby pressed.

"I'm twenty-eight," he replied.

"How many people work at your hedge fund?" she continued.

"Between fifty and sixty people, I think," he responded unassumingly.

"What questions can we answer for you?" I interjected, realizing Gabby's questions were getting more and more personal.

"We've already run your credit," Michael stated. "So I guess I just would like to know how long you want to lease the place."

"My boss told me I would be here a minimum of four years, so do you want to do a four-year lease?" I asked.

"Oh," he said, sounding a little surprised. "I was planning on selling this property in a couple of years, so maybe we could start with a two-year lease at $3,800 a month and see what happens after two years."

"What do you think the rental rate will be in two years if we extended the lease?" I asked.

"I have no idea!" he countered. "I'll be fair with you, but the market at that point in time will determine the rent. I was going to sell this property, but the market is taking a dump right now, and I'm not a fan of losing money on real estate."

"Just out of curiosity," I asked, "what would this sell for on today's market?"

"Probably somewhere between $1.5 and $1.7 million," he answered. "But I paid $2 million for it three years ago, so I'm hanging on to it for now."

We asked Michael if he would clean the carpets upstairs, and he agreed. Three days later, we signed a two-year lease.

Once we were moved in and comfortable, we started exploring the area by taking long walks around the village. This was a beautiful yet small community of gently sloping hills and massive homes that overlooked the Pacific Ocean.

Small, expensive specialty shops dominated both the small shopping centers at opposite ends of the town. The streets were lined with beautiful light fixtures, all of which had baskets of exotic flowers hanging below their halogen lights. Large, healthy palm trees were everywhere you looked. With a year-round temperature averaging seventy degrees, this was some of the most sought-after real estate in California.

Unfortunately, we soon found that most of the residents in the area were so intoxicated with their self-importance that it became almost comical to Gabby and me. The number-one activity in the community seemed to be "one-upping your neighbors."

Being more boisterous and more garish than anyone else when having dinner at one of the many fine dining establishments in the area was expected. Those loud conversations were inevitably centered on current stock prices, newfound IPOs, conservative politics, his or her golf or tennis game, exotic travel (past and planned), and, of course, fine wine.

There were no homes for less than $1.5 million in Newport Coast, but several sold for between $15 and $20 million while we lived there. We didn't really make many friends. We weren't socially inept, but we didn't seem to fit in to any of the clicks or tight-knit groups we met. We simply didn't measure up to the standard of excellence or wealth that was expected to become a part of this community.

I would never have dreamed that Gabby and I would be living among the rich and famous, but it was as much our choice as it was theirs not to participate or become trapped in this elitist lifestyle.

This was a community where only beautiful people could live. It was as if there was a sign on the city limits that forbade those who were of a hefty build, afflicted, or were raising less-than-brilliant children from living here. These lesser types could drive through town, stop to get a cup of coffee, a soft drink, or have a meal, if they kept moving and didn't stay for more than seven days at a time.

If you did see a large-bodied person more than once, it was safe to assume that he or she was in the upper echelons of society and wealth. The only thing that seemed to trump appearance in this self-absorbed conclave was net worth.

The cars, for which I have a personal affinity, were unlike any other place I'd lived or visited. It was not unusual to see three or four Aston Martins, Ferraris, Lamborghinis, Audi A8s, Bentleys, or Rolls-Royces on the short ten-minute drive to my office. The $50,000 and under cars were designated as first cars for the local high school kids.

The women were always in full makeup, even when making a quick trip to the grocery store. Most housewives dressed like movie stars, always dressed in high-fashion clothing as they wandered the pristine aisles of the only grocery store on the hill, inspecting overpriced broccoli in stiletto heels.

We had only lived there a month when I stopped at the Starbucks to get a coffee to take with me to the office when I had one of my most unforgettable experiences in New Port Coast.

I liked to stop at a specific Starbucks in the Newport Coast Plaza because it was close to my home. I don't know if I'm really telling the truth about my reason for stopping. I may have enjoyed watching the exotic cars pulling up and parking while their owners got in line with me for a quick espresso before heading out to fight the battles for that day even more.

I saw a beautiful Rolls-Royce Phantom pulling up outside as I stood with several people deep in line to order my coffee. I didn't really pay attention to the person getting out of the car as I continued checking e-mails on my iPhone.

As the line moved forward, I looked up to see several people staring at me. I smiled, and several of them gave me an abbreviated wave. I politely waved back. As more people turned to look at me, I wondered what they were smiling about.

I turned to see what was behind me, and I was staring at the stomach of a very tall African American man. I looked up at him, and we both smiled. "I thought everyone was smiling to me!" I said. "But they were probably looking at you!"

He chuckled and said, "You're probably right. I get that a lot." Then he asked, "What's your name, man?"

"Michael Larsen," I said, putting my hand out to shake his. His hand swallowed my own, but he didn't squeeze to hard as we shook hands. "What about you?" I asked.

The smile instantly disappeared from his face. He was shocked that it was even a possibility that I didn't know him!

After a couple of seconds of silence, I finally said, "I was just screwing around with you! I know you're one of the Los Angeles Lakers! It's nice to meet you!"

He started to laugh and gave me a little punch in the arm. "You had me, man!" he began. "I couldn't believe anyone in this town wouldn't know who I am! You got me good, Michael!"

After receiving my coffee, I said good-bye and exited the building. It was the first and last time I would see him while I lived in Newport Coast—well, except every other night when the Lakers played on TV.

I always knew when the Lakers were playing at the Staple Center, because on the nights they played home games, I would hear his helicopter heading home from LA as it flew over my house at one or two o'clock in the morning.

CHAPTER 21

Things were moving along nicely for Gabby and me since moving to California. Gabby had done her magic, and the condo looked great once she'd finished decorating. We absolutely loved the weather. The forecast never seemed to change. "Another beautiful day in Newport Beach! Highs in the midseventies with a five-mile-an-hour breeze coming off the ocean, and still no rain in sight!"

We were like kids again because there was so much to do and so many points of interest to explore relatively close by. Every weekend felt like we were on vacation as, one at a time, we checked off the places and attractions we wanted to visit.

Work, although challenging with the addition of the new properties in the portfolio, was going reasonably well. I spoke with Jeff Hall two or three times a week, and he seemed pleased with the numbers coming from our area.

In my first three months, we'd hired two potential regional managers and four district managers, all in areas where I'd determined we may need to make some changes in the future. One of the potential regionals was here in Los Angeles, and though I didn't have a place for her currently, she was entirely too talented not to hire her.

In her previous position, she'd supervised several more locations than I currently managed. It was obvious that in as little as a year, she would be able to replace me at the divisional level. I had asked her to join us for a two-day tour with Jeff Hall, and he had been very impressed with her as well.

After our tour, when I was dropping Jeff off at the airport to fly back to Seattle, he commented, "You know she could take your job someday."

I smiled and responded, "I hope she does! Hopefully not in the too near future. But if I were hit by a rogue meteor or some other catastrophe, I think you'd have a pretty good backup to fill my position."

Jeff smiled, shook my hand, grabbed his luggage, and headed into the terminal.

It was a beautiful Saturday morning. Gabby and I had just entered the admission gates at Knott's Berry Farm when my cell phone rang. Looking at it, I saw it was Harper Anthony calling. We stopped walking. I told Gabby it was Harper and then answered the call.

"Hey, Harper! How are you?" I said, excited to be hearing from her.

Before Harper could respond, Gabby said, "I hope nothing's wrong!"

"I'm pretty good!" she exclaimed. "But Jack hurt himself again!"

"What happened?" I asked. "Is he OK?"

"Well, it's kind of a long story. Do you have time to talk now?" she asked.

"Absolutely!" I responded. "We're not doing anything special. Tell me what happened."

"I don't know if we ever talked about it, but I own a cabin on an island on a lake by the name of Big Lake. It's about a three-hour drive north of Anchorage," she began. "Well, Jack got tired of making that drive, so he took some flying lessons. He got his pilot's license, and we bought a small four-seater airplane. We installed pontoons on it so we could make water landings.

"We've flown to the lake several times, but frankly, the wind coming off the lake scares the hell out of me when we're landing!" she said. "Well, he took off work yesterday and decided to fly up to the cabin to do some fishing this weekend. The wind was really bad, and he crashed the plane into our boat dock."

"Is he all right?" I asked.

"He broke his arm and two ribs. I guess he did quite a bit of damage when he landed because the plane ended upside down on the dock, half in and half out of the water. A neighbor saw the crash and jumped into his boat and went over to help. He ferried Jack to dry land and then drove him to the hospital."

"That's terrible!" I said, all the while, Gabby was talking into my other ear.

"What happened?" she kept saying over and over.

I took the phone away from my face, looked at Gabby, and said, "Jack crashed an airplane. Give me a minute and I'll tell you the whole story!"

"Oh my god!" she said, her hand involuntarily going up to cover her mouth.

Putting the phone back to my ear, I said, "Sorry, Harper, Gabby wanted to know what happened."

"That's OK, I understand," she responded. "But that's not the end of the story."

"What else?" I asked.

"They took X-rays and did an MRI to see if there was any internal damage," she said, her voice starting to break for the first time. "Jack has a mass of tumors on his left kidney and a small tumor on his liver. They're going to take a biopsy of the tumors tomorrow and see if they are cancerous. The doctor said that it would be rare if they weren't, but he still wanted to verify the diagnosis before making the final call." Then she began crying.

"Would you like me to come up? I could be there by tomorrow," I said.

"No. No, I don't think that's necessary," she responded. "Jack's mom and his sister are already on their way here. Let's see what happens with the biopsy first. I'll call you tomorrow with the results."

"How is Jack doing with all this?" I asked.

She chuckled into the phone. "You know Jack! He said we should look on the bright side! He should have been killed in the plane wreck, so every day he's alive from here on out is simply another bonus day!

"He actually tried to convince me that God wrecked his plane so he would have to come to the hospital and discover something more serious was wrong with him!"

We both chuckled, and I responded, "Sound's like perfect Jack Anthony logic to me!"

"I'll call you after we get the test results back," Harper said, her voice again turning serious.

"Thanks for calling," I replied. "Tell the big lug we'll all be praying for him. Don't forget to take care of yourself too! Eat something, get some sleep, and we'll talk tomorrow." We both said good-bye and hung up.

"You'd better call Jacob and let him know what's going on," Gabby said as I was putting my phone in my pocket.

"I'll do that tonight from home," I answered. "Let's get out of here. I'm not in the mood for Knott's Berry Farm anymore. Let's go home."

Neither Gabby nor I slept much that night. We were both tossing and turning and couldn't seem to shut our minds off. Finally, I got up as quietly as possible and went out into the living room. I grabbed a bottle of bourbon and a glass and was just sitting down on the sofa when Gabby walked out of the bedroom, tying her bathrobe shut as she approached me.

"Grab a glass!" I said as she was walking by the cabinet where we kept our liquor and drinking glasses. She stopped, picked up a glass, and a second later, was beside me on the sofa. I poured a small portion of bourbon into both glasses, and we each took a sip, sitting there in silence.

"Do you think Jack has cancer?" Gabby asked timidly.

"Probably," I answered. "They can take out the one bad kidney, and he can live with just one kidney. But cancer of the liver is a much scarier proposition. I just hope his liver is OK, or he and Harper are going to have some hard times ahead."

Gabby didn't ask any more questions as we sat there in silence again, finishing our drinks.

"Let's go back to bed and try to get some sleep," I announced, putting my empty glass on the coffee table and getting up to head back into our bedroom. Gabby got up and followed me, and we both crawled back into bed.

At about 10:00 a.m. the next day, my cell phone rang. I immediately picked it up and said hello, not checking to see who was calling. I was surprised to hear my brother's voice on the line, since we very seldom talked to each other over the phone.

"I'm calling because I have some bad news, Michael," he began. "Mom went to church last night instead of this morning because she and a couple of her friends were going to a flower show in Riverside today. She hadn't gotten up yet by 7:00 a.m., and she'd told me they were leaving at 8:00 a.m. I knocked on her door, and she didn't answer, so I opened it and told her she needed to get up."

He was silent for a few seconds and then said in a voice filled with emotion, "I walked over to her and shook her shoulder, and she didn't wake up. I felt for a pulse in her neck, but I immediately knew she was gone once I touched her cold skin."

Neither one of us spoke for a lengthy moment. "Do you know what happened yet?" I asked with very little emotion in my own voice. I was in shock as I tried to digest the horrible news. My consciousness seemed to be trying to block this information as not being factual.

"The EMTs said she had a heart attack in her sleep," Ronnie responded. "Based on how relaxed her body was lying on the bed, they said she never knew what hit her or felt any pain." Ronnie sniffed loudly, trying to keep it together while we continued our conversation.

"Where is Mom now?" I asked.

"They're doing an autopsy to confirm it was a heart attack, and I'm making arrangement to have her moved to Weaver's Mortuary when they are finished."

"I'll drive home this afternoon and let you know when I'll be there," I said. "Be sure you call the pastor at her church. They will want to know about this. We can talk about funeral arrangements once I'm there."

"Sounds good," Ronnie responded. "Love you, Michael."

His ending comment caught me a little off guard. We hadn't exchanged that affectionate term in thirty plus years to each other. "I love you too, Ronnie!" I repeated, and then we hung up.

I could feel the tears forming as soon as the call was over. Gabby walked from the kitchen into the living room where I was standing.

Seeing the tears in my eyes starting to overflow, she said, "Was that Harper? Have they gotten bad news from the biopsy?"

"No, it wasn't Harper," I replied. "It was my brother. My mom had a heart attack and passed away last night." The shocked expression on Gabby's face summed up exactly how I was feeling at that moment.

She rushed over to me and wrapped her arms around me in a tight embrace. "I'm so sorry, sweetheart! I'm so sorry!" Then she was kissing my face as she continued to apologize for something she had absolutely no control over.

"Are you leaving for Beaumont today?" she asked. "Do you want me to come along, or would you rather go without me?"

"Yes, we'll leave this afternoon," I responded. "And, of course, I want you to come with me!" I paused for a moment and then asked, "Will you do me a favor?"

"Certainly!" she replied.

"Will you call all the kids and let them know about my mom? I don't expect any of them to come to the funeral—make sure they all understand that. If Jacob wants to come, he can, but again, it's certainly not required."

"I'll call everyone right now," Gabby said, her voice letting me know there was a sense of urgency to comply with my request.

"I'm going to go outside for a while," I said dejectedly. "I need a few minutes to get my head around this."

"I understand," Gabby stated flatly. Then she turned and walked into our bedroom.

I walked over to the clubhouse and pool area in the center of the condo community. As with almost every day here, it was warm, sunny, and not a cloud in the sky.

I sat on the end of one of the many lounge chairs, folding my arms and resting them on my knees. I watched as several kids were swimming and playing in the pool. Some were accompanied by parents, while another group seemed to be playing a game of tag with no adult supervision. It brought a smile to my face to hear them all laughing, squealing, and having so much fun.

Three lounge chairs over, an older couple, probably grandparents, was sitting back in lounge chairs of their own, watching the same activities I was enjoying. The woman had placed her hand on top of the man's hand, which rested on the arm of his chair as they watched the kids frolicking in the water through dark sunglasses.

There it is, I thought to myself. Today is a testament to the true circle of life. You're born into this world, and if you're fortunate enough, you enjoy a happy childhood. Then the children become parents and teach and love their own children. Although less involved than the parents, the grandparents sit on the sidelines and cheer for both their children's and grandchildren's successes until they have served their purpose and are finally taken to heaven for the great family reunion.

My mom and dad were together now. I knew in my heart that they were both happier now than when they'd been separated by death for a short period. Someday, I would hopefully be blessed to join not only them but also generations of family I'd never known on earth.

There was no need for tears now. This was a joyous moment that needed to be celebrated. I got up from my lawn chair and turned to head back to the house, a contented smile on my face.

I made a call to Jeff Hall to let him know I would be out of town for most of the next week. I didn't know if I would speak with him or be leaving a voice mail since it was a Sunday.

His cell phone rang twice, and then he answered it. "Jeff Hall," he said, identifying himself.

"Mr. Hall, this is Michael Larsen," I replied. "I'm sorry to bother you on a Sunday, but I needed to let you know I won't be at work most of next week. My brother called me earlier today to tell me my mother had a heart attack and passed away."

"That's terrible!" he interrupted. "I'm so sorry for your loss! Take as much time as you need to be with your family. I remember when my mother died, and it was horrible! It is so hard when you lose the matriarch of the family—it's just awful!"

"With your permission, I'll give Wendy a call and ask her to fill in for me while I'm out," I said.

"No. No, don't do that," he reacted rather forcefully. "I have some real concerns with Wendy right now. Speak with your new-hired bench regional, and let's see how she does when given the chance. Once you're back, we can discuss Wendy, but for right now, just concentrate on your family and forget about work. Again, I'm so sorry for your loss!"

"Thank you, sir," I said. "I'll keep you updated when I'll be back."

We said our good-byes, and I disconnected the call. As much as I tried, I couldn't stop thinking about what concerns Jeff might have about Wendy. Her numbers were good, her staffing was according to plan, and her expenses were in line with the budget she'd been given. I simply couldn't put my finger on anything she'd done to cause the CEO concern.

Gabby and I had just gotten into the car and were getting ready to start our trip to Beaumont when my cell phone rang again. We weren't even out of the driveway yet, so I shifted back into park and left the car running while I answered the call.

"Hi, Michael," Harper said. "Hope I didn't catch you at a bad time?"

I didn't have the heart to tell her she was the second bad news call I'd been on today. "No! Gabby and I were just leaving the house," I answered. "What's the news?"

"Good news and bad news, I guess," she responded. "It wasn't a tumor on his liver—it was a cyst. But there are cancer tumors on his kidney," she continued. "They want to operate this coming Friday and see if they can save the kidney. At the same time, they'll remove the cyst on his liver."

"How are you doing?" I asked.

"I'm scared to death, but other than that, I'm doing OK," she said with a nervous chuckle. "Having Jack's mom and sister here helps. At least I have people to talk with who are as concerned as I am about Jack."

"I'll ask you again, do you think I should come up there?" I quizzed.

"No. No, I really don't," she responded. "Jack's mom and sister are going to stay for three weeks, so they can help me once Jack is released from the hospital. We'll be fine. I'd rather you come visit when Jack's home and needs some moral support."

"OK," I answered. "But if you guys need anything, don't hesitate to call."

"I won't," she said. "Can I say hi to Gabby before we hang up?"

"Of course!" I responded. I held out my phone for Gabby to take and said, "Harper wants to talk to you."

"Hi," Gabby said after taking the phone. Then she listened while Harper did most of the talking. There was an occasional "Yes" or "I understand" or a muttered "Uh-huh," but it was obvious Harper was dominating their conversation.

Finally, it was Gabby's turn to speak. She looked nervously at me before saying, "I don't know if that will be possible. Michael is taking this week off, and I doubt he can take more time off this month or next because of his job commitments."

Then she was listening again until it was her turn to respond. "Well, maybe if Jack feels like it, you guys could come down here and stay with us for a while. Michael will work during the day, but we could all be together every evening and on the weekends. Besides, I'm a better tour guide than Michael is anyway! I'd love to show you guys some of the special finds we've made since moving here."

She was listening again and then snapped her head around to look at me as panic overtook her expression. "You should talk with Michael about that," she said, putting her hand over the phone speaker and handing it back to me.

I started to take the phone from her hand, but she held it tightly. She said in a small voice, "Harper wants to know why you're taking off work this week. I don't know what to tell her!" Then she let go of the phone, and I brought it up to my face.

"Hi, Harper, me again," I said calmly. She asked me the same question she'd asked Gabby. I didn't want to lie to her, and as difficult as it was, I decided to tell her the truth.

"Well, all I can say is yesterday and today have been pretty rough days for me!" I stated firmly. "First, I got the call from you about Jack. Then this morning, my little brother called me to tell me my mom had a heart attack and passed away!"

"Oh my god!" Harper said involuntarily. "I'm so sorry!" she continued. "Why didn't you say something when we talked earlier?" she scolded.

"You've got enough to deal with right now!" I responded. "You don't need any more on your plate. We are on our way to Beaumont to make the arrangements for the funeral."

"Oh, I am so sorry!" she repeated. "I'll be praying for you and your family tonight!"

"Thank you," I answered. "Please call me Friday and let me know what the doctors say after Jack is out of surgery!" I said firmly. "Promise me you'll call!"

"I'll call," she responded, "I promise!" We said our good-byes, and Gabby yelled good-bye from across the car as we disconnected the call.

The funeral was beautiful. I was surprised by the number of people who attended. There must have been a hundred people from Mom's church and another twenty from her work. Art and Louise and their family were all there as well.

Ronnie was quite a bit more emotional than I was during the service. It only made sense; he'd lived all but the six years he was in the army with our mother. They'd become very close over the years, especially after Dad's death.

We had a reception at Mom's house, and for the second time that day, I was surprised by the large turnout. I heard so many great stories, most of them new to me, about her kindness and caring for others. I felt honored to be the son of such a well-intentioned and thoughtful mother as story after story was relived.

Gabby and I stayed to help clean up after everyone had gone home. Once done, Ronnie took a bottle of vodka out and filled three shot glasses. Handing one to each of us, he raised his and said, "Here's to the best mom anyone could have." Then looking up toward the heavens, he continued. "Tell Dad hi for us when you see him in the next life!"

We raised our shot glasses, clinked them against his, and downed our drinks.

Ronnie had several more shots of vodka while he and I reminisced about various experiences we'd had with Mom. He was smiling one minute, and tears were running down his cheeks the next, as he recalled different events that were special to him. I could tell he was getting drunk when his tongue started to get thick and he started to slur his speech. He also began repeating conversations we'd already had as we sat there.

As Ronnie continued to drink, his mood turned darker, and he started to express frustrations, not about Mom's death but about how screwed up he thought the world had become.

"The world is turning to shit!" he slurred. "It's probably a good thing Mom is gone so she doesn't have to see the decline of democracy everywhere.

"The Burmese military shot into crowds of people, including monks, to stop prodemocracy protests in Myanmar! They killed a shitload of innocent people!" He paused for a moment before continuing. "And no one did a damn thing to help those poor defenseless souls, not even us! Instead, we stuck another thirty thousand troops in Iraq to continue a war we shouldn't even be in!"

He poured another shot and quickly downed it. "Now we have thirty thousand more guys over there, and it hasn't made one bit of difference! Two of those radical assholes drove trucks right into the middle of Iraqi towns and exploded them. Five hundred dead Iraqis, and we couldn't do a damn thing about it!

"Now Bush has signed a bill to legalize eavesdropping of telephone conversations and e-mails of our own citizens! That's bullshit! It's just not right! I doubt our Founding Fathers ever had that in mind when they wrote the Constitution!

"And don't get me started on politics!" he spat out. "Nancy Pelosi, a liberal Democrat from California, becomes the first woman speaker of the house and will preside over Congress! Give me a friggin' break!

"Now, we have the first black man running for president of the United States, and he's a pacifist with no balls. All he does is apologize for America every time he opens his mouth! We screwed the American Indians. We screwed the African Americans because settlers brought slaves to our shores three hundred years ago! He's sorry our nation is so successful and other countries are not as prosperous!"

Ronnie poured himself another shot, and with a flick of his wrist, he quickly disposed of it. "The worst part is I think he's going to win because he's such a smooth talker! I really fear for the country if he becomes our next president!"

Gabby decided it was time to squash Ronnie's ranting. She suggested we all go to bed and get back together tomorrow before we drove back to Newport Coast. We all agreed, and Gabby and I went back to our hotel.

We met Ronnie at the restaurant next to our hotel the next morning at ten o'clock. He arrived about ten minutes late and sat down across from us, not bothering to remove his dark sunglasses once he was seated.

"How do you feel?" Gabby asked, a crooked smile on her face.

"You know how I feel!" he responded in a belligerent tone. "I feel like crap! Why didn't you guys stop me before I got completely shit-faced?"

Gabby and I looked at each other and chuckled, "We're not babysitters! You're a grown man! If you drink too much, you have to pay the consequences!" she said accusingly.

A small smile crossed his lips as he stared back at us through the dark glasses. The waitress arrived and asked, "What are you going to have, folks?"

Gabby started, "Two eggs over easy, whole wheat toast, a small orange juice, and a cup of coffee, please."

"I'll have the same thing," I added.

When it was Ronnie's turn, he asked for coffee, two orders of greasy bacon, rye toast, and a glass of tomato juice with two lemon slices on the side.

The waitress thanked us and started back toward the kitchen.

"Kind of an unusual breakfast," Gabby said, looking quizzingly at Ronnie.

"I need to soak up all that alcohol, and nothing does it better than greasy bacon and tomato juice," he responded.

Taking his sunglasses off for the first time, he looked at Michael and said, "I'm meeting with Mom's attorney tomorrow, and I'll have a copy of her will express mailed to you. I'll contact a realtor and get started selling the house so we can split the money."

"I don't want any money from the house! That's your home now!" I answered. "Have the lawyer put papers together so I can sign over my part of the house to you. You deserve that house, and it's yours to do with as you please!"

Ronnie's eyes teared up, and his lower lip quivered when he responded, "Are you sure that's what you want to do?"

"It's the right thing to do," Gabby said, a smile on her face.

"In fact," I said, "if Mom had life insurance that individually named us, I'll accept that, but everything else is yours! The furniture, the car, tools, everything!"

Ronnie looked gobsmacked, sitting there, staring back at us. "I don't know what to say!" he finally uttered.

"You don't have to say anything," I responded. "I don't need or want any of their stuff with the exception of a few family pictures to remember better days."

The waitress brought our breakfast, and we ate pretty much in silence. When we'd finished, I said, "Get papers drawn up for everything we've talked about here and send them to me. As soon as I get them, I'll sign them and send them back to you. It's important that we have legal documentation in case we need it for some reason in the future."

We all stood up, and Ronnie said, "I got this," as he picked up the bill the waitress had placed on our table. We all hugged, and for the second time in a week, we told each other, "I love you," before Gabby and I started for home.

I called to let Jeff Hall know I was in the office Friday morning. He had his administrative assistant set up a conference call for two o'clock that afternoon.

I dialed in to the conference call number I'd been given, and once I was connected, I identified myself. "Good afternoon, this is Michael Larsen," I stated confidently.

"Hi, Michael" came the response from Doris Young, our Human Resources director. "Jeff isn't on the line yet."

"Understood," I responded. "How are things in HR these days?"

"Busy!" she responded. "Jeff told me about your mother. I'm so sorry for your loss!"

"Thank you," I replied.

"My mother is getting up there in years, and I know that call is coming soon for me too," she continued.

Just then, a third person entered the call. "Hello!" Jeff said spiritedly. "Is everyone on the line?"

We both said hello and identified ourselves.

"OK!" Jeff began after our introductions. "Michael, about a week before you had to take some vacation time, Doris received an employee hot line call from one of our property managers in LA. The person stated that Wendy had a storage unit at her property, and for over six months now, she hasn't paid rent on her unit. Instead, she claimed that Wendy was going into the properties computer remotely and allowing her rent as if there was a customer service issue."

"As you know, Michael," Doris cut in, "a regional manager has the ability to allow rent to any customer one time per year. But allowing your own rent month after month is really nothing less than stealing money from the company. We have verified this and know she has allowed $1,287 rental income to her own account. We needed to bring you into the loop and ask you what your thoughts are on this situation."

I was stunned. All I could think about was what a stupid thing for a regional vice president to do! She should have known she would get caught!

I'd been silent long enough that Jeff checked to see if I'd dropped off the call. "Michael? Are you still on the line?" he inquired.

"Yes, sir, I'm still here," I responded. "I'm just trying to get my head around why she would do something so ridiculous!"

"Usually, people who do this sort of thing feel the company owes them, so they feel justified in taking a little extra from them," Doris stated. "I've been thinking about this quite a bit over the last couple of weeks. This started right after you were made the divisional, Michael. I think that maybe Wendy thought that should have been her promotion, instead of yours."

"That's an interesting but disturbing thought," Jeff interjected.

"Whether interesting or disturbing, it's stealing from the company that provides your income!" I said. "There is only one decision here. Wendy must be terminated as a lesson to everyone in the company that this is unacceptable behavior!"

"When do you want to do it?" Doris asked.

"I'll work on your time frame," I said. "When can you be down here so we can do this together?"

"How about Monday?" Doris asked.

"Monday works for me," I responded, feeling both angry and sick to my stomach all at the same time.

"Do you think your bench regional Laura is ready to step into her position?" Jeff asked.

"She's pretty new to our systems, but between her admin and myself, we can get her up to speed on the technical stuff. She already had the management skills necessary before she joined us," I responded. "I think she'll be fine."

"All right," Jeff said matter-of-factly. "Monday it is! Let's get this done and over with!"

Doris and I arrived at Wendy's office close to 11:00 a.m. I'd already checked her calendar for the day and knew she'd scheduled an office day for herself. She was standing next to the copy machine, waiting for some copies to finish printing, when we walked in unannounced.

Seeing us, she turned, smiled, and started walking in our direction. "This is a surprise!" she said, putting her hand out to shake.

Doris smiled back, shook her hand first, and responded, "It's nice to see you, Wendy."

Once they released their grip, I simply replaced Doris's hand with my own and said, "Wendy." Even though I tried, I couldn't force myself to smile.

Once Wendy released my hand, she put both her hands on her hips, still smiling, and calmly inquired, "What brings the two of you here?"

"We were hoping to get a moment with you in your office, if we could?" Doris answered; her smile now gone.

Wendy's smile was fading quickly as she tried to sound upbeat. "Sure! Come on in!" With that, she turned, and we followed her back into her office. Doris closed the door behind herself once all three of us were in the room.

"Please have a seat," Wendy said, pointing to the two chairs in front of her desk. She took her seat behind the desk as Doris and I seated ourselves. "How can I help you guys?" she asked, her hands relaxed on the top of her desk.

Doris pulled out a folder from her briefcase and placed it on our side of the desk. "Wendy," Doris began, "we need to ask you some questions about a storage unit you rent at our Pico Road location."

The color immediately drained from her face as she stared blankly back at us, saying nothing.

"You do have a storage locker at that location, don't you?" Doris pressed.

Wendy's eyes moved back and forth as she tried to think of the proper response. After a short silence, she replied, "Yes, I do have a small locker there with some of my mother's things and a few of mine in it. Why, is something wrong there?"

Doris leaned over and opened her folder, pulling out a copy of a computer transaction, and pushed it across the desk to Wendy. "It appears that you did a rent adjustment for customer satisfaction to your own space in February. Can you tell me what that was about?"

Wendy looked, first, at me and then to Doris, her eyes again moving from side to side while she searched for an answer. A crimson flush started at her neck and was quickly working its way up to her face as we waited for a response.

"I think that was because the roof had leaked, and many of the items in our unit were destroyed by the dripping water. Didn't I write a reason in the document?"

"You're looking at the document," Doris answered. "Did you put in a reason and I just missed it?"

Wendy studied the document slowly, and we both watched as perspiration began to make its way down the side of her face. "I guess I didn't write the reason," she said, trying to hand the document back to Doris.

Doris didn't take the document from Wendy. Instead, she opened the folder and pulled out a second document. Sliding it across the desk, she asked, "What was the reason for this rent allowance in March?" she asked. "I couldn't find an explanation on this one either."

Wendy picked up the second document and began to study it; her face was now fully flushed and damp with perspiration.

Before she could answer, Doris pulled out several more documents and slid them in front of Wendy. "Same question about the rent allowances for your space in April, May, June, and now July," she added.

Wendy's shoulders slumped in surrender. She looked, first, to me and then to Doris and pleaded, "I don't know what to say."

"Wendy," I said, "that's almost $1,300 in rent that you have allowed to yourself this year. Why would you do that?"

Tears formed in her eyes and started spilling over down her cheeks. "I don't have a good answer for your question. I guess when you got the divisional position, I felt like the company should have at least offered the divisional position to me first. My numbers were as good as yours, and I had more seniority than you, plus I was already here, and I know this market. Since I didn't get the promotion, I was angry, so I allowed the rent on my space to get back at the company for not at least offering me the job! Once I did that in February, I simply justified doing it month after month from then until now."

"Didn't you realize that you would eventually get caught?" Doris asked.

"I didn't really think about it," she responded. Then wiping her eyes and looking directly at me, she said, "I knew the minute I met you that you would create problems for me! I didn't want to hire you, but John Belk overrode my decision."

"You need to calm down, Wendy!" Doris said in a firm voice. "None of this is Michael's fault! He didn't ask you to steal! He didn't go to Jeff and ask for this job—Jeff came to him! You made a conscious decision to take money from the company you worked for, knowing it was against company policy!"

After a short period of silence, Wendy asked, "What happens now?"

Doris pulled more papers out of her folder and laid them in front of Wendy. "You are being terminated from the company," she responded.

Wendy brought one of her hands to her face and let out a loud cry. As she continued to wail, she mumbled, "I don't even get a second chance? I'll pay back the money! I can write you a check right now!"

"I'm sorry, Wendy," Doris replied, a slight note of compassion in her voice. Reaching back into the folder, she pulled out a payroll check. "I have your final payroll check here, which includes any unused vacation time you have for this year. Because the reason for termination was theft, you will also be forfeiting all the stock options that have been awarded to you."

Wendy wailed again after hearing she was losing her stock as well. She took a Kleenex off a shelf behind her and blew her nose, while Doris finished.

"I'll need all your keys that pertain to our business now," she stated. "Michael and I will help you move all your personal items to your car. Pictures, plaques, personal files, etc."

Wendy did as she was instructed, and an hour later, Doris and I watched her leave the regional office for the last time.

CHAPTER 22

We were just one week away from Christmas, and I asked my administrative assistant if I could take her to lunch sometime before Friday. She said sure, and we set up a lunch date for Thursday at 1:00 p.m.

It's been my custom to take each of my administrative assistants to lunch before Christmas beginning the first year I'd been promoted to the regional manager position. I always took each admin to lunch, gave them a card with a monetary gift inside, and thanked them for all their help throughout the year. It was always appreciated, and it made me happy to acknowledge their contribution to our team and to my successes.

I'd made reservations at a PF Chang's restaurant about ten miles from our office. This was the only reservation that I personally made all year, and I always kept the locations secret until the day of our lunch. Every other reservation, whether it be for meals, hotels, flights, etc., we're all done through the person I was acknowledging with our lunch this coming Thursday.

Karen and I arrived about ten minutes early. The waiting area was packed with people as I made my way through the crowd and approached the hostess. She looked up our reservation and then apologized and let me know that because of the volume of guests because of Christmas office lunches, we would probably be thirty minutes late being seated. She handed me a pager and told me we could walk around the mall outside of the restaurant, and she would page us when our table was ready. I thanked her and made my way back to Karen.

"It's going to be thirty to forty minutes before we can be seated," I explained to Karen.

"Do you want to go somewhere else to eat?" Karen asked.

"No, I think it's going to be pretty much the same story everywhere," I replied. "I guess we're not the only people having a Christmas lunch today!" I smiled, and she smiled back.

"The hostess gave me a pager and said we can walk around the mall if we want," I said to Karen. "Do you have any interest in doing that, or would you rather stay in here and wait?"

With so many bodies compressed together in the small waiting area, it was extremely noisy as I waited for her reply. She had to half yell her response when she answered. "Let's wait outside! This gives me claustrophobia!"

I took the lead and pushed through the crowd and headed to the door that led out of the restaurant with Karen right on my heels. Once outside, I let out, "Whoa! That is a lot of people! I'm glad we're out of there!"

"Me too!" Karen responded, looking back at me. We stood and looked around to see if there were any stores that might be of interest to visit while we waited.

"Oh, look!" Karen squealed. "An exotic bird stores! Can we go in and look around?"

"Absolutely!" I responded. "Let's see what they've got."

We were in the store for no more than five minutes when I saw this little ball of white down sitting in a cage toward the middle of the store. I was immediately drawn to it and stepped closer to inspect it.

Once I stopped at the cage, the little bird looked up at me and squawked weakly. It was all white, except for two mahogany eyes that were circled in what appeared to be baby-blue eye shadow. In that instant, I knew this would be Gabby's Christmas gift.

Gabby loved all animals, but she had always expressed a special fondness for birds. Several times when we'd see a flock of birds flying over us, she would say, "Don't you wish you could fly and be free like that?" as she watched them with a look of sheer amazement. She'd had a parakeet when she was a little girl, and she had talked several times about how much she loved her parakeet.

I motioned for Karen to come over and see my new friend. She walked to me and let out a subdued gasp. "Oh my god!" she said, raising one hand to her face. "That little thing is so beautiful! Look at the blue circles around its eyes! I don't know if I've ever seen anything quite like it!" Karen said, a huge smile on her face.

"I'm going to buy it and give it to Gabby for Christmas!" I stated emphatically.

"You are!" she answered, clapping her hands together like an excited small child.

"She is going to love him or her! I'm so jealous!" she replied gleefully.

"Let's find someone we can speak to about buying this guy," I said, looking around the store for someone who worked there. Spotting a middle-aged woman wearing an apron with the store's name on it, I made my way over to her.

"Excuse me," I began. "Can I ask how much you want for the little white bird in the center aisle?"

"She's already sold, and I have a backup offer on her if the first buyer doesn't take her," she responded gruffly without looking up at me.

"If she's already sold, why would there be a backup offer on her?" I asked with disappointment in my voice.

"Neither one of the buyers had the cash to take her home, so I gave them both a week to come up with the money," she responded. "If the first buyer doesn't come up with the money by close of business on Monday, the second buyer can have the bird on Tuesday, as long as they bring in the cash."

"What kind of bird is it?" I asked.

"Her name is Sweetpea, and she's an umbrella cockatoo," she responded.

"Can you tell me a little bit about her?" I asked.

"She'll grow to be about four times her size now. In a year or so, she will have a crown on her head that she can raise like an umbrella. The color of her features underneath her wings and under her crown is bright yellow. Everything else is stark white, except for the blue rings around her eyes. They will just turn a darker shade of blue as she ages. Come with me and I'll show you my own umbrella cockatoo."

Karen and I followed her to the back of her showroom, and she led us to a cage with a full-grown cockatoo. Opening the cage, she said, "Come on out of there, Willy!" When the bird didn't move, she put her hand into the cage and said, "Step up!" The bird immediately stepped onto her arm, and she carefully brought him out of the cage. He was stunning!

Once out of the cage, his umbrella went up, and we could see the yellow underside of the feathers in his crown. He was more like six times the size of the little white ball of down I'd fallen in love with earlier at the center of the store.

He immediately began to talk. "Bye, bye!" he said, opening his wings and flapping them like he was getting ready to fly away. Then he whistled and said, "What's cooking, good looking?" Karen and I both laughed.

"Does he say anything else?" I asked.

"Oh, god, yes!" she replied. "He has thirty plus words in his vocabulary."

"Are these high-maintenance birds?" I inquired.

"Umbrella cockatoos are probably the highest-maintenance bird you can buy. They require lots of attention, and they're very needy. They are easily bored, and when they're bored, they scream to get attention. They require a lot of human interaction, and like a dog or a cat, they like to be petted and sit with you all the time if possible," she said. "And they're picky eaters!"

"I think he is magnificent!" I responded once she'd finished.

Our pager started going off complete with flashing lights, which must have frightened Willy as he took flight and in a second was standing on top of his cage.

"I'm sorry," I apologized. "I didn't mean to scare him!"

"Not a problem," she answered. "As big as they are, they're afraid of everything until they become familiar with whatever scares them."

"Listen," I began, "we have to go eat our lunch, but I'd like to make you an offer, if I may?"

"What kind of offer?" she asked.

"How much are you selling Sweetpea for?" I asked.

"Fourteen hundred dollars," she responded.

"I'm going to write you a check right now for sixteen hundred dollars for Sweetpea. If neither of the two other parties comes up with the money, you can cash the check and I'll take her! Additionally, I'll buy a cage, all the supplies necessary, and her food from you if I get her!"

"I'm pretty sure one of those two customers will come up with the money," she responded, seeming unimpressed by my idea. "But I'll take your check, just in case."

"Can you call me next Wednesday and let me know if I got lucky or not, please?" I inquired.

"I'll call you a week from today," she answered, while she waited for me to write out the check.

As we were walking back to the restaurant, Karen said, "I didn't know you were such an impulse buyer. That was kind of surreal."

"I'm not!" I replied. "But it's like God himself told me we needed Sweetpea to complete our family! I loved that little bird, and I know Gabby will be ecstatic if we are fortunate enough to actually get her!"

After a great lunch, we returned to the office. Shortly after I was back in my office, Karen knocked on my door, stuck her head through it, and said, "Jeff Hall is on the phone for you, Michael." She backed out of the doorway and shut the office door behind her.

Picking up the phone and punching line three, I answered, "Good afternoon, sir! How are you today?"

"I'm fine, thank you," he responded. "How about yourself?"

"Good!" I answered enthusiastically. "Looking forward to the holidays! What can I do for you?"

"I'm calling all the divisionals to personally let them know I'm going to be retiring at the end of the year," Jeff said.

I was shocked by the news! "Wow!" I responded. "That's unexpected! When did you make the decision?"

"I've been thinking about it for over a year," he answered calmly. "I told the board of directors about this time last year that I wanted to retire. We've been looking for a suitable replacement all year."

"I assume by that comment that you won't be promoting one of the divisionals to your chair?" I asked tentatively.

"No, we won't be," he responded. "The board of directors and I feel it's time to bring in some new blood with new ideas to help take the company to the next level—someone who has already been successful in another industry and could bring some innovation to our company."

"I assume you've found such a person?" I inquired.

"We did!" he responded excitedly. "I think he will step in without much distraction and improve our operations almost immediately. His name is Shawn Meyers, and he was CEO for Sure Shed Buildings for about eight years. He will be leaving that position to take this assignment."

"I'm happy for you, Jeff!" I said, trying to act more excited than I was by the news. "You've done a great job building this company, and it's time to start enjoying some of the rewards you've reaped with your family and loved ones."

"Thank you, Michael!" he answered. "I'm not sure all the divisionals are going to feel the same as you do or be nearly as gracious! I know all of you wanted to be next in line for the CEO position. We evaluated each one of you, and our conclusion was that none of you really have the complete package necessary to step into this crucial assignment for the company at this time. As an officer of the company, I, along with the board of directors, needed to do what we thought was best for the company. I hope you can understand that."

"I do understand," I answered. "I'm looking forward to working with the new boss!"

"I know this is short notice and bad timing, but I'd like to have a two-day divisional meeting the week after Christmas on Tuesday and Wednesday to introduce everyone," Jeff stated sheepishly.

"It's between Christmas and New Year's, so it works for me," I responded. "I'd probably come in early on Tuesday and take a red-eye home on Wednesday night. Then I'd take the rest of the week off for vacation."

"Great!" he responded enthusiastically. "I appreciate your flexibility during the holidays! Oh, and by the way, if you talk to the other divisionals, don't say anything about our conversation. I'll be reaching out to all of them tomorrow. You're the first one I've talked with about my retirement. Please keep this conversation confidential, if you would."

"I won't say a word to anyone, sir!" I promised. "In case we don't talk again before Christmas, Merry Christmas to you and your family!"

"Merry Christmas to you as well, Michael," he responded, and then he hung up.

I sat back in my leather chair with my head resting on the plush leather padded pillow behind it as I tried to come to grips with what I'd just been told and how the news would affect me.

I was coming up on my ten-year anniversary with the company in June, and I'd just turned fifty-eight this year, both reasonably significant milestones in my life. Would I be working for someone younger than myself for the first time? Would the new CEO be sales oriented or cost control sensitive in his management approach?

Coming from a different industry, would he be open to suggestion, or would he employ a strictly top-down management style? Would we be doing more reports and be micromanaged, or would he be sales driven, wanting us out at the properties more often?

If I was honest with myself, I would confess to being apprehensive about building a relationship with a new boss at this point in my career. I also understood that the cards would fall where they fall, and it was up to me to play this new hand I'd been dealt to the best of my ability moving forward.

The next Thursday, with only two days until Christmas, I was working on a backup plan for Gabby's Christmas gift. I hadn't heard from the bird lady, and I could only assume Sweetpea was not meant to be ours and had found a home with one of the original offering couples.

I decided to drop by the Newport Coast shopping center and see if there might be something of interest for Gabby there. I knew there were several clothing stores along with two jewelry stores. Surely, I could find something unique that was still in my price range. I was just turning into the shopping center when my cell phone rang.

"Hello," I said, answering it.

"Hi, is this Michael Larsen?" the unfamiliar voice on the other end of the line inquired.

"Yes, it is," I responded.

"Mr. Larsen, this is Gail from Gail's Exotic Bird Store, and I wanted to speak with you for a moment, if I could."

"Absolutely!" I replied, not wanting to get my hopes up too much.

"We spoke last week about the umbrella cockatoo Sweetpea, and you gave me a check in case the other two parties that had offers ahead of yours couldn't meet the deadline I gave them," she said.

"Yes, I did," I answered excitedly.

"Well, the first lady couldn't come up with the money, and I haven't been able to get hold of the second potential buyer all week.

I thought I would call and see if you still want the bird before I deposited your check," she finished.

"Gail, this call has truly made my day!" I responded. "I absolutely want her! Please feel free to go ahead and deposit the check! What great news!"

"OK," she responded calmly. "I'll put all the paperwork together, and you can drop by anytime to pick up your papers whenever it's convenient for you."

"When can I pick up the bird?" I inquired.

"Oh, that's going to be a while," she said. "We are hand-feeding her four times a day, and I can't give her to you until she is eating real food."

"How long do you typically hand-feed them?" I asked.

"It will be a minimum of five but probably six more weeks before we can release her from the store," she responded.

I felt a huge wave of disappointment wash over me as I listened to her explanation. "I was hoping to give her to my wife for Christmas," I said dejectedly.

"You can still do that," Gail responded. "I'll have to come down here and feed all the birds on Christmas Day, just like I do every other day of the year. If you want, you can bring your wife in to meet her while I'm feeding on Christmas Day."

"That sounds wonderful!" I replied. "I can't tell you how much I appreciate this gesture on your part! It is going to make my wife's Christmas!"

"Just stop by when you have a minute so we can sign the papers and make this transaction legal," she added.

"I'll be there tomorrow!" I replied. Then we both hung up.

I slapped my steering wheel several times with exuberance and shouted, "Yes! Yes! Yes!" knowing this was going to be the best Christmas ever for Gabby!

As had been our tradition since the time Gabby and I had first become a couple, all the kids and grandkids opened presents and exchanged gifts with their immediate families on Christmas Eve. By about 10:00 a.m. or so on Christmas Day, everyone came over to our house, and we exchanged presents with our extended families.

This year was going to be very different in that everyone had to travel to Newport Coast if we wanted to celebrate as a family. Gabby had organized the travel so everyone would be together for at least a couple of days to visit, catch up, and enjoy each other's company. Our Christmas present to all the kids was to pay for all the airline fares if they decided to come spend some time with us. It hadn't been much of a hard sell to organize our first California family Christmas. It seemed everyone was excited to go for a nice warm walk on the Newport Beach in the dead of winter!

Jacob and Sophie had made the trip with their new daughter, Ellie. She was as cute as a button with dark complexion, lots of jet-black hair, and piercing brown eyes like both of her parents. They were proud parents as they showed off their beautiful girl to the family.

Thomas and Elise had come down earlier in the week to celebrate Christmas with the family, and they as well we're bringing another new grandbaby, Luke, along with our first grandchild, Michaela, to share the holidays with the family.

Luke was a sizable baby, and Elsie had confirmed that he'd been extremely hard to deliver because of his size. He didn't have the same big blue eyes that Michaela had, but he was a happy baby, always smiling and kicking when anyone was giving him attention or talking to him.

Aria and Todd were arriving midday Christmas Eve and were returning on a red-eye Christmas night for home. They hinted that they had some news for us and the rest of the family. I think everyone had a pretty good idea what the news was even before it was revealed.

Our granddaughter Michaela was up early, and she made enough noise to ensure everyone else was awake shortly before 7:00 a.m. on Christmas Day. Gabby and I woke up, smiled at each other, kissed, and said, "Merry Christmas." Then she stood up, put on her robe, and was gone, heading straight for the kitchen.

By the time I'd showered and dressed, everyone was gathered in the living room with hot drinks in their respective hands. Wishing everyone "Merry Christmas" and hearing it repeated back to me by six or seven voices all at once, I made my way into the dining room.

There were plates full of cut-up fresh fruit, fresh-baked cinnamon rolls, toast, juice, and hot coffee or cocoa, covering every available inch of our dining room table. I picked up a cup and filled it with hot coffee, grabbed a peeled banana, and walked back into the living room, taking my first bite of banana on the way.

I could feel my heart soften as I scanned the room and watched everyone sitting around and visiting while still in their pajamas or robes.

Elise was feeding Luke a jar of banana baby food, and by the mmm's and smiles coming from him, it was obvious he was loving his breakfast.

Ellie was laughing, kicking, and playfully watching a spinning mobile above her head that was accompanied by soft music.

Thomas had placed a pile of presents in front of Michaela, who was patiently waiting to be told she could start opening them.

I couldn't have been happier or prouder of our family as everyone gathered by the Christmas tree to enjoy the holiday.

Gabby and Aria came walking in from the kitchen, both carrying a cup of coffee with smiles on their faces, excited to be joining the festivities. "Where's Todd?" Aria asked. When no one responded, she turned and headed for their bedroom.

Everyone had started their conversations and visiting again when Aria stepped back into the living room, pulling her half-awake boyfriend behind her. He had on a pair of Levi's, a T-shirt, and no socks or shoes. It was obvious that he just been woken up and was trying to clear the cobwebs from his head. His hair was standing up in several places as he attempted to greet everyone through half-open eyes.

Everyone said "Merry Christmas" to him, and he responded in kind. "I'm going to grab a cup of coffee," he stated, moving slowly into the dining room.

"You didn't have to get him up," Gabby said to Aria. "It's Christmas! He could sleep in!"

"You're right, Mom," Aria replied. "It is Christmas, and we only have today to be with the rest of the family! He can sleep in at home when we get back! But for now, I want him involved with everyone!"

As Todd returned from the dining room, coffee in one hand and a cinnamon roll in the other, Michaela looked up at her mom and dad and asked, "Can I open my presents now?"

Before they could answer, Gabby said, "Of course, you can, sweetheart." She didn't wait for any other validation as she started ripping the wrapping paper off the first gift she came to. We spent the next hour with nonstop smiles on our faces as we all exchanged gifts and watched each other open them.

After we had cleared up the paper and used ribbon, Gabby went into the bedroom and came out with a box, handing it to me. "Merry Christmas, sweetheart!" she said in a loving voice.

I opened it and looked at a beautiful watch I'd been wanting for some time but didn't want to spend the money to buy. "Thank you, pumpkin," I said. "I absolutely love it!" I kissed her and gave her a warm hug.

Everyone was watching us, and finally, Aria asked, "Where is your gift for Mom?"

"It's not here," I responded. I instantly saw sadness in Gabby's eyes and a bit of contempt from everyone else in the room. "We have an appointment to go get her gift at 10:00 a.m. You're all invited to go along if you'd like."

Gabby's expression immediately changed to one of excitement. "What could possibly be open on Christmas Day that would have a Christmas gift for me?"

"I won't tell you what it is, but if you guess it, I will let you know you're right!" I responded. "In fact, you're all welcome to guess. But I'm betting none of you will figure it out until I actually give it to Gabby."

I spent the next twenty minutes saying the word "no." Is it a car? Is it a coat? Is it a new furniture? Is it jewelry? The closest guess came from Thomas, who asked, "Is it a new puppy?" Again, my response was a simple "No."

Once everyone had tired of the guessing game, Todd stood up and said, "I'd like to make an announcement, if I could." He pulled Aria up off the sofa and, while still holding her hand, said, "I've asked Aria to marry me!"

We all clapped and yelled congratulations as Aria showed off the beautiful diamond engagement ring on her left hand. Gabby was instantly on her feet and hugging her daughter. There were hugs, handshakes, and well-wishes all around for several minutes as we celebrated the news.

We were just sitting down again, coming off the news about the last wedding we'd have in the family for a while, when Michaela asked, "Do I have any more presents to open?"

We all laughed, and I responded, "I'm afraid you've already opened all your presents, sweetheart! Do you want to go for a ride and see Grandma's Christmas present in a little bit?"

She shook her head yes.

"OK, then," I continued. "Let's all get dressed and go see Grandma's present!"

Everyone was immediately up and headed in different directions toward their rooms. "We need to leave by nine thirty, so plan accordingly if you want to come with us!" I yelled as everyone exited the living room.

Thomas had rented an SUV at the airport when he and his family had arrived. With my car, Gabby's car, and Thomas's car, there was plenty of room for everyone. I led the way, while Jacob followed in Gabby's car, and Thomas brought up the rear of our little caravan.

We pulled into a completely empty shopping center parking lot, and I parked. After everyone was out of their cars, Aria said, "Michael, everything is closed! Are you sure this is the right place or that this was the correct time you were supposed to be here?"

"I'm pretty sure," I said, not sounding convincing.

Gabby just looked up at me like I was crazy, when I said, "Let's go look at your Christmas present."

The group followed me as we walked past business after business where lights were on, but clearly no one was working, and they were closed for the holiday. When we were standing in front of Gale's Exotic Birds, I calmly opened the door, and a bell rang, announcing our entry. Gale walked out of the back room and said, "Merry Christmas, Mr. Larsen!" Then she continued. "Wow! You brought quite a crowd!"

"Yes, I did," I responded. Taking Gabby's hand, I led her to the cage in the middle of the store. Stopping in front of the cage, I said, "This is Sweetpea, and she's yours now!"

Tears immediately filled her eyes and spilled over. "She is magnificent! What a beautiful baby!" By the time Gabby stopped talking, everyone was fawning over the little white ball of features.

"I love her!" Gabby said as she tried to touch her through the cage slats.

"Step back for a second, and I'll get her out of there for you," Gale said gruffly. "You can hold her—just be careful she doesn't poop on you."

Once the cage was open, Gabby reached in and picked her up slowly, putting the bird to her chest. Sweetpea looked up at her with loving eyes. "She's just precious!" Gabby said softly. "And look at those blue circles around her eyes! She's breathtaking!"

"Bring her with you and I'll show you guys what she'll look like once she's grown," I said.

Gail led the way to Willy's cage and opened the door. He stepped onto her hand, and she brought him out of the cage.

"Oh my," Gabby uttered, looking at the large umbrella cockatoo. "He's gorgeous! Will Sweetpea get that big?"

"Probably not," Gail answered. "But she'll get close to his size by the time she's two years old."

"How long do they live?" Aria asked.

"If you treat them well and feed them right, umbrella cockatoos usually live about seventy-five years."

The number brought gasps from almost everyone as they looked at each other in amazement.

"Will her features be the same color as his when she's grown?" Gabby asked.

"Except for a size difference, you won't be able to tell them apart by her third birthday," Gail answered.

"How do we take care of her?" Gabby asked.

"I'll teach you all about how to care for her by the time you take her home," Gail responded.

"I can't take her now?" Gabby asked dejectedly.

"No, it will be about five weeks before she can leave the store," Gail said. "I have to bottle-feed her and get her used to real food before she can go home with you. But you can come in and see her as much as you want. The more you're here, the better acquainted the two of you will become."

"I'll be here every day!" Gabby stated emphatically.

Just as Gabby finished speaking, Willy opened his wings, and the crown on his head went up. "See you later, alligator! After a while, crocodile!" came out of his mouth as he began flapping his large wings! We all laughed and were amazed by how well he pronounced the words. A few seconds later, wings still flapping, he repeated the phrase.

"That is so awesome!" Gabby said as she watched Willy and gently stroked Sweetpea. "I'm going to teach her to speak too!"

"Just be careful what you say around her," Gail warned. "They seem to pick up bad words faster than good ones. And they never forget once they learn a word!"

"With Gail's help, you'll need to pick out a suitable cage and a couple of perches for her to stand on when she is in other rooms, like the kitchen or your bathroom," I said, looking directly at Gabby. "This type of bird is a big commitment, and I hope you're up for the challenge, sweetheart."

Walking back to Sweetpea's temporary home, Gabby responded, "I am so up for the challenge! She's going to be my baby!"

Putting her back in her cage, Gabby just stared at her, a contented smile on her face. Leaning down, she began to sing to her new best friend, "Oh Sweetpea, won't you be my girl. Won't you, won't you, won't you be my girl!" The little bird watched her intently as she repeated the lyrics several times before quitting!

"I hope I won't have to listen to that every day for the next five weeks!" Gail said sarcastically. "OK, folks, it's time for you all to leave. I still have birds to feed, and I don't want to be here all day!"

We were almost all out the door when Gabby rushed back in and threw her arms around Gail. Gail went stiff as a board!

"Don't make a habit of that either!" Gail said, quickly stepping away from Gabby. "I'll take good care of your baby. There's no need for kisses, hugs, or songs! She'll be just fine."

Gabby simply said, "Thank you," and we all started back to the cars.

When we were a few stores away from the bird store, Aria said, "She's a real sweetheart, isn't she?" We all chuckled at her comment.

"Since we're out of the house already," I said, "how would everyone like to take a walk on the beach and maybe have lunch, if anything is open?"

There were resounding yeses from everyone. We loaded up in the cars, and twenty minutes later, we were walking in warm sand and very comfortable surf as it made its way up to our feet from the incoming tide.

That night, after we'd dropped Aria and Todd off at the airport and finally made it to bed, Gabby wrapped herself around me in a spoon position.

"Michael," she said, "I don't know how you thought of this idea, but that little angel is the best present I've ever received from anyone! I just love her, and I promise I'll always take good care of her! Thank you so much for my gift!" I smiled as she affectionately hugged me hard.

As it so often turns out, nothing is red hearts and candy canes all the time. True to her word, Gabby went into the pet store almost every day to continue bonding with Sweetpea. She spent an hour or two each visit, talking and singing songs to her new best friend. Unfortunately, Gail quickly tired of her daily visits and became a bit mean spirited when she confronted Gabby.

When Gabby would walk into the store, often she was met with "Don't ask me how she's doing! She's the same as she was yesterday!" Then she would walk away and attend to her other chores.

One day, I came home from work to find Gabby sitting at the dining room table, crying. I rushed over to her and asked what the matter was.

"It's that damn Gail!" she spat out. "I was singing my Sweetpea song today, and she yelled from across the store, 'How many times you need to sing that same damn song to your bird!' The store was full of people, and her hurtful comments embarrassed me!" She was quiet for a moment as she picked up a tissue and blew her nose.

"Well, that's horseshit!" I responded, feeling my anger starting to flare. "With the cage, supplies, and the cost of Sweetpea, we've probably spent $8,000 with her!"

I started to pace as my temper continued to escalate. "I'll go see her tonight, and we'll get this resolved quickly. She will not embarrass or disrespect you again! Not when we're responsible for contributing to her livelihood! We don't have to buy from her! There are other bird vendors in the area!"

"No, Michael!" Gabby rebutted. "I don't want another bird! I love Sweetpea, and I think we're really bonding! I'll just be glad when we can bring her home and not have to deal with Gail!"

I saw that Gabby could easily become upset with me if I confronted Gail over this issue, so I told her I would stay out of it and let her fight her own battles. She seemed pleased that I wasn't going to add fuel to the fire. I smiled, told her everything was going to be all right, and went to the bar and fixed myself a drink.

The next morning, I was waiting for Gail in front of her store as she unlocked the door to start her day. "Good morning," she said pensively. "I'm surprised to see you here so early."

I returned her good morning and followed her inside the store. I walked over to see Sweetpea and then walked into the back room where she was putting on her work apron.

"I understand my wife is making you crazy, singing to Sweetpea," I started.

The color drained from her face as she attempted to answer. "Well, she comes in here every day, and she talks and sings to that bird like she's human! And, yes, it is annoying and distracting for me while she's here."

"I came home last night, and Gabby was sitting in our dining room, crying because she said she felt like a little kid being scolded by a teacher in front of the class!" I said loudly, feeling the anger again building inside.

Gail made no response, so I continued. "We don't have to do business with you. There are other places that would be happy to have our business. You are the one who told her she could come in every day and bond with Sweetpea!"

Glaring at her, I said, "You only have two more weeks to deal with us coming in to see Sweetpea. My expectation is that you will be civil and not embarrass or say anything derogatory to my wife during that period. Trust me, we want Sweetpea out of your store as much as you do!" Putting my hands on my hips in a dominating stance, I asked, "Do we have an understanding?"

She shook her head affirmingly but made no reply. "I don't want Gabby to know we had this conversation either." I pivoted and started back to the front of the store without saying "good-bye," "go to hell," or anything else to Gail.

That night at dinner, Gabby commented that Gail had been nicer than normal when she visited Sweetpea today. "She must have been grumpy or was having a bad day yesterday," she said. "Because today, she seemed like a different person."

"That's great!" was all I said before changing the subject.

We'd had a huge cage delivered and assembled and then placed it where we wanted it in the living room. We were ready to finally bring home our little bundle of joy! She'd grown to double her size in the past five weeks, and her down was about 50 percent features now. She was starting to look like a bird finally!

We'd bought a second smaller cage and put it in a bedroom next to ours. Gabby had decorated the room, and it was officially Sweetpea's bedroom.

The day we brought her home, I had to leave for a meeting at our corporate office. Gabby assured me everything was going to be just fine as I left the house heading for the airport.

The next day, at about 6:00 a.m., Gabby called me on my cell phone, waking me up. "Hey," I said, answering the phone, "it's pretty early for a call. Is everything OK?"

"No!" she said sternly. "No. Everything is not OK! Sweetpea sat in her night cage and screamed all night! Neither one of us got any sleep! I don't know what's wrong with her! She has food, toys, I have a night light on, and her cage is covered with the same blanket she's had at Gail's store!"

After trying to absorb everything I'd just heard rattled off to me with machine-gun-like quickness, I responded, "It's probably more about different surroundings and a new environment than anything else."

"I took her out of her sleep cage and put her in the big cage in the living room this morning, and she's still screaming," Gabby said loudly. She hadn't needed to tell me that bit of information as I could easily hear Sweetpea in the background, and she was extremely loud!

"What do you think I should do?" Gabby asked, sounding completely frustrated.

"I have no idea," I replied with a chuckle. "I'm no bird expert!"

"Do you think you can come home tonight instead of tomorrow night so you can help me with her?" Gabby begged.

"No," I answered. "It's a two-day meeting, and I need to be here for both days. You're just going to have to handle this by yourself. If I was to give you any advice, it would be to first call Gail and see if this is normal behavior. And, second, get out of the house for a while and have a relaxing breakfast or lunch somewhere quiet. That's all I've got for you, baby!"

"OK," she responded, sounding like she was starting to calm down. "Thanks for listening. I feel better just talking about it." Just as she finished, Sweetpea let out the loudest screech yet, and we both chuckled once the deafening sound ended.

"Maybe a mimosa with breakfast," I added before saying "I love you" and hanging up.

In the following days and weeks, Sweetpea did stop screaming for the most part. We'd bought a book on cockatoos and found that sometimes, they just needed to scream. It was in their DNA, and they used the noise to scare off predators in the wild. So we got used to her outbursts once or twice a day as she forcefully exercised her lungs. We usually just left the room and let her scream to her heart's content for four or five minutes.

All the kids loved her, and she was always happy to see visitors. We discovered that she had a fondness for blondes and preferred females to males. She was always so sweet when a female member of the family approached her, lifting her wing and waiting to be stroked under it. She was much more cautious and apprehensive if a male figure approached her. Even with us, she preferred Gabby's touch to mine. If I moved too fast, she would fly back to her cage and wouldn't let me approach her for several hours, seeming to fear my hands specifically.

One Friday evening, about a month after we'd brought her home, I walked in the door, and Gabby said in a high-pitched voice, "Hello, Daddy!" Sweetpea was sitting on her arm, and she perfectly mimicked Gabby by saying, "Hello, Daddy!" We were both dumbstruck as we stood there looking at each other, stunned at how clearly she had said the phrase, and then we both laughed out loud.

CHAPTER 23

It only took a day for my worst fears to be realized with our new CEO, Shawn Meyers. He and I met during Jeff's introduction meeting between Christmas and New Year's Day. When Jeff introduced the two of us, Shawn smiled and said it was good to meet me as we shook hands.

Still holding my hand, his smile faded into more of a disdainful smirk as he added, "I read in your personnel files that you were in the army. When was that?"

"I was drafted and served in the Vietnam War," I responded.

"I joined the marines right out of college," he countered. "I was part of the Desert Storm campaign. Fortunately, by the time I enlisted, the United States knew how to win a war!"

He stared at me, waiting for a reaction. When none came, he continued. "While I was over there, I gained a lot of respect for the air force and their amazing capabilities. But the army guys, not so much. If I were ever to go into combat again, I'd take one marine over five army soldiers every time!"

I could feel my face starting to flush with anger, but as calmly as I could, I responded, "Well, I hope neither of us has to go back to war anytime soon!"

"That's easy for you to say," he snickered. "They won't be calling you up! You're too old to fight now!"

I was livid as I stood there and absorbed his personal attack. I wanted to hit him right in his smart mouth, but I decided today wasn't the day I was going to end my career with American Trust. Instead, I put on my best fake smile and said, "Well, then, I hope you aren't called back up to go to war."

Shawn let go of my hand and continued to study me, saying nothing. His eyes had narrowed into small slits as he stood there, waiting for me to do or say something else. Finally, he broke the silence by saying, "I'm sure we'll have plenty of time to talk on a more personal basis once Jeff's gone. Looking forward to working with you." Waiting for no response, he turned his back to me and headed in the direction of the next divisional he wanted to meet.

Working on day thirty-one under Shawn's supervision was no different than the first day we'd met. He was arrogant, vain, pompous, and egotistical, but he was also my new boss, and it was up to me to make all the necessary changes if this relationship had any chance of succeeding. Either that or I needed to seriously consider finding a new career.

At our first divisional meeting, we all presented budgets for the year and asked if anything needed to be changed or tweaked. After the last divisional presented, Shawn thanked all of us for our hard work on our plans. Then he simply said, "I'm on board with all these recommendations except for two areas. First, we need to cut our labor costs by 10 percent this coming year. And, second, we need to cut our spending budgets by 15 percent for the year. Other than that, everything seems to be in line."

Jim Donaldson, from the southern region, strongly protested the revisions. "I have twenty more locations this year than I had last year! How do I keep them all open if I have to cut my staffing dollars by 10 percent? And a 15 percent cut in spending means I have less money than I had last year in my expense budget—again, with twenty additional properties! That's damn near impossible to do unless we let the properties go to hell this year!"

"Jim," Shawn began after contemplating the feedback he'd just received, "just to make sure you understand, these reductions are not a suggestion—they are a mandate!" His eyes narrowed, and his voice raised as he continued. "The board of directors wants a higher yield for our stockholders. By the way, when I say stockholders, that includes everyone in this room! To accomplish the improved net operating income, we're going to need to start by cutting expenses. I think these initial cuts are a good start."

"You mean we could have more spending cuts before the end of the year?" Jim asked loudly.

"Well, I guess that depends on you guys," Shawn responded smugly. "We'll just take it quarter by quarter, and based on the results you achieve, we'll adjust accordingly. But I committed to the board that we would deliver higher income after expenses by the end of the year, and we will accomplish that goal! Are there any other questions?"

Everyone remained silent, but all eyes were fixed on our new leader. "OK, then," Shawn stated. "I would like to have your revised budgets to me by Friday. Hopefully, we won't have to do this again once the first quarter is complete. I have complete faith that all of you will make this work!"

"Is there anything else we need to discuss?" Shawn asked, looking into each person's eyes as his gaze traveled around the conference table. After a lengthy amount of silence, he began again. "We now have a plan. There are no reasons, only excuses, why this plan won't work! So get back out there and make this happen!" With that, everyone stood and started putting their papers, computers, and various reports in their backpacks or briefcases.

Jim and I were on the same floor at the hotel, so we rode up to our floor in the elevator together. Once the elevator door closed and the two of us were alone for our upward trip, Jim simply shook his head from side to side and said, "That's a damn stupid plan! Unless we stop hiring people and let the properties all go to hell, none of us will be able to live with these kinds of numbers!"

The door dinged and opened for our floor. We both stepped out of the elevator, and I said, "He's new to this business model, and maybe by the end of the first quarter, he'll have a better understanding of how much money it takes to operate these facilities."

"Michael!" Jim answered sarcastically. "Don't be so naïve! Everyone in that room was just set up to fail. Now all we can do is wait and see which one of us is the biggest loser!" Then Jim turned and headed down the hall toward his room. Not looking back at me, he said loudly over his shoulder, "I still need to pack! I'll talk with you tomorrow sometime!"

The flight back to John Wayne International Airport seemed much shorter than normal to me. Maybe it was because I'd spent the entire three-and-a-half-hour trip thinking about how we could lower our expenses by 15 percent and not hurt our business. I'd come up with a few good ideas and had been entering them onto my laptop when the flight attendant notified us that we would be landing soon. Closing my laptop and putting it away, I put my head back, closed my eyes, and rested for the remainder of the flight.

It was almost 7:00 p.m. when I pulled into our driveway. Once out of the car, I walked up on the porch, put my key in the door, opened it, and stepped inside.

I was instantly greeted by a "Hello, Daddy!" from Sweetpea, who was sitting on Gabby's shoulder. The words put an instant smile on my face as I responded, "Well, hello, Sweetpea."

Gabby had a huge smile on her face as I walked over to her and Sweetpea and gave her a kiss. As soon as we finished the kiss, Sweetpea made the same kissing sound as our lips separated.

Gabby and I both laughed. "That's a first!" Gabby commented.

As we continued to talk about my trip and Gabby's days while I was gone to the meeting, Sweetpea jumped down on the arm of the sofa and started rambling incoherently, wanting to be involved in our conversation. It was so cute that Gabby and I both started laughing as Sweetpea continued to speak gibberish as if she had something important to say.

Finally, Gabby said, "You're so cute, baby!" Then she leaned forward and gave Sweetpea a kiss on the beak. As she was pulling away, Sweetpea made the kissing noise again. "Thank you for the kiss!" Gabby announced, which sent Sweetpea into another tirade of gibberish.

"She makes a tough day much better, doesn't she?" I said, reaching over to stroke her wing. She sat there and accepted my affection but remained in an indistinguishable but animated conversation with us as her head moved around while she pontificated unintelligibly.

"She is truly amazing!" Gabby said, watching her with an expression of pure wonderment as her newest child and I interacted.

At the end of the first quarter, all the divisionals met at our corporate offices to go over results. Jim Donaldson had been correct; none of us had made the new performance goals for the quarter.

After Shawn came into the conference room and said good morning, he asked each of us to write down whom we thought our most promotable regional vice president was today, and if they were relocatable. He asked us to pass him the names and then had our CFO pass out piles of management reports to all of us.

Before we started looking at the reports, Jim Donaldson asked, "Where is Sam Ballard?" Sam was the divisional manager from the Great Lakes and Chicago area. It was very unusual to have these meetings without all five of the divisionals present.

I had also wondered why Sam wasn't here today. Was it a flight mix-up? Was one of his family members sick or dying? Was he ill? I curiously waited for Shawn's response as well.

Shawn looked at Jim Donaldson and simply responded, "Sam Ballard is no longer with the company."

We all sat there in complete shock upon hearing the news.

"Sam's expenses for the first quarter were 21 percent higher than his expenses for the first quarter of last year," Shawn began. "Since I'd asked for each of you to have a 15 percent reduction for the quarter, Sam's actual expenses were up 36 percent to goal.

"I called Sam and asked him what his plan was to offset this setback, and he responded that he had no plan in place currently to offset the increase. He went on to tell me that he would accomplish his net income goals through enhanced sales and rent increases to current tenants."

Shawn took a slow look at everyone in the room before continuing. "It is not your individual option to raise rents on existing customers—that's a corporate decision."

Then slowly scanning the room for a second time, ensuring everyone was paying attention, he continued. "We all stacked hands on our plan to lower expenses at our last meeting. Everyone agreed we would make it happen! If you have no plan in place to lower expenses for your division currently, I want to make sure you understand that is not acceptable! Because Sam had no plan and, apparently, he had no intention of making one, he was terminated yesterday, effective immediately."

No one commented on the news. I'm sure everyone would have liked to have expressed their thoughts, but we all remained silent. Most of the people in the room probably had the same thoughts running through their heads as I did. I didn't feel like we stacked hands on the new expense parameters; that was a top-down decree, and we were given zero input into the final decision!

"The reason I asked for your best regional vice president is so I can interview them and determine if they have the ability to move up to divisional vice presidents in the near future," Shawn stated flatly. "Hopefully, this is the only divisional vice president we lose this year, but we need backups in place in each of your divisions just in case."

Shawn's administrative assistant came in the room and handed him a slip of paper, bent over, and whispered in his ear. He looked at it quickly and rose to his feet.

"I apologize, gentlemen, but I have to take this call," he said. "Let's take a five-minute break, and then we can go over the quarterly results together. I'll be right back." He and the CFO both exited the conference room, which just left the four divisionals sitting in the room.

"This reminds me of that old Bob Dylan song," Jess Evers, the divisional manager that oversaw Texas and Florida, said. Then he began singing. "Things they are a changing," he bellowed.

Once he quit singing, Jim Donaldson said, "I told Michael at the last divisional meeting that we were all being set up to fail! This is a pretty screwed-up way to run a company! We all need to watch our asses if we expect to stick around!"

Fortunately for me, our California division had done the best at expense controls in the first quarter. We hadn't made the goal, but we were 5 percent down from our previous year's expenses, and we were the only division under the previous year's numbers. I didn't expect praise for the quarter, but I wasn't prepared for the next statement that came out of Shawn's mouth.

"Gentlemen," he began once he was back in the room, "you should all be pretty embarrassed that a guy who was in the fucking army and went to such a prestigious school as Fresno State was able to kick all your asses in the first quarter! I hoped you three were better than that!"

Everyone looked at me, wondering how I would respond to his outrageous comment. I was angry, but I stayed calm and decided to give this prick a taste of his own medicine.

"Thank you, Shawn," I responded, looking directly into his eyes. "I like to think it's not the branch of service you've served in or even the school you graduated from. Sometimes, the cream just rises to the top! The California division is getting better every day at managing our expenses! By next quarter, we should achieve the goals you've asked of us." I flashed him a fake smile and watched his jaw muscles clench and his eyes narrow as though he was peering directly into the sun.

It was a brutal two days, and each of us took our turn in the barrel as we defended our reasons for virtually every expense during the quarter. Most of the questions asked had obvious answers, but Shawn wanted to exchange verbal warfare with each of us to drive home his message.

By the end of the second day, I was mentally and physically drained. Before we were released to go home, Shawn assured us that we would be doing the same thing at the end of the second quarter.

We were just starting to get up to leave when Shawn looked at me and said, "By the way, Michael, since I don't have a divisional manager for the Great Lakes/Chicago division, I'd like you to supervise their expenses until we have a replacement for Sam. You've done such a good job in California that I'd like to see what you can accomplish with the worst division in the country."

Everyone stopped whatever they were doing and again turned to watch my reaction, knowing that my workload had just been doubled for the second quarter.

I zipped my backpack shut, slung it over my shoulder, and put the fake smile back on my face. "Whatever you need, boss!" I said. "I'm a team player!" I turned away from Shawn and exited the conference room.

On the flight home, I didn't dwell too much on how I would handle the new assignment. Instead, I spent most of the three and a half hours contemplating where I felt I currently stood in the game of life. Taking out a pad of paper from my backpack, I wrote "Bad" at the top left of the page and "Good" in the top center of the page. Then I drew a line right down the middle of the page, dividing the page in half.

I began with the Bad column first and started listing everything that I believed was adding negativity to my life.

1. Shawn Meyers – His promotion had caused me more mental stress and more hours spent at work since he'd become my boss.
2. United Sates politics – I hated how divided our country was becoming and how much further left we were moving with each new administration.

3. The world was a mess – There were multiple wars going on in almost every continent. Smaller conflicts were breaking out everywhere over religion, race, or human rights issues, killing hundreds of thousands of people.
4. God and Christianity, in particular, were under attack both in America and around the world. We were being told science has proved there is no God.
5. I wasn't spending enough time in the relationships that mattered most to me—family, my friends, and community service.

After I wrote these five items down, I laid my head back against the seat and wondered why I'd started with the Bad column first. Was I contributing to my own unhappiness by concentrating on the negativity in my life? Why hadn't I started with the Good column first?

I had a wonderful wife and family; none of us had ever been addicted to drugs or alcohol; no one had committed a crime or been to jail; our kids all had gainful employment; and we had a little money in the bank if we needed it for a rainy day. Compared to so many others in America, I was leading the perfect life!

The flight attendant's voice came over the loudspeaker, letting everyone know we would be landing in twenty minutes, which snapped me out of my self-absorbed reflection.

During my drive home from the airport, I tried to stop obsessing over my frame of mind and my struggle with negativity. After a couple of days apart, Gabby deserved better than to be greeted by a grumpy, obnoxious, moody husband.

I stopped by a flower store and purchased a dozen yellow roses, Gabby's favorite, and continued my drive home. The simple act of doing something nice for someone you love had already had a positive effect on my attitude. I felt myself smiling as I prepared to surprise my wife with the beautiful bouquet.

Walking through the front door, I was greeted by a high-pitched "Hello, Daddy!" from Sweetpea, who was sitting on top of her cage. I immediately smiled and looked up at her.

"Hello, Sweetpea!" I responded. "It's good to be home."

Gabby came walking out of the kitchen, drying her hands on a small kitchen towel as she approached me. "Oh, wow!" she shrieked. "Are those for me?"

"Well, as a matter of fact, they are," I responded as she stopped in front of me.

She kissed me, gave me a warm hug, and then stepped back, taking the bouquet from me. "These are simply beautiful!" she said, admiring her handful of flowers. "It's not my birthday, and it's not our anniversary, so why exactly am I getting flowers tonight?" she quizzed.

"You're getting flowers tonight because you are the most incredible woman I've ever known, and I am lucky enough to be married to you!" I replied.

"That's so sweet!" she commented, stepping in to give me a second kiss. While we were kissing, Sweetpea began talking again.

"Bye, bye!" she said loudly, followed by, "Hello, Sweetpea!"

I chuckled and said, "I've never heard her say that before."

"Me either," Gabby confessed, looking at Sweetpea, who was bouncing up and down on the top of her cage. "She's so smart! She picks up words much quicker than I thought she would, and she repeats them perfectly! When you're away, I talk to her all day like she's my best girlfriend! I just love her!"

Looking back at me, she gave me one more peck on the lips and said, "I'm going to go put these in some water, and then I'll finish dinner. Why don't you fix us both a drink and bring Sweetpea into the kitchen with you so we can talk about how your meeting went?"

"I'll do that!" I replied, knowing the last thing I wanted to talk about was our meeting!

After I had a drink in both hands, I walked over to Sweetpea's cage, raised my arm, and said, "Step up!" She jumped down onto my forearm like she'd been doing it forever. I walked into the kitchen and stood next to a perch, which was attached to a wide base with wheels under it that Gabby had rolled next to the sink. "Step down," I commanded, and Sweetpea jumped off my arm and onto her perch.

"I'm impressed!" I complimented Gabby. "She is really starting to follow commands. It appears you've been working hard with her!"

Before Gabby could comment, Sweetpea started bouncing up and down on her perch, flapping her wings, and again said, "Hello, Sweetpea!"

We both laughed, and Gabby responded, "Hello, Sweetpea!"

We had a nice dinner and great conversation for the next hour. Sweetpea put in her two cents' worth every few minutes as we talked. It was obvious that she felt the need to be included and contribute to the conversation.

I offered Sweetpea a small piece of broccoli, and she raised her left foot up to accept it. She looked at it for a minute before raising it to her beak and touching the vegetable with her tongue. Pulling it away again, she studied it, and then she brought it back to her mouth and began to eat it.

"That's another first!" Gabby chuckled and then continued. "Just by observing her, I've figured out that she's left-handed."

"Really!" I answered.

"Yes!" Gabby continued. "When I give her anything to play with, or when she eats and must use her claw to hold the food, she always uses her left foot. And at night, when she's tired and ready to go to sleep, she stands on her right leg and pulls her left foot up to her chest, folds her claw into a little fist, and keeps it there. Then she turns her head 180 degrees and puts her beak between the wings on her back and sleeps standing on her right foot!"

"That is so fascinating!" I commented.

"Let me help you with these dishes, and then we can go put her to bed together," I suggested.

"I'd really like that," Gabby replied. "Then we can have some alone adult time."

That night, when we were in bed, I held Gabby in my arms, and we lay there, both very content to be together. I was happier than I'd been all week. Before drifting off to sleep, I did something that I hadn't done in a very long time. I silently prayed and thanked God for all my blessings and asked him to watch over all my family members and equip them with his armor against all evil. I went to sleep with a smile on my face, and I can't ever remember sleeping better than I did that night.

The rest of my week went much better once I was home and working in my own office. On Saturday, the day Gabby was always able to sleep in, I was drinking a cup of coffee and going through e-mails on my computer when she came stumbling out of the bedroom. She plopped down next to me on the sofa and laid her head on my shoulder.

I'd already taken Sweetpea out of her night cage, brought her into the living room with me, and fed her breakfast. As soon as she saw Gabby, she became vocal.

"Hello, Sweetpea!" she said, flying over and landing on the couch right behind Gabby's head. She backed up until she could step down onto Gabby's shoulder and waited to be stroked by her momma.

"Good morning," I said softly to Gabby. "You look like you're still half asleep."

Reaching up, Gabby slowly and gently ran her hand over Sweetpea's raised wing and said, "Good morning, Sweetpea." Then she responded to me, "Good morning, sweetheart. Yes, I am still half asleep." She leaned forward and picked my coffee cup off the coffee table and took a quick drink.

We sat in silence for a couple of minutes as Gabby continued to stroke Sweetpea's wing softly. Sweetpea must have like it because she lay down flat on Gabby's shoulder and brought her left foot up to lovingly caress her beak gently.

"I know this may sound a little crazy," I said, breaking our silence. "But how would you feel about finding a church and starting to attend weekly?"

Gabby raised her head off my shoulder, gave me a questioning look, and simply replied, "Really! Are you serious?"

"I am," I responded. "I've been thinking about this a lot over the past few days. I want to get back to the days when my parents, Ronnie, and I went to church and thanked God for our blessings!"

"You and I have so much more than my parents had, and yet we don't take the time to say thank you before meals or worship and sing the praises of the one who gives us everything! I want to change that!"

"I'd love to go to church!" Gabby expressed eagerly. "I haven't really been to church except for Christmas Eve and Easter celebrations since my first husband died. I don't really know why. I just stopped going."

Looking into Gabby's eyes, I softly said, "I really think it would be good for us. It would also be a good example for our kids and grandkids to hopefully follow.

"With all the bad that is going on around us in today's world," I continued, "I feel like I really need to reconnect with Jesus Christ and replenish my soul and spirit on a regular basis, and I want the same for you, sweetheart."

Gabby laid her head back on my shoulder and responded, "I think that's a wonderful idea! Let's try a few churches and see if we find one we want to call our church home in the next few weeks. We can start tomorrow if you'd like."

Still laying her little body on Gabby's shoulder, Sweetpea picked up her head and said, "Bye, Bye!" Both Gabby and I chuckled at her input into our conversation.

We felt extremely lucky because it hadn't taken a very long time before we found a church that checked off all the boxes we were looking for. The church was in Santa Ana and only ten minutes from our home. They had four services weekly; one on Saturday night, and three on Sunday. It was a much larger church than either one of us had ever attended with an average of five hundred people attending each service.

We loved their music, a mix of contemporary songs and old Gospel hymns. We really enjoyed the lead pastor and his sermon delivery. We especially liked that he referenced to the Bible and shared with us how the ancient teaching applied to our lives today. The congregation was friendly and welcoming, but at the same time, we felt no pressure to get more deeply involved until we were ready to do so. We attended the church for almost a year before we became members.

Every Sunday, I left the service feeling energized and ready to take on anything that came my way during the next week. I was confident that I could take on anything that Shawn threw my way!

An unexpected bonus that I hadn't counted on was that Gabby's and my relationship improved and deepened as we spent more time together studying the scriptures. We studied the Bible at least two nights a week, and our discussions brought us both closer than we'd ever been.

During the next three years, I felt so blessed to be building a stronger relationship with the Lord while I watched the world around us crumbling at an ever-increasing pace. Whether it be natural disasters, wars, or issues inside our own country and government, things were changing so quickly and, in most cases, so horrifically that it was hard to keep up with the turmoil and strife.

In 2008, two significant natural disasters occurred. As many as sixty-eight thousand people were killed, and thousands more were injured or missing when a 7.9-magnitude earthquake struck three provinces in Western China.

Shortly after the tragedy in China, Cyclone Nargis ravaged Myanmar's Irrawaddy Delta and Yangon, killing seventy-eight thousand people and leaving another twenty-eight thousand missing and presumed dead. The twelve-foot tidal wave that developed during the storm was responsible for leaving over a million people homeless in its aftermath.

As well, man's inhumanity against his fellow man escalated in every corner of the world.

A truck bomb exploded outside a Marriott Hotel in Islamabad, Pakistan, killing fifty people and wounding hundreds of other citizens and tourists. Islamic terrorist took credit for the attack.

Hamas, a Palestinian terrorist organization, launched multiple rockets into Israel. Israel immediately retaliated with air strikes in Palestine, killing over three hundred people and wounding hundreds more. Israel targeted Hamas base training camps and missile storage facilities. The violence and animosity between the two factions continued to escalate after the attacks.

Ten gunmen carried out an attack on several commercial hubs in Mumbai, India. More than 170 people were killed, and another 320 were wounded or injured. Indian officials hinted that they believed Pakistan was complicit in these attacks, further straining relations between the two countries.

Rodovan Karadzic, the Serb president during the Bosnian War in the 1990s, was arrested and charged with genocide, persecution, deportation, and other crimes against non-Serb citizens and civilians. He was found guilty of orchestrating the massacre of over eight thousand men and boys in Srebrenica in 1995.

On the home front, the government began to intervene in the U.S. financial system, trying to avoid a national crisis. The Federal Reserve outlined a $200 billion loan program to let countries borrow U.S. Treasury certificates at a discounted rate.

The federal government approves a $30 billion loan to JPMorgan Chase so they could take over Bear Sterns, which was on the verge of collapsing.

The U.S. government announced a plan to loan General Motors and Chrysler Corporation $17.4 billion to keep the American auto industry from collapsing. The loan was intended to keep both business units afloat for at least three more months.

The California Supreme Court rules that same-sex couples have a constitutional right to marry and receive all the benefits of heterosexual couples.

On November 4, 2008, Barrack Obama won the presidential election by a landslide and becomes the first African American president in United States history. He was the one person who could unify the country and stem racial inequality in the United States.

As 2008 ended and 2009 began, the world seemed destined to continue its downward spiral. In Australia, a huge wildfire burns hundreds of thousands of acres, killing 181 people and destroying more than 900 homes.

Flight 447 disappears somewhere off the northeast coast of Brazil. All 228 people on board perished. The plane was never found.

H1N1 (swine flu) killed over 150 people in Mexico City, setting off a worldwide outbreak of the disease.

Sweden became the fifth European nation to recognize and legalize same-sex marriages in their country. The other nations were the Netherlands, Norway, Belgium, and Spain. It became obvious that the world communities were quickly shifting in their opinion and approach to same-sex marriages.

Two suicide bombers killed 155 people and injured 500 others in Bagdad, Iraq. This would be the first of many such attacks throughout Iraq in the years to come.

Israeli troops crossed their border into the Gaza Strip, launching a ground war against the militant's Palestinian group Hamas; 430

Palestinians died, while only four Israeli soldiers died in the battle. Israel claimed the Gaza Strip to now be part of the Israeli nation.

In the United States, the financial crisis worsened. American International Group (AIG) asked for and received a $61.7 billion bailout loan from the federal government. The government then provided an additional $30 billion to keep the insurance industry afloat, making it the largest bailout loan in history.

Chrysler filed for bankruptcy protection while entering into a new partnership agreement with a foreign car company, Fiat. It was the first time since 1933 that an American auto maker had been forced to restructure under bankruptcy protection.

Unemployment in the United States reached 8.1 percent in February. It was the highest unemployment rate since 1983. The U.S. Department of Labor reported that 598,000 jobs were lost in January alone. It was the highest number of job losses since 1974.

Bernard Madoff admitted to operating a massive Ponzi scheme that defrauded thousands of his clients of billions of dollars over a twenty-year period.

President Obama announces that he would be sending an additional thirty thousand troops to Afghanistan to fight Taliban insurgents.

In a speech in Cairo, Egypt, Pres. Barrack Obama called for a new beginning between the United States and Muslims around the world. He asked for new alliances based on mutual respect and common interests. The speech was not received very well in America. Those who were more on the right saw this as an apology that was not deserved to hostile Muslim nations and groups.

The high point of 2009 was the miracle on the Hudson. Captain "Sully" Sullenberger successfully landed flight 1549 on the Hudson River after a bird strike disabled multiple engines on his aircraft. All 150 passengers and the five crew members survived without injury. It was a glorious moment in U.S. aviation history.

As 2009 ended and 2010 began, it was more of the same. Massive catastrophic rains drenched Pakistan for two weeks, killing an estimated 1,600 people and displacing 14 million Pakistanis.

A 7.0 earthquake devastates Port-au-Prince, Haiti. The death toll rose to over two hundred thousand people. The infrastructure of Haiti was destroyed.

This was followed by an 8.8 earthquake that rocked Chile. Fatalities were relatively low, with some 750 people killed in the devastation. But as many as 1.5 million people were displaced from their homes in the aftermath.

At least three hundred people were killed, and hundreds more were injured during Cambodia's annual Water Festival. A densely populated bridge started to sway under the weight on it, causing a stampede and the eventual collapse of the bridge.

In another part of the world, street fighting between ethnic Kyrgyz and minority Uzbeks left over two thousand people dead. Because of the fighting, one hundred thousand people crossed the border between Kyrgyzstan and Uzbekistan, looking for asylum.

In the United States, we continued to live through a struggling economy. The United States experienced its worst economic period since the Great Depression. Over forty-four million people, or about 14 percent of Americans, were living in poverty.

Congress passed a bill called the Patient Protection and Affordable Care Act. It would soon be known by its simpler name, Obamacare. This bill was supposed to overhaul the American health-care system. It mandated that all Americans have health insurance at lower cost to the consumers. Those who chose not to have health insurance would have to pay a penalty through annual income tax filings for noncompliance. This program would become one of the most controversial topics of the Obama administration and was fiercely contested by the Republican Party.

A British petroleum (*Exxon*) oil drilling rig off the coast of Louisiana spilled approximately forty-two thousand gallons of crude oil into the Gulf of Mexico, creating the worst environmental disaster in U.S. history. It was eighty-six days before the leak was finally sealed. The cleanup was estimated to be in the billions of dollars.

Goldman Sachs agreed to pay the federal government $550 million in a settlement after being accused of misleading investors during the subprime mortgage crisis and the housing market collapse.

Thousands of rescue and cleanup workers at ground zero reached a settlement with New York City for $657 million. The money was to be used for health-care claims of those affected by the massive multiyear cleanup.

President Obama announces a revised American nuclear strategy that limited the instances in which the United States would use nuclear weapons. Part of the strategy included renouncing the creation of any more nuclear weapons. The president pointed out that an exception would be made for North Korea and Iran, even though both countries had violated the Nuclear Proliferation Treaty in the past.

The high point of 2010 was the rescue of thirty-three Chilean miners who were rescued after being trapped in a mine shaft one and a half miles underground. The rescue effort lasted for sixty-eight days, while the whole world watched the drama. All the miners lived in this epic rescue effort.

Very few of these events had a direct effect on my life or business, except for Obamacare, which raised our company insurance contribution rates dramatically.

The increased violence and terrorist attacks around the world concerned me a great deal. I was also beginning to see a concerted effort against the Christian religion around the world as well as here at home. Separation of church and state was being pushed constantly by liberal groups in the United States.

Elsewhere in the world, Christians were being killed for no other reason than for being Christians. The number killed for their faith had been estimated at fifty thousand people in 2010. Another five million Christians around the world were not allowed to practice their religion publicly. Christians would soon become the most persecuted faith group on the earth. Unfortunately, that distinction remains true today.

I didn't vote for President Obama, nor was I a fan once he took office. Every time he gave a speech to an international audience, he seemed to be apologizing for America's prosperity. He pledged to help struggling countries by sending billions of dollars in aid, while we had a very high unemployment rate and a record number of people living below the poverty line right here at home.

But I knew I was in the minority in my thought processes about the president. He and his wife were the "darlings" of the Democratic Party, and his approval rating was very high after his first two years as president. The mainstream media couldn't get enough face time with him and Michelle. They were on talk shows, news programs, and magazine covers every week, all with glowing commentaries on their performances and accomplishments.

As I had continued to age, I found myself identifying more and more with the Republican Party, and I even thought about possibly venturing into politics sometime in the future. But for now, my efforts were concentrated on my business and my personal job performance.

Since Shawn had taken the helm of American Trust, we'd lost a total of three divisional vice presidents who had all "moved on to pursue other opportunities." The first one was terminated. The second left American Trust to pursue a similar position with a competitor. The third, Jim Donaldson, had blown up in a divisional meeting and, before quitting, called Shawn names I'd never heard before.

Though Shawn and I agreed on very little, our division was one of his top performers, and whether he liked me, he respected my results.

I had been tasked with mentoring two of the three new divisionals. In fact, it seemed as though if there was extra work or a project that needed to be accomplished, I was always the go-to guy. I couldn't honestly tell if he thought that much of my abilities, or if he was trying to break me and force me out of the company. What I did know was that I always needed to be near the top in performance to be safe.

I had a large framed inspirational picture on the wall directly behind my desk. There was a majestic male lion lying in the wide-open plains on one side and a gazelle munching on grass in the same area on the opposite side of the picture. The caption underneath them was "Every day in Africa, a lion wakes up and knows it must capture the slowest gazelle if it wants to eat and survive. Every day, a gazelle wakes up and knows it has to outrun the fastest lion if it wants to survive. So whether you're a lion or a gazelle, when the sun comes up, you'd better be running if you want to survive!" This truly was the mantra that I lived by in business.

Shawn and I never grew close, but we had a healthy respect for each other's talents. Often, Shawn would make disparaging comments to me in front of the other divisionals that weren't necessary. But I'd learned over the years to respond politely with just a slight touch of passive-aggressiveness. We weren't friends, but even with the constant badgering, I knew I was an asset to the company and that, for the time being, he needed me more than I needed him.

CHAPTER 24

I was sitting on our living room sofa with my feet up on the coffee table when the telephone rang the first time. It was Thursday, and I'd been answering e-mails that I hadn't gotten to during the day. I looked up at the clock and saw it was almost 8:00 p.m. Putting down my computer and getting up off the sofa, I quickly made my way into the dining room and picked up the phone just as the third ring was completed.

"Hello," I said into the phone receiver.

"Hello yourself" came a familiar voice in response.

"Jack!" I answered with surprise and delight in my voice. "How are you? What's going on up there in Alaska?"

"We're all fine," he responded calmly. "As far as what's going on up here, nothing much. In fact, I'm a little bored, so I thought I'd give you a call and see what's new in your world."

"It's so good to hear your voice!" I replied. "How are you feeling now that you're finished with your chemo treatments? You are done with them, aren't you?"

"Oh, god, yes!" he stated emphatically. "I've been done with that crap for almost two months now."

"I thought you had to take chemo for twelve weeks?" I pressed after he responded.

"I did take it for twelve weeks," he answered. "And I've been off it for another two months." He paused for a moment before continuing. "We haven't talked for about six months!"

"Really!" I responded. "If that's the case, I need to apologize for not calling you for so long! Time is moving faster and faster every day that I get older. I can't believe it's been six months since we last spoke."

"Are things any better with you and your boss?" Jack asked.

"Pretty much the same," I answered. "We stay out of each other's way, and I try to do what he asks of me. I guess it's going OK because I still have a job. What about you? Are you back to work yet?"

"Yes, I am," Jack replied. "I went back right after I was done with the chemo. I was so happy to get away from the weekly chemo treatments, from home, and from the toilet in our master bathroom! I've never been happier to go to work in my life!"

"I'm truly sorry you had to go through that!" I answered sympathetically. "I can't even imagine how difficult that must have been."

"All I can say is that the toilet and I had a lot of meaningful conversation for three months," Jack stated. "The toilet didn't talk much, but it was a good listener while I constantly expressed my innermost thoughts."

"How's Harper?" I asked, changing the subject.

"She's pretty good," Jack answered. "I'm making an old lady out of her, though!"

"How so?" I asked.

"It was the damnedest thing," he commented. "One night we went to bed, and the next day when we woke up, her hair was almost completely gray! And I mean silver gray!"

"Are you joking again?" I asked. "I've never heard of that happening before!"

"No, I'm not kidding!" Jack responded, trying to convince me he was telling me the truth. "I'd never heard of it either! We went to see our doctor that same day, and he'd as well had never seen it before. He did some research and found out it was rare, but it did happen when someone was under an intense amount of stress! She stopped producing melanin because of the stress she was under, caused by yours truly. I guess it only happens to one in about five hundred thousand people, but it appears Harper held the winning lottery ticket on this one."

"How does she feel about it?" I asked.

"It's actually very attractive," Jack answered. "It took her a while to get used to it, but she gets so many compliments on her hair, that she's really starting to enjoy the color. I, however, have started introducing her as my mother instead of my wife!"

"Stop it!" I said. "I know that's BS!"

"Enough about us. How's Gabby doing?" Jack asked.

"She's good!" I answered. "Between grandbabies and Sweetpea, she stays very busy and seems to be as happy as a clam!"

"Oh, yeah," Jack responded. "I forgot about your bird. How's that going?"

"She owns us!" I answered. "We both love her so much! She brings joy to our house, and I'm so glad I got her for Gabby!"

"Wow!" Jack responded. "You sound like you're talking about an adopted kid, not a bird!"

"We both think of her as our baby," I replied. "She is spectacular!"

"That's really cool!" Jack said. "The reason for my call. Harper and I want to have a big party at our cabin on Big Lake this Fourth of July, and I was hoping you guys could come up and celebrate with us. It's a little over a month away, so you have plenty of time to plan. What do you think?"

"That sounds really fun!" I answered. "Of course, I'll need to talk with Gabby first, but I'm sure we can make it happen! You always seem to pick the busiest part of the move-in season for these fun events, so I'll have to beg my boss for the time off again."

"I said a big party!" Jack responded. "I'd like Jacob, Sunday, Thomas, and their families to come up too! The cabin sleeps sixteen, and six more can sleep in the boat if we need more room."

"That's a really generous offer, but all together, there are twelve of us now," I said. "That's a lot of mouths to feed!"

"Don't worry about that!" Jack responded. "You take care of the airfare, and we'll take care of the food and drinks! I'm going to ask my mom and sister to come up as well. I've already got a huge stash of killer fireworks ready for the Fourth!"

"That sounds so fun!" I answered.

"Come up for a week if you can," Jack said. "We might play a little golf. There's bald eagle sanctuaries and grizzly bears fishing for salmon that you can watch from a safe distance. Everyone will love those attractions. The lake is full of fish, and everyone can catch as many as they want! We'll clean them and have them for dinner that same day!"

"Stop selling!" I interrupted. "I'm in! I just need to see who else can go with us that week. I'll have an answer to you by this time next week, if that's OK."

"Sure," Jack replied. "We have three cars, so you shouldn't need to rent a car."

"Gabby is going to be so excited!" I sang out. "I'll call you next Thursday, and we can start finalizing the plans!"

"Sounds good," Jack replied. "Tell Gabby hello for us, and we'll talk again soon."

We both said our good-byes and hung up. I couldn't wipe the smile off my face as I went back into the living room and plopped down on the sofa. Looking at my watch, I realized Gabby would be home from Thomas's house in less than an hour, and I could hardly wait to tell her the news!

As soon as Gabby walked through the front door, I pounced on her with my news. "Guess who called tonight?" I began.

She bent down and kissed me and then, straightening up, and said, "I have no idea."

"Jack Anthony!" I responded excitedly.

A smile immediately lit up her face as she replied, "That's wonderful! How are they doing?"

"Everything seems to be fine," I answered. "Jack is done with his chemo treatments, and he seemed to be pretty upbeat during our conversation."

"That's great!" Gabby responded. "How's Harper?"

"She's good," I said. "Jack told me a crazy story about her hair, though."

"What?" Gabby asked, not understanding what I'd just said.

I relayed the entire story in detail to her over the next few minutes. She listened in amazement, putting her left hand up to cover her open mouth several times as she listened intently.

"I don't know if I think that's awful or if it's just strange," she said once I'd completed the story.

"Well, Jack says she gets lots of positive compliments on her hair color, and she's finally resigned to the fact that she still looks OK, even with the gray hair!"

"I'll bet it's beautiful," Gabby added. "What else did he say?"

"Well, he asked us to come up and spend the week of July 4 with them," I responded.

"That would be so much fun!" Gabby replied excitedly.

"I don't just mean you and me," I continued. "He wants the whole family to come up, grandkids and all!"

"What!" Gabby responded. "Where would we all stay?"

"He wants us all to stay at their cabin on Big Lake for the week," I offered.

"If everyone can go, that's twelve people," Gabby answered. "Where would we all sleep?"

"He said he can sleep sixteen in the cabin and another six in the boat, if necessary," I responded.

"Wow!" Gabby exclaimed. "I was picturing a small little log cabin. But when I hear that any place is large enough to sleep sixteen, I guess it's not that small. It must be huge to accommodate that many people."

"I'm sure it's very nice," I remarked. "So what do you think? Should we go, or do you feel we should think about this and talk to all the kids before making a decision?"

"Heck, no!" Gabby blurted out. "I say we go! If the kids can come, they're welcome. If not, too bad, but we're still going!"

"Sounds pretty cool, doesn't it?" I stated.

"I think it would be so fun!" Gabby answered. "Seeing the sun still up at midnight will be a pretty awesome experience too! I doubt any of us ever thought we'd see almost twenty hours of daylight in one day!"

"Why don't you start talking with the kids and let's see who can go?" I responded. "Once we know that, we can start working on flight arrangement. Make sure you tell the kids this is a free trip for them. We'll take care of the airfare, and Jack is covering the food, drinks, and lodging. It's a pretty sweet deal, and they'll be crazy if they don't take advantage of it!"

"Don't worry, I'll take care of everything on our end," Gabby replied. "I'll get started on calls and flight arrangements first thing tomorrow morning!"

The next day, I called my boss from my office. "Shawn," I began, "I wanted to keep you in the loop and let you know I will be taking the week of July 4 off for vacation. I'll make sure everything is caught up, and I won't leave any loose ends for others to deal with."

"You realize that is probably the busiest week of the moving season, don't you?" Shawn responded coldly. "Are you sure that's the best time for you to be taking time off versus being in the field with your teams?"

"My people are all self-sufficient," I replied. "Me not being here for a week won't have any effect on their performance or our move-in numbers."

"You're probably right," Shawn responded. "But I'm more concerned with the message it sends to the field. We ask them to not take any vacations during the moving season, and then we as upper management take time off? That's kind of like saying do what I say, but don't do what I do!"

I could feel myself starting to get angry, but I responded calmly. "There is no good time to take vacation in this business. We're planning for the busy season in the first quarter, we're in the moving season the second and third quarter, and we're planning our annual conference in the fourth quarter."

"If you recall, we all stacked hands on not taking vacation during our busy season at our first divisional meeting of the year!" Shawn snapped back.

"Actually, I don't remember that," I said with heavy sarcasm in my voice. "But if we did, none of the other divisionals got the memo either! I happen to know that at least two divisionals will be taking some vacation time during our busy season, and one of them will be gone for two full weeks in June!"

There was silence on the other end of the telephone. Without a response, I decided to continue. "I gave the company two weeks of unused vacation last year, and I'm not going to do that again this year. I have four weeks of earned vacation still to use this year, and I plan to use every day that I have accumulated."

Still no response, so I decided to end the call. "I'm sorry to have to rush off the telephone, but I have a new district manager interview scheduled, and it looks like she's here. I'll send you my revised July calendar by the end of the week. Got to go!" With that, I hung up my office phone and leaned back contentedly into my soft leather office chair, savoring the victory as a smile began to build.

When we touched down at the Anchorage International Airport, the weather could not have been more beautiful. Clear blue skies, a light breeze, and about seventy-two degrees outside. As we made our way toward baggage claims, we saw Jack, Harper, and Jack's sister all waiting for us. They were waving, jumping around, and carrying homemade signs.

Harper's sign read, "Welcome to Alaska!" Jack's sign simply said, "What took so long?" Both signs represented their individual personalities perfectly.

Jack's sister wasn't carrying a sign, and I was the only one in our family who had met her before. After introductions, greetings, and some heartfelt hugs, we all gathered our luggage and headed to the parking lot to begin our great Alaskan adventure.

We stopped by Jack and Harper's house in Anchorage to pick up Jack's mother and use the restroom before leaving for the lake cabin. More introductions and a quick tour of their home, and we were off again for the last leg of our trip.

The countryside was beautiful as we made our way toward Mount McKinley on an almost deserted three-lane freeway. "Is this normal traffic flow?" I asked Jack as we sped along at 75 MPH.

"Pretty much," Jack responded. "The freeways are busy about two hours in the morning and maybe an hour and a half in the evening. But even then, everyone moves along at 60 to 65 MPH, unless there's been an accident. Other than that, this is pretty much as crowded as our freeways get."

"It's sure not LA.!" I offered.

Jack looked at me and smiled. "No, it's nothing like LA. That's one of the reasons we love it up here."

After about two hours of driving through beautifully snowcapped mountains and some of the largest pine and fir trees I'd ever seen, we pulled off the freeway at an exit with a sign that simply said, "Big Lake." After another two miles, we turned off the paved road and started down a dusty dirt road. It was an extremely narrow road, and it didn't feel like there was enough space for two cars to pass if they were traveling in opposite directions.

After a few minutes, we broke out of the trees and into a meadow filled with wildflowers and grasses that were a couple of feet high on both sides of the car. After a couple of hundred more yards, the road ended at a sizable building that appeared to be a grocery store/restaurant/gas station combination. Behind the building was a marina with approximately sixty boats of various sizes and configuration. But what struck us all as unusual were the twenty to twenty-five pontoon float planes that were also tied to various docks scattered throughout the marina.

As we got out of the car, Jacob walked over to me and said, "You don't see that every day in the lower forty-eight states, do you?"

"No, you don't," I responded, following his gaze as we both watched the airplanes bobbing about on the lake.

"We can do this two ways," Jack said as we'd all grouped up in front of the store. "I can take everyone over to the cabin in one load and then come back with Jacob and take all the luggage over on a second trip. Or I can take half of you and your luggage over on one trip and then come back and pick up the second group and their luggage." After a brief pause, he continued. "Any preferences?"

It was silent for a moment, and finally, Gabby spoke up. "I think we should all go over on the first trip, and then you and Jacob can bring the luggage back on the second trip."

"I agree with Gabby," Harper added, which was followed by a chorus of agreement from others in the group.

"Sounds good," Jack said. "Then that's what we'll do."

"It's a good plan, but why don't Jacob and I stay here and take all the luggage to the dock and wait for you there until the second trip?" Thomas interjected. "We can get everything to the dock and lock up the vehicles by the time you make it back for us."

"That even sounds better!" Jack said. He turned and started down one of the dock walkways and shouted, "Let's get this party started!" We all followed him through the maze of boats and planes until he stopped by a twenty-eight-foot Sea Ray with a name on the back that read, "Fool's Gold."

The boat was much larger and better appointed than I had expected it to be. Several plush seats on the deck and an enclosed cabin that had a small kitchen, bed, and head for its passengers. Its inboard motor was covered by cowling at the rear of the vessel, and I was sure it must have had a V8 engine for power.

Jack jumped in, put out a step stool for everyone to use getting into the boat and walked up to the controls and started the motor.

Then he let it idle as he walked back and helped everyone aboard the boat.

Once we were all on board, except for Jacob and Thomas, he said, "I'll be back here in about an hour and a half to pick you guys and the luggage up. OK?"

Both boys shook their heads affirmingly, and Jack put the boat into reverse and started backing out of his slip into the wider channel. Once the boat had cleared the dock, he moved the handle forward, and it slowly turned and headed out into the lake. After he was five minutes away from the dock, he pushed the control handle all the way forward, and the boat quickly raised itself to a planning position and rapidly moved away from the shore, leaving a sizable wake behind us as we accelerated through the calm, crystal-clear blue water.

As I scanned the passengers, everyone had smiles on their faces as we gently bounced through the small ripples in front of the boat. Looking over to Jack at the controls, I watched his hair flying straight back as we sped toward our destination. I couldn't see his eyes through his sunglasses, but he too had a slight smile on his face as he seemed satisfied to captain his own boat.

We passed an abundance of small islands as we made our way west through the seemingly endless lake. Some islands had no inhabitants on them, while others had a single cabin. Still others had a small village of three or four cabins on them. It was clear people in Alaska liked the outdoors and took advantage of the life it offered.

After a thirty-minute ride, Jack started slowing down the boat as he headed for a specific island directly in front of us. Even though we were several hundred yards from the island, it was immediately evident that the cabin on it was larger than any we'd seen up to this point.

As we approached the dock, everyone looked at the float plane that was tied to it. On the side of the plane was the same name as on the boat, "Fool's Gold" in big gold letters. It was a pretty impressive sight as we slowed, and Jack prepared the boat for docking.

Once safely tied up, Jack put his stool back on the deck and started helping everyone off the boat one at a time. Before their parents could stop them, the grandkids went running off the dock and toward the cabin.

"Don't worry," Jack said, looking at Elise. "There's no place to really get in trouble here. It's shallow water all around the island except where the dock was built. The island is only twelve acres from end to end. They can explore to their heart's content."

Elise gave Jack an uncomfortable smile in response and started jogging after her kids, obviously not completely confident in what he was saying.

Jack and I went around to the back of the cabin, and he turned on a propane tank and then started a good-sized generator, which jumped to life on the second pull of the rope. He and I walked back around to the front where everyone was waiting on a very large deck that had several chairs and chaise lounges scattered around on it.

Harper opened the front door and stepped inside, followed by all of us. The inside of the cabin was massive! Huge exposed beams held up a high second-story log balcony with wood railings that looked down into the main living area. There were logs cut in half to make wide steps on both sides of the balcony leading to the upper floor with several bedrooms and extra bathrooms that were out of view from the ground floor.

There were three large sofas and four chairs in various areas of the great room. The kitchen was toward the rear of the building, but it had an unobstructed view of the entire great room. Large heavy glass windows were everywhere. They let in the sunlight and created beautiful views of both forest land and the lake, depending on which window you looked out.

Looking out one of the windows and admiring the view, Gabby suddenly yelled, "Look! There's a deer in the front yard!"

Everyone ran to the window to see the deer.

"We actually have four deer on the island," Harper commented from behind us.

"How did they get here?" Sophie asked. "Can deer swim that far?"

"We think they came over about three years ago when we had a terribly cold winter and the lake was frozen solid for several months," Harper answered. "We snowmobile out here in the winter across the ice, and that winter was the first time we remember seeing them. When the lake freezes, Jack brings out hay and grain for them, and there's plenty to eat on the island the rest of the year. They still run from me, but Jack can walk right up to them, and they'll eat out of his hand!"

"That is so awesome!" Gabby answered. "I sure hope we get to see that while we're here!"

"We brought all the supplies we'll need for the week out here yesterday," Harper said. "The refrigerator is stocked, but we need to let the generator work a little while so everything gets cold again." Pointing at them, Harper continued. "We have three ice chests in the kitchen filled with soda pop, juice, beer, and wine coolers. Everyone can help themselves to anything they want!"

Jack walked into the kitchen and grabbed two beers out of the first ice chest he came to and lobbed one over to me. He opened his and held it high. "To good times and great friends."

I raised my beer in response, and we both took long drinks off our cans.

"Now I'd better get back and pick up the boys and all our luggage," Jack stated matter-of-factly.

"Can you make it back safely before dark?" Sophie asked.

Jack and Harper both laughed at the question. Jack finally answered her, "It won't be dark until about 3:00 a.m. That's eight hours from now. So we should make it."

"Oh," Sophie responded, her face reddening after his response. "I forgot about that." Then she added, "Sorry for sounding so dumb!"

"It's not dumb!" Jack answered. "You just aren't used to twenty-one hours of daylight. But what will really seem weird to you guys is barbecuing at midnight with the sun still shining! We'll do it at least once while you're here just so you can get some pictures and tell your friends about it when you back home."

I walked with Jack back to the boat and asked him, "Do you need any help?"

He gave me a crooked little smile and responded, "No, I'm pretty sure I got this." He untied and threw both sets of lines securing the boat to the dock back inside the boat. Next, he took a quick little jump and was in the now free-floating boat himself. Walking to the front of the boat and the controls, he turned the key, and the engine started with a deep throaty roar. He waved good-bye to me with his free hand, while the boat turned in the water, and then he pushed the throttle forward, and within seconds, he was out of sight as he skimmed across the lake at full speed.

While we were talking and waiting for the boys and Jack to come back, Aria said excitedly, "Come here, you guys, and look at this!"

As we approached the window where she was standing, she said softly, "Walk slow, so we don't scare them!"

Before I got to the window, I heard several gasps as others were finally able to see what Aria was seeing. About twenty feet in front of the deck, Michaela, Luke, Matthew, and Ellie were standing perfectly still while two female deer were slowly walking in their direction. They stopped just a couple of feet from each other as both deer and kids seemed mesmerized.

"The deer won't hurt the kids, will they?" Elise asked quietly.

"No, they won't hurt them," Harper answered softly. "I've never seen anything like this!" she continued.

"I've got to get my camera!" Aria said, moving slowly away from the window as the rest of us stared at the spectacle before us.

Michaela slowly raised her arm, and her hand was literally inches from one of the deer's faces. The larger doe took one more tentative step toward her and bent forward, smelling her open hand. The move brought a little squeal of joy from Luke, causing both deer to quickly move a few steps away from the children.

They all remained standing there as Ellie and the two boys all raised a hand and offered it to the deer. After a few seconds, the two deer again took a few hesitant steps toward the kids, and both bent forward to smell the closest little hand in front of them.

"I've never seen anything like this!" Sophie offered softly, amazement in her voice.

"Oh my god!" Gabby continued. "This is just precious! I can't believe this is really happening!"

Aria had returned with the camera and was snapping pictures like a madwoman as she tried to memorialize this once-in-a-lifetime experience.

Suddenly, both deer straightened up with ears standing at full alert. They were looking at something behind the kids, but none of us could see what it was. They slowly turned and started back into the forest behind them. Seconds later, they were gone, and we all ran outside.

"Mama!" Michaela exclaimed. "Did you see that? Did you see what just happened?"

Elise was as excited as the kids when she responded. "I did see that!" she responded excitedly. "We all were standing at the window watching you guys making friends with the deer!"

"One kissed my hand!" Ellie blurted out. "He wasn't even afraid of me!"

We all started talking at the same time, reliving the experience we'd just witnessed, when I heard the growl of Jack's boat as it slowed and pulled up to the dock.

Looking behind the kids, I saw him and the two boys tying the boat up and starting to unload the luggage onto the dock.

"That's why the deer left!" I said loudly. "They heard the boat coming and knew it was time for them to go back to their part of the island!"

"I'll bet you're right," Sophie said affirmingly.

Heading toward the boat, I changed the subject. "Come on!" I said. "Let's give these boys a hand getting everything up to the cabin."

Before the adults reached the dock, all the kids had run ahead and were hysterically telling the story about the deer to their dads and Jack. By the time we reached them, Jack simply looked at Harper and asked, "Is this true? The deer walked right up to the kids and touched their hands with kisses?"

"It's true!" Harper exclaimed. "I've never seen anything quite like it in my life! It was simply magical!"

"How awesome!" Thomas added. "I wish we would have been here to see it."

"Don't worry," Aria announced enthusiastically, "I got about thirty pictures with my camera. I'm so glad I brought it with me on the first trip! You can watch their interactions on the camera screen now, and when I get home, I'll have pictures made and send them to everyone."

"Can I see the camera now?" Thomas asked.

"Sure!" Aria responded, handing the camera to him.

Jack and Jacob quickly gathered behind Thomas and watched as he scrolled from one picture to the next. It only took seconds before all three of them had huge smiles on their faces and began commenting on the event they were witnessing.

"That is so surreal!" Jack said as he watched Thomas flip through the pictures. "These are wild deer! But it's like they knew the kids wouldn't hurt them!"

"I think this is what heaven will be like," Gabby offered up.

"I think you may very well be right about that," Elise added.

Once all the gear was put away and everyone was assigned a place to sleep, the ladies started preparing a meal for everyone. We all ate around the large table, sitting on a log that had been cut in half to create two picnic-type benches. There were lots of talk about the kids and the deer, and everyone seemed to be in a great mood.

Jack said grace before we ate, and everyone dug into the food. The next several minutes were quiet as everyone became more interested in eating the scrumptious meal and less interested in talking.

Harper had made some chocolate brownies for dessert. As soon as the kids were finished with desert, they all wanted to go outside and play. They were excused from the table and ran out the front door together.

"Why don't we all go out on the porch where we can keep an eye on your youngsters?" Jack said. "Go on out there, and I'll be along in a minute. I've got a surprise for all of you."

We all got up, and leaving the table uncleared, we marched outside, and everyone picked their favorite chair or lounge and took a seat. The kids were all playing tag, and we all smiled as we watched them running around like little Indians, laughing and trying not to be tagged.

Jack came out of the cabin carrying a large paper sack, which he set down at his feet before taking a seat in one of the empty chairs. Reaching into the sack, he pulled out a small mesh bag with three small bottles in it. There was a label on the front, but it was too small to read from a distance.

Holding it like it was a pouch full of gold, he raised it up and said, "Ladies and gentlemen, this is the official drink of Alaska. If you visit here, it is required that you have at least one of these before you leave."

Slowly looking into each person's eyes as he continued to showcase the purple mesh pouch, he continued. "Everyone who drinks this compares it to eating a chocolate-covered cherry. It's meant to be drank after a meal, and we might as well get the party started by having one tonight."

"I'm not much of a drinker," Elise said softly.

"That's the case with a lot of people, Elise," Jack responded. "That's why this drink is designed to be downed in one gulp, kind of like you were drinking an oversized shot of something."

Jack stood up and started pulling individual pouches out and handing one to each person.

Gabby read the sign on the pouch and said loudly, "Duck Fart kit! This drink is called a Duck Fart?" Everyone laughed at her indignation as she offered up her comment.

"Yes, I don't know where the name comes from, but the drink is indeed called a Duck Fart!" Jack responded. "It's very important that the preparation be done in the correct order, so let's do this together. Open your pouch and take out the cup with the name Duck Fart on it. Now take out the little bottle of Amaretto and empty it into the cup." Everyone followed Jack's instructions and did as he asked.

"Now, take out the little bottle of Crown Royal and empty it into the cup with the Amaretto. And to finish the drink, take out the small bottle of Irish cream and empty it into the Duck Fart cup."

Once everyone had finished making their drink, Jack raised his cup and continued his instructions with a serious tone. "The last step is critical, so please follow my directions exactly!" Looking again at every face to drive home his point, he began again. "A Duck Fart must be drank in one drink! This is not a sipping drink! Once you put the cup to your lips, you must drink until you have drained your cup. Does everyone understand?" he said, again waiting for affirmation before continuing.

Elise said, "I'm not drinking this!" with a disgusted look on her face.

Jack glared at her for a minute before addressing her concerns. "Elise! If you don't drink it, you will bring bad luck on our entire vacation! Just down it like I asked, and it will simply taste like you ate a chocolate-covered cherry. More importantly, you will solidify that we have a good week without incident because of your participation!"

"She doesn't have to drink it if she doesn't want to!" Harper snapped.

Jack shot Harper a look but said nothing.

Before he could respond, Elise said, "OK! OK! I'll drink it! I don't want to be the cause for anyone's bad luck!"

"Thank you, Elise," Jack responded with a small smile. "I knew you would be a team player. OK, everyone, raise your glasses high. To friends and family, to loved ones past, present, and future, to good fortune and freedom from fear or pain, to life in Alaska, the last frontier! Now everyone drinks it all down at one time!"

Jack led, and everyone followed his example as they emptied their individual Duck Fart cups.

Once finished, Elise said, "Except for the burn from my throat to my tummy, it wasn't bad! And you were right! It does taste like a chocolate-covered cherry. It was really sweet!"

Several others commented on the drink, while Jack passed out bottles of cold water for each person. "This will stop the burning," Jack stated flatly. "If you feel like it, we can have another one at midnight. That's the tradition in the long days of summer."

We sat around and watched the kids play for about a half hour when Gabby tried to get up out of her chair and realized she couldn't. "I'm ready for bed, but I can't make my legs work," she slurred.

Elise and Aria roared with laughter at her comment. "I've had to pee for fifteen minutes," Aria added after she stopped laughing, "but I couldn't get up either!" Everyone burst out in laughter!

"You ass, Jack! I mean, you jackass!" Gabby said, barely able to keep her eyes open. "You knew we would all get smashed on your Duck Farts, didn't you!"

"Duck Farts," Elise repeated with a little chuckle, and everyone cracked up again like they'd just heard the funniest joke in their lives.

Harper raised herself from her chair and slowly staggered over to Aria. Grabbing Aria's arm, she said, "Come on, sweetheart, I'll help you to the bathroom." Her tongue felt so thick she hoped that Aria had understood her muddled words.

As they made their way into the house, Jack stood up and started to move. His equilibrium was obviously also affected. He took one step forward and then quickly had to take two steps sideways to maintain his balance. He tried to take a third step, but there was no more deck available, and he stepped off into thin air by the side of the deck. The only thing keeping him from falling to the ground four feet below was the handrail, which he was able to grab as he fell against it and bounced back onto the deck with a thud.

"Serves you right!" Elise yelled, followed by, "I'm sorry, I didn't mean that! Are you all right?"

Jack pulled himself back to a standing position with the help of the railing and started laughing. His laughs grew so ruckus that he started snorting when he tried to get air back into his lungs, which made the rest of us laugh right along with him.

Finally calming down enough to speak, he said, "Maybe we should all take a nap for a couple of hours and let our drinks wear off."

Jacob and I were in the best shape of the adults, so I added, "That's a good idea. Jacob and I will watch the kids and make them something for dinner while the rest of you sleep a little bit."

"Seems crazy," Jacob added. "But it's already 8:00 p.m. I don't think the kids need to eat again before bed. I think the bright sunlight is screwing with your internal clock, Dad."

"Well, then, we'll get the kids ready for bed in an hour or so," I responded.

There were no objections from anyone as, one by one, they moved into the house and went to their rooms for a nap.

Jack and Harper had thought about the long days of sunshine and had addressed the issue throughout the cabin. Over every window, there were pull-down blackout blinds. Once they were pulled down, they literally turned the room from day into night. The dark rooms made the sleeping so much more normal.

Jacob and I had put all the kids to bed and were sitting out on the deck when Jack came walking out of the cabin. "What time is it?" he asked.

Looking quickly at his watch, Jacob said, "Almost eleven thirty."

"Wow!" he responded. "I slept longer than I thought."

In the next thirty minutes, the rest of the adults came ambling out of the cabin one at a time. No one seemed interested in a beer, but everyone wanted a bottle of water to wet their dry mouths and quench their thirst.

"Well, it's 12:20 in the morning," Jack stated. "Anyone want to go for another Duck Fart yet?"

"I'm never having another one of those!" Elise said.

"They're certainly too strong for me to be interested in a second one," Gabby added.

"I could handle another one," Thomas interjected.

"Me too!" echoed Aria and Jacob.

"It depends," I added. "What did you have in mind for tomorrow?"

"You mean today," Jack corrected. "We're in the second hour of today already."

Looking up at the sun, which was starting to hang low in the sky, I said, "It's funny how much my sense of day and night are so strongly affected by the sun versus the watch on my wrist."

"So what are we going to do today?" I corrected myself.

"I thought it might be fun for the kids if we caught our dinner for tonight," Jack responded. "The lake is full of fish. There's rainbow trout, Dolly Varden, arctic graylings, and lake trout scattered all through Big Lake. I think we could catch enough to feed us all in less than half a day."

"That sounds so fun!" Aria exclaimed. "Can I go with you?"

"Everyone can go if they want!" Jack exclaimed. "We have plenty of gear, and it should be a beautiful day on the lake."

We were all filled with new excitement by the news about the fishing trip. But we knew we needed some more sleep if we wanted to keep up with the kids, who had been sleeping several hours already.

"Come on, Gabby," I said, offering my hand to help her up out of her chair. She accepted my help, and we made our way back into our bedroom, pulled down the blackout blinds, and were sleeping soundly in very short order.

"Hey, you two!" Harper said softly but firmly. "It's time to get up! You can't sleep all day!"

Gabby put her hand up to shade her eyes from the stream of bright sunshine coming through the bedroom door. "What time is it?" she asked timidly.

"It's just a few minutes past noon," Harper answered calmly.

"What!" Gabby yelled, jumping out of bed and looking for her Levi's. "Is everyone else already up?" she asked, a hint of panic in her voice.

"The little ones have been up for about four hours," Harper responded. "Jack made them pancakes and bacon for breakfast. Now they're outside playing, but they want to go boating and catch some fish! Everyone else got up at various times throughout the morning. Aria and Thomas just got up, and they're eating breakfast now. Come into the kitchen when you're ready, and Jack will make some fresh pancakes for both of you."

I'd been lying in bed with my eyes still closed, saying nothing while the two girls talked, but the smell of bacon cooking made me want to get up and get dressed as fast as possible. Suddenly, I was hungrier than I could ever remember being.

Jack had been correct about the lake having an abundance of fish. It was like we were fishing at a fish hatchery. No sooner would someone throw in a line than they would have a fish jumping out of the water with a hook in its mouth.

Everyone who wanted to fish caught at least one fish. The kids and grandkids were giddy with excitement as they reeled in fish after fish and brought them onto the boat.

Ellie caught the largest fish of the day, and Jacob had to help her reel it in because of the size and fight it was giving her. It was a beautiful five-pound Dolly Varden. Ellie was smiling from ear to ear as she held it up next to her, while everyone took pictures of her and her impressive catch.

It was the first time for all the kids cleaning fish. Jack made sure every one of them got blood on their hands and helped clean a fish, even if it was only for a few seconds.

Once the fish were cleaned and ready to cook, we decided to only cook half of them and save the rest for another meal during the week. After grilling the fish on a large outside grill, we took them inside to eat. Everyone loved the meal, and we were all stuffed before we finally gave up trying to finish them all.

Luke got up from the table and walked over to where Jack was sitting on the opposite side and tapped him on the arm. Luke's little belly was so full it protruded like a pregnant woman's.

"What's up, Luke?" Jack asked, looking down at him.

"I've had plenty of fish sticks before," he sang out, "but fish just tastes better when you catch it yourself! I love fishing! And I love you too, Uncle Jack! Thanks for taking us fishing today."

Jack couldn't answer him immediately as we all watched his lower lip start to quiver, and tears began dripping down his cheeks in a steady flow. Gaining a semblance of composure, he responded, "You are one heck of a good fisherman, Luke! And I love you too!"

Luke hugged Jack's arms, and the room was silent for a moment, with the exceptions of a few sniffs and sighs from those gathered around the table. There wasn't one adult that didn't require either a Kleenex or a napkin at the end of their sweet, heartfelt exchange. It was all I could do not to burst into tears as I took in the tender moment.

On July 2, Jack asked all the guys to go to bed early because he had another surprise for us the next day. The next morning at breakfast, he made his announcement.

"Ladies, you will be on your own from noon today until noon tomorrow. I and the other men on the island will be playing in a golf tournament for charity. I have taken care of the fees and have rented clubs for everyone who will be participating. I'll have Harper drop us off on the mainland, so you have the boat and aren't stranded here overnight, in case of an emergency."

"Sounds fun," Thomas said, "but why won't we be back here until tomorrow?"

"I'm glad you asked," Jack responded. "This is a little different than most golf tournaments in that the winning team is the team that plays the most holes in a twenty-hour period. Scores don't matter, just the number of completed holes. For every hole we complete, local vendors will donate ten dollars. That may not sound like much, but last year, we raised over $6,000, and this year we want to beat that!

"There are free drinks and free food throughout the event. You can drink anything from Gatorade to Duck Farts, depending on how serious you are about your golf game! My personal goal is to play seventy-two holes before I'm done. That's four rounds of eighteen holes every five hours."

Looking at everyone quickly, Jack asked, "Are there any questions?" When none came, he turned to Harper and asked, "Do you think you can get along without us for twenty-four hours?"

Harper shook her head from side to side and simply replied, "Please! You guys being gone is like an added vacation for all of us! We'll be just fine, thank you very much!"

"Be ready to leave in thirty minutes!" Jack bellowed as he turned to go back into his bedroom to change clothes.

The first eighteen holes were easy. Thomas, Jacob, and I were all still fresh. Jack was already showing signs of fatigue, and I doubted he would reach his goal of seventy-two holes.

After we finished our first round, we took thirty minutes and went into the clubhouse to have a sit-down lunch. We rested our legs, and everyone drank two or more bottles of water to hydrate themselves for the next round.

We teed off on the second eighteen holes at five fifteen and were pretty much on pace to making Jack's goal a reality. Before we'd left the cabin, Jack had offered each of us some of the smelliest mosquito ointment I'd ever smelled. We all declined, but Jack slathered himself in it.

It was 6:39 p.m., and we'd just finished the fourth hole as we walked through our first swarm of mosquitos. Between the fourth hole and the fifth tee, I must have been bitten by no less than ten mosquitos.

It seemed as if there were hundreds of them buzzing and circling my body as I stood in the tee box readying to tee off. I stepped away from my ball and swung in every direction with my arms flailing, trying to get away from the pest. "God, there's a lot of mosquitos here!" I said loudly in frustration.

When I looked at Thomas and Jacob, they were trying to swat them away as well. Jack, however, was standing with both hands on his driver, and there didn't appear to be a mosquito within ten feet of him.

"The mosquito is the state bird of Alaska," Jack offered up with a smirk on his face. "I offered you guys the best repellent available at the cabin, and there were no takers. If we stay out here all night, I'm going to guess each of you will have between twenty-five and forty-five mosquito bites on you." He chuckled as he relayed his dire message.

"Well, did you bring any of that lotion with you?" Jacob asked.

"I did," Jack responded.

"Unfortunately, there are conditions if you want to use it now," Jack answered.

"What kind of conditions?" Thomas interjected.

"You can use it now, but at the end of the round, you have to drink a Duck Fart as payment for the repellent."

"I'm not doing that!" Thomas said, anger in his tone.

"I will!" Jacob said while still swatting at the air with both hands, trying to ward off the little bloodsuckers.

"Me too!" I echoed. "Just get it out so we can put it on!"

Jack reached in his golf bag and handed Jacob a tube of the concoction he'd brought with him.

Jacob and I immediately started rubbing the ointment on all our exposed skin. Remarkably, the second it was applied, not one mosquito landed on either one of us. But Thomas was still flailing around and being bitten by the persistent pests.

We played one more hole before Thomas finally relented. "Give me the shit, Jack!" he half yelled. "I'll drink your damn Duck Fart!"

Jack smiled and handed him the tube of ointment.

When we finished the round, we again went inside the clubhouse to get something to eat. We needed to rest our tired legs and to get away from the constant loud buzzing of the mosquitos. Even though they weren't biting us, the noise was maddening!

After dinner, and to our surprise, Jack ordered four Duck Farts. The waiter smiled and returned and laid four untouched Duck Fart kits on our table.

"You don't have to drink one," Thomas said to Jack.

"Oh, I was always going to drink one," he responded. "I just hate drinking alone. So thank you, boys, for joining me!"

The alcohol didn't have that much of an effect on any of us until about the fourth hole of our third round. Thomas swung at his ball off the tee and missed it twice before hitting it thirty feet in front of us. We were all cracking up as we watched him make an ass of himself.

When it was Jacob's turn, he couldn't even get the ball to stay on the tee. After several tries, he dropped to his knees and, with both hands, was able to put the ball on the tee. As he got back up to his feet, he inadvertently kicked the ball off the tee as he was staggering to get his club. We were laughing so hard I couldn't breathe.

As we started to calm down and Jacob again dropped to the ground to put his ball on the tee, I heard Jack say, "Well, shit!" under his breath.

"What's wrong?" I asked.

"Well, either one of your ass clowns dumped a warm beer in my lap, or I just peed my pants!"

Thomas and I both were laughing so hard that we dropped and joined Jacob on the ground, rolling around and screeching like out-of-control little girls.

Another group came up to the tee, and we asked them to go ahead and play through because we didn't want to hold them up. The group consisted of four pretty serious golfers, and they looked at us with disdain as they took the tee.

After all four of them had teed off, I said a little too loudly, "Have a great game, guys." They all four looked back at us in disgust.

Jack stared back at them and said, "Bunch of old farts!" Again, the rest of us lost it and were dying laughing as they walked away.

We didn't make seventy-two holes. It was me who'd had enough, and somewhere around eight thirty the next morning, I said, "I'm done! You guys can keep on going, but I'm walking back to the clubhouse and sitting down for a while. My feet and back are killing me!"

"Thank God!" Jack yelled. "I didn't want to be the first to quit! Thank you, Michael. I'm done too!" It was an easy sell to convince Thomas and Jacob that we had played enough golf as we all made our way back to the clubhouse.

We turned in our gear, went into the lounge one last time, and sat at a table by the window where we could watch people coming up the eighteenth fairway to the green.

The server came over and took our order. Everyone ordered something light to eat, and we decided to cap off our golf marathon with mimosas. The effects of the Duck Farts had worn off several hours ago, and we were ready to have "a little hair of the dog" before leaving for the boat ramp.

"Look!" Thomas said. "Those old guys we let play through are coming up the fairway."

We watched as each of them hit on to the green and eventually sank all four putts. They all came together in the center of the green and bumped fists. Then they walked the short distance to the first tee.

"No!" I said loudly. "They can't be looking to play another round! They had to have just completed seventy-two holes!"

The first man teed off followed by the others in the group, and they left the tee area, walking at a pretty respectable pace up the first fairway.

"I bet every one of them is thirty years older than I am," Jacob uttered softly. "I don't know if I could actually play ninety holes of golf at one time, but they're going for it. That is impressive!"

"Are we ready?" Jack asked, getting up. Once he was standing, he let out a low groan. "My legs feel like spaghetti! That's a lot more walking than I'm used to!"

Everyone agreed as we slowly made our way back to Jack's SUV.

We arrived at our pickup point at about 10:00 a.m. "Should we call the girls and have them come pick us up early?" Thomas asked.

"I don't think so," Jack replied. "It's July 4, and everyone is going to be excited for a fireworks show tonight. We could be up late again. I'd suggest we just lie back and get a couple hours of sleep while we can! It's been a long night!"

No one responded verbally, but everyone slid down in their seats, and within minutes, there was light snoring coming from almost everyone.

When we arrived back at the cabin, we realized Jack had been correct. The kids were in hyper mode, running around and yelling like they were possessed by demons. They immediately came running up to us on the boat dock and wanted to start lighting fireworks. Jack simply smiled and said, "Not yet, guys."

All the adults congregated on the deck and took a seat, while the kids played on the flat area in front of us. We told the girls about our golf experience and were interrupted several times by their ruckus laughter as they listened. Then we made plans for our July 4 fireworks extravaganza later in the evening.

Knowing the sun would still be up regardless what time we had our show, we settled on lighting everything at 9:00 p.m. That gave us an hour for fireworks and an hour for the kids to calm down before going to bed at 11:00 p.m. In the meantime, we decided to give the kids sparklers every couple of hours to occupy their time and keep them smiling, while we all went inside to shower and clean up.

The fireworks show went off without a hitch! We took all the fireworks out to the boat dock, and Jack was the official lighter. He arranged his display in the order he wanted and simply walked from one item to the next once the previous item had been sent up into the heavens.

Sometime during the show, he had each one of the kids come down and help him light a special display. You could tell by the smile on their faces how proud they all were to accomplish lighting fireworks. He was so good with them!

When the show was over, we gave him a standing ovation, and he walked back up to the deck to join us, while Jacob and Thomas went down and cleaned up all the used and blown-up paper and debris on the dock. It was a very special Fourth of July for all of us.

Everyone had gone to bed, including Gabby and me, but I couldn't get comfortable and was having an impossible time trying to fall asleep. Not wanting to wake up Gabby with all my tossing and turning, I got out of bed and slipped on a T-shirt and a pair of shorts. As quietly as possible, I snuck out of the bedroom and then quietly continued through the cabin and out the front door onto the deck.

I stopped at one of the ice chests, opened it, and took out a cold beer. Sitting on one of the chairs, I opened my beer and took a long drink. It was between 2:00 a.m. and 3:00 a.m., and the sky was a deep shade of gray. I knew this was about as dark as it would get before the sun was out once again, announcing another new day.

As my eyes adjusted to the lower-than-average light, I spotted three deer at the edge of the clearing. They never moved as all three stood there like statues staring at me. Finally, one lowered her head and began eating from a bush in front of her. Soon, the others followed suit, and after a few minutes, they had made their way into the clearing and were much closer to the deck.

Suddenly, the doe in front raised her head, and her ears went up as she was alerted by a noise coming from down on the boat dock. The other two went on full alert as well, and all three were staring down toward the dock. I couldn't see anything in the direction they were looking, but they sure did. One by one, they turned and silently made their way back into the trees at the edge of the clearing from where they'd appeared.

Curiosity got the best of me, and I slipped on a pair of flip-flops someone had left on the deck and slowly walked off the deck, heading for the boat dock. I was going slow, being as quiet as possible when I arrived at the dock. Stopping and starting, I could make out the shape of someone sitting in a chair at the opposite end of the dock. It had to be one of us, but I couldn't quite make out which one.

As I got closer, Jack got up from his chair and turned to face me. "What are you doing up at this hour?" he asked.

"I could ask you the same question," I responded, continuing to move toward him. When I reached him, he pointed to a second empty chair and sat back down in his chair.

"I like to come out here and just sit sometimes," he said. "This is one of the most peaceful places in all of God's creation!"

I looked past him into the gray night and said, "I couldn't agree more."

Jack turned to face me and said, "Thank you for bringing your family up here to visit, Michael. It really means a lot to me."

"You're welcome," I replied. "Thank you for inviting us. Everyone has had a wonderful time. The only thing we didn't do was take a quick flight in your plane."

Jack laughed and looked at the plane behind us. "I'm afraid we won't be doing that," he stated. "I've been grounded."

"By Harper," I said, smiling back at him.

His face turned serious before he responded. "No, by my doctor." He paused for a long moment before continuing. "I'm dying, Michael."

I felt my breath catch in my throat as the words were uttered. I felt panic, pain, sorrow, and so many other emotions I hadn't expected. I sat there staring, unable to make myself talk or respond to him as my heart began pounding in my chest.

"The cancer's back," Jack said softly. "Can I have a drink of your beer?"

I leaned forward and handed him the can and watched as he drank the remaining liquid from the can.

"Well, you've got to fight it!" I was finally able to say. "When can you start chemotherapy again?"

Jack again smiled at me and said, "Chemotherapy won't work this time. The cancer's spread to my other kidney, my liver, and my pancreas. The oncologist said I have less than a 5 percent chance of surviving more than six months."

I could feel tears welling up and spilling from my eyes. "How is Harper doing with this?" I asked.

He looked at me for a long time before answering. "She doesn't know yet. No one knows except you now. I was hoping we could tell her and Gabby together before you guys go home."

CHAPTER 25

It was about eleven thirty at night as I sat alone in the dark living room, sipping on my second bourbon. Depending on flight arrangements, all the kids and grandkids would be, or were already here, in Newport Beach. Everyone except for me was in bed sleeping, readying for the events of tomorrow.

If tradition held, there would be a family walk on the beach; a friendly flag football game with both grandparents, the kids, and all our grandchildren; followed by a huge turkey dinner with all the trimmings. We would spend the rest of the day snacking, eating desserts, and complaining how full we all were while watching pro football on TV. That was usually followed by half of the clan taking a second walk, while the rest of us took a well-deserved nap.

Tomorrow was Thursday, November 24, 2011, Thanksgiving Day. It would be my sixty-third Thanksgiving. But unlike other Thanksgiving holidays, I wasn't excited about this one. I wasn't even thrilled that our entire immediate family was able to celebrate together for what might be the last time. The kids were pretty much grown now, and each of them had two sets of parents to appease during the holidays. Next year, Gabby and I had resigned ourselves that Thanksgiving would just be the two of us as the annual holiday rotation favored the second set of parents.

I'd had a difficult year, and I was finding it hard to feel thankful for much since last Thanksgiving. I think most of those feelings began with the news on our Fourth of July family vacation that Jack's cancer was back and that he was dying.

Jack and I had talked a minimum of once a week from the time we returned home from vacation through this week. As we remembered better days, I sensed he was getting weaker every time we spoke. His voice had become raspy, and lately, he couldn't finish a sentence without stopping to fill his cancer-filled lungs with a second breath.

When I'd talked with Harper on Monday, she'd let me know he was going downhill quickly now. He lost almost seventy pounds since I'd last seen him just five months ago. Hospice was now coming to their home for four hours every day to help her care for him. They bathed him, changed his bed, and gave him morphine packets, which he slipped under his tongue to help with the pain.

But through it all, Harper remarked that his spirits remained good. He never complained. He'd never gone through the anger stage or the "why me" stage in his dance with death. In fact, she commented tenderly, he says "please" and "thank you" more now than he did before the cancer returned. She said he also smiled and said "I love you" without fail each time she walks into his room.

As I listened, Harper had stopped talking for a moment, and I could hear her softly crying as she told me about the new normal in their lives. I could hear the exhaustion in her voice, but she was staying committed to her marriage vows—"For better or worse, during good times and bad, through sickness and health, for all the days we both shall live." My heart broke for her every time we spoke.

Jack's illness and eventual demise had put me in touch with my own mortality. When I was fighting in the jungles of Vietnam, I seldom thought about dying, even when we were involved in intense firefights with the enemy. But now, as I was entering the winter of my life and watching my best friend die, death was all I could think about.

I constantly wondered how much more time do I have. Will I go in my sleep from a stroke or heart attack, or will I suffer a slow and agonizing death like Jack?

Depression, which I'd never had to deal with in my life, suddenly had a grip on me, and I couldn't seem to shake it. Another irritation was that I didn't like the changes that were happening naturally to my body through the aging process. I was gaining five to ten pounds every year, and deposits of fat were quickly swallowing up what used to be muscle mass. I hated to look at my naked body in the mirror, and even worse, I hated for Gabby to see me naked with all my cellulite exposed and on display. I was only about twenty pounds overweight, but I was almost repulsed by the person staring back at me in the mirror after stepping out of the shower each day.

The other side of that equation was that I had no desire to run a couple of miles every day or go to the gym and work out two or three times a week. I'd been religious about working out up until I hit my midfifties. As I moved up the ladder, I found myself spending more and more hours at the office. I would go in no later than 7:00 a.m. to the office, and I seldom got home before 7:00 p.m. But rather than being out in the field daily, my duties became much more sedentary, and I found myself tied to a computer. I looked at numbers and was on the phone thirty times a day, talking with customers or with my direct reports.

By the end of the day, I just didn't have the desire or the energy to go work out, even though I knew it would benefit both my body and my mental state. So I made up excuses that I disguised as reasons why it was more important to spend what little time off I had with Gabby and Sweetpea.

Those feelings of self-loathing were accompanied by a loss of sexual desire. I found myself feeling less and less interested in having sex. It came to a head one day when Gabby asked me if I no longer felt sexually attracted to her. I explained that it wasn't her but, rather, me. Some of my lack of desire could be blamed on a reduction of testosterone that comes naturally with age, and some of it was attributed to my feelings of inadequacy because of the physical changes that were happening to my body.

She reassured me that she loved my body and still thought I was the most handsome man she'd ever known. I remember smiling and thanking her for her kind words and support, but I certainly didn't agree with her assessment of me.

In the last four months, I could feel myself withdrawing from everything I'd once held so dear. I grew more and more angry. I was angry that Jack was dying. I was angry that Gabby no longer thought I found her desirable. I was angry that none of the kids asked for my advice on major decisions anymore. I was angry that we didn't see more of our grandchildren. They were growing up so fast, and it felt like we were being excluded from participating in their development.

Over the last couple of years, I'd also grown to dislike my job and despise my boss. He was everything I loathed in a supervisor. He was condescending, arrogant, controlling, and more concerned about the stock portfolio than the people who were making our company successful.

After working together for several years now, he seldom asked for any input from me at divisional meetings. He would ask the younger, more eager divisionals what they thought, but seldom did he even look in my direction during roundtable discussions. Several times in the last year, he'd asked me when I was going to retire. He always added, "You've done a great job for the company, but you should think about retiring to enjoy your family while you're still physically able."

The badgering to retire had been a private conversation between him and me originally. However, as time passed, and I gave him no answer, he felt emboldened to repeat the dialogue at our divisional meetings in front of the other divisionals and the management team.

Soon, I stopped getting calls from other divisionals to talk about new ideas or just visit and compare numbers. The CEO had quite effectively isolated me from the rest of the herd, and I knew it would only be a matter of time before I would be forced to leave the company.

But it wasn't just Jack and it wasn't just my job that had put me in such a funk. It was also the world and national events that were driving me crazy. Still being a pretty strong Christian, I often wondered if what was happening around the globe was a sign of the end of times as had been prophesied in the Bible.

There was still more than enough natural disasters to go around. This year alone, a drought in East Africa had created a humanitarian hunger crisis in five African countries. The drought was the most severe these nations had seen in sixty years, creating a worldwide emergency. The rest of the developed countries in the world had to step in with food and aide to stop millions from dying of starvation.

At home in the United States, we endured one of the worst tornado seasons ever recorded. There were 137 reported tornados that killed 300 people in six states; 140 people were killed in one tornado alone as it tore a three-fourth mile path through the center of Joplin Missouri on May 22. The loss of livestock and personal property was staggering.

In August, Hurricane Irene moved up the eastern seaboard of the United States, killing forty-four people in thirteen states; 2.5 million people had to be evacuated to prevent more loss of life. Estimates for damage caused by Irene were well over $7 billion.

On the world stage, there were still wars and threats of wars throughout the globe. The Middle East remained very unstable, and now Syria, backed by Russian troops, was involved in a civil war that would kill over five hundred thousand people before its end.

Britain, France, and Germany released a joint statement that Syria's president, Bashar al-Assad, had lost legitimacy as Syria's leader, and they asked him to step down as Syria's leader. As a full-on genocide became a reality in Syria, President Obama also called for Assad to leave office.

On May 12, U.S. troops and CIA operatives killed Osama Bin-Laden in Abbottabad, Pakistan. He was the leader and mastermind responsible for the September 11, 2001, attack on the World Trade Center buildings in New York City and the Pentagon in Washington DC.

A movement that would become known as the Arab Spring began in Tunisia and moved west into Egypt. Egypt's citizens were protesting chronic unemployment and an increase in police brutality in their country. After a few months of unrest, Hosni Mubarak resigned as the prime minister of Egypt and handed power of the country over to the military.

Libya's interim government announced that former dictator Col. Muammar el-Qaddafi was killed by rebel troops in the town of Surt on October 20. Even after his death, there was fighting between separate Muslim factions trying to gain control of the government.

Fatah and Hamas, two Palestinian factions, united to form the Palestinian Liberation Organization. They dedicated themselves to opposing Israel and taking back Palestine territories they believed to be theirs through any means necessary.

The one good thing that came out of the Middle East this year happened in Saudi Arabia. King Abdullah granted women the right to vote in all elections going forward. In a country with a poor human rights record, this was thought to be a huge step forward for the women of Saudi Arabia.

In a different part of the world, terrorists were also at work. In Norway, terrorists exploded a bomb just outside of the prime minister's office in Oslo, killing eight people and injuring scores of others.

Two hours later, a terrorist gunman disguised as a police officer opened fire at a camp for young political activists on the island of Utoya, Norway, killing sixty-eight young people attending a convention and camping there.

Additionally, I was becoming increasingly concerned with the direction President Obama was taking our country. It appears he was apologizing for America's successes to the other nations of the world in his speeches. He had been in office for three years, and many of his decisions didn't seem to be in the best interests of the United States, but he sold his ideology to Americans like an accomplished "snake oil salesman." More social programs; health care for everyone; more government control; and a weaker, smaller military seemed to be the main pillars of his platform as he readied for a run at a second term.

In one of his speeches, President Obama declared that the border between Israel and Palestine should be the border of the two countries before the Arab-Israeli war back in 1967. Israel was furious with this proposal. It meant that Israel would lose 25 percent of their landmass, and because of the territory they would have to give up, they would no longer be able to defend their nation from attacks by other countries.

President Obama had run a campaign on several issues, and one of them was balancing the budget. He announced a plan to reduce the debt by $400 billion. After a year of haggling with Congress, a budget was finally passed. Unfortunately, the budget that was passed increased the national debt.

During the midterm elections, voters chose against conservative-backed measures and initiatives across the nation. Overall, the country showed strong support for a kinder and more left-leaning Democratic Party and the officials they'd voted into office.

President Obama signed an executive order determining that the Defense of Marriage Act was unconstitutional. This meant that the federal government would now recognize same-sex marriage as it did heterosexual marriage. Same-sex partners would receive the same rights and benefits under the law as their counterparts.

Occupy Wall Street protests erupted in New York City, Boston, Chicago, Los Angeles, San Francisco, Dallas, and Oakland. Thousands turned out to protest corporate greed, social inequities, and the disproportion between the rich and the poor. Hundreds of protestors were arrested when several of the protests turned violent as banks and buildings were vandalized or destroyed.

Arizona representative, Gabby Gifford, was among seventeen people shot by a right-wing radical while attending a constituent meeting outside a local supermarket in Arizona. Six people died as a result of the attack.

Squinting to see the clock above the TV, I realized it was now past midnight, and I thought about going to bed. Tomorrow was going to be a big day with the family.

I got up off the sofa and, with glass in hand, started toward the bedroom. I stopped to put the glass down on the bar but didn't take my hand off it. *Screw it*, I thought to myself. I'm just going to toss and turn for the next two hours before I fall asleep. I might as well have one more.

Grabbing the bottle of bourbon, I poured a pretty hefty shot into the glass and sat the bottle back down. I carefully made my way back to the sofa in the dark. I'd just sat down and taken my first sip from the glass when I heard a noise coming from the hallway. Seconds later, Jacob slowly walked into the dark living room. He was silently making his way through the living room, heading for the kitchen.

"What are you doing up so late?" I asked, a little louder than I had intended to.

He jumped, almost lost his balance, grabbed his chest, and in a whisper-yell shouted, "You scared the crap out of me, Dad! What the hell are you doing sitting here in the dark by yourself?"

"Just having a drink before going to bed," I answered.

"Turn on some light, then!" he responded, reprimanding me with his sharp tone.

"The light switch is on the wall on your left side," I answered. "If you want the lights on, then turn them on."

Jacob turned on the lights and stood there giving me his best angry face but saying nothing.

"Were you looking for something to eat?" I asked.

"Yes!" he snapped. "I was hungry, and I couldn't go to sleep."

"Help yourself to anything in the kitchen," I responded. "With tomorrow being Thanksgiving, the fridge is never going to be stocked any better than it is tonight!"

"Do you want something?" he asked with a calmer voice now.

I simply shook my head no, and he disappeared into the kitchen once the light was turned on.

Walking back into the living room with a large sandwich and a paper towel for a napkin, he plopped himself down beside me and took the first bite. Then saying nothing, he got up and quickly went back to the refrigerator and came back with a beer.

"Are you excited about tomorrow?" Jacob asked between bites of his sandwich.

"I can hardly wait!" I lied.

"Ellie is really excited to be here with her cousins and all you guys! She's been talking about Thanksgiving all month. Frankly, I'm glad it's almost over so we won't have to listen to it anymore!" Jacob snickered.

I laughed lightly with him and watched him finish his sandwich.

Talking a drink of his beer, he said, "You've been thinking about Jack?"

I shook my head affirmingly.

"Me too!" he responded. "He's been a huge part of our lives, and it's really painful to think about him not being around much longer."

"He's one of the best people you will ever meet," I answered. "If you want to pattern your life after someone, I'd suggest you try to be as good a man as Jack has been."

"He's been there for both of us when we needed him, that's for sure!" Jacob said. While still looking at me, he patted me on the shoulder and stood up. "He's lucky to have you as a friend too! I'm going to bed."

Before exiting the room, he stopped turned his head and said, "By the way, Jack is a wonderful human being, but I already have someone to pattern my life after. You're always going to be my hero!" He turned his head back and walked into the darkness of hallway.

I could instantly feel the tears coming. I felt my shoulders moving as I quietly sobbed, sitting there by myself. I cried for a good fifteen minutes before I was able to control my emotions. I hadn't cried like that since the night I sat on the porch with my father and we talked about Jessie and Vietnam.

Thank you, son, I thought to myself. *I needed that.* I needed to feel relevant to someone. I needed to get out of my own head and realize what a great life both Jack and I have lived.

I felt like I'd been in a rainstorm and the sky was black and I was getting soaked, but then the rain stopped and the warm sun came out, and everything looked clean and smelled fresh from the cleansing rain. After Jacob's comment and my cry, that was exactly how I felt.

I got up off the sofa and again headed for the bedroom. This time, I simply put the half-empty glass on top of the bar as I walked by. Tomorrow was going to be a big day, and for the first time this week, I was starting to get excited for Thanksgiving!

"Happy Thanksgiving!" little Matthew yelled as he ran up and wrapped his arms around my legs.

"Happy Thanksgiving to you too, Matthew!" I said, bending over to rub his head and softly pat him on the back.

I'd just entered the kitchen and was heading for a cup of coffee when I'd been ambushed by Matthew. Looking up at Gabby while Matthew was still holding tightly on my legs, I smiled and said, "Happy Thanksgiving, Grandma!"

She returned the greeting and, turning her back to me, poured me a cup of coffee. She handed it to me once Matthew let go, being careful not to burn either of us when she handed me the hot liquid.

Taking a small sip of the coffee to test for temperature, I asked, "How long have you been up?"

She smiled, kissed me on the cheek, and said, "About three hours. But everything is ready for dinner. I think I'll put the turkey in about ten o'clock so we can eat by two or three o'clock this afternoon."

"Sounds great," I responded.

Before I could say anything else, she interjected, "There're sweet rolls, yogurt, granola, juices, and some fresh fruit in the dining room. That's going to have to hold you over until we have our Thanksgiving meal."

"Sounds great!" I answered. "Are the kids up yet?"

"Jacob, Sophie, and Ellie got up right after me," she said. "They've already eaten and left for a morning walk about thirty minutes ago. Elise got up with me and helped get everything ready, and then she went back to bed. I'm watching Matthew, but Luke and Michaela haven't gotten up yet. Jacob took your car and went to the airport to pick up Todd and Aria." Looking over to the clock on the microwave oven, she continued. "They should be back here within the hour."

"Wow!" I said, taking another drink of my coffee. "You've got this day pretty well dialed! I'm impressed!"

She smiled up at me and said, "Now go get something to eat and then keep Matthew company so I can finish up in here." She gave me a kiss on the lips, a light pat on the butt, and turned back toward her kitchen counter and sink.

The day went off without a hitch. No one got hurt during the flag football game. The Thanksgiving dinner was fabulous. Everyone ate and drank their fill. The grandkids played all day, and I don't think I heard crying once from any of them. The Dallas Cowboys won, which made Jacob happy. After dinner, we all sat around in the living room and watched our first Hallmark Christmas movie of the season.

It was almost 10:00 p.m., and only Thomas, Jacob, Todd, and I were still up. The kids and the girls had all gone to bed, hoping to get a good night's sleep and plenty of rest before an early start to shopping on Black Friday!

They'd cut out their coupons, mapped the order of the stores they wanted to shop, and set their alarms to ensure they wouldn't be late and miss out on the best bargains available.

"You guys going shopping with the girls tomorrow?" I asked.

"Of course, we are. We don't have a choice," Jacob responded. "We are the chauffeurs, babysitters, and the packhorses tomorrow." Everyone lightly laughed but knew he was telling the truth.

"What time are you leaving?" I asked.

"Mom said breakfast is at 5:00, and we're leaving by 6:00 a.m.," Thomas answered.

"You boys better get to bed!" I said. "It sounds like you've got a big day ahead of you!"

"I suppose you're right," Thomas echoed. We all said our good nights and retired to our respective bedrooms.

The phone rang, waking me up the next morning. Glancing at the clock, I saw it was almost 9:00 a.m. I picked up the phone, wondering if something had gone wrong on the shopping trip, and said, "Hello."

"Hi, Michael, it's Harper."

"Hi, Harper, is everything OK?" I responded.

"Yeah!" she assured me. "Everything is OK. I just wanted to see how your Thanksgiving with the family went."

I pulled myself up into a sitting position in bed and answered, "It was a good day! Weather was nice, Gabby cooked a killer meal, and we even got a walk in on the beach!"

"Sounds like a pretty spectacular day to me!" Harper responded.

"How about you guys?" I asked.

"It was a good day," she said, not selling me with a lot of conviction. "Jack doesn't like turkey very much, so he asked if we could cook him a big rib eye steak for Thanksgiving. So we did."

"I'll bet he loved that!" I exclaimed.

"He said he liked it," she answered, "even though he only took two bites."

I didn't know how to respond, so I asked, "What about the rest of you? Did everyone eat steak?"

"No." She chuckled. "Jack's sister and mom made a traditional Thanksgiving dinner for the rest of us. Besides the three of us, the pastor and his wife from our church and Jack's hospice nurse all joined us for dinner. It was really nice to have a houseful of people for a change."

After a few seconds of silence, Harper said, "Listen, Michael, I think Jack is done fighting this battle."

"Should I come up there?" I asked.

"No! No, I don't want you to do that," she answered. "I know Jack doesn't want you to see him this way, and besides, you'll be too late."

"What do you mean?" I asked, not understanding.

"The reason for my call was to let you talk to Jack one last time," she responded, her voice breaking as she spoke. "Jack asked me to call you so he could talk with you, but only you. He doesn't want to speak to Gabby or Jacob. He thinks that would be too difficult."

We were both silent for a moment while I tried to process our conversation.

Finally, Harper said, "Jack had me invite the people who mean the most to him in Alaska here for Thanksgiving dinner yesterday. We ate, prayed, laughed, and said our good-byes before they left. Tonight, he wants me to fix him a peanut butter and grape jelly sandwich and serve it with two diet Cokes for dinner. His last dinner."

"You can't let him do that!" I yelled into the phone.

"Yes, I can!" she answered. "He's suffered enough. He has a full bottle of morphine packets, so he can self-medicate. He puts one under his tongue when the pain is too severe. By putting a few of those packets under his tongue while he drinks his diet Cokes, he will simply go to sleep and peacefully slip away. His mom, sister, and I will all be with him tonight. Those are his wishes, and I'm going to follow his wishes."

I had such a lump in my throat that I couldn't speak right away. After a moment, I asked, "What about a funeral?"

"He doesn't want a funeral," she answered. "He wants to be cremated and have his ashes scattered in Big Lake by our cabin."

"That actually sounds pretty cool," I responded before going silent again for a short time. "Can I talk to him now?" I asked.

"Yes, you can," she answered. "I'll call you tomorrow after everything is done. I'm walking into the bedroom now. OK, Michael, here's Jack," she said.

"Hey, little buddy!" Jack slurred into the phone. "What's happening down there?"

"Nothing new," I responded. "Just spending the holiday weekend with the family."

"That's nice," Jack replied. "Did Jacob bring his girlfriend with him?"

I instantly knew he was only half there by the question. Just five short months ago, he'd taken pictures and taught Ellie, Jacob's daughter, how to catch and clean a fish.

"Jacob actually married Sophie, and they have a little girl now," I said.

"No way!" Jack stated. "He's not old enough to be getting married! He needs to finish college first!"

"He did finish college," I answered. "He has his own business now."

"Wow!" Jack exclaimed. "I always knew that kid was going to end up on top of the world." He was quiet for a second before adding, "He's out of college? Damn, time passes faster every day, doesn't it?"

"It does," I answered. "How are you doing?"

"You know, Michael, I'm pretty damn good!" he responded. "I've lived a really good life. I met a wonderful girl who was crazy enough to love me and marry me. And I was blessed to meet my best friend at Fresno State."

I stayed silent, so he continued. "That's you, you dork!"

I faked a laugh and replied, "Oh! Well, you're my best friend too!"

"Yeah, I know," he said confidently. "We've had some great times together, Michael. You've always been there for me, and I've always been there for you. Do you remember kissing that girl at the Fresno State/Boise game? You were really going for it!" Jack started laughing, which turned into a horrible-sounding cough as he tried to breathe again.

"I remember," I answered. "Jack, is there anything I can do for you now?"

"No, not really," he said. "I think everything is taken care of. Maybe you could check in on Harper occasionally to see how she's doing."

"That goes without saying!" I responded. "We'll definitely keep in touch with her."

"Don't be mad if she hooks up with some other dude!" Jack said with a thick tongue. "She's still young, and I want her to find someone else. Life isn't meant to be lived alone!"

"You remember that cruise we went on?" Jack asked out of nowhere.

"Of course, I do," I answered.

"What was your favorite part of the cruise?" Jack asked.

"That's easy to answer," I said. "Meeting Gabby and falling in love with her. What about you?"

Jack thought for a moment before answering. "Really, my favorite part wasn't on the cruise—it was before the cruise. You remember that night when you invited Jacob and me to the Parma Restaurant in Fresno, and you asked me to go on the cruise with the two of you?"

I simply replied, "Yeah, I remember."

"Michael, nobody had ever done something that nice for me before in my life!" Jack shared. "You didn't want anything in return. You just picked up the tab like you were loaded, and I know you weren't." Jack stopped talking for a second and went into a coughing fit that lasted a couple of minutes.

When he was done, he said, "Anyway, that's when I knew we would be brothers for life. I love you and Jacob like you are my own blood. Except for Harper, you two are the best things that ever happened to me!" Jack started crying softly, but it quickly turned into another coughing fit.

I was crying too, but when he stopped coughing and was breathing seminormal again, I responded to him. "Jack, I love you, brother! Save a place for me on the other side, and I'll see you there soon enough. We all love you and respect you! Safe travels, my friend. Next time we talk, I hope it's in heaven."

"I hope so too!" Jack answered. "But you may want to clean up a few things if you want to get past St. Peter and through the pearly gates, buddy!" He laughed and then was coughing again. When he was able to talk again, he continued. "Love you, buddy! Now hang up and let me die in peace, you schmuck!"

"I love you too, Jack," I responded and disconnected the call.

I sat there for a few minutes, just thinking about our conversation. Finally, I got out of bed, hastily made it, and put on a T-shirt, shorts, and a pair of tennis shoes.

I stopped in the kitchen, put some grapes in my mouth, and looked through the drawers until I found a paper and pen. I wrote a short note for Gabby, telling her I'd gone for a walk but that I'd be home soon. I signed it "Love, Grandpa" and grabbed a muffin and a bottle of water, and in the next instant, I was out the front door.

Harper called me at about nine o'clock the next morning as she'd promised. Everything had gone as planned, and she sounded a little relieved that it was over. I asked her one last time if I could do anything to help, and again, she responded, "No, thank you." We said our good-byes and hung up.

I decided to keep Jack's passing to myself for the time being. I didn't want to ruin what had been a great Thanksgiving weekend by giving everyone the news today. I decided I would tell Gabby on Sunday night after everyone had left to go home. I would probably call Jacob when he got home Sunday night as well to give him the news. Gabby could have a conversation with the other kids on Monday to convey the news.

On Sunday night, after everyone had left for their own homes, I sat down on the sofa and flipped the news on the TV. Gabby came over and slumped on the sofa next to me and asked if I would give her a foot rub.

"My feet are killing me after a full weekend of kids, grandkids, cooking, and shopping," she said, laying her head on the arm of the sofa and putting her feet in my lap.

I simply smiled and started softly rubbing her feet. "You definitely deserve this!" I said. "Did you enjoy the weekend?"

She lay there with her eyes closed and a little smile on her face as she responded, "I had a really good holiday!" she answered. "But right now, this is the best part of the weekend. That feels heavenly! Don't stop until I fall asleep!"

Again, I smiled down at her completely relaxed body. "Harper called me yesterday," I said nonchalantly.

Gabby's eyes popped open as she asked, "Why didn't you say anything?" Before I could answer her question, she hit me with a follow-up. "Is everything OK? Is Jack having more issues?"

"No, not really," I responded. "Jack passed away yesterday."

Gabby shot up to a sitting position and yelled, "What! And you didn't tell me?"

"I didn't," I said calmly. "I didn't want to ruin everyone's weekend, so I decided to wait until tonight to say anything." I could see the anger in her eyes as she stared at me without saying anything. I believed she was trying to process my logic before going postal on me.

Finally, tears started streaming down her face, and then she began crying in earnest. She moved toward me, and I pulled her to my chest and let her cry as I gently rubbed her back. After a couple of minutes, she rose to her feet, went and got a tissue, and blew her nose. Then she dejectedly plopped back down on the sofa beside me.

"Poor Harper!" she said in a low voice. "She must be heartbroken! Do you think I should call her or wait a few days and let her grieve first?"

"I think it would be better if you let her have some time to herself right now," I answered. "Jack's mom and sister are up there, and they've got lots of things to get settled in the next couple of days. I'm sure she knows you're thinking about her."

"What happened?" Gabby asked.

Finding no reason to tell her the truth, I simply responded, "He went to sleep on Friday night and died in his sleep. Harper had prepared herself. She knew the end was near."

"When are you going to tell Jacob?" she asked and then added, "He's going to be crushed!"

"I'm going to call him tonight," I responded. "I wanted to tell you first and then call Jacob. I would appreciate it if you would talk with Aria and Thomas tomorrow for me. It won't be as big of a deal for them as they didn't know him as well as Jacob."

"OK," she said, wiping the remaining tears from her now red face. "You'd better call Jacob now."

"I will," I said, picking up my cell phone off the coffee table in front of us.

I called my boss first thing Monday morning and was surprised that he was already in the office at 7:00 a.m.

"Good morning," Shawn said, picking up his phone.

"Good morning," I responded in kind. "How was your Thanksgiving?"

"Same crap, different year," he said insolently. "I ran Friday, Saturday, and Sunday to make up for eating too much Thursday. I'm training for the marathon in Spain on the twelfth of December."

"Impressive," I commented.

"Thank you," Shawn responded. "It will be my fourth marathon this year. That's a record number of races for me in one year."

I'm sure he was waiting for me to react to his accomplishment with reverence and awe, but that wasn't exactly what I was passing out today. "That's a lot of time off work!" I said. "Do you take a weeks' vacation for each marathon?"

"If it's a race outside the country, I usually take a week with the travel and all. But it's just a Friday and a Monday off if the race is anywhere in the States," he responded. "A day to get there, two days for the race, and a day to get home."

It was peculiar to me that we were having a respectable conversation. I realized it was because we were talking about him and his passion, but nevertheless, we hadn't talked this long on personal stuff since he'd been here.

"Do your wife and family join you when you go to these races?" I asked.

"Sometimes, maybe 50 percent of the time," he answered.

"I can understand that," I replied. "After watching more than two times, I would imagine they'd get bored traveling and just watching you start the race and then waiting for you to finish seven hours later."

"It's never seven hours later!" he said sharply. "Five hours and twenty-two minutes is my average time," he said.

"Good for you!" I said dismissively. "Listen, the reason for my call was to let you know that I've decided to retire at the end of the year."

"Really?" he replied and, after a few seconds, continued. "Few things surprise me, but I certainly wasn't expecting that!"

"I've decided to take your advice and start spending more time with my family," I said. "Who knows, I might start training to run a marathon in my spare time!"

He made no reply at my snide comment, so I continued. "I decided over Thanksgiving that it's time for me to step down. You need some younger blood in here that is more subservient to your points of view."

"What do you mean by that?" he asked sarcastically.

"I don't mean anything by it," I stated. "I'm just the last of the old guard divisionals who would question your ideas or business decisions. The rest are already gone. They either were fired or resigned. This is your company now, and the people you've put in place won't disagree with any decision you make, whether they know it's correct. They will, as you so eloquently say all the time, 'stack hands' on whatever edict you decree."

"That's bullshit, and you know it!" Shawn yelled into the phone. "I'm glad to except your resignation! You've been a whiny thorn in my ass ever since I arrived. You have always questioned my abilities, and you've fought me on every decision I've made!"

"I guess it's probably because I wasn't a marine," I answered. "In the army, they taught us to think and not blindly follow. I learned that lesson well, so I've always questioned poor decisions."

"You pompous ass!" Shawn spat out. "I should fire you right now!"

"You can't fire me!" I said loudly. "But if you'd like, I can make my retirement effective today."

"I don't have anyone to replace you with at the moment, so you can stay through the end of the year," Shawn said, a little calmer now that I'd called his bluff. "Whom do you have to replace yourself?"

"No one," I replied calmly. "You used both of my bench divisionals for the last two divisional assignments in other parts of the country. Doesn't someone else have a bench divisional in training?"

"I don't think so," he responded sheepishly.

This was a huge problem, but secretly, I was laughing to myself on the inside. I just kept thinking, *You should retire! You should retire! No! Don't retire. I don't have anyone to replace you!* It was a classic case of the 7 P's—proper prior planning prevents piss-poor performances! This day was getting better and better!

"How about you stay through the end of January, so we can fast-track one of our highest-performing regionals to take your place?" he asked.

I knew it was killing him to ask, but I decided I was going to leave with the upper hand after seven years of taking his crap! "I'd like to, but Gabby and I have already made plans for a trip in January. My last working day will be December 23, because I'm taking the rest of the month off to use up my vacation time before I leave. Sorry!"

He said nothing, but I could almost feel the heat radiating through the phone as his anger intensified.

"I'll contact HR as soon as we hang up and get the paperwork started," I said calmly. Still no response, so I pressed him. "Do we need to go over anything else?"

"No!" he answered sharply. "I'll talk to you on the divisional conference call on Wednesday, unless something comes up before then." Not waiting for a response, he disconnected the call, and the line went dead.

"Hello, Daddy!" Sweetpea said loudly as soon as I walked through the front door.

"Hello, Sweetpea!" I answered back. "How was your day?"

Gabby came walking out of the kitchen, drying her hands on a towel, and said, "Hi! You're home early for a Monday after a holiday weekend! I didn't expect you until seven o'clock or later. What time is it anyway?"

Looking at the clock above the TV, I responded, "About ten minutes after four, if the clock is correct."

"I haven't even started dinner yet. Do you want a snack, because it's going to be at least two, if not three, hours before we eat dinner?" she asked. She had closed the space between us and raised her face to kiss me before I could answer.

After the kiss, Sweetpea flew over onto my shoulder and made her own kissing sound. We both smiled, and Gabby said, "Do you want a kiss too, Sweetpea?" She puckered up and stood on her tiptoes, and Sweetpea bent her head down to meet Gabby's. Once Gabby's lips touched Sweetpea's beak, the cute little cockatoo made the kissing noise again. We both smiled as Gabby pulled away.

"I'm not hungry," I responded. "But we could have a drink, and then I'd be happy to help you make dinner, if there's anything I can do."

Gabby turned and started for the bar. "Crown Royal on the rocks?" she asked as she walked away.

"Perfect!" I answered.

I took a seat on the sofa, and after fixing us both a drink, Gabby came over and took a seat next to me. Handing me my drink, she asked, "What should we drink to?"

I thought for a minute before raising my glass and saying, "Here's to retirement!"

She touched my glass with hers and responded, "To retirement!" We both took our first sip of our drinks. As we sat there in silence for a moment, letting the warm liquid hit bottom in our stomachs, Gabby asked, "When do you really think you'll retire?"

I looked at her and smiled. "I think my last day of work will probably be December 23, 2011."

Her smile disappeared, and her face went white. "You're not being serious, are you?" she asked, shock completely overtaking her now.

"I'm serious," I replied calmly. "I gave Shawn my notice this morning."

Gabby raised her glass to her lips and, in two gulps, drained its contents. "Can we afford for you to retire now?" she asked, a note of panic in her voice.

"I think so," I responded. "It depends an awful lot on what happens in the stock market, how long we live, and if either of us develops any serious health issues in our old age. But I'm pretty comfortable that we'll be OK."

"Did something bad happen at work today?" she asked.

"No. It's really a combination of things. Jack's death helped me reevaluate my priorities. None of us know when our time is up on this earth, and I want to spend the last few years of my life with the people I love.

"I want to spend more time with you holding hands while we take walks together. I want to see the kids and grandkids more. I want to go to dance recitals and little league baseball games. I also want to move back to the northwest so we can be closer to most of our family. Besides, it's too damn expensive to live here."

Gabby sat there in a daze as she listened to me. "So it doesn't have anything to do with work?"

"Well, maybe a little," I answered. "I don't really want to work for my horse's ass of a boss any longer either!"

Gabby laughed, got up, refilled her glass at the bar, and walked back to the sofa. Raising her glass in my direction, she said, "I'm so excited! Here's to retirement!" We bumped glasses and both took a drink.

CHAPTER 26

It was Wednesday, January 3, 2012, my third day of retirement, and I was already going nuts! Monday, January 1, seemed like a normal first day of the year. I watched college football bowl games well into the evening until my eyes crossed, just like I had for the past forty-five years.

Then it was Tuesday, January 2, and I woke up at 6:00 a.m. and, as was my habit, went into the bathroom and turned on the shower. I had taken out my electric razor and made one pass over my face as I concentrated closely on the guy in the mirror before I realized there was no need to be doing this.

I shut off my razor and put it down and then walked over and shut off the shower. I was gripped by competing emotions as I stared at myself in the reflective glass. The realization that I didn't have to deal with Shawn, upset customers, or employee issues any longer had me feeling ecstatic. But those feelings were offset by a sense of loss and thoughts of, what do I do with myself now?

I'd really done it! I had retired! I no longer had a job to go to every day. I officially had no source of income to rely on any longer. These revelations were accompanied by such a sense of finality that it felt uncomfortable and, quite frankly, a little scary.

Self-doubt kept creeping back into my subconscious. Had I made the right decision? Did we have enough money to live out our lives comfortably? How would Gabby deal with me being home all day versus seeing me a limited amount of time in the morning and evening most weekdays?

I went back to bed and stayed there until Gabby was awake. I got up with her and, for the most part, just tried to stay out of her way and observe what she did on a typical Tuesday. We didn't really talk much, but I was making mental notes of the order of her routines and when she did certain chores.

And now it was Wednesday morning, and as hard as I tried, I just couldn't sleep in. I tossed and turned until I finally woke up Gabby.

"What time is it?" she asked, sounding rather annoyed.

"It's about five o'clock," I answered.

"Do you think you could stop tossing and turning so we could both get some sleep?" she asked with a touch of irritation in her voice.

"I'm sorry, sweetheart," I replied as I turned away from her and tried to lie still. Ten minutes later, I got up and went out into the living room with my pillow in tow. I put the pillow on the arm of the sofa and laid my head down on it. I adjusted the pillow and tried closing my eyes again. I still couldn't fall asleep, but at least I could toss and turn to my heart's content here on the sofa without bothering anyone else.

I must have finally gone to sleep because I was awakened by the sound of the morning newspaper hitting our front door with a loud thud. The noise startled me, and I jumped awake after hearing the obnoxious sound. Looking at the clock through blurry eyes, I finally focused to see it was almost 8:00 a.m. I sat up, rubbed my hands over my face, and realized I still felt tired. I lay back down and started to think about what I wanted to do today.

Looking for my laptop computer on the coffee table, I again verified it wasn't there. This new life I'd chosen for myself wasn't a dream; it was my new reality.

I looked back at the coffee table again, only this time wishing the laptop was waiting for me. If it were, I'd check the move-in figures from yesterday and see how we were doing with collecting rents so far this month. Then I'd scan through the one hundred or so e-mails that had come in since I last viewed my computer screen and prioritize the order I needed to follow up on each of them.

Then I would get dressed, grab a cup of coffee and get something to eat, and off I'd go, heading to the office. The office would be bustling with people already, everyone planning out their day, or maybe even their week's activities before heading to their field locations.

But there was no laptop lying on the coffee table. There were no e-mails for me to respond to. There was only silence and solitude as I lay there staring at the coffee table and listening to the clock tick one second off at a time.

When Gabby got up, I had a hearty breakfast prepared for her. I'd gotten Sweetpea up prior to making breakfast and fed her. She'd been patiently sitting on her perch in the kitchen as I talked to her while making breakfast.

As Gabby sleepily entered the kitchen, I handed her the cup of coffee I'd poured for her when I'd first heard her moving around in the bedroom. I smiled and said, "Good morning!"

She responded in kind and then, looking at the breakfast on the kitchen table, asked, "What is all this?"

"I made breakfast for you!" I said excitedly.

She didn't smile but responded, "Sweetheart, thank you, but I don't normally eat breakfast, especially a huge one like this, except maybe on the weekends with you. If I ate like this every morning, I'd be as big as a cow."

She finally smiled at me, walked over and kissed me on the cheek, and continued. "This is so sweet of you, but please don't do this again. It's just a waste of food."

My smile faded, and I felt like I'd been sucker punched by the person I trusted most in the world. Delight turned to hurt, and I responded sharply, "OK, I'm sorry. I was just trying to be nice! I won't do it again!"

"Oh, don't be angry," she said. "I don't want to start our day like that! We just must establish some ground rules. Having you home all the time is going to take some getting used to and a lot of compromise by both of us if this is going to work. It's not just you but both of our routines have been interrupted by your retirement.

It's going to take a little time to understand each other and respect the other person's space and personal habits."

I smiled back at her and responded, "Of course, you're right! I just feel like a fish out of water! I don't know what to do with myself!"

She wrapped her arms around me and laid her head on my chest. "Well, the first thing you should do is sit down and help me eat this delicious-looking breakfast! It smells wonderful!"

After breakfast, I decided that I needed to get out of the house for a while. I didn't want to be underfoot as she tried to accomplish her normal Wednesday routine. Not knowing what that routine consisted of, I just wanted her to have some space and a little time to herself.

"I think I'm going to dust off my golf clubs and go to the driving range for a while," I said, trying to sound excited about the experience.

"That sounds fun!" Gabby commented. Getting up from the breakfast table, she continued. "You go ahead, I'll clean up here. When do you think you'll be home?"

"When do you want me home?" I asked.

"That's up to you, sweetheart," she answered. "I just want to know if I should have lunch ready for you at a specific time."

"Don't worry about fixing me lunch," I said. "I can take care of myself for lunch, and if I'm home, I can fix it for myself." Deciding that I needed to more clearly answer her question, I said, "I should be back by three or four o'clock this afternoon." Then smiling at her, I added, "Don't worry about you being home if you have something to do because I have a key."

Giving me a mischievous smile, she rose from table and responded, "Get out of here and go have some fun!" Then she walked around the table, kissed me, and started clearing off breakfast dishes.

As I was driving to the golf course, I wondered how long it had been since I'd even swung a golf club. Three years? Four years? Maybe longer? I saw a Starbucks ahead and decided to stop and have one more cup of coffee before I went to the golf course.

After ordering and receiving my coffee, I sat on one of the stools at the counter and slowly sipped my drink. Looking around the boutique coffee shop, I saw so many things that were familiar to me and a large part of my life just days ago.

People were on laptops doing who knows what with serious expressions on their faces. A man dressed in a nice suit was sitting at a table alone, obviously waiting for someone else. He kept adjusting his tie, ensuring it looked perfect, as he constantly stared at the front door.

A few minutes later, two men came into the coffee shop, and one of them walked over to his table, a big smile on his face. The other man went to the counter and ordered two coffees. The seated man rose to his feet, and the two men shook each other's hands. The man who'd been sitting at the table by himself handed a small folder to his new guest with what I assumed was probably a resume.

When the third man joined them, and after more introductions, they all talked and laughed for several minutes. Handing another folder to the second man, they began their interview.

I didn't try to listen to their conversation. Quite frankly, I didn't care one way or the other how the interview went. But I could recount doing that very same thing a hundred times in the past fifteen years. Lives would be affected one way or another based on this one conversation. For all of them, this was a critical moment in time.

I again felt a sense of the loss of self-esteem as I realized that, for me, this was just a stop at a coffee shop by an unemployed retiree who had nothing better to do today. Finishing my coffee, I stood up and exited the establishment and continued my trip to the driving range.

Once I arrived and changed into my seldom-worn golf shoes, I made my way into the office and paid for a large bucket of balls. There weren't that many people hitting balls as I approached the range—several women of different ages and two men who appeared to be older than me. I picked the perfect mat next to one of the men and far enough away from any of the female golfers to not embarrass myself. I couldn't see any sense in being outdriven by someone of the opposite, and supposedly, weaker sex.

I took a minute or two and stretched, hoping I wouldn't hurt myself since I hadn't done anything physical like this for an extended period. Placing my first ball on the tee, I took a slow practice swing and readied myself for the real thing.

I stood over the ball and mentally prepared to strike it. *Relax, breath, swing slow, and keep your head down*, I told myself. Pulling the club back and then slowly launching it forward, I watched as the first golf ball I'd hit in years took a straight and true flight, landing at the 250-yard marker.

The golfer standing next to me watched the ball flight with as much interest as my own. Once the ball stopped rolling, he simply said, "Nice ball!" not bothering to turn and look at me as he spoke.

I was elated! Nothing in my body hurt after the swing, and I'd hit the ball much better than I remembered when I was playing regularly! *I'm going to be playing a lot of golf*, I thought to myself.

Placing the second ball on the tee, I readied for my next shot. Just like the first, the ball went perfectly straight, just a few yards short of the first ball. *I need a little more power in my swing if I want to hit the ball further*, I thought to myself.

The third shot veered severely left, and the fourth an equal distance off center, only this time to the right. With each successive swing, it seemed as if I was getting worse at hitting the ball where I wanted it to go.

About halfway through the bucket of balls, I became aware that I was giving voice to my frustration. After hitting another poor shot, I caught myself saying, "Damn it! Slow down and stop trying to kill the ball, you idiot!"

Hearing my words, the golfer hitting balls next to me chimed in with a coaching tip. "I used to have that same problem," he stated.

"I finally figured out that it's not about the speed of the swing—it's about the tempo of the swing."

Having not solicited his advice, I simply looked up at him and remained silent. Placing another ball on the tee, I readied to hit it slower and with less force than the preceding shot. But because in my brain "far" meant "hard," I swung so hard that I missed the ball completely. The rush of air passing by the ball as the club missed it caused the ball to fall off the tee. I immediately looked over to see if the guy next to me had been watching. He quickly turned his head back and looked down at his own ball in front of him.

Shit! I thought to myself. *I must look like the worst golfer in history!* I didn't know if I wanted to bend down and put the ball back on the tee or just put my club back in the bag and leave without uttering so much as a good-bye.

While I struggled with my choices, the gentleman next to me turned completely around and faced me. Putting both hands on the club he held in front of him, he said, "Well, if you would have hit that ball, it would have ended up in China!" Then a smile crossed his face, and he continued. "Do you always swing that hard?"

I laughed nervously, partly out of embarrassment and partly because I knew he was spot-on. I'd felt a sharp pain in my lower back when I'd almost swung out of my shoes a moment ago.

He continued to smile at me and introduced himself. "I'm Scott, Scott Pruitt. What's your name?"

"Michael Larsen," I answered, putting my hand out to shake his.

He took my hand and shook it. "Michael," he said, still smiling, "I don't usually give advice, because I'm definitely not a pro and I don't like people telling me what's wrong with my golf game or my chipping or my putting. But I feel obligated to tell you that if you keep swinging that hard on every shot, there's about a 90 percent chance that you're going to break your fucking back!"

I found his delivery of the comment to be hilarious and immediately cracked up in a sincere laugh. I laughed for two full minutes. I laughed until my sides and stomach hurt from laughing. Finally, I calmed down enough to respond to him. "This is the first time I've swung a golf club in four years,"—and then I started laughing again—"in case you were wondering."

He watched me like he was watching someone who was losing their mind. "So why did you decide today was the day you were going to take up golf again?"

I decided to be honest with him. "I retired three days ago, and quite frankly, I don't know what to do with myself, so I thought I'd come to the range and try hitting a few balls."

"Well, you've got a good swing. The first few balls looked really good." Slowly smiling again, he continued. "But then you started swinging like someone was shoving a Taser up your ass! What the hell happened?"

Again, I broke out in a heartfelt laughing spree. I laughed until I had tears running down my face, and then I laughed some more. "I decided I wanted to hit the ball a little further, so I started swinging faster," I answered, trying not to go into another laughing fit.

"If you haven't played in four years, you probably need to work on your basics again before you try killing the ball with every swing. Would you like me to give you some pointers since neither one of us has any place special to be right now?"

"Thank you, Scott, that would be really helpful," I replied. "But I don't want to hit too many more balls today because I'm afraid I may have already hurt my back."

We both chuckled, and he spent the next hour helping me with my swing, tempo, and club head speed. By the time my arms and back were just about cooked for the day, I was hitting the ball consistently straight and reasonably long. I thanked him, and we exchanged contact information and agreed to meet here a week from today to practice again and maybe have lunch together at the clubhouse.

As I drove away from the golf course, I realized I'd made a new friend today, and I hadn't laughed like that for some time. Maybe retirement wasn't so bad after all.

My cell phone rang, and I answered it. It was a vendor wanting to know about payment on an invoice that was owed by American Trust Storage. I explained to him that I had retired from the company and gave him the corporate office's number, asking him to check with them. He thanked me, wished me a good retirement, and hung up.

I wondered how many more calls like that I would have to deal with in the coming months. How many vendors, recruiters, alarm system controllers, and municipalities had my direct cell number? I had no idea how many, but I knew it was a bunch.

The day was gorgeous as I drove north on the 101 freeway along the coastline. I stopped in Huntington Beach to grab a burger and take a walk on the almost deserted beach. After buying a burger and a drink, I took them and went to the farthest picnic table I could find and sat down to enjoy my lunch. I listened to the waves crashing onto the beach and watched the pristine blue water running up the sand, almost to my feet, before retreating into the ocean.

After I'd finished my lunch, I leaned back against the picnic bench, closed my eyes, and simply enjoyed the gentle breeze coming off the ocean. Seagulls screeching both close and in the distance were the only reason I didn't fall into a deep sleep. I felt so content just sitting there with the warm sun splashing down on my face.

"Hey, man" came a deep voice that startled me out of my utopian world. Quickly opening my eyes, I saw a tall, shaggy-haired, skinny man dressed basically in rags. "Can you spare any change, buddy?"

I looked both up and down the beach and realized there wasn't anyone else within five hundred yards of the two of us. Looking back at the man, I asked, "Are you hungry?"

"Yeah, a little," he said sheepishly.

"Why don't we walk over to that burger joint," I said, pointing to where I'd gotten my lunch, "and I'll buy you anything you want to eat?"

He looked at the small food stand and then back at me and said, "Naw, that's all right. I'll get something to eat later. I'll just take the money if you don't mind."

"Were you in the service?" I asked.

"Army," he responded.

"Did you go overseas?" I asked again.

"Two tours in Afghanistan," he responded.

"Is that where you got hooked on drugs?" I asked.

He shot me a look of disdain and said, "No. I got shot in Afghanistan serving my country. I got hooked on drugs in the hospital in Germany while I was recovering from the wounds, pain meds to start with and then street drugs once I got home and after I was discharged."

"Did you go to the VA and ask for help?" I asked.

"I went one time, but they couldn't see me for thirty days," he responded. "I never went back. I couldn't remember when my appointment was, so I just said, screw it!"

"Do you have any family?" I quizzed.

"Yeah, my family all live in New Jersey," he answered. "But we don't talk. They've pretty much disowned me."

"I was in the army too, at a different time, but the drug issues were the same then as they are now. Can I take you to the VA hospital and see if we can get you into a drug rehab program?" I asked.

"Naw!" he responded quickly. "I just want to live my life now." Looking back into my eyes, he asked, "So are you going to give me any money or not?"

I reached into my pocket and came out with a twenty-dollar bill. I held it out to the stranger and said, "I hope you get something to eat later. Don't forget to drink water or you'll get dehydrated out here."

He reached over with his dirty right hand and took the twenty dollars from me. Quickly stuffing it into his Levi's pocket, he turned away and started back down the beach. "Thanks, man," he said over his shoulder as he was walking away. "You're a good person."

"So are you, son!" I yelled back. "Thank you for your service!"

I watched him walk up the beach for several minutes, and then he turned up toward the highway and was gone. I wondered how many more like him were living out here in warm, sunny California—soldiers who had served and defended their country, only to be thrown out like trash once they got back home. It was tragic, and there wasn't anything I could do about it, I thought dejectedly.

Eventually, I walked back to my car and started for home. I couldn't stop thinking about the homeless man. What could I have done differently? How could I get him some much-needed help?

My cell phone rang, interrupting my thought process. "Hello," I said, answering the call.

"Good afternoon, Mr. Larsen" came the voice on the phone. "This is Jim Williams from the City of Pomona Sign Permitting Department. After an internal audit, it appears your permit for the sign on your property on Ninety-Second Avenue has been expired for some time now. I just wanted to give you a heads-up that you will be receiving a bill from us with a couple of years of back charges in the next few days. I would appreciate it if you would expedite the payment to avoid any further late fees."

"I'm sorry, but I no longer work for American Trust Storage," I answered calmly. "Let me give you the corporate number so you can give this information to the right people." I started to give him the phone number when he interrupted me.

"Couldn't you just pass this message along to the correct parties?" he asked, obvious irritation in his voice.

His condescending tone angered me. "I probably could, Jim," I answered. "But I'm retired, so I'm not going to do that. You can either take the corporate number and make the call yourself, or just send the bill and take your chances that it will be paid timely. So do you want the phone number or not?"

He didn't speak for a few seconds but finally responded, "Give me the number."

I gave him the phone number, repeated it once, and then disconnected the call without saying good-bye.

I immediately decided that I needed to stop by the nearest Verizon phone store and get my number changed to an unlisted number.

It took longer than I thought it would to have my phone changed over to a new number. But after a couple of hours, everything on my phone was like brand new. New phone number, new Gmail account, new browser, saved contacts, and saved document files.

I had the Verizon tech help me send a mass distribution text to all my family members, letting them all know my new unlisted phone number and my new Gmail account information.

I was excited because the last link between anything to do with American Trust Storage and me was now terminated. No more calls from anyone who didn't have my new unlisted phone number. I had accomplished a lot today, and I was ready to go home and tell Gabby about my day.

Just as I pulled into the driveway, my phone pinged, notifying me a new text had arrived. I looked at the phone and saw the e-mail was from Aria. Opening it up, it read, "Way to go, Dad! New e-mail, new phone number, a whole new life for you and Mom! I couldn't be happier for you guys. Love, Aria."

The message put a smile on my face, and the new freedom put a bit of a bounce in my step as I put my phone away and went into the house.

"Hello, Sweetpea!" greeted me as soon as I stepped through the doorway.

"Hello, Sweetpea." I repeated. "How has your day been?"

She flew over to my shoulder and started making the kissing noise in my ear. Then she said softly, "I love you."

I reached up and began to pet her under her right wing and responded in kind, "I love you too, Sweetpea!"

Gabby came walking out of the kitchen to greet me. "Hey!" she said. "How was your day, sweetheart?" She had closed the distance between us and moved her head forward to kiss me before I could answer her question. Sweetpea made her own kissing noise as our lips touched.

"It was good," I replied. "I had a very interesting day, as a matter of fact. Did you get my text?" I asked.

"Sorry, honey," she responded. "I haven't looked at my phone all day, and no one's called."

"Well, you look at the text, and then I'll tell you all about the day," I said.

"Now I'm curious," she said as she walked to her phone and picked it up off the coffee table. "You got a new phone number?" she said, surprised.

"Yes, I did," I answered. "Let me make us a drink, and then I'll tell you all about it."

"OK," she replied, sitting down on the sofa and waiting for me to bring our drinks over. "I can hardly wait to hear the stories!"

Scott Pruitt and I met at the golf course driving range the next Wednesday as we'd agreed, and after hitting balls for a couple of hours, we went into the clubhouse, and I bought him lunch.

I really enjoyed his company. He said whatever came to his mind, not caring if it offended anyone else or not. He was funny and loved to joke around with the bartender, waitresses, or anyone he knew who happened to be in the club.

Over the next few weeks, we met at the golf club two or three days each week, and I started hitting the ball much better. After we hit balls, we would either have lunch or go into the lounge and have a couple of drinks and a lot of laughs.

He introduced me to several of his buddies, and I started to feel like I was making a new batch of friends. Most of them were retired like me, and all of them called the golf club their home away from home. Almost to a man they used this place to get out of the house and not be underfoot of their wives during the day. We all told stories about our previous lives in the working world and empathized with each other when it was appropriate and laughed our asses off when we felt like it.

I started spending four or five hours at the club every day. Sometimes I'd hit balls, and sometimes we'd play cards, rummy mostly. I was younger than most of them, but I found myself being sucked into this pretty tight-knit group of old farts, and I liked it.

One day, Stan, one of the older gentlemen in the group, came in, and it was obvious he was upset. He ordered a double scotch on the rocks on his way to our table and took a seat where four of us were seated. The bartender brought the drink and set it in front of him.

Before she turned to go back behind the bar, he said, "Bring me another one, please." He raised the glass to his lips and drank it down all at once, smacking his empty glass on the table when he was finished. No one said anything as he sat there and stared at his empty glass.

The bartender brought a second drink, and he quickly downed it just like the first, still saying nothing.

Finally, Scott asked, "Stan, what's wrong, man?"

Tears started pouring out of Stan's eyes and down his cheeks. "Elsie died in her sleep last night. They think it was a heart attack."

"Oh, god, no!" Scott said, getting up and walking around the table to where Stan was sitting. "Oh, Stan," he said, pulling him up to his feet and giving him a tight hug. "I'm so, so sorry for your loss! She was such a good woman, and we'll all miss her!" They stood like that, both men quietly crying for a long moment.

I could feel tears starting to roll down my face as well watching the touching scene before me. Looking around, everyone including the bartender was teary eyed or was outright crying as they watched the two men embrace.

We spent the next three hours comforting our friend. He'd had too much to drink, hoping to kill his pain, when Scott finally said, "You need to get to bed, old buddy. Why don't you stay the night with Ann and me tonight?"

"No!" Stan replied sternly. "I'm going to sleep in my own bed tonight." He was slurring his words so badly that it was hard to understand what he was saying.

Scott looked at me and shrugged his shoulders, not understanding what he'd just heard.

"He said he wants to sleep in his own bed tonight. But one of us will have to take him home. He can't drive in this condition," I responded.

"I'll take him home and make him comfortable," Scott offered. "John, you drive his car home, and I'll bring you back to get your car once he's in bed."

"Sounds good," John responded. Everyone got up from the table, and each of us went our own way as Scott half carried Stan out the front door of the club.

That night in bed, I told Gabby what had happened.

She listened compassionately, and when I'd finished my story, she simply said, "That's so horrible. I feel so bad for that poor man."

Tears started running down my face as I said, "I don't know what I'd do if that happened to you. Promise me you won't die until after me, promise!"

"I can't make that promise," she retorted. "Besides, I want to go before you anyway."

I put my arm around her shoulders and pulled her close, and we fell asleep without any further conversation.

One of the advantages of hanging around a bunch of guys your own age or older is that you've all lived through the same time in history. We had all lived through Vietnam and then Iraqi and now Afghanistan. We'd all been involved or at least felt the strife and partisanship of the civil rights movement. We all could agree that we've had some great presidents as well as some that we weren't that proud of as representatives of this great country. We'd watched manufacturing dying a slow death as steel, aluminum, and automobile manufacturing left the United States to be manufactured in countries where there were much lower labor rates. We'd all watched as the very foundation that this country was built upon, "In God We Trust," was systematically being challenged and dismantled by various groups who wanted even more separation of church and state and to have all religion, especially Christianity, erased from the government.

But the most interesting bond the eight or nine of us had in common was a belief that the left-leaning politicians were leading us down the path of big government and toward socialism. All of us had strong Republican views and roots based on what we'd witnessed in our lives and how we'd been raised. We believed capitalism, not socialism, was the key to America's success.

These common beliefs made for some entertaining conversations over lunch or drinks in the clubhouse. As we expressed ourselves to others at the table, we often drew disapproving looks from other younger patrons who were obviously more middle of the road or left leaning in their own political attitudes.

Scott, our most outspoken group member, was the person most likely to confront a table of guys who were rolling their eyes at our conversation. If he saw them smirk or shake their heads negatively, he always addressed them.

"Excuse me!" he'd begin. "It seems you're interested in our conversation. Would you like to give us your thoughts on this subject?"

If the answer was no, he'd simply say something like, "I didn't think so."

If the answer was yes or sure, he always asked the same question. "First, can you explain to me why the police forces in this nation have been criminalizes by the Obama administration? Do you think he just hates cops, or is he trying to widen the racial divide by persecuting law enforcement?"

There were two possible outcomes to his question. One, they would say something obscene and turn away from us. Or, two, we would end up in an argument that usually turned into a shouting match until one side or the other started calling their opponents names.

After one particularly contentious encounter, I left the club in a pretty unhappy mood. I had long ago let my opinions be known about California's government and their left-leaning majority to anyone who would listen. And now Jerry Brown, the current governor of California, was proposing a $5 billion bullet train between Los Angeles and San Francisco. I thought the idea was the dumbest thing I'd ever heard, and I didn't want to donate one cent of my state taxes to the project.

Once I arrived home, I instantly accosted Gabby and said, "I'm ready to move up north where we can be closer to Thomas, Aria, and their families. I'd like to live in Washington if possible because they don't have a state income tax yet." Not giving her any time to think about my proposition, I followed up with "How do you feel about that?"

She just stood there wide eyed and finally said, "Hi, honey. How was your day?"

Later in the evening, after I'd calmed down a bit, we did have a constructive conversation and decided it was the right time to move out of California.

We made one trip to Portland, looked for houses in the area, and after two days of looking, decided on a home in Washougal, Washington, just across the border from Oregon. We made an offer, it was accepted, and two weeks later, we owned a new home in Washington.

The kids were thrilled and excited that we were moving back to the northwest, and quite frankly, so were we. We knew we'd miss the constant seventy-eight-degree temperatures, the walks on the beaches, but the offsetting benefits were worth the move. Not nearly as much traffic; no toll booths on freeways; gas would cost one dollar less a gallon; four distinct seasons every year; and we'd be able to spend so much more time with our kids and grandkids. We were both excited to begin our new lives in what we hoped was going to be our last move ever.

It was hard saying good-bye to my friends at the golf course before we left. I'd become close to them, especially Scott. I was going to miss our daily conversations on how to change the world and make it a better place. But I knew the conversations would go on with or without me there.

Moving day finally arrived. Gabby and I took one last walk on the beach as we were leaving Newport Coast for the last time. We'd decided to drive all the way up Highway 101. It followed the coastline and would take us through the Redwood Forest in Northern California. We planned a three-day trip, knowing our furniture and belongings would arrive at our new home in four days.

The most difficult part of the trip was being with Sweetpea in the car for three days. We had a small sleep cage with us for motels and nighttime, but during the day, she liked to sit either on Gabby's shoulder or her lap, or on whichever one of my arms that was holding the steering wheel. She was good, but she required so much attention that it was hard to really enjoy the ride and the scenery.

The trip was beautiful, and we arrived one day ahead of our moving truck, just like we'd planned. The next three weeks, however, were a pain. Putting everything where we wanted it. Hanging pictures and artwork. Organizing the garage and making space for the cars. We were exhausted by the time we had everything the way we wanted it.

What we hadn't anticipated was how much help the kids would give us, especially Todd and Aria. They came over to help any way they could most evenings after work and on the weekends. Todd probably saved my back by doing most, if not all, of the heavy lifting that needed to be done.

Once we were settled, I was back to square one of my retirement. No friends, nothing to keep me occupied; only this time, Gabby was in the same boat. I caught myself ordering Gabby around more than I knew was necessary. It took a toll on her, and eventually, she snapped back at me.

"Take off your divisional vice president hat," she would say when she'd had enough. "I don't work for you, and you're not my boss!" As usual, she was right.

We made friends with our neighbors but stayed pretty much to ourselves as we adapted to our new surroundings and lifestyle. I found a golf course with a driving range close to where we lived and began going there to hit balls a couple of times a week.

We found many beautiful well-groomed trails where we could walk hand in hand, most of them along the Columbia River. The Columbia River Gorge had been listed as one of the top-ten tourist sites in the United States. And they were right; the views and multiple waterfalls were breathtaking to behold.

But something was missing. We hadn't found a church yet that compared to our church in Newport Coast. We went to several different churches, but we just didn't feel called to join any of them. They simply weren't the right fit for us.

Both of us knew this was an important part of our life, and we kept searching the area for the perfect fit. And then we found it!

CHAPTER 27

"Good morning, congregation," the pastor said with a cheerful smile on his face. "Let us pray!" And with that, our weekly Sunday church service began.

We'd lived in Washougal for about four years. As the prayer ended and we were instructed to be seated, I couldn't help but look up and down the pew in amazement at our beautiful family.

It was Mother's Day, and all the kids came to church with us because they knew it was such an important part of Gabby and my life now. Even Jacob, Sophie, and Ellie, who was growing up to be a beautiful young lady, had flown up to be here for the Mother's Day weekend.

Jacob and Sophie's business had taken off and was becoming very successful. She had morphed into a very strong salesperson and was able to create more work than Jacob was capable of handling. They kept hiring extra people, and Sophie kept overselling their ever-increasing labor force.

I was very proud of our son and daughter-in-law. Not because they were successful business entrepreneurs but because their daughter was unquestioningly their number-one priority. Ellie played soccer, ran track, was an excellent snow skier, and loved the outdoors and camping. Every time we were able to watch her compete, Grandma would refer to her as our little warrior princess!

Although Ellie was competitive like her father, she'd also been blessed with an incredibly soft heart and empathy for those less fortunate than herself. She would give her own money to homeless people she encountered on the street. It was easy to see that she was genuinely pleased to help others in need. I always thought she might end up being a counselor or a social worker, working with the underprivileged in some way.

Seated next to us on the right side were Aria and Todd. Aria was the closest of all the kids with her mother. They talked on the phone daily, and Aria visited us twice as much as all the rest of the family combined.

I may have mentioned this saying before, "A son is a son until he takes a wife, but a daughter is a daughter all her life." The saying had never been more accurate than it was in our family. The boys and their families loved to be with us, and we enjoyed their company and loved them all, but our relationship with Aria was something special. She and her mother had been extremely close from the time she'd been very young. For some unknown reason, immediately after we'd moved back to the northwest, Aria had self-appointed herself to take on the role of our caregiver.

In the beginning, Gabby and I thought it was cute that Aria thought we needed someone to do things for us, someone to socialize with us, and someone to remind us to take our daily medications and monitor our health. But after a while, we realized that because we were no longer working, she seemed to believe that it was her turn to give back and ensure our happiness.

We finally had to sit her and Todd down and have a conversation to reassure them we were both fit and of sound mind and body and that we could take care of ourselves without assistance, at least for the time being. We didn't want to hurt their feelings, but we wanted them to understand that we still valued our independence.

They said they understood, but nothing really changed. When we would leave the house together, Aria, without fail, would ask one or both of us if we needed to take a hat to stay out of the sun or a sweater for later in the evening because it might get chilly. She was the sweetest daughter any parents could ask for as their child.

Further down the pew sat Thomas and his family. Thomas had been in medical supply sales for many years now with various companies and had moved up into a management position. Outside sales was still his first love, but he was adapting to managing other sales personnel and working at the next level, and he seemed to be very good at it.

To us, the most remarkable trait Thomas possessed was his patience and positive influence on his children. Michaela, Luke, and Matthew all loved and respected their father. He was a role model for them. He hardly ever drank alcohol, but when he did, it was never too excess. He never spoke poorly about anyone, even if they weren't his favorite people. He lived by the rule that if you can't say something nice about somebody, don't say anything at all. He never used swear words regardless how upset he was in any situation. And he walked the walk of a godly man, studying the Bible, taking his family to church, and teaching his children to render aid and compassion to those less fortunate.

Elise became a school nurse now that all three kids were in school, and she loved her job. The vocation was a perfect fit for her. Her compassion and empathy were exactly the right qualities to equip her for dealing with the physical and mental health issues high school students face daily. She became known on campus as Nurse Elise.

Michaela, their first child, had started dancing at the age of three. We went to recital after recital as we watched her skills improve every year. When she was about to graduate from high school, she informed her parents that she wanted to go to New York and try out for the New York City Rockettes dance team. Her parents were leery of letting their eighteen-year-old daughter go to New York City by herself but finally relented when she agreed to attend college while she was there.

She wasn't chosen to be a member of the Rockettes, but that didn't stop her from living her dream of becoming a dancer. She tried out and was chosen to be one of the dancers for the New York Knicks pro basketball team. She danced for two years and earned her associate degree before deciding to come home.

Once home, she enrolled at the University of Oregon. Michaela started her third year of college there and pursued a journalism major, aspiring to someday become a TV sportscaster. As part of her curriculum, she was chosen to be one of the sportscasters on *Duck TV*, a program available through the University of Oregon that broadcasted sports news to the student body through a private TV channel.

Luke, the second child, was graduating from high school and was planning on attending a small college in Bend, Oregon. He had no idea what he wanted to pursue as a career yet, but he wanted to get his college-required classes behind him, and then he would choose a major.

We had no worries about him. He'd proven himself to be a very good worker through the years, both around the house and in a couple of successful summer jobs. He was quieter than his siblings, but he was a great kid and always fun to be around. We attributed his quietness more to him being the middle child than anything else. He'd grown up to be a huge college and professional football fan and was the most likely child to want to watch a football game with his dad and grandpa.

Matthew was a crazy little guy who loved Harry Potter as a young boy. He'd read all the *Harry Potter* books by the time he was in the fourth grade. He was gifted regarding his intellect, but he liked to be goofy and took his intelligence with a grain of salt. At a young age, he had a crush on pretty much all of Michaela's friends, who were much older than him, and they all thought he was cute. He would take pictures with them and carry on meaningful conversations with them, and he was always the life of the party if she had friends over.

Even before Matthew entered middle school, he had become a strong and devout Christian. His faith was so strong that he'd had a pretty big influence on Gabby and me. Gabby and I were walking with him one day, and she asked him who his best friend was. His answer shocked us, but in a good way!

"Oh, that's easy," he said, responding to the question. "Jesus is my best friend. He's always with me."

Matthew had very little use for money. We began giving all the grandkids money for birthdays, and Matthew just put his into savings. We don't have any idea what Matthew will use that big brain for in the future, but my guess is that he will be involved in ministry at some point in his life.

"Let's all sing one of the old-time classics today before we dig into the word," the pastor said from the pulpit. "Turn to page 443 in your hymnals, and we'll sing 'Amazing Grace' together."

As the musicians behind the pastor began to play, we all started to sing along. Looking over at Matthew, I noticed that he wasn't looking at a hymnal, but he was singing loudly. I realized by the third verse that he didn't need a book; he knew all the words and verses by heart.

I don't know if I'd ever seen Gabby happier than on that Mother's Day. After the service, she must have introduced our family to fifty other families before we left. The smile never left her face, and her enthusiasm never waned as we entered the twenty-five-minute mark of introductions. She was so proud to show off her wonderful kids and grandkids. Finally, there was almost no one left in the church, so we exited and made our way to the cars and home.

Gabby and I had talked a lot about what we would do once we retired. Most of those plans revolved around travel and sightseeing tours. But the one thing I doubt any couple who is retiring takes into consideration is that your bodies are naturally wearing out. The aging process not only slows down your body and mind but also prevents you from doing tasks that seemed so simple only a few years ago.

We used to walk ten miles a day on the weekends when we lived in Seattle. Now, if we walked three plus miles, one or both of us would pay a heavy price in joint or muscle pain for the next couple of days.

I had no concerns about driving anywhere in Los Angeles and finding my way back home a few years ago. But now, I hated to drive in downtown Portland. The traffic bothered me. The aggressive drivers bothered me. And without an updated navigation system, I found myself either turned around or completely lost when we venture into a strange area or a new town. So we gradually started avoiding large cities and stayed closer to home, where I was more comfortable driving.

For Gabby, those feelings were multiplied by ten. Her car was five years old, and the navigation system wasn't accurate with new streets and freeway exits. The navigation had failed her multiple times, and she refused to use it. She very quickly reached a point where she would only drive in the areas around where we lived or those she was familiar with. For anything outside a ten-mile range, either I drove or she didn't go. Her fear of getting lost was so overwhelming that it had the potential to cause panic attacks.

I took her car into the dealer and had the navigation updated to current day maps, thinking that would solve the problem, but she still was uncomfortable with the system and preferred that I drive anywhere outside her known comfort zones.

I have been healthy all my life, but now that I was retired, my body decided it was time to self-destruct. In the four years we'd lived in Washougal, I'd had a hernia operation, two knee surgeries, a knee replacement, and a skin issue that doctors couldn't seem to figure out.

For two years, we went to dermatologists, nephrologists, hematologists, and gastroenterologists, and none of them could find out why my skin was so sensitive to light and the sun. None of them could tell me why my arms, face, and legs were covered with ugly leaching lesions. None of them could tell me why I felt so fatigued all the time and why I had a difficult time simply mowing the lawn without feeling like I was going to have a heart attack.

I was taking high doses of steroids for such a long time that I developed a "steroid hump" between my shoulder blades from overuse of the drug. Both Gabby and I thought I might well be dying.

The good news was that one of the nice perks of living in a metropolitan area is that there is usually excellent health care somewhere. For us, it was OHSU, the Oregon Health and Sciences University. The dermatologist that I saw at OHSU suggested that I try a new drug that had just been developed in-house. I began a trial with the drug, and within a month, the sores were gone, my energy was back to normal, and I was able to be in the sun without feeling sick. I got off the steroids, stopped all the other medicines, and felt better than I had in five years! It felt like God had performed a miracle on me!

We considered ourselves very fortunate to afford health insurance. But even with health insurance, the new drug would cost us $10,000 a year for the rest of my life. If not for Medicare and a supplemental insurance plan, the drug would have cost over $40,000 a year, and we wouldn't have been able to pay for it.

No sooner did I get back on my feet than Gabby started having severe pain in both her knees and legs. Again, no one could figure out what was going on with her body. We went to doctor after doctor without finding a resolution to her problem. Finally, an internist at OHSU determined that she had a neurological problem. He sent her to a neurologist who determined she had degenerative disks in her neck that would require surgery to correct. The surgery was completed, and Gabby began slowly overcoming the pain in her legs. She's still not completely healed, but we are able to again go on short walks together as she continues to recover.

It's one thing to be older and active, and a complete 180-degree turn to be aging and inactive. As I've said before, "Use it or lose it" comes to mind if you lose the ability to exercise and keep your muscles strengthened and toned.

Because of both of our physical issues and limitations, we found ourselves watching way too much TV. We mostly watched news programs, but the more we watched, the more we realized our country was dividing into two separate ideologies. The events of the last four years, both internationally and domestically, were disheartening, to say the least for us.

I don't know if I can honestly say things started to get more disturbing once we'd retired or if we were just spending so much time glued to the television that we stayed up to date on every natural disaster, every international conflict, and every political change and disagreement that was happening before us in real time.

I do know, however, that we both usually took the same side in most circumstances and on most events. We were empathetic to the horrors of war and destruction around the world, regardless if it was natural disasters or manmade atrocities. Conversely, at one time or another, we both found ourselves yelling at the television because we disagreed so strongly with the commentator or that TV channel's point of view.

We toned down our yelling at the TV on the morning of October 26, 2015. It was about 9:00 a.m., and Gabby had just gotten up for the day. I was sitting in the living room, drinking a cup of coffee, and petting Sweetpea, who was comfortably lying on my lap. The television was on Fox News, and Jeb Bush was being interviewed. He was pontificating on how unprofessional he felt Donald Trump was as a presidential candidate.

Gabby, who had been listening from the bedroom and was a huge proponent of change, didn't want another four years of the Bush family in the White House. She voiced her opinion loudly upon entering the living room.

"Just shut up, you asshole!" she yelled in the direction of the TV.

Immediately, Sweetpea jumped up, started flapping her wings, and very clearly said, "Shut up, asshole!"

Gabby's hand flew up to cover her mouth. I wasn't sure if the gesture was caused by astonishment or embarrassment for what she'd just said.

I looked at Gabby and, as calmly as I could, said, "Don't laugh, and just act like we never heard her say that! I don't want her to remember that phrase!" I could see a smile forming on Gabby's face, and I pointed a finger at her and simply said, "Don't do it!" She held her laugh.

Later, when just the two of us were out on the back porch, we laughed until or bellies hurt, and we could hardly breathe anymore. We made a pact that day to never swear in front of Sweetpea again.

After we'd calmed down, I said, "Wouldn't it be just our luck to have four couples plus the pastor and his wife over for a bible study, and while someone is praying, Sweetpea yells, 'Shut up, asshole!'" Gabby and I both lost it again as we envisioned the unthinkable scenario in our heads.

"Oh, dear God," Gabby said, looking up toward the heavens with her hands folded in front of her face, "please don't let that ever happen to us!"

The years 2013, 2014, and 2015 took a mental toll on us as we struggled with our physical issues and all the chaos that was happening around the world and at home. I can honestly say that Gabby and I both turned "old" in the blink of an eye during our first few years of retirement.

Some of the most disturbing events on the world stage in 2013 included a 7.7 magnitude earthquake that hit in Pakistan, causing hundreds of mud houses to collapse on sleeping residents. The estimated loss of life was 327 people killed.

Debris from a meteor hit the earth in Siberia, Russia. It fragmented once it entered the earth's atmosphere. The ten-ton meteor created a shock wave as it entered our atmosphere, traveling at forty thousand miles per hour. More than one thousand people were killed in the region.

Typhoon Haiyan, one of the strongest storms to ever make landfall, hit several islands in the Central Philippines. Tacloban, a coastal city with a population of 220,000 people, was destroyed. The typhoon affected more than 4.28 million people and over 270 towns and villages.

The roof of a large building containing several factories in Bangladesh collapses, killing approximately nine hundred people. Hundreds more were left missing in the rubble of the building.

On the world stage, international politics and confrontations between nations seemed to be escalating throughout the year.

Hugo Chavez, the president of Venezuela, died of cancer at fifty-eight years of age. Nicolas Maduro won a special election and became the presidential successor to Hugo Chavez. He was also a proponent of socialism, and his leadership followed in Chavez's footsteps. Unfortunately, the country continued its downward spiral, both economically and politically, under the new leadership.

Elsewhere, Russia granted Edward Snowden, an American citizen, asylum from the United States. Snowden had stolen and leaked information about U.S. surveillance techniques and information on both foreign and domestic citizens as well as other governments to the world.

In Kiev, Ukraine, hundreds of thousands protested, demanding Pres. Victor Yankukovich to resign. The protesters wanted to establish closer ties and relationships with Europe and Western nations and move away from their dependence on Russia.

In Egypt, the military deposed Egyptian president Mohammad Morsi and suspended the national constitution. Morsi and several of his inner circle were placed under house arrest during the military coup.

In the following weeks, police raided camps of protesters in Cairo, Egypt, where demonstrations had been going on since the ouster of Morsi. More than five hundred protesters were killed in the raids, and the military government declared a state of emergency for all of Egypt.

In North Korea, Kim Jung-Un stated that they would continue to develop nuclear weapons despite United Nations sanctions on his country. He also announced that they were restarting a mothballed nuclear reactor in Yongbyon. In response to these announcements, the United States deployed a missile defense system in Guam as a precautionary move.

Later in the same year, North Korea detonated a third nuclear bomb underground, defying United Nation sanctions. In a war of words, Kim Jung-Un threatens to launch a preemptive nuclear strike against the United States and South Korea.

In yet another part of the world, the Syrian government, in the middle of a civil war, attacked rebel strongholds in five separate areas of the country with chemical weapons. Graphic images of victims foaming at the mouth and with twitching bodies surfaced. Long lines of covered corpses also verified the death of as many as one thousand men, women, and children in the attacks. However, the Syrian president denied his army used any chemical weapons.

Later in the year, Britain and France reported to the United Nations that after an intensive investigation, they found the Syrian government had used chemical weapons multiple times against its own people.

President Obama stated that the use of chemical weapons by the Syrian government could lead to a military response from the United States if it ever happened again.

In Africa, El Shabab Muslim militants attacked an upscale mall in Nairobi, Kenya, killing 70 people and wounding an additional 175 others before they were forced out by Kenyan troops.

Things were no better at home in America.

In the United States, racial tensions were yet again raised when a jury in Florida found George Zimmerman not guilty of murder in the death of Trayvon Martin. The verdict sparked outrage, protests, and demonstrations in several cities throughout the United States.

Multiple bombs exploded near the finish line of the Boston Marathon. Three people were killed, and more than 170 others were wounded by shrapnel. Two young brothers with extremist Muslim ties were identified shortly after the bombing. One was killed in a gun battle with police, while the other was captured and held to stand trial for his crimes.

In response to the recent mass shootings of twenty first-grade children in Newtown, Connecticut, and twelve moviegoers in Aurora, Colorado, President Obama, in a televised speech, introduces proposals to tighten gun control laws in the United States. A fierce battle ensues as Republicans and various advocacy groups thought the new regulations infringe on our Second Amendment rights.

In his state of the union address for his second term, President Obama focuses on the role he believes government should play in stabilizing the middle class. Shortly after his speech, Congress raises the tax rate from 35 percent to 39.9 percent for anyone earning over $400,000 a year.

In another televised speech, President Obama becomes the first president to use the word "gay" when referring to same-sex couples. He compared the battle for same-sex marriage to past battles over gender and racial equality.

Gabby and I were starting to wonder if it was just our viewpoint, or was the world going to hell in a hand basket? So much had happened in this one year that it boggled our minds.

Four natural disasters seemed about the normal for most years, and the loss of life and property seemed comparable to previous years.

But on the world stage, humanity was almost constantly at war with itself. There were defining leadership and ideology changes in Venezuela, Egypt, Ukraine, North Korea, Russia, the United States, and several African and Middle Eastern countries.

Terrorism was also increasing with much more frequency throughout the world. Extremist groups, like the Taliban, ISIS, Boca Haram, Al-Qaeda, Hamas, Hezbollah, El Shabab, the Islamic Brotherhood, as well as other smaller groups, were again taking center stage as they tried to eliminate Western thinking, capitalism, and all other religions except their own. Though these radical views had been around for thousands of years on a smaller scale, after the beginning of the new millennium, these groups had exploded in size, creating chaos, death, and destruction in every corner of the world.

But the area that concerned us most were the changes slowly taking place in our own country.

Every time a person of color was shot and killed by a policeman, it was perceived to be a case of police brutality and was exacerbated by the news media, and even the president himself, as a possible racially motivated crimes. These views and opinions had a very negative effect on race relations throughout the United States, and you could almost feel the tension between the police and the African American community.

Capitalism was becoming a dirty word in America. If you listened to the government figureheads, we were becoming a nation of the "haves and have-nots." The thought processes seemed to be that the "rich get richer," and everyone else suffers in a capitalist society. Forced distribution of wealth through taxation and a redistribution of those monies seemed to be the goal of big government. We saw this as the first steps toward a socialist society, which hasn't worked successfully anywhere it's been tried so far.

The bedrock of our Founding Fathers, "In God We Trust," was beginning to be challenged daily throughout the country. Separation of church and state seemed to be the major concern of several organizations and government agencies.

There was a fundamental shift beginning to take place regarding same-sex marriage in the country. The large states and metropolitan areas lead the charge for equal rights for, as President Obama called them, gay couples. Those states in the south and the bible belt were mostly against legislation permitting same-sex marriage.

The country seemed to be dividing into two very distinct groups about both race relations and same-sex marriage. We believed President Obama's stance on both issues seemed to further divide the nation and helped drive a wedge between the two points of view.

I'll have to admit; I wasn't very pleased with some of the programs and processes the president had put into place during his first term. But being ever the optimist, I was looking for an improved second term that would benefit both the country and our sagging economy.

The year 2013 turned into 2014, and the most notable difference in the two years was that there were no natural catastrophes of consequence versus the prior year anywhere in the world.

However, on the world stage, there were more issues than in the previous year, especially in Russia, Ukraine, Syria, and parts of the world. But they were not the only countries to see armed conflicts or political oppression in 2014.

A judge in Egypt sentenced 529 people to death for the killing of a police officer during protests against the ouster of Pres. Mohammad Morsi. It was a stunning verdict that was met with international condemnation.

The Ukrainian government launched an eastern offensive in the Russia-controlled city of Sloviansk, Ukraine. As fighting escalated in the eastern Ukraine, the United States and Europe threatened crippling sanctions against Russia. In response, Pres. Vladimir Putin announced that he would withdraw forty thousand troops from the Ukraine border and help negotiate an end to the crisis.

When negotiations broke down, the Ukrainian Army starts taking control of several Ukraine border crossings by force. Approximately 1,130 people were killed in the fighting, including 800 Ukrainian civilians.

In response, Russia dispatches troops to Crimea and quickly took control of the area. The action by Russia sparks international rage and condemnation. In just a few weeks after the Russian takeover, Crimea voted to secede from the Ukraine and was formally annexed by Russia. The Ukraine pulled all its military and equipment out of Crimea, and it officially became part of Russia.

In another hot spot, Israel and Hamas militants went to war over the Gaza Strip. After seven weeks of fighting, 2,143 Palestinians were killed, mostly civilians, and more than 11,000 others were wounded or injured. An additional one hundred thousand Palestinians were left homeless. On the Israeli side, sixty-four soldiers and six civilians were killed in the fighting. After two more weeks of fighting, a cease-fire agreement was mediated by Egypt to try and put an end to the conflict.

In Nigeria, an Islamic militant group, Boca Haram, kidnapped 280 young girls from a school with the intent of making them sex slaves for Islamic fighters. The mass kidnapping sparked international outrage.

Members of the Islamic State of Iraq and Syria (ISIS) took control of the city of Mosul in Northern Iraq. Five hundred thousand people fled the city to avoid execution. ISIS took more and more territory in Iraq, including the largest dam in the country, and declared all their conquered territories to now be part of the new Islamic State.

The Taliban attacked the Army Public School and Degree College in Peshawar, Pakistan; 144 people were murdered, including 100 children. It was the most brazen and deadly attack by the Taliban in several years.

The United Nations Human Rights Council accuses North Korea of crimes against humanity and compares the ruling regime to Nazi Germany. Stunningly graphic descriptions and photos of the horrors endured by the 120,000 political prisoners in the country later emerged.

At home in America, President Obama authorized limited air strikes against ISIS. Additionally, humanitarian food and supplies were dropped to those who were fighting ISIS on the ground.

Members of ISIS captured and beheaded an American journalist, James Foley, and recorded it for the world to see. This was in retaliation for U.S. air strikes against the militant group. They captured, beheaded, and filmed a second American journalist, Steve Sotloff, who was on assignment for *Time* magazine in Syria. They again released the video for the world to view.

President Obama authorized increased air strikes against ISIS in Syria after a third victim was beheaded and filmed. This time, it was a British aid worker, David Hawthorne, who was killed.

Bahrain, Jordan, Qatar, Saudi Arabia, and the United Arab Emirate joined the United States in the campaign against ISIS. But ISIS continued to grow as other Islamic terrorist organizations pledged their allegiance and resources to them, including new terrorist groups from Egypt.

After years of negotiations, President Obama and Taliban leaders came to terms and completed a prisoner swap. The Taliban surrendered Sgt. Bowe Bergdahl, and the United States released five top members of the Taliban's leadership who had been serving time at the Guantanamo Bay maximum security prison.

President Obama announced that he would begin working with the Cuban government to resume full diplomatic relations between the two countries. The countries had not had a formal diplomatic relationship since 1961.

Defense Secretary Chuck Hagel announced that the Pentagon would be shrinking the U.S. military to its smallest size since before World War II. At the request of the Obama administration, the Pentagon was asked to prepare for nearly $1 trillion in spending reductions over the next decade.

President Obama announces major reforms to the U.S. surveillance programs. The NSA would now need court orders to surveil American citizens. The NSA would no longer be able to eavesdrop on leaders of allied nations. And, last, the NSA could no longer collect phone data on American citizens.

In the midterm elections, the Republican Party took back the majority in the U.S. Senate, basically creating a lame-duck Congress.

The Obama administration announced that the federal government would recognize the marriage of 1,300 same-sex couples in Utah, even though the state government did not. With federal approval in place, same-sex couples were now eligible for health benefits and joint federal income tax filings, the same as their heterosexual counterparts.

In a televised speech, President Obama announces that he was taking executive action to delay the deportation of five million illegal aliens from the United States.

It had been another year of instability in Egypt, Ukraine, Russia, Israel, Palestine, Nigeria, Pakistan, Iraq, Syria, and North Korea. If anything, there seemed to be less tolerance and more aggressiveness by a host of bad actors in 2014.

But again, our greatest concerns were about our leadership on the domestic front. Even though President Obama had reacted to the ISIS threat, his actions were limited. The terrorist organization was gaining a strong foothold in several Middle Eastern countries, and we were basically standing by and letting it happen.

We viewed the prisoner swap with the Taliban to be completely one-sided with a very poor outcome. The United States got back a deserter, and the Taliban got back most of their leadership who hated the West now more than ever.

The most frightening part of the year was the Pentagon talking about slashing the budget for our military forces by $1 trillion over the next ten years. It was as if no one in the administration was paying any attention to what was happening in the rest of the world. It certainly didn't seem to be the right time for a country that had become the policemen of the world to downsize their military.

And then it was 2015. Gabby and I found ourselves becoming more and more isolated as our bodies fought individual battles and outside activities became more arduous for both of us. We took walks on the river and enjoyed a good lunch out once or twice a week. But our desire to travel had all but disappeared in the last couple of years as our bodies began to betray us and terrorist attacks abroad became the new normal.

There was church and a few friends we'd made there, and there was family who were now busy raising their own families. And then there was news about a world that seemed to be in a death spiral.

Night after night, we watched and became more depressed as we witnessed violent crimes being committed daily, both around the country and right here in our own small community. It broke our hearts to hear about babies being killed by a mother's boyfriend or see another promising teen who died because of a heroin overdose.

There were a few feel-good news stories, but they were outnumbered ten to one by the bad news. Several nights during the month, we would eat dinner, watch the news, put Sweetpea to bed, and go to bed right after her, sometimes as early as 7:30 p.m. On those nights, I would hold Gabby in my arms, and we would lie there content to be safe and loved in our own little world where negative outside forces weren't allowed.

The year 2015 started with over eight thousand people dying in a 7.7 magnitude earthquake in Katmandu, Nepal. The severity of the earthquake destroyed buildings that were several thousands of years old. Several climbers on Mount Everest also perished in the strong quake.

Malaysian Airlines flight MH370 crashed in the Pacific Ocean and was never found or recovered. No one knew what caused the aircraft to crash. Everyone on board was presumed to be lost. Some months later, debris from the missing plane washed up on Reunion Island beaches. The disappearance remains a mystery to this day.

All 150 people aboard a German Wings flight 9525 died when the Airbus A320 crashed in the French Alps. It was later discovered that the copilot intentionally and deliberately crashed the plane into the side of a mountain.

Masked gunmen shouting, "Allah Akbar!" stormed the offices of the satirical magazine *Charlie Hebdo* and killed ten journalists and two police officers. The assailants took hostages, who were also killed in different areas of Paris, France, before they themselves were killed by police. The group was later identified to be an al-Qaeda group from Yemen.

ISIS terrorists attack tourists at a beach resort in a coastal town in Tunisia. Thirty-nine people were indiscriminately gunned down in the attack. On the same day, ISIS also orchestrates two other deadly attacks, one in France and one in Kuwait.

More than 2,400 Muslim faithful were killed during a human stampede outside of Mecca. It was the deadliest disaster at a haji in decades.

Late on a Friday night, ISIS extremists claim responsibility for coordinated attacks and shootings that kill over 130 people, leaving hundreds more wounded and injured in Paris, France. It was the worst terrorist attack in a European city in over a decade. Seven of the ten assailants were killed during the attack.

The French president declared war on the Islamic State, and days later, French fighter jets carried out waves of attacks on ISIS stronghold targets in Syria.

The attack sparked a heated political debate in Europe and the United States about what to do with the now 4.3 million refuges flooding into Europe from Syria. Those refugees that were fleeing Syria during this civil war were creating a crisis that had first gripped the Middle East and now was spilling over into Europe. Over four million refugees had arrived in Europe since the beginning of the year.

In the United States, Freddie Gray was arrested and thrown in the back of a police van in Baltimore, Maryland. Forty-five minutes later, he was fighting for his life as they arrived at the precinct. He died one week later. On the day of his funeral, violent protests broke out because of police brutality concerns. The protests quickly turned into riots in Baltimore before nightfall. The tension from the Baltimore incident went national, reigniting the Black Lives Matter movement. Six police officers were charged with crimes in the incident, but all six were found innocent of using excessive force, creating further protests and riots.

Nine African Americans were killed attending a prayer group gathering in a historic black Christian church in Charleston, South Carolina. The white man who shot the congregation members sat in their prayer session for over an hour before opening fire. The hate crime ignited a national conversation about racism in the South.

The U.S. Supreme Court struck down all laws that made gay marriage illegal in any state of the Union. They determined those state laws to be unconstitutional, making same-sex marriage legal in all fifty states.

Two radicalized citizens, a married couple, shot and killed fourteen people at a holiday party in San Bernardino, California. They had pledged allegiance to the Islamic State (ISIS) and were killed in a police officer shootout later that same day on a busy major California freeway.

On June 16, Donald Trump enters the race for the Republican nomination to be president of the United States. He pitches himself as the only candidate who could take the brand of the United States and make it great again. He also pledges to build a wall between Mexico and the United States to keep out rapists, murders, and drug dealers who were illegally sneaking into the United States by the tens of thousands.

By the time Christmas rolled around in 2015, Gabby and I had stopped watching nightly news every day. We made a pact to watch it on Tuesday and Friday evenings only. We also agreed to stay off all social media platforms except on the weekends.

I can't begin to express strongly enough how positive those simple changes made to our respective lives. We were happier, spent more time enjoying each other's company, and made a big decision about what we wanted to do with our newfound freedom and extra time.

We decided to become more involved in our community and to volunteer where we could help others less fortunate than ourselves.

Gabby became a hospice caregiver several days a week. She would travel to various people's homes who were terminally ill and sit and visit with them for hours. Depending on their religious backgrounds, sometimes they would pray together, or she would read to them from the Bible. To those who held no religious affiliation, she would simply talk with them and encourage them to share their favorite life stories with her. Often, she would rub their feet with lotion, make them a cup of cocoa, and try to help them be as comfortable as possible on her visits. But she always made the point that each one of them was a valuable person to society and that they should be proud of their individual accomplishments while they were here on this earth.

Hospice patients typically had less than six months to live. It seems like a short time, but it was enough time to develop a relationship. Gabby had wonderful relationships with all her patients and tried to steer them to the Lord, if they were open minded at all.

I have accompanied Gabby to twenty-four funerals so far. Without exception, the family members have thanked Gabby for her care, devotion, and empathy toward their loved ones.

She always says the same thing in response. "I gained so much from my relationship with your loved one. I am blessed to have known them in this life, and my greatest wish is that we will see each other again and renew our visits in the next life."

Hospice service didn't fit me well for a multitude of reasons, but I was determined to do something that would give back to our local community. Through our church, I signed up for our SCAT (Special Christian Action Team) Program. We would go to our warehouse and bag groceries for families in need of food and then deliver them to the families. I worked at this program two to three days a week.

After a very short time, Gabby became involved and wanted to help as well.

Many people think those who take advantage of these types of programs are lazy, unwilling to work, freeloaders that don't deserve the assistance. I'm sure there are a few out there that are trying to game the system, but in my experience, it was rare.

Just before Christmas in 2016, we were given the name of a single mother who had three children and had requested food from our program. Because of the time of year, we had collected toys for the holiday, and we would give each child a toy to celebrate the season along with the food.

When Gabby and I arrived at their apartment door, I knocked, and we waited for someone to answer. A young Hispanic lady answered the door and asked in broken English if she could help us. We identified ourselves and explained that we were here to deliver some food for them. Her face lit up like she had just won the lottery! We asked if we could bring in the food items, and she excitedly said, "Yes!"

We had four boxes of groceries and one box of wrapped Christmas gifts. There was one gift for her and one for each of her children. As we set the boxes down on the kitchen floor, Gabby offered to help her put the groceries away. She agreed, and Gabby opened the refrigerator to begin putting the cold foods inside. There was half of a bottle of apple juice and four individually wrapped pieces of string cheese in the refrigerator, and that was all! No meat, no milk, no vegetables, nothing else.

Her three small kids came running into the kitchen before we'd started putting the food away and dropped to the ground in front of the boxes. They didn't even look at the box with the presents in it. Instead, the oldest boy, who appeared to be five or six, pulled out a nice-sized red apple and held it up for his mother to see.

"Do you think we could split half of this tonight?" he asked, his eyes begging for a positive response.

"We might eat the whole thing!" his mother responded with a huge smile on her face. The kids all started jumping up and down in front of her at the news.

I heard my own voice catch in my throat as I started to cry. "I'll wait for you out in the car," I said to Gabby as tears streamed down my face. Before turning to leave, I pulled out my wallet and gave the mother all the cash I had, maybe fifty dollars or so, and said, "Merry Christmas!" Then I turned to leave.

Before I could get out of the front door, Gabby shouted for me to stop. Stopping and turning back toward the kitchen, I saw the young mother running toward me. She wrapped her arms around me and thanked me over and over for our kindness to her and her children.

After I'd finally broken free from her grip and was outside the apartment, I completely lost it. I don't know if I'd ever cried that hard before.

When Gabby finally exited the apartment and got into the car, she said, "That is the best Christmas experience I've ever had in my life. I feel like God led us to help that poor woman and her family. What a blessing to serve someone so deserving!"

I was still too emotional to answer her audibly, so I simply shook my head in agreement.

CHAPTER 28

Getting involved with the outreach programs that our church offered really opened our eyes to how much our country was changing as we moved through the new millennium. We were now at a place in our lives in which both Gabby and I considered ourselves to be Christians, capitalists, and conservatives.

Like hundreds of millions before me, I had walked down the road of life, and when I came to a fork, I'd been fortunate enough to take the correct path to more blessings than I deserved. However, as I'd aged and encountered new crossroads, the forks had started to blur a bit. It was more and more difficult to choose which was the correct path versus the path that satisfied someone else's agenda.

In my short time on this planet, I'd been witness to prayer being taken out of public schools and deemed unconstitutional in a case that went all the way to the Supreme Court, *Engel v. Vitale*.

The next year, in the case of *Abington School District v. Schempp*, the court decided against Bible readings in public schools along those same lines. Both cases were supported by Madalyn Murray O'Hair, an outspoken atheist. These changes were made in the latter half of the twentieth century to supposedly expand religious liberty for all public school children.

In 1980, the U.S. Supreme Court struck down a Kentucky statute that allowed every classroom to display the Ten Commandments in public school. This was again done to separate church and state. The first amendment was pointed out as the reason for not displaying the Ten Commandments. It stated that "Congress shall make no laws respecting an establishment of religion."

Education expert William Jeynes stated that there have been five significant negative developments in the public school system in the United States since those restrictions had been placed.

1. Academic achievement has plummeted, including SAT scores.
2. There has been a dramatic increase in out-of-wedlock births.
3. There has been an increase in illegal drug use by juveniles.
4. There has been an increase in juvenile crime.
5. There has been a deterioration in students' school behavior.

As these negative developments continued, the United States started to fall behind some of the other industrialized nations of the world in quality of education for the next generation.

One of the largest cross-national tests used to measure reading ability, math and science literacy, as well as other key skills among fifteen-year-old students is the Program for International Student Assessment, or PISA test. As of 2015, the United States ranked an unimpressive thirty-eighth out of the seventy-one nations in the world, according to a Pew research study. As little as twenty years ago, the United States was ranked number one against all other nations.

Another study known as the TIMSS has tested students in grades four and eight since 1995. The most recent test results showed that for fourth graders, ten countries out of forty-eight tested had higher math scores than the United States, while seven countries had higher science scores. The statistic was very comparable for the eighth graders tested.

According to the Program for International Student Assessment, the average reading literacy score for a fifteen-year-old student in the United States earns a ranking of twenty-four out of sixty-five countries ranked in that category. As well, the United States now ranks near the bottom among thirty-five industrialized nations in math at the high school level. The United States ranks seventeenth out of forty countries in overall educational performance.

I think this truly speaks to education expert William Jeynes's statement about the public school system. I also believe the "common core" approach that has been adopted by public school systems in forty-six states has exacerbated these problems.

Common core standards are a way to satisfy a state standard for specific subjects. It only attempts to ensure each student has a minimum of understanding of the subject. It does not reward outstanding achievement. I believe this process may have been the precursor to the introduction of socialism in our education system.

Once I graduated from college, it seemed as though there were only two choices given to every graduating student: either you moved on into the private sector and tried to become a capitalist using your newfound knowledge and grit to achieve great successes, or you stayed in the system as a support cell for the greater good of society and became a public servant in some way for the betterment of your fellow men or women.

I believe the socialist climate and agenda has been, and still is being, passed from generation to generation in our public schools and institutions of higher learning. Students who'd bought into the teachings of their socialist-leaning elders became teachers and are now forwarding their ideology on to the next generation. And with every generation, the new teachers want more control than their predecessors. They wanted more inclusion, more respect, better wages, better health care, more freedom to think independently, and more say in how society and government should be run and controlled. They also want less advice, argument, or debate from those who don't agree with their thinking.

Those who leaned more toward capitalism had children who were brought up to embrace the capitalist creed, "If you work hard enough, you can accomplish anything!" They built companies and businesses. They were the coal that sparked the fire for our country's economic dominance over the rest of the world.

Unfortunately, many capitalist take a dark path to acquiring their wealth. Some built their fortunes on the backs of those who were less fortunate and who were not willing to share their wealth. Others bribed, manipulated, or through other nefarious activities, cheated and gamed the system simply for personal gain with no regard for the people who were being negatively affected by their actions.

As is usually the case, the majority has been judged by the actions of the worst in this group, and capitalism is increasingly seen as the system that caters to the few wealthiest while ignoring the many.

However, I do believe that clean drinking water, the end of Ebola, and numerous other miracles of the twentieth and twenty-first century would have never been accomplished if it weren't for billionaires like Bill Gates, Paul Allen, J. Paul Getty, and a plethora of others who donated huge sums of their fortunes to improve humanity not only in America but also around the world.

All of us, regardless of race, sexual orientation, or gender, are born true socialists. In the first few months of life, we all are completely dependent on someone else for our welfare. Someone other than ourselves will feed us, bathe us, clean our poopy diapers, pick us up when we cry, and show us love. Newborn babies control absolutely nothing!

But as we start to mature and move through our life cycle, it is a natural tendency to break away from our socialist roots. At a very early age, kids will try to rip the spoon out of your hands so they can feed themselves. The older they get, the more independent they become, sometimes to their demise.

I would argue that most children are independent thinkers by the age of four. A year later, they are off to school, and their thinking is then heavily influenced by the school system.

In today's world, with most families relying on a double income to make ends meet, many of our children spend much more time with their teachers than they do with their parents and families.

The socialist message starts slow but remains consistent from grade one through college. "You can't have a cookie unless everyone else gets a cookie too." That will eventually morph into "You can't be truly successful unless you share all your successes and monetary gains with those less fortunate than yourself." To do otherwise brands you as a blight on society, someone who values money over people—an elitist.

As more and more children and young adults hear this, more and more of them fall victim to the socialist ideology. By the time your child graduates from high school or college, many, if not most, no longer think independently (although they believe they do). They have been indoctrinated into believing that making a great deal of money is bad, and those who do profit greatly from their labors are cheating society strictly to achieve their own financial gain.

I believe I first started seeing these changes when I was in college, fresh out of the army. It appears everyone was angry about something and felt their rights were being trampled on by others. Women were being discriminated against by men. Blacks were being discriminated against by whites. Alternative religious beliefs were being discriminated against by the Christian faith. Everyone was against us being at war in Vietnam. The socialist thinking in America at the time, mostly in academia, was angry and indignant to their capitalist counterparts.

Fortunately for capitalism, about 50 percent of these youngsters would realize by the time they were in their late thirties that everybody doesn't get a second cookie all the time. If you want a second cookie, you need to work harder, excel at your vocation, or change it all together to meet the dreams you've created for yourself. They will want new cars, homes to call their own, and the best possible environment to raise the next generation of children.

The other half will spend most of their efforts trying to improve everything for everyone. Teachers, politicians, and social workers will continue to chant the mantra of "All for one, and one for all!"

Government will grow larger, our national debt will increase, entitlement programs will expand, and we will ship American work overseas because no one is willing to work for less than what they think is a fair wage along with benefits and guaranteed retirement options.

I see our country moving further and further left every year. I see it in the people we elect to represent us. I see it in the debt we are willing to take on to fund various entitlement programs. And I see it in the erasing and abandoning of the very God this nation was built upon.

Sara Potter, CFA, VP, associate director, Thought Leadership and Insight, wrote an article about the increase in millennials and the decrease in baby boomers, which was very interesting. In the article, she states that according to the Census Bureau, as of 2015, the millennial generation has surpassed the baby boomers in size. There are 83.1 million millennials now compared to 75.4 million baby boomers.

Over eleven million baby boomers have died already, and moving forward, mostly because of age, they will die at a much higher rate than the younger millennials. That's not an abnormal phenomenon but, rather, a fact of chronology. The Greatest Generation, the generation before the baby boomers, only has about five hundred thousand people still alive today.

According to the Census Bureau, the millennials, although aging, will continue their population dominance until at least 2040.

Because of adverse economic conditions, a record number of millennials have moved back home with their parents. Millennials are witnesses to the Great Recession, which hit just as large numbers of them were graduating from college and looking for jobs. Older millennials also experienced the bursting of the tech bubble in 2001. The percentage of millennials that graduate from college and move back in with their parents as of 2015 is about 31 percent.

As a result, millennials' mind-sets have been shaped by the fact that they have had to live through recessions and tepid economic growth. This is in stark contrast to the baby boomers, who largely grew up during an extended period of American economic prosperity.

Through firsthand experience, millennials watched and saw that doing things the same way they had always been done worked out poorly during and after the recession for them. Consequently, they want to do things their own way, valuing job satisfaction over money.

The millennials have also brought a shift in the theology this country was founded on. In 1948, 91 percent of all Americans identified with Christianity. In 2015, that number has dropped to 75 percent. As the percentage of Americans identifying with a Christian religion has decreased, the percentage of those who identify with no formal religion has increased.

The percentage of Christians is highest among older Americans and decreases with each progressively younger age group. While only 8 percent of baby boomers state they have no religious affiliation, that number soars to 31 percent with millennials.

By a large number, millennials who now identify as "no religious affiliation" have made larger gains through religion switching than any other group. Nearly one in five millennial adults in the United States (20 percent) were raised in a religious faith household but now identify themselves as "no religion."

As an example, in 2004, a Sacramento-based emergency room doctor filed a lawsuit seeking to remove all references to God from U.S. currency. He suggested that "In God We Trust" placed a substantial burden on all atheists. It caused atheist to personally bear a religious message that is the antithesis of what they considered to be a religious truth.

My parents believed the baby boomers were ruining the world. They thought of us as self-indulgent and pulling further and further away from institutions that had been in place for centuries. Marriage, divorce, out-of-wedlock children, homosexuality, gender change, civil disobedience were all blamed on my generation by my parents. The older they were, the more we, baby boomers, were running the world into the ground.

I can't honestly say if my views have or have not been skewed by my age as well. But I know that when my parents were in trouble and didn't have a lot, the church was there to help in our hour of need, not the government. I also know that the most rewarding jobs I've ever been involved in had the word "volunteer" somewhere in the title.

And even if you don't believe in any religious affiliation, don't you think the Ten Commandments are still relevant to everyone? I believe God gave us the Ten Commandments because he wants us to lead good lives—lives that are peaceful, happy, and productive.

Billy Graham used to say in one of his sermons before his passing that if you read the Ten Commandments, which ones would you throw out? Would you abandon the commandments against murder or stealing or lying or adultery and unfaithfulness? Would you toss out the commandment to take care of our health and our environment by not allowing us enough rest at least one day a week? Would you eliminate the commandments against greed or neglecting the elderly (especially our parents)? I seriously doubt you would omit any of those because the alternative would be smothered in pain and chaos.

He went on to say, however, "I suspect your real problem with the Ten Commandments, or any other moral law in the Bible, is that you simply want to run your own life apart from God. But is that wise? God made you, and he knows what's best for you. Why do you deceive yourself into thinking you are wiser than God? For the first commandment declares, 'You shall have no other gods before me.'" I've listened to that sermon several times, and it always made perfect sense to me.

Something else that has always stayed with me was on a church billboard one day as I happened to drive by. It's a simply stated a fact in two lines:

Know God, Know Peace. No God, No Peace.

I don't think I've ever seen a more meaningful testament in so few words. Our lives would all be so much more fulfilling and simpler if we chose to simply follow this truth.

One day, Gabby and I were out for a walk, and a man was approaching us from the opposite direction. He had two medium-sized dogs on leashes, and the closer we got to each other, the more both dogs strained against their leashes to try and get to us. The man finally had to use both hands to hold his animals back so we could pass peacefully. As we walked by, he said, "Sorry about that! They just really like strangers!"

Two things struck me as we continued our walk. The first one I already pretty much knew; I don't really care for dogs, never have and probably never will. But the dogs reminded me of the relationship most people have with God.

Those dogs had never seen us before, yet they were willing to try and pull away from the one person whom they knew had fed them, bathed them, looked after them when they were sick, petted them, and loved them, all because they hoped something new and better was coming.

They don't know that I'm not a dog fan, yet they were willing to forsake their master, regardless the consequences, just to do what they wanted. The similarity between at least 31 percent of the millennial generation, and God is really no different.

I read somewhere that every person will have a positive, if not life-changing experience, by helping and changing the lives of seven people in their lifetime. Even though I've always felt the saying was crazy and had no factual or scientific backing, the thought has always stayed with me. I have wondered several times if I have had that effect on seven people yet, and if so, who were they?

Now that I'm nearing the end of my road, I've decided that I haven't had that effect on anyone yet, or I would know it. Now is my time for action. Gabby and I are committed to helping as many lost souls as we can in as many ways as we can. Our goal will always be to bring them to the Lord.

I've seen so many changes in my lifetime: diseases stamped out, mobile telephones with more computer power than our first manned space flights going to the moon, self-driving electric cars, and food delivered to your door within minutes of ordering it.

Likewise, I've been witness to so many human horrors in my short time on earth: the Jewish genocide, 40 percent of the world population starving, constant wars and struggles by nations for power over one another, and pollution that is choking our planet and destroying our oceans.

Do I fear for what the world holds for my grandchildren? Absolutely! But I also know that mankind is resourceful and can overcome obstacles, even the ones we create ourselves.

My story as a baby boomer is unique to me, but there are seventy-five million other baby boomers out there with their own life stories. I've tried to lead a good life, and I'm so grateful for my family and especially Gabby. We plan on spending whatever time we have left trying to help other less fortunate people in any way we can and laughing at our crazy but highly entertaining and lovable pet, Sweetpea.